Merry

P9-CQY-279

Love Brenda

OMAMORI

OMAMORI

RICHARD McGILL

BANTAM BOOKS

TORONTO · NEW YORK · LONDON · SYDNEY · AUCKLAND

O M A M O R I

A Bantam Book / September 1987

Library of Congress Cataloging-in-Publication Data

McGill, Richard.
  Omamori.

  I. Title.
PS3563.C363904   1987   813'.54   86-47910
ISBN 0-553-05204-7

Published simultaneously in the United States and Canada

PRINTED IN THE UNITED STATES OF AMERICA

FG   0 9 8 7 6 5 4 3 2 1

For Jenny
The keeper of my dungeon.

BOOK ONE
THE GENERATIONS
SUMMER

1936

The wind blows hard among the pines
Toward the beginning
Of an endless past.
Listen: you have heard everything.

SHINKICHI TAKAHASHI

CHAPTER 1

On a June day in 1936, marine clouds swept out across Nagasaki in a long gray shelf. Rising gradually from the west coast of Kyushu Island, Nagasaki, a small city of valleys and hills, was often referred to by travel guides as the San Francisco of Japan.

A high mountainous ridge divided two valleys into the old city and the new. The longest valley was the Urakami. There beat the heart of industrial Nagasaki. From the steep hills terraced with quaint residential sections, one could look down on the peaceful Urakami River and the tall smokestacks of modern factories.

Within walking distance of a large textile mill, Hosokawa-Napier, Limited, stood the largest Catholic cathedral in Japan, giving proof to the fact that thousands of Nagasaki's citizens worshipped as Christians. The chiseled stones that housed a faith brought to Japan from the New World and the high brick walls built to shelter modern technology had existed since the nineteenth century, when Nagasaki had been the first city in the empire to open its port to trade with the West. Cathedral and weaving mill gave testimony to the rebirth of this city. God's house remained secure, but not the house of a dynasty that had woven silk into cloth for more than sixty years.

Douglas Napier waited with his Japanese partner in the broad gravel yard of Hosokawa-Napier, Limited, listening to the familiar thunder of machinery from inside the mill. Having done everything in their power to keep the looms running, they now waited for the silence they both dreaded. After a few minutes the mill grew quiet.

Baron Tadashi Hosokawa looked at his American partner but said nothing. Together they watched the factory smokestacks exhale a wispy haze. The Hosokawa-Napier signature had been among the first to be written in smoke across Nagasaki Bay. Now the stacks expelled their last gasps, which were carried away on the same breeze that lifted the kites of children playing nearby.

Watching the children, Douglas Napier smiled. This was a city of kite enthusiasts, and each year during the kite festival, throngs of spectators dotted the Urakami Hills to view the display of colorful silk aerial creatures. Douglas recalled his own excitement when he had flown his kite there as a boy, the line singing out from the spool he gripped tightly, his young muscles tested by the heavy pull of his silk bird soaring to pierce a hole in the sky. The cheerful memory burst like a balloon, pierced by a sharp needle of sound, as suddenly the mill whistles screamed and men began flooding from the factory into the yard, streaming past their employers. As boys, the partners had stood here with their fathers, who knew every worker by name and would take time to inquire about each one's family. But now the mill employed too many men for that personal touch, and Douglas and the baron remained silent, like ushers at a funeral, as grim-faced Japanese trudged past them, wheeling their bicycles through the open gates of the mill yard.

Men whose forefathers had labored at the mill over the decades were now being sent home after a final day of work. The silenced looms were a shock to their ears, for the workers were accustomed to the incessant drone of the heavy machinery that had provided a comfortable living for them and their families. Once outside the gates, the stunned workers gathered together on the street. As the screaming whistles grew deadly silent, several men touched the pay envelopes they carried in their shirt pockets. Those final wages would not keep hunger from their doors for very long. One by one the men pedaled off for home under the low gray sky, the jingling of their bicycle bells echoed forlornly down the winding cobblestone street.

Together Baron Hosokawa and Douglas Napier closed the tall iron gates that had been forged in their grandfathers' time, when the mill's opening had ushered in the genteel age of the silk stocking. The baron inserted a large iron key, and its squealing turn in the lock marked the end of an era. His aristocratic face hardened as he said, "I wonder if these old gates will ever stand open again."

"Of course they will," Douglas said irritably. Only that morning the Kawasaki One-Hundredth Bank of Tokyo had cabled its refusal to grant the textile firm a loan. "We'll bring our proposal to the Yasuda Bank. Maybe its board of directors won't be so conservative."

"I don't mean to be pessimistic, Douglas, but we're running out of banks. And time," Baron Hosokawa commented dryly in English. He and Douglas had been classmates at Harvard, where the baron had acquired the high-toned accents of many of his instructors and fellow students.

"I'm sorry for barking at you, Tadashi." Tiredly, Douglas rubbed the bridge of his nose. "Well, let's get the wake over with," he said, and started across the deserted yard.

Nearing forty, Douglas Napier kept himself lean and fit with a regimen of tennis, racquetball, and laps in the swimming pool of an exclusive Tokyo men's club. Afternoons spent on the Yokohama golf course had bleached his ash blond hair and tanned his strong-featured face. His hardy masculinity made him appealing to both sexes. Women fluttered around him at parties, and inevitably his wife clung possessively to his arm, though Douglas was indifferent both to Angela Napier's jealousy and the attention paid to him by other women.

Douglas was six-two, but the baron was nearly as tall. Their eyes met briefly to share an intimacy founded in their boyhood. Entering the mill, they viewed the cleanup crew still at work. In the boom years for silk that followed the Great War, the mill's original red brick building had been expanded into this awesome brick-walled cavern, a city block long and nearly as wide. When they had run out of space, they had built a weaving mill in Kyoto to accommodate the surge in business. It was now one of the largest facilities for producing silk cloth in Japan.

Not twenty years before, Douglas Napier had taken a direct hand in constructing the Kyoto mill. Soon he would be forced to close those gates as well.

But it was here in Nagasaki that a dynasty had begun. The baron and Douglas halted before a wall of framed photographs that documented the history of their partnership. To its workers the Nagasaki mill had become part of tradition, and the men drew pride from this pictorial display that captured the aura of a bygone age. Brass plates on the picture frames were etched with the dates of each important occasion in the history of the mill and the lives of those who had served it until that day.

The images enshrined there spanned generations. Douglas Napier and Baron Hosokawa stood before them, transfixed, recalling childhood stories that brought the past to life in their minds.

Photography was still in its infancy that November day in 1871, when the founding fathers of Hosokawa-Napier, Limited, had posed for their pictures at the groundbreaking ceremony. Shinto priests had officiated over the proceedings, blurred figures in long white robes, captured by the photographer as they waved their streamer wands to purify the earth. Andrew Napier and his Japanese partner, both strapping young men dressed alike in western clothes, had posed proudly for the camera. Baron Fujio Hosokawa had struck a warriorlike stance. Looking at the sepia print, his grandson Tadashi could almost feel the old baron's discomfort in his tall black hat, his stiff shirt collar, and the tight, binding cut of a suit he had worn in order to show his willingness to adapt to the ways of his American partner. . . .

In the months since the two men first met, Fujio Hosokawa had grudgingly made adjustments to the white man's culture. As a Royalist samurai, he showed obedience to the decrees of his emperor's newly formed government. It seemed that Emperor Meiji wanted the Japanese people to absorb western civilization from the outside in, and they were ordered to cut off their feudal topknots and to exchange the traditional kimono for the modern dress of another world. Fujio gazed down at his high-button shoes and wished for the freedom of his thonged wooden geta. He felt constrained by his tailored wool pants. The velvet-cuffed jacket sleeves pinched his arms. Japan belonged to the Japanese, and by all rights he felt he should have posed for his picture wearing a formal kimono, stamped with the Hosokawa family crest.

Baron Fujio Hosokawa had attended the groundbreaking ceremony with mixed emotions. The benign *kami* spirits, whose presence had been felt dwelling in the Urakami Valley since the beginnings of time, now seemed to protest the wounds being inflicted by the excavators' picks and shovels. He almost cried out against this sacrilege as plows pulled by horses cleared the ground of its ancient trees and of rocks that had been smoothed by the centuries. His eyes misted over as he watched the escaping dust of ages. Bitterly, he looked into Andrew Napier's keen blue eyes and saw that they were filled with a sense of mission, as though it were his divine right to shape the soil of Japan to his own purpose.

Somehow Fujio managed to smile for the camera as his demonstrative American partner clasped an arm firmly around Fujio's shoulders. In the background stood the Urakami Hills; their slopes, as yet undisturbed, preserved the old Japan of Fujio Hosokawa's boyhood. He was a man at odds with the cultural upheaval being forced on his people. An exchange of ideas that would someday make Japan a power to be reckoned with was one thing. But for this proud samurai nobleman, the old ways of his ancestors, the Imperial Way, would always prevail, and no amount of change could shake the foundations of his long-held beliefs.

The beginnings of Fujio Hosokawa's personal misfortunes stretched back to 1853 and Commodore Matthew Perry's historic landing on Japanese shores. The mighty guns of America's "black ships" had terrified feudal Japan, and their arrival was soon followed by the landing of Russian and English vessels. But these events had been merely a trickle of things to come as Japan's locked doors gradually were forced open to trade with the western world. After unifying Japan in the middle of the seventeenth century, the ruling shogun had feared the spread of Christianity as a threat to his feudal government. And so for two hundred years the reigning Tokugawa Shogunate had barred trade with the West. The shogunate had preserved Japan's feudal society in strict isolation, a world unto itself, while Japan's traditions and mystical beliefs were held safely under a bell jar, like a fragile butterfly.

That was the world in which Fujio Hosokawa had been reared, and he had watched, horrified, as the bell jar's glass was finally shattered by the years of pressure exerted by ambitious foreign powers. It was as though a hurricane of time had come rushing into Japan to threaten all he held dear. Fujio had been prepared to wield his sword until the last white man had been driven back into the sea.

But his daimyo, Lord Mitsudara, had bowed to the realities. At his palace in Osaka, the lord held counsel before his samurai noblemen. Dressed in his full regalia, he unsheathed his long sword and pointed its glistening blade toward the Inland Sea of Japan, whose winds were bringing tall-masted clipper ships and steam-powered packets from many lands. Seated among his peers, Baron Fujio Hosokawa had listened sadly to the words spoken by his lord and master.

"These aggressive white men cannot be expelled by any means," Lord Mitsudara counseled his warriors. "Japan must bow or break, and I have refused to ally myself with those daimyos of other clans, who are prepared to take desperate measures. Through assassination, intrigue, and the use of arms, they hope to keep Japan for the Japanese. But even the shogun knows that feudalism is doomed."

"But, my lord," Baron Fujio spoke up, "these white devils will overrun us if we do not stand our ground against them and fight."

"No amount of bloodshed can alter the course of Japan's destiny," the lord answered strongly.

The anguish written on Baron Fujio's face was shared by his other samurai, but the lord was owed their absolute obedience.

In a gesture of surrender, Lord Mitsudara laid down his sword. "This is not defeat. It is an honorable surrender to the tide of change," he told his warriors. "The new challenges before us cannot be fought with our swords. Our fate is now in the hands of the gods."

It was not long before the daimyo's vision came to pass. The shogun resigned, and in the wake of that dark defeat, Lord Mitsudara pledged that he and his warriors would restore the emperor to the throne of Japan. Although just a boy, Meiji was regarded as a living god, and Lord Mitsudara shared the belief of many other Royalist daimyos—that only the emperor could shift Japan's course away from tragedy by negotiating hard treaties with the powers of the New World.

Less than three years after Meiji had been seated on the throne, ground was being broken in Nagasaki for the Hosokawa-Napier mill. The emperor had proclaimed that Japan's future rested in strengthening herself; the country could survive only as a modern industrial state and must master the techniques of western civilization. The samurai baron had taken his emperor's decree seriously, and it had resulted in the building of a weaving mill for Japanese silk.

Since he believed his emperor could do no wrong, Baron Hosokawa had reconciled himself with the new order of things. But he had not been prepared for the blow of another decree that divested the samurai of all privileges owed them by birth. In feudal Japan, social status had always been hereditary. Now the emperor had decided to borrow the principles of democracy from the West.

While the escaping dust of ages blew across the newly opened ground to make room for a weaving mill's foundation, Fujio Hosokawa thought back to the previous summer, when feudalism had been abolished. In one blow the foundation of his life—a foundation built from centuries of devoted service to his feudal lord—had crumbled. The old way was no more.

Although the baron retained his title, his family had lost their lord's patronage. To live on the yearly awards bestowed by him was samurai tradition. Daimyos had always shared the rice they collected as land taxes from the peasants. During lean years the rice was traded with the loathsome merchant class for money to pay off a samurai's debts. But with the abolishment of feudalism, Lord Mitsudara had no further need of armies. In a modern industrial state he, too, faced hardship, so the lord would pay no more tributes to his samurai.

With great sadness in his heart, Lord Mitsudara had shown obedience to the wishes announced by Emperor Meiji and disbanded his armies. Each samurai family was given a lump sum, which was to be a final settlement for all their years of devotion. Payment was in the form of the new government's bonds.

Men who had lived and died by their swords suddenly were like innocent children handed the responsibility of supporting themselves. The Hosokawa family belonged to the highest order of samurai, with lands of their own and land taxes to be collected from their peasantry. But the restoration of Japan would change all that.

As he said good-bye to his lord that summer, Fujio Hosokawa was painfully aware that the life he had known was now threatened with extinction. The baron had inherited his title at an early age, when his father was killed in a hunting accident. Lord Mitsudara had taken the young samurai under his wing and favored him above the others of his court.

"These are mean times for us," the lord imparted sadly, as he escorted Fujio to the road outside his palace gate. "I must send you home to Kyushu, but the ties between us will never be broken. I will always be your lord, Fujio. Whatever comes of this restoration, I expect you to seek my counsel as in the past."

"*Hai*, Mitsudara-*sama*." Fujio bowed deeply to his lord and master. A groom held the reins of his horse, and Fujio mounted for his journey home. Other homeward-bound samurai of the Mitsudara clan had gathered together on the road, perhaps for the last time.

It was a difficult parting among warriors who had been friends. Lifting his voice with theirs in a war cry, Fujio galloped off beside his mounted comrades as if charging into battle. Their horses thundered down the main road from Osaka until it branched out, and the riders separated, one by one, destined for faraway places.

All too quickly, the baron found himself alone. He watched the last of his comrades vanish down a road to the north. Fujio's journey put him on a course to the south, to the mountainous terrain of his birthplace on the island of Kyushu.

Soon after Fujio returned to his beloved lands, misfortune struck. A lightning storm set fire to the castle built by his ancestors. His family was evacuated to safety, and throughout the night, Fujio and his peasants fought the blaze with water buckets carried from the garden streams. Shifting mountain winds fought against their efforts, however, and it appeared the castle would be lost.

Risking his life, Fujio entered the flames time and again to rescue his family's most treasured possessions. These were not jewels or objects of art. What he carried from the blazing inferno were the silk battle flags, ancient swords, daggers, armor, and the awards for valor that had been earned by many generations of the Hosokawa clan. Just moments before the flaming rooftops of the castle collapsed, Fujio escaped with the last priceless treasures in his arms.

It was a night of grief as the baron and his family watched their home burn to the ground. At dawn its smoldering remains cast a black shadow across the land, and Fujio saw it as the harbinger of poverty. He had braved the flames to salvage the swords, flags, battle regalia, and the military honors bestowed on his noble ancestors. These sacred totems of his ancient lineage now lay spread on the scorched earth at his feet, and he stood there blackened by the smoke of the fire that had destroyed everything but the stone walls of his castle's foundation.

With reverence, he bowed to lift the long sword of one of his ancestors. Before leaving Lord Mitsudara's palace, he had surrendered a samurai's right to wear arms. Because of the fire and his emperor's decree, he had lost everything but his lands and the responsibility of his title. But Fujio Hosokawa drew himself up tall. His blood and bones were that of a samurai. Heredity could not be erased by official decree, nor by a fire.

The Hosokawa family moved into humble quarters once occupied by their servants. His family was used to luxury, and Fujio watched them suffer this indignity bravely and in silence. Their fertile mountain valley set deep in the agricultural heartland of Kyushu Island was favorable to silk farming, but not to planting rice. The government bonds they had received as settlement were quickly being eaten up in the bowls of his household. The Hosokawa family had never before relied on the silk farmed on their lands, but now it was all that stood between them and starvation. The next silk harvest would not be until the autumn, however, when the leaves of the mulberry orchards ripened with sap to feed the silkworms that wove it into cocoons.

Misfortune struck again, this time in the form of a government collector demanding taxes on the Hosokawa land to be paid in coins. A samurai baron found himself pleading for time in which to harvest the autumn silk. He was given an extension until the winter. But, he wondered, would his autumn harvest bring enough money to pay his debt?

Baron Hosokawa approached the local merchants with an estimate of his yield at harvest time. All of them shook their heads. The market was depressed, they said. The supply of silk was greater than the demand for export, and business was poor even in Japan, where the kimono was fast becoming a thing of the past. However, they agreed to take the next silk harvest off his hands as a favor to a man of his station.

Fujio seethed with anger as they named a price that would not satisfy the tax collector. From his daimyo's palace at Osaka, he had seen the horizon claimed by the masts of foreign ships, and he suspected Japanese silk could be worth its weight in gold if traded with the West. A message sent to Lord Mitsudara by courier brought a reply confirming his belief and advising him on a bold course of action.

As autumn drew near, Fujio Hosokawa vowed to keep the lands that had been paid for in the blood of his ancient clan. The changing laws of Japan had done nothing to improve the lot of his peasants, who still felt bound to him by the old feudal ties. They were puzzled by government decrees that ordered them to do one thing, then another. The fate of these simple people had always been intertwined with that of their baron. They were frightened. And so they looked to the baron for guidance.

The challenge Fujio set them was clear. To avoid calamity, the autumn silk harvest was to be increased as much as the land would allow. The land the peasants worked was owned by him, and the burden of paying the government land taxes rested solely on his shoulders. In the past, the peasants had served their baron as vassals, producing only enough silk so that they could live from one season to another, with no thought of the future. But suddenly the future was upon them. To survive this new age of commerce in Japan, they must now serve their baron as a unified working force. As free men and employees, Fujio promised them better lives. From that day forth, the Hosokawa lands would be managed by him as a business enterprise. The harvested cocoons would be sold at market to pay his taxes, and his profit would be shared with each family according to its yield.

Feudalism had discouraged incentive, but the Hosokawa peasants rose to meet their new challenge. The result was a bountiful harvest. On a brisk autumn day in 1871, those who worked the land stood bowing along its country roads as they had in ages past when the baron's ancestors had marched to war. That day, however, their baron was embarking on quite a different journey as he led a column of horse-drawn wagons loaded with silk cocoons. His destination was the silk exchange at the port of Yokohama, which had become Japan's center for export trade with the West and was located only a few miles from the new capital city of Tokyo, where his emperor held court over the foreign dignitaries whose ways had brought the Hosokawa family to the brink of ruin.

At the fishing village near his ancestral lands, Fujio's long journey began beneath the unfurling sails of a Japanese ship, which had been loaded with his rich cargo of silk. The winds favored his thousand-mile voyage from home. He was certain that the quality of his cocoons would impress the white traders. He intended to drive a hard bargain with them for a fair price. Nothing more. Nothing less.

But Fujio Hosokawa had never imagined the difficulties awaiting him as a novice silk merchant. At the silk exchange in Yokohama, he was plunged into a nightmare as he made his way through a greedy nest of vipers, lost in the dense smoke raised by the white traders' foul-smelling cigars and distracted by the clamor of their foreign tongues. In the confusion he wished for the companionship of his sword. But even its blade would command no respect among these foreign profiteers who were out to cheat him and who smiled falsely as Japanese interpreters conveyed their miserable offers. At the silk exchange, money alone was respected, and Fujio had barely enough to pay his expenses while attempting to strike the bargain for his silk harvest that would allow him to return to his waiting family with honor.

If ever there was a man in need of a friend, it was Fujio Hosokawa. The days soon became weeks, while unscrupulous foreign speculators waited for him to relent and lower his price. But the stubborn baron from Kyushu tightened his belt and steeled himself against those who would take advantage of him.

Time weighed heavily on Fujio Hosokawa as he walked the busy Yokohama docks. A deep depression now kept him from visiting the silk exchange, where the very atmosphere encouraged profiteering and quickly soiled the minds of those who came to trade with the Japanese. For days he watched the merchant ships come and go from this small fishing village where inns to house so many foreigners had risen virtually overnight. Every day the ships arrived in greater numbers, churning Yokohama Bay into white spume. Through narrowed eyes the baron searched the faces of the foreigners as they came ashore, hoping to find at least one who might deal fairly with him. But they all seemed cut from the same unscrupulous cloth, and the silk cocoons he displayed in the palm of his outstretched hand made him feel no better than a beggar.

He might have given up all hope if not for the tragic sight of other samurai who had actually become beggars. These were foot soldiers, *ronin*, who had also lost their masters. Once a samurai always a samurai, and these destitute warriors had no trade, no education. Their swords and daggers had been sold to buy food. Only yesterday samurai had ruled the city streets and the countrysides. Now these men were being made beggars by a nation they had proudly defended. If not for the silk farmed on his lands, Fujio might have become one of those men whose loss of face would lead them to end their lives in ritual suicide. The business of silk had spared him that fate. His honor was at stake, demanding as much of him as a fight on a battlefield.

Fujio Hosokawa entered the Shinto shrine near Yokohama's waterfront. There he paid homage to the gods, as his ancestors had always done on the eve of battle. As he knelt in prayer, he heard the bells of iron ships docking on the night tide. To preserve his honor he needed but one honest trader among the many now landing on Japanese shores. He placed a gift to his gods on the offering table. The small sack of rice was to have been his dinner. For that night his beliefs would sustain him; a samurai's courage was not found in his belly.

Early the next morning, Fujio Hosokawa marched inside the silk exchange building with his sample basket of cocoons. He was in unusually high spirits. As he walked through the crowd, a tall, sturdily built American jostled against him, causing Fujio to drop the basket. Then, incredibly, the foreign devil bowed politely and apologized in Japanese. The baron's response was a burst of laughter. Only the night before, he had petitioned the gods to send him just such a cultured white man as this. Here was a man whose respectful manner bespoke a fairness of mind. As the American smiled at him, Fujio saw no greed in the man's clear blue eyes. The baron introduced himself, and was pleased to find that the American responded properly in Japanese. It would be a relief to conduct business in his native tongue, but he guarded himself against being taken in by first impressions.

Andrew Napier was also relieved by the chance encounter. When they accidentally bumped against each other, he had been quick to recognize the fine quality of the silk cocoons that tumbled from Baron Hosokawa's basket. Now he was even more impressed by the yield produced on the lands of this aristocratic samurai. When Andrew's ship landed several days earlier, he had been surprised to find Yokohama already bustling with foreign speculators. Fujio Hosokawa's guardedness toward him was understandable after dealing with the profiteers crowding the silk exchange. Andrew might easily have taken advantage of the naive Japanese mercantile houses represented there, but his ambitions would not be served by turning a quick profit at the expense of those trusting people. He had burned his bridges behind him in America and had come to this new frontier to stay. And to make the most of his opportunity in Japan, he had made an effort to learn the language and customs of her people.

An inheritance from his mother had financed Andrew Napier's adventure. His father was a Bible-thumping, holier-than-thou Calvinist who treated his three sons no better than slaves born to toil in his New England woolen mills. Andrew, the youngest, had endured the old man's abuses only for his mother's sake. Andrew was a talented engineer, and the woolen looms he designed had enhanced his father's fortunes. Cold indifference, however, was his only reward.

Soon after his mother's death, Andrew had left New England for Japan with his inheritance in his purse and the plans for a revolutionary reeling machine for silk under his arm. Andrew knew that a samurai valued his honor above all else, and now he wanted the baron to know that he, too, was a man of honor. He priced the autumn harvest at its fair market value, and Fujio accepted the offer eagerly. His lands had been saved from the tax collector, and he was anxious to return home. But when the American pointed out that there was more profit to be made from the Hosokawa silk than the sale of a single harvest, the baron was intrigued enough to accept Andrew Napier's invitation to dine with him at his inn so that they could discuss what he had in mind.

The night before, Fujio had gone to bed on an empty stomach. Now he feasted. He was a man of substance once again. In the course of their conversation, a rapport was struck between men of East and West that allowed Baron Hosokawa to set aside his personal grievances. He realized that Andrew Napier was a young visionary with far more to offer than the baron had bargained for when he had set out from Kyushu.

Fujio scrutinized the American's plans for machines to weave the Hosokawa silk into cloth and blueprints for a mill to be built on Japanese soil. Andrew foresaw a promising market for Japanese silk textiles. Until Japan had reopened its doors to trade, silk from China had fed the hungering markets of America and Europe. The quality of Japanese silk was superior, but manufacturing silk material in America was costly. Were the cloth to be produced at its source with Japanese labor, it could be sold at more affordable prices in the West. Andrew Napier believed there was a fortune to be made in silk stockings.

The samurai baron knew little of machines, and less of ladies' stockings, but he was canny enough to see how the proposal Andrew laid out before him could return importance and respect to his family name. A dynasty of warriors held no station in a modern society. Gazing out the window of the inn at the harbor filled with merchant ships, Fujio envisioned the rewards of founding an industrial dynasty. Now money was station. He had learned a hard lesson dealing with the white profiteers at the silk exchange, and he began to feel a kinship toward the open-faced American who had befriended him.

Not a year separated the two men in age, and while Andrew Napier confided his innermost thoughts, Fujio Hosokawa listened and considered. This man had sailed to Japan, without wife or family, and sought to build himself a new life. His eyes glistened as he spoke of carving out a dynasty for his future heirs, a dynasty that would last for generations to come.

In the span of an afternoon, these two men of different backgrounds had come to share the same ambition. Each realized that his success hinged on what the other had to offer: Fujio Hosokawa needed a western partner to deal on an equal footing with the western world; Andrew Napier needed a Japanese partner if he was to strike a permanent claim on the soil of Imperial Japan. Although Japan had great need of foreign investors, at the same time the group now swarming across the shores struck fear into the hearts of the people. Other Asian nations had already fallen under the white man's domination by allowing vast parcels of land to be bought up. Those in power behind the emperor's throne had assumed an adamant stance against parceling off this "Land of the Gods" to foreigners. Emperor Meiji signed treaties with the western powers, but they were unequal treaties and in some cases favored a Japan that would govern over the lives of foreign guests.

Andrew Napier's desire to transplant his roots to Japanese soil held Fujio Hosokawa silent. The baron was a cautious man and he pondered the benefits and the pitfalls of such a partnership. Fujio had not yet taken a bride. But someday both he and Andrew would marry, and he weighed the consequences of joining their different races through generations of heirs, whose closeness would extend beyond the boundaries of a business relationship.

"Necessity will make us partners, Napier-*san*," Baron Fujio said, "but everything cannot be trusted to friendship. There are traditions to be observed." With a smile, he stretched one hand across the table and let it rest next to Andrew's hand so that the contrast in the color of their skin was evident. This polite way of "speaking" for their different races brought a nod from Andrew Napier, and the baron said, "I am thinking that certain lines must be drawn to protect both our interests now and in the future."

"Yes, we are different in complexion but of like minds, Hosokawa-*san*," Andrew told him, and both men shared a laugh.

They struck a bargain. Friendship would be tempered with wisdom. The capital city of Tokyo was not an hour's journey from Yokohama, and it was there that Andrew Napier retained legal advisers to set down on paper a partnership agreement in accordance with the Japanese law of the time.

The lawyers applied themselves for many days before the firm of Hosokawa-Napier, Limited, was created. Fujio Hosokawa would not think of signing any of the legal documents, however, until his American friend had been formally introduced to his family. The long journey south to Kyushu exposed Andrew Napier to the slow-flowing stream of Japanese life in a sheltered country province. He was a curiosity to the peasants, who had never laid eyes on a white man. The Hosokawa family were polite but aloof. Despite their misfortunes, they remained wedded to the past, and the necessity of Fujio's partnership with someone not Japanese made them wary. Eventually, Andrew's promise of restoring them to a comfortable life won the acceptance of all concerned, although no amount of charm could win the noble family's favor.

But here Fujio Hosokawa was the master. On a day marked by celebrations, Andrew Napier was given the honor of being the first white man to worship at the Shinto shrine of the baron's ancestors. Dressed in a Japanese kimono, Andrew knelt before his partner's gods to petition them for a successful business venture. Years ago Andrew Napier had been turned away from his Christian God by his tyrannical father's hand, and he believed in nothing but himself. Yet he showed respect for his Japanese friend's beliefs. Mutual respect for the preservation of each other's traditions was the covenant between the two men.

A grand feast was held in the baron's gardens, where colored lanterns illuminated the charred ruins of the stone castle. The festivities lasted far into the night. After they had drunk much sake together, Andrew entered

Fujio's humble rooms in quarters once occupied by the castle servants. Seated at a low table, they signed the documents of partnership as Japanese notaries witnessed the act.

Then Andrew Napier surprised his friend with a gift he had fashioned by hand to preserve the documents. Hosokawa-Napier, Limited, had been etched in gold leaf, in English and in Japanese characters, across the lid of a handsome metal box. Andrew had decorated it with intricate scrollwork and had also added the year of the company's founding.

"Please accept this box as a gesture of trust and goodwill between friends," Andrew said with feeling. "Some things felt between men can't be set down on paper, Fujio, but it would honor me for you to be the custodian of our written bonds."

"Your words have touched me, Andrew." Baron Hosokawa was impressed by his friend's craftsmanship and honored by his thoughtful gesture. Andrew handed him a key, thus giving their agreement into Fujio's care.

"I came to you as a stranger with a dream. Now it can be realized," said Andrew, tears filling his eyes in a rare display of emotion. "Thanks to your friendship, Japan is now my home."

As the first light of dawn touched the paper windowpanes, Fujio ceremoniously locked the box with its key. Only a serious breach in their covenant could dissolve the partnership, and neither man entertained any thoughts of future generations needing to unlock the box. They exchanged smiles, founders of a dynasty each one believed was destined to outlive him. It was bad luck for a man to pour sake for himself, so the partners filled one another's cups to toast the dawn of a new age.

The moment was too important for either of the new partners to think of sleep, so they strolled the gardens at sunrise, talking. Andrew Napier decided that work on the weaving mill should begin at once. Nagasaki was chosen as the building site. It was more than two hundred miles from the Hosokawa lands and the silk harvests that would feed Andrew's looms, but Nagasaki was the closest major port open to ships from the West, which would carry the mill's textiles to foreign markets.

Several days later, the partners arrived in Nagasaki. It was a sobering experience, for this was a city built of paper, wood, and stone, and Andrew Napier's heavy machinery demanded a sturdier construction of bricks, cement, and cast-iron beams. Men by the hundreds gathered at the building site, hoping for employment, but their skills belonged to a feudal Japan. Andrew saw the building of his mill as a monumental task.

Late in November, 1871, Andrew Napier rolled up his sleeves, and the work began. Andrew had to train a labor force. The Japanese laborers were quick to learn the art of brickmaking and how to lay the bricks in even rows plumb with the excavated ground. Metal pipes for the steam to run his machinery and the mill's cast-iron support beams were manufactured in a centuries-old foundry in which Buddhist temple bells had once been cast. The labor force he had trained was left to build the mill, while Andrew fashioned his machines, instructing Japanese craftsmen in the use of the modern lathes that he had brought with him from America. He worked on against mishaps and delays, driven by an obsession to succeed that tired Baron Fujio Hosokawa, who had little to offer other than his moral support.

Before that winter ended, the weaving mill of Hosokawa-Napier, Limited, had opened its gates and the roar of Andrew's machinery sent Baron Hosokawa packing for the quiet of home. His responsibility to their partnership lay with managing his lands. The baron returned to Kyushu accompanied by a learned Japanese gentleman who had devoted himself to the modern science of silk farming. Under the man's guidance, Fujio Hosokawa's workers were educated away from their ancient practices. Baron Hosokawa now channeled the self-discipline of a samurai into developing the full potential of his lands. Improving the breeding stock of the silkworm moth soon yielded more abundant harvests and a finer quality of cocoon. This occupied Fujio in Kyushu, while his American partner toiled in Nagasaki improving the breed of his mechanical looms.

Season followed season as Baron Hosokawa visited the Nagasaki mill with his abundant harvests of raw silk. They were cause for celebration, but Andrew Napier could not be pried loose from his thundering machines. He was like one of them, forever huffing and puffing. His machines were stopped to be oiled and greased, but Andrew stopped for nothing. His days were spent managing the assembly lines, his nights at his drawing board in the small office where he also ate and slept.

The looms he invented produced silk textiles far superior to those produced by the growing number of Japanese competitors, whose weaving methods lagged behind the times. America became Hosokawa-Napier, Limited's, strongest customer. Within a few years, the mill's exports of textiles as well as surplus raw silk had yielded a fortune.

But Andrew Napier was not satisfied. The baron grew increasingly distressed by his friend's relentless pursuit of still more wealth. He reasoned that female companionship might help cure Andrew's unnatural condition. But the only white women in Japan were the wives of foreign diplomats and businessmen, and any relationship with a Japanese woman of quality was out of the question. However, Fujio Hosokawa had no objection to his partner seeking the company of geisha girls or the Japanese women who served a man's carnal desires in Nagasaki's tenderloin district. On several occasions the baron suggested this, but Andrew Napier firmly shook his head to the idea. He seemed inured to pleasures of the flesh, and the baron could not lure him away from work even for a well-deserved holiday at the Hosokawa castle, which was being rebuilt with the riches they had earned.

After several years of unbroken toil, Andrew Napier at last gave in to exhaustion and was brought to a stop. Fujio Hosokawa used the moment to offer sound advice. "Both of us have channeled our energies to achieve the success we now enjoy," he told his weary friend. "Your solitary existence here at the mill has been most distressing to me, Andrew. Our fortunes are secure. A dynasty must have sons and heirs, and the time has come for us to take wives of our own races."

"Yes, we must have heirs," Andrew said thoughtfully. The mill whistle sounded to end another day of profits earned on his looms. As his workers flooded into the yard, Andrew stood at his office window and looked out across the yard to tall-masted ships setting sail in the distance. "America holds only bitter memories for me, and I have never had much patience with women, Fujio. But necessity calls me back to New England to choose a bride. And you? Has some pretty Japanese maiden caught your fancy?" He questioned his friend with a smile, and the baron laughed.

"*Hai*, a regal beauty wih fiery spirit, who has given me many a sleepless night." Fujio grew serious as he said, "Had my father lived, he would have chosen me a bride in the customary wedding match. However, I feel sure he would approve of my selection. The excellence of her bloodline promises me children worthy of the Hosokawa name."

Running both hands through his thick blond hair, Andrew sighed. "Breeding—yes. The woman I seek as a wife must also possess the qualities you speak of. I won't settle for less."

"Once again we are of like minds." Fujio surprised his friend by holding out an envelope stamped with the name of an American steamship line. "Please, accept my gift. I took the liberty of booking you passage on a swift ship. You have the finest stateroom aboard. Consider it a wedding present for you and the American bride you will bring back to Japan." He wagged the envelope and smiled. "Go before you are tempted to remain here with your noisy machines. The gods be with you on a safe journey."

Andrew Napier bowed to accept the tickets. "I shall miss you and my new homeland."

Andrew Napier sailed to America in January, 1875. He had left there an embittered young man, and during his years in Japan he had sacrificed every human emotion for the wealth he now enjoyed. Any spark of the love instilled in him by his compassionate mother had been snuffed out in that exchange. Andrew returned home only to choose a wife of hardy New England stock like his mother. His tyrannical father had died of a stroke soon after Andrew's departure for Japan. Freed of bondage, Andrew's two older brothers had lost the family woolen mill; it had financed their excesses. One was killing himself with drink, the other had become a drifter, taking jobs in the cotton mills of the South.

Andrew was a lonely man, incapable of reaching out to anyone. But women found him irresistible, and before long he won the heart of a very young well-bred beauty who seemed ideally suited to his purpose. The girl was mesmerized by the handsome adventurer's charming veneer and his exotic descriptions of a fairy-tale Japan, where she would live as a queen in the mansion that was being built for them in the hills of Tokyo.

"Dear Andrew, you make life in Japan as your bride seem a romantic dream come true," she said with a sigh. Fluttering his gift of a painted silk Japanese fan, the future Mrs. Napier shyly accepted his proposal of marriage.

Andrew Napier left nothing to chance. On his wedding night he energetically applied himself to the task of siring a son, and that ambition was quickly realized. When the newlyweds set sail for Japan, Andrew's bride, Louise, was already pregnant with his child.

Before leaving his adopted homeland, Andrew had laid careful plans. The Nagasaki weaving mill now functioned under the management of Japanese he had trained to replace him. Hosokawa–Napier, Limited, would open offices in the nation's capital, where he could better handle the executive demands of their far-flung business enterprises. In Tokyo, a grand Victorian mansion of Andrew's own design had been completed during his absence. He had built it to house his heirs in luxury, and it was there that his American bride gave birth to a healthy son.

But Louise Napier suffered complications in childbirth. When the doctors pronounced her unfit to give Andrew other heirs, he coldly turned his wife from his bed. To his narrow way of thinking, the woman had betrayed him, and forgiveness was out of the question.

Baron Fujio Hosokawa's Japanese bride had also given him a healthy son. But her second male child was stillborn, and her third child, a girl, died in infancy.

The future of the Hosokawa–Napier dynasty now rested with two male heirs and with the grandsons to be born of their seeds. Andrew Napier wanted nothing to do with his only child until the boy came of age to assume his duties. Through the empty years that followed, Andrew grew into a brooding figure, with graying hair, who stalked his Tokyo mansion feeling cheated by fate of having other sons. He lived only for his work, strengthening the fragile walls of his empire built on silk as he waited impatiently for the next generation to be born. . . .

And so, on a cloudy June day in 1936, the reflections of two grandsons, both grown men, were mirrored by a wall of glass-framed photographs in the silenced Nagasaki mill. Douglas Napier was the master of his grandfather's Tokyo mansion, and Baron Tadashi Hosokawa the master of the Kyushu lands where their grandfathers had signed a partnership what now seemed an eternity ago. To this day the documents that bound their families together had remained locked in the metal box fashioned by Andrew Napier.

Tadashi Hosokawa placed his arm around Douglas's shoulders, feeling moved by the changes that time had written on their faces since they had posed for the camera as Harvard graduates who had returned home to Japan with honors. That photograph was taken in the early 1920s and recorded another groundbreaking ceremony for the expansion of the mill whose gates they had locked today. The pictorial history ended in a family portrait. Douglas's and Tadashi's fathers stood beside the wives of their sons, who posed with another generation of small children. Frozen by the camera's unsparing eye, three generations smiled for their picture as if the prosperity they enjoyed would last forever.

Douglas Napier spread his tapered fingers across a glass display case that stood beneath the fading photographs. Preserved inside it was the first mechanical reeling machine designed by Andrew Napier. Its invention had helped to revolutionize the Japanese silk industry. The machine's cast-iron plating was a decorative work of art, sculpted by Japanese craftsmen in an age when beauty had served function.

Andrew's talent for invention had reasserted itself in his grandson, whose modern-day reeling machines sat bolted to the floor in long rows of glistening steel. Douglas Napier straightened his shoulders, feeling proud of his heritage. "If our grandfathers were alive today, they wouldn't give up," he told the baron. "They'd find some way to get our message across to the bankers."

"Yes, I'm sure that—" Baron Hosokawa was interrupted by a loud clang.

Douglas turned and, with Tadashi following, raced down the hall to a large room where a gigantic loom was being prepared for storage with a coat of grease. A mechanic had dropped some tool down its intricate mechanism. Douglas shouted at the man, then angrily threw off the jacket of his white summer suit and rolled up his shirt-sleeves. He scrambled up the work ladder, then reached down inside the clockwork maze of cogs and gears. Douglas Napier was a passionate man, and a good deal of that passion had always been channeled into his love affair with machines.

Watching his friend, the baron sighed inwardly and flexed his manicured hands, which had never been soiled by grease. Like his grandfather, he detested the clamor of machinery and did not take much enjoyment in the financial end of the business. In his heart, Tadashi Hosokawa cherished the samurai ideals of feudal Japan, when his ancestors had scorned money and never handled it. The economic necessity of engaging in business had turned the Hosokawa barons into silk farmers and merchants. Fujio Hosokawa had restored importance to their family name, but not at the cost of his samurai spirit. His long-held beliefs had lived on through his grandson.

Baron Hosokawa and Douglas Napier had inherited a legacy they were compelled to preserve. Like their grandfathers before them, Tadashi and Douglas formed a perfectly matched partnership in which American drive and technological ingenuity were coupled with Japanese industriousness and a respect for the land that produced the world's finest silk. This balance struck between them as partners still held true, although their dynasty now faltered.

Baron Hosokawa viewed the mill's final production output stacked high against the old brick walls. Fat spools of silk thread and wide bolts of cloth would eventually become kimonos for Japanese of wealth, sashes to add pomp to military uniforms, and flags to be waved at parades.

Silk had financed Japan's industrial revolution and once had been the balance of the country's trade with the West. But following the Great Depression of 1929, the luxury market for Japanese silk had collapsed, and the Japanese economy continued to suffer from that crippling blow. Some of Japan's exported goods were experiencing a boom. Tin windup toys, novelties, and porcelain vases were far cheaper to produce than silk textiles. The export price of raw silk had dropped by fifty percent, and no amount of cost shaving could bring a profit to the company books. America had been Japan's most important customer. The baron and Douglas had kept the mills running, gambling heavily on the future of that powerful nation's economic recovery under President Roosevelt's New Deal. The American market did show some promise of making a rebound, but that might not be for years, and Hosokawa-Napier, Limited's, gamble had drained their coffers dry.

These were calamitous times in which nations had no money to spend on frills. But here and abroad, governments were building up their military defenses. After boldly seizing Manchuria several years before, Japan had walked out of the League of Nations. Its territorial ambitions in China could be realized only by force of arms. Abroad, Adolf Hitler was rearming the Rhineland.

Yes, military-related industries were flourishing, Tadashi Hosokawa mused, passing his hand across the bolts of silk. Light as a feather and strong as steel when skillfully woven on his partner's looms, no other fabric could be manufactured into parachutes. In fact, he and Douglas had invested much of their personal fortunes in developing a prototype of a new parachute. It was now being made and tested by the Karlstadt Works in Germany.

The baron never once doubted the rightness of turning his silk into the material of war. If successful, their parachutes would also be manufactured in Japan and could one day serve to defend his country in a time of crisis. As a samurai loyal to his emperor, assisting to build up the might of the Japanese empire would bring him honor. But Douglas Napier's ambitions for their firm had nothing to do with patriotism.

His friend's only allegiance was to the business of their dynasty, Baron Hosokawa told himself, as he watched Douglas step off the work ladder. After wiping the grease off his hands, Douglas turned on the loom's master switch.

Assured that the loom was working, Douglas abruptly cut the power. Without silk to feed its appetite, the uproar of the machine was purposeless. Slinging his jacket across one shoulder, he approached Tadashi. Mastery over his complex machines had offered some escape from a personal life over which Douglas felt he had no control. Now even the machines had failed him, and he felt betrayed. "Give me one year to reverse the tide, that's all I ask," he railed against the stillness. "God helps those who help themselves, my mother used to say. Well, we've made all the right moves to get ourselves out of a dying market, and I refuse to believe our efforts won't pay off."

"From your mouth to the ears of the gods," Baron Hosokawa said in a reverent tone of voice. "Shizue will be meeting your son when he arrives on Kyushu this afternoon. I've asked my daughter to visit the shrine of our ancestors with Max, to petition the gods for a successful business venture. Perhaps their intervention will open the eyes of our bankers."

Douglas smiled at the mention of his son. "Max took it like a man when I confided what we're up against. The boy's growing up so fast."

"One can't still the hand of time," his partner said. "Wealth in itself is nothing, Douglas. Our true fortune is in the love of our children, and that can't be bought."

"Yes, you're right." Douglas ran his fingers through his hair as a voice echoed back on itself in the cavernous mill.

Their harried office manager was standing in the doorway. "The tax examiners are impatient to begin," he informed the two men.

"There in a moment!" Baron Hosokawa sighed and massaged his eyes. "These tax auditors are vultures, ready to spring at tasty morsels found in our ledgers."

"We've nothing to hide, Tadashi," Douglas said reassuringly. "Keep a cool head. If these pen-pushers from Tokyo decide to play rough, I can handle them. Civil servants have small minds. But forcing us into bankruptcy would cause them to lose the land taxes we pay on our facilities," Douglas continued, hoping to calm his partner's frayed nerves as they walked to a vaultlike steel door built to dampen the roar of the assembly lines. Across its threshold lay their executive offices in which the company's books were about to be scrutinized by a small army of government clerks who now stood bowing at desks stacked tall with ledgers.

Baron Hosokawa mopped sweat from his brow with his handkerchief. The tax examiners settled down behind their desks, adjusting their eyeglasses, fussing over the paper rolls in their adding machines, opening the company ledgers to scan the inked figures in silence. There were certain to be questions directed at both partners, and Douglas Napier anticipated a long afternoon spent in the company of these fussy government clerks.

As he waited, Douglas's thoughts turned to his son, Max, who would be spending his summer on the peaceful Hosokawa lands far to the south of this mill, where their dynasty now faced its greatest challenge.

CHAPTER 2

It was silk the Napier family owed its fortunes to, and seventeen-year-old Maxwell Napier wore a white shirt of the finest quality silk as nobility wore their family crest. As he stood on the deck of a Japanese steamer, the ocean breeze played with the ends of his thick blond hair. His tan Bond Street riding breeches and hand-crafted English boots drew stares from the poorly dressed native passengers, but his disarming smile quickly put them at ease.

Max's was the third generation of Japanese-born American sons in the Napier-Hosokawa dynasty. His boyhood years had been divided between two homes a thousand miles apart. The long winters were spent in Tokyo, while summer vacations were always spent at the Hosokawa home on the island of Kyushu.

It was a two-day journey from Tokyo by train and steamer. As he neared his destination, Max gripped the bow railing, his lean, muscular body stretching with anticipation. The ragged, wave-battered coastline was part of his earliest memories. Now the steamer entered a serene bay, and he could glimpse the distant mountains that rose out of Kyushu's agricultural heartland. Baron Tadashi Hosokawa's valley dominion lay nestled among these mist-shrouded peaks, its land and castle seemingly untouched by time.

Max regarded the dark volcanic rock that rose from the shoals of a quaint centuries-old fishing village. High on the rocky half-moon cliff above, tiny houses peeked through pine and cypress trees molded by the wind. Kyushu's inhabitants favored the color blue, and the pyramiding blue tile roofs of a sacred pagoda seemed to tie the land and sky together.

As the steamer approached the shore, Max combed back his tousled hair and called out to the big man waving at him from the dock. "O-nami!"

Well over six feet and built like a sumo wrestler, O-nami wore a black *happi* jacket, white cotton trousers, and a wide leather belt that seemed to be holding his enormous girth together. This samurai's ancestors had served the Hosokawa barons in feudal Japan, and he himself was regarded as one of the family. O-nami meant "great waves," a name that suited this huge man who barreled toward the steamer as it drew hard against the pier.

As Max stepped onto the pier, O-nami greeted him with an enormous bear hug. Max gasped for breath as O-nami cried, "Ichiban!" greeting Douglas Napier's son with the word used to mean "number one" in all things. "So much more of you than last year."

"Have a heart, O-nami. I'm no match for you!" Max laughed with the friend who now held him at arm's length and regarded him affectionately.

"Hah, you have grown some, but still you must look up to me," O-nami said in his booming voice. He pounded the boy's shoulders, his jovial spirit showing in his twinkling, deep-set eyes. His round, fleshy face caused his features to seem childlike. He wore his jet-black hair in the ancient manner, combed back tight and looped in a topknot. There was more gray in it than the previous summer, Max observed, but the salt added little to his years. "Ah, it is good to have you home again," O-nami said. Although he spoke English well, he felt more comfortable conversing with Max in Japanese. "Give me your baggage." O-nami gathered up the boy's suitcases and set off with a long stride. "Shizue is fetching our horses from the stable."

As they walked, Max scanned the busy street for Baron Hosokawa's daughter and son, who were always on hand to greet him. "Isn't Kimitake with her?"

"No, Ichiban is at home, being punished for his poor grades at school and under orders to spend his vacation studying with private tutors." O-nami showed no favoritism between these number-one sons and heirs to a dynasty. He addressed them both as Ichiban, which often led to confusion. "The baron is so hard on the boy." He made a long face and shrugged. "His son may not be your equal as a scholar, but Ichiban has other fine qualities."

"This past year, Kimitake's had nothing but girls on his mind," Max confided wryly. The two boys were the same age, and as close as blood brothers.

O-nami halted before some shuttered warehouses that faced the main street. "Our supply wagon will take your luggage from here, Ichiban," he said, depositing everything on a deserted loading dock. "What can be keeping Shizue?" he wondered, shielding his eyes to the sun.

HOSOKAWA-NAPIER, LTD. TOKYO-KYOTO-NAGASAKI was painted in Japanese characters and in English letters on sun-bleached wooden signs that squealed on their hinges above the warehouses. Max viewed the dusty loading docks, remembering better summers, when tons of raw silk had rolled out from there to fill the cargo holds of steamers bound for Japanese ports that, in turn, fed the trade routes to Europe and the States. Today the raw silk harvested on the Hosokawa lands mostly gathered dust here and at other depots located near the firm's Nagasaki and Kyoto weaving mills.

With sadness Max observed the long, slow-moving lines of people on the street ahead. They were hoping to sign up for work on the farmlands of Kyushu. His heart went out to them—homeless men, women, and children, blown across the miles with the changing seasons to bend their backs in other men's fields only for enough rice to fill their dinner bowls. "I've never seen so many in search of work," he told O-nami.

"Life grows harder with each passing year." Hands on hips, O-nami sighed heavily, and his large chest sagged. "We have no work for them until the next silk harvest."

In the fall workers would be needed to harvest the Hosokawa mulberry trees, whose leaves would be rich with sap to feed the silkworm moths' insatiable appetites. Seeing the hunger in their faces, Max knew that these people could not wait until then, and he wished he could help them in some way. He watched as they shuffled quietly in lines, carrying their bundled possessions. Those lucky enough to find work were being herded into horsedrawn wagons for their overland journey. It was hot for the beginning of June. Some men had stripped to the waist and tied *haki-machi* around their foreheads to catch the sweat. Women and children, their loose-fitting clothes laundered to threads, shielded their heads from the sun with tattered straw hats and faded cotton bonnets.

Max brightened at the approach of Shizue Hosokawa. She was mounted on a frisky chestnut gelding. In one hand she held the reins of two horses, another chestnut and O-nami's massive black stallion. Shizue sat a horse well. She was wearing a black-and-gray English riding habit tailormade by Japanese seamstresses, and her lustrous raven hair was swept up out of sight beneath a stylish black derby, raked at an angle that showed off her delicate profile. From a distance Shizue Hosokawa might have passed for a woman who had reached the age of consent. It was a ladylike look this beautiful fifteen-year-old girl had recently taken great pains to cultivate.

She reined her horse and dismounted with the regal bearing of a noblewoman. Shizue regarded Maxwell Napier affectionately. She had not seen him since the visit she had made to Tokyo for her birthday early the previous spring, when, for the first time, they had flirted with each other. The boy Shizue had roughhoused with in summers past had suddenly grown into a strikingly handsome young man. Today, her outfit had been chosen to impress him with her own blossoming maturity.

"Max, *o-kaeri-nasai*," Shizue said, welcoming him home. Ordinarily she would have rushed to kiss him on the cheek, but when they'd last met this fond greeting between friends had excited her in a way it had never done before. So instead, she coyly modeled her new riding habit. "It's the latest fashion abroad. I had it copied from the pages of *Vogue*." She was impatient for some compliment to reward her efforts. "Don't be shy, Max. What do you think?"

"Very becoming, Shizue. But isn't it a little dressy? Or have you planned a fox hunt?"

His amused laughter brought a scarlet blush to Shizue's cheeks and put sparks into her large dark eyes. In the past, Max had quite innocently teased the spirited young beauty. But she was no longer the tomboy who insistently tagged after him and her brother, Kimitake, and refused to be excluded from their play. No matter what outrageous challenge the boys had designed to get her out of their hair, Shizue had always persevered. Max admired her spunk. Now she regarded him with a look of womanly displeasure.

"Only kidding. You're very beautiful, Shizue." He said it as if he were making that observation for the very first time. But he had always thought her beautiful, had always seen her as more than just Kimitake's little sister. "It's a smashing outfit." He smiled, at a loss to put into words the emotions he felt. "Am I forgiven?"

"Of course, forgiven." Impulsively Shizue threw her arms around him. All that spring her moods had been as changeable as the winds. At her boarding school in Kyoto, she would pose before the mirror while the emerging woman stood at odds with the spunky girl who had dogged Maxwell Napier's footsteps in summers past. Those bittersweet memories often led to tears. Then she would sprawl across her bed, confessing things to her diary about her new self and her love for Max that started her giggling as she did just now. "Oh, Max, sometimes I take myself too seriously. But you always know how to make me laugh." She kissed his cheek. "There," she said. "Now I've properly welcomed you home."

"Well, since we're handing out kisses," said Max, lowering his face to hers, wanting to kiss her on the lips. But awkwardness stifled his desire, and he settled for kissing her smooth cheek, lingering against it and inhaling the sweet fragrance of lilac water that scented her hair. It was a familiar scent that called up memories. Once Shizue had surprised him with a kiss on the lips. Then she had been only twelve, a girl in pigtails who ran off giggling as he stood dazed by her boldness.

"Mount up, or we will lose the daylight," O-nami told them.

Max reluctantly moved away from Shizue. They exchanged a lingering glance before taking the reins of their horses. Max's chestnut gelding was the twin of Shizue's mount, born three years earlier. They shared a love of horses, as well as a love of the Hosokawa lands and its gracious people, who sang as they worked in the tall wooden houses where the silk was spun. Even as young children, the two had enjoyed sharing many things that did not interest Kimitake.

Max tightened up on the reins of his frisky horse. "Mercury is eager for a run," he told Shizue. As a colt Mercury had winged over high fences, leading the stablehands a merry chase, which had earned him the name of the Roman god.

Shizue's horse had black eyes that sparkled like stars. She had named him Vega, after a star in the Milky Way that shined brightly every summer at the festival of Tanabata. As they mounted, Shizue gave Max a smile. But her smile faded as a baby's cries shifted her attention to the gaunt-faced children among the migrant workers who crowded the village street. "So many hungry children. They suffer most from this depression," she told Max. "Papa telephoned me from Nagasaki. He and your father have decided to shut down our weaving mills. I could hear how heartsick he was over putting the men out of work."

"I know," Max said soberly. "Was there any news from the banks about the loan?"

"Papa didn't say, Max. But he asked me to help by petitioning the gods for a successful business venture. I felt you'd want to pray at the shrine with me this afternoon."

"Sure." Their eyes met, and Max put thoughts of family business from his mind. This would be their last carefree summer together. After another year of school, he would enter Harvard with Kimitake. He dreaded the prospect of leaving Shizue and Japan.

O-nami's stallion grew skittish. "Let us be on our way," he said, turning his mount from the village to lead them up a steep, narrowing path that the horses had to climb single file.

As Shizue followed Max, she observed how his silk shirt clung tightly across his muscular back and broad shoulders. Not until that day had she been struck by the sensuous powers of this fabric that united their two families.

Soon the village and the sea were behind them. It was yet some distance to the shrine, and as they rode, an ever-changing panorama unfolded before them. Locusts buzzed in luxuriant fields, where only the mushroom-shaped straw hats of peasants could be seen floating magically through the tall grass. Here and there bright pools of wildflowers painted the mountainsides, and low-drifting clouds rimmed the cone of a slumbering volcano. On rolling foothills neatly mapped out with row upon row of leafy plants, women wearing bonnets and cotton aprons tended Kyushu's prized green tea.

Life here seemed little changed from ages past, when Shizue's warrior ancestors had marched to battle along the precipitous mountain pass their sure-footed horses now climbed. Once they were through the pass, O-nami suggested resting the horses. As Max dismounted, the wind billowed his unbuttoned shirt, exposing his well-developed chest. Seeing this, Shizue sighed. Max helped her dismount, then stood regarding her. He had a rather boyish grin on his face.

"Well, Shizue, it looks like another summer of fun." He smiled, but her face grew serious.

"My, it's hot," Shizue said, and removed her gabardine jacket and the ascot at her throat, then folded them across her saddle. She found herself unable to meet the gaze of his clear blue eyes.

While her noble samurai family engaged in the industry of a modern world, Shizue still remained bound to the traditions they had lived by in centuries past. This drew a fine line between the Hosokawas and the Napiers, who had never mixed their blood. And yet the love welling inside Shizue for Max Napier felt so natural and right.

When the horses had drunk from a nearby stream, O-nami urged the youngsters to remount. His stallion took the lead, and the riders galloped off through woods of tall cedar that splintered the afternoon light.

Max slowed to allow Shizue's gelding to climb an uphill trail beside him. He could not help observing how her tailored silk blouse clung to her breasts. Feeling awkward, Max said the first thing to enter his mind. "Have you made many new friends at school?"

"Oh, a few. They're all nice girls but very immature," Shizue said, running her tongue across her lips to make them sparkle. "I didn't want to leave home, but Papa said it would do me good to associate with other young ladies of breeding, and I could only bow to his wishes." Shizue's mother had died some years before, and until the previous year, her father had kept her at home with him, where she was schooled by private tutors. "My finishing school at Kyoto is such a bore," Shizue continued. "We're taught the proper things to one day please our husbands. Everything but how to cook, which is considered beneath our stations." Her shoulders lifted on a weary sigh. "We're treated like silly idiots who aren't capable of thinking beyond marriage and babies."

"I'll bet you're the prettiest idiot there." Max laughed, and she smiled at him sweetly. He wanted to say so much more, but the love shining for him in her eyes brought a lump to his throat. "At my school the curriculum is tough. Only those who make high grades will be admitted to the universities," he said, lacking the courage to speak his heart. "I feel sorry for your brother, being cooped up studying all summer. Kimitake would get better grades if his head wasn't so easily turned by girls. He has a way with them, and not one pretty face escapes him."

"And you? Hasn't any pretty face distracted you from study?" Shizue inquired lightly, secretly dying for his answer. "Be honest with me."

"Only yours, Shizue," he confessed with feeling. "The spring dragged on. I couldn't wait to see you again. Did you think of me?"

"Yes, often." She could not help blushing. Nervously she smoothed the wisps of hair at the nape of her neck. Stern tutors had instructed her in the obligations owed her noble lineage and had attempted to curb her spirit. They had told her there was folly in being a headstrong woman and that her heart must never rule over her good judgment. But Max's desiring eyes now challenged all that. "Oh, dear, the sun's already turned your face pink," she said, changing the subject. "You should have worn a hat. If only mine weren't so small, I'd give it to you."

Max rubbed his cheek and smiled. "The Napier men don't burn. We tan like a bird in the oven."

The woods opened to a broad sweep of meadowland combed by mountain breezes. Farmers signaled the riders to halt while a convoy of mechanized tractors roared across the dirt road ahead. Their steel engine heads were stamped with the Mitsudara brand. Shizue knew the powerful industrialist who manufactured them, and, irritated, she looked away as the noisy intruders drove past. Lord Daisetz Mitsudara was more than just a friend of her father's. Back through the ages and until the abolishment of feudalism, the Hosokawa barons had served the Mitsudara clan. Her staunchly traditionalist father still held with the old samurai ties of love and implicit obedience owed to his daimyo. As a result, the Hosokawas socialized with their lord while a current of subservience ran beneath the surface.

The Mitsudara tractors reminded Shizue of her intense dislike for that man. Until the year before, her family had always resided in a wing of the Napier mansion when visiting Tokyo. But on her last birthday, the lord had asked them to be guests at his sprawling Tokyo home, which reminded Shizue of a dark, gloomy palace. Baron Hosokawa had been flattered by the invitation, but Shizue had hated the idea of being under the same roof with Lord Mitsudara. His eyes had regarded Shizue as though she were some rare object he wished to add to his family treasures.

One afternoon she had come upon her father and the lord huddled together in the garden like conspirators. Before they had seen her standing there, she had overheard the lord speak her name and that of his only son, Jiro, a cadet at the military academy. Then both fathers had noticed her and suddenly lapsed into silence, staring at her in the most unsettling way. It had not been her place to question what lay behind their partronizing smiles, but she could not forget the incident. Traditionally, Japanese marriages were arranged between consenting fathers of suitable families. She was not yet of age to be pledged in marriage, and the Mitsudaras were far above her in station. Still, the possibility of such a match with the lord's son gave her a chill.

Just then Max startled her with his touch. "What's this?" she asked him.

Leaning from his saddle, Max stuck a yellow wildflower in her derby hatband and cocked his head. "Something to brighten up your gloomy face." He grinned.

"How sweet," Shizue said, and smiled. She touched the flower's petals, cheered by Max's simple gift plucked from the hillside.

"What were you thinking about?" he asked.

"Oh, nothing important." She returned his smile. Lord Mitsudara's ugly tractors plowed up meadowland, flushing birds into flight, and she was determined not to let any further thoughts of that awful man darken this fine June day.

Soon all signposts of civilization vanished, and the riders were swallowed up in a wilderness of spectacular beauty. This was Hosokawa land, a forest preserved against the hand of progress, untraveled except by monks and wise old hermits, who came to meditate and to gather herbs. The overhanging branches of trees threw a canopy over the path. The song of cicadas vibrated in the still air, and the crystal water of mountain springs trickled down through shaded areas of lush fern. The riders drew up under dappled pools of sunlight, dismounted, and allowed their horses to drink at a rocky stream, where they knelt to quench their own thirst with cupped hands.

Max splashed water on his face and ran his wet hands through his hair. "What I wouldn't give for a swim."

"That must wait until we have visited the shrine to pay respects to the *kami*," said O-nami. He hoisted himself onto the saddle, then led his companions away through the stillness of the forest.

"Listen," Shizue said quietly. She heard laughter in the bubbling brooks, voices whispering in the rustling leaves. She knew that benevolent presences were watching over them. From earliest childhood she had known the *kami* spirits who dwelled in these clusters of mossy rocks, haunting the age-twisted trees and taking flight with the mountain mists that drifted down through the peaceful forest. *Kami* were the spirits of the earthly departed and those of innumerable deities who shared life alongside the living. This ancient Shinto belief gave Shizue a sense of permanence in a world fraught with uncertainty. To her *kami* were not fairy-tale creatures. Affirmations of faith in their existence were found throughout Japan at countless shrines erected wherever their special aura could be sensed.

"I must change into something more suitable for petitioning the *kami*," Shizue said "O-nami, did you remember to pack my kimono in your saddlebag?"

"To be honest, I would have left home without it if not for Yufugawo's watchful eye." Laughing, O-nami slapped his leather saddlebags. "Ah, what a good wife she is."

Max and Shizue laughed with him. Yufugawo was, indeed, a good wife to the baron's majordomo, and very dear to both Shizue and Max. Shizue expertly guided her horse down a steep mountain trail to the dense thicket near the valley floor, and Max and O-nami followed. Through the trees they could glimpse the shrine only a short distance away.

"I'll change clothes here," she said, dismounting. O-nami handed over his saddlebags. "You two stand watch."

Max bowed in the saddle. "Honored to guard your chastity, Hosokawa-*san*. No Peeping Toms will get past me."

Shizue struck a dignified pose, then marched into the thicket. She laughed softly to herself over Max's joke. The thought of him stealing a peek while she disrobed excited her. As children they had bathed naked with their parents in the steaming tubs of the Hosokawa castle *ofuru*, where business and family matters were discussed. That was the custom.

The tradition. But Max's American-born mother had never once shared the bath. All those years Angela Napier had lived in Japan aloof to its customs and people. She had been educated abroad, was fluent in French and German. Yet she hardly spoke a word of Japanese—or pretended not to. Shizue suspected that the woman understood more of the language than she let on. No matter, she liked Angela Napier very much despite her cool facade. So did the baron, and that was that.

As for bathing naked with Max, her father had put an end to that custom three years before, when Shizue's breasts first began to develop. Baron Hosokawa had explained that she had reached an age when girls must display a certain modesty, for older boys were naturally curious. Now, as she undressed, Shizue heard a sound and quickly folded both arms across her breasts, then glanced out through the dense thicket. It was only a doe, startled by her movements. Shizue smiled. Max was too much the gentleman to steal a peek, she decided, and hurried to dress.

Gold threads wove a delicate iris pattern in the white kimono that Shizue took from O-nami's saddlebags. Woven of the richest silk, it had belonged to her mother, who had died when Shizue was barely six. The exquisite kimono, with its delicate flower pattern, was one of many handed down to her, along with her mother's priceless jewelry. They were keepsakes reserved for special occasions.

The proper method of dressing in the kimono was considered an art, and Shizue wound the vermilion obi around her waist, artfully fashioning it into a splendid bow at her back.

Next she arranged her hair. Shining and black, it was the texture and sheen of spun silk. It had never been cut and cascaded well below her waist. That morning O-nami's wife, Yufugawo, had painstakingly braided and coiled it up into a crown so that it could be worn under her riding hat. Shizue disliked the childish braids. After unraveling them, she used her mother's delicate tortoiseshell combs to create a soft, womanly hairdo that might have been worn by ladies of the court in some bygone age.

Tucking her fan inside the folds of her obi, she stepped into lacquered wood clogs with white silk thongs and bent to unwrap the scarf that protected a twig cut from the sacred *sakaki* tree. Around its delicate leaves she had folded zigzagging strips of white paper. This twig would be her symbolic offering to the *kami*.

As she emerged from the thicket, Max was dazzled by her beauty. O-nami blinked as if he had seen a ghost. "Each year you become more like your mother." His voice was wistful, and Shizue looked away.

"Do you really think so?" she asked demurely. Indeed, everyone in the castle household had become aware of Shizue's striking resemblance to the late baroness, who had been much loved by them all.

Shizue handed O-nami a sum of money wrapped in satiny white paper tied with flaxen string. Such material gifts were always accepted in advance when requesting the performance of special rites. "Ride ahead with Max to alert the priests so they can prepare."

Max shook his head and grinned. "I'll walk with you."

O-nami started off alone, tethering their riderless horses behind his black stallion. Max walked slowly beside Shizue, observing her hips swaying sensuously beneath the silk. He recalled her being dressed in a child's kimono at parties in the castle gardens not so very long ago. Then she had been merely a little girl who played at being the grand lady, flirting with him from behind her tiny fan. Now Shizue was a young noblewoman, proudly marching to worship the ancient gods on the sacred ground of her family's ancestral shrine.

The country road they walked along wandered through quaint, somnolent villages where the Hosokawas had long ago carved their domain out of the wilderness. Max could almost see their ghostly shadows wielding their long swords in combat, spilling the blood of their enemies at the gates of the shrine's *tori-i* archway. As they reached it, Shizue seemed to draw inside herself. The wooden gateway separated the sacred from the secular world. Passing with Shizue beneath its horizontal crossbeam, Max felt the power of the ages separating them. He respected her deep beliefs. But Shinto was a mystical religion only a Japanese could embrace, and he did not share her devotion.

Shizue prepared to present herself to the enshrined spirits venerated within the compound's low cypress-wood walls. A Japanese worshipped his ancestors because his existence was owed to all those who had come before him. Pausing on the path, Shizue faced the small burial ground where the Hosokawa war dead of centuries past were interred. She bowed in solemn homage. These days, only priests who served this shrine enjoyed the honor of burial in its sacred grounds, upon which stood wooden pavilions used to prepare offerings of food for festive celebrations. A young priest appeared, wearing his formal white robes and tall black hat, and carrying a wooden bucket, spilling water in his haste. O-nami puffed behind him and waved to signal that everything had been arranged.

The main building was a simple structure made of cedar. It consisted of an offering hall, sanctuary, and inner chamber, housed under a thatched roof that was pierced by the wooden horns of its crisscrossing rafters. A flight of stairs led to the offering hall, and O-nami sat on a stair and removed his boots.

"Make haste," he whispered to Shizue. "The chief priest is feeling his years today and longs to return to his bed."

The young priest drew water from his ablution bucket with a bamboo dipper, trickled it over the worshippers' fingertips, then handed them pieces of white paper to dry their hands.

Dirt was an evil disliked by the gods, and after Max received the symbolic purification rite, he left his dusty boots by the stairs. "I don't have a coin for the offering box," he told O-nami, who dug one from his leather purse.

Breezes strummed a rope made of twisted rice straw and paper streamers which hung between the entrance pillars. O-nami's topknot barely cleared this sacred *shimenawa*, which dispelled evil spirits. One's prayers were to be focused on personal protection from misfortune. But Max could not center his thoughts on anything but Shizue as she entered the offering hall in her white *tabi* socks. She tossed a copper coin into the slatted wooden box there and rang the bell that hung above it, an act that served to calm the mind. Inclining her head, she offered a silent prayer, then bowed twice and twice clapped her hands to acknowledge the *kami* presence.

Shizue was like another person, unattainable to Max in this hushed, otherworldly atmosphere. With the sacred *sakaki* twig solemnly clasped between her hands, she glided toward the sanctuary. She seemed to be almost in a trance.

The sanctuary walls were bare of ornaments. An offering table constructed of raw cypress sat before two sealed doors that were kept locked except for special rites. The chief priest was already there attending to the duties of his high office. Well past eighty, he had a gaunt face that hung like a wrinkled sack beneath his tall black hat. Once the worshippers had seated themselves on straw mats, he muttered something to his female assistant, who held the gift of money O-nami had ridden ahead to deliver. A young maiden of the village, she wore a vermilion skirt under her white kimono. A length of black hair, tied with vermilion ribbon, trailed down her back as she placed Baron Hosokawa's generous donation on the offering table.

The old priest stood over Shizue, clearing his throat several times before his raspy voice broke the stillness. "Your father, the baron, is well?" She nodded and the priest regarded Max. The priest's pin-dot eyes grew cold as he asked, "And your parents, Napier-*san*?"

"*Hai*, they are well, *guji-san*," Max replied evenly. He was the fourth generation of his family to kneel here and display their respect for the Japanese gods. Yet in the eyes of this aged priest, he remained a *gaijin*—a foreigner. Elsewhere in Japan Max was at peace and in harmony with the surroundings of his birthplace. But in this barren sanctum sanctorum of the Shinto religion, he felt alien. Visiting the temple never failed to be an abrasive, wrenching experience. Today he had the urge to seize Shizue by the hand and flee that musty fortress of tradition. But the pull her religion exerted on her ran deep. There was a beatific expression on her oval face like that of a nun sworn to the holy vows of a mystical order. Max lowered his gaze, attempting to still his heart. Each second seemed an hour in the oppressive silence.

Petitioning the *kami* for a successful business venture required a formal ceremony that differed from province to province. Here sticks of incense were lighted to begin the rites. Inhaling the incense, Shizue closed her eyes. The musky scents invoked for her the presence of her ancestors.

The chief priest removed his purification wand from its wooden stand and faced the worshippers one by one, waving its streamers of white paper and flax over his bony shoulders from left to right, then back again. As always, Shizue lost all sense of time and place as she stared up at him through the haze of burning incense while his wand stirred the ribboning layers of smoke. Then the worshippers prostrated themselves, and the old priest bowed deeply as he swung open the doors to the inner chamber. He uttered an elongated, ghostly *ooing* sound, which never failed to send chills up Shizue's spine. Sacred objects symbolic of the divine *kami* presence resided within this inner chamber. It was not permitted to view them, however, and a heavy white silk curtain remained drawn across the entranceway.

The worshippers sat upright as the young priest joined voices with his elder, incanting prayers in classical Japanese, a language understood only by scholars. Their indecipherable words were buried in antiquity, their voices guttural sobs that rose and fell with the smoking sticks of incense.

Shizue felt herself floating on the tides of litanies passed down through the ages, while her mind spoke the prayer learned at her mother's knee. "Mine is the mother seed through which the Hosokawa bloodline flows as an unbroken river. Like the willow, I must bow to the wind, but always so with dignity. I am the brightest flower in my father's garden. No less samurai than my brother, at birth I was blessed with the deeper dimension only a woman can know. I call upon the *kami* to guide my innermost thoughts, so that I may be worthy of their love." The familiar words flowed on through her mind as smoky streamers of incense permeated the sanctuary.

Next, the old priest was handed a printed scroll. After unrolling it with a ritualistic flourish, he began to read aloud the special prayer that included the date and names of those in attendance. When he had finished, Shizue was jarred out of her trance by his hand tapping her shoulder. Bowing low, he whispered a reminder of the duties she had quite forgotten while floating on the calm sea of her beloved mother's memory. Piously, she stepped forward to place her sacred twig on the offering table. As the most important worshipper, she presented the gift to the gods on behalf of Max and O-nami, who remained seated behind her. Then she bowed, offering a silent prayer for their dynasty to prosper as it had in the past.

Her gaze went to the brocade banners mounted on wooden poles that flanked the offering table. Gold silk brocade bags attached to one standard contained a metal mirror and a *magatama*, a string of polished stone beads. A short sword also encased in gold silk brocade hung from the second standard. Shinto was the national cult. The mikado was worshipped as a living god descended from the heavens, and these symbols of his imperial regalia were treated as sacred objects. Shizue had been taught to regard them as symbolic of virtues. The sword stood for courage, the jewels for charity, and the mirror for wisdom, since it honestly reflected what it saw.

Worthy virtues difficult to attain, thought Shizue, resuming her place beside Max. His clear blue eyes mirrored both her youthful vanity and her beauty. Looking deep within them, she could not remember a single moment when she had not loved him. Lately she had spent far too much time at her mirror without seeking the wisdom to temper her heart's desire.

The incense sticks sputtered and died. She prostrated herself while the chief priest bowed deeply, once again uttering his spine-tingling *ooing* sound as he closed the inner chamber doors.

The priests silently withdrew, leaving the young maiden to perform the *naorai*. At festivals the worshippers would eat together with the *kami* at elaborate feasts where there was much drinking and laughter. But for today's rite, the sacred feast consisted merely of sipping rice wine served them by the young maiden.

The sanctuary was hot, and Max longed to be free of its walls. Taking Shizue by the hand, he said, "The ceremony is over," and began gently pulling her away. She followed him in silence; the ceremony still held her in its thrall. Her Shinto faith was strong, thought Max. But like most other Japanese, the Hosokawa family also worshipped in the Buddhist faith. He looked up at the rooftop of the local Buddhist temple, which was set on a hill overlooking the shrine grounds. It was a far more cheerful house of worship, he reflected, a place for dancing at the summer festival of Obon.

The Napier family was Protestant, but Max was more Buddhist than Christian, and the same could be said of his father. Their family tree had taken root in the East long ago. At times he felt more like a Japanese than an American.

He reached his arms to the sky and inhaled the fresh mountain air. "It's good to be in the open. I spend the winters dreaming of Kyushu."

Shizue smiled in response, and Max was happy to see that her solemn mood had broken.

"Let's buy a fortune," she said, stopping at the wooden stall nestled just inside the *tori-i* gateway. A fortune box had been placed among the religious objects on display. Before leaving the compound, it was customary to draw a number from the box and receive a printed oracle. "My friend will pay," she told the peddler.

The elderly man's eyes twinkled with enjoyment as his customers drew numbers from the box. Max handed the man a yen note. "Have you no coins, *danna*?" he asked Max, holding the yen in one shaky hand. "Business is poor, and I cannot change a bill so large."

"Sorry, nothing smaller. But please, accept it as payment for your services." He bowed, not wanting it to appear an act of charity that would bring the man loss of face. He and Shizue were given folded paper oracles.

Shizue quickly unfolded hers. "Good fortune is foretold!" she brightly exclaimed. "What does yours say, Max?"

He looked at it, smiled, and said, "The same." If bad fortune were foretold, Shizue would buy charms to guard him against harm.

Max twisted his paper oracle around a twig of an old nettle tree. Its branches were decorated with the good fortunes received by others who had visited the shrine. It was believed that by leaving the fortunes there, one petitioned the gods for their fulfillment. To Max it was a charming Japanese custom. Shizue, however, took the matter seriously and stretched for the highest branch she could reach. Ever since they were children, no branch but the highest would do for attaching her paper fortunes. As always, she twisted the paper around it, then closed her eyes to make a secret wish.

Watching her, Max felt a sense of protectiveness. His earliest memories were of guarding Shizue against scraped knees and elbows, breaking her falls from trees, and drying her salty tears with his fingers. He was the older, the man, and she had always followed his lead. Perhaps she always would, he thought.

Quite suddenly, he and the baron's daughter had become friends in love. Having made her wish, Shizue opened her eyes to Max, and they shined with love for him. He glanced away, painfully aware that their lives were united by fragile threads. She was a Hosokawa and a samurai, dressed for worship at her ancestral shrine. He was a Napier and an outsider, bound by the rules laid down by his own ancestors. The dynasty of their parents had been founded on a covenant of mutual respect for the two different races. That covenant forbade their children from ever becoming more than friends.

"I wish I knew what you were thinking," Shizue ventured in a small voice.

Max walked beside her under the *tori-i* archway, leaving the spirit world. But Shizue's ties to the tradition of ancient Japan could not be left on the path behind them, and the word *love* stuck in Max's throat. "Do you really place so much faith in wishes?"

"Why, of course," Shizue answered, disappointed by his reply. The look on Max's face told her what he had really been thinking. As they walked down the quiet country road, she snapped open her painted silk fan and fluttered it with girlish impatience. "Oh, not that I believe wishing will make it so," she told him. "But wishes help set my mind to some goal." She had just wished that Max would boldly take her in his arms and send tradition up in puffs of smoke. There was a sweet huskiness to her voice as she said, "Life is pointless unless you decide what it is you want and go after it. No matter the challenge. I sound so brave. But from the moment you arrived, I haven't been brave at all. Perhaps some things can't be wished for—or hoped for, Max. Your eyes tell me how hard it is not to speak of what both of us are thinking."

Max desperately wanted to embrace Shizue. Instead, he put his hands inside his pockets, thinking it was wrong of him to encourage their desires. "We know each other too well to lie about our feelings." He felt confused, and suddenly apprehensive.

"You're so very beautiful," he said softly, then bent down and covered her lips with his.

Everything they felt they expressed in a long, lingering kiss, which stirred the promise of a glorious union. At last Shizue drew away and leaned her head on Max's chest. She sighed, dazzled by the power of her first kiss.

Then the flapping sounds of priestly robes broke the spell. The young priest who had officiated at the rite appeared waving a scroll. He bowed and held it out to Shizue. "The record of your petition to the gods, Hosokawa-*san*. In his haste the chief priest carried it away to his bed. Please convey his warmest regards to the baron and his wishes of good fortune in your family's new business venture."

"Thank you, *guji-san*." Shizue accepted the parchment with trembling hands. The *tori-i* gateway behind them cast a dark shadow across the ground at her feet. Suddenly Shizue felt imprisoned by forces that could never be challenged.

Seeing the expression in her eyes, Max shivered. Her silence spoke of obligations she might never escape. He longed to reach out to her, to kiss her again. But another kiss would not bring down the walls of tradition.

Suddenly Shizue turned away. "Come," she said softly. "O-nami is waiting."

At the Nagasaki weaving mill, Douglas and Baron Hosokawa had grown short on patience while enduring the tax examiners' questions, which were spaced out between long periods of silence broken only by the clattering sounds of adding machines. Unraveled spools of white paper littered the floor. As yet not quite half the company's books had been picked over by the tireless auditors.

"Your wife is on the telephone, Napier-*san*," the office manager announced, holding the receiver out to Douglas.

"All right," Douglas said curtly. He carried the telephone as far from the auditors as the cord would stretch. "Angela, this is bad timing. Is it anything important, or can it wait?"

Douglas's wife responded in a strained voice. "I'm concerned over you, darling. Isn't that important enough to take a few moments away from business? Has there been any word from the bank?"

"Another turndown," Douglas answered. Hearing her sigh, he said, "Stop worrying. I'll pull us through."

"Yes, I believe you will. But I'm under a great deal of stress, and it's lonely for me here in Tokyo with Max on Kyushu and you there in Nagasaki. I miss you, darling." Angela paused and waited for a response. There was none. Her voice sounded hard as she broke the silence. "The Karlstadts cabled us from Germany. They've booked passage to Japan and are scheduled to arrive the second week in July. Oh, I can't wait to see our friends. Tokyo is stifling. How I loathe the summers here. If only we hadn't been forced to cancel our vacation abroad."

"Listen, Angela, I've got my hands full." Douglas glanced over his shoulder at the examiners who had gathered around their chief and were conferring in hushed voices. "Go shopping or something to take your mind off things," he told his wife. "It isn't the end of the world."

Angela Napier laughed nervously. "Perhaps you're right. A new hat might help to sweep away the blues. See that you eat properly, Douglas—and give Tadashi my love."

"Yes, dear. Talk to you later." Douglas hung the receiver on its hook. Angela's concern was wasted on him. His wife had been born to wealth, and he felt she was terrified of losing her social status. She never traveled with him on business; it was an arrangement Douglas had encouraged for reasons of his own. The cable sent from Germany was uplifting news that he shared with his partner. "This means Heinz Karlstadt has achieved our goal and is bringing some tangible results to Japan."

Baron Hosokawa loosened his necktie. "I can only hope for the best," he said. "We can't dig deeper into our pockets without risking everything."

Douglas settled on the high stool at his draftman's table. They had gambled heavily on developing their new parachute at the manufacturing facilities of the Karlstadt Parachute Works in Germany. But even the successful results of that gamble might not guarantee them a loan.

The government auditors ended their conference. This time all their questions were addressed to Baron Hosokawa. Japan had a class system much like that of England. Under the Emperor Meiji, the classes had been redefined and established by law into the nobility, the gentry, and common people. The baron's noble lineage still commanded respect in the tax vultures' eyes. He met their questions wearing his charming smile.

Douglas Napier glanced down at his drawings of new machinery that needed capital to be built. An American newspaper printed in Japan for the U.S. community lay beside the sketches. The *San Francisco Guardian* was folded back to a picture of Adolf Hitler. The Führer currently enjoyed great popularity with the world press and often granted interviews such as this one carried by an international wire service.

Hitler spoke warmly of his ties with Japan. Communism was a threat to both their nations, he stated, and they were negotiating an alliance to deter its spread. Germany's chancellor made good use of the press as a platform for bolstering his image as a man of peace who had no ambitions on the territories of his European neighbors. Germany's defenses were only being strengthened to repel Communist aggression, and Hitler promised he would fight that enemy until the bitter end.

Douglas threw the newspaper into the wastebasket. He felt uneasy about selling his talents to Nazi Germany, even though it was now his only customer. There was no market for his combat parachutes in

America, Great Britain, or France. The military armaments of those democracies were hopelessly obsolete, yet those same countries were not interested in newer, up-to-date equipment. Only Hitler's general staff seemed to recognize the advantages of paratroops in modern warfare.

It was on his vacation abroad in the summer of 1935 that Douglas had finally bowed to reality and entered a partnership with his friend, the German industrialist Heinz Karlstadt. At the time Douglas had rationalized that he was in no position to argue against an overwhelming flood of enthusiasm for Germany's dictator, who was credited with restoring order and economic stability to the fatherland. Economic circles in America and Great Britain welcomed Hitlerism. Such luminaries as the Du Pont chemical dynasty of America sought contracts with him, and other foreign businesses were gathered at the Führer's doorstep, competing for contracts. Hosokawa-Napier, Limited's, partnership with the German-owned Karlstadt Parachute Works granted them an edge in Hitler's game of playing one foreign investor against another.

But perhaps the Führer was not all he claimed to be, Douglas worried, rolling down the sleeves of his white silk shirt. He noticed a tiny spot of grease on the cloth. Silk had always held a fascination for him. Its versatile nature challenged his engineering skills, and he never tired of giving the fabric new shape, new weaves and textures. The fashioning of its threads into parachutes demanded a strength and resiliency that offered his greatest challenge. And yet he felt uncomfortable shaping the Hosokawa silk into parachutes for Adolf Hitler. He had a foreboding about that dark little man, and he did not trust him.

Suddenly Douglas was jarred alert by the tax examiners' abrasive voices. He looked questioningly at his partner, who threw up his hands. "I'm at a loss, Douglas. Perhaps you can satisfy these gentlemen."

"Well, gentlemen, have you found some error in our books?" Douglas masked his anger behind a smiling front as he came forward to stand over the chief examiner. "Kindly allow me to set your mind at ease." He slid an open ledger out from under the man's nose. "These figures are honest. You can't squeeze blood from a stone, and it's a pointless waste of our time and of yours to question what's clearly set down here in ink. Mostly red ink, you'll observe." He rippled the pages of inked figures into a red blur. "Hosokawa-Napier, Limited, has nothing left but its shares. Privately owned stock. Worthless paper until the mills are reopened. And they will be reopened soon, paying their fair share of taxes as in the past." Douglas closed one ledger and gently slid it back across the desk. "My partner and I wouldn't jeopardize our honor by cheating the government of a few yen."

The man squinted up from behind his thick glasses. "Our government has no wish to add to your business misfortune, Napier-*san*. We do not question your honesty, but a thorough audit must be done." He looked to the baron and shook his head. "The law is the law, Hosokawa-*san*."

"Of course one can't shirk one's duty." Tadashi poured himself a glass of water and nearly choked on it as a liveried chauffeur stepped inside the office. There was another entrance to the mill for the office workers, and the chauffeur had entered through it. "Yamaguchi—what brings you here?"

"Hosokawa-*san*." Removing his gray cap, the chauffeur bowed. "Lord Mitsudara wishes to see you and Napier-*san* at his office. Now, if it is convenient," he added, bowing again.

The baron exchanged a look of shock with Douglas. His lord had always been cool toward his American partner. "I know Lord Mitsudara doesn't like to be kept waiting, Yamaguchi," he said nervously. "But we're in the midst of an audit."

The chief examiner quickly rose to his feet. "Please, Baron, I do not think we will have further need of you. My respects to Mitsudara-*sama*. Please, do not keep him waiting."

Douglas put on his jacket as he hurried outside with his partner. "The lord must have watched us close the mill from his ivory tower."

Baron Hosokawa nodded. Two Rolls-Royce limousines sat at the curb. The baron's limousine was an inheritance from his father, and its sleek black chassis evoked more affluent times.

The Rolls-Royce that Lord Mitsudara had sent for them was custom-made. Its grillwork and interior appointments were gold plated, and the Mitsudara crest was embossed in gold on the door, which was now being held open by the chauffeur. Douglas eased back against the soft leather upholstery and eyed his friend's stoic profile. A glass partition between them and the driver made it safe to speak without being overheard. "After years of ignoring me, I wonder what's on the lord's mind," Douglas said. "Summoning us together can't be in the nature of a social call."

Baron Hosokawa's posture remained stiff. "We'll know what's on his mind soon enough."

CHAPTER 3

The limousine glided silently to the Mitsudara Steel and Arms Works. Douglas looked out his window at the impressive mass of buildings that dominated Nagasaki's industrial landscape. Daisetz Mitsudara's armaments supplied Japan's expanding garrisons in northern China; his engines ran Japan's industry; and his tentacles even reached across the sea to claim a large share of Manchuria's rich mineral deposits.

Lord Mitsudara was one of a small group of entrepreneurs whose *zaibatsu*—business cartels—controlled Japan's wealth. The source of the lord's *zaibatsu* was the Mitsudara Bank. However, for personal reasons, Baron Hosokawa had refused to call upon his lord's friendship to save the silk mills.

This was Douglas's first invitation to pass through the steel gates of the Mitsudara corporate headquarters. "It's even more impressive at close range," he observed. "All this power in the hands of one man. It must be an awesome responsibility."

"The power comes to Lord Mitsudara naturally, through his lineage, Douglas. But his great wealth was earned through cunning."

As the limousine braked to a stop, Douglas gripped his friend's arm. "He's after something. We're in a tight spot, Tadashi, but I don't expect you to compromise your honor."

"Oh, I'm sure it won't come to that." As the chauffeur opened the door, Baron Hosokawa pushed himself up from his seat. "No need to show us the way, Yamaguchi," he said, straightening his necktie.

Lord Mitsudara was a man of exquisite taste. A classical Japanese garden beautified the courtyard, and a high-tiered building resembling a pagoda housed his executive offices. His staff, all wearing kimonos, bowed as Douglas and Tadashi walked to the carved teakwood doors of an elevator. Its female operator kept her eyes lowered during the slow ascent. She was quite lovely, as were the two young women who greeted Douglas and Tadashi at the elevator, then escorted them down corridors decorated with flower arrangements. When they reached the lord's office, the two women knelt to remove the guests' shoes, exchanging them for straw sandals. Then they slid open the ebony-framed shoji. Beyond lay a vast room whose traditional furnishings created an ambiance of serene and understated luxury.

Lord Daisetz Mitsudara sat on a pillow behind his low ebony desk and made no effort to rise. A man in his fifties, he had a flabby body due to his sedentary ways. In his youth he had been an attractive man. Age and the stresses of power had made his face a fierce, scowling mask that was scored with deep creases around his eyes and down the length of his flaccid cheeks. His graying head remained bent over some papers while his owlish aide bowed and gestured for the visitors to seat themselves on plum-colored shantung pillows. The lord wore a black silk kimono decorated with the crest of his ancient clan.

Humming under his breath, Lord Mitsudara used a sharp-tipped bamboo brush to sign a document, which he handed to his aide, who was then dismissed. After the doors slid shut, the lord looked up at Baron Hosokawa and gave him a sparse smile. "Tadashi, how good of you to come. And you as well, Mr. Napier." His bushy eyebrows arched disdainfully as he addressed Douglas. He removed his thick reading glasses and said, "So. The burdens of business are heavy today." Rising on a groan, he circled the desk in his white *tabi* socks. "A cigar is in order. My physician says they will be the death of me. But the good doctor does not have an empire to run, and a man must have some rewards." Lord Mitsudara offered cigars from the gold humidor on his desk. "Havana," he said.

The baron accepted one and inhaled its aroma. "Excellent quality, my lord."

The lord's downturned mouth showed displeasure. "Why so formal? I asked you here as a friend, Tadashi. For some time now, I've kept silent while you struggled on alone. Tadashi's pride and honor are at stake, I thought. Otherwise, he would have come to me, rather than seek the help of common strangers." His nasal voice underscored the word *common*. He paused, smoothing back wisps of gray hair on his balding head. "Now that you've been forced to shut down the mills, I felt compelled to take action. As your lord and your friend, it's my obligation to spare you from total disaster and the inevitable loss of face."

"Business and friendship are a bad mix, Daisetz," the baron said. Then he added quickly, "Naturally, I appreciate your good intentions. But things aren't as serious as all that."

"What I'm about to propose isn't a handout, Tadashi. Money is tight, and I intend to drive a hard bargain," Lord Mitsudara said testily, then turned to offer Douglas a cigar. "Mr. Napier?"

"Thank you, I don't smoke," he said, eager to hear more but sensitive to the baron's discomfort. His partner was tongue-tied by pride, so Douglas spoke for him. "I assume the lord knows our true situation and it's useless putting up a front."

"Exactly so, Napier-*san*." Lord Mitsudara used a gold cigar clipper, then rolled the tip of his Havana between his thick lips. He held its blunt end to the desk lighter's flame. Finally, he spoke. "You plead with the banks in vain, gentlemen. All of them lack the vision to finance your new venture." Pulling on the cigar, he prolonged the tension before speaking again. "Mr. Napier's partnership in a Japanese firm is most displeasing to the banks' boards of directors. There is much anti-American sentiment in business these days, Napier-*san*. We sink ever deeper in the quicksand of this Depression created by your imperialist United States. And worsened, I might add, by President Roosevelt's insensitivity to the needs of a hungry Japan."

"My family's contributions to Japanese industry give me every right to do business here," Douglas said evenly. "This is my birthplace, and I've always put business before politics."

Lord Mitsudara offered a dry smile. "A difficult posture to maintain. If peaceful solutions aren't found to rescue us from this quicksand, war in Southeast Asia and on the European continent may be an inevitable outgrowth of our dissatisfactions. Meanwhile, distrust of one's neighbors and the fear that they might be the first to strike has made the military marketplace rich with promise," he said. "Your decision to enter it now is wise. But your necks are on the chopping block. Hosokawa-Napier stock and your personal fortunes combined aren't sufficient collateral for the millions you require. However, I know a good investment when I see one. My *zaibatsu* flourishes because I'm not afraid to take calculated risks." With his cigar he gestured at the baron and heaved a drawn-out sigh. "If only you hadn't been so reluctant to come to me, the wheels of progress would already be set in motion."

Tadashi managed to smile. Despite what his lord had said about sparing him loss of face, his status was diminished in a single stroke. To refuse the lord's proposition on any grounds was now unthinkable. "A regrettable mistake," he apologized.

"Dismiss it from your mind." Lord Mitsudara circled back to sit behind his desk. "Little takes place that I don't know about. My staff has thoroughly studied this proposal you submitted to the banks." He held up the documents in question, shifting his eyes from one man to the other. "These parachutes you hope to manufacture will cost more to develop than you have estimated. The undervalued Japanese yen puts us at a disadvantage against the German mark." He dropped the papers to his desk. "Even so, your partnership with the Karlstadt Parachute Works in Berlin is paramount to success, considering that the parachutes most widely in use today owe much to Herr Karlstadt's innovations. His facilities can be retooled to produce your first prototypes, saving us time. And then the master blueprints can be duplicated at your weaving mills here in short order. Yes, time is money, gentlemen." The lord made a clucking sound. "Herr Karlstadt faces bankruptcy unless his outstanding loans with the German banks are paid promptly. More millions, to be paid out in reichsmarks before we can begin to rebuild."

Douglas looked at the baron, but his drawn face expressed nothing. "If I may speak for us both," he ventured cautiously, encouraged by the lord's nod. "Heinz—Herr Karlstadt—is a shrewd businessman. But his civilian-related parachute business was hit hard by the Depression, and he lost out to another German firm that had enough capital to take advantage of Hitler's rearmament policy. The Gessler Parachute Works now owns the German Army's contracts." Douglas's deep voice was tense, and he took a moment to calm himself. "The Gessler parachute is inferior to the one I've designed. We control production of our raw silk and can manufacture them for less. I've also designed high-speed machinery that will mean fewer hours on the assembly lines. Back us up, and a year from now we'll demonstrate the superiority of our parachutes for Hitler's general staff."

Baron Hosokawa stirred from his inertia. "Yes, the Gessler Works can't possibly compete." Drawing on his cigar, he waited for some response from his lord. It was not forthcoming. "Well, since you've made such a thorough study of things, there's little else we can tell you."

Lord Mitsudara pressed a button on his desk, then leaned back slightly. "My terms aren't negotiable, gentlemen. I intend to protect my investment by taking an active role in this venture. The Mitsudara Bank will issue a note payable within three years. To free you from undue pressure, I'll defer an interest rate of twenty-five percent until that time. A hard bargain, but equitable under the circumstances. Agreed?"

"Agreed," Baron Hosokawa said quickly. Douglas weakly echoed his agreement. To him, the terms were bitter. He accepted only out of deference to the outmoded samurai ties that still bound the baron with his lord.

"Now, to the schedule." The lord rolled his cigar between the fingers of one hand, using the other to flip through his desk calendar. He had assumed power over those seated opposite him and rewarded himself with a smile. "Mr. Napier will leave for Germany. By this time next year, he will have accomplished what must be done in Berlin. Tadashi will manage things in Japan. While labor is so cheap, it's good business to increase raw silk production and add to your stockpiles for future use. An airstrip will be constructed on the Hosokawa lands. Once we become operational, my cargo planes can speed the silk to your mills here and in Kyoto to meet the military contracts we so confidently anticipate." Lord Mitsudara stood and walked to the window where he looked out over his empire. "Field Marshal Göring has already laid the groundwork for our success. Not long ago, his police paratroops were most effective in dispatching Communist cells active in Berlin, and Hitler was quick to recognize the value of adding airborne assault forces to his arsenal."

"We don't have to sell the Germans," Douglas put in forcefully. "But

Japan hasn't kept pace with the times. Most of the military budget goes into bolstering ground troops and strengthening the Imperial Navy."

"Japan is a nation of borrowers." Lord Mitsudara turned from the window and tapped the cigar against a green jade ashtray placed on a slender rosewood table. "We still look to the West for innovations. Our military attachés in Germany recently witnessed a demonstration of the new Heinkel bombers armed with incendiary bombs. Their impressive showing has convinced our general staff that modern warfare will be fought and won from the air. I've been given contracts to manufacture the engines for new Japanese bombers similar to the Heinkel." Rocking back on the heels of his stocking feet, he gave the other two men a superior grin. "So you see, gentlemen. Sell your parachutes to Hitler's army, and you'll soon sell them to the Japanese."

Douglas Napier felt drained. The baron sat beside him staring off in space as though numbed by the sudden end of their financial ordeal. Douglas reminded himself of other priorities. "Heinz Karlstadt has booked passage to Japan," he told the lord. "We'd hoped the proof of his results there would help sway the banks. Now his journey seems unnecessary."

"Not at all." Lord Mitsudara smiled. "I had it in mind to summon Herr Karlstadt to see for myself what sort of man I'm doing business with. Yes, his journey is well timed. I'm most eager to have a look at this evidence of your progress in Berlin." He looked toward the office doors as they were slid open from the outside by serving girls, who then knelt there with trays of sake and cake. "Now, if you'll excuse us, I'd like to speak with the baron in private."

"Certainly." Feeling slighted by the abrupt dismissal, Douglas stood up. "Might I ask the lord when his bank note will be issued?"

"With all speed, Mr. Napier. I may be some time with the baron. My chauffeur is at your disposal."

"Thank you. I'll be at our hotel suite, Tadashi."

One of the serving girls responded to Lord Mitsudara's hand wave, and Douglas followed her down the corridors of power where his friend had saved face by showing obedience to his daimyo. The enduring traditions of Fujio Hosokawa's Japan continued to orchestrate the lives of Andrew Napier's heirs, in business and in personal matters. Douglas wondered what his life would be like if those two men had never met.

Lord Mitsudara had his pound of flesh, but Douglas Napier tried looking at the bright side. At last the new machines of his design would become a reality, and the mill workers could be promised their jobs back within a year. But the Kyoto mill still had to be closed for the present. The next day he would board the train with his partner for the five-hundred-mile journey to that city. It was another three-hundred-mile train trip from there to his Tokyo home.

A sweet-smelling perfume worn by the lord's serving girl turned his thoughts to affairs of the heart, and Douglas longed to be free of business obligations. His good fortune had no meaning until it was shared in the arms of the woman he loved. For now he would have to content himself with her silky voice over the telephone lines bridging the distance between them.

Behind the closed doors of his lord's inner sanctum, Baron Hosokawa accepted sake but had no desire for the cakes. In a sugary voice, Lord Mitsudara inquired about his family. Outwardly their friendship seemed unchanged, which somewhat offset the embarrassment Tadashi had suffered while talking business. "My son is a constant source of disappointment," he confessed, not for the first time. "It wounds me to punish Kimitake. But what else can a father do?"

Lord Mitsudara savored his wine at length before answering. "Sons must be guided with a firm hand. Be stern and resolute, Tadashi. Blood will tell in the end." His interest shifted to the pretty young woman who refreshed his drink. "Ah, perhaps I should have remarried. But since my wife's death, I've grown too old and set in my ways. Wives can be a thorn in the side, but mine was a treasure. Sadly, her frail constitution was passed on to my firstborn son, Gentaro. Outwardly he was the picture of good health. That he should be called to join the gods in his infancy . . ." Touched by the memory, tears welled up in his eyes. "Why grieve over what can't be undone? My secondborn son is sound in every respect. Better to have one son than be cursed with nothing but daughters. Some day Jiro will inherit all this, and I will have grandsons and heirs to continue our bloodline."

Smiling now, the lord said, "Your daughter has the fiery spirit of our samurai mothers. That is why I chose Shizue over all the other worthy suitors for my son's hand. Yes, I have great expectations for the eventual union of our two bloodlines. When we spoke of this some months ago, I was distressed by your reluctance to settle on a binding marriage agreement between us. Have you given the matter any thought?"

Baron Hosokawa quietly set down his cup. He could not hope to strike a better match for his daughter, but he could not easily give Shizue away in marriage, either. She was his joy, his priceless treasure, and her happiness meant everything to him. "It breaks with tradition to pledge my daughter before she comes of age," he said at last. Even the old samurai ties did not bind him in this respect. The balance of power now shifted over to him while Lord Mitsudara impatiently tapped his fingers on the table. "Jiro's a wonderful young man. But Shizue is still my little girl. When she matures, it would honor me to reconsider your proposal."

"Really, Tadashi, why leave it up in the air?" the lord flared. "I'm plagued by fathers with daughters of a higher lineage than yours who refuse to take no for an answer. I want those nagging suitors off my back."

His manner softened. "Do be sensible, old friend." Shaking his head, the lord uttered a perplexed sigh. "How can I make even you understand the burdens of power? My household is cursed with worthless relatives who feast on the fruits of my labors. They are old and dried up. I long to hear the laughter of grandchildren. Knowing my only son and heir will have Shizue for his wife would grant me peace and rid me of this temptation to choose him another wife already of marriageable age. So"—he sighed again—"you see my dilemma, Tadashi. If you want what's best for your daughter, act on it now."

"The lord honors me in speaking so candidly." Baron Hosokawa paused to consider the risk of losing this match. The lord's son was a charming, handsome youth and Shizue might find love with him, as he himself had found love with the wife his father had chosen for him. But once Shizue was pledged, he could break the agreement only at the cost of his honor. Even so, perhaps he was being too cautious.

"Well, I am waiting for some reply."

"I'll give the matter more thought," Baron Hosokawa said, avoiding the lord's eyes. His thoughts were of home and the daughter who had inherited his wife's great beauty. The striking resemblance Shizue bore to Sumie both haunted and comforted him. His widower lord had taken mistresses over the years, but Tadashi could let no other woman into his life, and only Shizue's presence helped fill the void. "If I should agree to this match, then you and Jiro must promise to say nothing. I want Shizue to enjoy what's left of her childhood. I don't want her burdened by the knowledge of such an obligation."

"Of course, why trouble her pretty head?" Lord Mitsudara chuckled. "So. Business and friendship are not the bad mix that you had feared, eh, Tadashi?"

Baron Hosokawa shook his head and felt obliged to laugh. It seemed that his daughter's petitioning of the gods had been answered, and when he returned home, he would visit his ancestral shrine to give offerings of thanks.

CHAPTER 4

It was evening, and Baron Hosokawa and Douglas Napier relaxed in the steaming bath waters of the Miyako Hotel's *ofuru*. Douglas was quiet and withdrawn. Closing their Kyoto mill had kept them in this ancient capital city of Japan for several days. The firm's mills here and in Nagasaki had operated under Japanese managers and required little personal attention from the owners, who stayed at hotels while there on business. Just over three hundred miles away, the Tokyo office opened by Andrew Napier remained the hub of his grandson's operation. Japan's modern capital was also the financial capital of the empire, the conduit through which all important business flowed to the outside world.

Baron Hosokawa looked upon the Napier mansion in Tokyo as his home away from home. He visited with his friends often, even though the recent decline in business made his presence in Tokyo unnecessary. He would miss Douglas and Angela when they went to Germany. He knew they would be gone at least a year, and he wondered if perhaps that long separation between friends was the reason for Douglas's brooding silence. "Douglas, what's troubling you?" Tadashi asked. "You've hardly said a word all day."

"Natsu telephoned me this morning." Douglas dipped his head under the water for a moment and then surfaced. Combing back his wet hair, he said, "She was in a cheerful mood over some good news. I promised her I'd leave tonight for Tokyo on the overnight train. Natsu wants me to come to the tea shop."

"The tea shop?" Baron Hosokawa repeated. He shared a secret with Douglas. His friend's love affair with a Japanese woman often vexed him, but he never solicited information and never offered advice. "She must have good reason to make such a request of you, considering the difficulties of your situation," he commented softly.

"It's not much to ask of me. I'm grateful for having Natsu's love on any terms."

"Yes, I understand."

Douglas felt touched by his friend's look of sadness. He wished this lonely widower's term of mourning would draw to an end. Tadashi was a virile, attractive man, and there had been a number of lovely women who had sought his attention over the years. But none of them had produced sparks. The baron's interest in marrying again had steadily waned. "How do you manage it?" Douglas felt compelled to ask. "I respect your grief, Tadashi, but how can you go on year after year alone?"

"I have my memories. So long as they remain intact, no other woman can live up to them." Baron Hosokawa fanned one hand across his eyes. Sumie's loss had snuffed his masculine desires. In the years since her death, Douglas and Angela Napier had spent all their summers abroad, while he had remained at home with their children, keeping to the castle that preserved the memories of his beloved wife. "Soon it will be the festival of Tanabata, an event that was very special to my wife." The sadness in his eyes disappeared as he said, "I'd be grateful if you and Angela would visit the castle to celebrate Tanabata with me and our children, as we did when Sumie was alive."

"You can count on us," Douglas answered from the heart. "It will be like old times." Glancing away, he reflected on his wife's need for travel abroad. As a girl, Angela had been educated in the finishing schools of Europe. She preferred European society to that of her American birthplace, and she thought Europeans far more civilized than the Japanese. "I wouldn't have spent all these summers away from Japan if not for Angela," he told the baron.

"Yes, I know. But she's been a good wife to you, Douglas. I know that hasn't been enough, and I realize how hard it is for a man's heart to be split in two." The two friends exchanged understanding smiles. "I'm at the mercy of sentimentality. There aren't many summers left for our youngsters to enjoy as children. I'll leave for home tonight as well."

"Sometimes I wish we were boys again," Douglas mused aloud. "There are times when I'd like to rid myself of responsibilities and obligations."

The baron placed a hand on his shoulder. "We were born to them, Douglas. Our company is once again on solid ground. We can only go forward and hope that what lies ahead may give us both peace of mind."

Midday was a busy time at the Cherry Blossom Kissaten in Tokyo, where Natsu Yoseido, dressed in the cherry blossom print kimono of a tea maid, cheerfully waited on her customers. Natsu moved gracefully from table to table, aware of her beauty but not given to vanity. It was a day like any other in the life of this small tea shop that stood on the Ginza. But for Natsu Yoseido it was a day that held the promise of answering her most cherished hopes. Past summers had always been lonely for her. Each year the man she loved took his American wife abroad to escape Japan's steamy climate, and he did not return to his home in Tokyo before the first rusting leaves of autumn.

Natsu gave thanks that the summer of 1936 would not separate her from Douglas Napier. Quite suddenly this had become a season of good fortune to be shared with her lover, who had telephoned when his train from Kyoto had arrived in Tokyo. She anxiously looked out the shop window, expecting him to be here at any moment. A friendly voice startled her.

"Excuse me for being so forward, Madame Yoseido," said the man seated alone at a window table. "But today there is a radiance about you that I have not seen before."

"You flatter me, Tamura-*san*," Natsu said, smiling. Everyone addressed her as Madame. Long ago she had put an end to the unwanted advances of her customers by telling them that she was a married woman.

Hideo Tamura was wearing an expensive business suit and was immaculately groomed. He always read at tea, and that day an open book sat beside his cup. For some time now he had come to the shop daily and seated himself at one of the tables Natsu was serving.

Natsu could tell that the homely middle-aged gentleman loved her from afar. But he was too retiring for her to regard his obvious longing as more than a harmless flirtation. "Allow me to refresh your cup, Tamura-*san*."

"Yes, you are simply radiant," Tamura observed, closing the pages of his book. "Would it be too bold of me to inquire as to the cause of so much loveliness?"

"It's my son," Natsu answered him, feeling moved to share her happiness. "He graduated from Tokyo University several weeks ago, and we learned yesterday that he won first prize in the journalism competition sponsored by *Mainichi*. My son's been awarded a position on the staff. Oh, I'm so very proud of him!"

"My!" Tamura removed his glasses, surprise widening his small eyes. "It is hard to believe one so young can have a grown son. *Mainichi* is an excellent newspaper, and you have good reason to be proud. So, your son is a journalist. My, my, that is a surprise. Indeed, journalism is also my profession, Madame. Yes. I am often called upon to lecture at the university. Perhaps I have seen your son there."

Natsu daintily rested the teapot on its serving tray. "Perhaps."

"As editor-in-chief of *Nippon Shimbun*, many students ask me to read their writings. I cannot possibly read them all." Tamura extracted an embossed business card from his wallet and cleared his throat. "However, I do what I can to encourage young talent," he said. "Please take my card. Before your son accepts employment at *Mainichi*, why not send him round to me? Have him call for an appointment first."

"I had no idea you were such an important man," Natsu said, accepting his card. If only Hideo Tamura had spoken of his occupation before, it might have spared her son a great deal of torment, she thought.

Now this homely man's eyes made her uncomfortable, and she regretted having been so familiar. "Can I bring you something else, Tamura-*san*?"

"Yes, another of your excellent cakes, if you please." He was putting on his glasses as Natsu suddenly stopped and stared out the window. Tamura followed her gaze and saw a tall blond man stepping from a taxi. "Do you know this man?"

"Our accountant." Natsu quickly signaled for another tea maid to take her place. "I must go. Yoko has no head for figures, and I manage the account books." She rushed to the office door at the rear of the crowded shop, pausing long enough to say to Yoko, the owner of the shop, "Douglas is here. Please send him to the office."

"*Hai.*" Yoko rubbed her coarse red hands together and watched the street door. Though she employed Natsu, Yoko's relationship with her was that of a close friend. To love Douglas Napier was Natsu's curse, Yoko told herself, fearing that his visit could bring her friend only more grief.

For various reasons Douglas Napier had not been back to the tea shop in many years. When he had first set foot inside the Cherry Blossom Kissaten, it had been the summer of 1914, and electric bulbs had illuminated the pink glass sign hung over its door. Now the shop's name was molded of pink neon tubes. Entering beneath the tinkling brass bell, Douglas felt as if he had stepped back through time. Everything was as he remembered it when, as a young man, he had sat at the corner table under the warm glow of painted silk lanterns, holding hands with Natsu and whispering vows never to be parted.

The past melted away before Yoko's aging face. With a downward wave of one hand, she made the typical Japanese "come here" gesture to Douglas. "The years have been kind to you, Yoko," he lied.

"Save your charm for Natsu. She is waiting in the back office. You must remember the way," Yoko added with pointed innuendo.

"Is Paul with her?" he asked tensely.

"No, she is alone."

Douglas soberly opened the office door and saw Natsu. She was as unchanged as this pleasantly furnished back room with its narrow wooden staircase that led to the small apartments overhead. Here they were to have been married before a Buddhist priest. In one of the cozy apartments above, Natsu had given Douglas her virginity. And now she occupied those same rooms with her son, Paul.

"Darling! How I missed you." Natsu rushed to embrace him. "Oh, Douglas, it's so good to feel your arms around me again. I couldn't bear the days without you." She looked up at him. "Each day we're apart is like a tiny moment of death."

"For me as well, dearest." He kissed her soft lips and then stood gazing down into Natsu's warm, all-knowing eyes. "Tell me about our son."

Natsu smiled. "Our son," she said proudly, "has won first prize in the *Mainichi* journalism competition. He's been given a position on the staff."

Douglas's face lit up. "That's wonderful news!" he said. Then his expression grew serious as he looked up the staircase. "Is Paul here now?"

"No, he's left for the newspaper office to meet the editor. Oh, if only you could have seen his face when the messenger arrived with the announcement of his prize." Natsu bent back in Douglas's arms and laughed. "Our son's been floating on air ever since. I'd nearly given up hope that he would find a job with any newspaper in Tokyo. Now, at last, his ambitions can be realized. Douglas, I know in my heart this is the right moment for you to see him again." She put her arms around his neck. "We have so much to be grateful for. It seems all my prayers have been answered. Doors have suddenly been opened to both the men in my life. Now our son has a future, and your business problems are over. I feel like a giddy young girl."

"You'll always be that in my eyes." It seemed an eternity since Natsu had laughed in his arms, and Douglas spun her around the room. "Still light as a feather. How I adore you."

"Please, all this excitement takes my breath away," she pleaded. The color drained from her cheeks, and she felt a wave of dizziness. "I couldn't get to sleep last night—and the shop has been so busy." Hiding her discomfort behind a pretty smile, she flitted away to the mirror on the wall and pinched both cheeks to bring the color back. "Giving the right appearance is so important in getting a job," Natsu said, changing the subject. "I pressed Paul's best suit and bought him a new shirt and tie. His handkerchief," she worried. "I hope I didn't forget to put a clean handkerchief in his pocket."

The smile faded from Douglas's face. He could share Natsu's joy, but he doubted this turn of events would help bridge the chasm that separated him from his son. Some years ago, Paul had severed all contact with his father. This tea shop was Paul's home, and his parents met elsewhere when time permitted them to be together.

Douglas recalled the hostile scenes played out in years past whenever he came to visit his son. For years a fabric of lies had kept Douglas from knowing that he had a son. They had discovered each other too late. The past had deeply wounded Paul, and he could not be reached by all of Douglas's protestations of fatherly love. Indeed, Douglas would not have come to the tea shop that day if not for Natsu's belief in miracles. "Is this a gift for Paul?" he asked, eyeing the colorfully wrapped box on the desk.

"It's a birthday present for Yoko's son that I've promised to mail to his army base." Natsu rested her head against Douglas's shoulder, and he put his arms around her. "I've planned a celebration dinner for Paul. I wish Toru could be here with us. Our son has been lonely since his friend joined the army. Only yesterday they were boys, playing together in the street outside this shop."

"Lately I've felt time slipping away too quickly. I feel like I'm trying to hold on to a greased pole." Douglas bent to kiss Natsu's lustrous black hair, which she had swept up with tortoiseshell combs. Inhaling her perfumed fragrance evoked the memory of blissful nights they had spent together. "My favorite perfume."

"Haven't I always worn it when I'm with you?" she replied, standing on tiptoe to receive his kiss.

"My darling." Douglas's lips brushed the flawless skin of her cheek. "When I'm with you, nothing else seems to matter."

"Yes, it's a gift we give each other."

As Douglas rocked Natsu in his arms, her perfume took him back in time to Paris, where he had discovered this fragrance. He had brought a crystal decanter of it home for her, and ever since she had worn Black Narcissus only for him.

"Your thoughts are troubled. I can feel them running through me," said Natsu, shivering.

"I was thinking that we've never been separated for more than the summer. And now I have to go to Germany for a year. Sweetheart, I don't think I can survive the loneliness of a year without you."

Natsu quickly put her fingertips to his lips, silencing him. "No sad thoughts today. You look exhausted from your journey. Come sit here and relax."

Douglas surrendered to the spell of her loving gestures. Natsu removed his jacket and loosened his tie. He rested on the office sofa, and she slid an ottoman under his feet, then knelt to remove his shoes.

Seeing Natsu in the kimono of a tea maid was a painful reminder to Douglas of all she had given up for him. When they met at their Tokyo apartment to share precious hours together, Natsu wore the lovely garments of an upperclass Japanese woman. Douglas's eyes swept the room. Returning there after so many years reminded him of the luxuries Natsu had denied herself. As his wife she would have wanted for nothing. But as his mistress, she refused to accept anything. She was considered dead by her wealthy parents and ostracized from Japanese society for bearing a Eurasian child. It seemed a thousand summers ago when their parents had torn them apart, leaving Natsu alone to suffer the trials of raising an illegitimate child. She had raised Paul with dignity and had borne the burden of loving, and being loved by, a man who was married to someone else.

Natsu pulled back Douglas's shirt collar and massaged his neck. "Why so tense, darling?"

"I'd like to trust your heart, but Paul could make a scene when he finds me here," he answered wearily. "I'd give anything to make a fresh start between us."

"Please, don't torture yourself," Natsu said softly. "Our son promised to hurry back after his interview to tell me everything. Rest your thoughts, my dearest," she continued as she gently massaged his temples.

"All his bitterness will be forgotten when he returns home. Yes, everything between you will be changed. You'll see."

"How well your touch knows me," Douglas said, closing his eyes and relaxing under her loving hands.

Natsu and the tea shop were in Paul's thoughts as he excitedly made his way through the Tokyo crowds. The editor of *Mainichi* had personally telephoned Paul to set up the appointment. Now the young man hurried along a broad street to meet the editor. Until that day he had been like the jobless men who brushed past him looking grim-faced and lost, drifting aimlessly through the sunny afternoon.

Paul glanced up at the fissured tile rooftops of antiquated Oriental structures, survivors of the old Japan. They had put on bright new faces, but expansive display windows and sizzling neon signs above their revolving doors made the buildings stand out like vain dowagers, whose heavy makeup only advertised the ravages of time.

As Paul halted beneath the tall shadow of *Mainichi*'s modern offices, he felt full of hope. Japan was engaged in a battle for its very existence. The government, institutions, and even the old traditions were being challenged by change, and Paul believed this to be a time of opportunity. His generation might alter the nation's destiny. He would take part in Japan's grand epoch, he thought, checking his reflection in the plate glass street doors of the office building.

Straightening his necktie, he felt gratitude for his mother's loving touches. Natsu had seen to it that he would make a good first impression. Perhaps appearances were important, but his talent had won this victory, and he entered the newspaper's splendid lobby, buoyed by winning the prize that had opened these doors to him at last.

He gave his Japanese name to the admission guard. "Akira Yoseido. I have an appointment with city editor Kusaka-*san*."

The guard regarded Paul suspiciously before he searched the names on his appointment log. "Tenth floor, Yoseido," he said with a snarl.

Paul ignored the man's unpleasant attitude. A child of the Tokyo streets, he had fought hard to rise above the stigma of his mixed blood, and he had reason to hold his head high as he boarded an elevator. The white-gloved operator stopped his rising car on every floor. Reporters entered and exited, their staccato exchanges and breathless tempo increasing Paul's excitement. At last the elevator doors parted on the tenth floor. He stepped into the reception area of *Mainichi*'s vast city room and stood listening to its dynamic heartbeat—telephones jangling, men pounding typewriters, history being written on an orchestra of teletype machines.

A scratchy voice rose above the clamor. "Who let you in?"

Paul confronted the little clerk who gawked at him from behind the reception counter and loudly identified himself. "Akira Yoseido. The city editor is expecting me."

Ordered to wait, Paul watched the clerk stalk off to knock on the door of a glass-enclosed office that looked out on the pressroom. Saburo Kusaka's name was stenciled on the door. Paul shifted anxiously as he saw the fat, balding city editor light a cigarette. Whatever the clerk said—and Paul was certain he knew what it was—caused the city editor to rush from his desk to peer out through the glass partition. Paul's stomach churned. Then Kusaka wheeled around and shouted at the clerk. It was obvious to Paul that the editor had not known the winner of their competition was a Eurasian, and the flustered clerk ran more than walked from his office.

"Regrettable. Most regrettable," the clerk grumbled to himself. He reached for the telephone on his counter. "Go in, Yoseido. The editor will see you now."

As Paul was buzzed through the reception gate, he overheard the clerk ask for the security police. The city editor was right to anticipate trouble, Paul thought. Now that his dreams were within his grasp, he had no intention of forfeiting his prize without a fight. Kusaka mimicked a friendly smile, and Paul was told to close his office door. "Kusaka-*san*. Honored to meet you," Paul said icily, and bowed.

"A pleasure to meet our prizewinner." Kusaka's throaty voice resonated with controlled passion, and he gestured at a tubular chrome-and-leather chair imported from Germany. "Please, sit down."

On the editor's desk Paul saw his competition entry, bound in a maroon cover. Kusaka flipped through the typewritten pages, no doubt, thought Paul, stalling for time until the security police arrived to back him up when he withdrew the prize. Paul decided against playing into the enemy's hands by showing his outrage. Instead, he said in an even voice, "I put a great deal of thought into selecting my subject, Kusaka-*san*. Committing ourselves to a war in China would bring Japan to a turning point that ultimately might lead to a broader conflict in Southeast Asia."

"An interesting approach to our imperial ambitions. Of course, without experience, journalism is merely an exercise." Kusaka spoke with the cigarette clenched between his lips, one eye on the glass door behind Paul. "Your dissatisfaction with the course of Japan's destiny should be curbed. Yes, there are injustices. But after all, politicians are by nature corrupt, and your idealism belongs in the classroom, Yoseido-*san*."

Paul half-rose in the chair. "I value your criticism. But you spoke quite differently about my work over the telephone."

"Control your temper. The decision of our judges is final, and the prize is yours." The editor nervously cleared his throat when Paul's mouth dropped open with surprise. Kusaka stood up in order to have a better view of the pressroom. "However, I'm afraid the position we offered you is another matter."

Paul turned and saw two burly men dressed in black uniforms halting just outside the office door. Sweat rolled down the back of Paul's neck. "Kindly explain yourself," he demanded.

Saburo Kusaka's manner grew unctuous. "Times are hard. Circulation is down, and I've been forced to reduce my staff. Otherwise, we would gladly give you employment. Ah, but surely this prize will help you find work elsewhere. You understand my position, I am sure."

"I understand only too well." Despite the security guards' threatening presence, Paul rose and stared into the hate-filled eyes magnified behind gilt-rimmed glasses. "You can't dismiss me so easily. *Mainichi*'s circulation is on the rise. Every day thousands read what you print, and I want a voice in that!" He wiped his sweaty palms on his trousers and managed to keep his anger in check. "I'm willing to beg for that opportunity." Kusaka seemed prepared to hear him beg and quietly lit another cigarette. "Over the telephone you said I have a rare gift for words. If my mixed blood offends you, then let my words speak for themselves. Give me the chance to serve Japan and prove that spirit is stronger than blood."

"Yes, you have talent. Enviable talent. But you forget your place," Kusaka stated acidly. "A less belligerent attitude would serve you better. Teach if you can and leave Japan's future to the Japanese." He smacked the contest entry folder shut. "The prize is yours, Yoseido. Had you honestly expected more?"

"Goddamn racist!" Consumed with rage, Paul took hold of Kusaka's lapels. Instantly the two uniformed men charged into the office. Paul refused to unhand Kusaka, struggling against the guards' efforts to restrain him until a billy club was slammed hard across one side of his head, and the room went black.

"Take this mongrel away, and see to it he doesn't show his face here again!"

Kusaka's rasping voice was a distant echo as Paul, semiconscious, was dragged off between the security police, through the city room, and into an elevator. Once the doors had closed, the police beat him with their fists. His refusal to cry out only encouraged them to strike harder. But he suffered the pain in silence until they dragged him from the elevator and down the fire stairs to an alleyway door, where he was tumbled into the trash.

Paul got to his knees and held on to the alley wall for support. His ribs ached. Blood stung his eyes. When his vision cleared, he stared back with hatred at the security guards, who circled him menacingly, twirling their billy clubs.

The largest man jabbed Paul's ribs with his club. "What a devil behind those eyes," he said, laughing. "Get going, troublemaker! And don't come back unless you want more of a beating."

To Paul the busy street was a pinpoint of light at the end of a long, dark tunnel. Hugging the alley wall, he staggered toward it. The evening edition was being run off on the newspaper's giant presses, which filled the alleyway with their throbbing roar. The smell of ink drifted down from open windows high overhead. Paul envisioned the miles of newsprint being spun into words.

As a lonely child he had turned to the companionship of books. Shunned by his classmates, he had found the means to express himself through words. Words were anonymous. The color of their meaning stood apart from the color of a man's skin, and the voice behind them could be powerful. This was not the first time Paul had been attacked for attempting to assert his Japanese identity. As he listened to the presses trapped within the brick walls, he swore that one day their thundering would belong to him. He vowed to bring down the barrier erected against him because of his father's blood.

As Paul emerged from the alleyway, he was overcome by a wave of nausea. His mother had always seen to it that there was a freshly laundered white linen handkerchief in his jacket pocket. Now he used it to clean his face and hands, then set off, holding it to the side of his throbbing head. It was nearing the rush hour, and he was jostled by the street crowds. He felt himself being pushed toward Ueno Station. He glimpsed the neon sign of a bar, thinking whiskey might help ease his pain. Then someone shouted his name, and Paul saw a welcome face in the crowd. "Toru!" he addressed the sturdily built young soldier. He had never been more glad to see anyone in his life. "Why didn't you telephone you were coming home on leave?"

"It was to be a surprise." Yoko's son dropped his canvas suitcase to the sidewalk and took Paul by the shoulders. "What happened to you?"

Paul laughed shortly. "A slight misunderstanding."

"Your sarcasm isn't amusing." Toru's narrowed eyes searched the street. "Show me who did this, and I'll even the score."

"We're no longer children. I can fight my own battles."

"Not from the looks of you, my friend." Toru had a large, craggy face and wide-spaced, piercing eyes that had scared off even the bravest challengers when the two young men were children. But there was an open, generous side to his nature that showed now as he grinned at Paul. "Whoever roughed you over knew their business. I think Dr. Amano should have a look at that bump on your head."

Paul forced his shoulders back. "I'll be all right," he insisted, though the effort pained him.

"Stubborn as always." Toru lifted his suitcase. "I have a week's leave and a month's pay in my pocket. Come to the bar and we'll feed that bump some hard whiskey."

"I was headed there when you showed up." Hiding his discomfort, Paul enviously regarded his only real friend in the world. "You've made corporal," he observed, tapping the new insignia sewn on Toru's khaki uniform. "Congratulations."

"Yes, I'm fine samurai material. A born warrior," bragged Toru as he winked at two pretty girls walking past. "But commissions go to the gentry, not bastards like me. If not for an accident of birth, I'd be wearing an officer's uniform."

"At least an accident of birth hasn't prevented you from realizing your ambition."

"My aim isn't nearly so high as yours," Toru pointed out. "Tell me what really happened to rate you such a beating."

Paul recounted his experience. Yoko's son was almost four years his senior and was like an older brother to him. "I'm putting Kusaka's name high on my list. Someday I'll make him pay for this," Paul said at the end.

"What a glutton for punishment." Toru slung a brotherly arm around Paul's shoulders. "Why not set an easier goal for yourself? To become a journalist isn't the only thing in the world."

"Maybe so. But like your soldiering, it's what I was born to be, and I'm not about to give up." Paul threw a fist at the air, then winced and lowered the hand to his aching ribs.

Toru nudged him through the bar doors. "Come on, you look pale. Let's get you a drink." They sat down at the bar. "Two whiskeys," Toru told the bartender. "Doubles! And be quick about it, we're in a hurry."

Paul stared at the whiskey as it was poured into two glasses. "Today I had a lot of idealism kicked out of me, Toru. If there's a war in China, my pen will celebrate our victories. Who knows, I may even help to make heroes of you and your fighting comrades."

Toru laughed at the notion. "Then I wish you luck, my friend. Let your pen help make a hero of me, and perhaps I can earn the commission denied me by lowly birth. Hang a ceremonial sword around this waist with your fancy words, and we'll sit down over a fine wine, and laugh at our past misfortunes. Drink up, I'm eager to see my mother."

The whiskey burned as it went down. "I'm not used to hard liquor," Paul said.

"It's good for the blood," said Toru. He paid for the drinks, and then the two men walked outdoors. "Two bastards like us have got to be tough to survive. Each day after training, I soak my fists in brine. Now I can run the edge of a bayonet across my knuckles and not feel the pain." Suddenly he ducked behind a lamppost and made one hand into a gun. "Bang! You're dead!" Laughing broadly, Toru blew on the end of his finger as if it were a smoking gun barrel. "As always, you forgot to take cover from the enemy. You always dropped your schoolbooks and ran for cover too late. You never learned to keep one eye alert for a surprise attack. It could have saved you that beating, my intellectual friend."

"Yes, you're right." Paul smiled weakly as he recalled how the two had played war together. "That's why you're the samurai and I'm left stranded here alone with ink on my fingers."

"We'll ride the rest of the way home." Yoko's son half-carried Paul along to the trolley and virtually lifted him aboard with one strong arm.

*　　*　　*

At the Cherry Blossom Tea Shop, Hideo Tamura had lingered for some time over his afternoon tea, watching the closed door to the back office, curious about what was taking place behind it. Now Yoko gave him his bill. "Our charming Madame Yoseido seemed rather excited by the arrival of your accountant," he said. "I judged him to be an American."

Yoko only nodded, and Tamura counted out money from his wallet. The large tip he left on her tray was Natsu's reward for enduring his flirtations. "How generous of you, Tamura-*san*." Yoko glanced past him out the window and suddenly put both hands to her face. "My son, Toru! Ah, what a grand surprise!"

Tamura looked out the window at her soldier son. "The young man with him appears familiar," he observed, unable to recall where he had seen the Eurasian before.

From the street outside, Paul watched as Toru charged into the shop and lifted his mother off her feet. Yoko's son had always been the center of attention for the regular customers. Paul, however, never entered the tea shop. That would only have created ugly gossip and been bad for business.

After the violence he had suffered, his long-standing concession to racism nearly crumbled before the shop's forbidden front door. With effort, he turned to walk away. Just then Tamura came out of the shop. Paul recognized him instantly. Some months earlier, following a lecture Tamura had given at Tokyo University, Paul had pressed his best writing on *Nippon Shimbun*'s editor-in-chief. But nothing had ever come of it. Unfortunately, the man now appeared to remember him.

Paul attempted to gather together his torn jacket sleeve. Tamura acknowledged him with a nod, but Paul was too embarrassed by his soiled appearance to speak up. He experienced an intense pain in his head and passed one hand across his eyes as he walked down the alley between the tea shop and the neighboring building. He could feel *Nippon Shimbun*'s editor watching him from the street. How he despised the bigotry that had always forced him to enter his home by the back office door like one of the kitchen help.

Whiskey and the aftershock of his beating caused Paul's surroundings to spin as, with a groping hand, he took hold of the rusty doorknob. He staggered across the threshold, dizziness blurring his vision. Douglas Napier's face rippled before him as if viewed through melting glass.

Natsu was pouring Douglas tea, and the pot almost dropped from her hand. "My God!" she cried out in shock.

Paul moved away from her outstretched arms and stood unsteadily, glowering at his father. "Who invited you here?" The throbbing in his head made it impossible for him to shout his hatred. "You did this to me. This mongrel face is what your sins brought into the world. Thanks to you, it's a target for the fists of stupid bigots." Paul's rebuke sounded weak as he grabbed on to the back of a chair for support. "Well, now that you've had a taste of the living hell I'm cursed to—get out."

Natsu choked back tears. "But the prize."

"Worthless! The city editor saw what I was and said there won't be any job." Paul sent the chair spinning away and regained enough balance to cross to the sofa. "A beating was my reward when I demanded justice. Get out," he said to Douglas. He eased his head against the sofa pillows. "Your presence only makes things worse. And don't call for the doctor, Mother. It's only seeing *him* again and the whiskey I drank that's making me sick. I don't need babying."

Douglas confronted more of himself in Paul's battered face than had been captured in the photographs of their son that Natsu had given him over the years. He ached for this boy whose love he had never known. Reaching out, he attempted to comfort Paul. "Please, let me help you. The men who did this deserve to be horsewhipped. I'll call the police."

"The police will only take their side, Douglas," Natsu said, fighting to calm herself. "I'll get ice for his head."

"No, don't leave me alone with him." Paul roughly pushed his father's hands away. He wanted to lash out at him, but that would only bring more suffering to his mother. "You've denied me an identity. After what you've seen, can you blame me for despising you and the half-brother who's stolen my birthright?"

He covered his eyes with his arm and took deep breaths until his thoughts were clear. "You're not entirely blameless, Mother. Since you couldn't control your impulses, the least you could have done was to pick someone Japanese as your lover."

Paul's arm dropped to his lap, and his eyes condemned Douglas Napier. "I don't mind so much being a bastard. I could forgive you that. But I can never forgive you for not being a Japanese."

Tormented by guilt, Douglas sadly recalled the moment he had first laid eyes on this son. From their first encounter, Paul had been cold to this man who suddenly appeared to claim a portion of his mother's love. Finally, after years of angry exchanges, he had slammed the door in his father's face. That had been more than six years ago. When there was not enough money for Paul's college education, Douglas had insisted on paying for it, and Natsu could not refuse. But their son was unmoved by Douglas's generosity. If Paul would have allowed it, Douglas would have given the boy everything money could buy—fine clothes, expensive cars. More, he would have lavished love upon him. But Paul would have none of it. And it was not in Douglas's power to grant the unhappy young man another identity.

"Everything I've done has displeased you," said Douglas, resting both arms down at his sides. "I realize it's useless to beg for another chance. But if you could let go of the past and meet me halfway, I'd do everything to be a real father to you."

"I'm not moved by the guilty remorse on your face. Don't come back here again, or I might do something both of us would live to regret." Paul pushed himself up from the sofa and crossed to the wooden staircase. Holding on to the railing, he took the steps one at a time.

"I must tend to Paul's bruises," Natsu said.

She started after their son, but Douglas stopped her, cupping her lovely face between his hands. "He doesn't want to be babied. Damn it all. I feel so helpless. It's been hell keeping my distance from him, not even attending his graduation for fear he'd see me in the crowd, lose his temper, and spoil that happy occasion for you, dearest. I've had nothing of Paul but your snapshots, and I've worn them thin, every last one."

"Despite all he said, I feel Paul misses you more than he lets on."

Douglas brought her close. "Maybe we were wrong to leave things as they were. Married to you, I could have broken through his resentment. Natsu, I want you with me always. We have so little time together, and the apartment we've shared is like a prison for our love."

"We can't have life on our own terms, Douglas. Be content with holding on to what we have." Natsu's fingertips traced the deepening lines of his troubled face. She loved him more with every passing year, and even Paul's travails had not diminished the intensity of her adoration of Douglas Napier. "Paul's life is a nightmare. I've lost count of the beatings he's taken. We must free him of this suffocating existence. Perhaps Baron Hosokawa could do something. Despite his rigid beliefs, he bears no animosity toward our son."

"He'd like to help. But Tadashi hasn't any influential friends in the publishing field."

Natsu went to the desk and picked up a business card. "Hideo Tamura. A regular customer of mine." She related their brief exchange but told Douglas nothing about Tamura's flirtations. *Nippon Shimbun*'s editor-in-chief seemed to hold out the only ray of hope. But if she implored him to assist her son, what might the man ask of her in payment? she wondered, turning his card in her hand.

"Approach him if you like, but I wouldn't build up hope of him being any different from the others." Douglas took her into his arms. "Paul's grown into a man with fixed ideas. I don't regret having come here today. Seeing him was worth the punishment of his accusations."

"When can we be together again?" asked Natsu, kissing him tenderly.

"Very soon," he promised. "I can't make excuses to Angela my first night home." Douglas sighed heavily. "Now that the family fortunes have taken a turn for the better, she'll be in one of her party moods. If not for Max, if not for the love of that son, I'd . . ." His thoughts were left unspoken. "Well, I should go and leave you with Paul."

Natsu smiled at him. The wife and son with whom she shared her lover were only names. She did not want to know more about Douglas Napier's family than was absolutely necessary. Life for her and Paul would be infinitely worse if not for the curtain she had kept tightly drawn between their world and the privileged world of his father.

"You look faint, sweetheart," Douglas said, concerned. "I'm afraid our son demands too much of you."

"I'm all he has. Paul has been crushed, but it mustn't defeat him." She bid Douglas good-bye with a lingering kiss.

Her son's needs ruled Natsu's heart as she climbed the stairs to their cozy apartment above the busy shop. Its rooms were a convenient haven between shifts. But, lately, climbing the short flight of stairs exhausted her.

She heard Paul running water in the bathroom. The door was closed and she knocked. "Can I be of help?"

"No! I'm washing the filth off myself," he replied in a voice full of anger. "Has Douglas gone?" Paul had never referred to his father by any other name than "Douglas."

"Yes."

"Good riddance!"

Natsu Yoseido wearily sat on the side of her bed. The needs of those she loved were always placed above her own. But this day had tried her faith. She watched orange fingers of afternoon sunlight reaching through the window to touch the objects she kept on her bedside table: her Bible, rosary beads, and the framed photograph of her as a young mother standing on the steps of a Tokyo church with her growing child.

The photograph, taken on the day her son had been christened Paul, was faded by the light of many summers. She had embraced the Catholic faith at a point of desperation in her life, and the Christian religion had sustained her over the years.

The building was very old, and its floor trembled when Paul entered his mother's room. He had changed from his soiled western clothes into a kimono. Paul often wore the traditional kimono as a statement of his birthright, an announcement of his Japanese blood and a denial of his father's seed. As he stood before Natsu, he fingered his bruised cheekbone. "Another day of brutal rejection, Mother. I should have known it would end this way."

Confronted with his utter desperation, Natsu sadly shook her head. "You mustn't lose hope. There's always tomorrow," she told him.

"Don't you see? Being cheated of my prize leaves me standing in the cold to face the same old lie. So sorry, Yoseido, but the position you applied for was given to someone better qualified." Paul hammered the telephone. "What hypocrisy! I'm more than qualified, but they don't see beyond these eyes. *Mainichi*'s editor was like all the rest. To small-minded men like him, I'm nothing but a lowly *ainoko*, a half caste who should be satisfied pulling a jinrikisha through the Tokyo streets like some beast of burden." His voice grew hoarse with emotion. "Well, maybe I should give up my ambitions and settle for wearing a coolie hat."

Natsu fought back tears. "Your bitterness won't change things. Paul, if only you'd put your faith in God."

"The name on my birth certificate is Akira, Mother! The Christian

name you baptized me with long after the fact is one curse I'm not forced
to live with!"

"In the eyes of Christ, you are Paul," she said.

"Your God, not mine." Paul crossed to the lacquered wood writing
box on his mother's dresser. Angrily he opened the lid and removed the
letters stored inside. "The proofs of your sins, Mother." He threw the
letters across the floor. "You might as well know that I read them all!
Years ago."

"How could you?" Natsu grew rigid with shock. "I taught you to
respect my privacy. Those letters were never meant for your eyes. Oh,
Paul, there's no sin in being in love as I was. There's only beauty in words
exchanged between lovers," she said quietly. "Your father and I were so
very young. You judge me too harshly."

Paul softened at her words. As he looked down at her, he thought that
she seemed so fragile. The years had been kind to her, and she still looked
lovely. At that moment he saw her as the helpless girl of her love letters.
His mother had given up everything for him and had never complained.
"Mother, forgive me." Paul dropped at her feet and buried his head in her
lap. He felt sick over the awful things he had said. "It's Douglas I hate.
He's the one I want to punish, not you."

Natsu called on the courage that had always sustained her. "All this
hatred," she said, stroking his dark brown hair. "I realize what life is for
you. It hasn't been easy, but you were raised with honor, and somehow
we'll find a way. You must stop living in the past. You must build on the
future and never look back."

"I have no future," Paul said angrily, standing up. "My degree in
journalism counts for nothing. I can't even get a job as copy boy. And I
owe it all to my father's blood."

Natsu stood and reached out to him, but he refused her touch. She felt
the torment in his hazel eyes that sparkled with flecks of blue inherited
from Douglas Napier. Nature often favored Asian characteristics, and
there were some Eurasian children who could pass as pureblooded
Japanese. But in Paul, Caucasian and Japanese characteristics had fought
each other. His complexion was that of his mother. His aquiline features
were those of his father. To Natsu's loving eyes, her son was a handsome
blending of East and West, although, sadly, her vision of him was not
shared by most others. "I've prayed with all my heart for someone to see
only your talent and give it an opportunity to grow," she said.

"Prayers won't help! You've lived a lie. My father cheated us of
everything, and one day I intend to make him pay."

"You judge your father unfairly. Douglas and I weren't given any
choices. The decisions were taken out of our hands. When time permits,
we seize a tiny bit of happiness together. Surely you can't begrudge us
that," Natsu pleaded. "It's all I ask of him, Paul. To expect more would be
living a lie."

"I'll never forget standing in this very room as a little boy who suddenly had a total stranger pushed in his face." Paul turned his back on her and stared at his reflection in the bedroom mirror. "A father with cold blue eyes and no color in his hair and skin. A rich man who abandoned us both for years and took another woman as his wife. I remember how often he came here trying to win me over with gifts. He barged into our lives and took advantage of your love, while he left me behind here at night, fatherless and alone. It's true that sometimes he drove us to the country for a day together. We played ball and rode horses. But I could feel how ashamed he was of being seen with his Eurasian son."

"It wasn't at all what you think!" Natsu exclaimed. She recalled that shocking and painful day when her son was first presented to his father, a shy boy of seven, whose existence had been kept from Douglas Napier by a cruel fabric of lies. "Douglas never meant to hurt you. When your father came to us, it was too late for regrets—too late to correct the wrongs done to us by others." Time and again she had pleaded for his understanding, but the wounds he had received left him permanently scarred. And yet she no less stubbornly lived on the hope that he could be reached, that he could find it in himself to forgive his father. "Paul, for your own sake, you must stop clinging to this child's vision of the past."

"That isn't so easy, Mother." Tears ran down Paul's cheeks as he embraced her. "You've given me so much love, but it isn't enough. Even you can't know what life is for me. All these years I've kept my promise to you by remaining silent. I've protected Douglas's American wife and my spoiled half brother, but it's spared us nothing. I wonder what they'd do if I knocked at the door of their fancy home and politely introduced myself!"

"Paul, no!" Devastated, Natsu watched him storm from the room. She called to him in vain as he raced out of the apartment and down the stairs.

From her window on the Ginza, she watched Paul rush away under a darkening sky of clouds. Where was he going? Natsu anguished, fearing the injury his anger might cause. While earning his degree at Tokyo University, her son had been consumed by an obsession to graduate first in his class. He had achieved that goal only to find his ambitions stifled. Douglas's visit had rekindled old threats of taking revenge. If he exposed his father's infidelity, people would be hurt. True, she and Douglas shared their love in secrecy—but not for selfish reasons. They had to protect the feelings of others innocently caught in the web of the past.

Natsu calmed herself, knowing that Paul's love for her would not permit him to make good his threat. Wearily she gathered up her love letters and returned them to the box. As she did so, one wrinkled envelope caught her eye, and she removed the letter. The paper reeked of time lost between lovers. The words written to her by Douglas Napier as a young man bound for America had once given her false hope. Now they were faded ink on brittle paper. She knew this letter's contents by heart.

It began to shower. Rain streaked across the windowpane as Natsu was transported back in time to another rainy summer's day. As the raindrops rolled down her window like tears, she saw herself as a girl of seventeen waking to the call of Zen monks on their morning rounds as they begged alms outside her father's house. . . .

The child growing inside her womb made her dizzy and light-headed that morning. It was girlishly romantic of her not to have told Douglas; she wanted her pregnancy to be a surprise that she would announce on their wedding day. Only her kindly spinster aunt had been taken into her confidence.

Like other young girls of her station, Natsu was forbidden to walk the city streets unchaperoned. Her lonely old aunt delighted in playing this role with her niece, often going with her shopping and to the cinema. The woman had a loving soul and permitted a secret courtship to blossom between Natsu and the handsome American young man who had approached them on the street one spring day. His clear blue eyes had only met with Natsu's once before, at a party she had attended with her parents at the home of the Hosokawa family. The Yoseido family also did not believe in intermarriage. Natsu knew her father would reject Douglas as a suitor. Raisuke Yoseido's authority over his daughter was absolute. But she felt compelled to follow the dictates of her heart.

And so all that spring and summer of 1914, Natsu and Douglas met secretly, breaking with both their parents' unyielding traditions. Very soon the summer would end. Douglas was obligated to leave Japan to attend Harvard, which would mean they would be separated for years. But they had decided they were too much in love to allow that separation to occur.

There were many servants in her wealthy father's splendid house. Natsu passed among them that morning, softly humming a lullaby to her unborn child. That afternoon her aunt was to chaperone her to the place where she and Douglas would be wed. Marriage was an act of defiance to unite them forever. Natsu knew that their parents would be angry and hurt at first, but her love for Douglas Napier had fired her passion to break the chains of tradition, and Natsu naively believed that everyone would simply accept the situation once her baby was born. In a few short hours she would be a happy bride, Natsu thought, smiling to herself until she reached the family sitting room.

Suddenly, her father loomed up before her like a menacing bird of prey, flapping the winged sleeves of his black silk dressing gown. He took his daughter by the wrists and pulled her inside the room while her mother quickly closed the doors. Her aunt was seated there, moaning words of regret that stabbed Natsu's heart like a knife. Tears streamed down her mother's lovely face as well. Her daughter had missed her period, and Madame Yoseido's knowing eyes had recognized the symptoms of morning sickness. Natsu's aunt had already broken under Raisuke Yoseido's interrogation, confessing everything.

"You have seen the last of that white scoundrel!" her father announced in a fit of rage. "Douglas Napier's parents were equally appalled. We agreed to put an end to this affair by sending the boy to Harvard immediately. The Napiers sailed for America with him at dawn—aboard one of my merchant ships."

Natsu refused to believe it was so. But she was given no chance to speak. Her father bore down on her, shouting that no one wanted her mongrel child, that her shame would be promptly washed away by the family doctor.

"Your pregnancy will be aborted, along with the disgrace you have brought our household," Raisuke Yoseido trumpeted. "You have shamed us, Natsu. If a word of this should escape these walls, I could never strike a proper wedding match. I intend to choose you a Japanese husband worthy of your station. Dr. Kinoshita will be here shortly. You will do as he says." Her father spread his arms out wide, and his voice grew hard as he said, "Defy my authority again, and I will disown you. You will be dead to me then, Natsu. Dead to us all, and one can only mourn the loss." His cold eyes left no doubt of his sincerity.

Natsu sobbed, but her mother and her aunt offered no support. They submitted to this ultimatum in mute defeat. Suddenly Natsu was consumed by anger. Hurling herself at her father, she clawed at his face. Raisuke Yoseido staggered back, stunned and speechless, thin rivers of blood running down his cheeks. To Natsu, an ugly mask seemed to hide his once fatherly features. She screamed and lashed out at him again, but the cruel mask he wore could not be torn away, and she stared at his blood under her fingernails, horrified by what she had done. Then she turned and ran. Deaf to her father's shouted threats, she ran out of the house past the gawking servants.

Thunder rumbled in the street outside as she ran, mindless of the pouring rain, fleeing the oppressive bondage of her home. Natsu ran until her lungs felt about to burst. Finally, she collapsed against a building. Gradually, as she caught her breath, she realized she was leaning against the window of an American steamship company. In the window display she saw a slate blackboard on which the sailing schedules had been written in chalk. Next to the blackboard was the model of an ocean liner, painted with reds, whites, and blues. As she stood there, she began to accept the shattering truth. Douglas, too, was a prisoner of his American father's traditions. Faced with their children breaking with tradition, the two fathers had united: Douglas Napier had been forced to sail from Tokyo at dawn, put aboard one of Raisuke Yoseido's fleet of merchant ships to prevent him from ever seeing her again. At that very moment her lover was being pulled beyond the reach of her arms to a distant world across the sea.

Somehow Natsu found the strength not to return home. She walked on without any sense of direction, her lustrous black hair matted by the rain. Eventually she found herself standing on the Ginza, the broad boulevard that took its name from the coins once minted there. It was a street of department stores, cabarets, and shops, an avenue of blinking electric signs.

Cherry Blossom Kissaten winked at Natsu in pink lights from a sign just across the street. All that summer she and Douglas had met inside the cozy tea shop, and the widowed proprietress and her daughter, Yoko, had become sympathetic friends. The robust Yoko had a heart of gold. Despite their different stations in life, the two young women felt for each other as sisters. Natsu quickened her step. The Cherry Blossom Tea Shop held her only promise of sanctuary from a suddenly hostile world.

The tinkling brass bell above the door announced her arrival. Seeing the expression on Natsu's face, Yoko wordlessly embraced her tearful young friend.

"Oh, Yoko, Douglas is gone—gone to America."

Weeping with her, Yoko said, "I feared this was so. A messenger came to the shop early this morning with a letter from Douglas."

Natsu pulled away from her friend. "Where is it? Oh, give me his letter quickly."

"I put it here for safekeeping." Yoko hurried to bring Douglas Napier's letter from the cash drawer. "He hoped you would come to me. There is a note on his envelope telling me not to bring this to your home," she said, placing it in Natsu's trembling hand.

Natsu knew her father would have destroyed the letter. She shivered, thinking how her father now planned to destroy her baby. Yoko sat down with her friend at the same corner table where Douglas and Natsu had so often held hands and promised never to be parted. Offering thanks to the gods, Natsu read Douglas's letter.

Douglas wrote that he loved her more than life itself, but that he was unable to stand up against his father. Through his words, Natsu felt her lover's torment. She understood how impossible it was for him to defy his father by marrying her that day.

"Dearest," he wrote, "our happiness must wait until I can stand on my own, freed of my father's hold over my life. That means earning my degree at Harvard. My darling Natsu, will you wait for me? After searching my heart, I don't feel I have the right to ask you to wait for so long, but our only chance for happiness rests on your decision."

A love such as theirs could not be diminished by time, Natsu told herself. But what of her baby? Both sets of parents knew of the pregnancy, but there was no mention of it in Douglas's letter. Surely their parents had conspired to keep the truth from him. Otherwise, he would never have abandoned her.

Clutching the pages to her breast, Natsu said to Yoko, "I'm determined to have my baby. I will write to Douglas and tell him about my pregnancy. Then everything will be changed."

Yoko sadly shook her head. "Natsu, you are dreaming. I fear even knowing of your child cannot bring Douglas Napier back from America. What will you do then?"

"Wait for him." Natsu folded the pages of his letter, taking hope from Douglas's promises of happiness in the future. Perhaps he was lost to her for now, but she was convinced that one day he would return to claim her as his bride. Tightly grasping hold of Yoko's hands, she made a decision that would forever alter her life. "Douglas loves me, and I must be prepared to wait until he completes his education," she said, with more courage than she felt.

But staring down at her soft, fine-boned hands, Natsu grew frightened. She was the daughter of a wealthy man, educated in the social graces, trained only to serve a Japanese husband of equal station. Yoko's hands were red and coarse, the hands of a serving maid. Clinging to them, Natsu begged for work serving the customers. Tradition would make her dead to her parents, but she was prepared to sacrifice them and the luxuries of her past life, rather than give up her unborn child. For this child of love, she would gladly endure anything.

"I desperately need money and a safe place to live where I can care for my baby," she pleaded with Yoko.

"This love was not meant to be," Yoko answered. She was a few years older than Natsu and had also given her heart away to her first love. Her young man had been a sailor, who was tragically lost at sea before they could marry. Now the child she had given birth to out of wedlock appeared at the door in the back of the tea shop. Before he could run to his mother, his grandmother lifted him up. She understood what was taking place between the two friends and carried off her three-year-old grandson.

"Natsu, go home to your parents," Yoko implored, as her son vanished behind the closing rear door. "I speak from experience. What you feel now can only lead to hardship. Douglas is gone from your life. As my mother often says, '*Shikata ga nai.*' There is nothing you can do about it. Return home and spare yourself a life of grief."

"No, my mind is made up. I see no regret in your eyes, only love for your child." Natsu intensified her grip on Yoko's coarse red hands. She had fled the security of home with nothing but the clothes on her back, but to return there even for her wardrobe might weaken her resolve. She was now almost two months pregnant and time was her enemy. "I'll stop at nothing to keep my baby. Douglas's baby. Oh, please, Yoko, I have no one else to turn to but you."

Yoko was silent, thinking of her own innocent bid for happiness. Natsu, too, had risked everything for love and had lost it all. "How can I refuse you?" Yoko said at last, putting her arms around her distraught friend.

Later on that rainy summer afternoon, Natsu began her new life by writing two letters. She knew that it would take weeks before her letter reached Douglas across the vast distance separating them, weeks more of waiting to receive his reply. Yoko delivered the letter Natsu wrote to her parents and, in just a matter of hours, returned to the tea shop with their reply. Her father's words were no surprise, but no less wounding: The door to home was now permanently barred to her. Natsu had made her choice. The warm affections of Yoko and her mother soon made the Cherry Blossom Kissaten Natsu's home. She found joy in helping to care for her friend's child and looked forward to the day when she would have Douglas's child.

As time passed, Natsu felt the baby stirring in her womb. Each day she watched the mail for Douglas's letter, but she waited in vain. She was possessed by the fear that Douglas had taken ill. Surely something dreadful lay behind his failure to respond to any of her letters or even the cablegram that, at great expense, she had sent her lover.

One day Douglas's father appeared at the tea shop. Julius Napier had just returned from America, and Natsu was stunned by his announcement that he had taken measures to sever all communication between her and his son.

He issued Natsu a cold warning. "I won't permit you to interfere with the plans I have for my son! There is no way you can blackmail Douglas with this bastard child. I hold the upper hand, and you won't ruin his life as you have yours. Douglas won't return to Japan for some years. I'll see to that," he said arrogantly. "Remember what I've said. There's no future for you, Natsu. Don't attempt to force yourself into my son's life, or we'll have words again. Good day."

Her tears had no effect on Julius Napier. He left her weeping at the tea shop door. Only the movements of her unborn baby gave Natsu the strength to endure.

Over the years Douglas's father, prompted by fears of what Natsu might do when his son returned to Japan, had paid Natsu other visits. She might have hated Julius Napier, but she realized he was no different from her own father. Both men were blinded by tradition. Still, it was only years later that Natsu was able to forgive them . . . .

Just then Natsu's visions of the past were erased by a stabbing pain that took her breath away. Twenty-two years had elapsed since that fateful day when Douglas Napier had sailed to America. Now the summer ghosts dissolved before her eyes on the rain-sheeted windowpanes.

As the pain subsided, Natsu fell across her bed and closed her eyes, afraid it might strike again. For weeks she had felt drained of energy by her concern over the futures of her son and his father. The bank loan would solve Douglas's problems. But their son's ambitions as a journalist could not be bought for any sum of money. Despite all her efforts, she could not fight the stigma of Paul's mixed blood. After he had graduated from the university, one of his professors had recommended him for a teaching post there, but even that was cruelly denied him. His prize had seemed the answer to her prayers. Oh, why had God not answered them? Natsu anguished.

"Natsu?" Yoko called to her softly. "Are you there?"

"Yes, resting," she answered.

Yoko entered the darkened bedroom. "Toru has come home on leave."

Natsu lifted her head from the pillow. "How marvelous. Paul has great need of him. Something terrible has happened."

"*Hai*, my son told me everything. They met in the street after Paul was beaten."

As Yoko leaned down over her and placed one hand on her forehead, Natsu gave thanks for this tirelessly devoted friend. "I feel so helpless."

"You are feverish." Yoko's kind eyes showed concern. She was now a round matronly woman much like her mother, who had passed on a few years before. Yoko also had made many sacrifices for her illegitimate son. From time to time there had been men in Yoko's life willing to overlook her youthful mistake, but she, too, had loved only once and had never married. "Even with a fever your cheeks are so pale," Yoko said. "I will telephone Dr. Amano."

"I'm just a little tired," Natsu said, smiling up at her reassuringly. She recalled the night Yoko had brought Dr. Amano to this room, where he had delivered her son into the world. He was a man without hatred, whose tender hands had nursed Paul through the illnesses of childhood, and she had come to look upon Dr. Amano as her friend. His office was only a short walk from the tea shop. "Really, there's no reason to visit the doctor. Now, not another word. I won't be treated like an invalid," she told Yoko.

Just as Natsu rose from the bed, another brutal stab of pain assaulted her. Its passing left an intense throbbing deep inside her abdomen. Natsu explored herself with trembling fingers, unable to locate the exact spot where the pain had struck and frightened by what might have caused it.

"I am taking you to see Dr. Amano now," Yoko said firmly. Natsu did not protest. She held tightly to Yoko's sturdy arm, although she wanted Douglas there beside her, wanted his strong arms to support her dizzy passage down the staircase. In her pain Natsu relived the birth of their son, when she had wished for the sound of Douglas's voice telling her everything would be all right. He was never there when she needed him most.

CHAPTER 5

Clinging to her friend Yoko's arm, Natsu Yoseido descended the wide stone steps of a Tokyo hospital. More than two weeks had passed since she had experienced the pain that had taken her to the doctor. Dr. Amano had immediately ordered a number of tests, and that morning she had been called to the hospital to hear the results. Natsu had nearly fainted when Dr. Amano explained that there was a growth in her stomach, a tumor pressing on a nerve. That was the cause of her pain. X rays showed the tumor to be quite large.

Dr. Amano had sadly confessed that he was helpless to do more than ease her suffering with drugs until she submitted to surgery.

"Only after the growth is removed and biopsied can we be absolutely sure if it is malignant, Natsu. Cutting it out will end your pain, but I must tell you that the chances of it being benign are small. I do not want to give you false hope," Dr. Amano had explained, preparing her for the worst.

"And if it *is* malignant?" Natsu had somehow found the courage to ask.

"If so, we have a fight on our hands. The cancer will spread. But we will fight it, Natsu. Our medical knowledge is limited, but rest assured I'll do everything in my power to keep you with us."

Natsu had wept in Dr. Amano's arms, but now her tears were spent. As she and Yoko walked, life seemed to continue on as before: butterflies played around the city trees, and lovers strolled hand in hand to Hibiya Park.

Natsu halted Yoko. "No one else is to know of this," she said firmly. "If I am to die, those I love would suffer needlessly by knowing of my illness. I as well, Yoko. It would destroy what time is left to me to watch the pain grow in their eyes."

"But you cannot keep this tragic news to yourself," Yoko insisted, eyes red from crying. "The truth will come out when you enter the hospital for surgery."

"No. Dr. Amano must respect my feelings." Natsu removed the fan tucked inside her pink obi and snapped it open decisively. "Paul will be told it's only minor surgery. And I won't enter the hospital until Douglas leaves Japan." Only the other night she had nestled in Douglas's arms at the Tokyo apartment they shared, hiding her pain as he spoke of his business affairs. He had hoped to remain with her in Japan until the summer ended, but Lord Mitsudara was pressuring him to begin his work in Germany. Very soon now they would be separated. "My illness mustn't stand in the way of Douglas's future," she told Yoko. "He's left the city with his wife to visit Baron Hosokawa, and we'll have so little time together when he returns to me. I want to cherish every precious moment. My surgery can wait. The new drugs Dr. Amano prescribed will dull my pain, so Douglas need never know."

Her eyes filling with tears, Yoko hugged her friend. "The years between us make it impossible to deny your wishes. But perhaps the doctors are wrong, Natsu. Perhaps the tumor is benign and the surgeon's knife will make you well again."

Natsu soberly shook her head. "I wish it were so, but I've learned to trust what my heart tells me. I know it is cancer. And I'm even grateful to God for the pain. Without it my cancer would have gone undetected until it was too late even for the treatment that can prolong my life."

Yoko wiped away the tears. "Why do the gods always take the decent ones? You deserve better."

"I'm not afraid of death," Natsu said. "Be brave, Yoko." Natsu smiled. "Learning of this has given me a clear sense of purpose, and as always, I'll need your support to help me see it through."

"It is hard for me to accept this." Already experiencing a sense of loss, Yoko searched Natsu's pretty face. Nothing there spoke of the disease that threatened slowly to consume her. "Despite what your heart tells you, we must not give up all hope."

"Time is the best I can hope for," Natsu said. "With radium treatments, Dr. Amano can grant me a few more years of life. Time enough to see my son realize his ambitions."

She looked at the dainty silver wristwatch Douglas had given her. "Tamura-san will be coming to the shop for his afternoon tea. Several times he's inquired about my son's career. He's in a position to help Paul." Natsu thoughtfully walked on with her friend. The offices of *Nippon Shimbun* stood just down the street from Hibiya Park, where she halted Yoko and said, "The way Tamura-san looks at me has made me uncomfortable about approaching him. But now I must turn to him for help. I can't speak about this at the shop. I'll telephone the newspaper and ask him to meet me in the park."

"What?" Yoko regarded her friend with shock. "But Tamura-san has designs on you. To approach him, to ask that he help Paul, can only lead you to more grief."

Natsu impatiently fluttered her fan. "My mind is made up. He isn't an ogre, Yoko. He's a cultured gentleman."

"Underneath his fancy manners there is a man like any other," argued Yoko. "Please, reconsider before you rush into this."

"Oh, don't you see? The very thing you fear may encourage the man to give Paul a chance." Just then Natsu felt a stabbing pain. "I mustn't fail my son," she said breathlessly. "I'm going to call Mr. Tamura—now."

Natsu ignored Yoko's protestations and entered a nearby phone booth. Hideo Tamura was so excited at hearing from Natsu that his voice cracked. But she could not afford the luxury of having second thoughts, and she invited *Nippon Shimbun*'s editor-in-chief to meet her in the park. He said he would leave his office immediately.

While Yoko returned to the shop, Natsu sat waiting on a park bench near the fountain, formulating what she would say. By the time she saw the man hurrying eagerly toward her, she was prepared.

"Some last-minute business, Madame Yoseido," Hideo Tamura apologized, pulling down the vest of his black silk business suit. "Otherwise, I would not have kept you waiting."

"Please, sit down, Tamura-*san*." Natsu forced herself to smile as he sank beside her on the park bench and tugged at his trouser legs to keep their razor-sharp creases from wrinkling. "I appreciate your giving me this time," she said. "My son is in a desperate situation, or I would never presume on your good nature. What I have to say comes from the heart and is not easy for me to confess." She raised her open fan to just below her eyes, then fluttered it ever so slightly. "I ask only that you listen with an open mind." Natsu paused to wet her dry lips with the tip of her tongue. "I trust you are a man of honor and will judge me fairly."

Hideo Tamura's homely face reflected great inner turmoil. Nervous, he clasped his hands together. "I'm honored by your trust in me, Madame Yoseido. To be frank, it has always puzzled me how a woman of your obvious breeding has come to wear the kimono of a tea maid." Clearing his throat, he said, "It may surprise you that I know quite a bit more of things than you may think. Akira Yoseido, your son, is of mixed blood. Not long ago, we had a brief encounter at the university. The writing he pressed on me at the time was buried in my files, unread. After I encountered him again outside the tea shop, I decided to read it. He has a most impressive talent. No doubt you have sacrificed much for your son's education. But perhaps I'm mistaken and this isn't the same young man?"

Lowering her fan, Natsu collapsed it and held it tightly. Tamura's knowledge spared her a great deal. "No mistake," she said. "Paul is his Christian name. He's all I have, and no sacrifice is too great for him." At that moment she no longer felt it was necessary to give this man a full accounting of the past. Instead, she confessed just enough to gain his sympathy, never identifying Douglas Napier by name.

When she grew silent, Hideo removed his Panama hat and stared back at her for a moment.

"Help my son. I beg of you," she pleaded.

"I feel overwhelming compassion for you, Madame," he answered earnestly. "Yes, I will do what I can for your son. *Nippon Shimbun* employs only pure-blooded Japanese, but as editor-in-chief, I wield a great deal of power."

"Oh, I can't tell you what this means!" Natsu pushed aside her personal fears in order to voice the obvious question. "How can I ever repay your kindness?"

Hideo Tamura pulled out a handkerchief to wipe his perspiring face. "I must confess that I've worshipped you in silence all these months. If not for your son, I would never have found the courage to tell you."

Natsu pretended surprise. "I'm flattered—and shocked!"

"Mine is a lonely life." Hideo's voice lowered almost to a whisper. "Women find my outward appearance unattractive. But there are inner qualities, Madame."

His expression pleaded for some encouraging response. Natsu opened her painted silk fan fold by fold. "The gentleness in your eyes speaks for that," she said, looking at him. Suddenly she felt chilled—passion had replaced the gentleness.

"Forgive my boldness." Hideo quickly looked away. He realized his eyes had revealed too much. "Love is a powerful force. I recognize my shortcomings, but given time, perhaps my feelings for you will pave the way to a fond relationship." Turning his straw hat round and round in his hands, Tamura wiped its sweatband with his handkerchief and sighed. "The American who visited you at the tea shop is a handsome man. Although you did not say, I assumed this was Paul's father."

A sudden thought prompted Natsu to speak a lie. "Yes. But our affair ended long ago. Now there is no one else in my life."

"There is no one?" Hideo leaned closer to her. "Say nothing more of the past. All I ask is the opportunity to know you better in the future."

"I accept your proposal of friendship, Tamura-*san*." Natsu fluttered her fan while deciding the role she must play. This drab little man might quickly lose interest in Paul if she discouraged his hopes. A job was not enough to secure her son's future; only a powerful mentor such as Tamura could advance his career. "Since we've been entirely honest with each other, I'm tempted to ask something more of you. But I lack the courage. Yes, it's far too much to ask."

"Please, let me be the judge of that," he was quick to answer.

"Well, since you insist." Natsu told herself that it was not a sin to deceive this man. She would give him companionship while using her charm to hold off his desire. In that way she would please him without injuring his feelings. "My son harbors resentment toward his father that can only injure me and others," she began. "I pray that he'll come to realize how guiltless his father is." Suddenly she found herself speaking in a tone of desperation, for another stabbing pain had filled her mind with thoughts of death. Without the love Douglas could give him, their son would be left alone in the world. "If my son believed that his father's influential friends played some part in your decision to assist his career—

well, that might help bring them closer together. Perhaps my son's forgiveness can't be bought with a lie. But we all live on hope, Tamura-san."

"Say no more." Hideo reached out to touch her, then pulled back his hand. "Natsu—if I may address you so?" Her jaw quivered as she nodded. "Since we're to be friends, you must call me Hideo." He rose from the park bench and bowed. "It would please me to serve your hopes. I'm without family, and Paul will be treated like my own son. Tell him what you will, and I'll gladly be his silent mentor."

"Your generosity leaves me speechless." Tears welled up in Natsu's eyes. "You're a fine man." She felt compelled to offer him some small degree of hope. "You've made this a happy day for me. Deeper feelings are often found in friendship, Hideo. Given time to know you better, who can say?"

Hideo visibly brightened. "Yes, intimacy between us can't be rushed, Natsu. We have all the time in the world."

The pain she had experienced a moment before reminded Natsu how little time there actually was. "When can you act on Paul's behalf?"

"At once. Would you honor me with your presence at dinner this evening?"

"Yes, Hideo." She could not refuse, and Hideo Tamura set the hour and place. "Now, I really must return to the shop." Natsu excused herself with a bow. She was eager to tell her son the good news.

Natsu walked toward the park gates. The heat of the sun made her dizzy. Pausing by a small stream, she bent to wet her handkerchief, then pressed it to her forehead. How very much like the mountain streams of Baron Hosokawa's castle gardens, she mused, remembering the thrill of her first meeting there with Douglas Napier. Often she longed to revisit those fragrant gardens of a bygone summer. Had life gone differently for them, when the festival of Tanabata was celebrated a few days hence, she would be standing in those castle gardens with Douglas as her husband.

But it was better not to entertain such thoughts, Natsu told herself, walking on. Yet, while the city pulsed with noise, she let her spirit travel far away to join Douglas Napier in the gardens of their youth, beyond the sounds and smells of Tokyo, beyond the sacrifices of her days spent without him. She had asked Yoko to be brave for her. But when Douglas returned from Kyushu Island, Natsu knew that she must find the courage to bear her illness alone in silence until they were separated once again by the oceans.

Angela Napier held to her floppy-brimmed summer hat as she stepped off the train at a rustic village depot. The wind caused her beige silk dress to cling to her tall, slender body. She was annoyed. Douglas had booked first-class sleeping accommodations for them, but she had not slept well during the thousand-mile journey from Tokyo to this remote prefecture of Kyushu Island.

The wind was so strong that Angela was unable to open the dainty silk parasol she carried to shade her creamy complexion from the sun's harmful rays. "Oh, this wind! Here, Douglas, take this off my hands before my hat blows away." She thrust the parasol at her husband and looked up the village road that wended through brown fields of parched grass. "There's Tadashi's car!"

Douglas waved with Angela's parasol. O-nami honked the horn of a very dusty Rolls-Royce, whose dirty whitewall tires kicked up a storm of dust as the limousine came to a stop.

"Douglas! Angela!" O-nami called to them. He threw open the car door and hurried toward the couple.

Douglas embraced the baron's majordomo with affection. Angela Napier was much more reserved, allowing herself to be hugged but not responding in kind. "Please, let's get into the car," she said. "I'll never understand why no one waters down the road. I can't wait for a bath to soak the dust out of my pores."

"The baron sent me with a chilled bottle of your favorite white wine," O-nami said. "It is in the bar compartment." He managed to grab up all their expensive luggage, then heaved everything inside the trunk, and shut the lid with a loud crunch.

"How thoughtful of Tadashi," Angela said.

Douglas helped his wife into the limousine. Two crystal glasses sat chilling with an uncorked bottle of Riesling in a silver bucket of melting ice. Douglas poured wine for them both.

"Thank you darling," Angela said. "What a blessing! I'm so dehydrated."

"The heat wouldn't get to you as much if you didn't fight it," he said, handing her a frosty glass of wine as O-nami started the limousine. Douglas watched his wife take a sip, then flutter her attractive green eyes and sigh, shifting the position of her long, slender legs. From the day he had brought Angela to Japan as his bride, he reflected, she had remained only a visitor, estranged from its climate and its people.

"O-nami, must you drive so fast?" she complained, unable to find a comfortable position on the hot, dusty seat. It was yet some twenty miles to the Hosokawa lands, and she anticipated every jarring twist and turn along the antiquated road, little changed since sword-bearing samurai had marched along it on foot. "It seems silly to come all this way for so short a visit," she said to Douglas. "With the Karlstadts due to arrive in Tokyo in only a week, it would have been more sensible to decline Tadashi's invitation."

"Angela, bringing our families together to celebrate Tanabata means a good deal to him," Douglas replied. "Things aren't always as we'd like them to be."

"I'm not being insensitive—just practical. Hold my glass, please. I'm desperate for a cigarette." Wounded, Angela stared at him, then took a monogrammed gold cigarette case from her purse. After returning home from closing the mills, her husband had been somber and withdrawn. Lord Mitsudara's loan was cause for good cheer, she thought, and yet Douglas's mood was dismal at best. En route to Kyushu he had completely ignored her. Now, as she lit a cigarette, she felt angry and neglected. "Darling, I wish you'd tell me what it is that's bothering you so much."

"Business," Douglas answered, pausing to sip his wine. "Our arrangement with Lord Mitsudara isn't to my liking. His loan has just cleared with the German banks. Time lost is money lost, he told me from on high. The Karlstadts won't have much of a visit. We'll be returning to Germany with them the first week in August. I've booked passage for us on the Trans-Siberian Railway."

"But that's wonderful news." Angela took comfort in their escape from Japan. For Angela Napier, the civilized world began at the port of Vladivostok, where she sailed each year to board the train for summer holidays abroad with her husband.

Douglas said nothing more and turned his attention to the vista slowly unfolding before him. They were descending the steep road to Baron Hosokawa's fertile valley. Clouds hugged the jagged mountain peaks that circled the valley floor. The rolling foothills were a tapestry woven in blowing grass. From this height the miles of mulberry orchards appeared as forests of miniature bonsai, and the tall thatched-roofed wooden houses where the silkworms spun their cocoons were like clusters of sunflowers patterning the meadows. Shipping their tons of raw silk overland to the mills had always been a costly operation. Douglas agreed with the lord's plans to construct an airstrip here, but he regretted how it would deface the beauty of the land.

"I must admit, Tadashi's castle is like a charming fantasy," Angela observed, leaning forward in the seat for a better view. The castle's peaked blue tile roofs soared among tall pine trees. It was the beautiful Japanese gardens surrounding the castle that made it appear so extraordinary, Angela observed. Silver streams of mountain runoff created mossy green islands, which were spanned by arching bridges painted a bright vermilion. "I always feel as if time has stopped here," she said.

Douglas nodded. "Yes, this place always seems unchanged." In his boyhood, he had enjoyed listening to stories told by Tadashi's father of legendary battles fought against warlords who had wanted to add the Hosokawa lands to their dominions, and stories of family misfortunes after their home was destroyed by fire. The Hosokawa castle, with its tiered turrets and spacious apartments, was a reconstruction of the original structure built sometime in the seventeenth century. It might have forever lain there in ruins if not for the partnership that had enabled Fujio Hosokawa to restore the castle.

That had been more than sixty years ago. Since then the castle had undergone extensive remodeling. Its electric wiring, telephone lines, and modern plumbing had been artfully concealed to preserve its antique look.

"What elegance and serenity," Angela said quietly, resting her head back to gaze from the slowly moving limousine at cherry trees lining the broad road. Suddenly she grew pensive. From the day Angela first arrived in Japan as Douglas's bride, Tadashi and his lovely wife, Sumie, had showered her with warmth and affection. The strain of living in Japan might have been too much for her if it had not been for the Hosokawas. Although she placed a high value on Tadashi's friendship, it was Sumie's presence that had drawn her to this castle, and since Sumie's death, Angela's visits had become rare.

Angela looked at her husband. "Returning here brings fond memories of times we spent together when Sumie was alive," she said. "The two of us spent many quiet afternoons in these gardens, while our children napped in their rooms."

"Yes, Sumie's death was a great loss to us all." Douglas's fondest memories of the castle gardens were of the spring afternoon when he had first laid eyes on Natsu. Visiting here would shorten what time was left him with the woman he loved, and he was bereft over their being separated for an entire year.

O-nami stopped the limousine and opened the rear door. Douglas got out, then helped Angela from the car. He surveyed the grounds, searching for his son. "I guess Max is off somewhere enjoying himself," he said.

"*Hai*, youngsters thrive on fun," O-nami said. "There is little enough time for play in one's life."

"I'd gladly relive the carefree days Tadashi and I spent here when we were boys. It didn't take much to please us then."

"Men lose the knack of how to play," Angela commented bitingly. During the past weeks, her husband had worked late at his office almost every night and often did not return to her bed before dawn. He wearily ignored her desire to make love. "Your work has always come first, Douglas. Oh, well," she said, sighing, "I don't suppose I'm the only wife whose husband has taken business as his mistress."

His wife's sigh touched Douglas with guilt. She had been a good mother to their son and deserved more of him than he could possibly give in a life divided between two women. "Angela, I'm sorry for neglecting you so much of the time. But I'm under a lot of pressure from Lord Mitsudara to clear up our affairs here." Douglas made an effort to atone for his neglect with a husbandly kiss.

Angela smiled, and her green eyes sparkled. "Apology accepted, darling." She removed her floppy-brimmed hat, and the cool mountain breeze lifted her wavy auburn hair. "The climate here is a refreshing change from Tokyo. Let's get settled in and relax until dinner."

Servants scurried ahead with the luggage. Straw slippers were neatly laid out for them at the castle's open door, where O-nami's buxom wife, Yufugawo, bowed a greeting. She was dressed in a colorful silk kimono. "*O-kaeri-nasai*. Welcome home."

Angela regarded Yufugawo's woeful expression. "Is something wrong?"

"A family matter, Angela," she replied in English. "The baron is occupied in his study and will see you at dinner." Yufugawo was in her early forties, but she looked older than her husband. She narrowed her eyes as O-nami asked if the baron's son had gotten himself into trouble again. "And if he has, that is for his father to deal with privately," the woman snapped, and folded her arms across her ample bosom. "The servants have prepared your rooms," she told Douglas, smiling fondly as he kissed her cheek. "Max went riding with Shizue hours ago. Ah, those two lose track of the time together."

Angela had a soft spot in her heart for this childless woman who had become Shizue's surrogate mother and was the girl's traveling companion on visits to Tokyo. "I'm simply exhausted from our journey," she said, embracing Yufugawo. "Please have the servants draw my bath, then come to me so we can talk."

Yufugawo responded immediately, moving gracefully for a woman of her size as she instructed the household servants. Angela walked up the polished staircase, while Douglas remained below. The Hosokawas' spacious rooms were elegantly furnished in the traditional Japanese style. Their sliding doors lay open to the castle gardens. Douglas noted that the door to the baron's study was closed.

He turned to O-nami. "It seems we've arrived on the heels of a dilemma," he said. "Has my son been enjoying himself?"

"*Hai*, but there are things on his mind." O-nami looked away from Douglas. "He is a boy nearly grown into a man, Douglas."

Douglas nodded thoughtfully. "When Max returns, tell him I'd like to speak with him. I'll be in the garden."

Outside, Douglas glanced up at the windows of rooms he had often shared with his wife. But it was Natsu who haunted him as he walked the familiar garden paths, retracing the footsteps of his youth.

In his study Baron Hosokawa was seated in courtly fashion behind an impressive desk carved of ebony imported from Ceylon. His spine grew rigid against the high-backed ebony chair three generations of barons had occupied while dealing with peasants like the foreman seated opposite him. The man had come to lodge a complaint against his master's son. The baron had thoroughly interrogated Mr. Okamoto, hoping to trap him in some falsehood that would clear Kimitake of any wrongdoing, but the man held stubbornly to his story. In one of the barnlike sericulture houses, he had found Kimitake attempting to seduce his virginal young daughter. Okamoto had intervened before the act could be consummated, and now he asked for justice.

"I suggest serious punishment for the boy to discourage further advances toward my daughter," Okamoto said.

Tadashi Hosokawa rose to his feet, looming over the employee who had forgotten his place. "I'll decide his punishment without any help from you, Okamoto-*san!*" He began pacing the study.

Everything in the room remained as it had been since his grandfather, Fujio, had rebuilt the castle. Silk battle flags framed in glass hung on the walls. Helmets, weapons, and suits of armor were displayed in specially designed cases. Honors awarded the Hosokawa family for service to their daimyo and princely gifts awarded to them for service to the shogun's court lay on velvet-lined shelves in ornately carved rosewood cases.

These family treasures, which had been carried from the flames by his grandfather before the castle burned to the ground, were considered sacred. Even during the time of hardship that followed, the Hosokawa family would rather have starved than part with them. Tadashi found their presence a constant source of pride and a constant reminder of the Hosokawa honor.

"My son must have a chance to speak for himself," the baron announced. He called to his aged secretary, Akihiri. "Bring Kimitake here! You'll find him with the tutors."

Baron Hosokawa stationed himself at the open door. Soon his son appeared in the corridor beside Akihiri. Kimitake froze at the threshold, shocked at the sight of the man who was seated inside. He swallowed hard.

"Well, Kimitake, it seems you already know what this is about. Get inside," the baron ordered. Quickly he shut the doors. "I've heard Okamoto-*san*'s story, and now I'll hear yours. And it had better be the truth."

"Yes, Father." Kimitake had inherited his father's strong-featured face and tall, muscular build. Girls found him very attractive, and Kimitake took advantage of their attraction. "I don't know what Okamoto-*san* has told you, but his daughter is a little tease. I'm not the only boy she's lured into the sericulture houses. I swear it by my honor, Father."

Baron Hosokawa relaxed his shoulders. He knew when his son was telling the truth. "In my judgment, Kimitake isn't entirely at fault. Speak up, Okamoto-*san*. Is your daughter's loose morality common knowledge or not?"

Okamoto rubbed his face with calloused hands. "Everyone on the land can testify to my daughter's chastity, Hosokawa-*san*. She is not a harlot," he insisted. Then he looked at Kimitake and moaned. "How can you speak such a lie?"

"Look to your daughter for the truth, Okamoto-*san*," countered the baron, now showing sympathy for the man. "A father is often the last to know. I won't call in character witnesses and make this incident a subject of embarrassment for us both. Go home. Make her tell you what happened again, and this time look deep into your daughter's eyes."

Okamoto appeared about to argue the point, but then he bowed deeply and said, "*Hai*, I will follow your advice."

Kimitake could not help smiling as the foreman left in defeat. "Thanks for believing me, Father. Well, I'd better get back to my studies." He turned toward the door, but his father reached it first and barred it with his arm. He regarded his son sternly.

"But it wasn't my fault," Kimitake protested. "You said so yourself."

"There are two sides to every truth." The baron heaved a weary sigh. "Sit down and we'll examine what you've done." Anger and sternness had always failed him in the past, so he tried to be patient.

"Okamoto's daughter may be the harlot you say," Tadashi said, circling the boy, "but that's no excuse for your dishonorable behavior." He paused. At such times as these, the baron felt frustrated. To date, no amount of effort had brought out the qualities of Kimitake's noble lineage. "What am I to do with you? A boy of your station consorting with peasant girls!"

"But, Father, how could I resist this proof of my manhood with such a willing partner?" Kimitake offered a sheepish grin. "After all, a man must get his experience somewhere."

Tadashi threw up his hands in disgust. "Don't patronize me with drivel about proving your manhood! This distraction from your studies threatens to make you an ignoramus, unworthy to inherit my title and lands!" Suddenly at the mercy of his temper, he gestured toward the Hosokawa regalia. "Look around you and be ashamed before your ancestors. I've suffered your lack of self-discipline long enough. Your sister's everything a son should be. Shizue sets a worthy example that you'd be wise to follow. Our family crest printed on your kimono isn't just decoration. It's put there as a reminder of the obligations owed our bloodline."

Kimitake bowed his head. Shizue had always been treated with favoritism, he thought. Not since he had been young had he received any displays of fatherly love. His father had ceased to show him any warmth since the death of his mother, and now he felt chilled. "I've tried my best to please you, Father," he said.

"Your best isn't good enough." The baron weighed his next words. Sons required a stern, unwavering hand, he told himself, recalling Lord Mitsudara's advice and wondering if Jiro had been so aggravating at Kimitake's age. "I'm confining you to the castle grounds," he announced. "Work harder at your studies. I want to hear nothing but praise from your tutors. You've another year to qualify for entry at Harvard. Make the most of it." He crossed to his desk and sat down. "Max's parents should have arrived by now. Be on your best behavior, Kimitake. Don't embarrass me." With a wave of his hand, Tadashi excused his son from the study.

Kimitake was furious. While he was cooped up indoors sweating over his studies, Shizue and Max were outdoors horseback riding and enjoying archery and fencing. "It isn't fair!" he shouted at the top of his voice, then thought better of adding to his punishment and silently walked to the classroom, where his tutors were waiting.

Shizue raced Max home on horseback across a meadowland to a sparkling stream. The vastness of the Hosokawa valley often led them to surprising places, and that afternoon they had discovered a wondrous new site. It was hidden from the world by a dense forest of bamboo, whose loud rustling in the wind muffled the sounds of a nearby waterfall. What could be heard of its faint sounds guided them through the tall bamboo to a natural archway formed by two willow trees, whose boughs were joined together like the arms of embracing lovers. Beyond this cathedrallike entrance lay a sheltered garden oasis, where a wild yellow rose called kerria bloomed. There Max and Shizue swam in the cool crystal waters of a rocky reflecting pool as time drifted away with the buzzing tune made by the fairy wings of dragonflies who skimmed the water lilies. Then the lowering sun had reminded both Shizue and Max that his parents were arriving that day, and they had reluctantly left the beautiful spot, promising to return there.

Now they raced each other to the mountain stream whose tributaries nourished the castle gardens. Shizue was the first to reach the sloping banks, where she reined up, laughing as Max trotted his twin chestnut gelding down to her a moment later. "I suspect you let me win," she said. "Mercury has more spirit in him than that."

"Not his fault. You're the better rider." It pleased Max to let Shizue win. "I'm no match for a beautiful samurai on horseback," he said while helping her dismount.

After they had let the horses drink, Max sank to his knees at Shizue's feet. "Your wish is my command, my lady," he said, inwardly pained by the truth in his words. "I'm just a lowly peasant groveling for your kind words and your pretty smiles."

Shizue laughed. "Max, do get up!"

Suddenly Max dropped all pretense. "Your beauty leaves me weak," he confessed in a voice barely above a whisper. "I can't go on like this, pretending nothing's changed between us. Shizue, I've tried to hold back my feelings, but I can't go on just playing at being in love."

"I know, Max," she said softly.

"Shizue, I love you!" Max rose to his feet and brought her against him. "You do love me?"

"Oh, yes." Neither one had dared speak that word until that moment, and his boldness had her trembling as she murmured, "I love you as much if not more."

"Then we've got to face up to things."

"No, I don't want to question what loving you means, or think what's standing in the way," she implored. "Please, Max, just kiss me."

With that kiss, Shizue surrendered her heart to Max. When he released her, she clung to him, resting her head against his chest. For those brief moments, nothing else existed but their love.

"Being in love is all that really matters," said Shizue, gazing up into Max's clear blue eyes. "You're so beautiful." He was obviously embarrassed by her words, and she laughed. "Yes, a man can be beautiful. As a boy you were irresistible. That's why I tagged after you and made such a nuisance of myself."

Max shook his head and laughed. "Kimitake and I did everything to get you out of our hair. But no matter what we did, you always managed to keep up with us. No wonder I love you so much." He bent down and kissed her again.

At last Shizue pulled away, her cheeks on fire as she spoke his name, "Max—I've never wanted anyone but you. No one else will ever have me."

Max cupped her face between his hands. "I couldn't hope for more than that."

"Then we must live on hope." Just then her fiery spirit ignited in one flash of resolve. Their love, she thought, could conquer anything. "Whatever may come between us, I'll take my courage from you."

"Holding you like this, nothing seems impossible," he said, and kissed her tenderly again. Soon they heard the toll of iron bells echoing out across the valley. Their call was a tradition of the Hosokawa lands, announcing the beginning and the end of each day's work.

"Your parents must be wondering where we are," Shizue said. It had come as a shock when her father had told them that the Napiers would be leaving Japan before the summer was over. "It's awful about you going away so soon," she pouted. "We'll have only this month together."

Max skipped a pebble across the stream. "I don't have any say in the matter. I'll be living in Berlin with my parents' German friends and finish my schooling there." He caressed Shizue's cheek. "A year in Germany with only your letters. Our future seems only a dream." Suddenly Max saw in Shizue's eyes the same glimmer of fear he had seen the day they had first kissed near the shrine of her ancestors.

"Our families have never been apart for very long. Papa will be so much lonelier," she said. "Especially when I return to boarding school."

"Do you think he'll ever marry again?"

Shizue shook her head sadly, then changed the subject. "We mustn't be late for dinner."

As they mounted their horses, Max thought about Shizue's father. Under the influence of a loving wife, he might soften to their cause. The obligations he expected of his daughter posed an ominous threat to the fulfillment of their dream. But at last their feelings were out in the open. He knew that Shizue was counting on him to slay the dragon of tradition, and as they turned their horses for home, her expressive eyes regarded him as though he were her knight in shining armor.

"Tomorrow I'll fix a picnic basket, and we'll return to that lovely place we found today," she said.

"Yes, I'd like that." Max smiled back at her and urged his mount into a gallop through the lacy boughs of the mulberry orchards. Misty clouds drifted with the smoke that rose from the chimneys of tiny houses scattered like acorns among the foothills. Peasants waved at the riders and Max waved back at them, calling out their names. As a young boy, Max's heart had anchored itself in this beautiful valley. It was his real home, the place he longed for during the winter months of school in Tokyo.

When the riders arrived at the castle and dismounted, stable grooms took charge of their horses, and Shizue raced Max to the stone steps, where they sat pulling off their boots. She looked up at the face of the moon just becoming visible in the sky overhead. At the end of this first week in July, there would be a full moon to celebrate the festival that was so very special to her father. "I can't remember the last summer your parents were here with us for Tanabata," Shizue said.

Before Max could respond, O-nami appeared in the doorway. "Your father wishes to have words with you, Ichiban. Alone, in the garden."

"Coming," Max said. Once O-nami had turned away, Max gave Shizue a quick hug. "I'll see you at dinner," he said, then left her sitting on the steps.

Douglas was lost in thought as he sat under the boughs of an old cherry tree. Suddenly his son's voice brought him back to the present. "Max!" He stood with open arms to embrace his son. Max kissed him on the cheek. The boy had not yet outgrown that display of his love, but holding him at arm's length, Douglas observed a change in his son's eyes. "I've missed you, Max. Your mother's resting upstairs, and I thought we'd have a talk just between men."

"Sure, Dad."

"You're looking fit. Is everything all right?"

"Well, not exactly." He had always turned to his father for understanding. Now he wanted to tell him about his love for Shizue. However, the words stuck in his throat. "I've got a serious matter to talk to you about," he began awkwardly. "I couldn't tell you over the phone, but discussing it now isn't any easier."

Douglas mussed the boy's sunbleached hair. "Come on, son, we're old pals. Whatever is bothering you can't be so bad."

Max inhaled a deep breath, then said quickly and loudly, "I'm in love with Shizue, and she feels the same way about me." Douglas Napier's face registered his shock. "I'm glad you're here, Dad," Max went on. "I couldn't have held this inside much longer. Dad—I need your advice."

"That's a tall order," he said, too stunned for ready answers. Douglas had been almost the same age as his son when Natsu won his heart with a love that could not be denied or reasoned away. "I must admit this takes me by surprise," he said, and tried to smile. "Let's walk a bit. I think better on my feet."

Max felt relieved when his father put an arm around his shoulders. "I've never been so sure of my feelings," he said earnestly. "But I can't see straight."

Douglas was more personally affected by this turn of events than he wanted to show. "I can understand that," he said. "We'll take a look at the facts, and try to sort things out."

"I knew I could count on you, Dad."

They walked for a time in silence. Douglas grew outwardly calm, while a myriad of personal feelings raged inside him. His own emotional vulnerability conflicted with his role as a parent. He would have to be very careful in addressing the needs of his son. "I won't suggest what you feel for Shizue isn't love," he said at last. "Falling in love for the first time is a serious matter. You're an intelligent boy, but emotions are confusing—especially at your age."

Max lowered his eyes to the ground. "Agreed."

Douglas wished to spare his son from suffering as he had under the tyranny of an insensitive father. "Of course, there are problems to be faced" was all he said, and Max nodded. "But as things stand now, they can only add to your confusion. The best advice I can give you is to behave sensibly and not rush into things. Oh, I know it's going to be hard on you, but Shizue's very young, and since you're older, it's your responsibility to keep a level head. So, these are the facts." He paused for a beat. "Shizue is responsible to her father, and a father's rights can't be opposed by his children until they come of age. I've always trusted you to do the right thing, Max. In this case, there's nothing you can do but wait." His son's sober face was a painful reminder to Douglas of his own helplessness and anguish at the same age. "Listen, the bottom line is clearly drawn. We'll be going to Germany soon. Unfortunately, you have no choice but to wait. I realize this is a very difficult time in your life, and I know it will be very hard on you."

"Yes, it will," Max said, passing one hand across his brow. "But I'll get through it somehow."

As he looked down on a garden stream that rushed over the mossy-green faces of rocks, Douglas felt the pull of time joining his past with the present. He brought Max against him. "I'm proud of you. Be patient and things will work themselves out."

"Thanks for not treating me like a kid, Dad."

"I know you too well for that." Douglas met his son's trusting eyes and felt some relief. The problem was smoothed over, but far from solved. "Come on, it's getting late. Time we changed for dinner."

As Max walked on beside his father, he contemplated what had passed between them. Lights flickered on at the castle, and he glimpsed Shizue standing at her bedroom window. He was sure no other man on earth had ever known such happiness and bittersweet pain. Then Douglas put an arm around his shoulders, and it served as a reminder that he was still a boy who needed his father.

* * *

That evening before dinner, Angela Napier swept through the upstairs corridor wearing a pretty *yukata*. While in their homes during the summer, most Japanese wore this loose cotton garment, which resembled the kimono but was cooler. It was favored for beauty as well as comfort. Angela felt that wearing the *yukata* was appropriate dress when visiting the Hosokawas on Kyushu, though she never wore it at home in the city of Tokyo.

The baron stepped from his rooms to greet her. "Angela! Always a delight for my eyes and a lift for my spirits. I can't tell you how much having you here for Tanabata means to me," he said.

"Dear Tadashi, you'll make me cry if you go on." Angela hugged him, then glanced inside the bedroom that was unchanged since Sumie's death.

Shizue appeared in the corridor. She was wearing a new pink skirt and blouse. "Shizue, what a treasure you are! My, how you've blossomed since the spring."

"Do you really think so?" Shizue came forward, modeling her outfit, and then threw her arms around Max's mother in a girlish display of affection. They both laughed. "I'm not quite a woman yet, though," she confided demurely.

"At your age, I was also in a rush to grow up," said Angela, smiling. "Now I take forever at my vanity mirror. But cosmetics are no substitute for your blush of youth. Enjoy it while you can."

Douglas Napier appeared beside his wife and received a warm welcome from Shizue. He was struck by her maturity. Seeing her radiant smile added to the poignancy of his son's confession. Douglas wondered if Tadashi knew of Shizue's love for Max.

Kimitake sulked into view. He was very fond of Max's parents, but he'd had a bad day. Standing there, he kept both hands in the trouser pockets of his white suit. "Good evening, everyone," he said solemnly.

Then Angela gave Kimitake a hug, and he smiled. Next he warmly took Douglas's outstretched hand.

"What's keeping my son?" Angela wondered. "I haven't seen him since we arrived." She went to rap at the door of his room. "Maxwell, are you dressed? Everyone is ready for dinner."

Max opened the door and hugged Angela warmly, receiving a kiss on the cheek. "Hello, Mother." He loved his mother, but she had always been less demonstrative with her feelings than his father.

Angela glanced up at her tall son. "Just like your father. Always late dressing for dinner," she said, wiping her lipstick off his cheek with a handkerchief. "You look so healthy, Maxwell. Being here seems to agree with you."

Max smiled. If she only knew how much, he thought.

Just then the dinner bell sounded from below, and O-nami and his wife appeared. "Ah, I am hungry as a bear," O-nami announced in his booming voice. Everyone laughed, and together they descended the stairs for dinner.

The intimate dining room reflected the exquisite taste that Sumie Hosokawa had brought to the castle during her lifetime. As in summers past, the sliding glass doors of the outer walls had been removed. The room's muted shades of rose, beige, and white lent an airy atmosphere that blended into the gardens beyond. The focal point of the room was a low, oblong table of lacquered wood, whose deep blue color shimmered like a pond beneath the silk globes of Japanese lanterns suspended from the ceiling beams. Family and guests sat on blue silk pillows around the table.

As usual Shizue was seated next to her father. One long-stemmed flower displayed in a fluted glass vase occupied the place where Sumie had once sat.

Kimitake sent Max a gloomy look his friend had come to know well. Neither boy felt talkative. Throughout dinner, Baron Hosokawa reminisced about other family gatherings. When he fell silent, Angela Napier kept the conversation alive telling witty stories of her summers in Europe with the Karlstadts.

"Maxwell, you should devote some time to brushing up on your German," she told her son. Although Angela never meddled in her husband's business affairs, she had taken a direct hand in their son's education, insisting he become fluent in French and German so as not to be at a loss when the time came for him to socialize abroad. In that sense she was a designing mother. A number of her French and German friends had teenage daughters, one of whom might eventually be a suitable wife for her son.

Max shrugged. His eyes met Shizue's, and for a few moments they simply gazed at each other.

Then Tadashi looked around the table, tears welling in his eyes. "Ah, my heart is full on this night when we're joined here once again in friendships ripened with the years." He sighed and touched the flower that decorated the place where his wife had always sat. Now he looked at Douglas and Angela Napier as he reflected on the deaths that had brought tragedy to both families. Over the course of the last thirteen years, his parents and those of his friends had passed on. His gaze lifted to the gently swaying silk lanterns as he remembered his mother weeping on the day his father's body was carried into the castle by workers. His father had been a man not yet fifty, a man of great physical strength, who insisted on personally overseeing everything on the lands. Baron Kenji Hosokawa had been inspecting the construction of a new sericulture house, when the scaffolding collapsed under him. The fall had broken his neck. Tadashi's widowed mother had seemed to suffer the loss bravely, but grief had snuffed out her will to live. Not a year after Kenji Hosokawa's burial, his widow had died in her sleep. She had no history of heart disease and the doctors could give no medical explanation. Her heart had simply stopped beating.

Just then, the baron felt his own heart skip a beat. He understood the depths of a grief that had claimed the life of his mother. Once again he looked at those seated quietly around him at the table; they were waiting for him to speak. "Yes, some faces are missing from our family circle," Tadashi said, his voice made hoarse by emotion. "But the memories of loved ones are never forgotten. They still dine with us here, living on through the faces of our children."

"*Hai*, that is so," Yufugawo said. "Before long, grandchildren will sit here among us, sharing in the gods' good fortune."

Angela laughed rather nervously. "I've never given a thought to becoming a grandmother. Not so soon. Not at my age!"

"There have always been firstborn sons to carry on the family tradition," said O-nami, washing his food down with sake.

"Well, that's one tradition I'm in no hurry to embrace," Angela replied, pushing away her untouched dessert. She preferred the haute cuisine and wines of Europe to Japanese food. Tadashi had thoughtfully provided an excellent French wine for her at dinner. After finishing the wine, Angela turned to her husband. "The long journey has worn me out. Would you mind very much if we retired early, darling?"

"I thought we might have a game of bridge," Douglas said.

"Another night." Angela leaned close to Douglas and said, "I feel this splitting headache coming on. Be a dear and rid me of this awful pain with those marvelous hands of yours."

"All right." Douglas could tell what lay behind his wife's pleading tone of voice, and it was not one of her headaches. He said good night to everyone and patted Max on the shoulder. "Sleep well, son."

"Perhaps we should all turn in, so we can get an early start in the morning." Baron Hosokawa rose beside Shizue and put his arm around her waist. "I thought we'd tour the facilities, Douglas. I've several improvements in mind, and it's the last opportunity we'll have to consult on them before you leave the country. We'll make it a family outing."

Kimitake visibly brightened. "I'd like that."

"You'll concentrate on your studies."

The boy threw down his napkin. "Yes, Father."

Douglas Napier climbed the stairs with his wife. In the coolness of night the castle walls made creaking sounds not unlike those of the Napier mansion, which was nearly as old. He usually took a glass of brandy at bedtime, and the servants had left a decanter on a table in their upstairs sitting room. "Join me in a nightcap?"

Angela nodded and closed the outer doors. "It's so peaceful here," she said. As he was pouring, she walked up behind him and put her arms around his waist. "No city traffic. No office to call you away from home with demands that keep me waiting there alone in our bed until all hours of the night."

"Angela, must you harp on that again?" Douglas turned sharply, breaking her hold. He held a brandy snifter out to her. "I'm in no mood for a quarrel—or for romance."

She snatched the glass from his hand. "I see! And when, pray tell, can I expect to be given some consideration as your wife? Honestly, if it isn't business, it's some change of mood. What brought it on this time?"

Douglas crossed to the window that faced out on the gardens. "Father and son business. I had a talk with Max while you were resting."

"And?"

"There are things a boy doesn't discuss with his mother. Why not leave it at that?"

Angela groaned in exasperation. "Not that tired refrain again. This isn't entirely a man's world, Douglas. It was I who endured the labor pains to give you a son. I've devoted my best years to raising him properly and have every right to know what's bothering him." She glared at him. "Well, I'm waiting!"

"Since you must know, Max and Shizue are head over heels in love."

"Good Lord!" Angela collapsed into an easy chair, gulped down her brandy, then lowered the glass to her lap. "I saw this coming when Shizue visited with us in the spring. And the way she and Maxwell looked at each other at dinner tonight—well, I should have paid more notice to what was going on."

Douglas ran one hand through his hair. "We can't stop them from being in love," he said. "These things just happen."

"Is that all you have to say?" After fortifying herself with more brandy, Angela paced back and forth. "Of course, we've no reason to take his boyish infatuation so seriously," she decided at last. "Shizue's far too level-headed to lead Maxwell on. Even so, I don't think we should permit their summer romance to continue. Tadashi will agree, I'm sure. He wouldn't want to see either of our children hurt by allowing this puppy love to get out of hand." Angela stopped pacing and sighed. "Maxwell hasn't been exposed to many girls. A year or so in Europe will open his eyes. Thank God, they're still too young really to fall in love. Otherwise, I could only pity them both."

"How can you know what they feel for each other?" Douglas said angrily. "If you'd seen the emotion on our son's face, you wouldn't be so damn glib about what he's going through."

"Your behavior to me is inexcusable, Douglas." Angela's eyes filled with tears. "Max is all you care about. Sometimes I think you have no feelings for me at all. Sometimes I wonder why you ever married me."

Douglas made no effort to stop her as she fled into the adjoining bedroom. The sliding doors rattled shut behind his wife. He thought better of going to Angela with an apology. He had worn that word thin between them. As a mother, she had every right to voice her opinion, but he knew that Angela's meddling could only make the situation more painful for their son.

Douglas knew, too, that he himself would have to approach Tadashi; fathers were more equipped to handle this type of situation. He decided to act on it immediately. Going downstairs, he found the baron in his study pouring himself a nightcap.

"Trouble sleeping?" Tadashi inquired. "Would you like a drink?" When Douglas shook his head, the baron continued. "I don't recall when exactly I acquired this taste for scotch whiskey, but it helps me get to bed."

"While we were at Harvard," said Douglas. Then: "I have something to say, Tadashi. Maybe you'd better sit down."

Baron Hosokawa settled in the chair behind his desk. "I'm listening."

"My son and your daughter are in love."

Douglas's statement came as no surprise. "So I've observed for myself these past weeks. I expected Max would confide in you sooner or later. As it happens, I saw you speaking with him in the garden."

Douglas sat down across from his friend, startled by the calm response of this guardian of Japanese tradition. "I did what I could to spare the boy's feelings with sound advice."

"That's most reassuring, Douglas." The baron took a sip of his drink. Max had been raised as a Japanese, he thought. In spirit, the boy had something of the blood and bone of a samurai. But the color of his skin could not be discounted, much as he himself would have wished it otherwise, and his eyes sadly met Douglas's as he spoke.

"I was alarmed by this at first," the baron said. "But I've since had time to give the matter a good deal of thought. Growing up together, they have mistaken their natural bond for love. They're both well aware it can't lead to anything. Max is a gentleman, and Shizue"—his face lit with a smile—"well, I know my daughter. She's strong-willed and spirited, but not headstrong. I've said nothing to her. In my opinion it's best for us to stay out of it, Douglas. Our interference might only strengthen the bond. Better to keep cool heads and smile benignly until you leave Japan with Max." He smiled at Douglas. "I know you don't want the boy tortured as you were. But this is a far cry from your own youthful affair with Natsu; the circumstances are quite different. Max and Shizue would never jeopardize the bond of love and respect between our families."

"Maybe a separation will alter their feelings in time," Douglas answered uncertainly. "I can't find fault with your judgment. But Angela could be a problem. We've just had an unpleasant scene over this. Given her way, she'd separate our children now and complicate the situation."

"Angela's heart is in the right place," the baron assured his friend. "Tell her what I've said, and she'll give in to reason."

Douglas watched his friend stifle a yawn, secure in his beliefs and at peace with his thoughts.

Douglas, however, was feeling far from peaceful. Tadashi had bowed to his friend's enduring love for a Japanese, guarding the secret of Douglas's infidelity and accepting things as they were. His samurai code demanded that loyalty to their friendship. But the same code of honor would turn him against Douglas if his friend dared to challenge everything by divorcing Angela and taking Natsu Yoseido as his wife.

"I shouldn't have left Angela in such a state," Douglas said, and bid his friend good night.

Even if Max had fallen in love with a Japanese girl other than this nobleman's daughter, Douglas wondered if he himself would give his blessings to a mixed marriage, knowing what hell the children born of it would face. The thought of Paul's stifling existence haunted him. To promise Max any future with Shizue would be cruel. He remembered the fabric of lies his own father had woven to destroy all his youthful hopes and dreams. Julius had made his son believe that Natsu had bowed to tradition by marrying a Japanese and was lost to him forever. Julius Napier's deceitful acts had held his son at Harvard, where the years spent apart from Natsu had determined their separate fates.

Wearily Douglas thought of the double life he had been forced to lead once he had learned the truth. He was being unfair to both women in his life. Certainly not by design. But that did not minimize the injury done them. To Douglas his wife existed in the shadow of his great love for Natsu. He had an affection for Angela and a respect for the way in which she had raised their son. Perhaps he did love her in small ways. But no man could split his heart in two. Angela had never stood a fair chance to vie for the rapture he might have brought to their marriage had Natsu not entered his life first.

That night Douglas felt the eroding effect of years of living a lie. As he returned to his wife, he longed for the ecstasy of Natsu's scented body clinging to him in the act of love. Not many nights of sharing were left them when he returned to Tokyo.

He found his wife in bed lying facedown on her stomach. The floor groaned under his weight, and she stirred, faintly calling his name.

The unspent fury Douglas had left her with fought with the desire she felt as he reached out and touched her. But anger melted under the caresses of his strong hands, and as always Angela surrendered her wounded pride to her love of this man.

Morning brought an unexpected visitor to the Hosokawa castle—Ibo Shigeta, an aide to Lord Mitsudara. The lord had a thorough knowledge of Hosokawa-Napier, Limited's, weaving mills, but his knowledge of their silk-farming operations was not yet thorough enough to satisfy him. Ibo Shigeta had been sent from Nagasaki by the lord in order to report on the baron's facilities in greater detail. He could only stay the day.

The disagreeable-looking man admitted that he knew nothing about silkworms. "However, business is business, and I am here to gather more facts of your operations, Baron," he informed Tadashi in a raspy voice.

Baron Hosokawa was irritated and did not try to hide it. Lord Mitsudara had forced his aide on him unannounced for a report he himself could easily have supplied if asked. "My facilities are best seen on horseback, Shigeta-*san*. Do you ride?"

Shigeta pulled on his nose. "I shall manage, Baron, if the horse is tame."

"I will have the grooms choose a suitable mount," said O-nami, hiding his amusement.

The baron saw no reason to cancel the family outing, so the grooms saddled horses for everyone. Shigeta was introduced, and then O-nami helped him to sit on a swaybacked mare. Shizue found him a comical figure, and she laughed with Max as the man tightly gripped the reins of the docile old animal, which remained well behind the other horses.

Angela was in high spirits and cantered beside Douglas, who seemed to her to be in one of his better moods. At breakfast together in their rooms, he had reopened the subject that had led to their quarrel the night before. Tadashi's reasoning won her over, and yet in the light of day she observed how taken Max was with Shizue. Perhaps more so than could be forgotten in a year's time. She realized that, for the first time in his life, her son might be hurt. Angela glanced at her husband and forgave him his anger, for it had grown out of concern.

Baron Hosokawa drew everyone to a halt. "We mustn't leave Mr. Shigeta behind." He could not help laughing at the man's tight-lipped look of determination as he bounced up and down in the saddle. "Ride beside me, and we'll set a slower pace," he said.

"Most grateful, Baron." Ibo Shigeta lowered his straw hat against the sun. "What are those tall wooden structures I see everywhere?"

"The sericulture houses, where our silkworms spin their cocoons in season," answered the baron. "Silkworms thrive on sunlight and fresh air. Blight is a constant threat, so these houses are kept spotlessly clean."

"I will not trouble going inside them," said Shigeta. "I will, however, want the total number of these houses and the silk yield of each for my report to the lord."

"Certainly." Baron Hosokawa forced himself to be patient as they rode on. "My lands yield two harvests each year, in the spring and fall. Our enormous production is unrivaled by the other independent silk farms of Japan," he said with pride. "It would take more than a day for you to see everything."

Max and Shizue urged their horses ahead, delighting in the fine day. Peasants tending to the mulberry orchards smiled and bowed. Their children played nearby, flying kites in the meadows and diving into clear streams. Summer was a time for erecting new sericulture houses whose cocoons would be harvested by the millions in autumn. Riding past them, Tadashi was reminded of his father's death. In the years since then, he had kept away from the construction sites until the scaffolding had been pulled down.

At noon the party rested for lunch in a shady grove of fruit trees, where servants had laid out straw mats and artfully arranged the food. Then they continued on the tour. In the late afternoon the baron led the riders to a rocky hillock on which had been built a modern laboratory. The sprawling stone and glass building would have been more at home on some university campus. From that vantage point one could see for miles. Squat-shaped buildings with tin chimneys poking from their thatched rooftops lined the riverbanks to where the waters snaked around the distant foothills.

Groundskeepers took charge of the riders' horses, and Shigeta groaned with relief at being out of the saddle. "A most impressive sight, Baron. So many buildings on this river."

"Those are our steaming houses," Max said, pointing out the churning waterwheels that powered boiler systems. "The chimneys are quiet now, but they raise up giant clouds of steam night and day at harvest time. Then it's a race between Mother Nature and the nature of business. The silkworms must be steamed to death at the time of imago, before their larvae become fully mature moths. The emerging moths would tear the silk filaments of their cocoons, and we couldn't reel the silk for handling on the looms."

Baron Hosokawa stood back smiling, deferring to Max's energetic talk on the subject of sericulture. Douglas's son had not inherited his father's talent for machinery. Instead, he had a feeling for the land that was more Hosokawa than Napier. What a fine son-in-law Max would make if only he were Japanese, Tadashi thought sadly.

"You are a bright young man, Napier-*san*," the lord's aide complimented Max. "Now, I would like to observe the silkworms at their spinning, if you please."

"Sorry, but that can't be arranged. The silkworm's life cycle coincides with the harvesting of our mulberry orchards," Max explained. "For weeks their larvae gorge on the fresh sap of our mulberry leaves. Then a secretion of their glands converts the sap into the silk they spin."

"Come inside the laboratory," said the baron to Shigeta. "I want to show you the underground vaults, where we keep the family jewels." He winked at the youngsters, and they laughed.

The lord's aide fussed with his spectacles. "Of course, you are making a joke."

"No, it's quite true," the baron said. "These eggs are the family jewels. You see, through genetic engineering, my scientists have perfected a unique strain of silkworm superior to other breeds farmed elsewhere in Japan. Duplicating our breeding stock would require many generations of matings. If the eggs preserved in my cooling vaults were destroyed, we'd have no silk harvests for years."

"Forgive me, but it seems unwise to keep these eggs all in one place."

Shigeta jotted something down in his pocket notebook. "Suppose there is a fire?"

"No chance of that with all the safeguards we've taken," Douglas assured the man as they entered the laboratory. This was Max's element, he thought. His son had always shown a special interest in living things. As a boy he had collected injured creatures of the forest, nursing them back to health. Angela felt that Max should be encouraged to follow a career in medicine, but Douglas liked to think that father and son would one day work together as a team in the weaving mills, as the Napier generations had done before him.

Angela covered her nose with a handkerchief. "Oh, what a smell," she complained, as they entered a huge glass-walled room where lab technicians were seated at long benches. "All these men bent over bubbling test tubes and peering through microscopes. The silkworm moth was here long before them and their tamperings. Honestly, one shouldn't presume to improve on God's creations."

"That isn't so, Mother." Grinning, Max surveyed the magic at work and said, "Bombyx mori is a fragile, vulnerable creature entirely dependent on us for its survival. Its lineage would perish if not for the isolated, germ-free environment that's provided here when they mate. We've genetically altered their natural mating habits to assure the continuation of future generations."

"So, you *have* improved over nature," Shigeta quipped.

Max's eyes sparkled. "We've only assisted in that process, Shigeta-*san*."

The man scratched his head. "But if you steam the mature moths to death to preserve their cocoons, where do these eggs in your vault come from?"

Shizue stifled her amusement and said, "Several thousand males and females are spared from the steaming houses and are chosen for mating." She turned away and giggled.

Tadashi stood silent as Shizue's giggles kindled memories of his playful little girl who had brought so much laughter into her parents' lives. Now her resemblance to Sumie stirred the depths of his unending grief. "I seem to have lost the thread," he responded to Shigeta's questioning voice.

"The family jewels," he huffed, using his handkerchief to polish the lenses of his glasses. "The mating of the species, bombyx mori."

"Yes, genetic manipulation gives us control over what takes place," the baron continued. "In the wild the female silkworm moth flies off to lay her fertilized eggs in hidden nests, where they're hard to gather and exposed to disease and hungry predators." He turned to Shizue. "My daughter can speak with authority on the subject."

"Yes, Papa," Shizue answered, bowing dutifully. "Our special breed of female moth emerges from her cocoon without legs, Shigeta-*san*. She can't fly without them, and the males fly from one mate to another while the earthbound female drops her fertilized eggs by the thousands, here on antiseptic beds," she explained. "The female moth is bred only to carry on her lineage, and her brief existence ends soon afterward."

Max spoke to fill the silence. "After the eggs are examined for germs and proofs of genetic excellence, we store them in the vaults carved out in the bedrock below." He led the way down a winding stone staircase.

"Only the worthiest eggs gathered from last spring's matings are preserved here to be hatched next fall," Douglas added. He had engineered the underground vaults himself and took great pride in his accomplishment. "The vaults are fireproof. Ventilating and cooling systems preserve the eggs at an exact temperature and humidity. There's a backup system of gas-operated generators in the event of a power failure."

"How can they all be counted?" Shigeta wondered, his voice echoing back through the cavernous maze of illuminated cooling vaults, in which eggs of microscopic size glistened like diamond dust. "Baron, my head swims."

"Allow me to keep it afloat with an accurate inventory for your report."

The earth suddenly trembled, and Max reached out for Shizue as dust rained down from the rock ceilings. "Just a minor earthquake," he said calmly.

Shaking, Angela put her arms around her husband. "I'll never learn to live with these dreadful earthquakes that shake Japan."

Douglas stroked her hair, experiencing a fondness toward his wife built on their years together. "No reason to panic. The walls are reinforced with concrete and steel. Do you remember that summer we visited Sicily with the Karlstadts? An earthquake shook our hotel so hard the plaster fell crashing down around us while we crawled under the furniture."

"Well, there's nothing to crawl under here if the ceiling should come down on our heads," Angela said, hurrying toward the stairs.

Shigeta was not far behind her. "I quite agree, Madame. We could be trapped in the event of an aftershock."

Baron Hosokawa kept talking to allay everyone's fears as they climbed for the outdoors. "Our ancestors believed that other natural occurrences were foretold according to the hour of the quake. There's a doggerel verse about this. 'At twelve o'clock it means disease. At eight or four 'tis rain. At ten 'tis drought, while six and two, of wind are token plain.'"

Angela stepped into the open air, relieved and exhausted. "I do hope the castle hasn't been damaged."

"The quake wasn't serious enough for that, I'm sure." The baron stood back viewing his laboratory. "No damage here. Let's return to the castle and relax over cocktails."

"A dry martini would be heaven," Angela said, sighing. She put one foot in the stirrup of her saddle. She was not much of a horsewoman, and her thighs ached.

Suddenly wind gusts swept the valley floor. Shigeta's hat was blown off his head and away down to a ravine, where it landed in a rushing stream. Annoyed by its loss, he glanced at his wristwatch. "Just past six o'clock. The wind foretold by your verse is quite punctual, Baron. A coincidence, no doubt."

Baron Hosokawa held down his own hat. "I wouldn't dismiss it as merely that." To the baron, Japanese tradition was founded on the wisdom of ancestors; for him, tradition was an anchor in a changing world fraught with uncertainties.

"Still time for a swim," Shizue told Max, and raced him to mount their twin geldings. Mercury was the faster horse, and she urged Vega to pursue him with more intensity than the horse had to give. "Admit you let me win in all those races!" she called out to Max.

"Admit how much it pleased you!" he called back to her, and laughed.

Laughing with the youngsters, Douglas patted the mane of his frisky stallion. "Just look at them race! Born to the saddle and carefree as the wind!"

"How beautiful they are in their innocence," Angela said, sharing her husband's delight.

Shigeta anxiously wound his wristwatch. "I must have those figures you promised, Baron, and then hasten to board the train for Nagasaki."

"What a shame you can't stay for dinner," the baron said politely, although he was secretly relieved. The old samurai ties of obedience had already been strained by the terms of the bank loan. The lord had assumed dictatorial powers, ordering Douglas Napier to Germany sooner than both partners cared for. Tadashi was not in the habit of being dictated to, and the fact that Lord Mitsudara had forced Shigeta on him signaled the lord's intentions to exercise his power as he saw fit. "Please, convey my best wishes to Lord Mitsudara, and ask him to telephone me at his earliest convenience."

"Yes, Baron."

As Baron Hosokawa watched the man labor to board the old mare, he was no longer amused. Business was intruding on friendship, and he was reminded of Lord Mitsudara's forceful entreaties to have him pledge Shizue in marriage to Jiro. As she and Max raced on horseback to the nearby woods, the baron looked over at Douglas. His friend's wistful expression spoke for an attachment with the past. It seemed Douglas could not separate the fondness between their children from his love affair with Natsu. The baron could only feel sympathy for Natsu and her son. Now Angela Napier caught his eye with a mother's worried look, and he felt torn by the secret he had kept from her over the years—one that divided his loyalties between husband and wife.

"Tadashi, are you quite sure we're doing the right thing for our children?" Angela leaned from her saddle to ask him.

"Yes. Set your mind at rest." The baron smiled at her in a way that closed the subject to further conversation.

CHAPTER 6

The first week of July had drawn to an end, and that night would bring a full moon over Kyushu Island. Shizue and Max led their horses to the stable at the close of another day shared in the place where the kerria bloomed. Their muscles ached pleasantly from swimming in the pool. That night's festival was dedicated to lovers, and Max held Shizue's hand while cheerfully whistling a tune from their childhood.

They were unaware of being observed. Baron Hosokawa had been strolling the winding pathways of his gardens, when Max and Shizue walked into view. Infatuation or love? he wondered, watching them. It was not uncommon for a young person's first romance to be with a childhood friend, and he smiled at the thought. In the years to come, he was sure that his daughter and Douglas's son would look back on their love as just a sweet memory.

Over the telephone from Nagasaki, Lord Mitsudara had apologized for sending his aide unannounced. His friendly conversation had smoothed the baron's ruffled plumage. But the lord had restated his impatience to have grandchildren and had hinted he was on the brink of choosing for Jiro another bride, a girl of higher lineage who was already of marriageable age. Still the baron remained undecided, once again telling the lord that he would give the matter of a wedding pledge further thought.

Now he called to her. "Shizue, come here a moment." She left Max on the bridle path and rushed over to her father. "Lord Mitsudara has invited us to his summer home on Lake Biwa. His son Jiro will be vacationing from the military academy. I'm sure you'll enjoy his company for what remains of this summer."

"But, Papa!"

"Now, now, don't pout. This invitation won't shorten your time with Max." The baron cupped her worried face between his hands, deciding that her feelings for Maxwell Napier might wane all the more easily if a relationship with Jiro Mitsudara were encouraged during Max's absence. While they were at the summer house, the baron decided, he would observe Shizue and Jiro together. If the chemistry between them appeared favorable, then he would approach his lord to strike a binding match. "In the morning I must go to Tokyo with Max's parents on business and to meet their German friends," he told her softly. "You and Max will join me there the first week in August to say good-byes. We'll visit Lake Biwa after Max has left Japan."

"Oh, you're such a dear papa." Shizue squeezed him hard before running off to join Max. She told him of the lord's invitation, but, although she was uncomfortable about having Jiro Mitsudara as a companion, she kept that to herself.

"Looks like we'll have a clear sky for stargazing," Max observed. He had until the end of the month to spend with Shizue, and he pushed from mind all thoughts of being separated.

Left alone, Baron Hosokawa was in a reflective mood as he walked the gardens. Pausing under the window of the bedchamber once shared with his wife, he remembered other fading summer afternoons such as this when the garden rang with the laughter of their children at play and Sumie lay nestled beside him after making love. Her contented sighs still haunted the bed he now slept in alone.

His fireworks experts were busily engaged along the garden streams, preparing a dazzling display for later that evening. Baron Hosokawa crossed the footbridge to a small island paradise. This was Sumie's final resting place, and the baron had enshrined her grave with a stone statue of her likeness. Here the jasmine were in full bloom, perfuming the air. The moon showed its round face in a gray-blue sky overhead as he strolled among the flowers.

"*Komban-wa*, Baron."

"Good evening, Minami," Baron Hosokawa said to the head gardener, who hovered around the bushes with his pruning shears. "You tend the garden with reverent hands, old man. But soon the light will be gone. Please cut jasmine to place at my wife's shrine and rest your tools until another day."

"Her favorite flower," Minami remarked. He was partially crippled by arthritis and had cut off the fingers of his gardening gloves to allow his swollen joints greater freedom of movement. "I always sense Madame's presence here when the jasmine are in bloom. Has her passing been nine years?" He shuffled around the flowering bushes in search of their worthiest blossoms, then halted to snip the stems with his shears. "Tragic when the gods call one so young," he said, as he placed the jasmine cuttings in a straw basket.

Minami had tended the gardens when Tadashi rode their paths on his father's shoulders. Over the years he had come to value this man's peasant wisdom and now freely voiced his thoughts. "Sumie's death was like a chill wind howling through my castle. She had a rare gift with people, and everything here revolved around her warmth. After I sent Shizue away to school, there were times when my loneliness seemed to rattle the castle windows. But I could never bring another woman through its doors as my wife."

"A wise man tempers his grief by numbering his blessings, Baron. Shizue is her mother reborn. As much like her as the flowers blooming once again on these old vines. Who could tell them apart if we did not count the seasons?" Minami bowed and placed the straw basket of cuttings on Sumie's grave. "Ah, at times I think even the gods are lonely when the sun leaves their heavens. Life is pain, but the earth we walk upon is warm and yields many lovely things." It hurt the old gardener to straighten his back. Gazing up at the face of the moon, he massaged the painful joints of his gnarled fingers. "Even the moon in all its beauty is a cold, lifeless thing compared to these earthly flowers. And yet even the jasmine cannot match your daughter's beauty or the comfort you must take from her presence."

"Even so, my son's puzzling lack of character robs me of peace. Kimitake's tutors claim that he's applied himself since I last punished him. But he hasn't risen above the level of an average student." Baron Hosokawa bowed his head to the gardener, who was stooping to lift a faded cloth sack of tools. "I'm weighed down by concern," he confessed. "Despite what his tutors say, I know the boy has more in him than to settle for passing grades. It's disappointing when Kimitake smiles, thinking he's pleased me and hoping to be rewarded for his sorry efforts. My wife would know how to reach our son. If only she were here to advise me."

Minami smiled, his face alight with memory as he shifted his sack of tools across one scrawny shoulder. "Her presence resides here at the shrine you erected in her memory. While tending the flowers around her statue, I sometimes think I hear her voice speaking my name. Who can say if it is her spirit or only the wind?" The old gardener began walking across the footbridge. "Good evening, Baron."

"Good evening," the baron said, distracted. His gaze was fixed on the moss-covered stone figure that marked his wife's grave.

In the terrible thrall of his grief, Tadashi had broken with tradition by refusing to have Sumie buried with his ancestors in the Buddhist temple grounds. In her lifetime she had come to this place in the garden each day to meditate and to write poetry. This was where she belonged. He had committed Sumie's poems to the earth with her after Shinto priests had purified her final resting place with their wands. Here, Baron Hosokawa still sometimes heard the solemn cadence of the priests' drums as they led Sumie's mourners across the vermilion footbridge.

He had commissioned a master stonecarver to create a statue of Sumie. In the final days of her illness she had wasted away to skin and bones, and he had wanted to remember her as she was on their wedding day. The graceful likeness of Sumie was clad in the flowing robes of her wedding kimono and the bridal headdress that would one day be passed on to her daughter. There was the slightest suggestion of a smile on her delicate oval face, while her large almond-shaped eyes gazed out from the stone as if in silent prayer to the gods.

Her last gifts to him had been a smile and words of love. She had died so courageously, he thought. No samurai in battle could have given death more of a fight.

Neglecting the graves of one's dead was considered an unpardonable sin, and every growing thing around Sumie's shrine was treated by the gardener with special care. Two stone lanterns placed at either side of her grave were kept filled with oil. Every night the baron lit them, using matches that were kept by the grave in a tightly sealed metal box. That evening, after lighting the lamps, Tadashi sank to his knees before Sumie's statue. He took the jasmine from the basket and arranged the flowers in the tall bronze vase at the statue's feet.

"Tonight is the festival of Tanabata, my beloved. I've planned a fireworks display, and not long from now you'll be showered with bright colors." The baron went on to tell her all the events of that day just as he had always done while she had lived. "Perhaps I'm too hard on Kimitake. But I lack the insight you once gave me. My father was also a stern taskmaster, and without you I seem to become more like him with the passing years. It's so hard trying to raise our children alone. I have no fears about failing Shizue as a father. But, dearest, I shrink at the thought of failing in my duties to our son. Won't you help me?"

Sadly the baron looked up at Sumie's statue. In the span of less than a decade, the elements had given her likeness the look of antiquity. Moss grew around the statue's windward side.

To the baron, Sumie was the sphinx gazing out across the valley floor. Winds had eroded her lips but not her enigmatic smile. In that stone smile were locked the unconfessed mysteries of death and of life in the spirit world of their ancestors. But speaking to Sumie's statue had only made Tadashi feel more alone. "Oh, why did you leave me?" he cried. "There's no end to my grief."

Just then, Kimitake appeared at his mother's garden shrine. Although the tutors praised his recent efforts, the baron had remained unmoved, and his son had been drawn to the shrine to rekindle the memories of Sumie's loving touch, a touch that was denied him by his father.

Baron Hosokawa's sobbing riveted Kimitake in the well of darkness just beyond the burning lanterns. He had never seen this vulnerable side of his father's nature, and suddenly Kimitake was overcome by tears. He rushed into the light, desperately hoping to be taken in from the cold. "Papa—*ogisan*, forgive me for always disappointing you," he pleaded, throwing his arms around his startled father. "I miss Mother too. I'll work harder at my studies. I'll be the son you've always wanted."

Baron Hosokawa interpreted his son's emotional outburst as a sign that Sumie's spirit had witnessed his despondency and was answering his plea for help in dealing with the boy. Feeling closer to Kimitake than he had in many years, he said, "You're forgiven, son. Lord Mitsudara has invited both you and Shizue to vacation at his summer home. Perhaps some time off from your studies will do you good."

"Thank you, Father." Kimitake clung to him, feeling loved. "I couldn't have asked for a better reward."

Abruptly the baron stood up. "Don't mistake my softness as a license to fall back into your lazy ways, Kimitake." The baron found it difficult being so firm, but he was afraid that his son might think he could get around his father with another such display. Tadashi told himself that his sternness was in Kimitake's best interest. "Have fun. Refresh your mind before returning to school in the fall. Then I'll expect results."

Kimitake rose to his feet slowly. "This time I really mean to succeed, Father. You'll see." He shuddered at his father's return to coldness. "Thank you again for letting me go with Shizue. Will you be joining us there?"

"When I can." The baron was touched by his son's look of desolation. "If I seem harsh at times, bear in mind that I want only what's best for my children." He patted Kimitake's shoulder and offered a sparse smile. Then he glanced at Sumie's face of stone and once against fell prey to his emotions. "Go dress for dinner. I wish to be alone with your mother. You have her presence here to thank for this reward."

He watched his son cross the footbridge. Freeing this moody boy from study was an act of the heart he might live to regret, he thought. Gusting winds snuffed the lantern light. For a moment Baron Hosokawa thought he heard Sumie calling him. Then he remembered what the gardener had said. Perhaps it *was* Sumie's voice speaking his name and not just the wind stirring the tree branches over her grave.

Guided by moonlight, he walked the paths. Servants were festooning the gardens with colorful paper lanterns. He had felt warmed by Douglas and Angela's visit. Theirs was a friendship that helped him through the empty years. That night at Tanabata there would be fireworks, entertainment, and laughter. But without Sumie to share them with, Tadashi knew that playing the convivial host would be a trial.

Yufugawo entered Shizue's bedroom to find the girl sitting before her vanity mirror, pouting. She was not yet dressed for dinner. There was an expression of maternal concern on Yufugawo's face as she asked, "Why not share your thoughts with me, child?"

Shizue shook her head. "They're too private even to share with you."

"Do you think me blind? Everyone in the household can see you are in love with Max."

"I suppose it's naive of me to think it didn't show." Shizue turned and placed her arms around the woman, burying her face in Yufugawo's bosom. "Obviously Father hasn't said anything because Max will soon be going away. Oh, I'll be lost without him. Those European girls will throw themselves at him, and one of them might make him forget about me."

Yufugawo rocked her surrogate daughter. "Your beauty will put them all to shame," she said. "I want you to be happy, child. Time will answer your feelings for Max. Who can say what the years ahead may bring?" Caressing Shizue's anguished face, Yufugawo grew tearful. "There is still baby fat on these cheeks. You should be gay and enjoy the festival tonight. Now, hurry and dress."

Shizue confronted her reflection in the mirror. There *were* some annoying traces of baby fat in her cheeks, she thought. "I want to wear something mature," she announced, going to search her wardrobe closets.

Holding a summer dress against her with one hand, Shizue tugged on her braided crown of hair with the other. With Yufugawo, Shizue usually got anything she wanted. But the woman was adamant about preserving those girlish braids. "I'm tempted to take the scissors to these myself," Shizue said.

Yufugawo planted her hands on her hips and made a huffing sound. "I will dress your hair with flowers and allow you to wear lipstick. At that I draw the line!"

July was a month marked by festivals. Tanabata Matsuri was the first of these on the lunar calendar and was celebrated on the seventh day of the seventh moon, when the stars Vega and Altair shone brightly in the night sky.

Celebrating with fireworks was a custom of the Hosokawa household, and everyone applauded as skyrockets burst high above, showering the gardens with colored lights.

There were different versions of the story behind Tanabata, but they all centered around a common theme. That evening Baron Hosokawa sat among a gathering of the household's youngest children and told the story of the festival. The children listened, innocent wonder shining in their eyes. "According to a very ancient legend, a boy of fifteen and a girl of twelve had wed and lived happily ever after into old age. One could not live without the other, and after they had passed away in each other's arms, the merciful gods raised them up into the heavens together as the girl star Vega and the boy star Altair, who now dwell on opposite banks of the Milky Way."

The baron paused while his audience gleefully held their ears against a loud bombardment that showered fireworks across the starry heavens. "This is the Celestial River, where the Supreme Diety bathes every day," he continued, pointing to the Milky Way. "Since the lovers had been mortals, they are forbidden to pollute the river by bathing in it." He made a sad face and rolled his eyes. "Throughout the year they can only gaze longingly at each other from across this river's opposite shores. But," he said, grinning as he lifted one appealing little girl onto his lap, "on this one day of the year, when the deity descends to earthly temples to hear the Buddhist chanting of the sacred scriptures, the boy and girl stars enter his river to be happily reunited. And that is why we celebrate Tanabata Matsuri."

The baron finished to applause, which gave him much pleasure. "A treat for everyone," he announced, handing the children chocolate candies wrapped in bright cellophane.

Angela bent down and whispered in his ear, "How lovely, Tadashi. I know this occasion is one of sadness for you, but you're a dear to be so thoughtful of these children."

His eyes misted over. "Sumie told the legend better than I ever could."

"I'd forgotten it until now." Angela looked to her husband seated under a tree and sighed. "I once believed in happily ever after."

Tadashi smiled at the children enjoying their chocolates. "You're an incurable romantic, Angela. It's something we share in common."

"At times I suspect you know all about me," said Angela, brushing his forehead with a kiss. She felt an intimacy with Tadashi Hosokawa that often moved her to the brink of sharing her most private thoughts. But she could never bring herself to speak them to a man. "Yufugawo is motioning to me. Your daughter has a mother in that woman."

"Yes, she's been a comfort to Shizue. I've come to lean on her understanding way with my daughter more with each passing year."

Standing off by a garden stream, Max held Shizue's hand as the last sparkling, multicolored showers flickered out against the black velvet foothills. Max's thoughts were of Shizue. He desperately wanted to experience more than handholding and lingering kisses. That afternoon as he held her in his arms, he had sensed that Shizue felt the same way. Had he acted boldly, she might have cast aside her strict teachings. But she was like a fragile blossom, and he was obligated to protect what they both dreamed of sharing in another season of their years.

And so that night he could only inhale her intoxicating fragrance. Exercising restraint was his first sacrifice to loving her.

"Oh, look, the procession is beginning," Shizue said.

The household servants and their eldest children now filed across the garden in a slow-moving procession. Each year they shared in the festivities. They wore brightly colored *happi* jackets and carried candlelit lanterns strung from bamboo poles. As they walked they sang a romantic ballad of their sheltered country prefecture.

It was customary to observe Tanabata with poems honoring the celestial couple's renewal of eternal love. Like her mother before her, Shizue had composed a poem dedicated to the star-crossed lovers. Max was not much of a poet, but he had written a tribute to mortal love.

Beneath the swaying cone of light cast by a servant's lantern, Max handed Shizue the lines he had set down on blue rice paper, and she silently read what he had written:

How I cherish thoughts of our being like the celestial couple,
Happily wed from youth into old age.
Thoughts of it crowd into my mind.
And this coming year without you, separated by the oceans,
I will be like the blind in a snowstorm of stars.

Shizue touched Max's words to her blushing cheek. She recalled the day when she had tied her white paper fortune to a branch of the shrine tree. Then she had wished for Max to boldly take her in his arms and send tradition up in puffs of smoke with his kiss. They had found love together. Now she felt sick with despair at the thought that soon it would be beyond her grasp. Max's mother assisted Yufugawo in handing out poems printed on colored papers. The poems were read silently, then shared among the guests. After enjoying them it was customary for everyone to stick these tributes to eternal love on the stems of bamboo plants that had been placed around the castle gardens. Shizue looked around her as everyone there participated in decorating the bamboo with colored paper. But that night the tradition seemed only a charming custom to this woman-girl who yearned for so much more.

"Your poem is too special to be left here in the garden," she told Max. While her father watched her, Shizue could only stamp the imprint of her lipstick kiss across Max's tender words. "Keep it with you as a remembrance," she whispered, handing it back to him.

Max felt stunned by the longing in her eyes. Celebrating Tanabata had underscored the pain of being separated, and he carefully folded his poem scented with her lipstick kiss, then tucked it inside his dinner jacket pocket.

Douglas came forward and put his arms around their shoulders. "Why these gloomy faces? Your vacation isn't over yet," he said cheerfully, walking them to the outdoor stage, where musicians tuned their ancient instruments beneath a canopy of silk lanterns. "Your father's outdone himself tonight, Shizue. It appears we'll be entertained by dancers."

Shizue's moodiness lifted. "Yes, Papa brought them all the way from Osaka, along with acrobats and jugglers."

Angela walked past the garden benches filled by excited children and their parents. "Shizue!" she called. "I've saved two seats for us. Douglas, there's another place for you to sit with Max."

Shizue thought Angela Napier looked especially beautiful that evening. As she sat down beside her, Shizue admired the woman's elegant black satin dress, her glossy alabaster complexion, and her subtle use of makeup that enhanced her beautiful, refined face. Angela had an air of majesty, Shizue thought. Nothing about her was ever out of place, and she always seemed to be in control. "How I admire you," Shizue confessed, fingering the braids in her hair. "I'm so afraid I'll never be a proper lady."

"Nonsense! You were born to it, Shizue."

Both women opened their painted silk fans and fluttered them in silence.

Shizue heaved a sigh. "A year is such a long time. I'll miss you."

"And I'll miss you," Angela said, touched by Shizue's sincerity. "But the months will go by before you know it." She closed her fan, remembering how long a year had seemed when she had been Shizue's age.

"Mind if I join you?" The bench rocked as Kimitake sat down on the other side of Angela. His expression was gloomy.

Angela patted his arm. "You look handsome in your dinner jacket," she said, knowing how he craved attention. Since the best schools for boys were in Tokyo, Kimitake went to school with Max and lived at the Napier mansion. Angela had done her best to make Kimitake feel wanted, but she could not fill the void created by his mother's passing. He never spoke much, but his dark eyes revealed a troubled soul. "Your father tells me you'll be vacationing soon at Lake Biwa," she said, hoping to draw him out.

Kimitake nodded. "I'll be boarding at school this fall semester."

"Take heart. Think of all the friends you've made there."

"None like Max."

"I know he feels as you do," Angela said.

Breezes rustled through the garden as the entertainment began. Angela nervously lit a cigarette, feeling the loss of her friendship with Sumie Hosokawa. She could not bring herself to visit Sumie's grave. Death frightened her, and even the beauty of Sumie's final resting place did not keep Angela from shivering.

Onstage, musicians plucked the silk-stringed kotos. They were accompanied by bamboo flutes. Love was the theme of the dance performed by two beautiful girls in dazzling silk costumes. Douglas saw Natsu and Shizue in the two lovely young women. What young man could resist the spell cast by the graceful dancers who seemed to float across the stage.

The past reasserted itself in the fairy-tale gardens where Douglas had first seen Natsu. Max turned to him just then, and Douglas felt a chill. Suddenly he saw Paul in the features of his other son and became painfully aware of how his seed had made the two young men half brothers. Recognizably so if they were side by side.

Following his visit to the tea shop that day, he had not been able to divorce Paul from his thoughts and had lingered for hours over the boy's photographs, which he kept in a locked drawer of his study desk.

Suddenly Douglas felt an urgent need to leave for Tokyo. His memories of the castle's fragrant gardens had withered years ago, but Natsu remained as fresh as its blossoming jasmine. His attention shifted to

Angela smoking a cigarette as the guests applauded the dancers. With the Karlstadts as their houseguests, his wife would be more demanding of his time. But he had become a master of excuses in a marriage held together by deceit.

Jugglers and acrobats now marched through the crowd of spectators, delighting the children with surprises pulled from their bags of tricks. Kimitake sulked as he watched his father giving paper party hats to the giggling children, putting one then another child on his lap and tickling their ribs.

Then the festival was over, and candles flickered in the silk lanterns carried by the procession of servants as they silently wound their way back to the castle through gardens flickering with fireflies. Shizue joined Max, and they walked off together.

Curious, Kimitake followed them. He halted in the shadows and overheard Shizue speaking words of love to his best friend. Beset with his own problems, he had been ignorant of their romance. Now this discovery both astonished and amused him.

"Max, I don't want this night to end," Shizue murmured, as the two of them stood gazing at the stars, their arms around each other's waists. The girl and boy stars of Vega and Altair shone like sparkling gems. Their one night of love would end soon, and they would be parted for another year by the celestial river. Suddenly the Milky Way seemed to Shizue as vast as the oceans that would separate the two of them. "Oh, Max, I don't want you to go away!"

Max would have kissed her if not for the baron calling his daughter's name. They turned, surprised to see Kimitake standing there in the shadows, smiling sheepishly.

"Time for bed, Shizue," her father said, approaching with the Napiers. "Come along with me. I'll need your womanly touch to help me pack for the journey to Tokyo. Left to my own, everything gets wrinkled."

Angela fluttered her silk fan. "Most men lack patience and throw everything together in a heap. Not Douglas. He's too fastidious. Everything in its place. Socks, handkerchiefs, neckties, all neatly arranged like the organs of his machines. Max takes after him in that respect."

Kimitake said that he wanted to talk to Max, so Angela hugged each boy and bid them good night. "My, you boys look serious. I suppose it's your age. Another year and you'll be entering the university." As she took her husband's arm, her eyes welled up with tears.

"Entrance to Harvard must be earned," Baron Hosokawa sternly reminded his son, then hugged his daughter close as the two of them walked away.

Kimitake remained behind with Max and suggested they go to his room for a talk. "I didn't mean to spy on you and my sister," he assured his friend. "But from what I saw, you're both on dangerous ground. Has my father said anything?" Max shook his head. "I didn't think so. In his eyes, Shizue can do no wrong." He bent to pick up pebbles on the garden path, then hurled them hard at the branches of a tree. "Is it really serious between you two?"

"Really" was all Max said.

Kimitake shrugged. "Well, I wish you luck. But you can be damn sure my father has other ideas for his precious daughter."

"Let's change the subject!" Max said. He pointed to a different path from the one their parents and Shizue had taken. "I'll race you!" Max was off and running.

Kimitake accepted the challenge, but could not overtake his friend. At the end of the path they stopped, gasping for breath and laughing. "I've been excused from studies until next fall, and that's a relief," Kimitake said.

"How did you manage it?"

"Passing marks from the tutors," he said, as they walked the remaining distance to the castle. "I'll never be much of a scholar, no matter how hard I try. Thanks to you, I've squeezed through school all these years. But that's what blood brothers are for." Kimitake peeled off his dinner jacket and loosened his tie as they entered the castle. "I wonder how my father would react if he knew we'd mixed our blood."

Max laughed as he thought about the incident. Not so very long ago the two boys had cut their forearms with knives and joined their open wounds to become like the blood brothers in a story they had read about the American Indians of the Old West. The ceremonial bond had been sealed in a Tokyo playground, where the two boys had applied war paint to their faces and staged a whooping tribal dance before their wide-eyed Japanese classmates.

Now they locked arms in that old ceremonial embrace. "Maybe at Harvard, we'll have some real Indians in our class," Max said, smiling.

"Harvard!" Kimitake made a long face. "It'll take a miracle to get me past the entrance board requirements. What I wouldn't give to escape that dungeon of higher learning. I don't want to think about it now. Both of us need to let off steam. What do you say to a kendo match in my gym?"

"Okay, you're on." Max and Kimitake took the stairs two at a time.

"Be on guard, Max. I've kept in shape after slaving in the classroom and can show you some new tricks." Playfully punching Max, Kimitake laughed. The two boys entered Kimitake's room to dress for their bout.

This was a boy's room: cluttered, messy, and filled with objects reflecting his interests. Kimitake excelled at sports. He brought to them a confidence and self-discipline he could not bring to his studies. Max surveyed the impressive arsenal of weapons mounted along the walls. Among them were rifles for skeet shooting, Japanese archery bows, decorative quivers, and steel-tipped arrows. The disorderly closets were stuffed with outfits for every imaginable sport. A collection of bamboo swords used in kendo was stored in wooden racks.

Kimitake never tired of looking at himself. The walls were covered with photographs capturing him in action as he wielded various weapons in competitions or used his bare hands against judo opponents. One corner of the room was kept neat. In happier times, when Kimitake's mother was alive, the baron had given him a samurai suit of armor scaled to fit a seven-year-old boy. Now this rare gift of love, replete with a child-size dagger and long sword sheathed in an ornate case, was worn by a black felt mannequin.

While undressing, Kimitake paused to touch the armor's shiny breastplate and the horned helmet stamped with his family crest. Suddenly Kimitake angrily shoved this childhood symbol of his weighty obligations as a Hosokawa and a samurai. As the mannequin crashed to the floor, Max felt sad for his friend but he said nothing. The two boys undressed silently. Then Kimitake posed before a full-length mirror, growling meanly and flexing his well-developed muscles.

Max was not quite Kimitake's equal in the martial arts, and he observed that his friend appeared to be building up for a fight rather than a sportsmanlike match. Kimitake dug fencing outfits from the closet and snarled as he flung one across the room at Max. The flowing black garments were designed for freedom of movement and padded in places most vulnerable to the impact of blows, but a hard blow might still crack bones.

"I think we should call O-nami here to act as referee," Max suggested, and Kimitake hurled a mesh face mask at him, loudly demanding to know what he was afraid of. "You look fit to kill," Max said. "I don't want my skull cracked open to satisfy what's eating you."

Kimitake stood back and grinned. "Instilling fear into the opponent is just part of the game." His face quickly vanished behind his own protective mask. "We don't need a nursemaid! Come on! I'll hold my blows according to the rules."

"All right." Max selected a bamboo sword and entered the gymnasium that adjoined the bedroom. Kimitake lurched away to prime himself for the fight, performing a series of practice maneuvers, slashing the air with a ferocity that left him breathing hard, his forearms glistening with sweat.

After Max performed the exercise with less murderous intention, the two boys squared off and bowed politely. Then Kimitake lunged, striking the first blow. He was lightning-swift, and Max was hard-pressed to parry his opponent's thrust. At a disadvantage, he retreated across the gym. Kimitake grew overconfident and relaxed his guard. He was shocked as Max suddenly became the aggressor, driving him back across the floor, landing blow after blow. Max swiftly retreated once again, forcing Kimitake to come at him. Now anger put his sparring partner off balance, and Max took advantage by suddenly launching a thrusting assault that landed several clean blows. Had the two boys been samurai wielding their long swords, the blows would have taken Kimitake's life.

"*Hai*, it is good!" O-nami's booming voice resonated over the boys' clacking swords. He had been the master who instructed them in the martial arts. Unseen by the boys until now, O-nami stood in the doorway from where he had observed the match. "Hold your swords!" he ordered the angry warriors, striding across the gym to separate them. "In combat, Ichiban would have fallen to the field. The match goes to Ichiban," he announced.

Kimitake took off his face mask. "Which Ichiban?"

"You know very well that it was Max who kept his head and did as he was taught. Attack swiftly and then withdraw like the wind. Temper is your weakness, Ichiban," O-nami admonished Kimitake. "If not for that, you would easily best any man."

"Don't preach to me about temper!" Kimitake stalked off to his room, venting his anger at its clutter with his bamboo sword. Such tantrums were nothing new, and O-nami dismissed this one with a shrug.

Max stood in the gymnasium confronting his reflection in the mirrored wall. He saw himself as a Japanese. But it was all costume. He lifted the fencing mask from his face and was confronted by the clear blue Napier eyes. That night he and Kimitake had fought as men, not boys. Watching as Baron Hosokawa's temperamental son used his sword to smash a glass-framed photograph of a boy at play, Max experienced a foreboding that blood brothers would not fare so well together as men.

In a few weeks time Max would leave these rooms drenched with the memories of his happy boyhood. Germany was a distant land where in outward appearance, he would blend with the city crowds. But his heart would always long for Japan, the country of his birth. Thinking of the year ahead, he was already homesick.

O-nami read his thoughts. "My heart is heavy, Ichiban," he said. "I would join my wife in Tokyo and send you off. Ah, but the city is a noisy place crowded with strangers. One look at this topknot and they would take me for a provincial peasant." O-nami laughed and slapped the topknot, which bound him to the past. "But we know better, eh, Ichiban?"

"Yes." Smiling, Max recalled the many things O-nami had taught him besides horseback riding and the martial arts. The man's boundless affection had helped shape Max's mind and his spirit, and the closeness they shared was evident now as Max fell into step beside him.

"Kimitake!" O-nami roared the boy's first name, a rare occurrence that gained his attention. "You have no cause to take your defeat out on the furnishings. Both number-one sons fought well and make me proud! Your muscles will knot unless they are soaked in the bath."

"Put me down, you great oaf!" Kimitake shouted as O-nami lifted him off the floor and carried him to the bath, as he had when the boy was just a child.

The evening ended with the three men soaking in the *ofuru*. Max ducked his head beneath the steaming surface, holding his breath as he had when bathing with Shizue when they were little. She had often won their test of lung power and would emerge giggling. They would spray water at each other until the grown-ups put an end to such playfulness. Their fathers would resume talk of business matters, while Shizue teased Max by making faces. Her little body had had no breasts to taunt him then. Now they were a constant source of beauty, which tempted his touch. What rapture it would be to know the feeling of her naked body against his.

After the three friends got out of the *ofuru* and dried off, they went to their rooms. O-nami bid the two boys a good night at the apartment he shared with his wife. It was located just up the hall from Shizue's bedroom.

Just then Yufugawo swept into view. She motioned for Max to be quiet, then silently entered the old nursery adjoining Shizue's room, to sleep in the bed there as she had done since the baron's wife passed on. Perhaps the girl he loved was still in need of this devoted woman's mothering, thought Max, lingering outside her bedroom door. How he ached to tiptoe inside, just to stand there watching her in sleep. But seeing her might destroy his restraint.

Max blew her a kiss and whispered good night to his sleeping beauty. It had been a night that had tested his mettle, and even after the kendo match, he needed some release. He changed his clothes, then headed to the stables.

Mercury kicked at his stall as if sharing his master's restlessness. Max saddled him and rode to his and Shizue's secret place, his keen senses leading him there through the bamboo forest that stood guard over the hidden oasis.

Its beauty was empty without Shizue, thought Max, as he sat by the silvery reflecting pool. He skipped a pebble across its calm surface. The widening circles ebbed away like his remaining tomorrows.

On this, one of the last nights of his boyhood, Max mounted Mercury again and headed back toward the castle, galloping across quiet glens and hillocks, taking delight in riding free with the wind in his face. His gelding's powerful hoofbeats echoed off the foothills. One year from now, Max thought, a concrete airstrip would scar these meadowlands and Lord Mitsudara's cargo planes would roar down across them, frightening wildlife whose dens and nests had lain there undisturbed since long before the wilderness was claimed by the greedy hand of man.

For Maxwell Napier it was the saddest of times. And yet part of him looked forward to the adventures promised by living in a foreign land.

When summer had begun, he had been fearful of loving Shizue and burdened by apprehensions. But now she had given him her heart to take away, and Max began mentally preparing himself to embark upon a journey that would bring him one year closer to taking charge of his own life.

CHAPTER 7

The Karlstadts had wired of their arrival on Japanese shores by steamship from Siberia, and now their boat train had pulled into Tokyo Station. Just as they were getting off, Angela came down the platform with her husband. "There they are! Inge! Heinz, over here!" she called, waving a handkerchief.

Douglas shared his wife's high spirits. There was a chemistry between the two couples that was rare. "Heinz! God, it's good to see you," Douglas said, rushing forward to greet him.

"Douglas!" Heinz Karlstadt pulled him into a masculine embrace. "What a journey we had on this Trans-Siberian Railway. I have blueprints with me, and a little surprise to demonstrate our progress in Berlin." Heinz was a tall, distinguished-looking man in his early forties, with dark hair graying at the temples. He enjoyed living well, and his waistline showed some thickening as he stood back grinning at Douglas. "Now, with money in the bank, we make our parachutes!"

Angela clung tightly to Inge Karlstadt, who was like a breath of fresh air to her. She evoked memories of the gay social whirl Angela had thrived on during holidays abroad. She and Douglas had first met the Karlstadts at a party in Rome six years before. Since then, they had traveled everywhere as a foursome on holidays, which always began at the Karlstadts' splendid home in Berlin. "Dear Inge, summer has dragged on like a dirge without you. I simply adore your outfit. Chanel, isn't it?"

"Why, yes. It amazes me how you manage to keep up with the latest fashions." Inge replied in an educated English accent with barely a trace of German.

Angela tugged on the fingers of her short white gloves. "Fashion magazines and the foreign cinema help preserve my sanity."

"The Paris fashions are splendid this year," Inge said. "Heinz insisted I buy out the shops."

Heinz laughed. "*Ja*, her steamer trunks are filled with pretty things. I have arranged for our baggage to be sent on later, Douglas."

Husbands embraced each other's wives, then Angela linked arms with Inge. "Well, now that you're here at last, I'll take you under my protective wing," she said, walking them away. "Japan is fraught with pitfalls for the unwary tourist."

"Angela, you make it sound as if we had set foot among savages." Inge Karlstadt gave a deep, throaty laugh and shook her head. "I am eager to experience everything," she announced. "Even the pitfalls you warn me against."

"I'm afraid your visit won't allow time enough for you to plunge yourselves into the Orient," Angela said, keeping pace with Inge's bouncy, effervescent step as they walked from the train station. She could not help being rather jealous of how Inge outshined her. The woman was breathtakingly lovely, with long golden hair streaked by the sun, huge blue eyes, and a disarming smile that exuded warmth. Inge Karlstadt was almost ten years younger than Heinz, an earthy woman, good at sports, and daring enough to climb the Swiss Alps with the men, while Angela preferred to sit safely in some chalet, warming her toes before the fire with a dry martini in one hand and a cigarette in the other.

Heinz paused on the street by Douglas's car and said admiringly, "I see you drive a Duesenburg." Clenching a monocle in his nearsighted right eye, he locked both hands behind his back. "*Ja*, a fine American motorcar. Its lines are more elegant than my German-built Mercedes. Does it handle well?"

"Yes, she's a honey." Douglas smiled and patted the long gray hood of the sedan. "Well, get comfortable, you two." He gestured at the roomy leather seats in back. "Get in, and we'll show you around. Japan is a far cry from Europe. But there are delightful surprises for the eye at almost every turn."

Angela seated herself up front beside Douglas. "It's just a short drive to our home in the hills. The servants have prepared luncheon for us in the garden." As the car started away, Angela turned in her seat to face the Karlstadts, who sat nestled together. "I was so sorry to receive your letter about the miscarriage."

"Inge and I have each other," Heinz said, and watched his wife grow sad. "This is enough."

"I have been thinking we should try again, *Schatzken*."

Heinz brought Inge against him protectively. He adored it when she addressed him as *Schatzken*—darling—in her sultry voice. "No, I will not risk losing you. Three times now I have worried through your pregnancies. And this last vigil was the most difficult."

"You could always adopt a child." Angela's comment brought an exchange of tense looks between husband and wife.

"An adopted child would not be the same," Heinz answered for them both, then abruptly shifted the topic. "It will be a pleasure finally to meet Baron Hosokawa. Too bad he has not chosen to travel to Berlin even once in all these years."

"Tadashi's a darling man," Angela told him. "He thought the four of us should have the afternoon together. You'll meet him tonight at dinner."

"And Lord Mitsudara. What sort of man is he to deal with, Douglas?"

"You can judge that for yourself, Heinz. He'll be dining with us tonight as well."

"We know the lord only slightly. I'm rather nervous about having him as a dinner guest," Angela confessed.

While Douglas pointed out the Tokyo sights, the Karlstadts cuddled like newlyweds. Angela was sad for Inge, but the woman's inability to bear children seemed not to affect the loving rapport between her and her husband. The couple's closeness served only to underscore what was missing from her own marriage, Angela thought. As her husband spoke of how Japan had changed since the time of his grandfather, Angela lit a cigarette, irritably puffing on it and wishing Andrew Napier had never sailed to this strange, forbidding land.

Inge squeezed her husband's arm. "What a charming city," she exclaimed. "The houses are nestled together like gossiping women whispering secrets."

"Tokyo is dreadfully overcrowded. You wouldn't find those rickety little hovels so charming on the inside," Angela said, sulking over her husband's decision to give their friends a tour of this city she so abhorred. It was a sweltering afternoon. Her upper lip was damp with perspiration, and her dress was sticking to her skin.

However, the downtown business and government district was not entirely without charm, and Angela identified the most striking landmarks. "This is the best Tokyo has to offer. Its shrines and temples are quite beautiful, and parks are tucked away here and there offering some relief," she told the couple, who exclaimed over the tree-lined moats surrounding the Imperial Palace. The newly built Diet rose on a small hill above the palace rooftops. In the background, the couples caught a hazy glimpse of Mount Fujiyama.

"A gray pall of industrial filth often hovers over Tokyo," Angela went on, "and we rarely see Mount Fuji. At its worst this is a cluttered, rather odorous city. Especially in the heat of August." She passed her perfumed handkerchief under her nostrils. "The Japanese have an absolute fetish for personal cleanliness, but I'm afraid that doesn't always extend to the gutters of Tokyo's claustrophobic streets."

Inge leaned out the car window, her delight undiminished. "Heinz, we must climb that mountain to the top. I want to taste the snow there."

"Then we will do this, Ingelein." Laughing, Heinz captured her in both his arms.

Angela said, "The Japanese have a saying, 'Fuji-*san* has what man needs but rarely shows: a warm heart, with a clear, cool head.'" Angela glanced over at her husband, who had withdrawn immediately on their return home from Kyushu a few days earlier. At the baron's castle he had been attentive and warmer than usual. Now his aloofness put her in a bad temper. As he steered the car along the Ginza, staring thoughtfully at the windows of a tea shop, she said irritably, "Honestly, Douglas, this isn't the time for a guided tour. My luncheon will be ruined." She turned to the Karlstadts. "An awful street," she said.

"But it is charming," Inge observed. "What about the people?" Inge asked. "Do you find them friendly?"

"On the surface, yes." Angela took another cigarette from her monogrammed gold case, then snapped it shut. "They bow politely and smile. I have no trouble getting along with my servants and the tradesmen. But with few exceptions, I've never been able to make friends with the Japanese," she said, tapping her cigarette on the lid. "I've always tried to judge people as individuals, not as a whole. But as a nation, Japan is exclusively for the Japanese. Perhaps it has to do with centuries of being isolated from the rest of the world. Foreigners are merely tolerated. And they ostracize anyone of mixed blood." Her remark caused Douglas to stiffen. "I doubt there's a more tight-knit society than the Japanese."

"What of your many foreign friends in residence here?" asked Heinz.

"Oh, we have a small circle of acquaintances." Angela smiled. "But my closest friends have always been in Europe. If I didn't escape there each summer, I'd surely go mad. Douglas and Max adore Japan. Having been raised here, they feel they belong. But for someone of my background, it's impossible to adjust."

Angela sighed heavily. She wished Douglas could understand what a sacrifice it was for her to live in Japan. Still, she knew her place was with him, and somehow she managed.

Douglas stopped the car at an intersection where a Tokyo policeman was directing traffic. In the rearview mirror he glimpsed Paul walking toward the tea shop. Natsu had been radiant with joy when they had met on the evening of his return. She told him that their son had found a mentor and would soon begin writing for *Nippon Shimbun*. The miracle had lifted the hatred from Paul's face, and his smile now reflected in the rearview mirror granted his father a fleeting moment of peace before the policeman waved him on.

"Douglas, please get off this dreadful street and drive us home," Angela complained. "Inge and Heinz must be starved. Over lunch we'll map out an itinerary," she turned back in the seat to say. "I must apologize for sounding so negative about Japan. I want your visit with us to be a memorable one."

The Napier family's Victorian mansion stood aloof and removed from the neighboring Japanese estates nestled in the city hills. From its gabled eaves one could look down through tall pines at Tokyo's lights, which shimmered like a sequined evening bag.

Lord Mitsudara had sent his regrets. More pressing business kept him from attending that night's dinner party for the Karlstadts, but he expected to pay a call later in the evening to meet them. Since this was also to be their introduction to Baron Hosokawa, Angela had planned a candlelight dinner in the formal dining room. Lord Mitsudara's august presence would have made it a stuffy, guarded affair, she thought, and his absence now brought a relaxed atmosphere so that her friends could get acquainted.

The baron and the Karlstadts had hit it off at once, just as Angela had known they would. She observed how handsome the men looked in their white summer dinner jackets. Seated beside Baron Hosokawa, Inge was especially ravishing in her low-cut evening dress. Tadashi was in one of his lighthearted moods. Inge's charms had completely won the man over, and throughout dinner he delighted in answering her questions about the culture of his native land.

Uniformed maids hovered behind the guests' chairs, a well-trained army commanded by the family butler, Morita. Angela was particularly fond of the stoop-shouldered old man, who now directed the serving of dessert with all the braggadocio of a Tokyo traffic policeman. Morita's pixyish presence was as much a fixture of the household as the opulent furnishings that had been shipped across the oceans from Europe aboard tall-masted clipper ships well before the century turned.

The mansion had been built with high ceilings to help dispel the heat of summer. Angela gave thanks for a pleasant evening breeze that entered through the dining room's tall open windows. The breeze tinkled crystal chandeliers that hung above the long rosewood dining table covered with a Belgian lace cloth.

Douglas sat at the head of the table, laughing at Inge's witty remarks. The Karlstadts had brought him out of his shell. Watching how thoroughly her husband enjoyed himself, Angela thought of the contrast between their gay life abroad and their gloomy winters in Japan, where nothing she did had such an uplifting effect on him. Even as the conversation took on a more serious tone, Douglas leaned back in his chair and startled Angela by warmly grasping her hand.

"And this Bushido you speak of," Inge asked the baron. "What exactly does it mean?"

"Oh, that is impossible to define in so many words, Frau Karlstadt." Baron Hosokawa thoughtfully twirled his wineglass. "How does one explain the soul of a samurai? A true samurai once made his sword his soul, and Bushido is the blood and bone of his spirit. Letters and arms are two accomplishments expected in our ancient code of honor. A samurai is incomplete without a well-rounded education in the philosophies and literature. Great emphasis is placed on cultivating his understanding of nature and the arts. We call this his *bumbu*. It's not enough for a samurai to be brave. He must also be taught gentleness. This gentle aspect serves to temper his courageous spirit. It is a strengthening factor, never to be mistaken for weakness, Frau Karlstadt." A servant bowed to refill his wineglass and the baron took a sip, then continued. "Before going into combat, the samurai must prepare himself to match wits with the enemy and heroically challenge death. After the battle is fought and won, he knows that many brave comrades will lie dead around him. On the eve of battle, his gentle regard for beauty allows him to pluck a flower growing in his campgrounds. He might be moved to compose a poem celebrating the life cycle that its blossoming symbolizes. This poetic moment serves to calm his spirit, while it places his existence in perspective with nature. All things are born. All things must die." Soberly the baron looked at Inge. "I have never been called upon to test my Bushido in war, Madame. But I've considered the possibility that my son may be called to serve his emperor in the not too distant future. If so, his honor and mine will be tested through his actions. Should Kimitake shame me by an act of cowardice, I stand guilty of having failed to imbue my son with the Bushido owed our noble bloodline. Then only seppuku could redress my loss of face."

"I have not heard this term before," Inge said.

"You of the West know it by another name. Hara-kiri." Inge looked shocked. "Yes, ritual suicide."

Inge gave a nervous laugh. "Ach, Baron. But you are having a joke with me," she insisted. "Surely taking your life as your ancestors once did is no longer demanded of a samurai in the twentieth century."

"I am not alone in still holding with that code," the baron said firmly. "While Japan's glib modernizers have relegated Bushido to nothing more than an archaic word, to me its obligations are as valid today as in my ancestors' time." The handsome baron grinned and reached out to pat Inge's hand. "My Bushido isn't so very different from your European code of gallantry, dear lady. Once your ancestors fought duels over a point of honor. Men of the West still place great store in their sense of honor. In the stock market crash of 1929, many who had lost face in business chose to take their own lives. Not so very long ago during the Great War, European officers who had shamed themselves in battle often chose an honorable death by suicide. The difference between our cultures is that your soldier-gentry put pistols to their heads, while dishonored samurai chose to die by the sword. Is that not correct, sir?" He smiled at Heinz, aware his point was well made.

"You are correct." Polishing his monocle with his handkerchief, Heinz stared vacantly into the flickering flames of the tall silver candelabra. "As a young officer fighting for Germany in the last war, I witnessed much best forgotten. There was a lieutenant in my regiment, a classmate at Heidelberg University. He committed a single act of cowardice under fire that led to the deaths of those serving under him. German honor demanded that he forfeit his life. He applied the coup de grâce behind closed doors with a Luger placed firmly at his temple."

Inge flung down her napkin. "Good heavens, Heinz, what an awful picture to draw at the dinner table."

"I quite agree," Angela said, appalled.

"War is the business that has brought us together in Japan," said Heinz. "There have always been wars and men to fight them—soldiers who need weapons such as the parachutes we intend to manufacture. That is a reality we all must face. But I cannot embrace the Nazi party. Fascism is like a dark force at work in my country, Baron. How the German people could elevate a megalomaniac like Hitler to power escapes me. However, he is the acknowledged leader of Germany," he added, shifting uncomfortably in his chair. "Although I disagree with Hitler's politics, I owe allegiance to the fatherland. Right or wrong, one's country is one's country." Suddenly Heinz stopped talking, aware of the concern in his wife's eyes. "And you, Herr Baron? What are your feelings about the political alliance growing between Germany and Japan?" he asked, then cleared his throat as the baron considered his reply.

"Whatever course Japan chooses to follow, I am clearly obligated to serve my country with honor," Tadashi said evenly. "My allegiance to Japan can never be shaken by politics." He smiled at Heinz and Inge. "As a matter of fact, here we look up to the emperor and down our noses at the politicians. However, I'm personally no fan of Hitler's, despite Japan's close ties with the Nazi regime."

"Do go on, Baron Hosokawa," Inge said, giving him her most charming smile. "We are curious to know more about your feelings toward the führer."

"Please, do speak freely with us," said Heinz.

"I for one would like to end the discussion here and now," Angela put in forcefully. "Why dwell on the so-called Little Corporal? The newspapers all agree that he's no serious threat to anyone."

"His talent for charming the press isn't at issue here, Angela." Baron Hosokawa looked around the table of sober faces. "Hitler is a gifted diplomat. Much to my dismay, there is a side to the man everyone seems to have ignored. Germany's head of state is a deplorable racist. Although I don't believe in intermarriage, there's no malice attached to my belief. It's simply a matter of observing the rules of society. However, the Führer has made a point of drawing a hard line between a superior race of Germans and all others. I feel sure he has no tolerance for the Japanese. After all, we are a 'colored' race. Our nations happen to share an enemy in the Soviet Union. Otherwise I doubt Hitler would extend his hand to us any more than he would to a Jew." The baron noticed that Inge had suddenly grown rigid. "Has something I've said upset you?"

"I was born a Jew," Inge said, tossing back her head as if the statement left her open to challenge. "Hitler's filthy propaganda machine spreads lies against Germany's Jews. But I am not impressed by his fanatical thugs and those who support their fear tactics. Most of my countrymen show better sense."

Heinz and Inge looked at each other for a moment, communicating their thoughts. Then Heinz addressed the baron. "Inge was orphaned when she was just an infant. The family who adopted my wife raised her in the Protestant faith. She is first a German. She is a Jew only by virtue of her birth certificate."

"That is so, *Schatzken*. I had never thought of myself as a Jewess until this vicious propaganda campaign made me realize it was my duty to acknowledge my ancestry." Inge's blue eyes caught fire. "Not that I go about shouting this fact to everyone. But I will not be intimidated by the Nazis into denying it."

"Darling, calm yourself," said Angela, waving the servants from the dining table. She had known of Inge's ancestry for years, but that night her friend had revealed a heightened sensitivity that worried her. "This isn't like you, Inge. Honestly, all this talk of anti-Semitism only lends importance to the bigotry of others. The less said about it the better. Morita! We'll take brandy in the library."

"Perhaps Angela's right," the baron said. "Why cater to the ignorant?" he told Inge, walking beside her as everyone crossed the mansion's grand foyer to the library. "The Jewish students Douglas and I knew at Harvard were fine scholars. Achievers. Like the Japanese, the Jews are bound strongly together by their ancient traditions. Throughout history they've endured persecution without relinquishing their beliefs. Hitler brands the Jews as being racially inferior, while their achievements in the arts and the sciences make his claims preposterous. As a nation of borrowers, we Japanese might profit from knowing the Jews better."

The Karlstadts now enjoyed a laugh; then Heinz turned somber. "Inge's Jewish birth certificate has made it impossible for us to adopt a child. We have tried, but the Nazi bureaucrats shake their heads and give us more papers to fill out." Noticing Angela's look of shock, Heinz said, "Since you last visited with us, our German courts have passed laws that deny the human rights of Jews."

"Paving the way for what, I wonder," Inge questioned under her breath.

Just then the clock in the hallway chimed the hour of nine. "I expect Lord Mitsudara will be joining us shortly," Douglas commented. "Morita, show the lord into the library when he arrives."

In the library, colorful leatherbound books lined the dark mahogany shelves that reached from the floor to the ceiling. The room was two stories high, with a skylight of stained glass. Douglas prized the knowledge gathered here, especially the books on engineering he had collected over the years. Balconies wound around the room, dividing the shelves into three tiers that were reached by means of a spiral staircase. Moveable ladders on each tier provided access to the books. On a massive mahogany desk, the blueprints Heinz had brought from Germany had been pinned down with antique glass paperweights. Library lamps with green glass shades illuminated the blueprints. Elegant wing-back chairs upholstered in green leather were placed around a large table. Morita circled the table silently, pulling out chairs for the men.

"These drawings of my facilities in Berlin show what progress we have made so far using your private funds, Baron," said Heinz, smoothing out ripples in the blueprints. "As you can see, there is yet much work to be done before we can manufacture our first parachutes. But with the financing from the Mitsudara Bank, this can be accomplished within a year."

Angela Napier observed Inge's detachment while the butler served everyone brandy in crystal snifters. As the three men went over the blueprints, Angela said to Inge, "Come, let's talk." She steered her friend toward a deep leather sofa, away from the desk. Inge distractedly turned a large globe of the world in its antique brass stand, then sat down beside Angela.

"What do you think of this venture between our husbands?" Angela asked Inge, attempting to draw her out.

"I do not see an alternative for them. And you?"

"I hate the idea of Douglas getting into any business having to do with war. But he hasn't solicited my opinion, and I've never meddled in his business affairs." Angela took a sip of brandy. "At any rate, the year abroad will do my son a world of good. Maxwell has always preferred spending his summer vacations here with Baron Hosokawa's children, and it seemed wrong to uproot the boy by taking him with us. Of course, Douglas and I missed him terribly. Now he's nearly a grown man." She stared wistfully into her glass. "I can't get over how mature he is. It makes me feel positively ancient. I had such a difficult time in childbirth that the thought of having another baby frightened me, even though I desperately wanted a little girl. But Douglas seems satisfied having an only child." Suddenly Angela realized how tactless she had been. "Oh, dear. How terrible of me to complain, when you've tried so hard to have a child. Is there no way you can adopt one?"

"Even the position my husband enjoys cannot bend German law."

"Having you victimized by these stupid hatreds makes me furious. I hadn't intended to raise this awful subject again, but how can the Nazis treat you so shabbily just because the word Jew is stamped on your birth certificate? What possible difference could it make to them if you gave some poor child love and a good home?"

Inge smiled at her friend's naivete. "One cannot appeal to the Nazi intellect, Angela. Men like Herr Dr. Goebbels have been taught to see the Jews as Shylocks and Christ killers. Ja, the beliefs parents preach to their children are not easily shaken."

"Yes, that's an awful fact of life one often tends to overlook. Parents do shape the minds of their young." Angela glanced across the library at Baron Hosokawa. At dinner, his talk of honor and ritual suicide had chilled her to the bone. "I was raised to show tolerance for others," she told Inge. "My parents were always so understanding of me. I was an only child, and they spoiled me. When they were alive, they visited Japan every year. Maxwell was very fond of them. Yes, having my parents in this house almost made it seem like home." She paused to light a cigarette. "Douglas's father was such a cold man. But his mother, Irene, devoted herself to satisfying her husband's needs. She was a kind woman. We grew close over the years—but there was never the closeness between us that I felt with my own mother. I can remember mother seated here in the library when she last visited Japan, curled up on the sofa with a book. How she loved to read. I often miss her when I'm alone here during the winter months. She died of pneumonia four years ago."

Saddened, Angela drew on her cigarette. She had spoken of her parents to Inge before, and she now silently reflected on their deaths. Her father, Charles Sommersby, had owned banks. He died of a stroke soon after the stock market crash of 1929 had wiped out his personal fortune. Her mother, Margaret, had always been a rather frail woman. Angela had inherited Margaret's beauty and her flair for dressing well. She fussed with the shoulder straps of her evening dress and said, "I don't think anyone ever fully recovers from the death of a parent."

"I was too young when my natural parents died to remember them," Inge said. "But I have only the most wonderful memories of the Christian couple who adopted me. They had also longed to have children of their own. My Heinz has such a giving heart," she mused. "He says nothing, but I know he feels cheated."

Inge appeared to be fighting back tears, and Angela took her friend's hand. "There, you have a wonderful marriage. Children aren't everything."

Morita appeared in the doorway. "Lord Mitsudara," he announced, bowing.

Angela stepped forward to welcome her important guest. The two had met briefly years ago, here at the mansion when she had given a party for Tadashi and Sumie Hosokawa's wedding anniversary. Now, the lord surprised Angela by kissing the back of her hand in the continental manner. "Your presence honors my household, Lord Mitsudara. Allow me to introduce our friends, the Karlstadts."

"Charmed." Lord Mitsudara took Inge's hand and kissed it in the same manner. "Your wife is a delight for the eyes, Herr Karlstadt. Regrettable that business kept me from dining with two such lovely ladies." He smiled and bowed. "Tomorrow evening you will honor me by dining at my home."

The blueprints did not escape his notice, and the lord put on his reading glasses. "My staff has scheduled time for us to make use of your short visit to Japan, Herr Karlstadt. Tonight, I have only an hour. Shall we get down to business, gentlemen?"

"We've just been going over the blueprints," said Douglas. "Morita, pour a brandy for the lord. Would you like a cigar?"

"I have my own, thank you." Lord Mitsudara sat down on the chair Morita had placed by the desk. Then he took out one Havana cigar from his platinum case. "Now, show me what you have done."

A cloud of cigar smoke rose over the men. Angela glided up against Douglas, craving the attention Inge received from her husband even while Heinz talked business. Their hands joined, their eyes met, his arm drew Inge close. She was a part of him, thought Angela as she walked away to have Morita pour her another brandy.

"Your progress is most pleasing," the lord complimented Heinz, pausing to draw on his cigar. "However, blueprints are one thing, their execution another. I was led to believe that you were bringing some tangible evidence to Japan."

"You weren't misled," Douglas responded before Heinz could reply. "Heinz has taken a step beyond these blueprints. As the lord knows, model building is essential to the development of new machinery. Working models of my new looms were assembled at the Karlstadt Works to produce a miniature of our parachute. We're about to witness a demonstration of it in action."

"So! I am eager to see this." The lord rubbed his hands together in anticipation. "Will the model function in these unscientific conditions?"

Heinz placed his monocle in his right eye before answering. "Most definitely. The butler will assist me in demonstrating this for you now," he said, and Douglas signaled for Morita to climb up the spiral library staircase. The man carried a metal cylinder. "The miniature paratrooper harnessed to the parachute canopy is scaled to the actual size and weight of a man armed for assault against enemy ground forces. The design of this model was tested in my wind tunnel with excellent results." Heinz called up to Morita, "Once you have uncapped the cylinder, the model is triggered for release."

"Men and their toys," Angela bristled. "My husband looks like a ten-year-old at Christmas."

Inge smiled and put her arm around her friend's waist to draw her back to the men. "Come, we must show some interest to humor them."

"Don't forget to release it gently, Morita," Douglas cautioned the old man. "Are you ready?"

"*Hai, dannasama.*"

"Then hit the silk!" Douglas called back. Morita leaned out from the top of the stair railing and released the model parachute. Lord Mitsudara covered his head, afraid of being struck by the fast-falling projectile. Then a small burst of white silk mushroomed overhead. For a split-second the miniature paratrooper jerked to a standstill in midair before the opening canopy lifted him upward toward the ceiling. Then he slowly descended, rocked by faint air currents.

Douglas gripped Heinz's arm. "It's like witnessing an actual jump!"

"There are yet aerodynamic problems to be solved," Heinz replied as the model completed its slow descent and quietly settled on the blueprints, where its silk canopy bubbled with trapped air. "Once that is done, our parachutes will be much more maneuverable than those of the Gessler Works. We could not accomplish this without Douglas's skills," he told the lord. "While in Germany, he can work more closely with my staff to help perfect our parachute and his new assembly-line machinery."

What Baron Hosokawa had just witnessed left him rather shaken. His gaze lowered to the toy figurine. "This parachute is something more than I had imagined, Douglas. I can't account for it, but standing here looking at the Hosokawa silk, its purpose seems twisted."

"Nonsense, Tadashi. It's merely cloth shaped to serve the needs of the times," the lord gravely intoned. "My congratulations, gentlemen. Can the model be demonstrated again?"

Heinz ran one hand through his hair. "*Ja,* but the packing of a parachute is an art, Lord Mitsudara. This tiny model would demand much patience and time, or it would collapse when striking the air. Paratroopers' lives will rest in the hands of workers trained to pack the chutes. Please, Douglas, examine how the canopy is constructed. This intricate stitching was accomplished on the models of your machinery—does it meet with your approval?"

Douglas was grinning as he draped one section of the translucent silk chute over the green glass shade of a library lamp. "It more than meets my expectations. A spider would envy such craftsmanship, Heinz. What your staff has done with the gores and the shroud lines is brilliant. On the drawing board it's hard to predict how machinery will perform. We're closer to achieving our goal than I thought. Our German competitor would keel over if he saw this."

Heinz shook his head and laughed. "I have taken precautions against spies. There are more guards at my gates than at the führer's offices in Berlin."

"I have no time for levity, Mr. Karlstadt," the lord stated bluntly. "My industries cover a broad spectrum, but the manufacturing of parachutes is new to me, so kindly define your terms. What is a gore?"

"One of these many triangular panels of which the canopy is constructed, Lord Mitsudara." Heinz used his cigar as a pointer. "Each panel is built of several smaller pieces stitched together. In this way, no tear will ever become larger than the piece in which it originates." He smiled. "For lightness and strength, even these shroud lines and the harness worn by our paratrooper are constructed of your fine Japanese silk."

The lord made a humming sound. "Japan has an abundance of silk, but, unfortunately, few other natural resources. My factories must rely heavily on imports of scrap metal, largely from the United States. Without it, the empire would have no backbone and sag like an old woman."

He stood from the library table and bowed. "Now I must bid you all good night. Dear ladies, forgive my brevity. When you visit my home here in Tokyo, we'll enjoy some leisure to speak of more than business."

Inge linked arms with Heinz. "It is disappointing to have so little time in which to explore your lovely country," she said.

Lord Mitsudara bowed to kiss her hand. "Travelers should leave a foreign land with something unsatisfied to prompt their return, Madame."

Morita saw their visitor to the door, and the atmosphere instantly brightened.

"The lord can be difficult," the baron told the Karlstadts. "As a czar of industry, he wears a heavy mantle of responsibility."

Inge changed the subject. "If only we could stay long enough to visit your castle," she said to the baron. "Do tell us about it and your children."

While the baron entertained her German friends, Angela lapsed into silence. The telephone rang, and Douglas answered it. It was Max. Father and son spoke for just a few moments before hanging up.

"It was a bad connection," he told her. "I'll call him back from the study."

Angela watched her husband enter his study, which was located across the foyer from the library. Although she was curious to know why Max had called, Angela was above listening in. For a time she sulked over being excluded from that rapport between father and son. Then she left her guests to themselves and crossed the foyer to Douglas's study, where she hesitated at its closed door.

Douglas was seated at his desk, phone to his ear, listening to his son talking about his trials with love. With his free hand, Douglas drew Natsu's face in a sketchbook. Using a pencil, he shaded in her lustrous hair. He kept no photograph of his lover, whose image was indelibly etched in his mind. When separated from Natsu in summers past, Douglas often breathed her to life by sketching her from memory in familiar poses and outfits. More than once Angela Napier had almost caught him in the act. But on their travels abroad, he had always found it relaxing to fill sketchbooks with fanciful drawings—circus clowns, menacing dragons, and imaginary machines—as well as sketches of people. There was no way she could have known whom he was drawing from memory. Still, he would quickly turn the page on Natsu's likeness and begin to draw something else pulled from his fertile imagination.

Now Douglas sat up abruptly as his wife entered the study without knocking. He quickly closed the sketchbook. Later he would destroy this drawing of the woman he loved. "You're handling things well, Max. Now get some sleep." He put the receiver back on its hook. "Angela, shouldn't you be with our guests?"

"They're getting on famously without me. How is Maxwell?"

"Bearing up," answered Douglas, trying to appear casual as he placed the sketchbook inside a desk drawer. "I can't do more for the boy than be a good listener."

"He's fortunate having you as a father. It's petty of me to feel left out." Douglas stood up, and Angela put her arms around his neck. "Lord Mitsudara's visit was an eye opener. Now I realize the terrible burden you've been working under. Darling, at times I behave like such a witch. I'll try harder to be more understanding of you from now on." She smiled with that promise.

"We're both a little short-tempered." Douglas kissed her lightly on the mouth. "Will you excuse me to our friends? I have some work to do before turning in."

Angela tarried at the study door. "Don't be too late."

"I won't." Douglas observed his wife's long-legged walk. She had preserved her alluring figure. Angela was a woman of quality, he thought. Her effort to reconcile their differences stung his conscience.

He poured a whiskey at the bar and drank it neat. He looked up at his father's portrait, which hung over the marble mantelpiece, still ruling over the room to which Douglas had been summoned on one bitterly remembered night more than twenty years ago. The painter who had rendered Julius Napier's likeness had accurately captured the disdainful expression in his eyes.

Douglas retreated through time, once again seeing himself as the cowering young man his father had marched from this study up the mansion's broad staircase to Andrew Napier's kingly bedchamber. Grandfather Andrew stared out at him from a mountain of bed pillows. Withered by illness and looking far older than his seventy years, the bedridden patriarch no longer had the capacity to voice his wrath on the matter of his grandson's falling in love with a Japanese. Julius Napier's voice spoke for him.

"You'll not attempt to see that girl again or have any contact with her whatsoever," Julius said firmly. "You'll meet the obligations of this family and its business as I have, or be disowned. There's no alternative open to you, Douglas. Natsu Yoseido's father won't give his daughter to a mixed marriage. She's under age, so she can't make the choice. In any event, such a marriage would be doomed from the start. Doomed to a life of hardship here and in every country abroad. Japan is your home, but this family is your only claim to the life you've enjoyed here. Your first allegiance is to serve the mills. Without them, you're nothing. So, get these ideas of defiance out of your head. I'm removing you from temptation by cutting your time here short. We'll leave Japan in the morning, and this affair must be forgotten. I'll hear no more of it. And don't think of turning to your mother, Douglas. As in all matters pertaining to your future, she must abide by my decisions."

With tears in his eyes, Douglas stood there listening, his youthful hopes of marrying Natsu dashed to pieces by his father's ultimatums. His American-born mother, Irene, had been brought to the Napier mansion just as his grandmother had, chosen by Julius to fill its rooms with heirs.

Like the first Mrs. Napier, Irene had fallen short of her husband's expectations. She had given him a son. Why she had failed to bear him other children was a subject never spoken of in Douglas's presence. His mother was a loving woman, but that love was not returned by Julius. His father's word was law, and Douglas knew his mother would be helpless to act against it on her son's behalf.

Douglas had never known his grandfather to show emotion. Now a stroke had paralyzed Andrew Napier. He could only blink his staring eyes to communicate his approval of what had taken place at his sickbed. In another year, while Douglas was in America, this heartless old man would die.

As a child growing up in this house, Douglas had only vague memories of his grandmother, Louise, as a shadowy recluse who had kept to her own room and never left it until the day of her death. Andrew Napier had raised his son without love, shaping Julius's character to serve only his dynasty. Julius was now taking over the role of shaping the next generation to serve the mills, no matter what it cost.

That painful voyage at sea and the loneliness of his student days at Harvard had long been stored away in some deep enclave of Douglas's mind. He had no wish to recall that period in his life. But tonight it fought to be remembered, and he was carried back to his years of exile on American shores . . . .

For Douglas those years had blended together, meaningless without Natsu. He attended parties, but had always kept his distance from the young women there, until one fateful autumn evening at the start of his senior year when he attended the birthday party of a Harvard friend.

Douglas was standing alone on the veranda, thinking of Natsu, when a feminine voice called his name. He turned to see Angela Sommersby gliding toward him.

"What a bore you are, Douglas Napier," Angela chided him, and boldly took his arm. "It's positively unhealthy, all this brooding."

"Angela Sommersby, isn't it?" She was wearing a mint-green dress that complemented her emerald eyes, and Douglas acknowledged her attentions with a strained indifference that made her laugh.

"Oh, you know very well who I am," she answered tartly. "We've attended the same parties time and again. Why, I've practically thrown myself at you to gain some notice." Sweet, romantic music drifted through the doors that opened onto the veranda, and Angela swayed with the beat. "Well, Mr. Napier, I do have my pride. Since I've taken the first step, the very least you can do is ask me for a dance."

Douglas had not returned to Japan in the summers, and his father had given him every reason to believe that Natsu was lost to him forever. But he remained faithful to the haunting memories of their love. Now this perfumed Boston socialite was in his arms, and the sexual desire pent up inside him for Natsu suddenly made Douglas weak with passion.

Angela's arms tightened around his neck, and her body swayed sensuously against him long after the music had stopped. Douglas kissed her hard. She did not resist or question his urgency when he pulled her down the garden path into the darkness, where he kissed her hard again and again. He desperately wanted her, but she allowed him to go only so far.

Angela Sommersby made it clear to him that she was not some fast coed eager to leap headlong into a torrid first affair. She expected to be courted properly, and in the weeks that followed, she doled out her favors, teasing Douglas to the brink of madness. When Angela at last decided to surrender herself to love, Douglas arranged their accommodation at a country inn, where he registered as Mr. and Mrs. Napier, telling himself this tryst would never come to that.

With Angela's long legs twined around him and her sultry voice whispering, "Yes, Douglas—oh, yes, yes," their lovemaking dazzled him. He could not get enough of Angela Sommersby, and in the passionate nights that followed, his memories of Natsu grew dim.

At social affairs, Douglas came to enjoy being seen with this fashionable young woman on his arm. Angela could be witty, and they laughed easily together. As the autumn waned, they became an item, dancing close together, openly sharing kisses for all to see. As Christmas vacation neared, Douglas realized that Angela meant more to him than a casual fling. And yet Natsu retained possession of his heart. If not for that, he might have hoped to find lasting happiness with Angela as his wife. She spoke seriously of marriage, and he knew it was unfair of him not to break off with her. But his good intentions were lost to the fire that this outwardly cool socialite aroused in him. Ultimately, the decision to marry her was taken out of his hands when Douglas was summoned into the presence of his father.

Julius Napier sat behind the desk in his Boston hotel suite and announced to his son that he had come from Japan to attend a wedding. "The Sommersby girl is excellent breeding stock, Douglas," he said, preoccupied with unfolding the pages of his checkbook. "Her father wrote me, and I've since spoken with her parents, who've every right to be concerned over the seriousness of your affair. Talk of such things gets around, Douglas. You'll stop having your way with Angela and marry the girl before your graduation in June. She's agreeable to it, and marriage won't interfere with your studies. It will give you a more solid base." Julius scribbled his signature across a check, then ripped it off and blew on the wet ink. "This gift should wipe out your debts and settle you into some nice Boston apartment with your new bride. I hadn't intended to punish you with limited funds while you were at Harvard. It was only to prevent you from bolting to Japan and causing injury to Natsu and her husband. I did what any father would do to keep his son from making a damn fool of himself." Imperiously, he sailed the check across his desk, barely making eye contact with Douglas. "Natsu's marriage to a husband of her own race is a happy one. When I last saw her, she was a contented wife and mother. And now you'll settle down with a proper wife to start a family of your own."

"Generous of you, Dad." Douglas slowly folded his father's check. The news of Natsu's marriage to a Japanese three years before was just one lie in Julius's web of deceit, which his son had come to accept as the truth. His father's arrogant look rekindled bitter memories of his last night in Japan. But Julius might have chosen him a less agreeable wife, and he surrendered to his fate.

His father shuffled the papers on the desk. "Naturally, your betrothed will expect a formal proposal of marriage. I suggest you do it at once, so we can set the wedding date."

On the day before Christmas, 1917, Douglas Napier and Angela Sommersby were married at the Boston church of her parents. The nave was turned into spring by a profusion of hothouse flowers. The Great War was still raging "over there," and several of the groom's college friends attended the wedding in uniform. Some had enlisted, others had been drafted. Julius Napier had forbidden his only son and heir to enlist, and Douglas's number had so far not been drawn from the bowl of President Wilson's draft lottery. The armistice to be signed in November of the following year would spare him, but his best man, dressed in the uniform of a second lieutenant, would lie dead in the muddy trenches of Europe.

As the marriage vows were exchanged, Douglas's mother and Mrs. Sommersby had wept. Their husbands wore broad grins and congratulated themselves on a sound match. The newlyweds posed for photographers, kissing and smiling through the bombardment of exploding flash powder that foretold a tempestuous marriage . . . .

Suddenly Douglas Napier was pulled from his bitter recollections of the past by the sound of his wife's laughter in the foyer. He had raised up his father's ghost, and now it vanished, although in Douglas's mind there was something of the past yet unaccounted for. He walked over to a shelf and picked up an old scrapbook.

Over the years, his sensitive and good-hearted mother had catalogued mementos of the Napier family's travels abroad—picture postcards, theater programs, pressed flowers—which she carefully pasted into albums. The last pages of the book contained several yellowing newspaper clippings.

They were French newspaper accounts of a fatal motoring accident that had occurred near the white sandy beaches of the Côte d'Azur. To Douglas they were an epitaph for his parents. Witnesses at the scene had described how Julius Napier had swerved his expensive gray sedan to avoid running down a stray dog and had lost control. His car went over a cliff and crashed on the rocks below, instantly killing him and his wife. Douglas had never understood what could have prompted a man like Julius Napier to risk personal injury to avoid killing a stray dog.

Douglas had pasted those clippings in his mother's scrapbook. Perhaps he had never come to terms with the reality of his father's death, he thought now, and kept the articles as proof. Julius Napier had passed on to his son an empty legacy of wealth. His tyrannical rule over Douglas's life had ended eight long years ago. Yet the event had changed nothing.

Douglas returned the scrapbook to its place on the shelf. His finger traced across the dates stamped in gold leaf on the spines of the other albums. Tonight his parents' sojourn through life seemed ancient history doomed to dust on the study shelves.

Perhaps wealth was a curse, Douglas told himself. So far, only the founding fathers of the dynasty had lived into old age. Andrew Napier had died at seventy-one. Baron Fujio Hosokawa had passed on nearing eighty. Glancing at Julius's portrait, he wondered if his father would have softened with age or grown harder like Grandfather Andrew. Both men had been the cause of much unhappiness. And yet, Douglas's memories of this house were not all unhappy ones. When he was a boy, his father had seldom been there to take a hand in raising him, and his grandfather had no time for children. Douglas's mother had virtually a free hand in her son's upbringing. Irene Napier had encouraged his artistic talent and his scholarship at school. Yes, he was Irene's child, Douglas thought. She had a wealth of understanding for the needs of a growing boy. She had taught him the meaning of love.

Douglas sat down at his desk, remembering his joy as a new father, cradling his infant son in the upstairs nursery. Being a father to Max had made the years worthwhile. He recalled his son and Tadashi's children playing hide-and-seek, giggling while they ran through the house. When they were very little, Douglas had made a project of remodeling the mansion's spacious attic. He had transformed it into a playroom for rainy afternoons. Often he would climb up the attic stairs to visit Max, Shizue, and Kimitake, who drew him into their games.

It was true the mansion also held bitter memories for him, Douglas reflected. But the old house gave him a sense of continuity. Its rooms linked his own boyhood with that of his growing son. Angela felt no attachment to this house whatsoever. But like the weaving mills, Andrew Napier's mansion was an inheritance willed to Douglas with the obligation to preserve it for the next generation.

He was a Napier, to the manor born. Julius's death had passed the reins of industry into his son's hands. But Douglas's stock in Hosokawa-

Napier, Limited, had been earned by the sweat of his brow. His vision had bought the firm a new lease on life. And tonight's demonstration of his new parachute had justified all his sacrifices to the business.

He heard the voices of his friends calling it a night. Then Baron Hosokawa knocked at the study door, and Douglas crossed the room to open it. "I can see you enjoyed the evening."

"Yes, the Karlstadts are fine people," Tadashi said. "I agreed to climb Mount Fuji with them. Haven't done it since we were boys."

Douglas watched Angela going upstairs with the Karlstadts, and he lowered his voice. "Helping Angela entertain them would be a great favor to me."

Understanding his friend's needs, the baron nodded. "Surely, Douglas. I'll do what I can."

"Thanks. A nightcap?"

"No, I've had more than usual. Good night."

Douglas crossed to his desk and flipped the pages of his calendar. With Tadashi on hand to help entertain the Karlstadts, he could use work as an excuse for sharing precious time with Natsu. Less than three weeks were left them. He yearned to be with her now and lifted the telephone.

"Hello?" It was Paul. As Douglas was hanging up the phone, he heard Paul ask, "Mother, is that you?"

It was rare for Paul to answer the phone, and Douglas knew it would have been pointless to talk to him. Douglas looked at the clock on the fireplace mantel. It was eleven o'clock. He wondered where Natsu could be at this late hour. She always retired early and kept the phone near her bed in anticipation of his calls. Taking the sketchbook from his desk drawer, he tore up his drawing of her and sent the pieces into the wastebasket. He glanced up at his father's portrait. Art played tricks on the eye, he thought. His father seemed to be mocking his unhappiness from the grave.

It was close to midnight as Natsu made her way along the Ginza. She was troubled by a guilty conscience. She had spent that evening in Hideo Tamura's company, enduring the love in his sad eyes throughout the lingering dinner date. She had dated him several times while Douglas had been visiting with the baron. That night he had insisted on escorting her home, but she coyly refused, saying it was unwise for her son to learn of their arrangement. Natsu had decided to ask Paul to invite his employer for dinner at their apartment. In this way he would accept her friendship with Hideo as purely a matter of showing gratitude. Otherwise, her son might suspect that Douglas had a part in assisting his career. Before leaving Tamura, she had reminded him of his promise to remain Paul's silent mentor, and he had bowed again to her wishes.

Even at this late hour the establishments along the Ginza were open for business, advertising their entertainments with colorful splashes of neon light. Natsu walked down an adjoining street to the Roman Catholic church. She had first been drawn there one winter's night after Douglas's father had visited the tea shop. Then Natsu had nearly collapsed from grief when he announced his son had taken an American woman as his bride the year before and that she was expecting their first child. Julius Napier's motives were obvious. In the passing years he had tried to buy Natsu's silence with financial support for her and Paul. He had good reason to fear her actions when Douglas returned to Japan, but she could not be bought off. Now he had no reason to offer money. He knew that Natsu's enduring love for Douglas would keep her from injuring him and his pregnant wife with the truth.

If not for her son, Natsu would have ended her life on that wintry night, as she left the tea shop to wander aimlessly. Then, through the tinsel of falling snow, she had glimpsed the church windows warmly aglow. Natsu paused under them now, viewing the stained glass angels floating across a heavenly blue sky, heralding the birth of Christ on their long golden trumpets. Below them the Virgin Mary cradled the infant Jesus in her lap.

On that eve of desperation, Natsu had suddenly rushed inside the cathedral doors, always open to worshippers. She had encountered a kind priest, whose beliefs she had ultimately embraced. Through those beliefs she had found peace and serenity.

Father Watanabe was the parish priest. He often wandered the aisles at night, talking to and comforting those in need. Natsu saw him walk by, then sit in the last pew, his head bowed in silent meditation. Before approaching him, Natsu reflected on a confession made to this priest long ago. Adultery was a mortal sin, and Father Watanabe had told her that she must give up Douglas Napier. She had wept, feeling unable to make the sacrifice demanded by her faith. She clung to the belief that her love for Douglas was not a sin but a holy sacrament—as binding as any marriage performed in the sight of God.

"Oh, Father, I can't live without Douglas," she had pleaded with him in the confessional. "Don't ask me to choose between my love for Christ and my love for this man. Others committed sins against *us*. If not for that, Douglas and I would be man and wife. Oh, surely, my love for him isn't a sin."

"I can offer you the sympathy of a friend, Natsu," he had answered. "But as your priest, I am bound by my holy vows. The faith you have chosen to embrace cannot be bent to serve your rationalizations, my child. Think of your immortal soul and do not see this married man again."

Sobbing, Natsu had refused to make a promise she could never keep. That would truly have a been a sin. She had not gone to confession again. Still she worshipped as a Catholic in this church, believing that a merciful God would grant her the understanding that His priest could not give.

Father Watanabe was only a man, Natsu thought, rising to her feet. He continued to minister to her troubled soul with a quiet acceptance, as if waiting for her to find her way back along the right path.

Natsu walked over to him. "Father," she said quietly, "I need your help."

He glanced up at her from his meditation and smiled. "Sit here beside me."

Natsu stroked the silk scarf covering her head. First she told him of Hideo Tamura's one-sided love. She went on to tell him about her illness and of her decision to spare Paul from knowing how very ill she was. "I know it's cancer, Father," she told him, "even without the biopsy. I know this as I knew my faith in Christ on the day He first entered my heart."

There was a look of sadness on the priest's kind face as he met her eyes. "Natsu, I speak as a friend," he said softly, so as not to be overheard. "Giving your companionship to Mr. Tamura is not wrong. The man cannot hope to force his feelings on you, and he must settle for friendship, or lose even that. But keeping your illness from Paul *is* wrong. Natsu, you are his rock, and if you have cancer, then he must be given time in which to prepare for your death."

"Oh, I can't, Father. Please, pray for me." Pale and shaking, Natsu stood and hurried out of the church before the priest could say more.

For an instant, Natsu's faith faltered. Her son had accused her of living a lie. Had she coveted Douglas Napier's love too deeply, asking nothing for herself at the expense of her son? Had she been the cause of Paul's resentment toward his father?

"Oh, dear God," she prayed aloud, "when it's time for me to go, let me quietly slip away without regrets or too much pain. Let my son embrace his father in their shared hour of grief, and I'll come to you happily, rejoicing in that bond."

CHAPTER 8

Servants hurried about the Napier mansion preparing for a dinner party. Angela felt rather giddy with the anticipation of leaving Japan the next morning. Even the heat of August could not dampen her spirits as she went over last-minute details with Morita. All her Tokyo society acquaintances would be in attendance to bid farewell to the Napiers and their German friends.

Max had returned home from Kyushu, and the Karlstadts took an instant liking to him. Especially Inge, who had quickly adopted Angela's son with an affectionate charm that made it impossible for his mother to be jealous.

Looking forward to an entire year abroad, Angela viewed the floral arrangements she had ordered to liven the atmosphere of the stodgy, mahogany-paneled rooms. She would be glad to see the last of them.

"Everything seems in order, Madame," said the butler.

"Thanks to you, Morita." Angela saw the unhappiness on the old man's face. The house had never been closed for so long a time. Now its servants would be dismissed, while Morita stayed on as caretaker. "I do hope my husband finishes his work at the office before our guests arrive," she said, stepping around the dining room table to adjust the place cards. "We'll seat my son and Shizue opposite the Karlstadts. And Kimitake beside his father. It might encourage some conversation between them."

Just then, Max, Shizue, and Kimitake entered the house, trailed by Yufugawo, who always assumed the traditional role of Shizue's chaperone on ventures into the city streets.

"Enjoy your afternoon?" Angela inquired.

"Oh, yes," said Shizue. "We went to the cinema to see Greta Garbo in *Camille*. She was so lovely. I wept at the end."

"Too much kissing," her older brother countered, making a face.

Angela grew mindful of the time. "We're dressing tonight, children. Evening wear. Dinner is promptly at eight."

Yufugawo sighed. "Ah, the city heat has swelled my feet to twice their size. Go along, Shizue. I will be up in a moment."

Max held Shizue's hand as they climbed the stairs. He felt desperate to be alone with her. At the cinema she had cuddled against his shoulder, but Yufugawo had kept a watchful eye on the couple. Kimitake had also intruded on their last afternoon together. Max wanted to spend the eve of their parting alone with Shizue. "With the house full of guests, we can slip away together and not be missed," he promised her.

Shizue squeezed his hand, still in the thrall of a movie romance.

Hearing them, Baron Hosokawa appeared at the door of his room. "Max, I have something to give you," he said, inviting the boy inside. "A going-away present. It's very old."

Max bowed and accepted the silk scroll tied with black tassels. He was touched by the baron's gesture. Carefully, Max unrolled the scroll, then smiled with delight. It was a painting of the Hosokawa castle, its gardens, and the misty mountain peaks in the distance. "I'll treasure it," Max said, moved to tears.

The baron placed both hands on the boy's shoulders. "I know what it's like to be homesick. Good-byes are difficult. But soon you'll return to us," he said, then turned away in silence.

Max was left standing there, experiencing an uprooting that was softened by this painting of home. The baron had fathered him through the summers of his boyhood. Max knew that his love for Shizue might lead to hurting her father, but he could not imagine them ever becoming enemies.

The Cherry Blossom Kissaten was crowded with soldiers in uniform. Natsu served their tables, annoyed by the boisterous laughter of Toru's young comrades. Yoko's son had trained them for combat, and the next day their outfit was being shipped for duty in China. All but Toru, who sat brooding over his fate.

"I have a hunch you might see action there," Toru addressed his comrades gruffly. "Good training cadre are needed at home, my commanding officer told me when I asked to sail with you. Ah, but I'm fed up wet-nursing rookies at target practice against imaginary Chinese! If there's any fighting to be done, I want to be in on it from the start. What I'd give to ship out for China in the morning!"

Natsu felt faint. A searing jolt of pain sent the tray in her hands crashing to the floor. Douglas was also leaving Japan the next morning, she thought. More than three weeks had passed since her tumor was discovered, and the pain's intensity was weakening her resolve to keep her illness from him.

Toru quickly stood up and put his arms around her. "Natsu, are you sick?" he asked.

"It's nothing serious," she told him. "Only a benign cyst pressing on a nerve. I'm entering the hospital tomorrow to have it removed." Only the other day she had spoken the same lie to Paul. "You mustn't neglect your friends, Toru."

"You mean more to me than these ugly faces." Toru hugged her, then lowered his voice to a whisper. "I haven't seen much of Paul. How's he faring in his newspaper job?"

"Oh, Toru, he's a different person. I expect him home from work any minute now."

"Good! I'm eager to celebrate his good fortune."

Natsu smiled up at her son's only real friend. Paul had accepted her lie, but if she suffered a painful attack in Douglas's presence, he would never be so easily deceived. Following her lover's return from Kyushu, they had spent a number of evenings in each other's arms at the apartment, where she kept an unmarked vial of pills to dull her pain. That night would be their last together. A night to remember. If the tumor was cancerous, she would begin a series of treatments that she hoped would add months to her life. Precious days to share with Douglas when he returned home one year from now. Natsu comforted herself with that thought as she bent to pick up the tray of broken dishes.

Yoko rushed to her side. "Natsu, leave this to me! Go upstairs and rest," she insisted, placing her coarse red hands on her hips and refusing to hear any argument.

It was already growing dark as Natsu climbed the stairs. Yoko's second-floor apartment was roomier than hers on the floor above. Lacking the strength to climb another flight, Natsu entered its cozy sitting room to rest on the sofa there. She put one arm across her eyes and drifted off to sleep, mindless of the time until Paul's and Toru's voices sounded on the stairs. Natsu looked at the dainty silver watch Douglas had given her. In a few short hours she would be in his arms.

"Mother?" Paul called as he walked up the stairs.

"I'm here in Yoko's apartment," Natsu called back. "I was resting between shifts and fell asleep," she told Paul as he entered the sitting room with Yoko's son.

"Toru wants to take us to dinner."

Toru pounded his friend on the back. "Yes, we must toast this journalist's success."

"I can't this evening," Natsu begged off. "You two have a wonderful time."

Paul grew sullen. "I know where you'll be, Mother." Only her pained expression kept his anger at bay. "Nothing's changed because of this job. I didn't ask for Douglas's help in getting it, and he has no right to expect anything of me."

Natsu wearily shook her head. It seemed that Hideo Tamura's willingness to support the lie she had told her son might come to nothing. "Paul, your father realizes he can't buy your love," she said softly. "He did what any father would do for his son."

"Douglas's actions come too late for me to be grateful," Paul responded coldly. "Go to the apartment he keeps for you. Do as you please, Mother, but leave me out of it!"

Natsu made no effort to hold Paul there. Her son stormed down the stairs, followed by Toru. She felt a stab of excruciating pain, and the room began spinning. Dr. Amano could end her pain, she thought, struggling against her dizziness; she must go to him.

Somehow Natsu managed to exit the tea shop. The pain assaulted her in wave after wave, and it was torture for her to walk the distance to Dr. Amano's nearby office.

Stumbling inside, she gasped, "I must see Dr. Amano." The room spun, fading to black as Natsu passed out.

"I warned you against overtaxing yourself at work, Yoseido-*san*."

Natsu heard Dr. Amano's comforting voice, then felt a needle jab. She became aware that she was lying on an examining table.

"The morphine acts swiftly," he said. "But it is not a cure. As you've just discovered, one's body and mind can tolerate only so much pain."

Natsu felt the morphine beginning to take effect. Mercifully her pain relented. The drug induced a weightless feeling. "How long will the effects last?"

"Eight hours—perhaps more."

"What time is it now?"

"Time you entered the hospital for surgery," Dr. Amano answered sternly. "I should never have agreed to delay it."

"After Douglas sails. After tonight I'll do everything you say," Natsu promised him, willing herself to sit upright. "He might still be with me when the morphine wears off. The pills you gave me no longer have any effect. Can you write me a prescription for something stronger to relieve the pain?"

"There is no relief other than surgery." A gentle-mannered man of sixty, Dr. Amano was sympathetic as he reached out to hold Natsu there. "Enter the hospital now. The man you love has a right to know the truth. Lies cheated you out of sharing your joy when you gave birth to his son. Now you are denying yourself his comfort. And for what?"

"For love," Natsu answered in a hazy tone of voice. "Your friendship is a blessing. Thank you for respecting my wishes." She smiled, numb to the touch of his hands. "I must be going."

Natsu rode in a taxi to the apartment she and Douglas shared. Reclining against the seat, she turned her face to the open window. There was no relief from the wilting heat. Natsu fluttered her fan, trying to stir a faint breeze. The disease and the heat were weakening her. The next day Douglas would be enroute to Europe, and she would face surgery without his comforting presence. Already she could feel the miles stretching out between them.

"The apartment house on your left," Natsu told the taxi driver. "This was the first time Natsu had ever arrived at the apartment in her tea maid's kimono, and she experienced some embarrassment while unlocking the street door with her key. Outwardly the building was a rather dingy, sidestreet apartment hotel. But the suites were clean and modern, suited to the tastes of businessmen who lived alone and kept to themselves. The staff catered to the needs of Japanese and European bachelors. There was no likelihood of Douglas encountering anyone of his social circle at this nondescript building.

Natsu crossed the lobby to the elevator. "Madame." The elevator operator bowed. He had worked there for years and was startled to see this fine lady clad in a serving uniform. However, he said nothing as the car rose to her floor.

Natsu was shocked by her drawn, sickly face reflected in the oval mirrors on the elevator walls. Nothing in her apartment wardrobe could distract Douglas from her pallor, she thought. Before he arrived she must create a deceptive candlelight aura, she decided, as she hurried from the elevator car's merciless, glaring light.

Paul sat beside Toru at one of the many bars on the Ginza. Around them men talked excitedly of the Civil War in Spain. Hitler and Mussolini had acknowledged General Franco as Spain's new leader by pledging the support of their Axis powers. The bloody conflict had erupted only weeks before, and the wire services flooded Japan's press with accounts of the fighting, which divided brother against brother. Paul's thoughts were of his half brother who would be traveling abroad in style. *Nippon Shimbun*'s business section had carried news of Hosokawa-Napier, Limited's, bid for a place in the burgeoning military market. In the event of a broader war, thought Paul, the company would profit handsomely.

"To your talent with words, which will someday make you a man of importance!" Toru exclaimed, tapping whiskey glasses with his friend. "Fate has granted you a powerful ally in this editor Tamura."

"My talent speaks for itself, Toru." A little drunk, Paul set down his glass and said angrily, "Eventually someone like Tamura-*san* would have recognized my talent without being pressured by Douglas Napier's influential friends." Paul had no reason to question his mother's lie. "Well, it's the least he could have done," he continued. "When I think of his hands on my mother, it makes me want to tear down the door of his fancy house and expose the man for what he is!"

Toru shook his head in disapproval. "What good is vengeance?" he argued. "Accept this opportunity and concentrate all that energy on securing your future."

Paul thought about that while Toru paid for their drinks and they walked out into the street. "Maybe you're right about my father. But I wish that bastard would stay in Germany for good," Paul told the strutting army corporal who raked his cap, distracted by girls in the passing crowd. "*Nippon Shimbun*'s editor seems genuinely interested in my career, Toru," he continued. "But since the day I reported for work, his staff has made it clear they're out to get me. More than once their baiting put me on the verge of a fight. Oh, they'd like nothing better than to brand me a half-caste troublemaker."

"Keep your wits about you. Use those brains to write circles around them, and they'll be forced to show you respect," Toru assured him with a laugh. His attention shifted to another very attractive girl walking their way. She returned his smile, and he quickly moved in to engage her in conversation. They spoke for a minute. Then the girl looked Paul over and shook her head.

Toru returned to say, "A pity she has no friend so we could make it a foursome. Oh, well, there are other fish in the sea. Come along with us, and we'll catch one for you."

Paul's expression was glum. "One look at me and girls shy away. I'd only spoil your evening, Toru."

"Have you never been with a woman?"

"No."

Toru noted the pain in his friend's admission and then regarded the girl, who waited under a streetlamp for him. "Not so pretty after a second look," he lied. "At your age, never to have experienced the pleasures of a woman is a crime. We'll initiate you into manhood at some brothel. My treat."

"Not with prostitutes, Toru. I want love to play a role in that experience." Paul managed a smile. "It's bad manners to keep the girl waiting. Go on."

"Wish me luck," Toru winked. Cocksure of himself, he put an arm around the girl's waist and gestured at the dance hall across the street.

The celebration had all too quickly fizzled out. Paul's loneliness was especially painful as he walked on, passing other young couples bound for the Ginza's flashy nightspots. His step was a bit unsteady from the whiskeys he had drunk. His gaze met the narrowed eyes of a policeman coming his way, swinging a nightstick. Seeing the policeman reminded Paul of the beating he had been given by *Mainichi*'s security guards, and he clenched his fists while the policeman faced him off as if anticipating trouble. Abruptly, Paul lowered his head and stalked away, pushing through the pedestrian traffic, attempting to burn off all the bitter encounters he had suffered because of his father's seed.

Paul boarded an electric tram whose street tracks wound partway up into the Tokyo hills. He had not told Natsu of his frequent visits to the Napier mansion over the years. She had given him a bicycle for his tenth birthday, and he had first pedaled up these hills then to spy on the Napier family from just across the street, waiting for a glimpse of his father's

American wife and their blond-haired son. Over the years he had seen Max coming and going countless times.

Paul had nearly cracked under the strain of watching his half brother grow from a child in short pants to a boy in expensive trousers. Once he had almost charged across the street, wanting to shout Max's name and end the anger and frustration of existing in the shadows.

Paul had not been drawn to the Napier mansion since entering college. His determination to excel at the university consumed even his animosity toward his father. But that night it was the image of his mother in Douglas's arms that brought him to a tram stop in the city hills. His pace up the quiet hillside streets quickened. He was obsessed with the need to draw open the curtain Natsu had kept so tightly closed against those who resided in the luxurious Victorian mansion he now faced. Yet he halted short of the forbidden front door, which now seemed a more imposing barrier than the forbidden street door of the Ginza tea shop.

The whiskey he had drunk with Toru had given courage to his anger, but the effect was wearing off. The Napiers were entertaining friends, and liveried chauffeurs stood talking near limousines parked along the circular front drive. Tokyo's wealthy dwelled like gods in this Olympus above the teeming city. During the day their servants came and went on bicycle or on foot. The sidewalks were deserted now, and there were no walls built around the Napier mansion or dogs to keep out trespassers. Paul did something he had never done before: He squeezed through the row of neatly trimmed hedges that circled the grounds.

On the other side of the hedges was a spacious English garden. Paul walked toward the sounds of voices and laughter that drifted out across the flagstone path leading to a broad veranda whose balustrade and lattices were richly draped with ivy and climbing roses. The veranda doors stood open to the night air, and stone steps wound down from it to the shade trees, where Paul halted.

There were no servants nearby to bar him from disrupting the festivities and exposing everyone inside to the truth. But suddenly Paul realized the consequences of his actions. Satisfying his thirst for vengeance would betray his mother, and she might never forgive him.

He decided he could not risk being discovered. Two figures were stepping onto the veranda and he barely had time to hide among the trees.

Thorny rosebushes circling behind him pricked through his trouser legs and held him there. Unable to withdraw, but safely masked by the darkness, he stood watching his half brother stroll along the veranda with a beautiful Japanese girl.

It was as if Paul were seated in the front row of a darkened theater watching two actors onstage. Maxwell Napier spoke in a warm masculine voice surprisingly like his own. The years had altered this young man he once spied on as a boy. The resemblance between brothers now struck a raw nerve in Paul. He wrestled with the fires of his hatred as the regal

Japanese beauty hung on Max's every word. Clinging to his arm, she gazed up at him, her large eyes filled with love.

At the university, Paul had been exposed to other attractive young women of high breeding. But none, he thought, were the equal of this exquisite girl. Her elegant evening dress made it hard to judge her age. Sixteen? Yes, not more than sixteen, but he was certain that she had already claimed the hearts of many men. Even before Max spoke her name, Paul knew she was Baron Hosokawa's daughter.

Paul feared his labored breathing might give him away. There was his brother, the blond and suntanned gentleman, taking the samurai noblewoman into his arms to dance as a waltz was played on the piano inside. From what he observed, it seemed that Maxwell Napier's wealth raised him above the racial barrier. Paul had never been more painfully aware of his lowly station and the curse of his mixed blood.

Max held Shizue Hosokawa close as they danced, whirling her round and round. Just as the music stopped, Paul was torn by an overwhelming fit of jealous rage. He took hold of a tree trunk with both hands to control himself, and the branches shook.

"What was that?" Shizue broke away from Max and leaned out over the veranda railing. "Something moved in the trees."

"Only the breeze," said Max.

"No, I feel as if someone's there watching us."

Paul dared not move. He heard the flap of wings. Then a nightingale fluttered up from the branches overhead.

"There's your prowler." Max laughed and pointed at the long-tailed bird gracefully sailing across the treetops. A male nightingale was calling to his mate from the neighboring garden, serenading her with the distinctive notes of his love song.

Shizue cocked her head to one side, listening. "How free they are to come and go as they please. If only we had wings."

Max brought her close. Over the past few days in Tokyo, Max had lived each moment with Shizue to the fullest, quietly storing up memories of their hours together to sustain him over the long drought to come. Another year would pass before he'd hold Shizue again. There was so much he wanted to put into words, but he could only ask her for a kiss.

Shizue, too, had taken each moment together as a cherished gift. But tonight Max's kiss meant good-bye, and she clung to him possessively. "Oh, I want time to stand still."

"And I'd set the world spinning faster if I could," said Max. "That would shorten our year apart." He smiled as Shizue's fingertips traced his face. "We'll go on loving each other through our letters. We'll exchange snapshots, and I'll carry you with me here, in my wallet next to my heart."

"Oh, promise me you won't change too much." Shizue pressed her face against his chest, listening to his heartbeat. "You're too handsome as it is, and I love you just as you are now."

Angela Napier stepped outside, diamonds and emeralds glittering at her neck and wrists. "Maxwell, it's rude to keep Shizue out here all to yourself. Inge is going to play for us again. She's such an accomplished pianist." She sighed. "Your father telephoned to say he'd be working at the office through most of the night. He's had no time to himself, and we must be understanding of him. In his absence I expect you to act as the host to our guests," Angela told her son.

Playing the voyeur violated Paul's soul. Watching from the shadows, he felt less than a man. As Maxwell Napier guided Shizue through the veranda doors, Paul realized he could easily lose his heart to her. Once everyone was inside, Paul turned, pulling his trousers free of the thorns. As he fled from the garden and along the deserted sidewalks, he regretted that he had returned to the Napier mansion and wished he could erase the memory of what he had witnessed.

But Shizue's beautiful face flashed before his eyes like the afterimage of a brilliant light. Paul told himself his desire for Baron Hosokawa's daughter was only jealousy over her love for Max. Yes, he would seize that love from Max Napier if he could. But he did not belong to their glittering world of jewels and white dinner jackets; he had been born to the lower depths of Tokyo.

A sudden thought caused Paul to stop and glance back at the mansion. As a Japanese, Natsu had been barred from entering its front door as Douglas Napier's wife. Max and Shizue were also bound by their dynasty's covenant. He realized he had witnessed two naive children playing with matches. Turning downhill toward the tram stop, he felt momentary satisfaction over the pain his half brother would surely suffer for daring to love a Japanese. But Shizue would suffer as well. As a noblewoman, she could never hope to have Max even in the kind of backstreet romance that Natsu had settled for all these years.

Paul had nearly choked when Angela Napier spoke of her husband's business keeping him from home. Somewhere in Tokyo's oppressive bosom, Paul thought, his mother shared a love nest with Douglas Napier. Paul did not know the address, but its existence was no less real for that.

Paul boarded a tram car, then sat, pressing the palms of his hands into his bleary eyes, trying not to think of how it was between lovers when they met. He would not sleep that night. Even as a boy he had never been able to sleep alone above the tea shop when Natsu's bed was empty on nights such as this.

Douglas Napier was mentally and physically exhausted from the chores of last-minute business demands. When he entered the two-room apartment he shared with Natsu, he was pleased to find it softly lit with candles. She had an unerring gift for knowing his mood even before he walked through the door. "Natsu?"

"I'm in the bath, darling!" she answered from the bedroom.

Wearily, Douglas reached for the telephone and then remembered he had already made his excuses to Angela. He had spent the better part of a lifetime telephoning excuses to his wife from this apartment, he thought.

In a reminiscent mood, he viewed the familiar surroundings and tried to assess the years he had spent there stealing what happiness he could. No memento or photograph had found its way here to speak for two people in love. Oh, Natsu had added some personal touches: print curtains on the windows, candlesticks and pretty table settings, and satin pillowcases and sheets for the bed. But suddenly Douglas was struck by the hotel apartment's look of anonymity. No furnishings had been purchased by its occupants. Just the spartan necessities rearranged by the hotel maids on their rounds. The rooms were like a hideout. Time spent there had always been too brief for them to notice more than each other. To Douglas, Natsu's presence made the drab quarters sparkle like a jeweled temple. How he dreaded being separated from her, denied the love he had always found in her waiting arms.

He had said nothing to Natsu about his son and Shizue falling in love. He decided that might only sadden her. She had enough on her hands dealing with her own son. Douglas took a manila envelope from his jacket pocket and placed it on the telephone table before entering the bedroom. He was surprised to find the bathroom door locked. Usually he would join Natsu in the tub. "Sweetheart, is something wrong?"

"No! Tonight is special," she answered him cheerfully, watching the doorknob turn. "I want to make myself beautiful before coming to you. Give me another few minutes, darling. I've laid out your dressing gown. Do you like the candles?"

Standing on the other side of the locked door, Douglas laughed. "It's like being in church. Pretty, though." He yawned. "Soft on the eyes."

Natsu pulled the bathtub plug. The morphine injected by Dr. Amano kept her floating weightlessly above the earth and beyond all pain. She sat up as the bathwater drained from around her firm, youthful figure, draining away like life itself, she thought, and shivered. She heard Douglas moving in the bedroom as she stepped out of the tub. Numbed though she was, her image in the mirror spoke for the illness that consumed her body. She prayed her pallor would escape notice in the dim candlelight.

Carefully she applied makeup to enhance the illusion of good health. She was barely able to feel the touch of her own hands or the soft bristles of the rouge brush she used to add color to her cheeks. Natsu's senses were so muted that when she dabbed herself with Douglas's favorite perfume, it smelled to her like ether.

Finally, she had done all she could. She put on a silk dressing gown and prayed for courage. Then she switched off the glaring bathroom light and opened the door. Douglas stood naked before her. "Can you stay the night?" she asked.

"Yes, sweetheart. I've set the alarm for six."

As Natsu stepped into the bedroom, Douglas came toward her. *Solid, built to outlast me*, she thought.

"Natsu." He spoke her name like a benediction, undressing her where she stood, his lips caressing her unblemished skin. "If not for you . . ."

"Hush, my darling," she said, the silk curtaining down around her ankles. Douglas lifted her in his arms and carried her to the bed, where he lay her down across the satin sheets.

"Never leave me," he whispered in her ear.

"Never, darling," she promised.

She was unable to experience the feeling of rapture when Douglas entered her. It was as if her body were dead, and Natsu was forced to rely on memories of other times when his mouth, his strong yet gentle hands, had made her come alive.

Later that night she lay cradled in Douglas's arms, feeling him drift into sleep while she listened to the bedroom clock ticking away what little time was left them.

The morphine's effect dwindled like the flickering candles, and she was left awake in the dark, feeling faint twinges of pain. Her lover would not be there the next day, anguishing through the hours of her surgery. The surgeon's knife might leave gruesome scars. She had not thought of that until now. For one last night her body was unblemished and pressed against Douglas. Would he sleep with her again this way? Would he still make love, caressing her scarred body with his mouth and tongue, or would her disfigurement repel him when he returned?

Natsu remembered spending cold winter nights with Douglas's arms wrapped around her, his body keeping her warm. Sometimes during the lonely summers, she would come to the apartment to feel near him. Lying across the satin sheets, she would count the days until his return. How cold the satin was to her skin now, as if the coming winter without Douglas were already upon her. Her skin tingled as her senses slowly awakened from their morphine sleep. Now she could smell the perfume scenting her body and mingling with the comforting scent of her lover's smooth, warm skin. The return of her senses would soon make her vulnerable to the pain. But for the moment she felt blessed by the delirious sensations of being held and protected. She and Douglas seemed to be one heart beating, and his deep, even breathing gently rocked Natsu to sleep.

Without any memory of having slept, she woke to a stab of pain. She glanced at the bedside clock. It was fifteen minutes to six.

Natsu thought of the virulent attack of pain that had sent her to Dr. Amano. If the pain struck again with such force, she would surely cry out. But to wake Douglas now and send him away without any excuse was unthinkable. The alarm bell would ring at six, and she silenced her fears, drawing on her faith for strength.

Natsu bit down on her lower lip as a jolting spasm made her flesh seem on fire. While Douglas had made love to her, she was insensate to his touch. Now her senses were in flames. His arm rubbed across the stiffening nipples of her breasts. He made a sound, turning away on his side.

Quietly she slipped from the bed. Daybreak touched the window near the bathroom medicine cabinet where she kept the unmarked vial of the drug prescribed when her tumor had first been diagnosed. It lacked the potency to be of much help to her now, but it was all she had. She ran tap water into a glass. Pain constricted her throat, and she gagged but managed to swallow several pills.

"Oh, dear God, hold back my pain and grant me strength," she prayed, gripping the bathroom sink for support while asking only for enough time in which to bid her lover good-bye.

By the grace of God, the terrible assault ended. But she knew the pain was only temporarily submerged, likely to strike again at any moment. Natsu returned to the bedroom. Douglas slept through the ringing alarm, and she gently prodded him. "Darling, wake up."

He groaned, rubbed his eyes, and sat up. "Oh, no. Is it six already?" he asked, leaning back against the pillows.

"Yes, I'm afraid so." Natsu bravely snuggled up beside him while her mind was in a turmoil.

"You're such a tiny thing. I could almost tuck you in my pocket and carry you away." Douglas chuckled at the thought.

"I couldn't leave our son," Natsu said. Suddenly she thought of her impending operation. People often died in surgery. What if she did not survive? Suddenly all her fears became focused on Paul. "Paul has no one else to love but me." Just then Natsu felt another stabbing pain. She gasped for breath, hiding her face against Douglas's chest. "Everything we suffered was for Paul," she said, hoping her voice did not betray her. "If anything should happen to me, he'd be utterly lost in the world." Mercifully the pain abated, but she felt chilled as she waited for it to strike again. "I fear for Paul's future. Even if he achieves success, people may still treat him differently. You must promise me not to abandon him." She had not told Douglas of the lie that had led Paul to believe his father was responsible for his newspaper job. How could she justify Tamura's generosity without raising unanswerable questions? she thought. "A year is such a long time and your promise will give me peace of mind," she said, managing to smile. "Humor a mother's fears. No matter how many times Paul may turn away from you, promise me you'll never stop reaching out to him. Oh, dear God, I pity our son if he never finds it in his heart to accept you as his father."

"Yes, I promise." Douglas cupped her face between his hands and kissed her mouth. "Time is such a cheat. I want to stay here and cover you with kisses." Natsu ran her fingers through his hair. "It seems we're forever saying good-byes." He cradled her tightly against him. "If anything happened to you, I'd have no reason to live. I love both my sons, but it's us that makes everything worthwhile."

"I know," she said, fighting back tears.

While Douglas hurried to dress, Natsu remained in bed, sensing the imminent approach of devastating pain. "Never forget me," she said in a small, frightened voice.

He smiled. "You'll never be far from my thoughts." Douglas buckled the strap of his wristwatch, mindful of the time. "Don't see me out the door. Get some rest. Yoko can manage without you for once."

"Yes, I *am* tired."

"There's an envelope on the telephone table. Open it after I've left. Of course, I'll write you every day."

"I shall live for your letters."

Douglas bent over the bed and caressed Natsu's hair. She prayed that he would not see the ravages of pain in her face. Taking his hand, she kissed it, then held it to her cheek.

"I love you, my darling," Douglas said, gently withdrawing his hand from her grasp and putting both arms around her. He drew her to him, and they kissed lingeringly.

Natsu clung to Douglas, not wanting to let him go. "God bless," she said.

He gave Natsu one last kiss, then stood up and smiled. "God bless." There were tears in Douglas's eyes as he turned away and left the room.

As Douglas Napier walked out of her life, Natsu bravely fought the pain. She stuffed a fist in her mouth, fighting not to scream until she heard the hall door close. Then she groped her way to the bathroom, unable any longer to muffle the screams that would have held Douglas there. She opened the vial. Her hands trembled, spilling the contents across the bathroom floor. Going down on her knees, she picked up one pill after another and swallowed them, only to cough them up in a puddle of vomit.

She felt alone and abandoned. There was no hand to reach for, no kind voice to comfort her as she struggled to her feet, bathed in a cold sweat.

She managed to walk to the living room, where she telephoned Yoko. "Douglas is gone. I must get to the hospital. Please—come here and help me."

"Your voice sounds so weak. Put a cool compress on your forehead and rest," Yoko told her friend. "I will get a taxi and be with you in ten minutes."

"Yoko—how would I ever manage without you?"

Natsu cradled the receiver and saw the manila envelope Douglas had left on the telephone table. She recalled him leaving another envelope at the Ginza tea shop an eternity ago. That yellowing letter kept as a keepsake had come apart in her hands. These inked lines of Japanese characters were still fresh, and the business stationery they were written on was rich to the touch.

"Don't be angry with me, darling," she read. "I'll rest easier knowing that you have this money in the event some emergency arises during my absence. All my love and devotion, Douglas."

His Berlin mailing address and ten crisp one-thousand-dollar bills fluttered to the table from Natsu's ice cold hands. That day the pain of death would be cut out, she thought. If by the grace of God she did not die under the knife and the cancer was not too far advanced, then her treatments would be expensive. What irony in her lover's parting gift.

Natsu drew open the curtains on Tokyo's morning skies. How many other sunrises were left her? she wondered. She grasped the small gold cross she wore on a chain around her neck and asked God to be merciful. She wanted to live; she wanted to feel Douglas's gentle touch again; she wanted to experience the serenity of old age with her lover's hand in hers in the twilight of their years.

"Dear God," Natsu prayed, "I want to live."

BOOK TWO
THE LEGACY
SUMMER

1937

Like the pearl of dew
On the grass in my garden
In the evening shadows,
I shall be no more.

LADY KASA (THE NARA PERIOD)

CHAPTER 9

Shizue woke to the songs of birds in the garden outside her bedroom window and stretched out catlike beneath the satin sheets. She felt warm with expectancy as she languished over a vivid dream in which Max had already returned from Germany to take her into his arms. He was on his way home. One year had swept past since their good-byes, and she envisioned Max traveling aboard the Trans-Siberian train, speeding closer to Japan with each beat of her heart. Just one more day of waiting and he would pass from the realm of her dreams into reality.

Shizue sighed and sat up in bed. Staring at her reflection in the mirror across the room, she put the backs of her hands under the soft hem of her shoulder-length hair and lifted it to the high cheekbones of her oval face. There was no longer the slightest trace of baby fat. Tilting her head to one side, she wondered how Max would see her now. The excitement generated by his homecoming caused a tingling sensation down to her toes.

"Enough daydreaming, child." Yufugawo entered to part the bedroom curtains. "It is past ten, and the lord's son will soon be arriving home."

Shizue sat there pouting. Once again she was Lord Mitsudara's houseguest in Tokyo. His son, Jiro, had just graduated from the military academy, and today was his homecoming. Soon a party would be given in his honor, and she would be obligated to attend as his date.

"Jiro is such a handsome young man," Yufugawo chatted on, fussing about the room. "Anyone with eyes can see how pleased the baron is that you and Jiro get along so well. I think your father has romance in mind for you."

"Oh, don't be silly. Jiro is charming and pleasant company. Nothing more than a friend." Shizue fell back against the pillows. Indeed, she could not help liking the young army cadet. But now she felt certain her father must have been approached on the matter of a marriage agreement between them. He had obviously hoped to nurture their relationship by arranging for her to spend each school holiday in this dreadful house, where Jiro was always conveniently home on leave. She was grateful that she was not yet of age for any binding agreement to be made between their fathers. "I'm aware what Papa's been up to by throwing us together time and again," she told Yufugawo. "But there's not the remotest chance of sparking a romance with Jiro. This party in his honor won't be given for days. I suspect Father brought me here early to welcome Max home, just so he can observe if we still love each other. Well, he'll soon discover that what we feel isn't just childish infatuation."

"Love indeed!" Yufugawo pursed her mouth. "You are old enough now to lock these girlish thoughts of Douglas Napier's son away inside your diary for good, and give some mind to your obligations."

"Yes, I'm old enough to know this is love!" Rising from the bed, Shizue took the robe Yufugawo handed her, then stifled the woman's lecture with an obstinate look. "I've no quarrel with my other obligations, Yufugawo," Shizue said as she put on the robe. "But love is a matter of the heart, and tradition has no place in it," she announced, then brightly spun away with outstretched arms. "Oh, I can't believe Max will be here tomorrow! Not another word about Jiro. I'll need a new summer outfit. Something sophisticated."

"You have more than enough dresses to choose from, child."

"I've outgrown these old things," Shizue complained while rummaging through her wardrobe. "Oh, I'm sure those European girls dress in the latest fashion. They must have spoiled Max terribly," she worried. Max hardly had written anything about his social life in Berlin, dismissing it all as "uninteresting" and filling his letters with brooding descriptions of an alien land he could not wait to leave.

Shizue pulled one dress after another out of her wardrobe. None of them pleased her, and she let them fall to the floor. Finally she chose a dress, then took silk stockings and French lingerie from the dresser drawers. "We're going on a shopping spree, Yufugawo. I want to look special for Max."

"Very well, you shall have your way with me again." Yufugawo stroked Shizue's lustrous hair and recalled how she had wept on the day her precious girl had insisted that she cut the braids that bound her to childhood. "Less fortunate girls would be overjoyed to own your cast-off clothing." Yufugawo groaned, stooping to pick up the garments Shizue had dropped on the floor.

Shizue dressed quickly, then sat at the vanity brushing her hair. The bedroom was furnished in French provincial antiques. Nothing in Lord Mitsudara's rambling manor house was new. To Shizue, roaming its rooms was like touring a museum. The upstairs rooms were given over to the western world, except for one wing that paid homage to the lord's personal preference for things Japanese. There, and in the labyrinth of corridors connecting the ground floor rooms below, priceless Asian artifacts were displayed and the servants moved about in *tabi* socks speaking in hushed tones as if afraid to stir the cobwebs with their voices.

"I'm ready to leave." Shizue checked her appearance in the vanity mirror, then stood and picked up her purse. "Hurry, Yufugawo."

"But you must have something to eat."

"There's no time for breakfast. If I'm here when Jiro arrives, he'll keep me talking for hours."

Shizue opened the bedroom door to a corridor that was lined with antique clocks. Servants were at work inserting keys in the clocks' ornamental faces to wind their mainsprings. Lord Mitsudara prided himself on being punctual, and clocks throughout the mansion chimed the quarter hour, the half hour, the hour. Shizue had a fearful vision of the lord as an enormous human clock churning out money in time with the phalanx of swinging pendulums.

Synchronized to within a split-second, the household clocks bonged and chimed the hour of eleven. Shizue held her ears as she raced down the stairs, fearing that someday she might be imprisoned there as Jiro's wife. "Oh, do hurry," she told Yufugawo.

"Such energy!" Yufugawo toddled behind her, out of breath. "Take pity on your elders, child."

A servant informed them that Lord Mitsudara and the baron had taken the limousine. "The other family cars are also in use. I will get you a taxi," he said. Rushing ahead of them through the house gates, he blew on his tin whistle to stop a cab.

Settling down in the seat beside Shizue, Yufugawo prepared for an arduous day of standing. "Your father must be at the Napier house, arranging things for their return," she said. "The baron keeps so much stored up inside him. Having Douglas and his wife away for so long in Germany distressed your father. Ah, his life is lonely. For his sake, I hope the Napiers will remain here at home, where they belong."

Shizue nodded, distracted by the thought that Max and her brother would sail to America when the summer ended. Perhaps the time had come to assert herself. She could never openly defy her father, but perhaps he would respond to a heartfelt appeal.

As she gazed out the window at Tokyo Bay, the sight of ocean liners sailing to far-off ports emphasized the unfairness of her situation. How cruel it would be to have her reunion with Max end in tearful good-byes with no real future in sight to sustain them both.

Loving him was an awesome challenge. Now Shizue was sixteen summers old, and she quietly weighed a child's subservience to her father against a young woman's need for independence.

Suddenly she noticed dense black smoke across the bay. "Is there a fire in the city?" Shizue asked the taxi driver.

"The wind blows from Yokohama to the west," the man said. "What you see comes from there."

"What would be burning with such an awful smoke?" Yufugawo wondered aloud.

*   *   *

Across the headlands twenty miles to the west of Tokyo Bay, smoke filled the morning sky over Yokohama Bay, and the captain of a rescue launch spurred on his crew as several dinghies came alongside.

"Get these men aboard!" the captain shouted. "And be quick about it!"

Paul had jumped aboard this boat, ignoring its captain's warnings of danger. It was one of a number of rescue launches that had been sent out to the burning decks of an American oil tanker. The tanker sat adrift not a mile from the Yokohama docks, and Paul worked with the launch crew, pulling trembling sailors from the sea and wrapping them in blankets. Some of them had been burned, while other survivors were gasping for breath, having nearly suffocated in the spiraling funnels of smoke.

A ring of fire boats pumped fountains of seawater onto the tanker's blazing decks. Tongues of orange flame shot out through the dense black shroud that now obscured both the tanker and any other survivors who might still be bobbing somewhere near its rusted hull. The fire could not be contained; it raged out of control. The tanker's explosive cargo could be set off at any moment and the fire boats gave up the fight, retreating with their engines at full throttle while Paul's launch was left heaving in their wake.

"Abandon the search!" the launch captain hollered above their screaming sirens. A line was thrown to a dinghy returning with survivors. As its crew rowed alongside the launch, her captain shouted, "Get aboard with those men and push that dinghy free—so I can make speed before the tanker goes up!"

Those who manned the dinghy were quick to obey. After getting on board with the survivors, the men in the dinghy threw off its lines, and the launch began its run for shore in a rain of ash. The deck was crowded with men huddled together staring at the distant funeral pyre that claimed their dead.

Paul spoke English and had questioned some of these men, who had been pulled from the jaws of death. Suddenly their blackened faces grew tense as the flames appeared to have been smothered out. There was no trace of fire in the billowing smoke. For an instant the smoke seemed to freeze. And then the illusion was shattered with a deafening thunderclap.

Paul held his ears and crouched low for cover as shockwave followed explosive shockwave. When he dared look again, debris and liquid flame were rocketing into the sky. The bay was churned into a stormy sea of whitecaps, rocking the launch hard.

A great wound in the sea was opening to swallow the tanker, while her spilled cargo floated across the surface as a molten sea of flames. Aboard the launch, some men crossed themselves; others buried their heads in their hands and wept. Paul felt compassion for them, but he also felt exhilarated. He had come near enough to feel the raging inferno's heat, he had choked on the screams of dying men too badly burned to take hold of their rescuers' lines, and now he faced the less courageous members of the press who had remained safely anchored to the Yokohama dockside.

Feeling baptized by what he had experienced, Paul was the first man off when the launch docked. He shouldered his way toward the faint-hearted staff photographer assigned to cover the story with him. "Did you snap any good pictures from here?"

The photographer winced at Paul's tone and said, "Mixed blood has touched you with madness."

Paul laughed. The photographer's barb was meant in jest; there was no hint of bigotry behind it. He urged the man into their press car. "Time enough to make the afternoon edition if I write while you drive."

As the two drove off, they passed a snarl of other reporters racing to get to their own cars. Competition among the Tokyo newspapers was stiff. Paul balanced his writing pad across both knees, determined to get his story to press ahead of them all. He penned a dizzying torrent of words while the car sped for *Nippon Shimbun*'s offices. Since the day its doors had opened to him, the editor-in-chief had guided his progress like a doting father. Paul's mercurial rise to full-fledged reporter outraged the racist staff, but their animosity no longer bothered him.

Without a moment to spare, Paul finished the last line of his story, blotting the ink with his shirt cuff as the braking car jerked him back in the seat. He was out in an instant. Grabbing the photographer by one arm, Paul dashed inside the office building and pulled his companion to the elevator. "Rush through prints of your best shots, and the beers are on me," he said on their way up to the city room.

"I don't drink, but thanks all the same. Crazy *ainoko*," said the photographer, laughing good-naturedly.

Though *Ainoko* was slang for someone half-blooded, the man had not spoken it in a derogatory way, and Paul wished there were more like him on *Nippon Shimbun*'s hostile staff. Shuffling the pages of his story into a neat pile, he grimly set his jaw and ignored the ugly stares that followed his march down the long aisle of desks. He knew that his power over these leering reporters lay in his talent and grinned at them before he knocked at Tamura's office door.

Hideo Tamura looked up from his desk as Paul entered. "You seem pleased with yourself," he observed. "Well, let's see what you have."

"I think it's first-rate."

"Rest your ego in that chair." Swiveling his desk chair, Tamura read what was handed to him. He rolled a sharpened pencil between his fingers but seldom put it to use.

Paul felt a deep affection for his mentor. Over this past year his mother had befriended Tamura out of gratitude and made him feel like one of the family. He was a frequent dinner guest in their apartment above the

Ginza tea shop and often escorted Natsu to concerts and the cinema. Paul had observed Tamura's lovestruck looks and the way his mother's coyness kept the man safely dangling at arm's length.

Paul never questioned his mother's feelings about the homely man. "Tamura-*san* is such a fine gentleman," Natsu would say after bidding him good night at their apartment door. Paul would return her pleased smile, believing this platonic relationship had brought some happiness into Tamura's life.

Now Tamura grinned up at Paul with approval. "A fine piece of reporting," he said. "But talent isn't everything. The audaciousness you displayed in going after this story distinguishes you from that pack of chair warmers."

Swiveling in his chair to face the office's glass partition, he gestured at his sedentary newsroom staff. "Shiny pants! The badge of mediocrity. Well, Akira, your story will show them up for what they are. American oil is absolutely vital to the Japanese economy, and yet they transport it to us in some unseaworthy tanker badly in need of an overhaul." He bent over the story. "These survivors you questioned bear testimony to the equipment failures that cost so many lives. I'm giving this front page coverage, with your byline."

"I don't know what to say." Paul could have embraced the man, but settled for warmly shaking his hand.

"You've more than earned the recognition," said Tamura. "Pictures?"

"Being rushed through now."

Hideo Tamura lifted his telephone receiver. "Don't just stand there, Akira. Get this to press or we'll miss the next edition."

To be given a byline was the fulfillment of Paul's dreams. By afternoon, all of Tokyo would know his name.

A copy boy rushed Paul's story to the linotype machines. Before very long his words would be set in type for the presses. Paul hurried excitedly down the hall to the art department, where two dramatic photographs of the exploding American tanker were already being processed into metal plates.

"Great shots!" Paul told the friendly photographer who had taken them not an hour ago.

"I've never worked so fast," he said, and looked at his watch. "We go to press in fifteen minutes."

The presses were being prepared to roll as Paul entered the hectic atmosphere of *Nippon Shimbun*'s gigantic pressroom. Its work crew scrambled about him in ink-stained aprons. The foreman wore a hat made of folded newspaper. Paul's arrogant look dared the man to question his right to be there when his story rolled from the presses.

Paul breathed deeply, enjoying the smell of ink. It seemed to take forever until the machinery finally came to life with a deafening roar. The speeding rolls of paper were a blur. To his ears, the pounding of the presses sounded like a chorus of a thousand voices singing his Japanese name as it was being printed on paper after paper. His pulse quickening, he bent down over the folded stacks of the afternoon edition and snatched up one copy. The ink was still wet on its front page as Paul folded the newspaper back to frame his byline. Akira Yoseido. There it was! His laughter was drowned in the roar, and he was jostled by men pushing handcarts. "This is my story!" he shouted, unheard.

The newspapers were bound, then stacked on the men's handcarts, which Paul followed to the loading dock outside. He walked down the line of delivery trucks parked there. "Whose route takes him to the Ginza?" Paul inquired.

"Mine does," one driver said.

Paul climbed in beside him. "Akira Yoseido."

The driver inclined his head at the folded front page that Paul held up to him. "So?" he sniffed, flicking his cigarette butt out the window. "Do I look like a taxi for hire?"

A worker called from in back. "Finished loading."

"I'm in a hurry," said Paul, ignoring the driver's frosty glare and resting his elbow on the window frame. Perhaps his accomplishment would return the glow to Natsu's thinning face. She had not looked well for some time. Dr. Amano assured him it was only a minor ailment. He trusted the doctor, whose reassurances had also calmed his fears when Natsu was operated on the previous summer. And yet his mother's strength and radiance seemed to wane with the passing months.

Paul got off the delivery truck at a newsstall near the tea shop and stood there watching its weaselish proprietor use his penknife to snip the twined bundle of newspapers. His eager customers helped themselves, depositing coins in a metal cup.

"Nothing of China," one disappointed reader loudly complained to his male companions. "Our soldiers killed at the Marco Polo Bridge weeks ago and not one shot fired back at those chinks to avenge them. What of Japanese honor while our generals there settle for a truce? We should declare war and run the Chinese through with bayonets."

Another man cut in on him. "Look here," he said, thumping Paul's front-page story to gain his friend's attention. "Fire aboard an American oil tanker. Unseaworthy, it says here," he said, snarling. "Those arrogant Americans send us little enough oil as it is, driving up the price of everything we buy."

Paul experienced a thrill as the man talked about his story. He started up the street, then suddenly halted. Baron Hosokawa's daughter was standing just outside the tea shop door. Paul watched Shizue stubbornly shaking her head at the plump gray-haired woman who was carrying several shopping bags. Weary, the woman tried prodding Shizue inside the shop, but the girl turned away, and her chaperone was forced to walk on.

Paul watched Shizue come toward him. She was even lovelier and more radiant than he remembered. In the year since he had first seen

Shizue while hiding in the darkness of his father's garden, her face had returned to haunt him time and again. Now she passed close enough for him to smell her perfume. He knew it was foolish and juvenile of him to be so stricken with emotion by this fleeting glimpse of the baron's daughter, but she was an extraordinarily beautiful girl. Fate had caused their paths to cross once again, and he felt compelled to follow her.

The two women stopped to window-shop near the busy entranceway of a department store. Pretending interest in the window display, Paul stole sidelong glances at Shizue, searching for flaws in her delicately chiseled profile. But everything about her was perfect. When she and her chaperone entered the store, Paul followed as if spellbound.

He stationed himself directly across from the circular glass counters where Shizue paused to examine the purse compacts on display. She was certain to notice him, he thought. She had only to lift her head to see him staring at her. No doubt this young noblewoman would stare back with cold indifference. Girls always did whenever he mustered courage enough to approach them.

Shizue picked up a tortoiseshell compact from the counter. She opened it and held its mirror to her face while smoothing one eyebrow with her fingertip. Masked from her vision, Paul relived that night when he had spied on her and his half brother. Someone's paper shopping bags scratched against his pant legs, and it was like the thorny rosebushes cutting off his escape while he watched two lovers dancing on a vine-covered veranda.

"May I be of assistance?" a sharp female voice inquired.

Paul blinked and looked down at the frowning store clerk. "Just browsing," he answered her shortly. He fingered the folded newspaper under his arm, wondering if his name in print would ever change the way people saw him.

Just then, Shizue's chaperone caught him staring. Suddenly he felt exposed. Turning, he began to push his way through the crowds.

"That young man seems to know you," said Yufugawo.

Shizue lowered the compact. "Where is he?"

"He was standing there a moment ago." Then she shrugged. "Men. They are all alike when it comes to a pretty face. Take hold of my arm and keep your eyes to yourself. You are at an age to turn men's heads. In my time they would never approach a lady without first being properly introduced. These days they take liberties. Especially city men and foreigners."

"Tell me about the young man who was staring," Shizue asked with curiosity.

"What is there to tell?" Yufugawo trudged past endless racks of summer dresses and wearily rolled her eyes. "He was *ainoko*. Handsome enough but too sure of himself."

Shizue admonished the woman. "Honestly, Yufugawo, it's wrong to snub your nose at those of mixed blood. People fall in love. Some are ugly and will have ugly children; some are of different races. What difference does it make so long as they're happy together and pass that love on to their children?"

"Life can be cruel to those who are different," Yufugawo said, plopping down in a chair to rest her sore feet. "I hope something here pleases you."

Not bothering to check the price tags, Shizue picked out several dresses. Across the way, she noticed a pregnant girl shopping for maternity dresses with her mother. Shizue judged the girl to be only about a year older than she. Parents determined when a daughter was mature enough for marriage, and seventeen was not considered too young by many Japanese. The young mother-to-be simply glowed, and she stood there, dreamy-eyed and unaware of being watched as she caressed her abdomen, as if feeling the baby stir. The husband selected by her parents must have pleased her, thought Shizue, envious of the girl's happiness. Shizue faced the store mirror and placed a dress against her slender figure, wondering if she would ever carry Max's child—a child of mixed blood.

Paul angrily bucked the Ginza crowd. His brief encounter with Shizue had rekindled old hatreds. Life had been tolerable while the Napiers remained abroad. Their imminent return to Japan would bring back his restless nights of pacing an empty apartment while Natsu slept in his father's arms. His privileged half brother would be fawned over by Shizue Hosokawa, while he himself would be haunted by the memory of her beautiful face.

Abruptly Paul halted in front of the tea shop. A concession to racism had always prevented him from entering the shop by its front door. That day he had proved himself as a journalist; he had earned the right to correct an old wrong by announcing himself as Natsu's son.

Paul rolled up the newspaper tightly. The Cherry Blossom Kissaten loomed up before him as the last bastion of racism he must storm. Doing so would help purge him of the bitterness of the past, he decided, taking a deep breath.

Heads craned at the Eurasian, whose entrance set the bell above the shop door jangling violently. Paul quickly looked past the small gathering of customers, searching for his mother. But she was not waiting tables. "Where's Natsu?"

Yoko stared at Paul, speechless with shock.

"Where's my mother?" he loudly demanded.

His question brought a hush over the room, and then the customers hunched across their tables buzzing to each other as though war with China had just been announced.

Yoko found her voice. "Natsu is resting—in the office," she told Paul.

A chair screeched back from one table. An elderly man rose to his feet. As the oldest there, he appointed himself their spokesman and motioned for silence with his walking cane. "I will handle this," he said in a rasping voice and slowly faced the intruder. "You say you are Madame Yoseido's son?"

"Yes!" Paul unrolled the newspaper and held its front page within inches of the man's challenging eyes. "Here is my name. Akira Yoseido. There's the proof if you can read."

"A common enough name," the elderly man said, slapping the newspaper away with the flat of his hand. "Liar! We simply won't allow you to speak such an outrageous lie. *Ainoko* upstart!" He pounded the floor with his cane. "Our Natsu is a lady of quality. Away with you, no decent woman's son!"

"My mother is a lady, yes!" shouted Paul, shaking his fist. "She's a lady forced to lower herself by serving ignorant bigots like you!"

"Half-blooded trash!" The elderly spokesman snarled, brandishing his cane. "Crawl back into the gutter where you belong, or those younger than I will give you a thrashing."

"You're all nothing but windbags, good for nothing but sitting on your behinds!" Paul wrenched the cane from the man's grip and sailed it to the far end of the shop. It clattered against the wall, barely missing Natsu, who stood, frail and tearful, just outside the office door.

"Paul, stop this violence," she pleaded softly. His shouts had wakened her from a nap, and she found it an effort to focus on what had taken place. Everyone waited for her to speak again, and Natsu forced a smile. "This is my son."

Mustering all her strength, she held her head high as she crossed the room to stand united beside her son. "I can understand your rage," she told Paul, hugging his arm. Natsu's heavily rouged cheeks served to heighten her pallor. Her son glanced down at her, and his anger was replaced by a look of concern. "Paul, I should never have used deceit, knowing what harm it has done you."

She turned to meet the stares of customers who had gathered around her. "And now all of you know my secret and my pride," she addressed the once friendly faces. "Yes, Paul is my shining source of pride. I should have made my son known to you long ago, and that is my only shame."

"Proud to call this *ainoko* your son?" The elderly spokesman was handed his cane by another man who had retrieved it, and now he aimed the rubber tip at Natsu like an accusing finger. "Your deceit has made fools of us. So, the truth is out, and we know you for what you are, Madame Yoseido. Word of this will spread quickly. Of that you can be sure."

"And what makes you her judge?" Hands on hips, Yoko glowered at them all. "Natsu is still a lady and is owed your proper respect. She has served you well and deserves better than your sharp, gossiping tongues as thanks. Which of you has not had his day brightened by her presence here? How dare you speak dishonorably of her? Natsu has more honor in the tip of her little finger than the lot of you put together. Leave my shop!"

She snatched up a broom and threatened them with it. "Into the street, and don't return unless it is with your apologies. Ingrates!" she cried, chasing the customers out her door. When the last man had run out, she turned to Natsu and Paul. "They are old men set in their ways. I, too, must bear the shame for being a party to this deceit. So," she sighed, leaning the broom to one side of the door. "Now it is undone." Yoko rubbed her hands together. "A thing of the past."

"All the ugliness can't be forgotten that easily," said Paul. "Shouting the truth wasn't satisfaction enough for all those years of sneaking home through the back door." He scuffed at the worn floorboards with his shoe. As a boy he had swept and polished those worn wooden slats after closing time. He had cleaned the kitchen and washed mountains of dishes. Those menial chores earned him a few yen, which he spent on books. Paul doubted that Douglas Napier's American son had ever had to earn a thing by the sweat of his brow. "The secrecy and deception we've lived with doesn't end here, Mother. Somehow my father's got to pay for what he's taken from us."

Natsu pressed his hand. "Please, for your own sake, surrender these feelings into God's hands and let His will be done. If your father is guilty of anything, God will punish him."

His mother's sermonizing only fed his determination to take things into his own hands. "I no longer believe in gods," he said. Then he softened when he saw Natsu's hurt expression. "Look, Mother." Paul bent for the newspaper he had dropped on the floor during his vengeful assault. "I rushed here to show you this. My first byline. Tragedy at sea. I was there in the thick of it. Tamura-*san* was very impressed."

"Is it true?" Natsu's eyes shone with joy. She gave Paul a long and tearful hug, then sat at a table and spread out the front page with trembling hands. She would have preferred to see his Christian name printed above the story. She tried to read, but her eyes lacked focus and the words ran together fuzzily. "I'm feeling a little dizzy," she said. "The excitement."

"I will get your medicine." Yoko rushed for the back office.

"Mother, you shouldn't be working so hard. Soon I'll be earning enough to support us both. I'll buy you a fine home and pretty clothes. All the things you've missed while sacrificing your life to that bastard, Douglas Napier."

It grieved Natsu to see her son consumed by hatred. Here was his name in print, tangible proof of the fame awaiting him, and even this miracle had done nothing to soften his heart. She smiled benignly, hiding the resurgence of physical pain that Dr. Amano had prepared her for. As she feared, the tumor removed from her abdomen the previous summer had been malignant. For some time after surgery she had not suffered any pain, but the cancer had continued its insidious spread, entering her lymph glands and now wreaking damage on her liver. She was in the final stage of the disease. Dr. Amano had done his best, and yet the cancer had spread quickly over the past few months. Now she visited the hospital frequently. The radium treatments had been intensified. With each one Natsu died a little.

"Paul, give me your hand," she said. "I'm so proud of you. But everything I'll ever need or want is here in this cozy shop. I live through you. Soon the world will lie open to you and you could be lost—swallowed up—unless you learn how to call upon others. Needing love isn't a weakness. Turning away from it, is. Your father—"

"He's the last person on earth I'd ever turn to!"

Paul's refusal to let go of the past threatened to destroy what Natsu longed for most. Her eyelids grew heavy. The ache she felt could only be dulled by the medication Yoko had gone to fetch. Nights were especially hard to endure. Just one night more until Douglas walked back into her life and she must hold on!

Extremely vulnerable to her emotions, Natsu fought back tears. "Oh, my baby, no one is self-sufficient. We can feed on our own resources just so long before we dry up."

Paul nervously ran his fingers through his dark brown hair. Just then Yoko came to the table carrying a tray laden with vials of pills. Paul observed the sadness in Yoko's eyes. Turning to his mother, he asked, "What made you cry out in your sleep last night?"

"A bad dream," Natsu answered unhesitatingly. Paul's questioning face made her taut. "So much fuss over a slight dizzy spell."

Yoko's unsteady hands caused the glass vials on her bamboo tray to tinkle noisily. "Dr. Amano warned you against too much excitement."

"Oh, he's such an old tyrant. Why these long faces?" Natsu took a deep breath and somehow managed to smile, although she was racked by another spasm of pain. "At the least sign of illness you both treat me like an invalid. Well, I won't have this happy occasion spoiled. Now, not another word from either of you."

"Take your medicine." Yoko handed her the water glass.

"So many pills." Natsu sighed, finding it difficult to swallow the various drugs while Paul watched her. "My celebrated journalist," she said, attempting to change the subject. "You've made me so very happy."

Paul ignored her comment. "Mother, I trust Dr. Amano's care, but maybe we should see a specialist for a second opinion," he said, shifting his gaze to Yoko, who avoided his eyes.

"This heat and the excitement," Yoko said, then managed to smile. "Dr. Amano would have your mother see a specialist if he felt it was necessary."

Paul would not be put off. "All the same, I'm going to talk with him again."

"If it will help put your mind to rest." Natsu stood up, but again she felt faint. "Invite Tamura-san to dinner. I'll prepare something special to show him my gratitude. Go and buy flowers for the table—and sake," she told Paul, taking his arm and coaxing him to the door.

"Are you feeling well enough to entertain?"

"Of course. This is cause for celebration. I'll take a nap before dinner," Natsu promised. Part of his father resided behind Paul's hazel eyes flecked with blue, she thought, linking her with Douglas across time and space. "Have Tamura-*san* come at seven."

"All right." His earliest memories of his mother were of clinging to her cotton kimono and inhaling its scents of tea and cakes. Embracing her now, Paul saw himself as that small boy with whom the other children refused to play, crying while anchored to her skirt.

The bell on the tea shop's door announced new customers. Businessmen dressed in wrinkled summer suits hesitated before entering the vacant shop. Obviously they had never visited there before, and Yoko stepped forward to greet them warmly.

"Business as usual," said Paul, kissing his mother on the forehead. Then: "You're feverish."

"It's only the medication." Mercifully, her pain had abated. Her secret was safe with Dr. Amano. God's will would determine when the truth would be revealed to her son, and she sighed deeply as Paul left. It seemed her son's ambitions would be realized. At least she had lived to bear witness to that much. But death stalked her ever more closely.

Other customers, some of them regulars, began to trickle into the shop. Natsu breathed easier now and went to wait on them. The shop grew busier, and Natsu carried her tray, serving the customers. She felt comforted by the hum of male voices. Her customers lit cigars and cigarettes as they relaxed from the trials of the day. This was her home, Natsu thought. The shop was like her sitting room, and she looked upon those she served as relatives come to call. In the apartment above, she had given birth to Paul, nursing him between shifts. Even through the worst of times, she thought, these old walls had provided a sanctuary from the hostile world just outside its windows. When death came for her, she wanted it to be here, not in the sterile atmosphere of some hospital room.

Doing what she had always done, Natsu mindlessly performed the familiar tasks that helped to span another long day of waiting. She seemed forever to be waiting for Douglas. Just one more night until he returned to her. The surgeon's knife had been kind, leaving only hairline scars. If she took care with the lighting, Douglas was unlikely to notice them when they made love. She smiled, strengthened by the thought of being in her lover's arms once again.

Gradually she wearied of serving her customers. Her hands made mistakes. It was a trial of sheer will to make them behave gracefully. But if death was watching her, she thought, let him know that she intended to fight his touch. Let him know that she intended to live to the fullest whatever time was left her after Douglas's return.

*   *   *

"*Arigato.*" Max thanked the shipboard waiter who refilled his wineglass, then held the man at his table to comment on the smooth sailing, merely for the enjoyment of speaking Japanese. A large contingent of Germans had boarded the Japanese steamer with him and his parents at Vladivostock. German businessmen, newspaper correspondents, and members of the Nazi diplomatic corps peopled the first-class dining room, where an ensemble of Japanese musicians entertained them with Viennese waltzes. After two weeks confined aboard the Trans-Siberian train, Max found it a welcome relief to be at sea. In his mind's eye, Max saw Japan as a glistening jewel hours within his reach. It was an overnight voyage to Tsuruga on the Sea of Japan. By morning, he would be home.

Seated at the captain's table, Max observed his mother's forced politeness toward the German couple who had made a nuisance of themselves throughout the journey, with their boring chitchat and endless rubbers of bridge. Christian von Hausten was a career diplomat, a card-carrying Nazi, and an oily-tongued Hitlerite. His heavyset wife spoke over him in an irritably high falsetto while her attractive seventeen-year-old daughter flirted with Max, despite his aloofness. There had been little room for escaping her while aboard the train. Even on the ship, Liesl von Hausten had managed to be seated beside him. As she toyed with her food, her foot made contact with his under the table. Max shifted his leg, and she responded with a giggle and a toothy grin.

"*Ach,* I am glad to see the last of Siberia," Christian von Hausten was telling Douglas Napier. "If not for the element of time, I would have much preferred the long voyage to Japan by sea. However, the journey by rail impresses one with the vastness of Mother Russia and gives us a lesson in why no one has ever conquered her." Von Hausten paused, using the napkin tucked under his chin to wipe his mouth before sipping his wine. "The Japanese proved themselves a nation to be reckoned with when the Imperial Navy defeated the mighty Russian armada at sea in 1905. But Japan wisely struck a bargain for peace. One would think that Stalin and his red tide of communism would bring the führer and Japan into an ever closer alliance against our common threat, Herr Napier. But privately, this necessity to—"

He quickly broke off, then switched over into German when the English-speaking Japanese captain turned toward their conversation. "To be quite candid," he said to Douglas Napier in German, "the Japanese are a funny race." Von Hausten smiled diplomatically at the captain, who showed no understanding of what he had said, then continued in his native tongue. "While they smile and bow politely, one can never be sure of what they are thinking. I would not put it past them to strike some bargain with Stalin behind Germany's back. But for now, we must smile and return their bows."

Max tuned out von Hausten's abrasive voice, which sounded very much to his ears like that of Adolf Hitler. During the year Max had spent in Germany, the Führer's voice had seemed a constant presence, broadcast

continually over radios and heard on loudspeakers echoing through the
streets. To Max's ears the harsh, guttural tongue of the German people
matched the sharp-edged Teutonic landscape. Several times he had
witnessed German Jews being singled out in the streets by Nazi thugs who
bullied them, hanging anti-Semitic slogans around their necks and forcing
them to sweep the pavement with brooms while spectators gathered to
laugh at the insult.

Max had come to detest the Nazi intellect. Beneath the surface glitter
of Berlin lay the squalor of poverty never mentioned in the almighty
Führer's rambling speeches, which preyed upon the gullibility of the
German masses, insisting they were a superior race. Curiosity had led
Max into the midst of mass rallies where Germans were whipped into a
fevered pitch bordering on insanity, lifting their arms together with
successive cries of "*Sieg heil.*" Many Germans did not support the Nazis,
but fear tactics silenced their protests.

At night a desperate gaiety prevailed along Berlin's Kurfurstendamm,
and some of that now carried itself over to the shipboard gathering of
Germans bound for Japan. Max winced, seeing them all as bawdy boors,
drunk on Hitler's concoction of the Master Race. On one occasion Max
had attended the Berlin opera for a performance of *The Valkyrie.* Hitler
was in attendance, and Max had watched the führer lean both elbows on
the crimson felt railing of his private box, a demonic sparkle in his eyes.
To Max he had been the devil incarnate, rapaciously peering down on the
heads of those he had consigned to hell.

Tonight Max could hear the roar of Hitler's legions in the Germans
seated around him, all talking louder than was necessary and erupting in
laughter when there was no joke. The overweight Frau von Hausten
nearly choked on her food while laughing at a German couple who were
tangoing across the dance floor with long-stemmed roses clenched in their
teeth.

Douglas Napier could not afford to make an enemy of this Nazi
diplomat, but he had difficulty being civil to the von Haustens. He was
thankful when a Japanese steward made his way through the dining room
loudly calling his name.

"*Kore!*" Douglas signaled the steward and was handed a wireless
printed on a folded sheet of yellow paper. Angela Napier's eyes questioned
the delay as he slowly unfolded the message just enough to read: 15 July
37—Berlin, Germany.

"Is it news from Heinz?" Angela inquired.

"From Berlin, yes," said Douglas. Well over a month before, the
German Army had tested his new parachutes. Hitler's generals were
impressed but remained maddeningly noncommittal. Douglas had caved
in from exhaustion and the loneliness of a year separated from Natsu.
Rather than wait it out in Berlin while the army made up its mind, he had
rushed for home by the fastest route. Success or failure? he wondered,
slowly peeling open Heinz Karlstadt's answer.

Von Hausten was aware of Douglas's business dealings and considered him a Nazi sympathizer. "Good news, Herr Napier?"

"The Wehrmacht has awarded us a contract." Douglas laid the wireless facedown. "Quite a handsome one," he added woodenly. He had won the gamble, and yet he felt little sense of accomplishment for all his months of labor.

Von Hausten pounded the table. "Steward, a bottle of your finest champagne! This calls for a toast. *Ja.* Herr Napier, I insist."

"Congratulations, darling!"

Douglas recoiled from Angela's kiss, and she drew back in her chair, wounded. His sudden urgency to leave Germany before learning if his efforts had brought success puzzled her. Now their fortunes were secure, but his distant manner told her that something other than business ruled his thoughts. During their months in Germany, the same glazed look had often shut her out. With each passing week, her husband had grown more withdrawn. In their twenty years of marriage, Angela Napier had never understood the reasons for his drastically shifting moods. Fire and ice, she thought. Tonight Douglas was showing his icy side. When the champagne was served, she raised her glass to him in a toast, smiling for the sake of appearances. *"Prosit."*

"Max, why do you sit there brooding?" Frau von Hausten nudged him playfully and laughed. "Dance with the young man, Liesl. Show some spirit."

"Ja, dance and be gay." Singing with the waltz music, Christian von Hausten came around the table and circled the youngsters' shoulders. "Come, we are only young once."

Virtually pulled from his chair by Liesl, Max felt trapped. On the dance floor he held her at a distance, the schooled gentleman doing what was expected of him. But she slithered up against him, her perfumed hair teasing his cheek. Despite an occasional flirtation with attractive European girls, his thoughts were only of Shizue. Even so, he was not oblivious to Liesl's softness, which aroused him. But it was a craving only Shizue could satisfy. For one year he had lived on nothing but Shizue's letters and snapshots of her lovely face that he carried in his wallet next to his heart.

When the dance ended, Max politely excused himself and went out on deck. The night air was cool, and a fine mist wet the railing he gripped.

Raucous laughter escaped through the opening dining room doors. Max turned and saw that his mother was unsteady from too much alcohol. His father supported her. Max could not hear the words they exchanged, but all at once his mother threw her arms around his father's neck and kissed him passionately. Max watched his father take her wrists and pry her loose. Douglas grew rigid as Angela raised her voice. His parents had always argued in private, and it shocked Max to observe the hostility between them now. When Angela saw him standing at the rail she went limp, and put both hands to her face like a kitten licking its paws. Max had never before seen her so vulnerable. Refusing her husband's touch, she weaved off toward their stateroom alone.

Douglas approached his son hesitantly. Privately, he had hoped that his son would become seriously involved with some European girl, whose love would have saved the boy the heartbreak Douglas had endured. But now both men yearned to be with the Japanese women they loved. "Feel like walking, Max?"

"Sure." Max paced alongside him. It seemed ages since they had talked father to son, and at eighteen he felt the right to assert himself. "What's wrong between you and mother?"

"Let's just say relations between us are strained," Douglas said, dismissing the subject.

"I've often wondered why you stopped with me. Didn't you want other children?"

"Hell, what kind of a question is that?"

"A perfectly natural one."

"Your mother had a difficult time in childbirth. It scared her from having more children." Douglas bristled, then suddenly caught himself acting the righteous father. His son was obviously reaching out to establish a more mature rapport between them, and he wanted that as well. "Some women just aren't cut out for motherhood," he confided uneasily. "Did you feel cheated growing up without brothers and sisters?"

"In a way, yes. I guess so," Max said honestly. "It's lonely at times."

Douglas slung one arm around his son's shoulders. "Look, I know how much you've disliked Germany. You enter Harvard in the fall. Kimitake will keep you company. And you'll make new friends. America should be a welcome change."

"To hell with Harvard. I mean it, Dad," he said emphatically, halting at the vacant rows of teakwood deck chairs. The steamer rolled in the crosscurrents that marked the halfway point of his voyage home, and Max gazed down at the foaming swells that washed against the ship's hull. "Now that Germany's behind me, I won't be separated from Shizue again."

"You've still got a lot to learn. Harvard is—"

"Another convenient way to put distance between me and the girl I love," Max finished for his father. "Let me explain what I'm feeling, Dad, or I'll explode."

"All right." Douglas took a swipe at a deck chair beaded with moisture, but his wet fingertips discouraged him from sitting down. "Let's have it."

"You want me to be the dutiful son and heir to Hosokawa-Napier, Limited. But you can't expect me to inherit your life if it means giving Shizue up. Dad, I'm not naive enough to believe her father will break with tradition without a fight."

Max locked the fingers of both hands together, pulling his knuckles as he sought to express his emotions. "Everyone is silent on the subject of intermarriage, while our families hug and kiss and count their profits as if it didn't exist. Why not face it, Dad? You may be his equal partner on paper, but Baron Hosokawa has the upper hand. Japan is his turf, and we're privileged Americans so long as we contribute to the business and don't make waves. That's what supports us in the elegant manner I'm guilty of taking for granted. Well, I've decided to take charge of my own life. Maybe you don't see things my way, but Shizue's love for her father is all mixed up with her feelings of obedience to the obligations she owes to her bloodline. She doesn't want anyone hurt, but it can't be avoided. By standing on my own ground, the baron will be forced to deal with me man to man. I know it wouldn't make a dent if you pleaded my case with him; it's something I've got to do for myself. Dammit! He's in control of his daughter's life. But we're in love, and that gives me every right to challenge his blindness."

Max was touched by the sadness in his father's eyes. "Dad, I've seen how unhappy you are. I don't know if it's because of Mother, or because of doing business with a tyrant like Hitler. Maybe you've been too busy to notice it, but I've grown up and I won't be pushed into honoring a bunch of senseless obligations just because it's expected of me."

"Yes, too busy," Douglas responded quietly. He thought back to their talk in the castle gardens one year earlier, when Max had accepted the restrictions of his youth. His son had since grown up and was now a man in love, a man whose impatience challenged Douglas's powers of persuasion. More fatherly advice would not solve the problem, and to confess that he also loved a Japanese woman, that there was a son—a half brother born of that love—would do more harm than good.

Douglas struggled with the truth as he watched the ship's foaming wake close the distance to Natsu's waiting arms. Finally, he broke the tense silence. "Your impatience is understandable, Max," he began rather haltingly. "Believe me, I understand exactly what it is you're going through."

Angrily shaking his head, Max just stared at his father.

"Don't make snap judgments without having all the facts." Douglas knew he was on dangerous ground and nervously cleared his throat. "There are things about my life you don't know. I made mistakes at your age that led to many disappointments and regrets." He paused, wondering if he had waited too long ever to change his life or atone for the injuries he had caused others. "But it's your future we're talking about, and you're not prepared to take on the world by a long shot. I'm your father. It's my responsibility to point out what I've learned from experience. Max, there are some obligations that can't be sidetracked." His tone pleaded for understanding. "Life isn't simply a matter of doing as we please. You've got to play by the rules. Society sets certain standards for us to live by, and they aren't easily broken."

"Meaning, hands off Shizue. Preserve the dynasty at all costs."

"No! Your happiness means more to me than the business." Douglas took Max by the shoulders. "I won't lecture you on the consequences of marrying out of your race. Hell, to keep any marriage going demands a lot of work. Listen, I'm in your corner. You can believe that much."

"I don't know what to believe," Max said. The sincerity in his father's voice was convincing enough, but Max could not see the expression in his father's eyes because the sea mist shrouded his face. "Every time we've talked, I've come away feeling as though you wanted to sweep the racial issue under the rug, Dad."

"You can't possibly think I'm a racist. God almighty, Max, haven't I always taught you that the Japanese are our brothers? When you turned to me with your feelings for Shizue, I didn't think it was necessary to voice my position against holding with this tradition. My hands are tied as well. Anything I might have said to the contrary would have been just so much talk. Would it have solved the problems facing you and Shizue if I lied about that? Well?"

"No," Max agreed, subdued as he waited for his father to continue.

"You've got a fight on your hands, that's for sure," said Douglas. "I can't argue against your right to love Shizue, but she's still a child and you're not much older, Max. Oh, I know you see yourself as a grown man ready to take charge. I was there once myself, don't forget. I lived through the same growing pains. Harvard, your experiences in America, will help mold you into a man. There's power in having a Harvard diploma. Your mother thinks you'd make a fine doctor. Study medicine if you like, but get that education under your belt. Listen, time is on your side. Shizue will be waiting when you've graduated. Talk things over with her. Make your plans for the future and stick to them. Remember that Shizue loves you, so you've won half the battle already. I don't want to break your spirit, Max. I'm just advising you to bend a little with the realities of life. You can count on me to back you up all the way."

Just then a loud group of Germans invaded the misty deck, marching past like soldiers. Douglas faced out to sea, reflecting on what he had told his son. "I had no choice about inheriting my father's life," he said at last. "I'd never push you into fulfilling that family obligation, son. Our stay in Germany has altered my view of things. There's a grimness closing in around us. It's not the same world that I was brought up in. I can't blame Tadashi for insulating himself from a changing world with the traditions of his ancestors. But he's only human, and perhaps time will open a chink in his armor. Set your goal on earning that diploma."

"Quite a speech," Max said.

"Think over what I said. Give it time." The ship's bell chimed. Douglas patted his son's shoulder. "I'd better see to your mother. She's in a state over nothing."

As Douglas walked away, Max hit the rail with his fist in frustration and cursed aloud. "Damn!" Maybe he did expect too much too soon, but facing up to the realities brought him a feeling of despair. Hands in his pockets, Max roamed the misty deck, trying to make some sense of it all.

* * *

Douglas passed a steward exiting his stateroom. As he entered the room, he saw a frosty martini pitcher on the vanity where Angela sat before the mirror.

"You disapprove," she addressed Douglas's frowning reflection while peering over the rim of her chilled glass.

"Drunkenness doesn't become you."

"Is that so? Well, drunk or sober, other men still find me attractive. Or hadn't you noticed how Christian von Hausten's beady little eyes devoured me? Imagine what it must be like, saddled to that frizzy-haired balloon of a wife." With a throaty laugh, she swiveled around on the bench. She was wearing an emerald green peignoir with a deep slit, which revealed her long, shapely legs. "Well, I've kept my figure. Wasted effort." Sipping her martini, she kicked off her satin pumps and then rested both elbows back on the vanity top, holding the glass in one hand as she watched Douglas undress for bed. It was true that some men grew more handsome with the years, she thought, and they damn well knew it. "Vanity, all is vanity," she observed. "What would it take to seduce you, hmmm, my vain peacock?"

"Playing the vamp doesn't become you either. Must you drink so much?"

"Oh, honestly, Douglas. You can be such a prude," Angela said indignantly. "Dry martinis are a sedative, darling. God knows how I need one." She turned away and poured another from the pitcher. Her auburn hair fell in ringlets across her forehead as she faced Douglas again. "For months now you've been so silent. So detached and ohhh so unavailable. Can't be reached." Her finger traced the rim of the glass. "I wonder if you hear a word I say. I wonder if you see me at all."

Douglas took a pair of silk pajamas from the drawer of his steamer trunk and began to put them on. "You know damn well what pressures I've been under."

"Distracted, yes. I've tried my best to be understanding of you. Never once complaining about the long hours given to your work in Berlin. Business first. And yet no trace of a smile now that the contract is yours. Why? Still no answer. Better not to speak at all, Douglas. Easier for you to pretend I don't exist." Angela shivered. "How grim you are tonight. Usually your spirits soar when we're returning to Japan. I can't account for your dismal mood. We've usually had such good times when we've been abroad, and there were even times when sex between us burned with something of the old fire. Now that seems to have fizzled out in you. Well, I'm still too young to settle for a yawning companionship."

"Must you harp at me?"

She dropped her voice to a husky growl. "These little tantrums don't become you, darling." Her sarcasm was wasted on him. Taking another sip of her martini, she said, "Do you remember how it was when we first met? We couldn't get enough of each other. After we married, everything was so perfect for us while we shared that charming apartment in Boston until your graduation. The months in Europe were perfect, too. Then your father cabled us, and everything began to go wrong. Almost from the day you brought me to Japan to live in that dreadful house. Oh, I detested Julius's hold on you and poor Irene. Somehow your mother always managed to smooth things over. Her kindness helped me to adjust. 'My son isn't like his father,' Irene told me. 'You and Douglas will build a happy life together here,' she reassured me. But you grew less attentive. I was pregnant with Max, and that did get in the way. But after he was born, nothing much changed for the better. Suddenly what we had together began to fall apart. It was as if something in Japan or . . ."

Angela quickly censored the thought. She had almost said "someone." But she had never caught Douglas with lipstick on his collar or wearing the tell-tale traces of another woman's perfume. Actually, she knew there was no woman among the western community enticing enough to turn his head. And taking a Japanese lover was simply out of the question; Baron Hosokawa would never tolerate it. Yes, her husband was faithful to their marriage vows. This offered little comfort, though, when he rejected her overtures in bed.

"I'm forever the dutiful wife, looking after your comforts while being ignored." The empty martini glass slipped from Angela's hand, rolling on the carpet at her feet as Douglas became a blur. "No one to blame but myself. I allow you to use me whenever it suits you. Have you ever asked yourself why?"

"You're my wife," Douglas said angrily.

"Oh, yes," she answered, putting one hand to her forehead. "Chattel, that's me. Conveniently taken to bed when it pleases the lord and master. Just as conveniently set aside afterward." Angela swayed on her bare feet, running both hands down the length of her peignoir. "Silk. How I love its feel next to my skin. How I abhor the breeding worms that bind us to Japan." She spun around, and in a burst of rage swung her arm wildly. Cosmetic bottles and the martini pitcher crashed to the floor. Holding on to the top of the vanity, she stared into the mirror. The first signs of age had written tiny lines in her creamy white skin. She had spared no time or expense to preserve her youthful complexion, and suddenly all her effort seemed wasted. Angry, choked by tears, she abruptly looked away.

"I don't know what keeps me with you, Douglas. You don't need me. I'm all alone and drifting. Marriage should be an anchor in life. Ours just keeps us drifting between two worlds without an anchor in either of them."

Angela's tirades were nothing new to Douglas. Alcohol often made her abrasive and overemotional. "It's the drink talking, Angela," he said, turning down the bedcovers, anxious to call it a night. "Why not get some sleep."

The dryness of his tone seemed to Angela like a slap in the face. "Just like that." She pushed her hair back from her forehead and watched

Douglas yawn. "Oh, it's infuriating the way you shut out anything you don't want to hear! Well, I'm wounded. Your indifference has wounded me time and again. I hurt, Douglas. I've tried being a good wife and mother. Have I failed you in some way? Is that why you treat me so shabbily?"

"Angela. It's all my fault." Douglas went to put his arms around her. "Listen to me. You've been a perfect wife," he said gently, moved by husbandly feelings. "This was a trying year. It's behind us now. Into bed with you." He lifted Angela up in his arms and carried her to the bed. "Tomorrow morning I'll fix you a prairie oyster that'll bring your head back down to size. You never could hold your liquor."

Angela whimpered. "You're right. It's the drink." The stateroom was spinning, and she never wanted Douglas to let her go. Part pride, part fear of rejection had prevented her from going down on her knees to confess her adoration of him. "Oh, damn, the world is upside down," she groaned, as Douglas tucked the bed covers around her. True to form, he smiled as though his ministrations had solved everything.

"Are you going to be sick?"

"Nuno. Sleepy," she slurred with a heavy tongue. "Very sleepy."

Douglas fluffed the pillow under her head, and she moaned. "Can I get you something?" he asked.

"Just turn out the lights."

He did so, then opened the porthole. The Sea of Japan held a distinctive aroma that brought him closer to home. He stretched out beside his sleeping wife and lay there staring into the darkness.

In the silence Douglas mused over what he had told his son about society setting certain standards to live by that were not easily broken. His own father had chosen him an acceptable wife according to those rules, and Angela was not always a thorn in his side. On a mental ledger sheet Douglas listed the assets and liabilities in a life divided between two women.

This past year, on brief holidays spent in Paris, Rome, and Switzerland, the Napiers and their son had shared some happy times with the Karlstadts. There Angela had shone on Douglas's arm, complementing his station, perfectly at ease in social circles that would never accept Natsu as his wife.

On the plus side of their marriage, sex between them could be good, she kept their household running smoothly, was a good mother to their son, a charming and gracious hostess at parties, and was blessed with a wit that was both sharp and amusing. He enjoyed the interesting mix of friends Angela's vivacity attracted. He and Angela were social creatures. As a couple they had nurtured friendships that Douglas valued highly.

Suddenly Douglas was struck by the terrible realization that he and Natsu had never been a couple. They had never been seen together, had never known what it was like to see their love reflected in the eyes of other people.

Restless, he got out of bed and walked to the open porthole, where he stared out at the sea. When Max was still a child, divorcing Angela had been out of the question. She would have been given custody of their son, would have fled Japan with him, and might have poisoned the boy's mind against his father. Now Max had grown up; his life would be changed, but not radically, if Douglas divorced Angela.

Then Douglas thought of Paul, who was also a grown man. Marrying Natsu might not change things between father and son. Perhaps Natsu had been right all along in believing the time for their happiness had long since passed.

With Japan growing ever nearer on the horizon, Douglas Napier felt the pull of his destiny rooted in those islands. He had sailed from them as a young man Max's age, weeping at the ship's rail, heartbroken and guilt-ridden for having abandoned the girl he loved. Tonight he was returning home from another long voyage with Angela as his wife. She was still very beautiful, desirable enough to build a happier future with someone else if she were free of him. His infidelity was grounds for divorce. But could he divorce himself from their years together? Would Natsu listen to reason if he approached her with that in mind? And how could he be fair to everyone concerned—most of all to his wife?

So many considerations now demanded his attention. Hosokawa–Napier's parachutes had been sold to Hitler's army, but Lord Mitsudara's loan could not be repaid for years. Baron Hosokawa's loss of face was at stake if Douglas reneged on his business obligations. His work in Germany had just begun, and Heinz Karlstadt was counting on his abilities to see it through. He had engineered this venture, and it was not in his character to be a quitter. No, he must finish what he had started.

That night Douglas stood poised on the brink of making decisions he had forestalled for many years. He could not continue hurting two women indefinitely. It would take time to sort things out, but somehow he must put his house in order at long last. He felt exhausted, like a long-distance runner who had reached the limit of his endurance, yet was straining to cover the remaining miles.

Moonlight danced and sparkled on the cresting waves of the sea. Very soon he would share these thoughts with Natsu. How he had missed their quiet moments together. Their love transcended everything. A covenant had kept them apart, but only as man and wife. Both had given up so much to the past, they had lost sight of the future. Somehow, he must find a way to end their years of self-denial.

CHAPTER 10

There would never be another day quite like this, and Natsu hummed as she readied the hotel apartment to welcome Douglas home. He had telephoned her early that morning before boarding his plane at Tsuruga, promising to come to her the instant he could free himself. Just to hear his voice once again made her giddy with joy. Kneeling at a low table in the living room, Natsu cut, bent, and twisted the stems of peony, iris, chrysanthemum, and lily. She had been taught the delicate art of ikebana as a girl, and she arranged the fragrant flowers in vases and shallow ceramic dishes to delight her lover when he stepped through the door.

Yoko was there to help. She hung wind bells at the open windows. A slight breeze stirred these chains of dainty tin bells called *furin*, whose metallic tinkle provided a cool sound to take one's mind off the heat. Though perspiration blossomed across Yoko's upper lip as she completed her task, she was cheered by Natsu's radiance. Her friend seemed reborn on this sultry July morning; she looked as fresh and bright as the flowers she was arranging.

Natsu flitted here and there, placing her artful creations around the room. Every twig and leaf portrayed a symbolic message, and each arrangement was judged by her discerning eyes, each given a final loving touch that sought perfection. The main parts of her floral compositions shot upward, representing heaven. Always there was a twig on the right in the shape of a V. This denoted man, and Natsu carefully bent one twig sideways just a fraction more, as it should be. The lowest twigs and branches on the left signified earth and she bent their stems only slightly to point upward. *Tengoku, chikyū, ningen*—Natsu spoke to herself while standing back to judge her creations for these essential ingredients. Any ikebana arrangement not embodying heaven, earth, and man was considered barren and lifeless.

Natsu would not permit death to take a foothold here this day. She had fashioned the floral displays as acts of love, and to her they symbolized the renewal of the life force she had felt glowing within her since she had arisen that morning. She took a final turn around the living room, then broke into a smile. "I want everything to be perfect when Douglas steps through the door. Only a few short hours more, and I must look my best," she told Yoko. "Sooner or later he'll suspect how ill I am. But Douglas mustn't see that in my face when he arrives. Not today, nor for as many other days as the Lord sees fit to grant me."

Gently, Yoko cupped Natsu's exquisite face with her work-roughened hands and spoke what was in her heart. "Love will make Douglas see you as unchanged." She still prayed to the gods of their ancestors for some miracle that would cure her dearest friend and companion, who had shared everything with her over the years. Perhaps Natsu's great love for Douglas would be stronger medicine than the doctors could provide. "For once you will obey me," Yoko said firmly. "Go make yourself pretty for him. Relax in the bath and leave the rest of these chores to me."

"Dearest Yoko, I'd be lost without you."

"And I without you," Yoko murmured to herself, misty-eyed as her friend left the room.

Natsu had visited the apartment often in Douglas's absence, touching the garments he had left hanging in the bedroom closet, lying in the bed where they had made love. So much had passed between them in the privacy of these rooms, she thought, so many cherished moments to be called upon over the lonely months of waiting.

While drawing her bath, Natsu took carved ivory hairpins from her jewel box. They had been a lover's gift on that day long ago when Douglas had promised to be with her always. Reveries held her at the bedroom mirror while she used the ivory pins to arrange her hair as she had worn it for him then. The previous night her sleep had not been broken by pain, and she had awakened feeling none of the usual aching discomfort or the extreme thirst that were side effects of her hospital treatments. Some color had returned to her thinning cheeks. The soft coiffure helped to minimize the ravages of cancer and she prayed that Douglas would see her as unchanged.

Alerted by the gurgling faucet, she rushed to the bathroom. The tub was near overflowing. As she bent to turn off the taps, the steam made her light-headed. When she stood up, a twinge of pain sent her to the medicine cabinet. Her efforts that morning had brought it on, she told herself. She recalled hiding unbearable pain the morning Douglas had walked out of her life. As she reached for the vials of drugs stored on the medicine cabinet shelf, she was stopped by the memory of the morphine, which had dulled her pain while rendering her insensate to Douglas's loving touch on their last night together. She had waited too long for this day to be cheated of his touch again by taking numbing drugs. Closing her eyes, she breathed deeply until the pain faded away. Douglas would question her if he saw so many pills, she realized. After her bath she must hide them.

Natsu brought the crystal perfume decanter down from its shelf. She dabbed a small amount behind her ears. When sleeping in the apartment alone, she had scented herself with Douglas's favorite perfume and dreamed of his warm body pressed against hers. Very soon now they would share an unspoiled time of joy.

Disrobing for the bath, she felt a sudden wave of nausea. The narrow bathroom window was just beyond reach of her hand. "God help me," she gasped, desperately in need of air. The room began to spin. All at once she felt a searing whiplash of pain that drove her back against the sink, and she grasped onto it, her body shaking from the pain's awesome force. She groped for the drugs with one violently trembling hand, sending the vials tumbling to the floor.

"Natsu?"

Yoko was standing in the kitchen preparing the evening meal the lovers would share. Natsu's high spirits were infectious, and she had been singing along with the radio. Then she had heard something. The crash of glass?

"Natsu?" she called again. There was no reply, and Yoko hurried to the bathroom. Shock froze her at its open door. Natsu lay there face-down. Pills were spilled everywhere on the white tile floor around her, and she appeared not to be breathing.

It was the shattering of the crystal perfume decanter Yoko had heard, and she stepped carefully around broken glass. The ivory hairpins had tumbled free of Natsu's hair. There was blood on the floor where she had fallen. Horrified, Yoko parted the hair from Natsu's face and saw blood trickling from her nostrils.

Natsu moaned, then curled one ice cold hand around Yoko's wrist. Thank the gods she was still alive, Yoko thought.

It was Paul's day off from the newspaper. He had slept late and had been jarred awake less than an hour earlier by Yoko's telephone call. Sobbing, she had stunned him with the news of his mother's collapse and a confession of how very ill Natsu was. His mother's terminal illness had been thrust upon him all at once; he had been given no time to prepare himself for death. Now he stood in her hospital room feeling his narrow world being torn apart at the seams. His mother lay in bed deathly still, her skin like wax. His tear-choked voice shattered the silence. "But she can't be dying."

Sweat rolled down the doctor's mournful face as he briefly turned to Paul from Natsu's bedside. Dr. Amano finished giving Natsu an injection of morphine, then stood back with a weighty sigh and set the hypodermic syringe on the tray held by the assisting nurse. "I've done all I can, Akira. Now I can only offer your mother a painless death."

"Please, don't let her die. There must be something you haven't tried. Some new drug," Paul begged of the man who had delivered him into the world.

Dr. Amano removed his glasses. "If only it were so. Natsu has put up a brave fight. Now we can only ease her suffering and wait." He pinched the bridge of his nose with his fingers as he looked away. "She may not live through the day," he said.

Natsu had surfaced from the blackness to hear Dr. Amano's distantly echoing voice and to perceive the fuzzy outlines of those gathered around her bed. She felt paralyzed, her eyelids terribly heavy as she struggled to let in the light. True, she felt no physical pain; her body no longer belonged to her. Death had sucked her insides dry, while her mind lived on within an empty shell.

Yoko saw her eyelids flutter. "Natsu, can you hear me? I have sent for your priest—Father Watanabe," she sobbed.

What of Douglas? Natsu's anguished mind cried out. In her bereavement had Yoko forgotten to send for him? She fought against the undertow drawing her down into a drugged oblivion, thinking that Dr. Amano had no right to force this painless death on her when she so desperately wanted the pain of wakefulness. Oh, dear God, she wanted her voice and her senses returned to her on any terms.

"Mother, please don't leave me." Paul sank to his knees.

Natsu had given her son the better part of her life. Now there was nothing left to be sacrificed to him, and selfishness took possession of her. Paul's useless tears and Yoko's hysterical sobs laid claim to her final moments. Yet Natsu clung tenaciously to life, wanting Douglas's arms around her, fearing that death would cheat her of even that tender mercy.

"Paul—come close . . ." Thank God, she thought, her faint whispers had been heard. "Bring your father to me," she implored him. "Go quickly. Bring Douglas!" She heaved a great sigh, her lover's name still on her lips as she felt herself falling back into the black void. Her hands weakly gripped the sheets. Distantly Natsu heard her son's voice trying to call her back from the vortex that was spinning her down and away.

Paul stood up, taut, at the bedside. His mother lay dying, and all she could think of was his father! She had not spoken a single word to comfort him, and he turned his wrath on Yoko. "Did my father know how ill she was?"

"No. She wished to spare you both," Yoko answered through her tears. Natsu's son had a right to know of his mother's decisions, and Yoko told him everything. But on the matter of Hideo Tamura, she remained sworn to secrecy. "I alone shared the burden of her suffering. Do not hold it against me."

Paul could only open his arms to Yoko and share his grief with her. "My mother's lost to us," he said. The woman was so bereft she seemed near swooning, and he helped her sit in a chair where she began to rock, oblivious to all but the pale countenance of her dying friend.

Had his mother the presence of mind to comprehend what she had asked of him? Paul anguished. His father had used up Natsu's life, and now that bastard would claim her dying breaths, replacing his own importance at the bedside. Not to bring Douglas would be a just punishment, he thought, torn between love and hatred.

Father Watanabe entered the room. He regarded Natsu with the quiet acceptance of a deep-seated faith. "Consider death as a release from the indignities your mother so bravely suffered in this world," he said to Paul consolingly. "Her goodness will soon be rewarded in heaven. Pray, my son."

Unable to speak the prayers taught him as a child, Paul mutely watched as the priest administered the last rites. Father Watanabe made the sign of the cross over the deathly still face of the woman who had always placed the needs of others above herself, never once complaining, never once asking anything of her son in return until now. All of Paul's capacity for love, all his faith and courage, had flowed into him from his mother. She was the source of all that sustained him, and he could find no consolation in the priestly utterances. They did nothing to stop her life from draining away before his eyes.

Cursing this God who was taking Natsu from him, Paul fled what had become a suffocating tomb. Payment was due on his mother's years of selfless devotion, and the circumstances demanded that his debt be paid in person. Attendants mopped the hospital corridors with disinfectant, but even the sharp odor failed to eradicate the corrosive stench of death that Paul carried with him outside, where he frantically searched for a taxi.

Rain was in the offing as Baron Hosokawa left the Napier mansion trailed by servants. "*O-kaeri-nasai*. Welcome home." He laughed and rather gruffly seized Douglas's hand as his friend stepped from the arriving taxi. "Well, you look fit as ever. And, Max, tall as your father now. Angela! Perfectly turned out in the latest Paris fashion. How do you manage to keep so young?" Grinning cheerfully, the baron embraced her. "Glad to be home?"

Angela gave him a continental peck on both cheeks. "I'm so glad to see you again, Tadashi. Are the children with you?"

"Only Shizue." Baron Hosokawa noted Max's eager smile. "Kimitake is vacationing at the seashore with friends. A reward for doing so well in his studies this past year. Forgive the mess inside," he said, affectionately twining Angela's arm in his. "You left Germany on such short notice. Lord Mitsudara has consumed most of my time with business matters, and I've run behind schedule opening the house. Heinz cabled us of your success in Germany, and the lord is eager to begin retooling our weaving mills in Japan at once."

Douglas glanced over his shoulder at the servants carrying their luggage from the taxi. "Everything's here in my briefcase and those blueprint cases." He noted some new faces among the household staff.

"A number of your old retainers found employment elsewhere," the baron said, as if reading his friend's mind. "These will prove satisfactory, I'm sure. Morita did the hiring."

"This awful humidity." Angela entered the cavernous Victorian mansion with loathing. The house was a beehive of activity, servants uncovering the furnishings, unshuttering the tall windows, and vacuuming the Persian rugs. "What a doomsday of noise!"

The butler bowed a greeting. "How good to have you back, *okusama.*"

"Thank you, Morita. I have a splitting headache. Silence those vacuum cleaners, and please bring me the aspirin."

Shizue had glimpsed Max's arrival from an upstairs bedroom window. Now she took one last look in the full-length mirror, making sure everything about her appearance was perfect. Her new dress was sky-blue silk, high at the waist and patterned with lavender iris. Its skirt danced up gracefully around her legs as she turned left then right, eyeing the seams of her silk stockings.

Flushed with excitement, she raced down the hall, then struck a calm pose to begin her slow, ladylike descent. The day before, she had coaxed Yufugawo to go with her to the cinema, and her grand entrance was inspired by a scene in which Bette Davis had glided toward her lover down a broad, grand staircase. "Max. *O-kaeri-nasai.*"

Seeing Max rush toward her, Shizue's composure dissolved. They met on the staircase landing, each hesitating for a moment, then drawn together in an electrifying embrace. "Oh, Max, I can't believe you're finally here!"

Baron Hosokawa stiffened, disappointed but touched by what he witnessed. He had brought Shizue to the mansion expressly to observe this reunion, for he wanted to reassure himself that the previous summer's romance had waned into a sweet memory. Last September he had pledged Shizue in marriage to Jiro Mitsudara after observing how well they had taken to each other while Shizue had vacationed at his lord's summer home. Nurturing their relationship over the past year had led him to believe that his daughter's happiness would be assured by such a match.

Now Shizue's large almond eyes invited another young man's kiss. There was too much sweetness in the moment for Baron Hosokawa to be angry. Shizue and Max seemed so pure and innocent, totally oblivious to those who watched their tender kiss. But then his daughter ran her fingers through Max's hair while his hands explored the curve of her spine. She lifted one foot off the landing, and her high-heeled shoe slipped off while her foot remained poised in midair. As she quietly lowered her face against Max's chest, the baron loudly cleared his throat.

Suddenly, the youngsters were aware of being watched. Shizue quickly bent for her shoe, and Max ran his fingers through his hair, attempting to pull himself back together. For an instant the baron saw their faces supplanted by those of another such couple, whose love had defied tradition. He looked to Douglas, who was lost in reveries of the past, and then he called up the staircase to his daughter. "Shizue, don't stray very far. The lord and his son expect us at lunch." He was smiling and calm in the face of a love that had not been outgrown. "My business here with Douglas won't take more than an hour or so."

"Yes, Father." Shizue feared a stern rebuke lay in store. Her father's calm manner seemed forced, and Angela's green eyes were wide with alarm. Max took Shizue's hand, and they quickly walked away.

Douglas consulted his watch, eager to free himself under some pretext. "Can't business wait, Tadashi? Two weeks of inactivity has put extra baggage around my waist, and I planned to visit the club for a good workout."

The baron knew exactly where Douglas was bound for. "Sorry, but I need to know something of your latest cost accounting," he said. "Lord Mitsudara insisted that you lunch with us. But I persuaded him to give you time in which to relax and set your personal affairs in order."

Sighing, Douglas shifted his briefcase from one hand to the other. "Let's get to it, then."

"Well, you're both remarkably composed, I must say," Angela bristled. "Aren't you going to have a talk with those children."

"Douglas and I will discuss the matter," Baron Hosokawa answered her.

The baron and her husband entered the study, closing the door behind them, excluding her. As Angela removed the stickpin from her floppy-brimmed summer hat, she thought about her son and Shizue. Anyone could see they were hopelessly in love. She resented being shut out from discussing the problem with the men.

Morita reappeared carrying a silver tray. "Your aspirin, Madame."

"Bring it into the sitting room." Angela left her hat on the foyer table, along with her short cotton gloves. Then she walked into the sitting room, where she collapsed, exhausted, on the settee.

"This oppressive heat. The house has a musty smell, Morita. Have the servants light incense. Sandalwood in the master bedroom. It's Douglas's favorite scent. He's overworked, and we mustn't trouble him with any trivial details. I rely on you to keep the chaos to a minimum."

Morita bent with his tray to serve her. The water was tepid, and the aspirin tablets left a powdery aftertaste on her tongue. "Good Lord," she groaned as the front doorbell rang. "Who on earth can that be?"

"The truck with your steamer trunks, *okusama*," Morita announced from the window looking out across the mansion's circular front drive.

"Oh, well, I'll see to them personally."

In another part of the mansion, Max led Shizue to the garden veranda in search of privacy. Servants were underfoot everywhere, and he was disappointed to find a small army of men pruning and weeding the neglected grounds. "No place we can be alone," he complained.

Shizue tightly hugged his arm, thinking that a year had gone by at last, and he was finally here.

"Come with me," said Max, drawing her to a corner of the veranda, where the ivy- and rose-covered trellis hid them from the gardeners.

For a moment they stood apart, drinking in the way time's passage had changed them both. Then they were in each other's arms.

As Max covered her lips with his, Shizue trembled. The passion in his kiss left her breathless. Leaning back in his arms, she took a moment to compose herself before speaking. "You've grown more handsome than your snapshots."

"And you're even more beautiful." Max smiled and caressed her shoulder-length hair. "The new look becomes you."

She danced her head side to side, letting her straight black hair swing back and forth, thrilled by his approval. "A present for my sixteenth birthday," she said. "I finally put my foot down and insisted that Yufugawo cut it. She carried on so. Her hands shook with the scissors. She put my braids in a fancy box as a keepsake. I honestly believe she'd glue them back on me if she could."

Max laughed with her. Their year apart had given him a manly look, and he had grown at least another inch taller. Even wearing her high-heeled shoes, Shizue's head just reached to his broad shoulders. His smile made her blush, and she stepped away before he could take her in his arms once again. "Let's walk in the garden," she said. "There's so much to say, but my thoughts are all confused from just being near you again."

"Same here." Max put an arm around her waist, and they strolled along the neglected garden paths. Shizue spoke of her school in Kyoto, where all her classmates were still forced to wear their girlish braids. Max spoke of his travels in Europe, of the Karlstadts and his parents' other friends. The small talk demanded little of them, allowing them time to adjust to the new sensations evoked by their hands touching and the lingering glances they exchanged.

Paul arrived at the Napier mansion by taxi. Distractedly, he paid the driver, then quickly followed the delivery men who were carrying steamer trunks up the driveway. One year ago he had lacked the courage to assault the mansion's tall front doors, Paul thought. Now the forbidden doors stood wide open to him. He stopped at the threshold, watching Douglas Napier's stylishly dressed American wife dismiss the delivery men after the last steamer trunk had been accounted for.

How often Paul had written a scenario for this exact moment! But now his mother was dying, and even his desire for vengeance paled against that fact. The butler blocked his way. "Is Napier-*san* at home?"

"And if so?" Morita brusquely challenged him.

Angela saw the young man shifting uneasily just outside her door. "Who is it, Morita?"

"Akira Yoseido," Paul announced himself to her rather timidly. "I have business—urgent business with Mr. Napier."

No doubt one of her husband's employees, Angela thought. "Don't just stand there, Morita. Show the young man in." The butler muttered some racial slur under his breath. Angela felt sorry for this somber-faced Eurasian. She thought him quite handsome and smiled. "Do come inside, Mr. Yoseido. My husband's in his study. My butler isn't usually so ill-mannered. Show our visitor to the study and announce him, Morita."

Paul removed his gray felt hat. Angela Napier bent to read steamer trunk tags while servants awaited her commands. All these riches should have rightly belonged to his mother, Paul thought. Now all his father's material wealth could not buy Natsu even a single day of life. Paul envisioned her pale face as she lay motionless in the hospital bed. Suddenly he had the terrible fear that she might pass away before he returned there with her lover.

"This way." Morita irritably motioned at the visitor to follow him. "The name again?"

"Akira Yoseido." The butler moved at a snail's pace. "Please, hurry."

"Show respect for your elders," Morita snapped, purposely taking time to straighten his black bow tie before rapping on the study door. He opened it only enough to show himself to Douglas, who sat at his desk. "A young man wishes to see you on urgent business, *dannasama*. Akira Yoseido."

"Get out of my way!" Paul shoved the butler aside. His father recoiled, looking as if he had just seen a ghost, while Baron Hosokawa spun around. Paul stood in the middle of the room. "Tell your servant to close the door, unless you want everyone to hear what I've come to say."

"Madame allowed this troublemaker inside, Napier-*san*."

Feeling weak in the knees, Douglas told Morita, "Do as he says."

"Yes, better do as I say!" Paul's voice reverberated through the cavernous study before its door closed behind him. "Don't fall down, Douglas. I didn't come here to make a scene. Nothing matters now that mother's so ill. She's in the hospital, unconscious—and soon she'll be dead."

"Oh, my God," Douglas mouthed the words, the blood draining from his face. "An accident," he said, as tears welled up in Paul's eyes. "What happened! Tell me!" he demanded, urgently reaching out to his son.

"No accident." Emotion choked Paul's voice while he raised up both his arms to fend off his father's touch. "Mother is dying of cancer, and you're the cause."

Douglas fell back, stunned, as Baron Hosokawa sagged in an armchair.

Paul wiped his eyes with one sleeve, but everything in the room bled together through a curtain of tears. "You're the cancer that's eaten her up. All those years of suffering your selfishness slowly destroyed my mother. But she called your name. 'Bring Douglas here'—she pleaded in a voice so faint I could hardly hear her," he painfully recounted, struggling against the tears that kept his father out of focus. "You fed on Mother like a cancer. If only it were I dying of your accursed touch. If only it were I and not her!"

"Cancer." Douglas bowed his head, barely able to speak the deadly word. Striken with disbelief, he refused to accept his son's pronouncement. "No, it's a lie!! You're punishing me with a cruel lie."

"Damn you! Even hating you as I do, I'm not capable of that!" Paul raised his fists in anger. But he had never been able to strike Douglas Napier, and he dropped both hands at his sides, while he assaulted his father with words. "Mother knew how ill she was before you left Japan," he said. "She kept the truth even from me. Yoko told me how she delayed the surgery that would have ended her pain and sent you away fearing she might not live to see you again. Oh, what a terrible price she paid for my silence and to keep your miserable fortune from going down the drain. Her sacrifice bought you the right to go on living in all this luxury." His words struck hard and deep, but his father's eyes were dry, not clouded by tears of remorse. "You're incapable of loving anyone but yourself!" Paul's shouted accusation echoed through the room as his gaze swept the expensive furnishings. "Well, now you'll rot in this fancy mansion, wallowing in guilt and self-pity. That's all that's left for you. Knowing that you failed my mother—failed us both. Knowing what could have been yours if you'd had guts enough to claim it."

Douglas suddenly felt lost in some vast, barren wasteland as he stood there alone in his bereavement, scorned by his son and unable to find release in tears. "Son—where is she? What hospital?"

There was nothing more Paul could say or do. Bowing his head, he answered, "She's being cared for at Tokyo Teikoku Daigaku. She might not live through the day."

Following Paul's volatile entrance, Angela Napier had stationed herself outside the study door with Morita, but most of what she could overhear of the young man's words was unintelligible. She heard Tadashi raise his voice, not in anger, but in what seemed to be a pleading tone. Suddenly Douglas charged from the room, his face ghastly pale. He ignored her presence, breaking into a run across the foyer. Baron Hosokawa placed a hand on the young man's shoulder. Not to hold him there, but more as a gesture of sympathy, Angela observed.

"Douglas! What's happening?" Angela cried. Her husband seemed to run faster. "Don't you dare leave this house without giving me some explanation!"

All the years of living a lie crashed down around him as Douglas raced out the front door and up the drive to his garage. Even Paul was forgotten in Douglas's race against death.

The baron ignored Angela's demands for an explanation, and she chased after Paul, barring the door to him. "What's the meaning of this?"

Angela softened when she saw the tears on the young man's cheeks. Not answering, Paul put on his gray felt hat and lowered the brim across the blue-flecked hazel eyes. "Who are you to come barging into my home, shouting at my servant, and upsetting my husband?" she asked in a more even tone.

Paul steadily fixed his eyes on Angela Napier, then took a deep breath and said, "I'm his son."

He watched her grope for something to take hold of as Baron Hosokawa pushed through the group of servants who had gathered by the door. The baron supported Angela with his arm. Paul quickly walked outside, glad to be free of his father's house.

In the Napier garage a mechanic hired to service the family cars was working over Angela's bright red Bugatti. "Which car can be driven?" Douglas asked, his tone urgent.

"The Duesenberg, *dannasama*," the mechanic said, wiping grease off his hands. "In perfect order and a full tank of gas."

"The keys?"

"There on the seat."

Douglas jumped behind the wheel. The canvas top of the sleek gray car was rolled down. He started the engine and floored the accelerator, tires squealing as he drove off.

Paul halted on the sidewalk, waving both arms and shouting at Douglas to no avail. The car sped away. He would have suffered his father's presence for a ride to the hospital. Cursing himself for not asking the taxi driver to wait, Paul ran downhill past the manicured hedges and high garden walls of the very wealthy. At that moment, he was no longer envious of the opulent world inhabited by his half brother and Douglas's American wife.

Identifying himself to Angela had given him no satisfaction. He could think of nothing but the precious moments Douglas might steal from Natsu before he reached the hospital. He saw no taxis on the main cross street and waited at the tram stop there for what seemed hours. It began to rain. Paul turned his collar up against the steady drizzle. Finally, a tram arrived and he boarded it. There was no relief from the withering humidity. Paul searched his pockets. For the first time in memory, his mother had neglected to place a freshly laundered handkerchief in the coat pocket of his suit. Suddenly he was devastated by the loss of this simple gesture of love.

The rain drove Shizue and Max indoors to search for a place where they could be alone until the baron finished his business with Douglas. They encountered Morita in the reception foyer scurrying about and clapping his hands to silence a gathering of whispering servants.

"Is something wrong?" Shizue asked.

"No, Hosokawa-*san*. But there has been a change of plans, and you will not be lunching with Lord Mitsudara," said Morita. "The baron and Madame Napier are in the study, not to be disturbed."

"Where's my dad?" asked Max.

"Gone to the city on some business." Morita bowed. He had said what the baron had instructed him to say to Shizue and Max. The servants under him knew their places, and his sharp looks sent them all scurrying back to work. "Shall I have the cook prepare a lunch for you, Max-*san*?"

"Yes, I'm starved." Max drew back his shoulders, delighted by this turn of events. "Well, Shizue, it seems we have the afternoon all to ourselves," he announced cheerily.

She faced the sealed study door. "What could be important enough for my father to cancel our luncheon with the lord?"

"Why trouble ourselves with that?" Thunder rumbled outside the windows as Max watched a driving summer rain turn the day dark and gloomy. Servants were hauling the steamer trunks upstairs. "Once we've found a quiet spot to settle down, I'll call on the house phone and tell you where to serve lunch," he told Morita, taking Shizue's hand and leading her away.

Behind the closed study door, Tadashi felt torn between two loyalties, to Douglas Napier and to his wronged wife.

Angela was in shock. Tears coursed down her cheeks and her mascara was smudged. The baron poured them both another brandy, then sat down across from her. In a soft-spoken manner, he had already related almost everything he knew about Douglas's youthful romance and its aftermath.

"Keeping this from you has given me many a sleepless night, Angela. I didn't ask to become a party to Douglas's secret," Tadashi confided hoarsely. "No, that obligation was forced on me by circumstances set into motion long ago."

Angela coughed on her brandy. "Men. How they protect one another and their secrets. Have you no idea what it is to discover that my trusted husband and my dear, honorable friend are both liars? Both hypocrites," she said in a brittle tone of voice. "Akira—that poor young man." She stared down into the glass, which she clutched between her quivering hands. "I can't get his face out of my mind."

"Yes, I know." Baron Hosokawa fortified himself with brandy, listening to the beat of the rain against the study windows before he spoke again. "When I last saw Natsu's son, he was a little boy," he said. "Some years ago, she adopted the Christian faith and had the boy baptized in the name of Paul. Over the years Douglas showed me photographs. But it was a great shock for me to see him face-to-face."

"His features do resemble my husband's," Angela said. "I didn't notice the resemblance when he first appeared at the door. But the instant he identified himself as Douglas's son, I was stunned into accepting the truth." She grew silent, waiting for Baron Hosokawa to reveal something more of Douglas's secret life.

"You should know," the baron said at last, "that while I shared Douglas's secret, I respected his privacy. I'm not your husband's keeper, Angela. I couldn't presume to dictate his actions, and he didn't ask for my approval. Since he's not here to speak for himself, this trial has been dropped in my lap. But it's unfair to hold me accountable for a breach of trust I had no choice about." Tadashi felt genuine empathy for all concerned. Only the man who loved Natsu could speak for the depths of what they had together, he thought. It was not for him to pass judgment on them. As a friend, he could only try to soften Angela's emotional distress. "I'll stay with you until Douglas returns to speak for himself," he said. "No matter what you may be feeling at this moment, never once forget that you're his wife. He conducted his affair with Natsu as a gentleman. The family unit was preserved. Angela, the better part of his life was devoted to you. He gave you and your son his name."

Abruptly Angela stood up and paced the floor in a tight circle. "Honestly, Tadashi, the consequences of his infidelity are far too cruel for me to be consoled by a legality. All these years of sharing Douglas with another woman. Where did you store that precious code of honor while you were hiding Douglas's sordid affair behind my back?"

The baron remained silent, and Angela fumbled with the cigarette box. She managed to extract one and, hands shaking, she lit it with the heavy crystal desk lighter. "Conducted himself as a gentleman. How dare you defend him!" Folding one arm across her waist, Angela took a deep drag of the cigarette, then angrily exhaled short bursts of smoke. "Douglas and this woman. How did they live?" she asked with difficulty. Seeing Tadashi's hesitation, she said, "Oh, surely he confided that much of their relationship."

"Douglas kept a small apartment. Naturally, I never visited there. But from what I understand, it was rather drab and located off some side street. It wasn't a pleasant set of circumstances, Angela. They couldn't take more suitable accommodations without running the risk of being seen by those in our social circle. Douglas went to great lengths to protect you and your son. I'm sure he and Natsu must have felt imprisoned, never going out together in public or enjoying the company of friends."

"Forgive me for not being moved by their sacrifices." She pulled on her cigarette, anguishing in silence over how very much in love Douglas must have been to sacrifice his creature comforts. "And his mistress. Surely she must have wanted more of Douglas than he gave her."

"Natsu was resigned to things as they were. She made no monetary demands for herself or their son. Except for allowing Douglas to support Paul's education, she and her son lived humbly on what she earned waiting tables at the Cherry Blossom Kissaten. She shared an apartment with her son above the tea shop, refusing to accept the personal luxuries Douglas's wealth could have brought her."

"Not a *paid* whore, you mean."

"Nothing of the sort. Natsu came from a well-to-do family. She's a woman of culture and refinement who suffered dearly for her mistakes." The baron massaged his eyes. "She's dying. Why torment yourself over the past?"

"To hear you talk, one would think she was a candidate for sainthood!" Angela crushed her cigarette in an onyx ashtray and stared at the cold-eyed portrait of Douglas's father hanging over the marble fireplace, thinking that his meddling was to blame. Now she understood why her marriage had begun to deteriorate almost from the very day she set foot inside this house. Her husband had loved Natsu even before they had met. When Douglas had asked her to be his wife, his Japanese lover had already given birth to his son. "I might forgive his whoring with some common prostitute. But never this!"

"Hysterics won't solve anything. More is at stake here than your injured pride."

Angela stiffened. "Obviously your first concern is how all this might affect our precious dynasty," she commented acidly. "Oh, yes, the family unit must be preserved at all costs. Business must go on as usual." She poured herself more brandy and lifted the glass in both hands, her fingers tightening around it as she tried to hold back her tears. "Douglas never loved me. I've suffered as his wife long enough. How I despise Japan and this house."

"Angela, you're too overwrought to be thinking clearly." Tadashi came toward her, his arms outstretched. "I know Douglas better than he knows himself. He could never go on without you. It's only natural you feel the need to strike back at him. But you can't throw everything away. Think of what that would do to your son and to all of us who love you."

"Leave me alone!" Wildly jerking around, she hurled her brandy glass at Julius Napier's portrait and watched the crystal shatter and amber liquid roll down his austere face. "Douglas brought me here to rot while he enjoyed the best of both worlds as if it were his birthright. All I ever was to him was breeding stock. A proper wife to bear him proper sons and heirs."

Her outburst had drained Angela of her strength, and in a weak, muted voice, she said, "I can't hold you responsible for being so loyal to Douglas. None of us is perfect. Upholding your code of honor leaves you vulnerable to making mistakes, Tadashi. Often we do more injury to those we love by wanting to spare them from things that can't be helped."

"Please, take the time to think of what's at stake before doing anything rash when your husband returns home."

"I won't have Douglas bringing his grief for that woman into my house!" Angela shouted at the top of her voice. She bolted to the study door and threw it open. "Wait here if you like. But hell can freeze over before I take him back when he returns. I'm leaving him, Tadashi."

As she rushed from the study, Baron Hosokawa crossed to stand in its open doorway. He watched Angela climb the staircase. Morita was coming down.

"I'm going to my room and don't want to be disturbed for any reason," she told the butler.

The baron felt drained. Natsu would never have wanted her death to bring a legacy of destruction. In Douglas's absence he was the head of this household and the guardian of a dynasty he intended to hold together by every means at his disposal.

"Morita, I'll be at work in the study," he called. "I will handle any telephone calls from there."

Douglas would stay at Natsu's bedside until the end, he thought, pacing to the study windows as the mantel clock chimed the hour of two. Marriage had given Angela the Napier name, but Natsu Yoseido was not a common mistress for lack of that piece of paper. She had been Douglas's soulmate, his most precious treasure, and his partner in a life built on stolen moments. Yes, Douglas would suffer no less than he himself had suffered when he had lost his beloved Sumie.

Suddenly, all the grief he had felt in the past was forced upon him once again by the tragic events of the day. He began weeping as the lines of an ageless poem wrote themselves across his mind. "To meet my love, I have no way. Like the tall peak of Fuji in Suruga, shall I burn forever?"

Dr. Amano was using the telephone at the hospital admissions desk when a tall American presented himself to the nurse there. The man wore no hat, and rainwater dripped off the matted locks of his graying blond hair as he urgently bent over the nurse and asked to see Natsu Yoseido.

"She is allowed no visitors, except for immediate family," the nurse informed him.

"I'm more to her than family," Douglas protested.

Dr. Amano stepped forward. "Napier-*san*, isn't it?"

"Yes . . ."

"Natsu is under my care." He bowed. "Dr. Amano. I have been her physician for many years. And her friend."

"What's her condition? Paul—my son—said that she had only a short time to live."

"I cannot say how much time is left her. Please, this way. Mind your step in those wet shoes. The corridor is slippery."

Douglas accompanied the soft-spoken doctor, who confided every painful detail of Natsu's courageous struggle for life. Douglas lowered his eyes to the dark whirling patterns that the blades of ceiling fans cast on the polished tile floors. "Will she know me?"

"I cannot speak for her state of mind," Dr. Amano said at the door to Natsu's room. "A pity you did not return to Japan sooner. She may not regain consciousness again before the end." Tears glistened behind his thick eyeglasses. "Natsu is very special. I have witnessed death many times, but in her case, it's the living who are to be pitied. I shall never forget her. Go and make your peace with her, Napier-*san*."

The floor seemed to pitch beneath his trembling legs as Douglas pushed through the swinging door into the darkened room. He stood paralyzed, just inside the door, unable to comprehend that the frail creature lying in the hospital bed was his beloved Natsu.

A nurse bent over her, performing duties with clinical detachment. The nurse charted Natsu's faint life signs and noted them on the clipboard that was hung at the foot of the bed.

Gasping for breath, Douglas moved forward and took hold of a chair for support. The nurse exited into the corridor. Without the squeal of her rubber-soled shoes and the rustle of her starched white uniform, the room was suddenly ominously quiet. In the icy stillness between him and the dying Natsu, his mind cruelly brought to life vivid images of their stolen moments together. Having known the ecstasy of her love, he would surely drown in the vacuum created by her passing, Douglas thought in anguish.

Hearing the sound of heavy breathing, Douglas turned to face a shadowy figure seated in one corner of the room. "Yoko," he whispered.

The woman acknowledged his presence with a resigned nod and said, "You have returned too late, Douglas. Too late."

Alone with her grief, Yoko rocked back and forth in her chair. Douglas sank in the vacant chair at Natsu's bedside. Her once fresh beauty was now dried up, like a delicate flower that had been pressed between the pages of a book. Her hands seemed translucent, colorless as the bed linen on which they rested.

"Natsu." Douglas spoke her name softly while taking her hand between his. It was so dry and thin he was afraid it might turn to dust. She had promised never to leave him, he thought. She was still so young. How could she be dying? It was absurd that she should die. His eyes filled with angry tears. She must not leave him this way, without ever knowing that he was there, without feeling his touch and hearing his voice tell her how much he loved her.

Desperately, he cupped her ravaged face and pressed his mouth on hers, trying to warm her cold lips with his kiss. "Natsu. I'm here with you, my darling. Natsu—Natsu," he breathed her name over and over, as his mouth caressed her icy cheek. "Dearest, I'm here," he called to her, and kissed each eyelid. At last he felt one flutter against his lips.

Natsu's head tossed on the pillow, then came to rest, and she opened her eyes to his face. "My darling." She uttered a sigh. Her eyelids felt like great weights. Her lover's voice had called her up from a wishful dream, and she was caught in limbo, not knowing if Douglas was real or only a drug-induced delusion. Weakly, her frail hands and arms established contact with what could not possibly be a dream. The reality of his touch miraculously tapped some reservoir of life that flickered within her like a tiny flame. "Douglas. Oh, my dearest. I prayed you would return to me in time. Oh—hold me darling. I've waited so long for this moment. Don't let me go."

"Never! I won't let you die," Douglas wept, clutching her to him. "Sweetheart, listen to me. I'll give up everything for our happiness. You can't die now. Live so we can be together as husband and wife. Live for me."

"Oh, my darling—don't grieve over what could never be. I've loved you more than life itself, but now it's over. You mustn't dwell in the past. Oh, your lips are like fire." Her sigh became a gasp. She could feel the heat generated by Douglas's touch. And with it the wave of a searing pain that made each breath torture. "Our son—remember what you promised me. Don't abandon him." She felt as if her lungs might burst. Natsu sensed death was about to claim her all too swiftly. "You're all he has," she said, her voice barely a whisper. "Paul's future is in your hands now."

"I'll look after him. I swear it."

"Paul—where's my baby?"

Just then Paul entered the room. "I'm here, Mother."

Natsu suddenly sat up in Douglas's arms. Her eyelids fluttered violently. "Paul. I can't see you. Come closer—here where I can see you—and forgive your father."

He was immobilized by her plea. How could she ask this of him? He twisted his rain-soaked hat in his hands. He wanted to scream, to tear Natsu loose from his father's arms.

"Paul—I love you. Oh, my baby—where are you?"

The heart-wrenching cry of a dying mother for her child uprooted him. Paul rushed to her bedside, terrified she was near the end but unable to find his voice. Natsu's eyelids ceased their violent fluttering. Her eyes blinked open wide, but the light had gone out of them. Paul looked into the unseeing eyes of the dead, and forgiveness died unspoken on his trembling lips.

Douglas held Natsu quietly for a time and then gently rested her frail body on the pillows. His fingers gently closed her fixed, staring eyes, and he surrendered Natsu's body to her son.

Paul flung himself across her remains, shuddering with sobs while Yoko continued slowly rocking in her chair and wept, pressing a handkerchief across her eyes.

Cut off from both mourners, Douglas could find no tears. Natsu's passing had extinguished all his emotions, and he was engulfed in a sea of emptiness, unable to find any outlet to express his grief. He sat at the death bed waiting to be overwhelmed by feeling, but he remained numb.

Douglas knew there was no consolation for him there. Mindlessly, he walked down the hospital corridor and through the door to the outside. It had stopped raining. Douglas stood shakily on the hospital steps, feeling like a tightrope walker balanced midway across the high wire at the point of no return. Paul had not forgiven him, and the way back to Natsu's son was no less treacherous than the way ahead to Angela and Max. He had neither the stomach nor the heart to bridge the awesome chasm between those who waited for him at home.

Douglas numbly got into his car and drove without any destination in mind. Was it chance or unconscious design that brought him to the Ginza? he wondered. He slowed to a stop at the Cherry Blossom Kissaten.

A chill went through him. He could have sworn he saw Natsu approaching him on this worn pavement outside the tea shop's locked entrance. The young woman was dressed in a colorful kimono, her hair swept up in an elegant though girlish fashion, much in the way that he remembered Natsu wearing her hair when they had first met. The girl was pregnant and halted to rest, putting down her shopping bags, then massaging the small of her back. Douglas saw her as the young girl he had abandoned, weary after a day's work waiting tables. He collapsed across the wheel, in pain and unable to cry. Only the night before he had contemplated ending his double life and freeing himself of lies. Now Natsu was gone.

The Duesenberg's idling motor evaporated beads of rain on the hood, and Douglas's eyes went down to the key ring dangling from the ignition. On the ring was the key to the apartment he and Natsu had shared. Their apartment was where he belonged, he decided. Perhaps there he might find some peace and put the past to rest.

It was a short drive from the Ginza to the weathered brick building. Douglas parked the car in his alloted space, then crossed the underground garage and rang for the elevator. Returning there reinforced the totality of his loss. Suddenly he felt defenseless against an onrush of memories. The white-gloved operator greeted him by name, but Douglas avoided conversation with the man during the slow ascent.

He got off the elevator and walked down the dimly lit hallway to the apartment. Slowly he unlocked the door and opened it. What greeted his eyes were the flower arrangements placed around the room to welcome him home. Stunned, Douglas left the key ring dangling in the lock. The fresh flowers that sweetened the air were evidence that Natsu had been there only that morning. A muggy breeze caused the wind bells strung at the open window to tinkle merrily. He envisioned Natsu joyfully at work arranging the colorful blossoms that had outlived her to greet him with the harsh reality of her passing.

He entered their bedroom. The air was permeated with a familiar scent that drew Douglas to the adjoining bathroom. He shuddered as he stood at its threshold, forced to bear witness to that awful moment of her fatal seizure. The crystal decanter of his favorite perfume lay shattered on the tile floor. Its contents had evaporated, but the lingering aroma evoked images of her body scented after the bath. Pills were scattered everywhere, spilled from their vials, many crushed underfoot.

Douglas clutched his chest, short of breath and bathed in perspiration as he envisioned Natsu struggling to reach for the drugs that would dull her pain. He could hear her cry out, could see her falling and lying there unconscious on the white tiles near a brownish splotch of dried blood. Her ivory hairpins lay on the floor. They must have tumbled from her hair, he thought. She had wanted to greet him wearing the gift he had given her on a long-ago summer day when he vowed that no power on earth would ever come between them. Only that morning she was preparing herself for love, when death had mercilessly struck her down. There were drops of dried blood leading to the bed. He looked away from bloodstains on the satin pillowcase, cotton swabs, an empty serum vial, and a hypodermic needle left on the night table by Dr. Amano in his haste.

There could be no comfort for him there. Natsu's ghost seemed earthbound, crying out for him to make peace with the past so that her spirit could be set free. But Douglas clung to her memory. He saw her everywhere and heard her voice in the wind bells, heard her footsteps beside him as he crossed for the whiskey decanter on the dining alcove sideboard. He draped his suit coat across the back of a chair, then carried the decanter and a glass to the sofa.

Seated there, he poured drink after drink. The alcohol shot through him swiftly, but it had no effect on his pain. The telephone glared at him as a reminder of how he had stormed from home, where he now imagined Angela pacing that house she loathed and asking Tadashi questions. He thought of Max; returning home to face his judgment would be the worst trial of all. But for the moment Douglas felt answerable to no one but himself.

It began to rain again. Refilling his glass, he sought oblivion in alcohol. Although it burned in his gut, he felt chilled to the bone. Natsu's son had wished he were dying in her place. In truth both their spirits had died with her.

Douglas waited for tears to come. But like Paul's forgiveness, they were denied him.

CHAPTER 11

Not for years had Max and Shizue climbed the creaking stairs to the attic playroom located in a wing of the Napier mansion that the Hosokawa family had occupied years ago on visits with their small children. Max opened the attic door, and its hinges squealed. As a young father, Douglas Napier had transformed this spacious attic into a playroom for his son. The room was filled with happy memories. There were hobby horses, chests of toys, and shelves lined with dog-eared storybooks the children had read while sprawled on the floor on other rainy afternoons. Even on gloomy days this room was a bright place because there were skylights placed between the rafters high above, as well as windows set low under the eaves.

Max closed the door behind them, relieved to be alone at last. The unused playroom was forgotten by Morita's cleaning force of servants, and time had woven cobwebs over a soft carpet of dust.

"Oh, Max, it's as if we played here only yesterday." Shizue crossed the room, touching its reassuring mementos of childhood. "Everything is just as we left it," she said, as she touched the elaborate puppet stage erected on a velvet-covered platform. "Remember what fun we had putting on shows for the grown-ups?" Circling the stage, she crouched out of sight behind its drawn curtain, rummaging through the wooden chests there.

"Are you hiding from me?" Max asked.

Shizue uttered a squeal of delight. "No! Stay where you are," she pleaded. "I have a surprise."

Max folded his arms across his chest and watched the embroidered velvet curtain draw open.

"Oh, oh," Shizue sobbed, manipulating a hand puppet's pretty face and tiny wooden hands. It was fashioned after the lifelike Bunraku *ningyō* characters used to act out the old Jojuri fables in Tokyo theaters. The puppet was richly costumed as the courtesan of a great lord. She had always been Shizue's favorite, and now she knelt sobbing beneath the silk cut-out moon and silver foil clouds that hung from strings. "Oh, I serve a cruel and jealous master," Shizue spoke for her courtesan in a high falsetto voice. "My lover promised to meet me here at the stream. We were to run off together to be wed. But I've waited here for hours, and the lord's soldiers must be searching for me at this very moment." Shizue shook the bowed puppet head and moaned, unaware that Max was silently creeping up behind her around the stage. "Oh, where can my lover be?"

Max cried. "Here I am!" circling both arms around her waist.

Taken by surprise, Shizue let the puppet slip from her grasp. Her laughter was husky, that of a woman. "Look what you've done to my beautiful courtesan."

"She'll survive."

Max whisked Shizue off her feet and sat her down in the old wicker swing that had been hung from the attic rafters. The swing's chains groaned as he pushed her high. "Tell me when you're ready to come back down to earth," he said, pushing the swing ever higher until Shizue's toes nearly touched the sloping skylight overhead. "Higher?"

"No, you win." She laughed. "Bring me down."

Max slowed the swing, then sat beside her, and they rocked together, gazing deep into each other's eyes. "God, how I love you," he said.

Raindrops rolling down the sloping skylight above them patterned Max's face with snaking shadows as he bent toward Shizue and kissed her. She felt utterly defenseless and missed his lips as soon as he withdrew them. Her fingertips explored his face. "I adore you, as well. Was there no one else for you this past year? In your letters, you seemed to be avoiding the subject of other girls." Shizue watched her question bring a momentary look of pain to Max's luminous blue eyes, and then he sighed.

"There was someone else," Shizue said. "I just knew it."

"No one to compete with you," Max replied. "Oh, there were lots of beautiful, well-mannered girls in Europe. Blondes, redheads, brunettes. The world's full of girls, Shizue, but I love you. Now and for always." Abruptly he got up and walked over to one of the windows set under the eaves.

"Max?" she questioned his silence.

Max loosened his tie. He continued to look out the window, observing a fine mist drifting through the rain-drenched pines. "I had it out with my dad about us," he said at last. "We talked last night, and his advice does make sense. But I'll let you be the final judge of that."

While he related their exchange aboard the steamer, Shizue picked at the graying white paint flaking off the wicker swing. The passing years had eroded everything here, she thought, even the fond memories she had tried to recapture only a moment ago.

"Well, there you have it," Max said finally, turning to face her. "I don't see any way to avoid a fight with your father. Last summer, you put all your faith in me. It's true, I'm the man and older. But it was naive of me to think I could take all the responsibility for us both, Shizue. We can't go on loving each other without facing up to the fact that others are bound to be hurt. Dad is on our side, but his hands are tied when it comes to dealing with your father." Shaken by the torment in Shizue's eyes, Max took her hands in his. "It won't do any good talking things out between our parents. Sooner or later, you'll have to make a choice between hurting me or your father, and I need to know if you love me enough for that."

On the verge of tears, Shizue brought Max's hands to her cheek. "It's not a question of my loving you enough. Oh, Max, I've already given you my heart. One year hasn't changed how I feel. But my father's in control of my life until I come of age. I can only live on hope and promise to wait until you finish your education."

Being with him again strengthened her resolve. "Papa isn't some dragon spitting fire and smoke in the path of our happiness. The world is changing, and the old ways must give in to the new." She quoted what Max had written her in a letter, then smiled brightly. "Oh, don't you see, being forced to make the awful choice you spoke of may never come to pass. I believe we'll find a way around Papa's objections."

"Maybe you're right," Max said, thinking that what he had asked of her was premature. "I can't help being impatient, Shizue. Maybe when I'm old enough to carry some weight with your father, he'll give in."

"Oh, yes, after you've graduated from Harvard, he'll see you differently." Shizue put her arms around Max's neck. "Father's never denied me anything. Yes, he's rigid. But love will bend him to our cause. That's my hope, Max. After the way we kissed on the stairs, no one can think of us as children. Papa will have to take us seriously. I'm sure he won't dismiss the incident without saying a word to me."

"And what will you tell him?"

"That my feelings are those of a woman. That he can't stop me from loving you without losing my love." Shizue heaved a long sigh, believing she had dealt with the problem as an adult. "Papa is stern, but he's also warm and sensitive. Eventually, he'll want us to be happy." Shizue smiled. "He'll have four years to get used to the idea when you're at Harvard."

Just then the house phone on the attic wall buzzed insistently. "It's Papa wondering where we are," Shizue said. "Oh, I don't want the afternoon to end."

Max answered the phone. "Morita? Yes, we're in the old attic playroom," he told the butler, then hung up the receiver and grinned. "That's a relief. He's sending up our lunch in the dumb waiter. Your father is staying for the afternoon."

"Thank the gods." Shizue drifted to the puppet stage and lifted her fallen courtesan, smoothing its human hair, which was done up with tiny ivory pins. "If only this were make-believe, we'd run away together and marry each other now," Shizue said, a wistful expression on her face. She rested the puppet doll inside the storage trunk beside a handsome wooden lover and a mean-faced lord. "He resembles Lord Mitsudara," she said, shivering as she closed the trunk lid. "I wish we were staying here with you in our old rooms. That awful man's eyes chill me. He tyrannizes his household, making everyone jump at his slightest command. Especially his son."

"I met the lord only once, years ago when he visited the Nagasaki weaving mill. But your description of him lingers on." Max brought her close. "You didn't say much about Jiro Mitsudara in your letters."

"There's not much to say. I like him as a friend." Shizue could not burden Max with yet another obstacle to their dream by voicing the suspicion that her father might pledge her to Jiro when she came of age. "It's like being children again, standing here with rain tapping against the skylights," she told him cheerily, changing the subject.

Then she reached up and fixed the knot of Max's loosened necktie. "Papa and Kimitake are always asking me to help them with their neckties. Men never can get it right." She sighed contentedly, smoothing down the wing tips of his collar.

The clanging bell announced that their lunch had arrived in the dumb waiter. Shizue lifted its door to remove the tray.

"Good old cook. The man's an artist with his sushi knife," Max observed gleefully. "Just look at those goodies."

"You set the table."

"Were we ever that tiny?" Max laughed as he pulled out the child-sized chairs around a small wicker table whose basket weave had parted company with its nails. "We'll just have to sit on the floor."

The attic floorboards were dusty. Max found some straw mats on the toy chests and rolled them out by the table. Even seated on the floor he and Shizue dwarfed the table like awkward adults at a children's tea party.

"Not one Japanese restaurant in Berlin. Japanese diplomats ate in the consulate, while I could only dream of a spread like this." Max quickly unrolled his napkin to get at the chopsticks inside. The cook had artfully arranged everything in black lacquered dishes. There were flowers in a tiny china vase. Vegetables around the raw fish were carved into graceful blossoms. "Mmmm! Now I know I'm home. Sea urchin, yellowtail, and squid. There's nothing remotely like this abroad. The Italians call squid *calamari*, but they fry it breaded, and it tastes like rubber inner tubes."

Shizue laughed, hungry but mesmerized by her lover's delight over the food. "I wonder what's keeping Papa here with your mother," she mused.

"Adult business," Max commented wryly, dissolving a green lump of horseradish in his bowl of soy sauce. "Dad made it clear I'm not ready to join the club." As he chewed on morsels of raw fish and rice clad in thin layers of seaweed, he uttered sounds that kept Shizue smiling. "Not hungry?"

"I'm curious to know what's taken your father into the city on this drizzly afternoon."

"I don't know," Max said. "Some business emergency, I suppose."

Shizue glanced around the room at the familiar childhood objects.

"Everything was so simple when we were children playing with these toys," she said pensively. "Being here makes growing up seem so final, Max. I don't want to leave these happy memories behind."

"Come with me." Max threw down his napkin, took her hand, and pulled her up with him. They crossed the attic to where a collection of fancifully painted wooden boxes had been stored. "Pay your respects to some old friends. You remember my rogues' gallery. Hans the Terrible Hun," he lisped, affecting a theatrical German accent and triggering the lid of a jack-in-the-box.

The gruesome head of Hans the Terrible, wearing a Wagnerian helmet of horns, popped up from his box unleashing puffs of dust. Douglas had carved this gallery of samurai warriors, pirates, mustachioed mandarins, snorting dragons, knights in armor, and white-bearded wizards. All of them had been birthday presents for Max as a child. Their painted faces had not seen the light of day in years. Shizue could not help giggling as Max triggered one jack-in-the-box after another. Douglas had given them eyes that rolled, lids that blinked, hinged ears and noses that wiggled, and lifelike mouths that now gaped open as though shocked to find themselves freed after being confined so long to the darkness of their boxes.

"Luke the Mute, speaking the only way he can by tooting on his flute," Max said, as the last character popped to life out of its dusty lid. Max stood back, remembering the glee he had felt while unwrapping these special gifts. None of the expensive toys his father had bought him were a match for these labors of love. "No offense to you other guys," he addressed the rogues' gallery, "but I always had a soft spot in my heart for Luke. It's his crossed eyes under those droopy lids. Sure, he's a dope. But a nice dope."

Shizue fondled Luke's pink-cheeked face. "Poor Luke the Mute, you're funny but sad." Shizue looked up at Max. "It's amazing how fresh their painted faces still look. Even the cloth of their spring necks seems brand new, as if your father had made them only yesterday." Someday their children would enjoy playing with them here, she thought. The wooden heads all seemed to nod agreement, their painted eyes fixed on her as if hoping for another generation of fun. "Don't close them up again, Max. Their funny faces are so happy to be free. Thank you for bringing them to life. They remind me of all the happy times we had here. We'll always have those memories."

"Yes." He gently nudged Luke's spring neck and watched the hinged wooden fingers play a painted silver flute. "I remember laughing until my sides hurt when he first flew out of the box. Makes me wish I'd inherited something of my dad's talent." Maybe one of their sons would, he thought to himself and smiled.

Max put his arm around Shizue. "Can we count on Yufugawo to slip you out of the lord's house so we can meet again tomorrow?"

"Yes, we'll picnic in the park together if it's a sunny day." Shizue leaned her head against his shoulder. "We'll be returning home soon. Oh, that reminds me—I've exercised Mercury. He's faster than ever, and O-nami just can't wait to see you."

"Same here." Max kissed the top of Shizue's head. "I like your haircut, but I miss seeing your pretty little ears," he teased in a whisper.

"I'll comb it up tomorrow if you like," she said, now much preferring the present to the past as Max bent down to kiss her.

Baron Hosokawa planted both elbows on Douglas Napier's study desk. He chewed the end of an extinguished cigar, one of several he had lit and half-smoked while waiting for his friend to return home. He had handled several telephone calls from women of Angela's Tokyo social set, chatting affably with them like some social secretary, excusing her on the grounds of fatigue after a long journey and promising that she would return their calls soon. Not an hour ago he had telephoned the hospital. Natsu's death had occurred at three that afternoon. He had not intruded on Douglas's grief by having him paged to the hospital phone. When Sumie died, time had stopped for him; he had refused to relinquish her corpse and vaguely remembered the doctors prying his numbed arms from his beloved, after which he lost all memory except for the unbearable pain of his grief. Now he anticipated Douglas maintaining a long vigil at Natsu's deathbed. Perhaps it would be evening before he returned home.

Earlier the baron had telephoned Lord Mitsudara, saying that family matters would keep him at the Napiers' indefinitely. To pass the time, he applied himself to the business papers Douglas had brought from Germany, since his lord would demand a thorough accounting of costs and an explanation of the master blueprints. But Tadashi's concentration was divided, and adding to his turmoil of the moment was his ignorance of engineering. His head seemed to spin as he looked at the blueprints.

As the mantelpiece clock chimed the hour, the baron sighed and put the blueprints back into their cardboard tube. Nature had created his silkworm moths, but nature had no hand in the enormous task of weaving their silk into parachutes. If Douglas went to pieces, their fortunes would be lost, for their project could not go forward without his engineering genius. Angela was sure to set off fireworks when her husband did return home, and the baron suddenly thought better of having his daughter exposed to that volatile display. Shizue's hours alone with Douglas's son in the old attic playroom must have added fuel to the fires of their infatuation, he thought, unhooking the house-phone receiver.

"Please bring Shizue downstairs," he told Max, who picked up the phone. "I want a word with you both."

He had Morita telephone for a taxi and paced the foyer until Shizue came down the staircase beside Max. "We're in the midst of a family crisis," the baron said, smiling as though his statement carried no threat. "I expect it to be resolved when Douglas returns home. In the meantime, I'll watch over things here."

Max distrusted the baron's overly pleasant facade. "When will my dad get back?"

"I have no idea," he answered, locking both hands behind his back. "There's a taxi waiting. I'm sending my daughter to the lord's house. Run along, Shizue."

"I'll ride with her," Max announced, taking Shizue's arm and not bothering to ask her father's permission.

Baron Hosokawa stationed himself at the front door as they drove off together. Actually he was relieved to have Max out of the house as well. There was a lesson to be learned from Douglas and Natsu's folly, but it was not some skeleton to be dragged out of the closet and rattled in the faces of the young. His daughter would marry Jiro Mitsudara when she came of age, and she did not require such a cruel example to make her honor that obligation. As for Douglas's son, Tadashi thought, he might benefit from a confrontation with the truth. But that was one thing his father must deal with himself.

The foyer telephone rang.

"I'll get that, Morita!" Tadashi rushed to lift the receiver. "*Moshi moshi*. Hosokawa-*san*, here. Douglas, I hoped it might be you," he addressed the slurred voice on the line. "Tragic. Natsu's death was so sudden and unexpected," the baron responded sympathetically. "Are you at the hospital?"

"The apartment." In a far less splendid ward of Tokyo, Douglas Napier drunkenly weaved across the floor, taking the telephone with him as far as the cord would reach. "Angela—what's the situation there?" he asked, only half-listening to the baron's succinct reprise of their conversation. That she knew about Natsu was a relief; that she planned to leave him did not seem to matter. "My guts are turned inside out. I'll be staying here for as long as it takes to feel something again."

"You mustn't just sit there alone with your grief," Tadashi said, his voice cracking with emotion. "Douglas, listen to me. When Sumie died, I told myself that no one else had the right to mourn her passing. I made the mistake of shutting everyone out. Even my children. But I was wrong to take it all upon myself. Of course, you need time before facing up to Angela and your son. She's taken a sedative. Max knows nothing as yet. Let me come to the apartment. It may help you to talk. Douglas, you're in no condition to look after yourself. Give me the address."

"No! I suddenly feel the need to talk, but you never really wanted to hear about this part of my life, and I don't want you here now." He paused to splash whiskey in his glass and take a drink. "I'm not alone, Tadashi. Natsu is with me. Everything we shared together here makes this sacred ground. I won't have outsiders profaning her memory by touching her things. The day I left for Germany, I held Natsu in my arms in this apartment. She pleaded with me not to abandon our son if anything should happen to her. I glimpsed her pain, but she excused it away as a mother's concern for her child. What horrible pain she must have hidden from me then. Dear God, if only I'd seen through her courageous act." Anguish over what might have been held Douglas silent while his gaze swept across the flower arrangements Natsu had placed there only that morning to welcome him home. Now they were dying, withered by the heat, their petals falling soundlessly to the floor.

Tadashi's voice through the receiver broke the silence. "Douglas, don't blame yourself. There's nothing you could have done," the baron said consolingly.

"Don't tell me I couldn't have done anything about it!" Douglas shouted. "If only I'd known she was dying—I'd have said to hell with the business and everything that went with it. I would have had a year to devote myself entirely to her. One year that would have lasted for a lifetime. God forgive me, I wasn't worthy of her love. Now it's too late. Too late even for remorse. Oh, dear God, I've lost her." Finally, Douglas began to weep. Holding the receiver against his chest, he sobbed uncontrollably until at last he had no more tears to give.

"Douglas! Are you there?"

He limply raised the receiver. "Natsu's gone from here now," Douglas whispered hoarsely. The wind bells at the open window swayed back and forth. His tears had set her earthbound spirit free, he thought. He could no longer hold her prisoner in these rooms as he had in life.

"Douglas, alcohol is a depressant," the baron said. "If you won't give me the address, at least don't try drinking yourself into oblivion," he implored. "Take a shower. Get some food in your stomach and sober up. I'll do my best to placate Angela and call you later."

"Don't want a nursemaid—or a friend," Douglas countered feebly. At last the whiskey was bringing the numbness he sought. But he had enough presence of mind to remember that the baron knew the telephone number at the apartment, a necessity in the event of some business crisis or trouble at home. "I'm leaving the receiver off the hook, Tadashi," he mumbled, and severed the connection. He stared down at the buzzing receiver, which he laid beside flowers arranged in a shallow ceramic dish. The falling petals would soon cover this buzzing annoyance, he thought, fanning his hand across the blossoms. Some petals stuck to his fingers, their sweet nectar brought back to life as he rubbed them together under his nostrils.

It was Natsu's aroma he desired, that heady combination of the scent of her skin and the fragrance of Black Narcissus. Douglas staggered to the bedroom. Sitting on the edge of the bed, he kicked off his shoes. His lover's scent still lived on these satin cases stained with her dried blood, he thought. Gathering the pillows against him, he imagined he held Natsu in his arms and passed into a drunken sleep the moment after.

Baron Hosokawa stood in the foyer of the Napier mansion, puffing on a fresh cigar. He felt frustrated. Although he had the phone number of the apartment, there was no way he could find out the address. Douglas had guarded his secret by listing the telephone under a false name. His brow creased in worry as Angela came down the staircase, a cigarette clenched tightly in the fingers of one hand.

"Douglas just telephoned," Tadashi told her. "Natsu Yoseido is dead."

"Dead," Angela responded to the news dully. The sedative she had taken made her thoughts fuzzy. "And Douglas?"

"At the apartment they shared. He's had a good deal to drink. I think he'll stay there for at least tonight, sleeping it off. He knows we've talked and asked that you be patient with him."

"Patient? Is that all he had to say?" Angela stormed into her husband's study. "That coward. Passing messages to you over the phone. Well, what's the number, Tadashi?"

The baron lifted his shoulders. "It won't do you any good. He's left the receiver off the hook, and I don't know the address."

Angela exhaled a stream of smoke at the desk telephone, then put the cigarette out. "I see. The rat's gone underground. Well, Douglas can rot in his secret love nest, as I've rotted here, making him a comfortable home to visit when he wasn't sleeping with that woman. There's no reason to stay here staring at me as if I were some helpless waif, Tadashi. Your concern is touching but a wasted effort." She gestured to the study door. "If and when I need a shoulder to cry on, I'll ring you up."

The baron met her eyes and said sadly, "I'm hurt, too, Angela. Two people very dear to me have turned away from me. You're still in shock. Acting in anger can only do further injury to yourself and others. Think what effect the past will have on your son. Max will want to know where his father is. Say that you argued and he's gone off somewhere by himself to cool down."

"Oh, now you want me to act out a lie for my son!" Angela laughed caustically. "You have a lot of nerve asking anything of me. I remember how often you made weak excuses for Douglas's tardiness at dinner parties and all those sudden overnight business trips." She gripped one forearm so tightly that her fingernails almost drew blood. "I was mistaken to excuse you on the grounds of divided loyalties. Good Lord, my husband has come and gone as he pleased based on my trust as his wife. This is entirely my affair, Tadashi, and I'll do as I damn well please with my son. I won't be manipulated by the concerns of a dynasty that's shown me nothing but deceit and contempt. Morita will see you out."

"Yes, I've outstayed my welcome. But I know how much you love Douglas, and despite what you're feeling for him now, dissolving your marriage won't come easily."

The baron watched the hardness drain from her eyes; he saw the pain there. "Angela, you can't deny your love for Douglas or turn him out just because it's been challenged," he addressed her softly. "I've nothing more to say. That's a decision only you can make."

Angela turned her back to him and nervously lit another cigarette.

Without another word the baron left the study. As he crossed the foyer, Morita hovered at his elbow. "Don't bother seeing me to the door. Look after Madame Napier and her son. If something arises that needs my attention, ring me at the lord's house immediately."

Morita bowed low. *"Hai, Danshaku-sama."*

The baron smiled. Very few Japanese still addressed the nobility in the feudal manner, showing absolute respect. After taking his hat from the ornate brass stand, the baron left the Napiers' house. He could do no more. The future of their dynasty rested on the slender shoulders of an angry woman and a grief-stricken husband who had isolated himself somewhere in Tokyo's sprawling bosom.

Angela saw the list of names that the baron had left for her on the desk pad. The women who had telephoned were quick to pass around any bit of gossip. She trusted Morita implicitly, but there were new servants in the house, and what they had witnessed could spread quickly among the help of other households.

Now waves of anger swept over her. She had already searched through her husband's steamer trunks, finding no shred of tangible evidence of his mistress. No letter tucked inside his suit pockets forgotten. No photograph carried with him to Germany as a remembrance. Natsu was nothing more than a name. How could she feel a thing about his Japanese lover's death? Angela looked down at the study desk where her husband had often conducted business. Its drawers were always kept locked. "Against the servants," he had told her. Not until that afternoon did she have reason to question his word.

Just then Morita appeared in the doorway. "Is there something I can do for the *okusama*?" he asked.

"Yes, bring me the household keys so I can unlock the desk."

"Only your husband has these keys, Madame."

Angela studied Morita's face. He had been her loyal right hand for so many years that she could not imagine his lying about the desk keys. The sturdy brass letter opener would serve her purpose.

"That will be all, Morita! Well?" she questioned when he did not leave but stood there with downcast eyes. He was sad for her, his wrinkled face creased with sympathy, but his station prevented him from speaking what he felt.

Angela mustered a smile, recalling how Morita had fawned over her when she had first arrived from America. He had patiently instructed her in the Japanese ways so she would not prove an embarrassment to her husband. She had so wanted to please Douglas then, when love had first taken her across the waters to this wretched land. Now she stood before Morita, the wronged wife, and she was touched by his moist eyes.

"I'm sorry for snapping at you," she apologized, wanting to dispense with the formalities of servant and master just to hear a few kind words. But she knew he would be embarrassed, even offended if asked to forget his place. "As always, I rely on you to keep everything here running smoothly. Tell anyone who telephones that I'm exhausted—much too busy with reopening the house to chat over the phone. I won't have a scandal disgracing my household. Somehow we must keep up appearances. For the time being, we'll simply go on as usual."

"*Hai, okusama*. Do not trouble your mind." Morita pulled out the handkerchief from the pocket of his gray pinstripe butler's apron and wrinkled his small nose while blowing it hard. "Max-*san* has gone out with the baron's daughter. When he returns, I will inform him that dinner will be served at eight. Punctually, as usual." He bowed deeply. "Shall I close the door, Madame?"

"Yes, please." Angela's eyes filled with tears. Oh, she wished Inge Karlstadt were here. Tadashi had offered her his shoulder to cry on, but she would not soon forgive his deceit, and she felt desperately in need of her only trustworthy woman friend. But pride would make it impossible to confess her husband's infidelity even to Inge. She stood in the study, alone with her fears.

Japan had become her only real home. There was nothing for her in America, where Sommersby was nothing more than an old family name remembered with respect. The Boston line had died out years ago, the grand house on Beacon Hill sold and its contents auctioned off soon after her mother's death. Love had completely uprooted her. Oceans and years removed from the Boston of her happy childhood, she had lost contact with family friends and her college sorority sisters. Correspondence between them had been reduced to a trickle of cards exchanged at Christmas—drips of water from a leaky faucet. It was as though she had never lived a past other than here, in what to her was a darkly oppressive mausoleum.

She had taken her husband's name, she thought bitterly, and all that went with their marriage vows—especially "for better or worse." Suddenly she was overwhelmed with rage. Douglas had brought her to Japan under false pretenses. Who was this Natsu? What had made her so desirable? She must find out.

Picking up the letter opener, she attacked the locks on Douglas's desk drawers. Natsu! Some evidence of that phantom lover must be hidden inside the drawers. Letters to give her a voice. Photographs to give her a face.

The locks were old and not difficult to spring after inserting the tip of the letter opener in the space between drawers. Frantically she yanked open one drawer after another, sifting through their contents with increasing frenzy. Business papers. Sketchbooks Douglas had filled with drawings of machines. Supplies. Angela dumped the contents of the drawers on the floor. Finally, she pried open the bottom drawer. Inside was a thick black leather folio.

Angela recognized it as part of a desk set she had given Douglas on his graduation from Harvard. Taking it out, she touched his initials embossed in gold leaf on its cover, remembering the pains she had taken with the clerk at an exclusive Boston shop where the folio had been custom-made. Untying its faded crimson and gold silk ribbons, she hesitated a moment. Then she opened it.

Photographs. But they were all of a boy. Angela searched in vain for another face, but she saw only Douglas's son by Natsu, as he grew from an infant into the young man who had appeared that day at the mansion. The edges of the photographs were worn from handling. Douglas must have sat there often, looking at Natsu's son, Angela thought.

Determined to find at least one photograph of Natsu, she emptied the folio's leather pockets. There was an account book. Its dated entries stretched back a number of years. Tuition fees, clothing, schoolbooks, and other academic supplies: the education Douglas had paid for was all listed in neat columns. His mistress had asked nothing for herself, she recalled Tadashi saying. Angela held the proof in her hands. That woman's son stared back at her from snapshots. He bore a great resemblance to his father—and to Max. How thoroughly Douglas had covered his tracks, she thought, except for these sentimental keepsakes. She threw them on the floor.

But as angry as Angela was, the photographs had touched a sympathetic nerve. She felt saddened at the death of this young man's mother, and she felt pity over the tortured lives Natsu and her Eurasian child must have led. And she felt utter contempt for the husband whose selfishness had allowed him to put all the tokens of his double life into this graduation present she had given him as a happy young bride.

There was a checkbook in the folio's deepest pocket. Douglas's personal account with the Mitsubishi Bank of Tokyo. All of the stubs were for checks written out to Paul for his last year of education. She might have dismissed them, but one stub flipped by that was different from the others. It was dated the summer before, made out to a Tokyo apartment hotel for one year's lease paid in advance. No address, but she could find the location of the hotel in the telephone directory.

Her husband kept a telephone directory in the study. Angela quickly turned its pages. The love nest where Douglas was in hiding seemed to jump at her from the printed page, which she ripped from the directory. Kawano Apartments. Not half an hour's drive from her home. Angela marched to the foyer. She wanted to go to his love nest and slap Douglas across the face. Then she stopped. It was beneath her to chase after her unfaithful husband. She was the injured party! He must come to her in this loathsome house, where her suffering had begun.

As she was standing there, the front doorbell rang. Perhaps it was Douglas, she thought. Suddenly she was concerned with her appearance and confronted her reflection in the foyer's gold-framed mirror. Her hair was a stringy mess, she thought, and she had wept so bitterly that her eyes were puffy and unattractive. She would not give Douglas the satisfaction of seeing her in such a ghastly state. But Morita was already opening the door.

At that very moment, Angela Napier reckoned with the most awful truth: she still loved her husband. Even after what he had done, she could not stop loving him or control the panic that was eroding the vindictiveness in her heart. Then Max walked inside.

"Forgot my keys," he said. "Is Dad home yet?"

"No." Angela had built up her hopes and felt deflated. She could only think of how badly she had been hurt and how desperately she wanted to hurt Douglas back. Their son had always enjoyed his love, and she could strike a blow at him through Max. However, she might alienate her son in the bargain—and such underhanded methods were beneath her.

She began to cry as Max questioned her about his father's absence. "You'll only hate me for telling you," she pleaded. "We argued and I don't know when we'll see him again."

"Look, whatever it is, I'm old enough to be told." Max put an arm around her shoulders. Angela was his mother, but also a woman in distress, and he took it upon himself to take care of her. "Honestly, Mother, whatever it is can't be that bad."

Angela weakened to his masculine caress and in a shaky voice said, "I'm afraid it is. But there's no way of keeping this to myself. No way of keeping up appearances, even for your sake. Come into the study. We'll talk there."

Max was stunned when he entered the study and saw the damaged desk, the overturned drawers, sketchpads, and a number of photographs scattered on the floor. "Mother, what happened?"

Angela stooped to gather up the photographs along with her courage to identify the boy in them. "Sit down. What I have to say isn't easy. Your father hasn't been honest with us. I've been hurt beyond caring, but I'll try to be understanding of your feelings."

Dropping in the red upholstered chair near his grandfather's portrait, Max grew somber. "Let's have it," he said in a resigned tone of voice much like his father's.

"Your father's had an affair with another woman. A Japanese. Natsu Yoseido." Angela struggled for some balance between the wronged wife's vindictiveness and a mother's love. She told him everything she knew. As she spoke, Angela was faced with Max's shock and his disbelief. "Paul—her son—has refused to have anything to do with your father for years. All Douglas had were these photographs of him, no doubt taken by his mother." Finally, the proof of all she had said was passed from her cold, damp hands to those of her son. Max was moved to tears.

"Oh, Max, I'm so sorry," Angela said. One betrayal did not justify another.

Max said nothing. His half brother's snapshots, the account book, the apartment house name written on a check stub, all these bits of paper spoke for the roots of his father's unhappiness. Douglas had fallen in love with a Japanese. Suddenly the lives of father and son had struck a parallel that brought Max closer to Douglas than ever before. His father was guilty of infidelity, but Max could think of nothing but his father's grief and pain. Douglas was mourning the woman he had loved since his youth, and Max could not judge his father's actions.

"There's a lot we don't know, Mother. You have only the baron's version of things. Dad hasn't had a chance to defend himself. Aren't you worried about him?"

Angela responded with a sparse nod. "God knows, I wish it were otherwise. Tadashi said he'd been drinking. He's taken the apartment phone off the hook, and I can't go to him there. It's absolutely impossible for me to do more than wait." Her manner hardened. "There are limits to what a woman will do."

Suddenly Max had been presented with a brother he had never known, and he rested the evidence of Paul's existence on the desk. The check stubs bore his brother's Japanese name, Akira Yoseido, but their father's seed was written clearly on this young man's face, altering the complexion of Max's life and promising repercussions that overwhelmed him. "Maybe I should go to Dad," he said. Confronted with Angela's vulnerability, he felt out of his element, incapable of offering her more than a young son's love. "Mother, I can't take sides between my parents. That wouldn't be fair to either of you."

"Oh, I've never felt so helpless and confused. Max, you're my baby. You're all I have."

Max was surprised when his mother reached out to hold him tightly against her. She had always been an attentive and concerned mother, but she was seldom demonstrative. He recalled standing on the ship's deck only the night before, witnessing the tense scene between his parents. Their hostility to each other and his mother's vulnerability had shocked him then. Now he knew the cause of their unhappiness, and his mother's need for his support shifted his compassion for his father to her. "Would it be easier for you if we went to Dad together?"

"Thank you for asking, but no." Angela smoothed the hair at his temples with a caring hand. "Forgive me for wanting to hurt your father through you. I know how you've looked up to him, and I wouldn't want that changed for the world. You're right not to take sides. His or mine. You're the one thing that makes all the years seem worthwhile."

Max faltered before asking, "Do you love him?"

Angela stepped back. The anguish his question brought into her eyes answered for her. Turning away, she said, "I simply can't cope with it all. Go to your father if you want, but he isn't likely to welcome an intrusion on his grief. Even from you."

Without a word, Max turned and left the room.

Angela wondered if Douglas would bar the door to his son. Perhaps he had drunk himself into a stupor, and Max would return home without talking to his father. She had unintentionally cast her son in the role of a go-between, and now she felt petty and small.

Morita was so fastidious, she thought. The glass she had hurled at Julius Napier's portrait had been swept up and the brandy wiped from his cold face. "Julius, you gloating bastard. If there is a hell, I'm sure you're roasting on the spit." Glaring at the painting, she dug her high heels into the plush pile of an antique Chinese rug. "You think you've won, that I'm trapped here for good. But you're only dust and bones."

That day a new Napier had entered the dynasty, hat in hand, Angela reflected as she walked out of the study. The covenant with tradition had been broken long ago, and she wondered if the dynasty could withstand this challenge. Seeing Morita in the hallway, Angela said to him, "I'll dine alone, Morita. I've no appetite, but one must keep up one's strength."

Given an audience of Morita and several other faithful family retainers, Angela proudly climbed the staircase to dress for dinner.

Mihoko, the kind-faced old woman who had been her personal body servant for nearly twenty years sponged Angela's delicate skin while she lounged in a deep pink-veined marble tub, staring at its gold-plated faucet that was molded into a grinning dolphin. Never speaking, the old woman gently scrubbed her mistress's feet, then helped her to step from the bubbly bath water and gently blotted her body dry with fluffy terrycloth towels. Angela vacantly went through the motions of lifting each arm to have her underarms powdered. When the servant brought Angela her pink satin robe and matching slippers, Angela shook her head, walking out of the humid bathroom to the relative cool of the master bedroom. There she sat naked before the Chippendale vanity. With a cigarette burning in one hand and a dry martini held in the other, Angela allowed Mihoko to brush her auburn hair. Not a single gray hair as yet, Angela observed.

"You may go," Angela said when Mihoko had finished. "I'll dress myself."

Setting the martini glass down, Angela put out the cigarette in an ashtray, then began rummaging through the velvet-lined traveling case that held her jewelry. She tried not to think of Douglas being with her son. Taking out a teardrop emerald necklace, she draped it around her neck and fastened a matching bracelet around her wrist. The faceted stones picked up the color in her frosty green eyes, which were less puffy after the soothing compresses she had applied.

She intended to appear at dinner looking absolutely smashing, if only to prove to herself that she could get on quite well alone, free of Douglas, an independent woman who could survive a divorce with her pride intact. If by some slim chance he did return that night, she thought, let him discover her stone cold sober and dressed to kill. The thought caused her to push the martini glass away. And then she took hold of it, experiencing a sinking sensation as she drained the glass dry. The ravaged face in the mirror belied her foolish efforts to put on a front. None of her expensive cosmetics or skillful use of them could paint over her wretchedness.

Even if she left Douglas, she would always belong to him—always be a Napier. What Angela Sommersby wanted most in life had been denied her by the randomness of fate. That night, as she sat before the mirror naked, wearing only the Napier family jewels against her creamy white skin, she felt branded by their ownership forever.

CHAPTER 12

Intermittent showers sent pedestrians running for cover as Max taxied to the Kawano Apartments. His concern for Douglas sent him hurrying from the taxi, and he bumped into the opening umbrella of a tenant who was coming out of the lobby door. Once inside, however, Max hesitated; he wasn't sure he should barge in on his father unannounced. His personal need for contact warred against Douglas's desire for solitude.

An elderly stoop-shouldered man was seated behind the lobby desk playing go with one of the tenants. There was no telephone switchboard, just pigeonholes for the mail and a rather antiquated brass intercom call box hung on one wall with buttons to buzz the apartments above. Max scanned the numbered paper nameplates that listed the occupants. Most of them were illegible, yellowed, and the ink faded by age.

"Napier-*san*'s apartment. Would you buzz it, please," Max asked the clerk who finished his moves on the go board and chuckled gleefully at his opponent's sour face. The clerk looked the visitor up and down.

"I'm Napier-*san*'s son."

The clerk knew the intercom buttons by heart, and he held the flat black listening device to his ear as he hit one button. "No reply," he said after a moment.

"Keep trying. I know he's in," Max insisted.

The incessant buzzing roused Douglas from his drunken sleep. He staggered through the dark rooms, bumping against the furniture, wanting only to silence the call box. His fingers made contact with its earpiece, and he yanked it off the hook. "Don't want to be disturbed," he mumbled.

"Your son is in the lobby," the clerk said.

"Not possible," Douglas mumbled, totally disoriented. He dropped the earpiece, leaving it dangling from its cord. Then, vaguely, he perceived Max's voice buzzing from the earpiece. How his son had found him paled against the fact that he was there. His son had come, not his wife. The earpiece spun, eluding his grasp as he heard Max ask if he was all right. Supported by the wall, Douglas spoke into the intercom. "Max—I don't know what to say."

"Dad, I'll understand if you won't see me now. Mother told me about Natsu. I just had to find out if you were all right." Max exhaled a deep breath. "I'm worried about you."

"Son—I'm very drunk." Douglas warmed to the voice that carried no animosity. *This* son had not turned against him. "Come up. Just for a few minutes. Haven't got strength to talk much." He hung up the intercom and staggered to the door. As he snapped open the lock, he began to shake all over.

Shivering and thirsty, Douglas was in no condition to make his way to the kitchen water tap, and the opened bottle of scotch on the cocktail table was empty. It pained him now to think of the deceit that had been forced upon him while he kept this half of his life a secret from Angela and her son. He noticed the telephone was still off the hook. He had used bribery to have its number listed under an assumed name, but he had been required by law to present his passport when renting the apartment some years ago. However, the hotel staff minded their own business. To them, he was just another tenant. Yes, he and Natsu had been safe here, Douglas thought—perhaps too safe, while he had promised himself a different tomorrow, which would never come to pass.

"Unlocked," Douglas called out weakly when his son knocked at the door. As Max opened it, he struggled to get to his feet. "Son, don't turn on the lights. Eyes can't take it." His speech grew ever more slurred while he fought to maintain his equilibrium. "Wrong to let you see me like this."

Douglas stumbled when Max embraced him, and Max had to hold him up. "I love you, Dad," he said, in tears. Taking one of his father's limp arms, Max put it around his neck. "Let me help you to the bed."

Douglas's head hung down to his chest. "Next room."

There was enough light coming through the windows for Max to find his way, and he sat Douglas on the edge of the bed. "Is there a kitchen where I can make you some coffee or tea?"

"Need sleep." Fighting to keep his eyelids open, Douglas tousled his son's straight blond hair. "Can't talk now. Enough you came. Enough you care."

"Dad, I'll get you undressed and spend the night here," Max said, loosening his father's belt buckle.

"No—don't want that." Douglas's hand went down on Max's, and he began to sob. "Natsu's gone. Can't talk about her now. Leave, Max. Please, go." He took hold of Max's lapel, and just for a moment he stared into his son's eyes. "Angela knows nothing. You both deserve to hear the truth. Give me a day or so. Go home. Keys. Find keys to lock the door. Do this for me, Max." Douglas fell back across the bed. "Need sleep. Finished with whiskey. I'll eat something in the morning."

Max bent over his father. He was dead to the world. Max wanted to disobey his drunken plea, but he knew that when his father woke, his state of mind was unlikely to be much different. As Max's eyes adjusted to the darkened rooms, he glimpsed enough of the tragic past to feel like a trespasser. His father had settled for this when he might have challenged tradition and won.

Max found Douglas's keys on the cocktail table, then quickly left and locked the door. The key to his father's car was also on the ring, and the elevator operator told him there was an underground garage.

Tokyo had always looked its shiny best following the summer rain, Max observed as he drove from the garage. His curiosity to know more about the past brought him to the Ginza. As he pulled up at the shuttered tea shop where Natsu had toiled as a waitress, he saw two figures in silhouette poised near the brightly lit apartment window above. He guessed that one of them was Paul. The other was a heavyset woman. Holding each other, they rocked back and forth, sharing their grief.

The tea shop's pink neon sign was dark. Max saw customers gathered outside the shuttered entrance, where a long paper banner announced its closing due to Natsu Yoseido's death. Several regulars of the shop, obviously shocked and distressed, voiced their tributes to a lady Max would never know. Natsu's loved ones vanished from the upstairs window, and he stifled his yearning to establish contact with his half brother.

Max slowly drove away, wondering what effect the past would have on his and Shizue's hopes for the future.

He steered a course for Lord Mitsudara's estate. When he had taxied there with Shizue some hours ago, they had kissed just outside the tall iron gates. Now the glass lanterns on the gates were lit, and liveried guards stood by the open entrance, admitting the limousines of the guests the lord would entertain at dinner. No one entered without a formal invitation.

Max parked at the curb and tried to see inside the gates. Lord Mitsudara had always remained aloof to the Napier family. As a child, Max had never been invited to this house with the Hosokawa children, who attended Jiro's birthday parties and other social functions. He had never even met the lord's only son. From what Shizue had told him, an undercurrent of subservience had existed in her family's relationship with Mitsudara. But it struck Max that her visits there over the past year had brought the two families closer. Sitting outside the gates, he experienced an uncomfortable feeling about the lord's increased hospitality toward nobility of a lower lineage. A man who wielded such enormous power over others was not in the habit of handing out favors without seeking something in return.

Max squinted into the gold-plated headlamps of a Rolls-Royce limousine, which cruised up to the guarded gates. He glimpsed Shizue riding with a young army cadet lieutenant. Yufugawo sat in the limousine wedged between them, the ever-present chaperone, unable to do more than turn her head in profile as Max sounded his horn. Shizue faced out the rear window and saw him seated in the open-topped car. The worn expression on his face told her something was wrong. He watched her ask Yufugawo for permission to go to him. O-nami's wife shook her head.

As the limousine cruised on through the parted gates, Jiro Mitsudara looked back through its rear window at Max. Their eyes met for the very first time. The lord's son acknowledged Max Napier with a nod, adjusted the visor of his cap with one white-gloved hand, then faced away. Max took an instant dislike to Jiro for being so good-looking and so free to enjoy Shizue's company. He stared at the closing iron gates, feeling as if the girl he loved were being confined to some forbidding institution. He decided to telephone Shizue later that night. He wanted to share his emotions with her in person, but that afternoon the baron had made a point of separating them. He was likely to restrict her movements from now on.

As Max reached home, it began to rain hard. Angela's fire-engine-red Bugatti sports car was missing from the garage, and the other cars there were covered with soiled tarpaulins, yet to be serviced by the mechanic.

Morita, his face pinched, greeted Max at the door. "Your mother left the house some time ago."

"Where did she go?" Max asked.

"Your mother did not say," he answered, taking Max's hat and shaking off the rain.

The cook had prepared dinner, but Max had no appetite and went to his room. Like his father, he was an orderly person. Unlike Kimitake's cluttered room in the Hosokawa castle, Max's room was spartan. The walls were bare except for framed prints depicting quiet forest and mountain scenes that evoked the baron's lands. He had collected these, as well as two centuries-old Japanese bronze horses, which decorated his dresser top and writing desk.

Max slipped on his old baseball mitt. That sport was very popular in Japan, and he had become an avid fan as a boy. Growing up, he had spent many hours playing sandlot baseball with his schoolmates. He had missed those sandlot games during his year away. He picked up a baseball and began hitting it into the glove, experiencing a boyish satisfaction.

Thinking back on his boyhood, he grew sentimental for the past, and leaving his room, he climbed the rickety attic stairs for the second time that day. Lamps with metal shades had been strung across the attic playroom rafters, and they cast pools of yellowish light on the floorboards. One by one, Max set his rogues' gallery of jack-in-the-boxes in motion. Their painted wooden heads bobbed on their colorful spring necks. The father whose talented hands had given life to these fanciful creatures as acts of love could be forgiven almost anything, thought Max. Then, remembering himself as the possessive child cleaving to the security offered by both his parents, he grew despondent. His parents had given him so much, while Natsu and her son were denied everything. Even when Douglas confessed his version of the past, perhaps nothing in it could justify abandoning Natsu and his other son.

Sadly, Max bid good night to the carved wooden characters, putting each to bed in the darkness of its box. At some future time their comical heads would pop out again, delighting other children. His and Shizue's. He intended to make her his bride and succeed where his father had failed. He intended to seek out Natsu's son, to bring Paul into their lives and somehow make up for the years of secrecy and neglect.

Standing in the attic surrounded by the shadows of his boyhood playthings, Max glanced down at Shizue's fingermarks traced across the dusty lid of a trunk. He raised the lid on her beautiful courtesan puppet resting between its handsome lover and its mean-faced lord and master. No matter how these puppet lovers were rearranged, the villainous lord came between them. Shizue's father was only a baron, yet his tyrannical rule over her life was like that of this feudal puppet lord. Max turned him facedown inside the trunk before slamming its lid.

Angela Napier peered through the windshield of her car at a side-street Tokyo apartment house. She had cruised past it time and again, over a period of hours, wondering if Max was there with his father or if Douglas had refused to see him. If she did lower herself by going inside, she wanted Douglas all to herself. Just coming this far had made his affair with Natsu more painfully real to her. Still, she wanted Douglas badly enough to fight for him.

She pulled the car to a stop at the lighted entranceway, then gripped the wheel with her kidskin driving gloves; she was held in the car by her sense of pride. He might be there all alone, she thought, drunk and sleeping it off in the bed he had shared with Natsu. If so, it was now his bed of grief and pain. But if she went to Douglas, not in anger but in love, she might yet win out over Natsu's memory.

Angela decisively got out of her car, then turned up the collar of her tan raincoat as she entered the summer downpour. The tiles of the apartment house walkway were slippery. She lost her balance and twisted her ankle. Straightening up, she winced in pain but continued walking toward the plate-glass lobby door. She tried to open it, but it was locked. Angela looked in on the vacant lobby, which was carpeted in a greenish color. The carpeting was worn dark in a trail that led to the elevator, where its operator sat dozing in an overstuffed chair. The dingy atmosphere put her off. She had not imagined that the love nest would be so shabby and depressing. Her finger went to the button of a night bell, but she could not bring herself to ring it. She never should have come here to have it out with Douglas, she thought, reaching down to massage her twisted ankle. What he felt for Natsu was powerful enough to bring him down in the world to this decrepit Tokyo apartment house, and she stood no chance of fighting that here, even with a magnanimous display of understanding.

She limped to the comfort of her shiny red sports car and slid into its glove-soft leather seat. Douglas had put her through hell, she thought. All day she had alternated between feeling contempt for him and love. But now she knew that she could not go to him in his apartment like some cardboard saint, willing to forgive and forget purely on the basis of her love. No! The next move was his.

Angela switched on the ignition. The engine stalled, and she lightly pumped the gas pedal as Douglas had taught her to do. He had bought the Bugatti for her one summer in Rome, and patiently taught her how to handle it while they toured the Italian countryside. Along the route to Naples she had accidentally stripped the gears and stranded them both in some backward village where livestock ran in the unpaved streets. She had burst into tears, and Douglas had taken her to him and laughed them away. He must have loved her then; he must have loved her just a little. Angela had thought there were no more tears left to shed, but she wept with the memory of that night when they made love in the sweet-smelling hay of an Italian barn. Next morning they sat in these very car seats, breakfasting on wine and cheese while horses towed them through miles of vineyards.

That was one summer in Italy not so very long ago. The summer memories of Europe outshone those wasted winters spent with Douglas in Japan, and she fought to hold on to the happy memories. But this was unromantic Tokyo, not a charming cypress-lined country road of Italy. Here the gutters overflowed with summer rain, and her tires swerved on the debris washing down the streets. She did not bother to drive to the Ginza tea shop where Natsu had shared an apartment with her lover's bastard son. Knowing more about either of them could only make things worse. Angela's curiosity ended at the love nest.

She was out of cigarettes and crushed the empty pack, then flung it out the car window. Her mother had abhorred women who smoked. That same mother had reared her with a demonstrative affection she herself had withheld, perhaps jealously, from the son who enjoyed all his father's love. Well, we are what we are, she thought. If it came to a custody suit, Max was now of age to choose the parent he would live with. She risked losing both her men.

Tadashi had been so sensitive when they spoke on the telephone before she drove to the apartment house. He had suggested a trial separation as an alternative to a clean break and had become agitated when she informed him that she had told Max of his father's infidelity and that her son's sympathies were with Douglas. All this, she said, was unlikely to discourage Max's designs on Shizue. Then the baron had quietly stated his intention to put a stop to things.

Before learning of Douglas's deceit, Angela would have sided with Tadashi. All at once she had become furious with the baron for meddling. "You're no better than Julius Napier," she had rattled back at him over the line. "Oh, you can forbid Shizue to see my son. The poor dear child will obey you, I'm sure. But that won't stop our children from loving each other. Both of them will be irreparably damaged as a result of the hold you enjoy over your defenseless daughter."

Perhaps there could never be happiness between lovers of different races, thought Angela, as she honked the car horn, warning some pedestrians who were hurrying across the street. A beautiful young Japanese woman and her lover fled across her headlight beams. She was like Sumie's ghost, Angela thought. The baron's wife had been her only Japanese woman friend in all these years. She and Sumie had been like sisters.

As Angela drove toward the Tokyo hills, past quiet mansions, she thought about the women who resided within. Women were soft and scented creatures, she mused, who comforted their men after arduous play with the adult toys of politics and industry. To Angela, a woman's concept of time was charted by the motions of her man: waiting to be held, waiting to hear his words of love, waiting to share the hours of her day spent apart from him. A woman's concept of place and her sense of belonging was focused on her man's ever-constant presence in her life. And when Douglas had not been with her, his presence still ruled her sense of time and place. Her sense of belonging.

Like Sumie Hosokawa, Angela had cared for her husband, had placed his comforts and those of their child before her own. But unlike the baron's happily married wife, she had only been a partner to a husband who led a double life.

Angela wondered if Natsu had loved Douglas as much as she. If so, she could only pity the woman; her final year must have seemed an eternity of waiting.

Angela could not bring herself to return to the Napier mansion. She drove past it and took the turns of the winding hillside roads at breakneck speed. She had no idea how long she drove, but when the needle of the dashboard temperature gauge shot to the red danger mark, she finally eased up on the accelerator and headed back toward home.

As she pulled into the driveway, Angela noticed that her husband's sleek gray Duesenberg was parked in the garage. Had Douglas returned, or had Max driven the car back after visiting his father? she wondered. Angela got out of the Bugatti and limped to the front door.

Morita had waited up for her. "Is my husband at home?" Angela asked.

"No, the *dannasama* is not here," Morita replied. His kind eyes searched Angela out for news of Douglas. She shook her head. "There's nothing more to be done tonight. Go to bed, Morita."

The first Napier wife had still been alive when Morita came to serve the household. Angela had never met Grandmother Louise, whose travails had made her into a white-haired recluse bound to her bed. The second Napier wife brought here from America had not fared much better. And now, Angela reflected, she was the third victim in line. After bidding Morita good night, she climbed the stairs to her son's room.

Angela looked in on her sleeping son. Max had kicked the bed covers off. In some ways he was still the boy Douglas had nightly tucked into bed with a kiss on the forehead. Poor Max, caught in the middle between his parents. Angela decided it was unfair to wake him and ask questions about his father. She went to her empty bed, which had already been turned down by her servant. A Parisian nightgown lay on the bed. Morita had seen to it that yellow tea roses were arranged in the antique vases, and sticks of sandalwood incense, Douglas's favorite, were left burning to chase out the musty odor of rooms shuttered up for a year. Suddenly she imagined her husband making passionate love to Natsu. She remembered how often he had turned away from her advances, and she thought of all those nights she had spent here alone, while another woman slept in her husband's arms. That night Angela would have traded away every single luxury she enjoyed to exchange places with Douglas's tea maid, if only for a single night of bliss.

She refused to feel sorry for Douglas. Regardless of what he had to say for himself, he had quite plainly been the architect of his own destruction. Angela lay down across the bed, the ire aching in her bones. Folding one arm across her eyes, she began to sob.

Retiring to his guest room at Lord Mitsudara's house, Baron Hosokawa was also besieged by concerns. After dinner, his lord had sifted through the account sheets and blueprints his chauffeur had collected at the Napier mansion. An incident that had taken place in China some days before had encouraged the lord's belief that war was imminent. Twice, shots had been exchanged between Chinese and Japanese forces at the Marco Polo Bridge. The Chinese general Sung Chi-yuen, commander in chief of all Chinese forces in North China, and General Gun Hashimoto, commander of the Japanese garrison there, enjoyed a friendship that had so far kept this incident from destroying the flimsy peace erected after Japan had seized Manchuria several years before. But Lord Mitsudara was confident that these friendly generals could not hold their troops at the gates of peace much longer. He had demanded Douglas Napier's attendance at a business conference early the next morning so the master blueprints could be put into effect, preparing the Japanese weaving mills to profit from the likelihood of war.

Baron Hosokawa pacified his lord by simply stating the truth: marital strife between Angela Napier and her husband would make Douglas unavailable for business. Naturally, the cause behind it was private, not to be spoken of. There were times of personal crisis in every man's life that must be waited out, the baron had said.

"Time lost is money lost," Lord Mitsudara had said angrily. He enjoyed no power over Douglas Napier other than the terms of his loan, but he needed this man's talent, or he stood to lose millions, and he was not in the habit of being made to wait by anyone.

The lord held the marriage bond as sacred. Divorce for a Japanese was unthinkable. Lord Mitsudara was above being touched by any scandal that might take place in Tokyo's western community, and he had curtly suggested to the baron that Douglas put his troubled household in order promptly and get back to work.

Baron Hosokawa set his own mind at rest knowing his aggrieved friend would eventually honor his business commitment. But there was one problem the baron intended to deal with and eliminate that night.

A short time before, having gone to Shizue's room, he had been held outside the closed door by what he overheard of her telephone conversation with Max. He might have barged into her room, but Douglas's son had already dragged Shizue into the past and so Baron Hosokawa had exercised a father's prerogative by listening in on another phone. Hearing Shizue speak words of love to Max was painful to his ears. The baron realized that neither Shizue nor Max had been shocked to their senses by the revelation of the tragic past, and he felt it was his responsibility to set his daughter straight.

As the baron changed into his dressing gown, he recalled how well Shizue got on with Jiro Mitsudara that evening at dinner. He was more certain than ever that her happiness would be served by the binding marriage agreement he had entered into with his lord. He had not seen fit to tell Douglas of this. No, this was a father's private affair, shared only by the lord and his son, who were sworn not to breathe a word of it to Shizue. His daughter lacked the wisdom to know what was best for her, he thought. Years hence she would thank him for striking such a perfect match.

He crossed the hallway to Shizue's guest room and knocked. "Shizue?"

"Come in, Papa." Shizue was sitting up against the pillows, her knees raised to hold an open book of poems. She looked sadly at her father, who seated himself at the foot of her bed. "I know you're cross with me for the way I kissed Max," she said, closing the book. "I've been expecting a lecture on my obligations."

"There's no need of that, since you know them so well," he answered, smiling. "I'm not cross with you, Shizue. I'm disappointed. You should know that I listened in on your telephone conversation with Max."

Shizue lowered her knees and reached for her handkerchief on the night table. "*Ogisan*, it's all so sad."

"Death is always reason for sadness." He doted on being called "papa," and as he looked at Shizue, he saw her as the child she once was. Years ago he had been able to make her laugh by lifting her in his arms for a ride into the sky. How her laughter had blessed him then. Now the child and the young woman faced him tearfully, inseparably one and the same. Baron Hosokawa responded in a gentle manner. She had been taught well, and there was no need for a display of strength on his part. "I bear no animosity toward Natsu or her son," he told her. "My sympathies are with those who were hurt by this tragedy. It may dissolve a marriage, but life goes on. Our families will survive."

"I wept for Natsu as if she were my dearest friend. I love Max." Shizue felt her heart pounding up in her throat as she confessed her love for Max to her father for the very first time. "We're deeply in love, and I'm torn between you, Papa."

"Max is a fine young man, but I'm the father who brought you into the world, and that carries an obligation your mother would have shared with me now, had she lived. Sumie would be sitting here with me on your bed, smiling as she always did in times of strife." Baron Hosokawa folded both hands across his lap to display the gold signet ring stamped with his family crest. Japanese men were not given to wearing jewelry, but Sumie had given him the ring on their wedding night, a token of their vows, and he had never removed it. "I don't stand alone between you and this love you profess for Douglas's son. No, everything you are and were taught to be stands with me. All this is what tears you between a father and a lover not of our race. Natsu Yoseido was a young lady of breeding who defied her father by turning from the ways of our ancestors. The consequences were a lifetime of torment and a son torn between two races. Love isn't all passion and romance, Shizue. Marriage is children, and no amount of love given a child of mixed blood can spare that child the cruelty of others." He searched her eyes a moment, then asked, "Would you have such a child on your conscience?"

She answered without hesitation. "If it were Max's child, yes." Her father was so soft-spoken, smiling when she had anticipated his anger. All her resolve was melting away as he just sat there giving her a patient smile. She had expected him to call her a child, to insist that the love she felt was only transitory, an early blossom that would wither with the passing seasons. Confronted by his gentleness, Shizue was at a loss for words. "I can't give up all hope," she said at last, caught in the undertow of her obligations. "Papa, the past doesn't change how I feel toward Max. If only you gave your blessings, we'd be happy, I know. You've never denied me anything."

"That's so. Except for this one thing. Don't deceive yourself by thinking the world is any different from that which shunned Natsu." Shizue began to cry. "Now, now," he hushed, rising to embrace his daughter. "It's difficult for me to end your dreams. Trust me to know what's best for my little girl. Max is older than you—nearly a man. I'm afraid he's acting irresponsibly by encouraging your hopes, just as his father did to poor Natsu." Tenderly stroking her hair, the baron heaved a sigh. "I'm afraid that I must forbid you to see him again."

Willful and defiant now, Shizue pushed him away and sat up shivering against the pillows. "I won't be forbidden. I'm a woman, not a child. How can you pretend to love me and be so cruel?"

"A father's act of love can often seem cruel to one so young." Baron Hosokawa's concern extinguished the brief flare of anger that Shizue had heard in his voice. "I thought I knew my daughter. This defiance is something I've come to expect from your brother. Shizue, I've spoken to you from my heart. I don't wish to be your jailer, nor do I wish to punish you for disobedience, but I must act in your best interests. I've been forced to punish Kimitake so many times, but never out of cruelty. The gods know, it's hurt me more than it has him." Perplexed, he once again sat at the foot of her bed, weighing his next words. "Being a parent is a trying vigil, and perhaps a thankless task. Forgotten when the fledglings leave their nest. Some leap rashly over the edge only to take a hard fall testing their wings. What sort of father would I be if I didn't gently nudge you back into the nest? You say you're a woman. Perhaps so. Perhaps I'm guilty of wanting to prolong the childhood of my little girl. Perhaps the time has come to treat you as a woman."

"Oh, yes, Father!" Shizue thought he was softening to her cause and wrapped both arms tightly around her upraised knees. "I'll do anything you say. Only promise to give some thought to my happiness."

"So like your mother when we were betrothed. I've only your happiness in mind, Shizue." Tadashi suddenly felt exhausted as he went to cup her beautiful face between his hands. "Have you really outgrown childhood? Yes, I think so. We'll talk of this again in the morning." The baron turned and walked to the door.

"Oh, I can't possibly sleep," said Shizue, bounding off the bed to hold her father there. "Papa, I love you so much. Please don't forbid me to see Max."

"Shizue, your persistence leaves me no choice," Tadashi said, soberly meeting her anxious eyes. "I might have come to you in anger, as the threatening, outraged father intent on laying down the law. But that law is in your blood and bone. As surely as you are my daughter, you are a Hosokawa and a samurai. So, it serves no purpose to raise my hand and voice to you. Tradition must be served, and I'll hear no further arguments to the contrary. Now, give me your hands. I have something to say that's important to your future."

"Father?" She questioned his look of firmness while his touch on her hands remained gentle.

"You are the most precious thing in my life. But even if I loved you less, my duty would be the same. I've chosen you a suitable husband. I've pledged you in marriage to Lord Mitsudara's son. And so, these feelings for Douglas's son must be forgotten."

"No, it can't be true!" Shizue stared up at him, her eyes blazing. She had suspected this all along but had always pushed it from her thoughts. Horrified, she watched her father's lips move but was deaf to his voice. Her life was suddenly no longer her own. He had pledged her into the slavery of a loveless marriage. How she wanted to hate him for that. But she could only shake her head back and forth, knowing it would do no good to defy him with her screams even if she could find her voice. Deaf and dumb, she felt his hands let hers go. Sobbing uncontrollably, she ran to throw herself facedown across the bed.

"There, you'll find love with Jiro. I firmly believe that your happiness lies with him."

Her father attempted to console her, but Shizue only wept more bitterly. Then she heard the door to the adjoining bedroom squealing open on its hinges.

"Little one," Yufugawo said, reaching out her arms and hugging her.

Years ago her father had called upon Yufugawo to mother her, and Shizue clung to the woman now, like the child who had once fallen at play and scraped her knees. But her long braids had been sheared off; the umbilical cord had been severed. She had professed to be a woman in love, not this sniveling child who sobbed for her papa to take back the awful thing he had said. "Father, you can't mean it. You haven't given me away."

"You're still my little girl, Shizue," he reassured her softly. "The marriage agreement won't be honored until you come of age. Go to sleep. Everything will look brighter in the morning." The sleeves of his dressing gown rustled while Baron Hosokawa stood at the open door to the hallway, gesturing for Yufugawo to come to his room. "When she's calmed down," he whispered, then walked away.

"Oh, go away!" Shizue protested to Yufugawo. "I just want to be left alone to die."

The woman drew back, wounded. "Such talk."

"Go and tell Father that I'd prefer to die!"

After Yufugawo left, Shizue hugged a mound of pillows, convinced no other woman on earth had ever known such suffering. All at once she held the tragic past responsible for this nightmare, and she began beating the pillows with her fists, growing more desolate with each useless blow. She had been forbidden ever to see Max again. Surely her father was telling this to Yufugawo at that very minute and the woman would obey his edict.

Her tormented thoughts now revolved around what Max had told her about the past. Natsu was a far more courageous woman than she had proved to be that night. Natsu had defied her father, had defied tradition, bravely enduring every hardship imposed on her because of her love for Douglas Napier. But the woman had been pregnant with his child. Their love had been consummated, and bearing that child had strengthened Natsu's conviction.

Shizue got up from her bed. For a fleeting moment she thought of giving her virginity to Max, conceiving his child out of wedlock to break the marriage agreement. She knew, though, that the loss of face to her father would ultimately destroy her love for Max. She glared back at her tear-streaked face in the mirror. She was fatally bound to her teachings. This was a nightmare she would not wake from in the morning.

Shizue picked up the telephone to cry her heart out to Max. But he was helpless as well; it would do no good weeping to her lover over the phone, she thought, and cradled the receiver. Suddenly she realized something that made her feel better: time was on her side. The marriage agreement would not be honored for years. A real woman would not be whimpering over her fate, defeated and resigned to losing Max without a fight. A real woman would be more resourceful, she told herself, using the time to come up with a solution.

She assumed a courageous pose before the mirror and confronted the young noblewoman in her looking glass. The mirror never lied, she thought. It reflected exactly what it saw. She was a Hosokawa and a samurai. Her ancestors were not given to displays of weakness—nor to losing. She put a robe around her shoulders, then quietly slipped downstairs to the household *kami-dana*.

The *kami-dana* was an altar to the gods. Many Japanese homes had these high shelves on which a miniature Shinto shrine was placed for private worship. These wooden shrines were set up either in the garden or in a clean, quiet corner of the house. Its size and the number of sacred objects on display varied according to the head of the household's faith and finances.

Lord Mitsudara's shrine was quite large and decorated with tiny lanterns, a traditional mirror, and sprigs of the sacred *sakaki* tree, which were placed in delicate porcelain vases on either side. A talisman of the Grand Shrine of Ise was placed vertically within the shrine. There were also talismen for the guardian *kami*. On another shelf below the *kami-dana*, talismen for the Mitsudara ancestral spirits were kept in a box. Since dirt was an evil disliked by the gods, the altar place was kept spotlessly clean.

Shizue approached the lord's *kami-dana* feeling in harmony with her surroundings. In all the house, only this room devoted to private worship seemed free of Lord Mitsudara's chilling presence. One could always call upon the gods for help and strength. Using the cedar ablution basin, Shizue washed her fingers and dried them with a slip of white paper that she took from a box beside the silk floor pillows. Fresh fruit was delivered to the house daily, and she reverently placed a ripe plum on the shelf as her offering to the *kami*. Then, seating herself on a pillow, she bowed in silence, recalling the words of the prayer Sumie Hosokawa had taught her. "Like the willow, I must bow to the wind, but always so with dignity. No less a samurai than my brother, at birth I was blessed with the deeper dimensions only a woman can know."

Bowing in silent prayer, she asked the *kami* to guide her innermost thoughts and make her wise beyond her years. Then wisdom came to her as a faint whisper. Her emotions had been too easily manipulated; she had tried to fight her father's will by falling back on tears, when she should have stood up to him with dignity. Shizue bowed twice, and twice clapped her hands to acknowledge the *kami* presence. The illumination she asked of them was to be found within herself, she decided. That night her heart had ruled over her good judgment, and she must not allow it to do so again. In order to have her heart's desire, she must gain control over her emotions and put her intelligence to work.

Yufugawo was waiting in her bedroom, but Shizue did not question her surrogate mother. Her father had made his intentions perfectly clear. Now she would exercise her womanly right to prove difficult. She would simply refuse to leave her room, refuse to have her emotions dictated to, and would sit there meditating until she found the insight to deal with them. Her father could not punish her more than he already had, and she grimly set her jaw, determined to stage a show of strength and not to speak a word about this awful pledge to Max over the telephone.

"I knew nothing of this marriage pledge until tonight, child." In tears, Yufugawo clasped the bodice of her robe. "I was ignorant of the past as well until your father confided this to me just now. Ah, your heart is wounded, I know. But time heals all wounds."

"It isn't so!" Shizue dropped across her bed. "Father's never stopped mourning my mother, and there can never be another woman for him. I think he's forgotten what it is to be young and in love." Yufugawo bent to stroke Shizue's hair as the young woman fought against giving in to tears. "Dear Yufugawo, there's a generation between us. I can't make you see how wrong Father is, chaining me to Jiro Mitsudara for the rest of my life. If I can't reach his heart, then I'll defy him. Otherwise, Max will marry someone else, and we'll both spend the rest of our days apart—wanting each other. And all because I'm a Japanese."

Yufugawo had no answers, only love for this woman-child who was like her own flesh and blood. "You and Max have grown up like twin vines linked around a single tree, child," she said. "Max is rooted deeply beside you in the soil of our lands. Uprooting one vine will surely cause the other's leaves to rust. But the gods have always favored you, little one. Place your trust in them."

Shizue sat up and hugged the woman tightly. "Oh, you feel as I do. Loving Max is so natural and right. If only Father would open his heart to me as you just have."

"My heart has always been open to you, Shizue. Sleep here in my arms as you once did. Shall I sing you a lullaby?"

"Yes. Rock me to sleep one last time." Feeling her eyelids grow heavy, Shizue rested in Yufugawo's arms. "The marriage pledge has ended my childhood. Tomorrow I'll come of age before my years."

"Perhaps it is so." O-nami's wife crooned a lullaby from their ancestral lands, observing how angelic Shizue looked as she gave in to sleep. Yufugawo reflected that as a child the baron's daughter often woke in the night crying out for her mother. But it was she, Yufugawo, who came to rock her back to sleep. Perhaps childhood had ended for her. Still, a mother's vigilant care was unending.

When she was sure Shizue was asleep, Yufugawo gently lay her down on the pillows. She made sure a light was burning and then left the door to her connecting room open as she had always done.

CHAPTER 13

Douglas Napier felt chilled as he woke, alone. He reached out across the bed sheet, his fingertips stroking the smooth satin, with only the memory of Natsu's silky skin to remind him of her passing. He had lost all track of time, and now he struggled to his feet, his mouth dry, the clothes he had slept in foul-smelling and damp with sweat.

In the kitchen he brewed green tea. Max had visited him again. Was it yesterday? No matter. He sighed as he carried the teapot to the dining alcove, where he sat at the table. Max had hoped to draw him out about the past, but Douglas had sat as now, withdrawn and remembering, while Max spoke of his mother, who was too proud even to telephone her husband here. Douglas could not breach the chasm between them by simply lifting the receiver. He saw himself as a man balanced midway on a high wire, teetering at the point of no return. Behind him lay the void created by Natsu's passing; ahead were only the broken pieces of his tempestuous marriage.

So he remained in limbo, crippled by a feeling of dislocation as he uncapped his fountain pen and sat reading over what he had so far managed to set down in a letter to Angela. His letter was not merely some painfully expressed apology written to spare him an ugly scene. He made no attempt to garner her sympathy or to offer evidence in his defense. The words so painfully strung together on paper were an outpouring of all the things he had thought and felt but had not been free to say to her until now.

Douglas began to write again, baring his soul on paper. Although his grief and guilt were not lessened, he experienced a gradual catharsis, as each new line brought him closer to the damning truth about himself. He had no right wallowing in self-pity for having failed Paul and the woman he loved; he could not erase the wrongs suffered by the dead. Paul might never forgive him, and Douglas's need for atonement was focused on the wife who might offer him redemption. Perhaps Angela would feel even greater contempt for him not speaking these words to her in person; perhaps he could not rebuild his life with her on any terms. Resting his pen, Douglas saw Natsu dying in his arms, imploring him not to live in the past, not to put himself through torture over things that could never be.

Someone knocked at the door. Max had the key, and Douglas had forbidden the hotel maids to enter. If it was Angela— He ran both hands through his unkempt hair. "Who is it?"

"Yoko."

Douglas opened the door, and Yoko froze, shocked by Douglas's appearance. He looked like a derelict one would hurry past on the street. The apartment reeked of him and of rotting food. Yoko looked to the kitchen, where the meal she had been preparing for his homecoming still sat on the counter swarming with flies.

"I telephoned you last night. Do you not remember?" she asked, entering the apartment and closing the door behind her. "The burial is tomorrow." Douglas's face was pasty gray, and there was no emotion whatsoever in his voice as he asked where Natsu's funeral would take place. "Our Lady of Mercy Cemetery in Kichijoji. The services will be in the chapel there. Some months ago I assisted Natsu in making arrangements for this day. *Hai*, she wished to spare you and her son the added grief of attending to such matters," said Yoko. "Natsu instructed me of her last wishes, and I have come for her things."

Douglas followed Yoko to the bedroom closet, bowing his head as the woman brought out one of Natsu's embroidered silk kimonos and matching house slippers. They held memories of their nights spent together in the apartment.

"Natsu wanted to be dressed in these, and I was to fix her hair with the ivory hairpins you gave to her." Yoko laid the clothes across a chair, then went to open Natsu's jewel box, searching for the hairpins. Suddenly she looked up, covering her mouth with both hands as she recoiled from the memory of Natsu lying on the bathroom floor.

Yoko walked into the bathroom. Nothing there had been touched since the day of Natsu's death, and tears rolled down Yoko's cheeks as she stooped over the glass shards of the shattered crystal perfume decanter and picked up the ivory hairpins. "She wanted to be scented with your favorite perfume," the woman sobbed. She could not recall ever seeing a label on the perfume decanter. "I do not know the name," said Yoko, rising to question Douglas with her tearful eyes.

"Black Narcissus. French." He brought the money clip from his trouser pocket. "Go to the Sato perfume shop near the Imperial Hotel. I often bought it for her there."

Yoko shook her head angrily. "I want nothing from you." Just then she felt the small hairs rise at the nape of her neck. She strongly sensed Natsu's presence here, judging her, and quickly put out a hand to accept Douglas's money. "Natsu wished for her remains to be viewed at the cemetery chapel," she said. "The viewing will begin there at ten in the morning." She walked into the bedroom and carefully bundled Natsu's clothes in the folded cloth *furoshiki* she had brought with her.

"I want to remember Natsu as she was," said Douglas, following her.

"Then come for the mass at noon. Her coffin will be sealed."

"Paul will resent my presence. I don't want her funeral turned into a battleground. It's a sacrifice Natsu would understand," he added hoarsely.

"This son Natsu leaves behind can never grant you what is not in his heart to grant. But respect for the dead will hold his tongue. Douglas, you must come." Yoko touched his arm, moved to forgive the past. "You were Natsu's happiness and her sorrow. She freely chose her path and is beyond sorrow now. Her spirit will not find rest unless you stand beside her son at the grave."

He nodded. "How is Paul getting on?"

"I cannot speak for him." Yoko's coarse red hands tightened around her cloth bundle as she gazed at the other personal effects of her friend. Silk kimonos, lace negligees, satin slippers, tortoiseshell brushes and combs. One year ago, when Yoko had arrived to take Natsu to the hospital, Natsu had scented herself with her lover's perfume to feel Douglas near her and had dressed in one of the outfits suited to the station to which she was born. "Even in her pain, Natsu maintained her dignity," Yoko said. "While you shut yourself up with her ghost, Paul has run away. I am alone. He moved out two days ago, taking none of his mother's things from the apartment—just his clothes and the books he had collected over the years. Your other son visited the shop only this morning. He wanted to see Paul and pleaded with me for his brother's address. I pretended ignorance. I say, let the gods decide if these two should meet. Ah, I will not return here again." With one hand she wiped the tears from her cheeks. "It is for you to dispose of these things." Yoko sighed mournfully, then let herself out the door.

Douglas carried the jewelry box to the dining alcove table, where he sat laying out the contents of the box. Angela was diamonds, emeralds, and rubies. Natsu was tortoiseshell combs, jade, silver, and delicate gold pieces. With their gracefulness and charm, these gifts suited her. Without her to wear them, however, they were lackluster and cold. Meaningless objects except for the poignant memories they stirred. He decided that after the funeral he would not return for Natsu's belongings.

It struck him that no one owned anything. People just borrowed objects for the term of their lives—such as these rooms he had leased. Another occupant would follow, new paint would be applied to the walls, and their old memories would be covered up. Then what he and Natsu shared here would cease to exist. The objects he had given Natsu had no importance; the memories did.

Douglas put the jewelry back into the box, then finished writing his letter to Angela, which he put into an envelope and sealed. Another day shifted into evening while Douglas sat in silence, thinking about his sons, what bearing they might have on each other's lives, his obligations to them both. He did not hear Max enter the darkened apartment, and he was startled when Max turned on the lights.

"Dad, how long are you going to just sit here in your own filth?"

Max received no answer. His father stared fixedly at an envelope on the dining table, and Max felt compelled somehow to bring him out of his grief. "See here, I'm going to take charge. A bath, a shave, and a good meal are what you need," he insisted. "While we're out, I'll have the maids clean up here. I'm going to look after you until you're ready to come home."

Douglas managed a smile. "I'm touched by your concern. Sit down, Max. You've been patient with me and we'll talk now. I want to tell you about Natsu."

Max pulled out a chair and asked anxiously, "Are you up to this?"

"Yes." Standing the sealed envelope on end, Douglas observed how fat it was with words meant for Angela's eyes alone. What was owed his wife and what was owed their son were two different things. If he could spare Angela anything, it was the poignant remembrances of his long-enduring love. Max regarded him with a straightforward, rather boyish eagerness.

"I've already passed judgment on myself, son. Given my circumstances, you might have reacted differently, but it's over and done with now. Hindsight is worthless. All my guilt and remorse fit neatly in one hand." Douglas weighed the letter in a hand made steady by having unburdened his conscience on paper. "This letter to your mother is my first step toward bringing the past to a close," he said. "Writing everything down seemed the best way to set the record straight. It will give your mother time to reflect on things I couldn't possibly express in a shouting match. There's been enough misunderstanding between us." He put the envelope aside and got to his feet. "I'm worn out and restless. A nasty combination. Would you like a drink? Whiskey on the cocktail table."

Max removed his hat and put it on the table. "No, thanks. Tell me about Natsu."

"Where to begin," Douglas wondered aloud, rolling his sleeves up another notch as the memories unraveled to lead him back through time. "I first saw Natsu at Baron Hosokawa's castle. The gardens were decorated for a feast to celebrate his father's forty-second birthday, his *yakudoshi*, and his family and close friends had gathered there to honor him." His hand played against the wind bells. Then Douglas pressed his fingers to his weary eyes. The past vividly took shape in his mind, and he no longer heard the sound of his own voice unfolding his story that had begun in the castle garden.

"Natsu was sitting with a group of girls under an old nettle tree. They were singing songs to entertain their host. Natsu was so very lovely, I simply couldn't take my eyes off her, and she sensed me staring. When the singing ended, she glanced my way. The other girls all giggled behind their fluttering fans, but Natsu kept her fan in her lap. She smiled, not in the least bit shy. My knees felt weak as I started to approach her. In those days the conventions were strictly observed. To speak to a young lady of her social standing without a proper introduction was unthinkable. Still, I just had to learn her name and find out where she lived so that I could see her again.

"Suddenly her fan went up as a warning signal. Her mother crossed the garden. 'Natsu,' she said, 'your father received a business cable, and we must leave for Nagasaki at once.'

"On that afternoon, Natsu outdazzled the spring flowers blooming along the garden path. My whole world had been changed by a glance. A smile. I knew this was love. And without exchanging a single word, I knew that Natsu loved me too. I followed her into the crowd of guests, where her father stood conversing with his host, who addressed him as 'Yoseido-*san*.'" Here Douglas paused, remembering Raisuke Yoseido as a tyrannical figure of a man. "Natsu dared to sneak a backward glance at me, then vanished under the shade of her mother's bamboo umbrella. This glance didn't escape her father's notice. Obviously he saw how lovestruck I was, and he gave me a murderous look, then turned and hurried Natsu and his wife aboard a horsedrawn carriage. It was clear that he didn't welcome my attraction to his daughter. But nothing could stop me from seeing her again. As I watched her carriage leave, I felt heartbroken."

As Max listened, he removed his suit jacket and hung it across the chair back. "Later, I checked the guest list," Douglas continued, totally immersed in the past. "Natsu's parents lived in Tokyo. I copied down the address. That was in the spring of 1914. I was your age. Natsu was not quite seventeen."

In his mind's eye, Douglas saw himself as a young man Max's age—a strapping blond, blue-eyed youth who was helplessly in love with a Japanese. "I knew what I was up against from the start. Natsu's parents would reject me if I formally approached them asking to court their daughter with the intention of marriage." With a deep sigh, he settled on the sofa, and Max moved from the dining alcove to sit beside him. At that moment Max was to Douglas just a vague presence set apart from his vivid remembrances. Douglas saw himself as he had looked in the spring of 1914, wearing a striped blazer and a straw boater hat, waiting outside the gates of Raisuke Yoseido's magnificent house in Tokyo.

Douglas picked up the thread of his story. "Natsu's father owned a fleet of merchant ships. His daughter led a guarded existence, schooled by private tutors and bound to her home by the strict conventions imposed upon young ladies of her class. Even if I were a Japanese, I couldn't just knock at her door asking to see her. Her father would have been outraged and would have slammed the door in my face.

"And so, day after day I waited near the gates to the Yoseido house, hoping for just a glimpse of Natsu. Finally, my patience was rewarded. How my pulse raced as she stepped gracefully through the open gates chaperoned by her spinster aunt. Natsu's eyes rested on me for an instant. They showed delight, love, and hope. I followed the two women at a proper distance, building up my courage.

"The elderly aunt had eyes in the back of her head. All at once she turned and confronted me. I pleaded my cause. The woman could tell how much in love I was with her niece, who now pleaded with her as well just for an afternoon together."

This memory brought a fleeting smile to Douglas's face. "As it happened, this kind-faced but rather homely woman was a romantic at heart. That spring afternoon was the first of many that Mr. Yoseido's older sister allowed us. Having never had a suitor, she found pleasure in assisting her niece's bid for happiness, and she grew ever more permissive.

"One rainy spring day, we took shelter inside a tea shop on the Ginza, and it became our meeting place from then on. All that spring and into the first weeks of summer, we met at the Cherry Blossom Kissaten. Its proprietress and her young daughter, Yoko, took a fancy to us. Natsu's aunt would remain there chatting with Yoko's mother, while we were free to go off together."

In his mind, Douglas roamed the Tokyo of yesteryear with his arm wound tightly around Natsu's slender waist. "During those hours we spent alone, we realized how deeply in love we were." Douglas's voice lifted softly, filled with the wonder of those remembered afternoons. "We wanted to be married, but we knew our parents would never permit that, and we'd be prevented from meeting again if they found out. To make things worse, we knew that when the summer ended, I'd leave Japan to attend Harvard, and we would be separated for years.

"We were dizzy with love for each other." Douglas was suddenly aware of the son who sat beside him, desperate to hear it all. "What is there to say? Our hearts took control. It was a rainy afternoon when we climbed the stairs to the apartments above the tea shop. We had nowhere else to go, and Natsu felt as I did. Our thoughts were only of each other. The world around us ceased to exist and we . . ."

Douglas never finished. The rapt expression on his son's face threatened to disperse the phantoms conjured up from that long ago day, and Douglas slumped back against the sofa, closing his eyes, reliving a moment in time that belonged only to him and Natsu.

He would never speak to anyone of his memory of consummating their love in the cozy sitting room above the tea shop. Douglas remembered the urgent movements of Natsu's loins and the silken texture of her lips caressing him. His eyelids fluttered. There was no pain, only pleasure in the memory. He wanted it never to end; he wished to remain suspended forever in this unending dream of love.

The blast of car horns on the street below interrupted his reverie. "Dad?"

He felt Max's hand gripping his shoulder, calling him back to reality. "I seem to have lost the thread," Douglas said, pressing his son's arm.

"Please, help me up. My legs are like rubber." He leaned on Max for strength, aged by grief.

"Maybe you should lie down," Max suggested, his voice cracking.

"No, no, I've been flat on my back too long." Douglas crossed to the bedroom by himself. He paused before the bedroom closet and caressed Natsu's garments, holding the material to his face while the past came alive again as if woven into the scented silk threads.

Max stood in the doorway. "From what you've said about Natsu's aunt, she was very much like Yufugawo," he ventured.

His father nodded. "She encouraged us to take our happiness. 'Your parents gave you life. Life is to be lived, not sacrificed to their old ways,' she told us.

"We decided to marry without our parents' consent," said Douglas, finding it hard to speak of events that had caused him so much pain. "Natsu's devout aunt knew a Buddhist priest, a kind old man who agreed to perform the ceremony in the back room of the tea shop. In another week I'd sail for America, and we had to act quickly.

"Natsu was pregnant, but I didn't know of this at the time. It was a secret she shared only with her aunt and Yoko. Natsu planned to announce it to me as a surprise on our wedding day. But fate intervened to stop us from marrying. If not for her innocently kept secret, everything might have been different. Only years later did I learn the truth. I heard it from my father in a long overdue confrontation between us two years after I returned to Japan. The rest of the truth I heard from Natsu when we were reunited and I first laid eyes on Paul."

Douglas ran both hands through his hair. "It took me years to piece together everything that had taken place behind our backs," he said, sitting down on the side of the bed. "Natsu's mother had observed her daughter's morning sickness. Her father went directly to my father, and both men conspired to put an abrupt end to our affair. It was decided that I wouldn't be told of Natsu's pregnancy. The Yoseido family physician would abort this unwanted child, and I was to leave Japan at once, without ever seeing her again."

These were bitter recollections, and Douglas's voice took on a hard edge. "Even though I wasn't told of Natsu's pregnancy, I didn't capitulate without first standing up to my father. It was useless effort. Your grandfather threatened to cut me off without a cent if I disobeyed, and I couldn't have stood on my own at the time.

"I desperately wanted to take charge of my own life," Douglas told his son, who nervously shifted before him as their eyes joined to search one another out. "Yes, I felt the same things you felt when we talked aboard the steamer," he said. "But I wasn't free to tell you all this. Your grandfather pointed out to me that married to a Japanese, I couldn't hope to find anything but menial work in Japan, since, of course, I would no longer be part of the family business. And if I took Natsu to America, we'd face the same discrimination against interracial couples. We'd live in poverty and end up despising each other. Julius cleverly turned my love for Natsu to his advantage. How could I, a boy of almost eighteen who had never done an honest day's work in his life, take this well-bred girl down into the gutter with me? I was defeated by fear of not only destroying her life, but everything that we felt between us. So, I agreed to give her up—but only for then, I told myself. Natsu had just turned seventeen. I decided I'd let my father pay for the education that would prepare me to take her as my wife. Then I'd fight all the rotten things he threw in my face! What were four years apart, weighed against a lifetime together? Those were my thoughts on the night before I sailed to America. I wrote Natsu all this in a letter, asking her to wait until I could earn my own way. I had my letter delivered to Yoko at the tea shop, knowing Natsu would visit there for the comfort of her friends.

"Yes, I asked Natsu to wait for me, even though I didn't feel I had the right to expect so much of her. I never received a reply to that letter, or any of the others I wrote her from Harvard," he told Max. "My father saw to that."

Douglas slowly shook his head. "He realized that Natsu's decision to have her baby could be a powerful threat to his plans for my future, and he personally saw to it that she couldn't reach out to me through any means. My housemaster at Harvard was told to intercept all mail and any cables sent me from Japan, and paid handsomely to confiscate any letters I posted to Japan. There was no telephone service to Japan. I lost count of how many letters I sent Natsu—addressed to her home and to Yoko at the tea shop. When we found each other again, she spoke of waiting day after day for a letter from me.

"Julius was clever. In the winter of my freshman year, I was allowed to receive one special letter from Japan. I believed that it was written to me by Natsu's father, who said that his daughter had married a Japanese and was expecting a child. Natsu lacked the heart to write me of this, the letter said, and had asked her father to do it for her. He ended the letter by telling me that any further mail he received from America would be destroyed unopened.

"I held that letter in my hands, devastated by its contents. Everything about it seemed genuine. But your grandfather had dictated it. Much later, he admitted to having it written by one of his secretaries in a hand I wouldn't recognize.

"There I stood, chained to my study desk at Harvard, nearly ten thousand miles from the woman I loved and completely at the mercy of your grandfather's plot. And he saw to it I was kept there on a short leash," Douglas said bitterly, gripping the sleeves of his silk shirt. "I could draw money from the bank, but only enough for my immediate expenses. Julius must have patted himself on the back for thinking of everything. Toward the end of my freshman year, your grandfather made a timely descent on my dormitory, with news from home. I was devastated when he said that he had seen Natsu with her Japanese husband, and she was radiantly happy. Actually, Natsu had just given birth to Paul, and your grandfather had visited her before leaving Japan. Knowing that one day I'd return to Japan, he tried to buy Natsu's silence with an offer of support for her and the child. He wanted her to move to another city, where there was no possibility of our paths ever crossing again. But Natsu couldn't be bought off, and he feared what steps she might take in the future. So, he made it a point to spend a great deal of those years with me in America. For business reasons, he said. But he became my jailer, making damn sure I wouldn't bolt to Japan and find him out." Now Douglas rested his voice and heaved a deep sigh. "I believed I'd lost her. The great distance between us helped ease the pain, but I never stopped loving Natsu." Tears mixed with the sweat in the deep pockets underneath his eyes. "But when I met your mother—well, I was attracted to her, and your grandfather more than approved of the match."

Douglas refrained from saying more about Angela. He sat on the edge of the bed, thinking of Natsu's narrow world; its boundaries had been this apartment and the Ginza tea shop. "Four long years of study in America. Then you were born soon after I returned here with your mother."

Max could feel the depressing weight of those years as his father stared off into space. His very existence was owed to a conspiracy of lies, and Max wrestled with the thought of being an unwanted child. But he had glimpsed Douglas's tormented soul and was incapable of condemning his father. "How did you discover the truth, Dad? Did Natsu contact you?"

"No. Your grandfather visited Natsu shortly before I returned home, to announce my marriage. He showed her photographs of the happy couple and told her we were expecting our first child. Marrying Angela accomplished what his money couldn't buy. He knew that Natsu's love for me would hold her silent. But from the moment I set foot back on Japanese soil, I thought of her constantly. I was tortured by the desire to see her again. Then you were born."

Douglas visibly brightened with that memory. "I became the proud father of a baby boy. Love at first sight. I cradled you in my arms, and life took on a new meaning. I thought of Natsu, believing she was married with children of her own to think of, and that seeing her again could only bring us pain." Sorrow darkened his face. "But the urge to seek her out grew and grew. There's no way to describe what I felt when I confronted your grandfather, demanding to know where Natsu and her husband lived."

Douglas's voice was a whisper. " 'Why, the little tart will serve you tea at the Cherry Blossom Kissaten. Natsu's a tea maid there, and you'd be sweeping the floors if not for me,' your grandfather said. Oh, he was so sure of himself and of his power over me now that I had a wife and son! I could have strangled him with my bare hands when he laughed." Breathing hard, Douglas buried his face in his hands. "He admitted to no guilt. He was convinced he'd done a father's duty. He'd alienated my affections years before and he cared nothing about my feelings for him now, and so he told how cleverly he'd pulled the strings. He never thought I'd go to the tea shop. I'll never forget seeing Natsu wearing the uniform of a tea maid, smiling through her tears as we embraced."

"Dad, you weren't to blame for any of this," Max insisted, pulling Douglas close as if their roles were reversed and the sorrow was his. "You don't have to say more."

"Max, I've failed two women, and I want you to hear it all."

"All right. I understand." He released his father and looked at him.

As he spoke, Douglas was lost to the demons of his guilt. "Soon after, we found each other again, Natsu said that she felt we couldn't alter the course of our lives. She believed the time for our happiness had passed. Her life was what it was, and she expected nothing of me but my love. Natsu exonerated me—but the damage done was too great. I remember standing before Paul, realizing justice for us had come too late. The three of us were imprisoned by the past. Bars had been erected between us that no man could break down. Oh, I could reach out to them between the bars—but I could never make up for the lost years. No, she and Paul remained hostages of your grandfather's lies. No ransom could buy them back. No price could be placed on the cost of their suffering."

A single tear welled in the corner of one eye as Douglas pressed his son's arm and said, "Your half brother never accepted me. He saw me as an intruder who was guilty of abandoning him and who suddenly reappeared only to steal his mother's love. Paul hates me for not being Japanese. Natsu sacrificed everything for him, clinging to the hope that he'd forgive me."

Douglas was silent for a moment. Then he said softly, "Dearest Natsu, you were always the one who gave more." He looked at Max. "I should have taken a stronger stand against all her rationalizations. Instead, I simply resigned myself to them."

Douglas slowly got up from the bed and walked to the dining alcove. Max followed. "I don't know where the years went. All those wasted years after your grandfather died, doing what was expected of me, while Natsu was always here for me to turn to. I'm flawed, Max. I think you would have survived a divorce. Even as a child you were a scrapper." Smiling, he tousled his son's hair. "I settled for what Natsu and I had together here. But deep inside, I yearned to turn the past around on its ear."

How many days had passed since Natsu prepared these rooms for his homecoming? Douglas wondered silently. "Her last act of giving was to hide her pain," he said wearily. "She might have held me here to share in her dying, but she freed me with a lie so that I could go to Germany to save the family fortunes. Lies. Black or white, they breed like roaches. Kill one and a dozen more crawl from the woodwork." He turned to Max. "Don't judge your future by my past. Unlike your grandfather, I'm not standing in the way of your happiness with Shizue. I know Tadashi's forbidden you to see her; we spoke over the telephone last night. I don't remember much of what I said. Something about a son not suffering for the sins of his father. Something about these being different times, and how wrong he was, behaving like a feudal patriarch, treating Shizue like a prisoner in the lord's house. Something about not standing in Angela's way if she decides to leave me. And business—yes, that commitment must be honored. Max, we're men of honor. Tadashi's love for his daughter is twisted to suit his old beliefs. While she's underage, he can lay down ultimatums. In the years to come, maybe she'll find the strength to overturn his dictatorial powers."

"I can't base my hopes on maybes," Max said, suddenly furious as the parallels between his life and his father's seemed to narrow into a single line. "What happens to me while you hold the dynasty together by honoring your business obligations?" he questioned shortly. "It seems I'm doomed to inherit your life no matter what I do."

"Listen, Max. What I said about getting a sound education still applies. Soon I'll return to Germany, with or without your mother. I'll have my work as my escape. But there's nothing for you there and nothing you can do by staying here at home." He seated himself at the dining table, picked up his fountain pen, and, in a draftsman's precision hand, printed Angela's name across the sealed envelope. "Why not make good use of your time? Give Harvard a year or so. And get any notion of repeating my past failures out of your head. The circumstances are different. It's your decision, son. You're your own man now." He extended the envelope. "Would you deliver this to your mother?"

Max swallowed hard. "Sure." He lifted his jacket from the back of the chair and put the envelope in its pocket.

"I'll need a change of clothes," Douglas said. "Natsu is being laid to rest at noon tomorrow. Our Lady of Mercy Cemetery in Kichijoji. I can't go there looking like this. Would you bring me some clothes from home?" He smiled weakly. "Your brother will be at the funeral. I promised not to abandon him. But whether he accepts that or not is his choice." Douglas pictured himself standing at the grave, reaching out to Paul in love, only to have his hand pushed away.

"Dad, let me take you there. You're in no shape to drive that far, and I'd like to see my half brother."

"The cemetery's no place for you to meet," Douglas countered. Then, seeing the urgent expression in Max's eyes, he relented. "I understand. All right. Drive me there. Only, please, don't attempt to force yourself on Paul."

"I know better than to intrude on his grief. I'll wait for you outside the cemetery gates."

"Fine." Douglas looked around the room. "At last, I'm ready to make peace with the dead. I'll clean up and check into a hotel for the night."

Douglas took Max by the shoulders. "Angela's been a good wife. I've done what I can to write all those feelings down in that letter. She's suffered a lot thinking there was something lacking in her, and I've set all that straight. I've promised her a great deal if she'll take me back, Max. What I owe to Natsu's memory, and to the years Angela devoted to me as a wife, tear me apart. But the three of us have always been a family. I'm telling you this now man to man. Max, I never regretted having you. Don't ever think that you weren't wanted, don't ever think that you had anything whatsoever to do with all this. I love you, son. And I wouldn't exchange all the hurt and pain caused by so many lies for one hair on your head. It's over now. What's left belongs to the living."

Emotion flooded through Max as he kissed his father on the cheek. He needed time to sort out his own feelings.

It was a rainy evening much like the one when Max had first visited his father at the apartment house. As he drove, Max's thoughts were of Shizue. He felt that nothing good had come from his father unveiling the past—Shizue seemed more unattainable than ever. Two generations of Napier men had chosen Japanese lovers. Tradition had kept Douglas from Natsu, and it threatened to keep him from Shizue.

His thoughts turned to Paul, his flesh and blood brother, who was half Japanese and half American. Tomorrow their eyes would meet for the first time and perhaps some good would come of the past after all. Perhaps brothers would be immunized to the disease that had isolated them from each other.

Flashes of lightning struck against the sky as Max parked at his home and glanced across the deserted street. An image stored in the dark recesses of his mind suddenly sprang to life. He remembered seeing a young boy straddling a bicycle just across the street from the driveway. The boy was Eurasian, some years older than Max, and he stood watching him return home from school. Now Max recalled that same boy as a recurring presence over the years. He was sure it was Paul. The boy's face was always twisted as if he held some grudge against Max. The animosity in his face had made him look different from the snapshots Angela had pressed into her son's hands a few days ago. Max recalled once curiously venturing toward Paul. But Natsu's son had quickly mounted his bicycle and begun pedaling off. A book had tumbled from the handlebar basket, and Max had picked it up, waving it high, shouting for the boy to come back. But Paul had sped away downhill, and Max had no memory of ever seeing him again.

As Max left the car in the driveway and hurried inside the house, he wondered how often Paul had spied on him without being seen. He imagined the young man's rage over being denied his birthright, and Max now feared that Natsu's son was poisoned by a venom of envy and denial that would prevent them from ever becoming true brothers.

His mother was seated alone at the far end of the banquet-length table in the dining room. She wore no jewelry except the diamonds on her wedding finger. Her face was scrubbed clean of makeup. Attired in a simple black dress, her hair combed back tightly in a severe bun, she looked like a widow in mourning. Max watched her cut a tiny morsel of food with a knife belonging to her finest silver setting. "I've been with Dad," he announced, and slipped the envelope from his jacket pocket. "He asked me to deliver this."

Angela set down her knife and fork, then dabbed her lips with a rose-colored linen napkin and regarded her son. Her eyes, however, were far from cold. The green in them caught fire as Max placed the envelope on the burnished rosewood dining table. "A letter. How civilized of your father. Morita, set another place."

A serving maid pulled out a chair at one side of the table, and Max sat down, not in the least hungry but accepting a glass of wine. Heinz Karlstadt had selected a number of bottles from his private stock and given them to the Napiers as a bon voyage present. Max wondered at the stamina of this proud woman. In the midst of her crumbling marriage, his mother had instructed Morita to uncrate this vintage wine to accompany her solitary dinner.

"How is your father?" she asked, attempting to sound matter-of-fact. Douglas's letter sat beside her elbow, untouched.

"Emotionally drained but sober, Mother." Max disliked being cast as their go-between and irritably waved off the serving maid. "Nothing else for me."

Angela bolstered herself with another glass of German wine. "Morita, dismiss the servants."

After the room was cleared, Max watched his mother tear open the envelope. He observed her as she read each sheet, then shuffled through them to reread certain sections. Douglas had told him something of its contents, but his father's wish to salvage their marriage and the things he promised Angela as atonement seemed only to add to her despair. Angela bowed her head. Suddenly, angrily, she squeezed the pages into a tight ball. Her lips began to tremble, and she clenched the wadded paper to her mouth and quietly sobbed.

"Dad told me he wanted to set the record straight between you," Max said, feeling helplessness and compassion as his mother lowered the balled-up pages with trembling hands and dropped them on her dinner plate.

"Oh, your father's set everything straight so far as he's concerned," she said flatly, fighting back the tears. "He's so eloquently damned himself. But that isn't enough of an accounting to undo all the hurt. You've every right to know that he's asked to be given a second chance, but he won't contest a divorce if that's what I want. No, your father won't fight me. He feels he's lost the right to hold me to the marriage vows he's broken. He's offered me a blank check as a divorce settlement."

Angela pressed her dinner napkin to her eyes like a veil. How dare Douglas throw money at her to absolve his guilt? And using this letter to plead with her for a chance to make amends was the worst insult of all. He would come to her after Natsu Yoseido was laid to rest, hat in hand. "When do they bury his mistress?" she asked her son.

"Tomorrow at noon."

"Where?"

Max did not answer right away. His father had good reason not to offer this information in the letter. "It's a Catholic cemetery in the suburbs." He felt obliged to volunteer at least that much.

"Oh, she was a Catholic! How convenient for her to confess her sins and have them forgiven." Furious, Angela picked up the crumpled papers and held them to the flame of a candle in a silver candelabra. "I object to your methods, Douglas. You won't be left off the hook so easily," she vowed.

The pages burst into a bright red ball of flames, which she dropped on the table, where it burned a ring in the polished veneer.

"Your father has a clever way with words, Maxwell. It seems his mistress's son inherited something of value to offset all the ugliness of mixed blood. I'm told he's a talented journalist—brilliant, in fact. Well, so much for words." She watched the letter burn itself down to black ashes. "I don't place much store in words. No doubt your father thought they would help soften the blow. Much to the contrary, his words are only ashes. Feathers darkening the air. You think he's done his best? Yes, I can see that in your Napier eyes. Never forget that the Sommersby blood also flows in your veins, Maxwell. We were a close-knit family, given to forgiving and forgetting the bad taste of others. If you've forgiven your father, that sensibility is due to my blood in you. There, I've spoken to you as an adult." Bowing her head, she massaged the polished chair arms over and over.

"I'm taking Dad a change of clothes for the funeral," Max interjected in the tense silence. "Is there anything you want me to tell him, Mother?"

"Nothing."

"Anything I can do for you?"

Angela shook her head, then carefully lifted a crystal wineglass in one pale, trembling hand. "You're right not to give me the name of that cemetery. I might be tempted to degrade myself by going there to make a scene." She paused to sip the wine. "Have Morita help you select what's required from your father's wardrobe. His dark blue serge is appropriate. White shirt, maroon tie, black oxfords, and something to dress up his handkerchief pocket." Catching herself in the act of being the dutiful wife, Angela laughed sarcastically. "Force of habit," she told Max. "Years of seeing to your father's attire. Black socks. Don't forget his socks."

Max left to pack a bag of clothing suitable for attending a funeral, and Angela Napier crossed the hallway to the sitting room. Wineglass in one hand, a lit cigarette in the other, she gave in to the luxury of self-pity. The next day Douglas would walk through the door to suffer a personal accounting. She might strike him, but violence was a useless weapon against the beaten man of his letter. Might as well strike the dead, she thought, stifling the urge to pick up the telephone. There were few Catholic cemeteries in Tokyo's suburbs. She could easily locate it by placing a few calls. Oh, but it would hurt Natsu's son more than it might hurt Douglas if she arrived to shout invectives over the woman's open grave. Besides, the dead could not hear her anger.

And yet, attending Natsu's funeral was the closest Angela would ever come to a confrontation with the other woman. Perhaps viewing Natsu Yoseido's corpse laid out in the casket would provide the catharsis that she so desperately sought, to justify picking up the torn threads of her life with Douglas.

Agitated, she paced the floor. The woman wronged, the woman so often scorned by her husband's apathy, the woman cheated of that loving rapport Natsu must have enjoyed in her place. Douglas had written a glowing accolade to her wifely and motherly performance of twenty years. He had taken all the blame, all the guilt upon himself, but he had not written one word of love for her. She felt so defeated, so defenseless. Her love for him still dominated her, leaving her weakly clinging to her place here as his wife.

It had rained off and on throughout that day as it often did at that time of year. One clear sultry day followed by one day of rain. The predictability of the Japanese climate offered no relief, few surprises. From the sitting room window Angela watched her son swing a suitcase into his father's car. Max saw her standing there. Bubbles and distortions in the old glass windowpanes conspired with the rain to make her son appear a rippling duplicate of Douglas Napier. Twenty years melted away before her eyes as Angela turned from the window.

She would not use their son to carry some vindictive reply. Tomorrow she would see Douglas herself. Tomorrow she must face the ultimate moment of truth. If there were no limits to her love for Douglas, she would know it then.

CHAPTER 14

Early morning sunlight shone down through the chapel's stained-glass windows as Yoko knelt alone over Natsu's open casket, applying face powder, rouge, and lipstick to the face of the dead woman. She had given the embalmer a photograph of Natsu to work from, but he lacked the knowledge to add the personal finishing touches. As she worked, Yoko chatted on about inconsequential things, just as the two women had done in life. She had already swept up Natsu's jet-black hair, dressing it with the ivory hairpins. After she finished applying the makeup, Yoko anointed Natsu's hair and folded hands with her lover's favorite perfume. Yoko tucked the crystal decanter under the white satin pillows, then stood back and observed how lifelike and at peace her dear friend looked. Soon the mourners would arrive to pay their last respects to the dead, and Father Watanabe would stand before the altar cross to petition his Christian God on behalf of Natsu's immortal soul.

But this was a Japanese soul, Yoko thought, glancing up from the rosary beads that had been placed in Natsu's hands. Though the trappings of this chapel were pleasing to her eyes, Yoko saw no objects to speak for the Japanese gods of their ancestors. If this Jesus was a loving god, then he would make room for them. Yoko secreted a Shinto talisman and Buddhist prayer beads in the satin folds of the casket. The day before, she had paid a Buddhist priest to write a *kaimyō* for the deceased. One's soul could not reach "the better world" without these posthumous declarations inked in Japanese characters by the priest's brush on a slender piece of white paper. Yoko read the beautiful message aloud. "Heroic disciple to Buddha residing in ravine full of sunshine and nightingales." Then she carefully rolled the paper and slipped it inside one sleeve of her dear friend's kimono.

Bowing her head in prayer to the Amida Buddha, Yoko contemplated Natsu's divine release from earthly pain and sorrow, until the tolling chapel bell intruded on her solitude. She was now at peace and smiling as she pressed her lips to the face of the dead. *"Sayonara,"* Yoko said quietly.

Paul entered the chapel with Yoko's son, Toru, who had been granted leave from his military duty to attend the funeral. Paul carried flowers he had purchased at the cemetery stall. Their petals were misted with water and gave off a sweet scent. As he bent over the casket to brush Natsu's forehead with a kiss, there was some stronger fragrance that he inhaled. His mother had always carried this perfume scent home after sleeping with his father, and Paul's eyes fixed narrowly on Yoko.

"It was her wish," she told him. Weak in the knees from having knelt for so long, she leaned on her son for support, and he helped her to the front pew. She sat down between Toru and Paul.

Other mourners began to arrive. Yoko had posted a notice on the shuttered tea shop door, and many of her regular customers filed inside the chapel after leaving their shoes at the open doors. Paul confronted the sorrowful faces of men who had turned against Natsu the day he had stormed the tea shop. Today their eyes showed no animosity. All of them bowed. They had come to pay their respects to the lovely tea maid who had added a ray of brightness to their days, and their petty hatreds were set aside to honor his mother's memory. As each man passed before her open casket, Paul silently forgave him.

The pews soon were filled with mourners, but Paul was not yet reconciled to death. As the attendants closed the casket, Paul rose up. For one panic-stricken moment he feared his mother would suffocate, and he very nearly rushed forward to pry open the coffin lid. Then Yoko's touch on his arm and Father Watanabe's singsong voice beginning the mass brought Paul to his senses. He sat down, tearfully bowing his head.

Several times during the mass, Paul glanced back to the crowded doorway for signs of his father. Toward the end of the mass, he saw Hideo Tamura squeezing his way inside. *Nippon Shimbun*'s editor removed his straw hat. He was wiping its brim and his perspiring face with a handkerchief when he was jostled from behind by Douglas Napier. Tamura's face showed contempt, and he glowered at Douglas's faintly whispered apology. But Douglas did not notice. From across the chapel his eyes locked with his son's.

Paul faced away, stunned by how much his father had aged. Perhaps guilt was punishment enough, he thought. At the end of the mass, Father Watanabe motioned for him to step forward.

"Choose your pallbearers, my son."

Paul was handed a straw basket filled with white cotton gloves by the young altar boy who had assisted in the mass. Toru slipped on one pair, then held the basket while Paul did the same. Four pairs of gloves remained. Paul searched out the mourners' faces. "Will you accept the honor of bearing my mother's casket?" he asked of two men dressed in business suits, who were younger and sturdier than the others. Then he reached the open doors, where he first extended the basket to Hideo Tamura. "And you, Douglas." The words stuck in his throat. Douglas Napier's dark, sunken eyes went from him to the last pair of gloves in the basket. "Mother would have wanted it," said Paul. The gesture was a painful concession to the forgiveness Natsu had pleaded of him before she had died.

Douglas's hands trembled as he put on the white cotton gloves. He followed his son to the sealed casket, where he took hold of one of the varnished metal handles. He thought of Natsu arranging for her own burial. Even in death she had refused his wealth, selecting a simple wooden box and a narrow plot of earth in a humble graveyard.

Marching on the opposite side of the casket from his father, Paul thought it was too fine a day for burying the dead. There were no storm clouds or gloomy sheets of rain to match his despair.

It was a rather steep downhill walk from the chapel to the open grave, and the pallbearers led the funeral procession at a snail's pace. Some of the mourners were dressed in the traditional kimono and shielded from the sun's heat under colorful bamboo umbrellas. They added a strangely festive touch to Natsu's funeral.

Douglas Napier stumbled, but there were sturdier arms to keep the casket aloft the remaining distance to the gravesite. Natsu had been so thin and frail in death, and yet her casket seemed an unbearable weight to him. At last the pallbearers set it down on ropes stretched across the open earth. He bowed his head while Father Watanabe spoke the final prayers for the dead. Before the ceremony ended, the priest sprinkled holy water on the casket lid. Douglas watched the breeze stir dust at his feet as Father Watanabe solemnly intoned the familiar phrase that lingered on in Douglas's mind. "Ashes to ashes, dust to dust." Then the cemetery custodian activated the hand winch that slowly lowered Natsu into her grave.

The custodian wore a cutaway morning coat and a black silk top hat. He dug a silver spade into the mound of earth heaped at the graveside, removed his silk top hat, and bowed while extending the spade to Paul, who sent a spadeful of earth down on his mother's coffin.

One by one the other mourners passed in a line, each in turn doing as Paul had done. Douglas looked on numbly. He could not yet bring himself to perform that final farewell. The mourners were silently departing; the last of them left the spade in the mound of earth.

"I'll join you in a minute," Paul told Yoko and her son. She turned from the graveside reluctantly. Hideo Tamura saw he was not wanted and joined Yoko for the uphill climb.

Douglas stood directly across Natsu's grave from their son. He wanted to reach out his hand in love, but the opened earth was like a black abyss yawning between them. "Son, I'm guilty of many things in your eyes, but you can't hold me responsible for your mother's death. Natsu feared for you being all alone in the world," he said in a voice choked with emotion. "I swore to her that I'd never stop reaching out to be a father to you. The hatred inside you has kept us strangers. Paul, give me a chance to know you. You're a grown man with a fine future before you. What you remember as a child is clouded by so many misconceptions. Your mother and I never deceived you. She would have been my wife if not for the lies that destroyed our chances. Maybe it would have hurt you less if Natsu and I had decided never to see each other again, but we loved each other too deeply to remain apart. Your mother had fixed ideas of her own, and our lives together were guided by those. Won't you please give me a chance? The animosity you carry is a punishing weight for us both. Please, let me try to at least earn your forgiveness."

"Don't expect me to offer you atonement, Douglas. Some things can never be forgotten. Never forgiven." Paul lowered his gaze to the dusty casket lid. "I've wasted enough years on hatreds and thoughts of revenge. All the pain I've suffered has left scars that won't heal. All those checks you wrote to pay for my education were just token attempts to salve your conscience. I should have refused to take your filthy money. It's all you've ever had to give me as a father. That and weekly afternoons in the country as a boy—far from Tokyo, where you didn't risk being seen by your fancy society friends. Why not admit that you were ashamed of your half-caste son?" His voice cracked as he recalled being driven into the countryside in his father's care to horseback-ride and picnic and play ball. He remembered hugging his father on a Sunday afternoon much like this one, when he, in his loneliness, had nearly surrendered to love.

"All last night I battled with my feelings toward you," Paul confessed haltingly. "The man who orphaned me as an infant, only to reappear with a claim of fatherhood he couldn't make good. You staked a claim on my mother's love, and when I was old enough to know the things you did together—it made me sick. I was tormented by those nights she lay in your arms. You must have known what hell that put me through—but I doubt you gave it a second thought." He paused, brushing tears from his eyes. "You can never atone for that blind spot in your character. Your atonement can't wipe away the disdain for me in everyone's eyes—the torture of having no woman to love and the trial of always having to prove that I'm better than the coolie society expects me to be. My future doesn't include you. I much prefer being alone in the world to that. My mother was the only link between us, and you're dead to me now. I'm burying you with the dead, and you no longer exist. Mother, forgive me," he whispered over her open grave, then swung around as his father reeled from his blistering rejection.

"Paul! I wasn't ashamed of you," Douglas called weakly. He could find no hidden reservoir of strength to buttress himself against his son's crushing rebuke. Paul stalked uphill toward the road and never looked back.

Feeling faint, Douglas sank to his knees. Taking hold of the silver spade, he dug a spadeful of dirt from the mound of earth and spilled it down on Natsu's casket, an unsparing formality of farewell.

Sunlight glared off the polished stone marking Natsu's grave. Before dying, she had visited the stone cutter to pick out a slim rounded slab of pink marble, almost the color of cherry blossoms. He squinted to read what was carved under the holy cross: her name, the year Natsu had entered the world, and the year and the day on which she had left it, just forty summers old.

Douglas's fingers traced the words that had been chiseled in the stone according to Natsu's last wishes. *Mother of a son. Paul Yoseido. Conceived in love.* "Conceived in love," he gave voice to her brief epitaph. Dear Natsu's every act had been conceived in love, he thought. He wept, clawing at the earth, humbled by her memory and damned by the son who had survived her. He had lost them both.

On the cemetery road, Hideo Tamura stepped forward to place his hand on Paul's shoulder. "*Osasshi-itashimasu.* A great loss," he said. "Is there anything I can do to help ease your grief?"

"Work is what I need, Tamura-*san.*"

"Work. Yes, of course, I quite understand." Tamura wanted to share his bereavement with Natsu's son, but he was not a demonstrative man, and he nervously cleared his throat. "Your mother was very dear to me."

"You were a dear friend to her as well." Paul looked back at his father kneeling at the graveside. He believed Douglas was responsible for his job with *Nippon Shimbun* and wished it were otherwise. He faced the editor who had treated him like a real son. "You don't look well, Tamura-*san.*"

"The heat," Hideo Tamura complained, quickly hiding his tearful eyes behind a handkerchief. "I shall always treasure Natsu's memory." He owed it to Natsu to continue acting as Paul's silent mentor. Also, he felt a deep affection for her son and knew that the feeling was returned. To regain control over his emotions, Tamura fell back into the more comfortable role of journalist. "If it's work you want, report to me first thing in the morning," he said. "The deteriorating situation in China made me late for the funeral. There are new reports of large numbers of Chinese troops being massed in North China." He paused to glance at Yoko standing nearby with Toru, whose face showed delight over the news. "Chiang Kai-shek has just issued an inflammatory proclamation from Nanking," Tamura continued, "announcing that he has no intention of surrendering another inch of territory to Japan's latest demands for his armies to stop increasing their garrisons. I'm afraid it's now become a matter of Japan either withdrawing its forces or engaging in war with the Chinese republic."

"It's time we answered these chinks with our bullets!" Toru exclaimed. His arms went up, holding an imaginary rifle. "*Pling, pling, pling!* Let all enemies of Japan fall before our guns."

Hideo Tamura shook his head at the cocky young army corporal. "So, you are ready to be a hero, brave samurai."

"Trained for battle to the point of madness, old man," said Toru. "My regiment has just been ordered to China. We sail tomorrow night."

Yoko gasped at this news. "Give us a smile, Mother. I won't shame you by failing in my duty to the emperor. You should be proud of me."

"Of course I am proud," Yoko answered her son, but her voice lacked heart. She contemplated a mother's lonely vigil while Toru threw out his chest and talked of at last seeing action. "Such talk has no place here," she interrupted him.

Hideo signaled for the hired car he had arrived in. "If Japan goes to war, there will be much bloodshed on both sides," he said ruefully. "May I give you a ride to the city?" he asked Paul.

"Thanks, but I'll take the train with Toru."

"I hope there will be no war," Yoko said, managing to smile for her son.

As Tamura's departing car churned dust along the gravel road, Paul spotted Max standing just outside the gates, and he clenched his fists. Yoko had told him of Max's visit to her tea shop the day before. "He's got a lot of nerve coming here," Paul commented darkly.

Yoko took Paul's hand. "Let it be. I am sure the boy came only to help your father and means no harm."

Toru eyed the young American. "So, at long last I get to feast my eyes on this privileged half brother you talked about so much." He slung a protective arm around Paul's shoulders. "I don't like the looks of him."

"If there's any trouble, stay out of it." Paul shrugged loose of Toru's arm, annoyed by the pathos in Max's face in response to his own pointedly hostile glare. Seeing Max again evoked bitter thoughts of being sworn to silence for so many years. Yoko's son had been more of a brother to him than this rich man's son, whose sleek gray Duesenberg was parked on the cemetery road. This was consecrated ground, and he would not disgrace Natsu's memory by venting his hatred against the pure-blooded heir who bore her lover's legal name. "We'll ignore him," Paul told his friends.

Max had promised himself not to intrude on Paul's grief. However, when his brother strode past as if Max were invisible, he felt driven by a sudden compulsion and chased after Paul. "Wait!" he called.

Paul ignored the shout, but Max caught up to seize his arm from behind. Paul turned and shouted, "I want nothing to do with you!"

"But we're brothers!"

"You're no brother of mine," Paul roared. He had never been capable of striking his father, but nothing prevented his lashing out at this young man who dared to call him brother. He assaulted Max wildly, swinging both his fists to land hard punches that made Max reel.

Max took a number of blows with his arms, keeping his guard up but refusing to fight back. He absorbed Paul's blows like a punching bag. Then a powerful punch landed squarely in his face, and Max went down on one knee, dazed and spitting blood.

"Stop," Yoko cried in a horrified voice.

Paul staggered back. He felt no sense of satisfaction. Their father deserved the beating Max had taken in his place, and Paul felt seared by his half-brother's blood wetting the knuckles of his hand. Violence had accomplished nothing.

He reached inside his jacket pocket for the handkerchief his mother had always put there. This was a loving touch he now performed himself. Wiping the blood from his knuckles, he told himself that Natsu would have been hurt by his act of violence. Max had not knowingly done him any harm, and Paul held out the handkerchief to his half brother in a gesture bordering on remorse. "Here! Wipe your face and don't force yourself on me again."

"I won't be discouraged by a punch in the mouth," said Max, still dazed and too dizzy to get to his feet. He accepted the handkerchief as a peace offering.

As Max dabbed his cut lip, Paul hurried away to catch the electric tram that was approaching its stop on the paved street below. Paul's words were more wounding than his fists, and Max was determined not to leave things at this. He found his balance, and ran for the tram car Paul had just boarded with his friends. But as he reached the stop, the tram was moving too fast for him to jump on. He read the destination sign and hailed a taxi.

"Kichijoji Station," he told the driver. Thoughts of his father made him look back at the cemetery gates where he had left the Duesenberg, the keys still in the ignition. His father was in no condition to drive home from the cemetery, but Max knew that if he did not board the same commuter train as Paul, he might not be given a second chance to reach out to him.

"Hurry," Max urged the driver, no longer able to see the tram car on the winding street ahead as the taxi braked at a crosswalk.

At the cemetery, Douglas squinted up at two men with shovels resting across their shoulders and *haki-machi* tied around their brows to catch the sweat. He rose on wobbly legs, brushing dirt off his trousers as the gravediggers bowed politely, asking him to leave so they could fill in the opened earth.

After an exhausting climb to the road above, Douglas stepped through the gates and saw his abandoned car. "Max?" he called, searching for his son on the street below. Douglas reasoned that his sons must have struck some rapport. Perhaps Max would fare better than he himself had. Yes, Paul might accept the hand of a brother who bore no guilt for the past. Then Natsu's son would not be alone in the world, as she had feared.

Douglas slumped against the fender of his car and looked at the rusting iron fence that separated the living from the dead. Natsu was now sealed for all eternity in the earth, while he lived on to face the empty silences, longing for the sweetness of her voice—lived on to endure the endless nights, longing for her touch. His only hope of atonement rested with Angela. Even given that new lease on life, Natsu would always own his heart.

He got into the car and started the engine. Paul had justly slammed the door in his face, he thought. He was guilty of claiming the greater portion of Natsu's love. Now he drove to Tokyo, where Angela waited. He had no idea what to expect from his wronged wife. Maybe some things could never be forgotten or forgiven, as Paul had said.

Paul relaxed back in his seat as the train departed from Kichijoji Station and picked up speed. Then he looked up and froze: his obstinate half brother had entered the car and was walking down the aisle. Max took a seat directly across from his. Paul stared sourly at him, then looked away. But he could not ignore the presence of those staring eyes.

"Some people have a nerve butting in where they're not wanted," Toru said loudly.

"Does he do all your talking?" Max inquired evenly. Paul ventured a sidelong look as Max tapped his shoulder. "We have unfinished business. Here and now, or at some other time, Paul. You decide." That said, he marched away to throw open the doors between cars and stepped outside to wait.

Yoko rolled her eyes heavenward. "If Paul goes, there will be more trouble," she told her son.

"He's goading you into a fight to get even," Toru warned, holding Paul down in the seat. "You got in a lucky punch. He blocked your fists like someone who's been well trained in the art of self-defense. Better let me handle him."

Paul shoved free of Toru's hold. "It's not a fight he's after. I'll handle this myself," he said, starting up the aisle.

Toru followed. "I'm keeping an eye on you all the same!"

Paul stepped outside between cars and banged the door shut on Toru, who stationed himself at the window, ready for violence. Paul took hold of the handrail opposite the one that Max held to steady himself. The rumble of train wheels and squeals of the car couplings were deafening.

They were the same height, of similar build, and their hawklike features and strong jawlines were cut from the same Napier cloth. Paul disliked the earnestness in Max's clear blue eyes. They were his father's eyes, only softer, Paul thought.

Max dug Paul's handkerchief from his jacket pocket. "Thanks for the loan," he said.

Paul glared at the white linen stained with blood and shook his head. "Keep it as a reminder that there's nothing between us but bad blood." The metal platform shuddered underfoot as he leaned in close to dust Max's jacket with his free hand. "So sorry for soiling your clean white suit, but you have no claim on me as a brother. The only thing we share in common is Douglas Napier. That bastard's laid enough claims on my life. Today I buried him with the past, and I want no part of his fair-haired son."

"You're entitled to your feelings, Paul."

"Well, since that's clear between us, there's nothing to be gained from pushing yourself on me."

"I want us to be brothers."

Paul responded with a scornful laugh. "Just like your father. You're used to having anything you want or need handed to you for the asking. I imagined you'd be spoiled. But your stupidity surprises me. I gather you've been told all about the past." Max nodded. "You don't know a thing," he fired back angrily. "You've lived in a vacuum, coddled and protected while I stood on the outside taking all the blows for your father's sins. You've heard a lot of words from him, I'm sure, but the pain behind them hasn't penetrated your thick head, or you wouldn't be standing here making stupid demands. You can never know me, and I don't want to know you."

Max took a determined stance, legs spaced wide apart on the rumbling metal floor. "The past isn't just a bunch of words to me, Paul," he countered strongly. "We were kept apart by lies. But we're brothers all the same."

"Allow me to set you straight on that!" Paul had waited a lifetime for this moment, and his voice shook with emotion. "Because you existed, I was forgotten. Everything was denied me because of you. I'm the first-born, I'm the rightful heir to your name, your position in life, and the keys to your high and mighty mansion. My father's mansion! You've occupied my space in it all these years. Even my childhood was sacrificed to you. Every toy you received, every fatherly embrace, every moment you spent playing with him, were stolen from me. Even the tailored silk shirts on your back were put there by me because I remained silent. You can't know what that does to a boy hungering to belong but forgotten and dumped on the street while another fills his shoes. A proper, pure-blooded white aristocrat!"

Max reached out his hand to touch Paul. "I'm sorry. You've shut our father out of your life, but please don't shut me out as well," he implored.

Paul shrugged off Max's touch. "No, we aren't the brothers you'd have us be," he said, fighting tears. "I'm a half-caste and a bastard. I can never be your equal. I can never belong in your white man's world. I can never take back everything you've taken in my place, or share these brotherly feelings you'd like to shove down my throat."

Just then, Paul saw Toru's angry face flattened against the window glass. The door started open, but Paul hammered it shut with his fist and shook his head at Toru. "Stay out of it!" he shouted, and placed his back against the door.

"There must be some way I can reach you, Paul. I realize how hard it's been for you because of me. I can't blame you for telling me off. I had no business forcing myself on you today; I showed no respect for your grief. I put my own feelings first," Max said, lowering his head. "Your mother's just been laid to rest, and I've come at you with my selfish needs.

Maybe I am spoiled and arrogant, Paul. I've never had to earn my own way as you have. You've succeeded with everything stacked against you, and I admire you for that. Maybe you've taken a lot of punishment, but you seem stronger for it. I could learn a lot from you. An older brother whom I can look up to." Now Max's head lifted to confront his brother's thoughtful silence. "I hope you'll give me another chance. The choices were made for us a long time ago, Paul. Other people's choices. They shouldn't bind us."

Paul was deeply moved by Max's sincerity. His half brother was nothing like he had imagined him to be. He slumped against the train car door, feeling the animosity draining out of him. For so long the object of his hatred, Max was now pleading for them to embrace and set the past aside. But that was not easily done, and Paul shook his head. "My better instincts tell me you can only bring more pain into my life if I let you in," he said.

Passing one hand across his eyes, Paul thought how Natsu's death had cast him into a well of loneliness. Soon Toru would be lost to him as well, far across the sea in China. That prospect deepened his sense of aloneness. The lonely child who still resided within him had been touched, and he could not spitefully shut Max out of his life. There were feelings here to be explored, he decided.

"You're very persuasive," he told Max, and almost smiled. "I didn't enjoy hitting you." He sighed in surrender. "All right, I'm willing to give you a chance. You don't share your father's guilt. He's guilty as sin, so don't try to defend him—or mention him in my presence. Understood?"

Max grinned and put out his hand. "Agreed. Let's shake on it."

Paul refused his hand. "Don't push things, Max. Maybe we can be friends after a time, but I don't know what it will take for me to feel like your brother."

The train slowed to make a stop.

Max awkwardly dug both hands into his pockets and managed a smile. "I'll just follow your lead, Paul."

"Good." Paul's eyes softened. He was the older and intended to play the dominant role. He knew Max wanted a more demonstrative display of acceptance, but that would have to be earned. "Let's get off the train here," he said. "I'm thirsty for a cold beer and need to stretch my legs."

Max accepted his brother's invitation. He stifled the urge to bombard Paul with questions. The contact he was desperate for had been made, and he felt grateful for that as they stepped onto the station platform.

Aboard the train, a bewildered Toru watched Paul standing on the platform chatting with his former archenemy. Slowly the train bound for Tokyo began to pull from the station. Toru felt a twinge of jealousy over being forgotten, and he returned to take the seat beside his mother. She was looking out her window, observing the apparent friendliness between the brothers.

"Natsu would be so pleased," said Yoko. "It is the gods' work, my son. But without Natsu there to guide Paul, he might yet seek revenge on his father."

From the train window she watched Paul and Max walking away. Natsu's passing had brought two sons together. Yet, the forgiveness Paul denied his father made her question if either son could be freed of the past.

Angela Napier lounged on the fluffy chintz pillows of her sitting room window seat facing the mansion driveway. She extinguished another cigarette in the ashtray filled with the butts of those she had smoked while waiting for Douglas to return. Her nerves were keyed to the breaking point, but she resisted the temptation to insulate her emotions with the chilled pitcher of martinis Morita had brought her.

Angela wore her sportiest summer dress, a white two-piece outfit of crêpe de chine with navy blue piping. Its accordion-pleated skirt fell midlength across her shapely legs. She glanced down at her silk stockings, carefully straightening them. When Douglas had first brought her to this house as his bride, she mused, his wealth had come from dressing women's legs in Hosokawa silk. Today, her marriage could be as easily destroyed as the fragile threads of her stockings—with one stroke of vindictiveness.

Angela struggled to compose herself. She had painted her nails the same color as her lipstick, a bright ruby red. She had taken great pains with her makeup and with her auburn hair, using a curling iron to turn it into ringlets, the style she had favored as a young bride.

The night before, she had made herself look like a widow, but that lackluster role ill-suited a woman with her flare for fashion. It seemed only fitting that she should re-create the chic, youthful image of her bridal years, to sweep out of Douglas Napier's life just as haughtily as she had first swept into it one spring night in Cambridge, when she had linked arms with a brooding young man, forcing him to take notice of her. The servants had already packed her steamer trunks. Angela had booked passage to San Francisco and reserved a suite at Tokyo's finest hotel, where she would stay until the ocean liner sailed. She had been married in Boston, and it seemed only fitting that the bonds should be broken there. An old girlfriend or two might extend her a hand in sympathy, while she endured the legal process of a divorce and retraced her girlhood footsteps on Beacon Hill. Perhaps there she would gain insight on where she had been and where it was she must go to make a fresh start. Perhaps she would never marry again. But she was determined to squeeze the most out of the rest of her life with all the gaiety and grace she could muster.

Her plans would buttress her against weakening to her love for Douglas. She lit another cigarette, thinking how she would miss Tadashi and his children. Otherwise, she had no roots in Japan. She reasoned that her son would attend Harvard. Perhaps she would take an apartment in

Boston to be near him for a time. His formative years were over, and her role as his mother would steadily diminish. Suddenly she felt an overwhelming sadness, as well as an uncertainty that she could carry out her plan to sever the bonds of matrimony to the only man she could ever love.

A roaring sound dissolved the composure Angela fought to maintain. Douglas's car braked on the drive. The long-awaited moment of truth was upon her. Her husband's face, haggard from grieving over another woman, added to her pain as she saw him walk to the front door. Douglas rang the bell like a visitor come to call. She heard Morita's rasping voice lift excitedly as he welcomed the *dannasama* home.

Angela experienced a stony rage that steeled her against feeling pity for the stooped-shouldered man entering the room. The new gray at his temples shocked her. His trousers and black oxfords were covered with dust. "How dare you come home to me, soiled from kneeling at that woman's grave," she addressed him in a high, quivering voice, pulling at the pleats of her skirt as she got up from the window seat. "How dare you go into hiding from me and think that everything could be neatly accounted for in a letter!"

"Angela, I'm sorry. My letter was just a first step—at least I'd hoped that would be the case."

Douglas stared through her with a glassy-eyed look of bereavement that made her own suffering seem inconsequential by comparison. Mirrored in those staring blue eyes, Angela could almost see the face of the woman he had only just laid to rest. Suddenly Natsu became terrifyingly real—more threatening to her in death than she had ever been in life.

"I'm glad she's dead! Goddamn you for taking everything I had to give and cheating behind my back!" She slapped him hard across the face and then jerked her hand away, shocked by what she had done. It was a futile act that moved her to tears.

"It's over between us, Douglas," she sobbed, pulling a lace handkerchief from the long white sleeve of her blouse and pressing it to the corners of her eyes. "You're a coward to ask to be taken back in a letter—and you're a cruel and hateful man to try to write off the years with a blank check. You've come home too late. If only you'd stood up for yourself like a man, days ago, I might have found some redeemable quality in you. Now it's too late. I'm leaving you."

Douglas took a few faltering steps toward his sobbing wife. Angela's slap had shocked him out of his numbing grief. While Natsu lived, he had failed to grasp the full extent of his wife's suffering, and he stood there as if seeing her for the first time. "Angela, I didn't mean to make things worse. I came here this afternoon to face what's coming to me. Maybe I should have done it days ago, but I needed time to sort it all out."

He slowly took in the luxuriously furnished sitting room. Over the years Angela had redecorated the mansion with draperies, paintings, vases, and innumerable other treasures collected on their travels abroad.

But this house, paneled in dark mahogany, fought her efforts and remained an overpowering presence, basically unchanged since he was a boy. "I should never have brought you here," he said quietly. "When we married, I was content," he told her. "We went well together. We were happy in Boston and on our honeymoon. Our marriage wouldn't have suffered if we had returned to America and built lives of our own there. Instead, I allowed Julius to pull me back to the weaving mills and to a confrontation with the past that hurt everyone concerned."

Angela stared at him, her green eyes welling up with fresh tears as if she, too, were touched by the happier times they had sailed away from long ago.

"Angela, I cannot stand in the way of a divorce if that's what you want. But ending our marriage won't solve anything. There are close feelings between us that will always be there. You've always been an important part of my life."

"Lies. Nothing but lies," she sobbed.

"No. I'm being honest with you. I'm guilty of being dishonest in the past, but we haven't always been unhappy." Douglas went to put his arms around her; Angela was more to him than a loyal mate. The randomness of fate had claimed the great love of his life, ending his years of unfaithfulness. He had come home to take his punishment, but found himself comforting his wife and moved to seek atonement. "You've given so much to our marriage, while I've only taken from you without giving very much in return," he told Angela, who no longer struggled in his arms. "Won't you let me try to make it up to you?"

"Oh, it's too late to make amends. Let me go," Angela cried out, twisting loose of his arms. - She sank down on the window seat. Vindictiveness melted to love, and she feared being won over by his plea. But for once she intended not to fall prey to her love for this man. "How I once trusted you." She spoke through her tears, pulling on her handkerchief with trembling hands. "But even our wedding vows were sworn to me on a stack of lies. How can I be expected to believe you now? All those years of sharing you with another woman. When I think how often you came to my bed directly from her arms, it makes everything we had together seem secondhand and dirty."

"Angela, there was never anything secondhand or dirty about my feelings for you." Angela was so beautiful, so healthy, and full of life, he thought. With the sunlight glowing behind her, she was an agelessly young vision that mocked the dead. Suddenly, he felt unfaithful to Natsu's memory.

"I'm afraid our marriage can't be mended, Douglas," Angela said quietly.

Douglas glimpsed a softening in her face. He sat down beside her on the window seat. "The years between us can't be so easily dismissed," he said. "Think of the good years we shared together. Angela, our marriage is worth saving. Try to find it in your heart to forgive me."

Angela found herself embracing him. A woman could forgive her man anything rather than lose him, she thought, struggling against the sudden desire to take Douglas back. Perhaps a man *could* love two women at once. When had he stopped telling her that he loved her? she wondered, hoping he would speak those words to her again. Running her fingers through his graying blond hair, she felt at the mercy of her lifelong crush on Douglas Napier. "You can be so vulnerable at times—so persuasive. It's always given you the upper hand with me," she said. "How often you held me, trying to make amends after we argued. I always gave in to you then."

"Through the years, I've tried to show respect for your feelings," said Douglas. "To find some balance that smoothed things over between us."

"Thank you for that reminder!" Abruptly Angela pushed him away. "Don't think you can twist me around your little finger the way you have in the past. You've put me through hell, and now you're expecting to be forgiven by playing on my emotions. Well, I'm not falling for those tricks, Douglas. You've juggled my emotions once too often!"

Angela's hand went across her moist brow as she searched for the right words to grant her at least some small degree of spiteful satisfaction. "These past days have made me see that I can get along quite well without you. You're a weakling, Douglas. A real man would have had the courage to admit his mistakes years ago, rather than cause so much suffering to others. A real man couldn't have lived all these years with so much guilt on his conscience. They say confession is good for the soul, but yours comes too late to be forgiven. If memory serves me, you wore the word *sorry* thin, as thin as the paper it was written on. What you've done is beneath contempt. Please correct me if I'm wrong."

"No, you're right. I don't expect forgiveness handed me on a silver platter. You've every right to refuse me," Douglas answered, slumping back in the window seat, a genuine look of pain on his face. "You've every right to hurt me back, Angela. Maybe I don't deserve another chance."

"Exactly so!" Angela fussed with the collar of her blouse. "You haven't the right to ask anything of me. I'm prepared to sue for a divorce and rid myself of you as quickly as the law will allow." Angrily her hands stretched the pleated crêpe de chine skirt flat across her lap. Somehow she had hurt Douglas after all, but she felt a lack of satisfaction that confused her. "Learning of your infidelity was the ultimate injury. The final insult! Something no woman could forgive. You'll have to offer me something more than a bleeding heart to persuade me our marriage is worth saving," she finished with a proud toss of her head. "At a loss for words, Douglas?"

Feeling defenseless against her charges, Douglas sighed and lowered his head. "What more can I say? I believe we both have needs that can't be satisfied by your running away. Needs that can't be summed up in so many words."

"I need more than you have to give," Angela said bitterly. Just one word of love would salve her wounds. Oh, how hard it was to cling to her pride while every fiber of her body wanted him back. She was too proud to confess her love, too frightened and proud to ask if Douglas had ever loved her at all.

"If it's forgiveness you so desperately need, climb down inside the grave with Natsu Yoseido and plead with her ghost to show you mercy. She was the great love in your life, and you used her as well."

"She was the first love in my life," Douglas addressed her hoarsely. He reached out and took Angela's hands. "Please, don't pull away. Let me explain what I feel for you," he begged. "For almost twenty years you've called me darling. You've picked out my clothes and lavished me with an endless stream of affection. We've argued over all the things that test a partnership between husband and wife, then kissed and made up. We've learned to accommodate petty disagreements and annoying little habits. We walked the floor with Max when he was a baby and delighted in watching him grow into a fine young man. We've made friends and lost a few along the way. We've traveled the world together. We've had a marriage, you and I. Natsu and I had none of these things, Angela. What I felt for her happened when I was very young. You and I met after I was led to believe she'd married another man and was the mother of his children. You were both women of great charm and grace, with giving hearts. Two incomparable women I selfishly took for granted. Natsu's dead. I've lost her, and her son was lost to me years ago. I doubt time will lessen Paul's animosity. But that's a punishment I'll bear alone. We have a son of our own to think of, Angela. The three of us are a family. We've had so many years of caring and sharing the good with the bad. All that can't be wiped out by a divorce."

Douglas felt drained. He let go of Angela's quivering hands and fingered the throbbing welt on his cheek. "I'm very tired. Tired of hurting us both. Tired of bringing so much pain to those I care about the most. Leaving me would allow you to start over. Angela, the blank check was offered to be fair. I just wanted to be fair."

"A price can't be set on fairness," she said flatly. His words had touched her deeply, undercutting everything she had decided the night before. She had struck him hard in a rage, and now the red welt on his cheek made her think how ghastly pale he looked. As much as she had been hurt, Douglas's physical condition still concerned her.

Angela sat erect. She teetered at the brink of saying she forgave him. But the words stuck in her throat like pieces of bone. "Perhaps our marriage wasn't made in heaven, Douglas, but it was a source of great happiness to me, until I was plunged into this hellhole of deceit. Good God, you've taken my youth, enjoyed the love of my son, and turned away from our marriage bed for the comfort of your Japanese harlot."

"She was never that!" Douglas said with a flash of anger.

Suddenly Angela felt a renewed sense of purpose. She had nearly been swayed by his clever words, but now she was struck by her husband's defense of that woman. "Look at you! Barely able to hold up your head. Ravaged by a grief that makes everything you've said about our marriage a sham." She twisted the diamond rings on her wedding finger. "Oh, how

I wanted you to beg to be taken back. Now it doesn't matter. You've sentenced yourself, Douglas. Why scream and raise my hand again to a condemned man? Anything I did would be a postmortem to our marriage. You've lost me. I'm divorcing you. My decision is final. Be honest for once and take what's coming to you like a man."

Exhausted, Douglas ran his hands through his hair. They had reached an impasse. "I need you, Angela. But I can see your hurt runs too deep for me to expect a reprieve."

With a great deal of effort, he crossed to the doorway of the sitting room and went out into the hall. "Morita, bring my hat. I won't be staying."

Angela shot to her feet. "How dare you walk out on me again! If anyone's leaving this dreadful house, it's I!" She marched past Douglas with her head held high, showing him all the determination she could muster. She intended to sweep out of his life as she had first swept into it twenty years before. But her posture lacked the spirited haughtiness of her youth. That was long since gone. She felt her spirit broken by middle age, and fears of growing old alone slowed her pace as she climbed the broad staircase and entered the master bedroom where other Napier women had taken refuge from unloving husbands. They as well had been bound to their places by one-sided love. Well, she would be the exception; she would not remain chained here "until death us do part."

Angela sat on the white silk upholstered vanity stool. Her steamship tickets to America lay on the vanity. Black steamer trunks, carefully packed by her maids, surrounded her. There was no excuse for delaying her cold march out the front door. Yet, she sat there drained of strength.

She regarded her reflection in the vanity mirror. Her cheekbones were smudged with mascara. She unscrewed the cold cream jar and mindlessly cleaned her face. Once she had stepped out the front door, there would be no turning back. The finality of that action kept Angela seated before the mirror, applying a fresh coat of makeup to her face, playing for time. Half her lifetime had been shared with the man she had just walked out on, she reflected, and here she was, sitting in limbo, painting on new eyes as if she were expecting to receive guests for tea.

As the minutes ticked by, Angela struggled against the thought of giving Douglas another chance. He had been her one and only love. Despite everything, she could not imagine life without him.

With shaking hands, she reached out to touch one battered steamer trunk that had held her bridal trousseau. It had traveled with her on a European honeymoon and across the seas to Japan when she had still felt like a glowingly happy bride, more completely in love than on the day she and Douglas Napier had exchanged their vows.

That memory brought tears to her eyes. She used her long fingernails to peel the trunk's thick wallpaper of travel labels down to one pasted there at the port of San Francisco. She had been pregnant with Douglas's child when a porter slapped on this sticker before her maiden voyage to Japan. As the expectant father, Douglas had pampered and caressed her. He must have loved me then, Angela told herself. He must have loved me on our wedding day to have sworn to it in a church before God.

"Angela?" her husband now called softly from the other side of the bedroom door. "I was worried about you. Are you ill? Is there any way I can be of help?"

Angela quickly dried her tears with a handkerchief before opening the door to him. "No, I'm not ill—just weary and rather confused about us," she said, thinking how devoted he could sometimes be to her needs. "Come in." There was a glimmer of hope in his eyes as she invited him inside.

"I've been thinking there's a great deal of truth in what you said about us having a marriage. Well, one is entitled to second thoughts, Douglas."

"And have you changed your mind?"

Without answering, Angela watched him sit on the edge of the bed they had shared. A plaintive inner voice reminded her that Douglas had confessed to needing her; he had pleaded with her for a chance to make amends. The unhappiness of sharing him with a phantom lover was over. Natsu had been buried today. She no longer existed except in Douglas's memories, and time would erode those into steadily fading images. The dead could no longer hurt her, she told herself. For the first time in her life, she had Douglas all to herself.

Angela nodded her head and whispered, "Yes, I've changed my mind." She seated herself at the vanity mirror. Her face was drawn, mocking her failure to set herself free of this man who came up behind her, so handsome even in his grief. "Don't think this is forgiveness," she felt compelled to point out.

"I'm grateful to be taken back on any terms," Douglas said with much feeling. "You won't regret it, Angela. We'll make a fresh start."

"Can we, really?" she asked softly, turning on the stool to face him. He took her hands and drew her up to him. Although his tender kiss of gratitude spoke for promises that would not be broken, Angela knew she had won him only by outliving the dead.

She grew rigid and pushed from his embrace. "Let it be understood that I won't settle for things as they were," she said tersely. "Consider this in the nature of a trial arrangement."

Douglas nodded. "Any other conditions?"

"Yes. Do your mourning in one of the guest rooms. And I never want to hear that woman's name spoken again. Or that of her son."

Angela hugged herself tightly. For now Douglas was vulnerable, but she feared he might revert to form once his grieving ended. Natsu's son had shut him out, yet she now saw Paul's presence as a threat, a lingering shadow from the past who would keep Natsu's memory alive. "Maxwell drove you to the ceremony," she recalled aloud. "This morning, he told me of his intention to become friends with his half-caste brother."

Douglas had given no thought to his sons until her reminder. "Max left without me. I assumed he went off with Paul."

"I refuse to be punished by any relationship between your sons,"

Angela stated firmly. "Of course I feel sorry for that young man. But I don't want his face haunting our lives. Max can do as he pleases outside the home, but tell him to keep this friendship to himself. If you're hoping to get at Paul through him, dismiss the idea. It's clear Natsu's son turned you out as a painful reminder of the past. He showed good sense. So leave it be, Douglas. I need time in which to adjust—if that's possible. Now, I have a splitting headache."

Douglas watched his wife pull the bell cord to summon Mihoko. Angela nervously began snapping open the hasps of steamer trunks as if he were no longer there. He left her alone and descended the stairs to his study.

"The *okusama* won't be leaving us, Morita," Douglas told the butler, whose old eyes misted over. "Ask the cook to prepare me a bowl of soup and bring it to the study."

"*Hai, dannasama*. Right away," Morita answered, rushing for the kitchen faster than he had moved in years.

Julius Napier's glowering portrait had stared at Douglas long enough from its gilded frame above the mantelpiece. He took it down and placed it on the floor, turning his father's cold face to the wall.

Max felt the need for privacy. He had returned home to find that his parents had begun to settle their differences. That pleased him but he failed to see how it had any bearing on his own problems. He had talked with Shizue on the phone the night before. She had tried to sound cheerful, but he sensed her depression and had the feeling she was keeping something to herself. He felt depressed—and angry—that Jiro Mitsudara could spend all the time he liked with her. The lord was giving a party the next afternoon, in honor of his son's graduation from the military academy. Max was tempted to crash those gates and make a nuisance of himself. Only that would make a bad situation worse, he thought.

Max sat at his writing desk thumbing through the calendar. He would have to sail in less than six weeks in order to reach Cambridge in time for enrollment. Shizue had promised to wait for him. Perhaps during the time he was in school, she would outgrow her father's domination. "Bound for Harvard," he jotted down in the last week of August 1937, determined not to leave Japan without seeing Shizue again.

Max opened the folio containing the writings Paul had given him to read that afternoon. Natsu's son had a quiet strength, an openness in his keen hazel eyes that had made it easy for Max to talk about himself. He realized now that he had carried the conversation while Paul just soaked it all in, nodding and offering occasional sparse smiles. Only when Max had described his summers spent on the Hosokawa lands did Paul break his aloofness and draw Max out about the baron's daughter. Afterward, he grew silent and grim-faced. Max recognized Paul's moodiness as that of a Napier. Though the two brothers had grown up in markedly different environments, Max detected similarities in their natures that defied explanation.

Max started to read one of Paul's articles dealing with financial cliques such as Lord Mitsudara's *zaibatsu*. He was excited by Paul's talent and impressed by his fury over the social injustices endured by the Japanese people because of a small but powerful minority.

Max shared Paul's ideals and felt proud to have such a brother. Had they grown up together as siblings, there might have been petty jealousies between them. Now they stood on unbroken ground as grown men, and Max foresaw no difficulties that could not be overcome. The day had taxed his mind. His eyes grew heavy, and Paul's writing slipped through his fingers.

Douglas knocked at the closed door of the master bedroom. Angela did not respond, and he entered the room cautiously. She was sound asleep facedown across the bed. An empty martini pitcher sat on the night table beside an open vial of pills. It was a hot, humid night, and she slept naked, half-covered by a satin sheet that caressed the lines of her shapely buttocks and legs. Her body smelled of the Parisian bubble bath she was so fond of.

She was the mother of their son, the woman who had made them a family, Douglas thought. On some future night he must return to this bed, prepared to perform his husbandly duties with more than the weary displays he had brought to their lovemaking over the last months of their stay in Germany. A year without the pleasures of lying in Natsu's arms had squelched his sex drive. Douglas was often guilty of calling upon Natsu's image to have sex with his no less beautiful wife. Natsu had been the only woman he had ever truly desired, and one could not conjure up the image of the dead to make love to the living.

Douglas slid a pair of silk pajamas from his dresser drawer, painfully aware of what was lacking in his marriage and of how difficult it would be to make good his promises to Angela. But he was home to stay. He would never return to the apartment he and Natsu had shared. That day he had locked the door, leaving all her personal belongings there. Without saying a word, he had handed the key to the desk clerk. Oddly enough, the rent had fallen due on that very day, as if fate had written an end to their destiny on the clerk's inked ledger book.

The grief suddenly ripped through Douglas, bringing on an attack of tears. He stumbled to the room adjoining that of his son. His love for Natsu was undying. For the rest of his days, he would be haunted by the beatific face of the young girl he had first seen in the castle gardens, where her mother's voice called, "Natsu!" and his knees had melted with the sound of her name.

CHAPTER 15

It was the afternoon of the formal party honoring Cadet Lieutenant Jiro Mitsudara. That morning Shizue had wept bitterly, called to task by her father for defiantly refusing to leave her room in the lord's house. The baron had ordered her to attend the party—and to be on her best behavior. Now fire had replaced the tears in Shizue's eyes, as she stepped into the festively decorated Japanese garden. She was still forbidden to see Max; the marriage agreement was still binding. But her solitary days spent in meditation had given her insight that might help solve that dilemma.

The shoji doors at the rear of the huge house had been removed, opening its rooms to the garden. No guests had arrived as yet. Shizue presented herself to the lord's mother, a dour-faced matriarch of eighty dressed in black silk. The woman stood at the head of a receiving line that included the other family elders. "Mitsudara-*sama*," she addressed the old woman respectfully, and bowed.

Lady Mitsudara's voice was irritatingly harsh and nasal, like that of her powerful son. "How lovely you look," she complimented Shizue. "I am glad to see the illness that confined you to your room has run its course. Your daughter is a delight, Baron."

"The kimono Shizue wears was handed down to her by my late wife, Mitsudara-*sama*," Baron Hosokawa replied, wearing a proud smile.

Shizue gracefully bowed to each family elder in the receiving line. Yufugawo had done up her hair with a gold fan-shaped comb, and she wore the peach-colored silk kimono embroidered with royal cranes, which had belonged to her mother. She wished Sumie were in attendance to offer encouragement; there was much Shizue hoped to achieve by attending this party.

Jiro Mitsudara was her official escort, and he greeted her with a friendly smile. "Glad to see you're feeling better. It promised to be a stuffy affair without your company," he whispered as she stepped into line beside him. "The guest list reads like the social register. Don't be nervous. Just smile and bow while I introduce you to the mighty."

"I'm not the least bit nervous." Shizue snapped open her fan and watched the first guests entering the garden, their invitations collected by a servant who announced their titles and names. Shizue had not seen Jiro since learning of the marriage agreement, and it was all she could do to stifle her impatience to talk to him about it as the guests began filing past them. As a woman, she had absolutely no say in the marriage arrangement, but the bridegroom did have some say in the matter. If Jiro objected to her selection as his bride, the agreement between their fathers could be broken without loss of face.

"Your daughter and my grandson go well together," Lady Mitsudara told the baron.

"Yes, Mitsudara-*sama*, well suited to one another." Baron Hosokawa enjoyed a place of honor in the receiving line due to the marriage arrangement. His lord had begun to treat him as a member of the family. But privately, he had come to have reservations about his future son-in-law. He knew Jiro in only the most superficial way and had made an effort over the past few days to know the young man better. Jiro was a charming conversationalist, but he spoke only of the arts, of music and literature, and could not be drawn out to discuss his military training.

Baron Hosokawa glanced down the receiving line to the young cadet, thinking that Jiro's delicate mannerisms were ill-suited to his lieutenant's uniform. Jiro's sugary voice lacked authority, and he detected an unmanly gentleness behind the soft brown eyes, rather than the firmness expected of a young samurai of his noble lineage. Of course, blood did not always tell on the surface. The baron pushed these negative observations from his mind. Jiro was a Mitsudara, and that guaranteed his fiber.

"Ah, General Hoshi." Lord Mitsudara greeted an old friend and introduced the gracefully aging warrior to Baron Hosokawa. "Have there been any new developments in North China, General?"

"None. Our commanding general there reports a quiet climate. Perhaps too quiet." General Hoshi smiled wryly. "Chiang's refusal to accept our latest demands has taken the quarrel between us beyond the talking stage, gentlemen. Japanese civilians in China and their property there must be protected; we have too great an investment to withdraw our forces. The next shot fired by either side will plunge Japan into war. Then we'll have need of well-trained officers like your son, *Koshaku desu*," he said to the lord, using the formal term of address.

The sun was at General Hoshi's back, and Lord Mitsudara shaded his eyes with one hand while saying, "Now that my son has earned his commission, his active duty must be deferred until he has earned his degree in letters at the university."

"The uniform he wears carries with it a sworn obligation to serve his emperor," the general reminded him.

"Naturally. But as a Mitsudara, he must fulfill the obligations of his Bushido," the lord pointed out rather shortly. "After he graduates from Tokyo University, I will proudly release Jiro into the service of his emperor."

"Your influence grants him that privilege," the general said in a grave tone. "I suppose we should make some allowances to nurture the accomplishments so revered by our chivalrous ancestors. Even in a time of war." General Hoshi's smile placated the lord, but when he looked down the line at Jiro, his expression became grim.

Shizue's feet grew tired from standing in the receiving line. Still, she graciously greeted what seemed to her an endless stream of the Japanese power elite and their wives, who were attired in the traditional kimono, as requested by Lord Mitsudara's invitation. Except for cadets and key officers of the Imperial Navy and the Army General Staff, all the guests were dressed in the traditional manner, and they slowly transformed the garden into a quaint picture of the past.

At last Shizue's ordeal was over, and Jiro offered her his arm. "I must talk to you," she whispered urgently. "In private."

"Whatever it is will have to wait until after the party," he said, leading her across the garden. "Father insisted that I invite some of my classmates, and I must spend time with them," Jiro explained as they approached the gathering of other cadet lieutenants in full-dress uniform. "I made few real friends at the academy. But these fellows are pleasant and offered some relief from the military rigors. Be a friend and act polite."

Shizue resented being put off while Jiro conversed with his classmates. Their young ladies were older than she and docile, fluttering their fans and speaking only of the fine weather and the beauty of the garden. They kept to themselves, away from the men and their political conversation. Shizue felt suffocated in the little circle of chattering, subservient women. Jiro acted no better than the other young men; he paid no attention to her whatsoever. As a Japanese woman, it was not her place to join them and render an opinion.

She glanced back across the garden at her ever-watchful father, thinking of what he had said that morning when ordering her to be on her best behavior. She snapped her fan shut decisively, then brazenly stepped forward to meet the cadets head-on. "You all look so handsome in your uniforms. How did you earn these?" she asked, touching her fan to the tallest cadet's shiny medals.

"Fencing. Marksmanship," he said, pointing to them and grinning proudly.

"I've never fired a gun, but I have been trained in fencing."

"Have you, really?" the cadet challenged her with a laugh.

Shizue stood up to him. "I could show you a trick or two."

The cadet bowed. "Name the time and place. That is, if Jiro has no objections."

She saw how annoyed Jiro was, but gave him no chance to speak. "If I bested you at kendo, what of your pride?" she teased the grinning cadet, who bowed again.

"I'd safely entrust it and my honor into your beautiful hands, Hosokawa-*san*."

Jiro quickly took Shizue by the arm. "You'll excuse us. Father expects me to mingle with his other guests."

"Another of Jiro's tactical retreats from the firing line," the tall cadet said mockingly, and the others laughed.

"What's gotten into you today?" Jiro hissed under his breath as he guided Shizue away. "Making a spectacle of yourself before my friends."

"I'll do as I please, Jiro. You don't own me yet."

"What is that supposed to mean?"

Shizue halted by a wooden bridge that spanned a fish pond stocked with *koi*. "I'm referring to the marriage agreement." Jiro's mouth dropped open in surprise. "My father told me you've known about it all along," Shizue said indignantly. "Jiro, I thought we were friends. How could you have kept this from me?"

"I was ordered by my father not to speak of the agreement."

"Orders!" Shizue huffed, snapping open her fan and following Jiro's nervous eyes across the garden to where their fathers circulated together among the guests. "I was ordered to behave like your classmates' mindless women, whose opinions count for nothing. But you might as well know that I have a will of my own. I don't love you, Jiro, and I'm opposed to this marriage pledge."

"Please, keep your voice down," Jiro said through clenched teeth, as several guests came their way. "This isn't the place to discuss it. Behave sensibly."

"Oh, I see. You're afraid I'll cause an embarrassing scene. Well, I'm not afraid of your father." Shizue closed her fan with a whack against the flat of one hand. "I refuse to carry on this pretense between us like some timid little mouse, Jiro." A show of defiance might give the lord cause to reconsider choosing her as his son's wife, she thought, angrily lifting the hem of her kimono to rush off along a garden path away from the guests.

"Wait!" Jiro chased after her. He nearly tripped on his ceremonial sword. Swinging it clear of his legs, he hurried on, catching up to Shizue at a grove of trees. "What do you hope to gain by making a scene?"

"Your attention." Shizue threw back her head and walked on. "We'll talk now, away from all these staring eyes."

"Oh, very well." Jiro quickly faced back across the garden, where their fathers stood craning their necks to see the couple. A number of guests had witnessed Shizue's temperamental display, and they also stared at Jiro. Embarrassed, he took a moment to feign a posture of manly control, then turned and marched off after Shizue.

★ ★ ★

Baron Hosokawa felt humiliated. His daughter and Jiro vanished from sight, and the women guests clustered together, beating their fans in rhythm with their gossiping tongues. Lord Mitsudara locked both hands together at the base of his spine and glared at the baron, who strained for composure.

"You're owed an apology and some explanation for this display. I'm guilty of spoiling Shizue with a father's love," the baron confessed nervously. "I decided it was time she was told about our agreement. She protested against being pledged before she came of age. I had thought my daughter was old enough now to be made aware of her obligation, but after witnessing this humiliating scene, I see that she's still a child whose head is filled with romantic fantasies of idyllic love."

"Is that all." Lord Mitsudara showed his relief with a thin smile. "My son will know how to handle the situation. When he returns with Shizue on his arm, it will silence those gossiping old crows. But my mother's displeasure must be addressed," he said, responding to the summons of her gestured fan.

Baron Hosokawa followed his lord's example and fixed a frozen smile on his lips. He passed among the guests as though nothing extraordinary had taken place. Flanked by the family elders, Lady Mitsudara held court over the proceedings from a high-backed chair upholstered in red velvet. The lord leaned close to smooth her ruffled plumage with an explanation. Then mother and son joined forces in a look that reminded the baron that he was beneath them in station.

"Your daughter must learn to curb her spirited nature," Lady Mitsudara announced, and the family elders around her nodded solemnly.

"*Hai*, I quite agree." Baron Hosokawa suffered a humbling bow. As head of the family, the stern old widow enjoyed the last word. "A month spent in meditation with the Buddhist nuns should grant her ample time for reflection."

"We can only hope this is so," the lord's mother retorted. "Our family's interests cannot be jeopardized by the immature caprices of a girl. Beauty can be a curse in disguise."

"Rest assured that my daughter will not in any way stir you to displeasure again, Mitsudara-*sama*." The baron withdrew, eyes to the ground, like a samurai of old leaving the court of his lord. He could not imagine what Shizue was up to, but he wished to stifle any further embarrassing displays of temperament.

The baron sought privacy, making himself comfortable at a garden table under the bowing branches of willow trees. Rice wine served to calm his nerves. Earlier that morning he had visited the Napier mansion, where Angela's outwardly relaxed manner gave him reason to hope their dynasty would soon be set back in order. Douglas had kept to his room, sending Max downstairs to say that his father would talk business when it suited him.

The baron understood Max's hostile attitude. The young man was entitled to know that Shizue was pledged to Jiro, but the announcement must come from her. His strict posture had seemed only to encourage her willfulness, the baron thought, and was responsible for today's humiliating display. A less stern approach would serve him better. He decided to free her to see Max. Once Shizue told him the truth, Douglas's son could only bow to Shizue's fate gracefully; it was the gentlemanly thing to do. The baron could not lessen the wounding effects of Shizue's farewells with Max, but it was kinder to both lovers not to prolong the heartbreak of living on false hope.

Baron Hosokawa asked a servant to bring Yufugawo to him. He would instruct the woman to give Shizue a free rein when she saw Max.

In another part of the garden, Shizue had breathlessly come to rest near walls that were overgrown with vines. She had led Jiro to this spot, where no guests were likely to venture. After plopping down on a warped wooden bench, she kicked off her shoes and dug her stocking feet into the cool grass. She plucked the gold comb from her hair to let it fall free around her shoulders. In the past she had enjoyed wearing her mother's clothes, but that afternoon she felt trapped in the traditions they represented. "What a relief to be myself again." She sighed and shook her hair from side to side.

Jiro removed his cap and stuck it under one arm. "And who exactly is that?"

"Not the submissive maiden of the past these clothes would make of me." She glanced up at Jiro's soft eyes. He bore little resemblance to his father, she thought. Tall and slender, his delicate features gave him a pretty-boy look other women might find attractive. "Well, now that we're alone, haven't you anything to say?"

"I'm not exactly thrilled about the arrangement either."

That was what Shizue had hoped for. "I knew you'd feel as I do."

"Unfortunately, my feelings don't carry any weight." He grew somber. "My father is set on the match, and nothing I might say will change his mind. It isn't the end of the world, Shizue." Jiro smiled charmingly. "Look at the bright side. We're fond of one another."

"Fondness is no substitute for love," she replied in an anguished voice.

Jiro stood himself at attention. "Marriage is a partnership. The business of forming a family unit. The continuation of the Mitsudara bloodline rests with me. As an only son, I'm obligated to marry a wife of suitable breeding chosen for me."

"Oh, you've memorized your teachings well. You rattle them off like a trained parrot!" Rising from the bench, Shizue flung her gold comb at him. Jiro flinched. The comb bounced off his chest and landed somewhere in the grass. "I'm sorry—but you make me so angry! These aren't your thoughts at all. Why are you so terrified of your father? Don't deny it, Jiro, I've seen how you cower in his presence."

Jiro's face revealed an inner turmoil as he ran one hand back and forth across his short-cropped military haircut. "Father's word is law," he confessed. "His firstborn son died in infancy, and the obligations my brother would have inherited fell to me. If not for that, I'd be free to devote my life to teaching and the arts. Father knows how much I detested the military academy. He's also well aware that I want nothing to do with the business world. But there's no escape from my responsibilities."

Shizue had prayed to the gods for help and guidance. Now she knew that Jiro's desperate desire to pursue a scholarly life rather than be dragged into serving the lord's financial empire was the key that might unchain them both. Her sympathies were with Jiro as she took his hand and said, "All those dreadful years earning a commission. Now the lord's expecting you to enter a loveless marriage without a whimper of protest. Poor Jiro. Your father orders you about like some little boy without a will of his own. It hurts me to see you so at his mercy. Are you prepared to throw your life away simply because it's expected of you? Are you satisfied with being nothing more than your father's helpless pawn?"

"I could ask the same questions of you, Shizue."

He crossed the grass to retrieve her gold comb. Shizue looked away, stung by the truth in his quietly spoken reply. "I'm only a woman, completely at the mercy of men and their decisions. I hate the limits imposed on my sex! But you have a voice, Jiro. You have the right to object to this match. If only I had that voice to speak for you. But I can shout and scream and no one would hear me."

"You're very beautiful," Jiro told her softly, then cleared his throat and put on his cap. He tugged the visor low so that it shaded his eyes from her scrutiny. "I admire your spirit, Shizue, but knowing what you want and getting it are two different things. Our lives were determined for us at birth, and you'd be far happier resigning yourself to this marriage, as I have."

Shizue fought back tears. "Oh, Jiro, I could accept your resignation if you loved me. But all we feel for each other is friendship, and it can never be more than that. Think how unhappy we'll be without love."

"All this talk of love from a girl of sixteen."

"What would you say if I confessed that I loved someone else? Loved him with all my heart and soul."

Jiro shook his head with an amused grin. "Shizue, you overdramatize everything. You're much too young to be taken seriously."

"But I *am* in love!"

"Silly girl." Jiro quickly took her chin in his hand. "So in love with love. Now, I've heard enough. You can keep at me all afternoon, and it won't change my mind. Your eyes are so sad. One would think the hangman had put a noose around that pretty neck." He shrugged and laughed. "We've two years until you come of age. Who can predict what may happen before we're called upon to honor our fathers' agreement? Here," he said, holding the gold comb out to her. "Fix your hair and we'll return to the party. Just a few hours of boredom to suffer though and then we can relax."

"If only you would take me as seriously as you take your male friends, we might spare ourselves a great deal of heartache." Shizue dropped to a seat on the garden bench. Jiro thought her too young to know her heart. To name Max as her heart's desire and confess that she hoped to marry a white man would only make him think she was simple-minded.

She took the gold comb from his hand. As she was arranging her hair, she desperately tried to think of a fresh approach. "Two years is a long time," she said. "You could meet a beautiful girl at the university. Someone more mature. You could fall in love with someone else, Jiro. What would you say to your father then?"

Jiro only laughed. "Suppose I got struck down by a motor car while crossing the street? That would solve everything for you with far less complications than my falling in love."

"I'd never wish for that! Oh, do be serious, Jiro," she pleaded.

"I don't feel like being serious. Drop this nonsense, Shizue. Love isn't everything. Falling in love with someone else can only make us both miserable. I don't want to think beyond the coming year." In better spirits now, Jiro looked up at the treetops. "After today I'm free of this stifling uniform. Free of the narrow military mentality I've been forced to endure while I've worn it. At last I'm free to use my intellect. I can't wait to meet my fellow students. I intend to enjoy the next few years to the fullest."

Frustrated by his attitude, Shizue knotted her hands together in her lap. "A carefree time for you," she said spitefully.

"Time is what you make of it, Shizue. Why dwell on the unpleasantness of the future? We'll go on just as if this agreement didn't exist. There's no reason for our friendship to change." Jiro's smile faded. "I imagine Father must be furious. I'll have to deal with a nasty scene unless you return to the party with me now, smiling as if the incident were smoothed over. Will you do that for me, Shizue? I ask it as your friend."

Shizue sighed deeply. "How can I refuse? I didn't think that you might be punished for my behavior. Am I forgiven?"

"You're far too lovely to ask that of any man." Jiro shifted his ceremonial sword and sank to one knee. "Give me your pretty little foot."

She surrendered her stocking foot into his hands. "Promise to think over what I've said."

"Yes, I promise. Friends must stand by each other."

Kind and gentle Jiro, Shizue thought fondly as he slipped on her shoes. She was unable to remain angry with him for refusing to take her seriously. It seemed she must resign herself to waiting for time to take its course. And yet she could not accept the helplessness of her situation. Suddenly she burst into tears. "I don't want to make you my enemy, Jiro, but I'm not a silly girl whose feelings can be laughed away," she sobbed. "I'm a woman. Stand up to your father. If not for me, then do it for yourself. Object to this match and free yourself before it's too late."

"Father would only put me in my place," Jiro answered, nervously searching the pockets of his uniform for a handkerchief. "I'm all thumbs around you. Like some awkward boy."

"You're a Mitsudara!" Shizue brushed away the handkerchief he offered her, refusing to be consoled. "The lord would respect you for showing the strength of your bloodline. Jiro—if you strongly object to me as your wife, the worst that can happen is that your father will say no. Oh, please, you must try to break this agreement for both our sakes."

Jiro looked away from her, a pained expression on his face. "You're asking too much of me."

"The courage is there in you," Shizue insisted. "I know I should be satisfied with your promise to think about it, but this fear of your father makes me afraid. You're an officer now, trained to show bravery in the face of the enemy. You wear the sword of a samurai, Jiro. You've earned the right to wear it, and your father can't dismiss your feelings as he has in the past."

"Perhaps I *have* been too timid," Jiro said in a brittle tone of voice. Sunlight glinted off the oiled steel blade of his ceremonial sword as he partially withdrew it from the ornamental sheath. "Perhaps Father's been waiting for me to show more spirit. If I thought there was a good chance of reasoning with him . . ." He left the thought unfinished, thrusting the sword blade back inside the sheath.

"Tears are a most persuasive weapon." He gave Shizue a charming smile. "Especially those of a beautiful girl. I'd like nothing better than to rid myself of Father's stranglehold on my life."

"Oh, then you'll go to him and object?" Shizue rushed to hug him, but her gratitude was premature.

Jiro's manner darkened. He stood Shizue at arm's length, then released her and snapped to a stiff military posture. "Maybe I do love you in a way. You're the only person I've ever confided in. At times I think you know me better than I know myself. Forgive me for laughing at your feelings. I meant no harm. You want to marry for love. I want to peel off my obligations like the layers of this military straitjacket. When and if I find the stomach to assert myself, I'll let you know."

"Thank you, Jiro. I couldn't have hoped for more."

"Then we'll return to the party as smiling friends?"

"Yes, we shall always be friends." Shizue felt pleased, believing she had won a small victory for her and Max.

As they walked back, Jiro was unusually quiet. When the party guests came into view, Shizue looked to their fathers, staring at them across the garden. She hoped that the lord's troubled son would eventually spare her a fate worse than death, and smiled as she had promised to do.

* * *

At sunset Lord Mitsudara's guests departed. Shizue had performed well, smiling until her face felt stiff. A few remaining guests tarried in the garden, conversing with the lord and her father.

Lady Mitsudara called to her grandson. "Jiro, I wish to speak with you."

"Yes, right away." Squirming, Jiro tugged at his high collar. "Grandmother can often be worse than Father," he told Shizue, excusing himself with a bow.

In their black silk kimonos, Lady Mitsudara and the family elders reminded Shizue of a gathering of vultures perched beneath the garden trees. The sour old group dismissed her and grimly watched Jiro approach. As his wife, Shizue would be at their mercy.

She decided to seek sanctuary in prayer and entered the dark, forbidding mansion.

Two ornamental windows were set high in the wall at either side of the household god shelf. The translucent panes caught the setting sun's fiery glare as Shizue sat before the *kami-dana*'s miniature shrine asking the gods to assist her once again.

"Shizue."

She gasped and turned. "Yufugawo! You scared me half to death."

"Your father spoke with me this afternoon," Yufugawo whispered, turning her head to make sure no servants were about. "He has decided to allow you to see Max tomorrow afternoon."

"Oh, is it really true?"

"Yes, child. Your father instructed me to chaperone this meeting before we travel home together. I will not make a nuisance of myself." She smiled at the joy lighting Shizue's face. "You can have this time alone with Max."

Shizue bowed twice and twice clapped her hands to acknowledge the *kami*, sure they had intervened on her behalf. Nothing less could have softened her father's heart. After Yufugawo left the room, she offered thanks in silent prayer, watching the ornamental windows twinkling like twin stars in the night sky.

Only a few weeks ago she had celebrated the festival of Tanabata, when the girl star and the boy star reunited to swim in the celestial river. The year before, Max had stood beside her in the castle gardens, witnessing the mystical union. This year at Tanabata she had stood alone gazing into the bright heavens, missing her lover's strong, warm hand. If Max sailed to Harvard with her brother, she would observe many turns of the celestial pinwheel without him. Another two full turns and she would come of age.

Shizue walked back to her room, thinking she might have only the next day with Max. Suddenly her father's motives became clear. His heart remained hard as stone; he was merely loosening his hold on the leash. He was compelling her to be honest with Max about her obligation to marry Jiro.

Jiro Mitsudara waited outside the door to Shizue's room. "Grandmother interrogated me," he said. "I suspect the old woman disapproves of my father's choice. If I should object to this match, she might side with me."

Shizue excitedly fluttered her fan over the encouraging news. The seed she had planted in Jiro was taking root. Yet, his sensitive eyes lacked spirit, and she could not openly court Lady Mitsudara's displeasure again without bringing loss of face to her father. "Well, it seems we've found a friendly enemy to our cause," she said, acutely aware that his sensibilities had undergone enough pressure for one day.

"Maybe so," he allowed. "Come to my room and I'll play you my new phonograph records from Europe. I ordered one album especially for you—the Chopin nocturnes."

"After I've changed into something comfortable." Shizue watched him walk off to his quarters, a most unlikely soldier even in his splendid full-dress uniform. Chopin's music was so romantic, she thought. She would curl up in a chair while Jiro played his phonograph. He would read her some of the poetry he had written, then pull out folios from his collection of Japanese prints for them to browse through until she yawned and excused herself. Yes, Jiro Mitsudara was pleasant company. They had similar tastes in a number of things that she did not share with Max. Fondness versus love. It was no contest. But had she not loved Max, then her father's choice of a husband might have pleased her.

Alone in her room, Shizue opened the dresser drawer that contained her diary. She fingered its gold lock and remembered the last thoughts she had written on the gilt-edged pages on the night before Max returned home. The girlish secrets they contained were now in the realm of keepsakes. She had outgrown them, but not her belief in the power of wishes. Wishes were like stepping-stones placed across a stream, she thought. One by one they would lead to what awaited her on the opposite shore. Tomorrow held too many unknowns for Shizue to lay careful plans. Love would dictate her response when she saw Max again.

Uncertainties fled from Shizue's mind as Max rushed toward her across the landscaped grounds of Hibiya Park. But Yufugawo came between them and embraced Max.

"If only my husband were here to see his Ichiban, now grown into a man." Yufugawo sniffled, recalling how she had once rocked Max against her bosom. "Ah, where has the time gone? Forgive an old woman's tears, but life is so short, so filled with uncertainties that now keep our families apart."

Max smiled. The woman's coarse black hair was grayer than he remembered it and her fleshy face sagged in folds. "Is O-nami well?"

"*Hai*, unchanged. While you were away, he often woke in the middle of the night, and I would hear his pen scratching the paper, writing you letters."

"Wonderful letters." Max glanced at Shizue, impatient to have her all to himself. "Too bad O-nami isn't here with you."

Yufugawo sadly pressed his arm. "My husband is like an old pine, rooted in the soil of Kyushu. In the city there is no room to stretch out his long limbs, and his large head bumps against doorways built for smaller men. O-nami will be so disappointed when you do not return home with us."

"Please, Yufugawo, we don't have all day," Shizue implored, seizing Max's arm. "You promised not to interfere."

"Go along." Yufugawo settled on a park bench, relieved to be off her swollen feet. The city heat always caused her joints to swell. Fanning herself, she sighed as the youngsters kissed, remembering when she was young and in love. "Return promptly at four o'clock. Your father will be here then to drive with us to the airport."

Shizue strolled off arm in arm with Max. "What a gorgeous day. I was so afraid it would rain and we'd be forced inside somewhere stuffy," she said exuberantly.

Max swung his gray felt hat in one hand and took a deep breath. "Why did your father suddenly allow us to meet?"

"It shocked me as well." Shizue thought about how her father was manipulating her emotions by this outward act of kindness. "Max, let's not spoil everything with questions. We've so little time to be together. Oh, I hate the telephone. Hearing your voice and not seeing your eyes is such a cheat. Last night all you talked about was Paul. There's so much you haven't told me about your father and Natsu."

"I know. I couldn't talk about that over the phone."

Max hurried them off the path, ducking beneath low-hanging branches to a shady glen of new mown grass. Here the park grounds dipped away from view of the city skyline, and they could not be seen by passersby.

As Shizue seated herself on a bench next to Max, she wanted only to be held in his arms until they were forced to say good-bye. She did not want to destroy all their hopes by telling him of her betrothal to Jiro Mitsudara. For now, Max's wish to share the past with her forestalled her confronting him about what the future might hold. "You seem uncomfortable about telling me everything you know," she observed, and managed to smile.

"Hearing this from me isn't the same as sitting with my dad in the apartment he shared with Natsu. But I want you to understand how their lives were manipulated by others," Max said, then began the painful task of recounting his father's story.

Max's timbrous voice and expressive eyes were those of a storyteller who was possessed by the sad fable he weaved. But the story was true, not meant to entertain, and Shizue wept at the end. Max put his arms around her, and both were silent, thinking of this story in terms of their own lives.

At last Max got up and dug his hands into his trouser pockets. "I've decided to go to Harvard," he said. "Dad isn't pushing me into it, but still I don't have any options. I'll sail for America as my father did, and yours will keep us apart until then. That much of the past is happening all over again, Shizue."

"Harvard is the other side of the world." Although there was a hot, humid breeze, Shizue experienced a shiver that raised gooseflesh on her bare arms. She massaged them, thinking of how Natsu had kept the truth of her illness a secret, while bravely sending her lover away to Germany. Often the truth could be so cruel, Shizue told herself, looking up at Max. She faced the hardest decision of her life. She could not tell him about the marriage pledge to Jiro. No, she decided to send Max away to America with hope.

"That rainy afternoon in the attic playroom, I told you Papa wasn't beyond my reach, that he would bend in time. Well, now I'm more certain than ever," Shizue said, her voice resonating with conviction. "Now I see that he's shown an understanding of how we feel by letting us meet like this. Papa didn't use the past as a lesson in obeying my obligations. No, he had only sympathy for Natsu and her son. It broke with his beliefs to guard your father's secret, but he acted out of love, and there's hope for us in that."

Silently she asked the gods for courage, afraid Max might see the truth about Jiro in her eyes. "Papa won't ever remarry. I'm his only comfort, and he's sure to keep me with him once I've finished school. Loneliness makes him so possessive. I'll be bound to him for years to come. Time is our hope, Max. It won't ever be too late for us," she promised him with all her heart. "I couldn't bear parting with you, knowing you'd lost all faith in our dream."

"Promises just aren't enough, Shizue." Max cupped her face between his hands. "I won't see you again before I sail, and what I feel can't be locked up inside me through all those months at Harvard. I love you too much for that." Time was running out for them, and he could no longer be the restrained gentleman. "Sweetheart, don't send me away again with only promises."

"*Anata. Itoshiihito.*" It was the first time Shizue had called him sweetheart, a term of endearment that increased the longing in her eyes. "My dearest, my beautiful Max." She gently stroked his hair. Only the bonds of her morality gave her pause before she said, "I want you to make love to me. I desperately want that as well."

Max kissed her with a searing intensity. Her lips opened to his mouth, and their kiss deepened. For the very first time Shizue allowed his strong yet gentle hands to explore the contours of her breasts. And then Max's hands found their way beneath her lacy satin bra. She stilled them from exploring her nipples. But his fiery touch on her flesh was too exciting to be fought, and her restraint melted. She wished that she were free of clothes and lying naked against him as she had so often in her fantasies.

Delirious, Shizue felt herself slowly sinking to the sweet-smelling grass. Max lay on top of her. They were a man and woman deeply in love, and nothing else existed for them.

Suddenly Max pulled away. Opening her eyes, Shizue stared up at him, questioning why he had stopped. Another instant more and she would have known what it was to hold him inside her.

Shizue heard the laughter of children. She heard the hollow thud of a bouncing rubber ball, then saw it rolling across the grass. Two small children ran toward them. The girl and boy regarded them with innocent faces, as Max helped Shizue to her feet.

The two children ran off to play catch, and Max lifted his hat from the ground soberly. Shizue brushed off her dress and fussed with her hair in an attempt to regain her composure. The interruption had come too abruptly, and she could see that Max's emotions were left dangling too.

Raindrops began to patter on the trees. Just a few drops of moisture from the passing clouds, but Shizue was suddenly conscious of the hour and of the fact that they were in a public park where others might have spied on them through the trees. Max had boldly taken the initiative, and she had willingly succumbed to their shared desire, their shared need to form a lasting bond against anything that might come between them. Now the moment was lost.

Silently, they looked at each other. Although Shizue's chastity remained intact, she no longer felt quite so virginal. By surrendering herself completely, she would have vanquished the forceful hold of tradition. Not her father, not the lord's power over him, would have threatened her once she belonged to Max as a woman. After today, she thought, they could never touch without desiring more. For the moment, though, they awkwardly avoided touching as Max handed Shizue her purse.

"It's almost four," he said as he nervously consulted his wristwatch.

There seemed nothing to say that had not already been said. Talk only choked their hopes, and walking together in silence did little to ease their difficult descent from the heights they had climbed.

Hibiya Park was an anomaly, landscaped partly in Japanese and partly in western style. Its winding paths offered sharp contrasts between two conflicting cultures. The overall effect was abrasive rather than serene. People dressed in the traditional kimono clashed with those dressed in western garb. One could feel the pull of opposing forces in the quietly moving stream of pedestrian traffic.

Shizue, still far from composed, stopped to use the comb in her purse as Max anxiously fidgeted with his necktie. It was just minutes before they must part. "Let's not say good-bye on such a gloomy note," she pleaded, pulling the comb through a snag in her hair. She picked a new mown blade of grass from its tortoiseshell teeth. "Oh, darling, those few moments were so wonderful."

"Miss your plane, Shizue," Max interrupted her, speaking urgently. "Let go of your father and give him something real to open his eyes. We can take a room at the Imperial Hotel and have tonight together."

"No, it wasn't meant to be." Shizue wound his arms around her waist, holding them tightly. "Father thinks the world of you," she said. "In time he'll give us his blessings."

"He'll never give in. Stop lying to yourself about that."

"If not, I won't hesitate choosing between you." She was shocked to hear herself say what might never be in her power to grant. If Jiro did not break this pledge, that awful choice would be thrust upon her. But now Max's eyes caught fire with renewed hope, and she could only reinforce it with another promise. "Max, I mean to have you no matter whom it hurts."

"If only you could prove those words today," he said. Gazing up at the cloudy sky, he felt a strange sense of foreboding.

Max's necktie was still askew, and Shizue straightened the knot. "I'll worry about you," she said, feeling strong and womanly enough to deal with the problem of Jiro on her own. "America's a frightening place, full of gangsters."

Max laughed ruefully. "Cheer up and give me one of those beautiful smiles to remember you by."

She did her best to please him. "Kiss me one last time so we can hold on to what we feel."

Max kissed her ardently, as if to bind Shizue to her promises and keep them from being carried off like wisps of smoke in the wind. "I adore you, Shizue. Hold on tight to the memory of this afternoon. I know I will. Through all the lonely days and nights without you."

Time had run out. It began to shower, and they ran along the path, huddled together under Max's suit coat.

Yufugawo anxiously twirled her colorful bamboo umbrella. "Hurry," she called to Shizue.

Lord Mitsudara's Rolls-Royce was pulling into view just outside the park entrance as Max whispered, "Sayonara." He held Shizue in his arms with an intensity meant to last him for the duration of his term at Harvard. "Have a safe flight home. I love you."

"And I love you." Shizue squeezed his hand, prolonging the contact until Yufugawo called to her once more. "Max dearest, I must go. Don't come to the car. Father might say things to spoil what we've had together. Sayonara," she said, and blew him a kiss before running to the limousine, where her father sat peering out the door, which was held open by the lord's chauffeur.

Yufugawo collapsed her umbrella, then accepted the baron's helping hand to climb inside. "Be gentle with the poor child," Yufugawo whispered to the baron.

"Get in out of the rain, Shizue," he told her.

All at once Shizue had doubts that her secret would be safe from Max, and she turned to watch him taking shelter under the park trees. Her brother was still vacationing with his friends and as yet knew nothing about the marriage agreement. Her father's aloofness toward Kimitake made it unlikely that he would feel it necessary to speak of this. But Kimitake told Max everything. She could not afford to trust so much to chance. Her father was staying on in Tokyo, where some slip of his tongue might expose Max or his parents to the truth.

"Please don't question me, Father," Shizue said, taking the seat beside him. "It was very hard to say good-bye to Max. I'd appreciate it if nothing more was said about this marriage agreement to anyone else." She prayed that fate would guard her secret until Jiro found his courage. Then Max would forgive her the deception that had spared them both. "I don't want this betrothal to Jiro made a subject of conversation. After all, it won't be honored until I come of age, and I'm entitled to enjoy some peace of mind until then," she told her father in a tearful voice.

"I'll respect your feelings in the matter." Tadashi was satisfied that both youngsters had come to grips with reality. He felt saddened by the faraway, wistful expression in Shizue's tear-reddened eyes. Even after telling Max of her betrothal to Jiro Mitsudara, thought the baron, his little girl still clung to her fantasy. He did not expect her to stop loving Douglas's son all at once. He would allow her to correspond with the young man. Gradually his little girl would settle for friendship and let go of her dreams, he thought, as he took her hand in his. "I'm proud of you, Shizue. I realize how difficult it was to do the right thing. But holding to Max on false hope was unfair to you both. Now he can go on with his life."

"Can he really, Papa?" Shizue sniffled, disliking herself for pretending to be her father's dutiful child. Her tears were genuine, and they led him to believe only what he wanted to believe.

Max waved his hat at the departing limousine, but Shizue did not turn to wave back from the rear window. The rain was like a badly needed cold shower, Max thought. His moment of passion with Shizue left him aching for her in a new way. He would carry this bittersweet ache of unfulfilled love to America.

As he walked on, the rain tapered to a misty drizzle, and he stopped to watch some youngsters play sandlot baseball. He wondered if his half brother had played baseball as a boy. He had arranged to meet Paul that afternoon, and Max boarded the underground railway to Ueno Station for the five-minute ride to Asakusa, a popular amusement center that was the Coney Island of Tokyo.

Paul's apartment was within walking distance of the amusement center, and Max had agreed to meet him on its main thoroughfare. Pleasure-seekers, not discouraged by the intermittent rain showers, stopped to look at the wares displayed in awning-covered stalls and eyed the cinema billboards. Max strolled the broad lane reserved for pedestrian traffic. It flowed toward the sloping tile rooftops of Kwannon Temple. Kwannon was a seventeenth-century Buddhist temple dedicated to the Goddess of Mercy. Feeling in need of mercy, Max strolled toward the temple grounds, window-shopping along the way. A charming display of Oriental objects caught his eye. He stopped outside the window of a curio shop, fascinated by the pieces set on a black velvet turntable. Antiquity preserved in jade, ivory, gold, and silver spun silently behind the rain-streaked window glass. One shiny object, a tiny elliptical ornament on which an intricate design had been etched, held him mesmerized, and he stood watching it slowly disappear from sight, then move into view again.

He entered the dimly lit shop. The air was layered with the pungent smoke of incense sticks burning in long-stemmed ebony holders. Max pointed to the object displayed on the turntable, and the shopkeeper removed it from the window display and set it on the counter on a black velvet jeweler's cloth. Max knew he must have it for Shizue.

The piece was a miniature work of art, just half the length of Max's thumb. In the center of the tiny ellipse was a bird whose feathers had the warm look of gold. Japanese characters were etched around either side of the bird's wings and set against a delicate motif of cherry blossoms. "What can you tell me about the piece?" Max inquired.

"It is copper and silver, inlaid against silver leaf," the shopkeeper said. Just a wisp of a man in his seventies, he perched on a high stool behind the counter. "This work is *shibuichi*, a method of working various metals used by master swordmakers of the eighteenth century. Such ornamentation was common to swords and daggers carried by samurai of that period. I can only assume this piece was executed by the artist to perfect his craft. Everything cannot be appreciated with the naked eye, *O-botchan*," he said, addressing Max as "young man." He held out a magnifying glass. "A good luck piece. These characters etched around the bird speak for happiness and good fortune. It is the bird, Hōō. Quite an unusual and animated depiction."

"Yes, that's what caught my eye in your window." Max examined the workmanship through the magnifying glass. The fabulous bird, Hōō, was the Japanese phoenix—a symbol of eternal life, as well as a symbol of undying hope. Inlaid in copper against the silver leaf, the bird seemed about to flap its wings and rise into flight. It was flawlessly engraved down to the quills of each feather and the sharp talons of one foot, which were curled around the blossoming branch of a cherry tree. Shizue's birthday was in early spring, when the cherry trees were in full bloom, Max thought. He envisioned her surprised delight at receiving this unique treasure.

While bargaining with the shopkeeper, Max turned the ornament over in his hand. The back of it was badly scarred. "It looks as though someone gouged the metal with a knife," he said. "Why would anyone damage something so beautiful?"

"No doubt this piece changed hands many times before finding a home in my shop. Perhaps an angry thief tested the metal for hidden gold. I'm afraid it is too deeply marred to be polished smooth."

"But this is perfect for what I have in mind," said Max. "Can you fix the piece so it can be worn on a chain?"

The shopkeeper nodded. "*Hai*, a setting can be made for it. Of the same shape, of course." Taking out a pencil and paper, he made a quick sketch. "This will cover the scratches and provide a small eyelet for the chain. Is it for a lady to wear?"

"Yes, someone very special."

"Ah, so, then you will want gold for both the setting and the chain. Expensive, but warmer against the skin than silver."

The shopkeeper brought out trays of antique gold chains. Max selected a delicate chain that complemented the ornament perfectly. Strong yet light as Hosokawa silk, he thought, weighing the chain in one hand.

After they had agreed on a price, the shopkeeper said, "To fashion the setting will require some weeks, young man."

"I must have it no later than the last week in August. Telephone me when the work is done." Max wrote down his number, and the old man bowed, promising to have the amulet ready by then.

When Max exited the shop, the late afternoon sky was clearing of rainclouds, and the sun was a brilliant orange color. In his mind's eye, Max saw himself in America, where his years apart from Shizue would be charted by this orange ball's risings and settings. Today he had found a keepsake that would help lift Shizue's spirits during his absence. The thought made him smile. He walked on through the crowds, bound for the gates of Kwannon Temple. His half brother was already there and waved at Max with a folded newspaper he held in one hand.

"You're late," Paul said rather irritably.

"Sorry, lost track of the time."

As the two young men walked on, Max began to talk freely about his good-byes with Shizue.

"While you were strolling in the park, I put in a hard day's work at the newspaper. Let's get something to eat," said Paul. He had felt a twinge of jealousy at the mention of her name. Unaware, Max continued to share his thoughts while they entered a restaurant.

Seated across the table from his half brother, Paul might have discouraged the intimacy of Max's confidences. And yet he felt helplessly entangled in the web spun by Max's need to express his emotions. Through his words, Shizue Hosokawa became a real presence who had entered Paul's life by the door he had opened to Max just three days ago.

After dinner, Max walked Paul to his nearby apartment, hoping for an invitation that was not extended.

"I'll invite you up some other time," Paul said, guarding his privacy.

The young men parted with a friendly handshake, then Paul entered the squalid building alone and climbed the stairs to his apartment. The books he had collected over the years were still in boxes stacked around the small rooms. A gloomy place, he observed, but far removed from the bitterness of his past, which haunted the rooms he had once shared with his mother. Being with Max tonight had helped take his mind off his grief, but Shizue's face haunted him now. He settled down at his writing desk and tried to lose himself to work. But it was no use. Thoughts of the baron's daughter destroyed his concentration.

In the days that followed, Paul's time was consumed by work at the newspaper. Max had no career to occupy his days and looked forward to evenings spent at Paul's small apartment now cluttered with the books unpacked from their boxes. Paul talked mostly about politics and literature and took it upon himself to correct gaps in his half brother's education. Max talked mostly about Shizue. One evening as he paced between the stacks of books on the floor, bemoaning the pain of being kept apart from Shizue, Paul became enraged.

"This racial covenant of your dynasty is the cancer that killed my mother! I'm fed up with all your talk about something that's a constant reminder of my past! Love has dulled your senses, Max." Paul tore open the door with a sweeping gesture. "I was wrong to think we could find something more in common than our blood. Go home to your satin sheets, where you belong."

Max paused outside the door. "Paul, I'm sorry. I just didn't think," he said quietly, afraid his insensitivity might not be forgotten.

"Go home!" Paul slammed the door, then grew angry with himself for allowing the past to destroy a friendship he could not afford to lose. He opened the door again and walked to the landing.

"Max," he called down the stairs to his half brother, who stopped. "Meet me tomorrow at noon. The American bar across the street from *Nippon Shimbun*."

CHAPTER 16

The American bar located across the street from *Nippon Shimbun*'s offices was a popular watering hole for the newspaper staff and members of the foreign press. As Max entered, he paused, observing Paul sitting alone at a table, hunched over a beer. From outward appearances his half brother seemed in a foul mood. Max approached the table warily. "Hi."

"Hi, yourself." Paul felt ill at ease as Max pulled out a chair and settled down across the table. "About last night . . ."

Max shrugged. "I had it coming to me."

"Want a beer?"

"No, thanks."

"Sorry for blowing up at you that way." Paul apologized with difficulty, averting his eyes as he lit a cigarette. Smoking was a newly acquired habit, and he coughed on the first drag. "I think it's past time I said a few things—private things about myself. You wouldn't know me any better for rehashing all the sordid details of my childhood. So, I'll make it short and to the point." His cigarette burned into a long ash before he spoke again. "I grew up running a bloody gauntlet. One fistfight after another. But that still didn't end the constant baiting I got from the other boys at school. Sometimes they ganged up on me, chasing me home up and down alleys like some stray dog." Paul's glass struck the table hard. "When I entered the university, life wasn't much better. I was rejected by my Japanese classmates and even by foreign students. Over the years, I grew a thick skin. Not quite thick enough when it comes to being rejected by women, however." Paul looked down at his glass. "That's another reason why it's hard for me to listen to your talk of being in love. You have Shizue, and I have no one. To women," he said softly, "I'm something of a freak."

"People can be stupid and cruel," Max said, saddened by his half brother's words. "Paul, you must have found intelligent people who weren't blind to everything but your mixed blood."

"Oh, yes, once in a great while there's been a friendly face in the crowd. Professors who encouraged my talent. Tamura-*san*, who gave me the opportunity to prove myself. Any success I enjoy is owed to him, and I've a deep affection for that man. He's been like a father protecting me from those hyenas." Paul motioned to the reporters crowding the long mahogany bar. "My fellow journalists, Max. Members of the press from around the world. They associate only with their Japanese colleagues who are pure-blooded. White or yellow, I'm not good enough for those bigots. To them, I'll always be looked down on, no matter how high I rise above the pack."

It was a noisy gathering at the bar. Max saw heads turn their way and then watched Paul suck in his lips as if physically assaulted by a wave of laughter.

"You're better than that group of drunkards," Max said.

"Try telling them that and see what it gets you. I once made the mistake of trying to join their exclusive club and was elbowed from the bar. So, I sit here drinking my beer alone." Paul signaled the waiter, then put his elbows up on the table and rested his chin on his hands. "Since we first talked, we've sidestepped the crucial difference between us. I invited you here to see how it really is for me. Not a pretty picture, but I've learned to live with it, thanks to my mother. Her love sustained me. I still can't believe that she's gone." He looked away from Max. "Sometimes I feel her presence watching me, imploring me to turn the other cheek to this crummy world."

The waiter appeared and impatiently flicked his bar towel. "You wanted me, mister?"

"What took you so long?" Paul snapped at him. "Bring me another beer. And one for my friend. Come on, Max, it'll help lighten the conversation."

"All right." Max observed the waiter, who picked up Paul's empty glass as if it might be contaminated. Until that moment he had not really paid attention to how others saw his Eurasian brother. Paul shrugged it off with a slight smile, and Max could only smile back, lacking the words to express his empathy.

A copy boy suddenly rushed inside the bar, calling Paul's name. "Tamura-*san* said to bring you right away," the copy boy said breathlessly, halting at their table to hand Paul a sheet of paper torn off the teletype machine. "There is fighting in China. We have bombed Langfang."

Paul seemed stunned by the news dispatch he read.

"Has war been declared?" Max asked, as the pay telephones at the far end of the bar began to jangle one after another, creating a stampede of reporters to answer them.

"I don't know!" Paul shouted back, and ran to the door.

Max followed him into the street. "Can I come with you?"

"Yes, why not!" Paul stopped on the curb, searching for an opening in the traffic. "Chinese and Japanese troops skirmished at the Langfang railroad station last night," he shouted, sharing what he knew, while Max zigzagged across the street with him. "Heavy fighting broke out. Japanese reinforcements were dispatched from the garrison at Peking. We bombed the Chinese barracks in a dawn raid. Langfang has fallen, and we've occupied the city!"

Paul shoved Max along to an elevator in *Nippon Shimbun*'s lobby. "Get this car moving!" he yelled at the elevator operator. When the doors opened on the newsroom, Paul said to Max, "Follow me!"

News of Japan's aggression in China had turned the newspaper staff into a jubilant crowd standing in the aisles between their desks. Hideo Tamura shouted at them for order, then made his way toward Paul. Paul introduced Max, but Tamura dispensed with the formality of a bow and took Paul by the sleeve, leading him to his newsroom desk.

"We're putting out an extra edition," Tamura said, speaking quickly. "Prime Minister Konoye has granted General Katsuki permission to protect Japanese lives and property forcibly in North China."

"Then we're in a state of war," Paul responded, rather dazed by the reality of what was taking place across the China Sea.

"Communications from the battle zone are poor," said the editor-in-chief. "We know that two Japanese divisions of reinforcements were sent to Shanghai and Tsingtao. Domei News Agency and our own sources there have wired us sketchy accounts of the fighting. I'm trusting you to work from these and what other scraps come in before our extra goes to press." Tamura motioned toward Paul's desk, which was littered with teletype messages and cables. "There's been no formal declaration of war with the Chinese republic as yet. But this could well be the start of an unlimited commitment of Japanese forces. Here's your headline, Akira. 'China Incident!'"

"The publisher returning your call!" Hideo Tamura's secretary called out.

"In a minute!" Hideo Tamura placed a hand on Paul's shoulder and said in a voice choked with emotion, "Today I'm fulfilling a promise I made to Natsu. Your words carry great power, Akira. Choose them wisely, and it will encourage our publisher to take a personal interest in advancing your career." His gaze shifted to Max. Paul had spoken of their friendship, and Tamura smiled. "Have a seat, young man. You're welcome to stay and watch your brother in action."

Max returned the editor's bow. "Paul, are you sure I'm not in the way?"

"No, relax and pull up a chair." Paul watched his mentor cross to the glass-enclosed office midway down the newsroom and lift the telephone. "*Nippon Shimbun*'s publisher is a powerful man," he said, heaving a deep sigh as he sat down behind his desk. "Sketchy reports like these don't add up to much of a story," he went on, sifting through the cables. "The story of a lifetime's just been dropped in my lap, and it's a bloody jigsaw puzzle with the essential pieces missing."

A fevered patriotism held sway over the newsroom. It seemed Japan had finally initiated a full-scale war with China, and everyone around Max rejoiced as though this would bring about a cure for all the nation's ills. Max loosened his necktie, in awe of Paul's calmness under pressure. He watched with fascination as the papers littering his brother's desk were annotated and arranged into a neat, orderly pattern. Then Paul covered his eyes with his palms. His concentration was so intense, Max could almost hear him thinking.

"Cable from Peking, Yoseido-*san*."

Paul's head jerked around at the copy boy, and he grabbed the cable. He scowled as he read it. "Seventeen planes participated in the bombing of Langfang," he told Max. "Chinese troops suffered heavy losses, and Chinese civilian casualties were heavy as well. But our sources at Peking don't know what the hell is taking place in the thick of the fighting. If I was in there, you can bet I wouldn't be sitting it out safely in a garrison fifty miles from the action waiting for the news to come to me!"

The sweep second hand on the newsroom clock now became Paul's taskmaster. Sketchy accounts of the battle lay spread out before him like a grinning skeleton in need of flesh, a heart, a soul, the voice to cry out against the carnage of what Paul believed was an unjust war. But his pen faltered. This was not the university classroom, where his youthful idealism had flowered, but the nerve center of a powerful newspaper controlled by a prowar publisher, and his own zealously held beliefs must be surrendered. Sacrificing the truth had him perspiring, his hands clammy while he fashioned a stirring account of Japanese victory in the taking of Langfang.

He played down the number of Chinese civilians killed in the bombing and lauded the Japanese pilots for showing heroism in the face of enemy artillery fire. Yoko's son might be among the ground troops who had seen action, and he recalled saying that someday his pen might help make Toru a hero. Now he imagined a loaded rifle in the young samurai's hands. Paul used this image to breathe life into his account of heroic Japanese infantry charging through the Chinese lines. His words would fan the fires of Japan's imperial expansionism. That was what *Nippon Shimbun*'s publisher wanted. As the last page of copy sailed into the desk tray, Paul sat back, exhausted from having traded his ideals in exchange for a step up the ladder of success.

Max had quietly sat there reading Paul's story as it took shape. Paul waited for him to finish the last page, then said, "Well, what do you think?"

"You compromised your ideals."

"Editorial policy!" Paul lunged across the desk, snatching the pages from Max's hands. "I don't need you to act as my conscience."

"Maybe you need to be reminded of all our conversations," Max answered in a challenging tone. "Only the ruling elite stand to profit from war with China. It will block the way to social reforms and slowly bleed the Japanese people dry. Those are your own words, Paul."

"Sorry, but I can't afford the luxury of crusading for my beliefs. I can't expect a rich man's son to understand what it is to work for a living."

Paul stalked off to the editor's office with his story in hand while Max became the target of icy stares from the newsroom staff. He could not overhear what was being said by the reporters who huddled together. One beefy man with fists like sledgehammers poked those around him. Then everyone faced Max and exploded with laughter. He rose to his feet, bearing the brunt of their bigotry as Paul's brother, but he was at a loss for how to redress this mild instance of what Paul had so long endured.

Paul exited Tamura's office. Ignoring Max, he went straight to the elevator. "Roof," he told the operator, looking away as his brother squeezed inside the closing doors. He held Max at bay with his scowl.

The car door opened onto *Nippon Shimbun*'s landscaped rooftop, where a small Shinto shrine offered a pocket of tranquility high above the roar of the city. Paul often sought the stillness there to recharge his energies. It had drizzled, and the wood benches were damp. He wiped the slats of one bench with his handkerchief, then sat down, stretching out his long legs.

"Allow me to straighten you out, Max," Paul said with authority. "Today my ideals came up against the hard reality of fact. There's no future for social crusaders in Japan. We've gone to war. That course is set, and the way to social reform is blocked. Before too long the doves in the government will be slaughtered. The Japanese press will become a propaganda machine like that in Nazi Germany, and our journalists will write what they're told to write." He lit a cigarette and dragged on it, exhaling puffs of smoke to underscore his points. "My career is on the line every minute of the day. *Nippon Shimbun*'s publisher is a war hawk. He dictates policy, and I'm not about to kiss my future good-bye. Wake up, Max. Your easy-come-easy-go life doesn't qualify you to act as my conscience. Hosokawa-Napier, Limited, stands to profit from this war, and you can't escape being corrupted, either. Your parachutes will be strapped to the backs of trained killers in uniform. Japanese and Chinese blood will be spilled to pay for the fancy clothes on your back and your Harvard education. Sorry if I disappointed you by selling out my ideals, but it isn't a matter of choice. Like it or not, you don't have any more of a choice than I do. So, don't play the righteous brother. Don't presume to be my conscience until you can put your own beliefs into action!"

The anger in Paul's voice challenged the tranquility of the rooftop shrine. He faced its lone worshipper, a gray-haired woman dressed in a black cotton smock who each day wheeled her cart through the newsroom serving tea and cakes. Her sad old eyes met his for only an instant, and he saw them as Natsu's eyes judging his actions.

"Today," Paul said softly, "I confessed things to you I've never told another living soul. Not to solicit your pity, but to gain your understanding."

"And I let you down." Max was angry with himself. "Who am I to question your decisions? Maybe life forces us to outgrow our youthful visions of truth and justice. The way you've been shunned, it's amazing you didn't give up your ideals years ago. Why should you give a damn for Japan and her people?"

Paul shot to his feet. "My people! I am Japanese. Natsu's blood runs in my veins, and that gives me more of a birthright here than you can ever lay claim to with your white skin!"

Max saw his brother truly for the first time, not as a Eurasian cursing his fate, but as a Japanese proudly asserting his identity. He soberly turned away. "I'm guilty of not recognizing that critical difference between us, Paul. Being denied your Japanese birthright must be the cruelest injustice of all. You opened up to me, and I hurled accusations at you. I always seem to do the wrong thing."

"Don't be so hard on yourself." Paul took Max firmly by the shoulders. "These things needed to be said. Hell, brothers can enjoy a friendly scrap now and then. We've missed having that as boys together." Paul tried relieving the tension with a laugh. "Come on, Max, don't hold back. Don't censor your thoughts just because I might bark at you again."

"Okay." Turning, Max asked, "What's your ambition? Fame? Power? To prove you're a Japanese by marching to war with pen and paper and becoming a hero of what seems to be the popular cause?"

Paul slowly nodded his head. "Yes, all those things. These are sad but exciting times, Max. This war is an awesome source of material to serve my ambitions. History is written by men like me, dipping their pens into the blood, not seated behind desks like cowards, but risking death beside soldiers in the battlefield. Wars cause everyone to rally around a common cause. My talent will bring down even the barriers erected against these eyes of mine, and I'd be a fool not to seize the moment. For once I want my fair share of this goddamn world. Yes, men are made or broken by wars. But I'm a survivor, Max. I'll come out of this as someone of importance, whose voice can't be ignored. Maybe then I can be a crusader for good in Japan."

"The price of success might destroy all the good in you," Max countered strongly. "Have you thought of that?"

"I'm willing to risk the consequences."

Blue-white lightning flashed across the Tokyo sky. Thunder followed like the distant thumps of artillery fire that Max remembered hearing the previous autumn in Germany while he had been bicycling in the countryside. Nazi tanks had blocked a crossroad, and he was forced to stop. He had watched as columns of troops marched to army maneuvers, their young faces tempered with the hardened steel of Prussian pride. Paul's face had taken on a similar hardness. His eyes were shining with the new sense of purpose he had exchanged for his old ideals. Natsu's blood exerted a strong force on her son, pulling him into the tides of war to prove he was a Japanese. At that moment, Max felt closer to Paul than he ever had—and suddenly he was also afraid for him.

For Max, the expanding conflict in China seemed to accelerate time as Chinese cities fell to the Japanese with lightning swiftness. In August, as Tokyo sizzled in the last dog days of summer, people in the streets were whipped into a patriotic frenzy, buying up newspapers that spoke of crushing the Chinese before the winter's snow.

An important errand returned Max to the Asakusa district and the curio shop near Kwannon Temple. Earlier, the shopkeeper had telephoned Max about the ornament he had purchased there some weeks before. As he entered the quiet shop the shopkeeper rose and bowed deeply. He brought out the amulet and placed it on a black velvet cloth, then waited expectantly for Max's approval. The ornament was even more beautiful now that it had been set in an elliptical yellow-gold frame. Max lifted it from the cloth, allowing the pendant to dangle from the delicate antique gold chain he had selected to complement its beauty. The craftsmanship more than exceeded his expectations. He sighed inwardly, feeling the specialness of this gift, and imagining the joy that wearing it would give Shizue. He held up the amulet like a necklace, delighted by the way the setting emphasized the sparkling copper plumage of the bird, Hōō.

"You are pleased, Napier-*san*?" the shopkeeper inquired.

"Yes, very much so." Max handed him a slip of white paper. "I'm having the amulet blessed as a charm by a priest at Kwannon. He wrote this invocation to be engraved on the back of the setting."

The shopkeeper studied the invocation. "I believe there is room enough to engrave these characters. Might I ask what the charm is intended to guard against?"

"Hata Sensei Ushiku is blessing it as an *omamori*, to guard against personal harm in one's journey through life."

The shopkeeper grinned and bowed. "Master Ushiku is revered by those of us who worship at Kwannon Temple. Because of his blessing, there will be much protection in your *omamori*, young man."

Smiling, Max consulted his wristwatch. "It must be blessed this afternoon. Will the engraving take long?"

"Twenty minutes." The shopkeeper clapped his hands to summon a pretty, young girl from behind a sliding screen. "Please, allow my granddaughter to assist you in selecting the gift wrappings."

Max judged the girl to be Shizue's age. He bent over the counter while she displayed satin-cushioned boxes, ribbons, and wrapping papers. For purity, he chose a plain box made of bamboo reeds. For beauty, he chose a rich-textured paper decorated with pastel water lilies, and finally a wide gold ribbon whose moiré pattern reflected the light. The shopkeeper reappeared, and his granddaughter sighed as she regarded the amulet. Smiling, the shopkeeper gently placed it facedown on a black velvet cloth.

Max examined the invocation now engraved on the gold setting, then looked up at the girl, who regarded him with questioning eyes. "It's a very special gift for a very special young lady," he responded, saddened by the thought that he would not be with Shizue to witness her delight, that he would not be there to fasten the chain around her neck and see how it glowed against her flawless skin. "Would you model this for me?"

The granddaughter happily obliged him. Her raven hair was cut to shoulder length, and she wore a print blouse open at the throat. She held the chain around her neck so that the amulet was shown off against her skin. The girl blushed, and her eyes were dreamy. Just for an instant Max saw her as Shizue. He thanked her, and she carefully set it down. "I'd like to write a gift card."

Max penned a love note to Shizue, which he slipped inside a fancy rice-paper envelope. The young girl sealed it with red wax that she dripped on the envelope from a square stick.

The amulet would be wrapped after Max returned with it from Kwannon Temple. There, for a small fee, it would be blessed as an *omamori*.

Max hurried the short distance to the temple. On the temple grounds he saw worshippers gathered around a stall that sold a variety of *omamori*s. This was a popular charm, purchased at the shrines and temples of Japan. Some of the *omamori*s were made of wood, others were only slips of paper. But all of them were inscribed with various invocations or with the pictures of deities, who guarded one against robbery, fires in the home, traffic accidents in taxis, and all manner of personal misfortunes. These on display were made of humbler materials than the gold of Max's amulet.

Taking it from his pocket, Max thought of the unusual nature of his request to have the priest bless it as an *omamori*. He paused to meditate before the large gilded statue of Buddha, whose benign face looked down on Max's gift to Shizue and seemed to approve.

"Napier-*san*." Hata Sensei Ushiku bowed a greeting. "You have brought the object to be blessed?"

"Yes." Max placed the amulet in Ushiku's outstretched hand. The priest was quite taken with its beauty. On his previous visit to Kwannon Temple, Max had talked with the owlish-faced priest at length before deciding on the nature of the blessing.

Now Ushiku bowed his clean-shaven head and blessed the charm. His concentration was intense; sweat ran down his skull. His prayers were offered silently, as if giving voice to them would shatter the spell of his communion with Buddha. Then he slowly raised his head and passed the *omamori* back into Max's hands as he spoke in a hoarse whisper. "One's journey through this life may burn briefly as a candle, or it may lead into the stillness and calm of old age," he said. "But one who is mindless invites misfortune, young man. One must think before one acts. It is not only the *omamori* that offers protection. The thought behind its blessing places one on guard against harm."

The priest's words echoed through his mind as Max exited into the bustling pedestrian walkway. The *omamori* was not unlike religious medals worn by Catholics, Max reflected. But his own faith was rooted in the beliefs of Buddhism. He turned and regarded the serene temple grounds. In America there would be no tranquil haven such as this temple, whose garden stones were worn smooth by the centuries. Suddenly his final hours in Japan were upon him. The next day he would be at sea, bound for Harvard.

Max returned to the curio shop, watching his *omamori* vanish within the carefully folded paper decorated with water lilies. The shopkeeper's pretty granddaughter sealed the small package with wax and bands of gold ribbon, then handed it to Max.

"A pleasure to serve you. Please, come again," she said, shyly lowering her pretty face.

Max left the shop and walked to Paul's apartment. Tokyo was sheeted with flags of the rising sun, displayed in support of Japan's involvement in China. The newspaper stalls were enjoying a brisk business. Headlines shouted news of Japanese bombing raids over Chinese cities and of Fascist bombings over Spain, where brother continued to fight brother in a bloody civil war. The year before, Mussolini had invaded Abyssinia unopposed by Great Britain. Hitler's troops had marched into the Rhineland with equal impunity, unopposed by Britain and France. The annexation of Austria was next on the Führer's agenda. While the super powers attempted to avoid going to war, pieces of the world were being given away to pacify the well-armed Fascist beast who grew steadily fatter and stronger. Max distrusted the logic of maintaining such a costly peace. To him it was like handing out appetizers at a dinner party. Rather than satisfying the Fascists' hunger, it only whetted their palates for the eventual feast to come. In many parts of the world, acts of aggression by Hitler and Mussolini were applauded, but with few exceptions, the West had condemned Japanese aggression in China. What served the ambitions of a white race seemed acceptable, Max thought, while the expansionist ambitions of an Oriental race were viewed as barbaric and uncivilized.

He entered Paul's apartment house, where two elderly charwomen knelt scrubbing the worn tiles of the vestibule. "I, too, have grandsons old enough to fight," one woman bemoaned as she rinsed her brush in the wash bucket. "These Chinese cannot feed themselves. So, how can conquering them put rice in our bowls?" The woman sighed woefully and shook her kerchiefed head. "If you ask me, this war trades bad for worse."

Her companion made a clucking sound. "There is nothing one can do about it."

"*Chin Chin Chidori*," the charwomen sang to lighten their burden. Max stepped around their soapy brushes, listening to this song from his childhood. Yufugawo had often sung it to him and Shizue.

As he climbed the stairs, Max's thoughts were of Kyushu's blue tile roofs, its fertile land capped in mist-shrouded mountain peaks, and Shizue confined there to what had been his second home in summers past. Sadly, he reflected on the all too brief rapture they had experienced while lying together on the sweet-smelling newly mown grass of Hibiya Park. Even the frustrating link of breathing his love to Shizue across the telephone lines would soon be broken. After docking in San Francisco, he might get through to her over the shortwave telephone pickup towers in Tokyo. Then all vocal communication would run out with the train rails to Boston, and he faced another year living on nothing but memories and letters.

Max knocked on Paul's door. There was no answer, and he knocked again. Finally, Paul opened it. Dressed in pajamas, he yawned and scratched his rumpled hair. "Worked through the night. On the graveyard shift again."

Max followed him into the tiny cluttered apartment. The bed covers were heaped in a knotted tangle. The stacks of books and periodicals seemed to have grown since Max's last visit.

"Tea or coffee?" Paul asked, lighting a match to the kitchen gas burner.

"Whatever you're having." Max set his gift package on the desk. Paul's landlord had raised his rent for the small cramped rooms in the rear of the shabby apartment house. Two dirty slivers of window faced out on a brick airshaft, and it was hard to distinguish day from night. The electric lights burned dim, flickering with the other tenants' demands on the poor wiring. Despite Paul's growing popularity, the newspaper paid him barely enough to get by. He had resisted Yoko's plea to move back into the cozy apartment above her tea shop. Paul's solitary existence in this drab place depressed Max, who was handed a chipped cup filled with black coffee.

An alarm clock ticked away the hour while Paul shaved and dressed. He talked of the war, steering away from what preyed on both their minds, until suddenly he blurted out, "Dammit, Max. I hate to see you go. Hell, I was just getting used to having you around. Look at me." Paul laughed as he looked down at his stocking feet, one blue, one brown. He turned to assault the dresser drawer. "So, you're going to Harvard for a privileged upper-class education. It's nothing to get maudlin and all choked up about. Where's that other sock?"

Max saw his brother's reflection in the dresser mirror. Paul's eyes were filled with tears. Max felt a lump in his throat. He wanted to embrace his brother, but Paul confronted him, dry-eyed now and grinning, the matching blue sock dangling in one hand.

Although the brothers had drawn closer, their relationship was still tenuous, and Max hesitated before saying what was on his mind. "I have a favor to ask of you, Paul."

"A favor?" Paul echoed as he bent to tie his shoelace.

"I'd like you to give this present to Shizue. It's a surprise, something special that I don't want to send through the mail. You can visit her when she returns to her school at Kyoto in the fall. I've talked about you so much over the phone, she feels that you're already friends." Max grinned.

"I know you'll hit it off together. You won't be so alone, and I'd feel better knowing that my brother's looking after the girl I love while I'm gone."

Paul raised his head, open-mouthed, while Max held out the small package tied with gold ribbon. Finally, he would meet Shizue, Paul thought. His brother's trusting smile was paving the way to their encounter, but Paul's personal desires caused him to hesitate a moment.

"Sure, I'll keep an eye on her for you," he said, trying to appear casual about what might prove to be his undoing as he stood up to accept the package. "Give me the address." He put the package on his desk.

Max jotted down her school address on the desk pad and the address of his Harvard dormitory. "You can write me here."

"Randolph Hall," Paul read aloud over his shoulder. "Sounds pretty fancy."

"Not from the way Dad described it. He and Baron Hosokawa roomed there as freshmen. Dad told me—" Max quickly broke off. Until that moment he had carefully avoided bringing their father into the conversation. "Sorry."

"He's your father. I don't think of him," Paul responded shortly.

Max shifted his gaze to some faded photographs and a leather-bound Bible on the desk. "Your mother?" he asked, taking the photographs in hand.

"Yes. Yoko paid me a visit with these things of my mother's, insisting I should have them."

"Your mother couldn't have been more than seventeen when this picture was taken." Until that moment, Max had only imagined the ravishing beauty who had captured his father's heart so very long ago. Natsu's all-knowing eyes stared out at him from the past, adding a deeper dimension to their love story and heightening his compassion for his father's and Paul's sense of loss. He was touched as he looked at the photograph of the young girl who had posed outside the Cherry Blossom Kissaten that summer of 1914 that Douglas had brought so vividly to life. His father must have snapped these pictures of Natsu and her spinster aunt. "She was very beautiful."

"My mother can't be judged from these faded snapshots. My mother was like a fragile flower. She never seemed to age through the years. Even when she grew so ill, her face was radiant, her skin like that of a young girl," Paul said softly.

He opened the Bible Father Watanabe had given his mother as a communion gift and removed his baptismal certificate from between the tissue-paper-thin pages. The yellowing certificate bore an image of the patron saint he had been named for. "She was a devout Catholic," he told Max. "My mother wanted me to accept her God. Her priest gave me instruction, and I accepted Christ only to please her. There isn't enough good in the world to prove the existence of this Christian God of love."

Closing the Bible, he pressed its soft leather cover to his chest. "I wish Yoko had never brought me these things. They only rekindle my grief—

they're like bridges linking me with the past. At her open grave, I told Douglas that some things can never be forgotten. Never forgiven. My mother's father is still alive. But he was incapable of forgiving her even in death."

"You never spoke of your mother's parents," Max said. "Did you ever have contact with your grandparents?"

"Yes and no." Paul rested his mother's Bible on the desk, observing how the gilt edges had been worn away by her years of turning to that holy book for sustenance. As he spoke, his calm surface disguised the stormy sea conjured up by what had been a dim memory. "I recall my mother dressing me in my best clothes. I couldn't have been more than three or four. Oh, she was so cheerful. We were going to see Grandpa and Grandma, she cooed to me sweetly, explaining that her parents had been away for a very long time. Grandfather's fleet of ships sailed the seven seas, and he often sailed on them, she said, trading silk for treasures. Secretly, she hoped that seeing his grandson would soften his heart. I remember being excited and nervous, clinging to my mother's skirt outside the gates to some grand house. I remember a servant appearing there, looming over us like some jagged mountain peak, while saying things that made my mother weep. I couldn't reach her cheeks to dry her tears.

"'Ogisan—Grandpa!' I cried and cried for him, but the bastard never showed his face, and my mother pulled me away by the hand. I remember her being sad for months afterward. I was too young to understand why we were turned away from my grandparents' house. That day, my mother realized the gates were closed to her forever. We never returned there."

Paul crossed to the discolored mirror and knotted his silk necktie. He had never before told anyone about that day. "I was twelve when my grandmother died. My mother took me to the burial. Her body shook as she wept. Those at the grave ignored us and her grief. I saw my grandfather for the first time. His eyes were gaping black holes, like the eyes of the blind, and he stalked past us both, his head bowed as if we didn't exist. Now he must be over eighty. He lives all alone. My mother's aunt died years ago, leaving her an inheritance my grandfather refused to pass on. I had thought he might attend my mother's funeral, but no, she was already dead to him, and the announcement I sent to his house was returned to me in its envelope. The flap was torn open. I assumed his tears bled the ink on my note."

Saying all this to his brother was a trial. Paul's hands trembled as he ran silver brushes—a graduation gift from Natsu—through his dark brown hair. "A few days ago I visited Mother's grave, and there he was— my grandfather—bereft of tears, handing money to the caretaker, instructing him to give extra attention to Natsu's gravesite. What a hypocrite!" Paul slapped the brushes together. "His honor was at stake if he neglected his daughter's final resting place. I stood back at a distance, watching this old man, aware of his loneliness and his pain. He turned and saw me, knowing damn well who I was. He expected me to come to him.

I was his grandson and the only heir to his dying bloodline. Grief made him weak to my presence. But just for a moment. Then his hands went out to thrash the air, as if erasing me from sight. He was dried up by age, wizened and stooped, and he leaned on his chauffeur as he climbed the hill to his car. I felt no pity for that sour old man. When he dies, I'll visit his grave to spit on the earth. Maybe there is a God after all. Maybe my grandfather's soul will be damned to hell." He put on his suit jacket. "Forget all this, Max. That part of the past had nothing to do with us."

Paul lifted his gray felt hat off the hook on the door. Pressing the crown with two fingers, he tried to smile as he regarded his sad-faced brother. "By this time tomorrow you'll be out at sea. I envy you going to Harvard. It's a university with an impressive history, and you'll be exposed to some exciting minds. Think of it as a turning point in your life, Max. You'll learn what it's like to be on your own. Don't worry, I won't forget to deliver your package to Shizue. First chance I get," he added soberly.

Just before his mother's death, Paul had stood close enough to Shizue to have reached out and touched her. But the past had created insurmountable barriers between them. To know her had been his fantasy. Now, when he carried his half brother's gift to Shizue, that moment he had so often dreamed of would become real.

"Come on, let's shake off the gloom and get out of here and enjoy ourselves," said Paul, wanting to embrace his brother but restraining himself. Indeed, he feared loving Max too much. Alone in the world, Paul had nothing to lose. Taking Max into his life also meant taking Shizue into it and he might be hurt, caught in the middle between his secret desires and two lovers who wanted him only as a friend.

Later that night, rain puddled up along the Ginza, reflecting its gaudy neon trimming as Paul and Max ducked for cover inside a taxi. After dinner they had gone to the cinema, laughing through a zany Marx Brothers film. But the newsreel that followed the movie had sobered them. It provided a riveting glimpse of the devastation wreaked by modern Japanese bombers on several Chinese cities. Both were pensive during the short ride that carried them past the Cherry Blossom Kissaten's blinking pink sign.

Paul coughed, snuffing his cigarette in the ashtray. Max looked worn and anxious as the taxi braked to a curb outside *Nippon Shimbun*'s offices.

"Well, this is good-bye." Paul's stomach felt tied in knots. "I'd be at the dock to see you off, but Douglas will be there. Good luck," he said quickly, and put out a hand.

Max gripped his hand firmly. But it was not enough, and he brought Paul close, his arm circling his half brother's rigid shoulders. "I'll miss you."

Without speaking, Paul eased away. In the cool blue fluorescent light

of the newspaper's doorway, he turned briefly to wave. Max wondered
how long it would be until they would see each other again.

The Napier mansion glittered just as Max remembered it in gayer times.
Morita was all smiles at the front door, where servants rushed to fetch the
departing guests' hats and evening wraps.

"Look, there's Max," someone called out before Max could slip up
the staircase unnoticed.

Angela had thrown one of her lavish dinner parties for Tokyo's
western society. It was a calculated effort to silence the whispers among
her acquaintances, most of whom she had avoided since returning to
Japan. She had accepted a handful of invitations just to keep up
appearances, smiling and explaining away Douglas's failure to attend as
"business demands." That night's affair had satisfied everyone that the
Napier marriage was not on the rocks.

Outwardly Angela was the vivacious hostess her acquaintances had
come to know over the years, but to Max's ears his mother's laughter rang
false as she clutched his arm to show him off to her departing guests.
Women whose names Max was hard-pressed to remember kissed his
cheek, commenting on how grown-up he was, while their husbands all
shook his hand.

Angela wore a tight black sequined dress. The Napier emeralds
gleamed at her throat and wrists. The emeralds advertised her position as
Douglas's wife and mistress of the manor. Especially so to the woman
who reigned over Tokyo's western social register, a buxom dowager of
British descent, who sighed as Angela approached her. "You remember
my son, Max."

"My, how grown-up he is," the woman observed, lifting her bare
shoulders as Morita draped them with a taffeta evening wrap sequined
with Japanese pearls. "A splendid party, Angela. You're to be complimented for handling things so well," she added with pointed innuendo,
glancing over at Douglas Napier, who stood across the reception foyer
conversing with Baron Hosokawa and Lord Mitsudara. "Your husband
isn't looking at all well."

"Overwork," Angela responded coldly.

Max wanted to break free, but his mother clutched his arm rather
desperately, keeping him at her side to help draw attention away from his
father. Douglas had lost a good deal of weight. The new gray hair at his
temples gave him a distinguished look, but his complexion was sallow, his
cheeks hollowed out, and the once keen blue eyes were dull and indifferent
to what took place around him.

Lord Mitsudara had attended the dinner party to talk business, not to
socialize. Baron Hosokawa's partner had shirked his business obligations
for nearly six weeks, and all that evening the lord had found Douglas
aggravatingly removed from his efforts to establish contact. "How much

work remains to be done in Germany after your return?" the lord asked him, straining for patience.

"I can't say." Douglas responded distractedly, then saw displeasure in the lord's eyes and did his utmost to give attention to what was being asked of him. "The job we began in Germany a year ago doesn't end with fulfilling our army contract, Mitsudara-*sama*," he said, addressing the lord formally. "Hitler's boys are hard to keep pleased. We've come a long way, but our German competitor won't sit still while we enjoy the edge. Unless Gessler improves the effectiveness of his parachutes, the company stands to lose its contract with the Luftwaffe to us. We're in a fight with Gessler for the lion's share and we've got to refine our parachute designs until they surpass anything our German competitor can manufacture."

Once, Douglas had railed against the silenced weaving mill and had been willing to give almost anything to finance this new venture. That evening its success meant absolutely nothing to him, and his voice was tinged with irony as he spoke again. "Your investment is safe, Lord Mitsudara. Hitler would like to keep German industry to the Germans, but the Nazis are determined to equip their airborne troops with the very best, and we've spared German pride by stamping Hosokawa-Napier parachutes with only the Karlstadt name. They'll soon prove superior when put to the test against anything produced by Herr Gessler's wholly German-owned firm. The German Air Force contracts are due for renewal at the end of this year. By then our parachutes won't be outclassed by any competitor, and world patent rights protect us against anyone stealing our ideas."

"It pleases me to hear such confidence, Mr. Napier." Lord Mitsudara rocked back on his heels. "I never for a moment doubted the profitability of our joint venture. My bank's financing of other military-related ventures has already begun to show dividends due to Japan's aggression in China. I seriously doubt Japan's course there will end as swiftly as the press believe. The public is drugged on Japanese victories, addicted to the heroism displayed by Japanese armies at war. Nothing short of total victory in China can satisfy the public's craving." He laughed. "Peace is such a bore."

Tadashi laughed with his lord, but it was force of habit rather than genuine amusement. "Unfortunately, I've had no success convincing the military that parachutes can serve as more than an escape device. Perhaps we should delay retooling our weaving mills here," he said, worrying out loud.

"This is a time for boldness, not for timidity, Tadashi," the lord said, frowning. "We are writing history, and we'll spare no expense upgrading your mills."

The lord glanced at Angela Napier, bidding good night to the last of her guests at the door. "We must move forward, Mr. Napier. This matter that so distracted your attention from business since returning to Japan," he whispered. "Has it finally been settled with your wife?"

"My private life doesn't concern you." Douglas's brusque response ruffled the lord. "Excuse me," he said, and crossed the reception foyer now emptied of guests.

Angela surrendered her son's arm as Douglas joined them. "What did you say to the lord? He looks as if you've stepped on his toes," she observed with an artificial smile.

"I told him to mind his own business," Douglas answered his wife, and put his arm around Max's shoulder.

"Well, Max, tomorrow's the big day. I'm going to miss you." Tightening his grip on Max, he proudly faced the lord. "I don't believe you've ever met my son, Max."

"I met him as a boy when I visited the Nagasaki weaving mill," Lord Mitsudara reminded him stiffly, and bowed. "A pleasure, young man."

Max took an instant dislike to the lord. "Mitsudara-*sama*. The pleasure is mine," he bowed lower than was necessary, privately mocking the lord's arrogance.

Lord Mitsudara took it as a compliment and chuckled. "Your son appears to know his manners, Mr. Napier."

Douglas ignored the lord's remark. "Max enters Harvard this fall with Tadashi's son. They're sailing tomorrow for those ivy-covered halls," he said nostalgically. That night he was able to ignore the dreadful circumstances surrounding his years at Harvard. That night he remembered only the best of what Harvard had to offer him as a young man Max's age.

"Daisetz," the baron said, "our hosts appear tired. Perhaps business can wait until after our sons have sailed."

"Very well! But in the future I'd suggest that family business be kept in perspective," the lord said sternly. "Mrs. Napier, my compliments to a gracious hostess for this splendid evening."

"Thank you, Mitsudara-*sama*." Angela kept up a smiling front as the lord took her hand to kiss it. "I shall have Morita see to your car."

"Well, Max, I gather you're all packed for the journey." Tadashi patted Max on the shoulder, trying to ignore the reaction he saw in the boy's eyes. Douglas's son loved his daughter, and he had separated them for their own good. Still, the baron could not help being moved by Max's bitterness on the eve of his departure from Japan. He remembered how his friend had suffered through the years of banishment from home and Natsu Yoseido. The baron's parents had never uttered a word to him about his friend's love affair with a Japanese. Douglas had chosen to keep it to himself, suffering in silence until Julius Napier's lies convinced him that Natsu had married a Japanese. Then his tearful confession had both shocked and angered the baron. For some time he could not forgive his friend's transgression. Only much later had he found it possible to offer Douglas sympathy.

Now the baron's gaze shifted from Douglas to Angela. He felt sure Max had told his parents that Shizue was pledged to Jiro Mitsudara, and he had anticipated some display of opposition, especially from Douglas. Yet neither parent had voiced a single word to him. He interpreted the couple's silence on the subject as resignation. After all, the marriage agreement was final and binding.

The baron's focus shifted back to Max. His daughter had asked him for privacy in which to deal with the painful process of letting go. And so, the baron viewed Max's refusal to speak of the marriage pledge as a further need for privacy. In truth, he was relieved not to have the subject opened to debate.

"You'll discover Harvard isn't such an unpleasant fate," he assured Max, saddened to have lost the boy's affections and hoping in time to win them back. "Kimitake wanted to stretch his summer holiday to the last hour. He's driving here from the seashore with his friends. My son's worked hard to pass the entrance requirements and I've rewarded his diligence with a new motor car. The New England countryside is quite beautiful. You'll both enjoy driving through the fresh country air as Douglas and I so often did after a rigorous week of study. Harvard's academic standards are high, but I'm sure you boys will look after each other."

"I don't need looking after," Max said, staring at the baron evenly. What a nerve this man had, Max thought, hinting that he expected him to pull Kimitake through Harvard, expecting anything of him after forbidding Shizue even to see him off at the docks. But this proud samurai believed he was in the right. A display of temperament would be wasted on the man, and Max held himself in check. "I understand your concern over Kimitake's performance at Harvard. But I can't influence my friend. He'll just have to look after himself."

The baron shook his head. "Max, I wasn't asking you to be his guardian. No, boys will be boys, but you are like brothers."

"The only brother I have isn't sailing with me tomorrow!" Max instantly regretted having said that. His mother grew rigid, while his father gave him a pleading look that stifled any further mention of Paul.

Lord Mitsudara was entirely preoccupied with business concerns. "I've a board meeting to prepare for," he announced, winding the stem of his gold pocket watch and comparing its face against that of the foyer's towering porcelain clock. "Three minutes slow."

Morita appeared just then, bowing as if on cue. "Your car is waiting, *Koshakusama*," he informed the lord. A hat in each hand, he extended them to the two remaining guests. *"Danshakusama. Kōshakusama."*

Angela saw both men to the door. "You must come again when we return to Japan, Mitsudara-*sama*," she said, her smile withering as he planted another wet kiss on the back of her hand. Finally, Morita closed the door, and Angela deflated like a leaky balloon. "I thought the evening would never end. I'm simply done in."

Max was uncomfortable in the silence between his parents. These days they seldom spoke to each other, or touched. Feeling estranged from them, he bid them good night.

"Good night, son." Douglas thought of his other son, hoping just for a glimpse of Paul at the Yokohama dock when Max sailed. After the next day he would lose even the secondhand contact with Paul that was provided by Max, who shared much of what took place between brothers.

Angela sighed heavily as she switched off the crystal chandelier. "Are you upset by what Max said about his brother?" Douglas asked her.

"Maxwell's friendship with him is an unpleasant reminder of the past. I can feel that young man's presence in the house with Max after their evenings together." She nervously fingered her auburn hair. "Tadashi's tyranny over his daughter was deserving of Max's anger. That poor girl won't even get to wave good-bye to him from the dock. Good Lord, she won't see Max or her brother again for years."

"Yes, it's unfair and pointless." Douglas put his arms around his wife, something he had not done in weeks. "Angela, I've been thinking of taking a short holiday in Paris before returning to the grind. Would that please you?"

"Paris is lovely in the autumn." Angela searched out his haggard face. While his period of mourning waned on, she had quietly watched over Douglas, ever alert for signs of his recovery. Now at last he showed a faint spark of surfacing from his loss and genuinely seemed eager to please her. "It's a wonderful idea, darling," she said, lavishing him with that term of endearment she had not used again until that moment.

"I missed hearing you call me that," Douglas said, observing how very beautiful she was.

"We've always had such good times in Paris. Heinz and Inge could join us there."

"I'll cable Heinz to make the arrangements."

"Yes, that would be wonderful. Inge's so good at chasing away the blues." Angela lapsed into a wifely comfortableness, linking arms with Douglas as they climbed the staircase together. Her vindictiveness had slowly died while her nerves grew frayed keeping Douglas from sharing their marriage bed. She felt so neglected as a woman, so terribly out of touch with her femininity. "You've grown too thin, Douglas. The French cuisine will help round you out again. Book our old suite at the Ritz. The one with that charming balcony overlooking the flower garden," she said, remembering holidays spent in those sunny rooms, and walks along the Seine.

Douglas nodded. With her arm linked in his, she felt the pull of happy memories when Natsu Yoseido had not existed for her. How desperate she was to recapture those times of innocence, and to embrace her husband once more with the total abandon of the young bride who had never wanted their European honeymoon to end.

But as they halted outside the door to their bedroom, Angela watched Douglas's smile fade. She would have invited him inside if not for his eyes drifting off as if she ceased to exist. Feeling vulnerable and neglected, she turned quickly and said, "Well, good night, then."

As she entered their room, she was startled by the touch of her body servant. The old woman was eager to perform her duties and retire for the night. "I'll undress myself. You can go to bed, Mihoko."

"Hai, okusama."

Mihoko exited, bowing, and Angela dropped across the bed, aware that it was too soon for Douglas and her to reconcile their differences by making love. She could never begin to rebuild her emotions in this house, she thought. Never in this bed, where Douglas had so often returned to her from the arms of his mistress. Perhaps the gulf between them would be closed in Paris. At the Hotel Ritz all her wounds might be healed by Douglas's hands caressing her naked body.

Angela Napier closed her eyes, remembering all she had enjoyed as Douglas's wife. Natsu Yoseido had enjoyed none of those things. Yes, she and Douglas had a marriage. The good times they had shared were enough to rebuild on. She sighed, convinced that happiness lay just within her grasp once Japan was behind her. Only then would she truly have Douglas to herself.

Well after midnight Max was sprawled across his bed with the telephone cupped to his ear. He and Shizue had talked themselves out but were incapable of severing the connection. That night her voice from Kyushu sounded very far away. Even O-nami's voice lacked its thunder when she put him on the line.

"Do not lose sight of Kimitake, Ichiban," he said in response to Max's decision that at Harvard it was "every man for himself."

"The baron thinks nothing of separating me from Shizue. Why should I be a nursemaid to his son?" Max responded angrily.

"Ichiban, we cannot all be scholars, and Kimitake will have need of you in this land of strangers. Never forget that you are brothers under the skin. I will write you. *Sayonara.*"

O-nami's voice trailed off, and Max could not bring himself to say good-bye. Then Shizue took O-nami's place at the receiver. "Say that you love me," he said.

"I love you. Forever and for always."

"If only I could hold you," Max said with longing.

"You can," Shizue told him in a tearful voice. "Just rest your head on the pillows and I'll do the same. Imagine me lying there beside you."

Max did as she asked. "It's no substitute for feeling you here in my arms."

"I know," she murmured. Her voice was husky over the telephone line. "Just close your eyes and picture us together as we were in the park. Each night while you're in America, I'll be holding you like this, remembering that afternoon."

"Are you still there?" Max questioned the drawn-out silence.

Shizue gave a languorous sigh. "Of course, Max. But it's late and the mountain air makes me so sleepy."

"You don't have to talk. Just keep the line open and hold me close to your pretty ear."

"I will, my *anata*, my sweetheart. This isn't good-bye. Only good night," she whispered to him softly across the miles.

"Good night," he whispered back. Leaving the receiver unhooked on the pillow beside his ear, Max heard the hiss that spoke for miles of cable stretching to his beloved Shizue.

From his adjoining room, Douglas had overheard his son's touching conversation. Restless, he slipped a robe over his silk pajamas to prowl the old house. Its timbers groaned and creaked in the stillness. His nocturnal prowlings conjured up the echoing voices and shadowy phantoms of the previous generations. Japanese believed one's existence was owed to all those who had come before. That night he felt the truth in that. The mansion's previous occupants continued to touch upon his life and those of his two sons.

That night the furnishings held a musty smell, and Douglas bid farewell to this mansion's ghosts. Everything there spoke for the unhappiness forced upon him by unloving men. For the first time in his life, he shared his wife's eagerness to escape from this land of the gods.

Sometime later, he looked in on Max, asleep with the telephone lying next to him on the bed.

"Dad?" Max peered up at him, sleepy-eyed.

"Go back to sleep, son."

"Paul won't be on the dock tomorrow morning."

"I had hoped to see him, even at a distance." Douglas's pained expression went unseen; Max turned away on his side, breathing evenly.

This youth bound for Harvard was all he had left, Douglas reflected, and it was hard for him to let go. "If only I could promise things would be different for you, son," he whispered softly, unable to tear himself away. He sat down in an overstuffed chair at his son's bedside.

Watching his son toss and turn in a young man's dream of love, all the pain of his own sailing to Harvard pressed in around Douglas. Max regarded crossing the forbidding boundary of tradition as a manly challenge. But Tadashi Hosokawa could not be fought. Everything hinged on Shizue's ability to cast off her obligations. As it had for Natsu, that act of courage would demand sacrifices.

Douglas went limp in the chair. The groaning weight of his continuing obligations to their dynasty weighed him down, iron chains forged by a bitter New Englander and a proud samurai well before the century had turned. His gaze went to Max's study desk, where he himself had once sat, tearfully writing Natsu words of hope. Their destinies had rested on a single letter he had left at the Ginza tea shop, and the reply to it, which he had never received.

Douglas stared into the darkness of his boyhood room. No such conspiracy existed between present-day fathers, whose children were free to open their hearts in letters, keeping their hopes alive. But sadly, nothing either of them wrote would carry more weight than a single feather in the down of their bed pillows that would lay oceans apart.

CHAPTER 17

Douglas Napier awakened to the morning light and to the sounds of Morita's gong announcing the breakfast hour. Douglas had passed the night sleeping in the easy chair near his son's bed, and now Max sat up, scratching his head, surprised to find his father seated there.

Morita rapped on the door, then entered, followed by maids carrying white wooden breakfast trays. It was the day of the sailing, and the clear, sunny skies over Tokyo broke into view as a maid drew open the curtains. Morita instructed the servants to lock Max-*san*'s trunks and quickly carry them downstairs to the steamship company's waiting truck.

"Will you be taking the Duesenberg to Yokahama, *dannasama*?" Morita asked of Douglas.

"Yes." A maid set a breakfast tray across his lap. On it was the morning edition of *Nippon Shimbun* and Douglas unfolded it to a lead article by Akira Yoseido. Paul wrote of a bloody battle raging on the China front. Max read a duplicate copy of the newspaper, which had been placed on his breakfast tray. This was not just another morning, thought Douglas. In a few short hours he would lose sight of both his sons. For a moment the three men were linked together by a newspaper story bearing Paul's Japanese name. Reading of a war-torn China, Douglas felt the pull of destiny altering their lives.

Angela appeared at the open bedroom door wearing a smart pink chiffon dressing gown. "Good Lord, there's no time to be reading the newspapers."

"Mother, the boat doesn't sail until this afternoon," Max reminded her, biting into a piece of toast.

"I've arranged a bon voyage party aboard ship for you and Kimitake. Noon sharp," Angela informed him crisply. "Do please get a move on, you two."

"I'm not in a party mood," Max said, lowering the newspaper to the breakfast tray. "Well, Kimitake will be on board to help me get through it." He stretched and yawned. "Kimi didn't sound much changed when we talked over the phone. He just barely got into Harvard."

"I'm surprised Kimitake qualified," Douglas said, taking a spoonful of soft-boiled egg. "He's a bright boy but lazy as sin."

"That's a fact," Max agreed. "Kimi has a talent for leaning on others. I'm sure he recruited some school chums to get him over the hurdles in my absence this past year. Well, most everyone cheats at school. My classmates in Germany considered it a fine science, a test of German efficiency applied against the watchful eyes of our classroom monitors," he added wryly.

"Have you ever played their cheating game?"

"No," Max said, taking a swallow of tea. "I'm blessed with one of those minds that doesn't have to crack a book more than once."

"I was the same way," Douglas said, then sighed.

"Maybe a shower will help shake off the gloom of saying good-bye." Max set aside his half-eaten breakfast and got out of bed. As he entered the bathroom and turned on the shower, he reflected that his next shower would be taken at sea aboard ship. San Francisco was a two-week voyage and Boston almost another week's journey aboard the cross-country train. The six-week round trip made returning home to Japan every summer both costly and impractical. He felt homesick already.

Kimitake Hosokawa was not thinking of his sailing that afternoon as he leaned out across the guard rail at Tokyo's Fuchu Racecourse, adding his shouts to the roar of the thousands who filled the spacious stands. The horse he had bet to win was now breaking from the pack, whipped by its jockey and taking the lead by half a length.

"*Dainamaito!* Come on, Dynamite!" Kimitake shouted, urging his horse on as the black stallion seemed to fly along the inside rail, coming out of the last furlong and now hitting the final stretch. There seemed no way Dynamite could be overtaken. Then suddenly the horse broke stride. Its jockey nearly took a fall as another thoroughbred streaked into the lead, flashing across the finish line while Dynamite shied in a storm of dust.

Kimitake faced away from the rail, cursing his bad luck. "Damn! He had this race in his pocket!"

"Some horse you picked," one of his friends complained loudly.

"Dynamite fizzled at the stretch," another young man chimed in.

Kimitake shrugged and viewed the clubhouse clock as his disgruntled friends threw their torn tickets to the ground. His summer vacation had been spent in the company of these young Japanese aristocrats. All of them would enter the University of Tokyo that fall, and he was envious of them. "There's just time to turn our luck around before driving on to Yokohama," Kimitake said. He consulted his race sheet. "Funnu looks like a winner at six to one," he told his four friends. "Sasajima, lend me another fifty yen."

Sasajima was wealthier than the others and leader of the pack. "I don't throw good money after bad."

Kimitake rose up to him indignantly. "I'm good for it."

Sasajima laughed. "Cool off. We've had our share of fun together, but now you're leaving us and the good times are over."

"America-*ryugakusei*," another friend said.

"Yes, the America-bound student. It's a shame you can't finish your schooling here with us," Sasajima said. "It won't be the same without you. Inagaki, pass the flask. Let's drink to friendship."

Inagaki was the buffoon of their pack, a chubby youth with a fat-cheeked baby face and bulging eyes. Uncapping the whiskey flask, he did a comical imitation of a drunk, which made them all laugh. "To friendship," he toasted Kimitake. Then the others joined voices with him to cry "*banzai*" three times for luck.

The flask was passed around and finally handed to Kimitake, who drained it dry. Surrounded by his fun-loving friends, he was promised a rousing sendoff as they all joined arms and marched to the racecourse parking lot.

Everyone but Kimitake, who was driving his new car, piled into Sasajima's open-topped roadster. "I'll race you to the dock," Sasajima called out from behind the wheel. "Let's see what your Alfa can really do!"

Ordinarily, Kimitake would have jumped to accept the challenge. But he had lived in dread of this day. He was in no hurry to reach the ship that would separate him from home and friends. Kimitake climbed into the sports car and drove slowly after them, courting the idea of missing his ship. Shizue would not even be there to see him off, and leaving Japan without seeing her again added to his depression. He had not been told of Shizue's pledge to Jiro Mitsudara. He believed that his sister was being kept at home as punishment for her romantic entanglement with Max Napier.

He pictured his father's anger at his lateness. If he missed the sailing, his father would only book him passage on another steamer. There seemed no way to alter his fate. His foot went down on the accelerator, and he swerved the car to speed past the roadster in which his cheering friends rode. He blasted his horn before leaving their car well behind him.

Kimitake's hands began to sweat as he drove the tree-lined ribbon of highway toward Yokohama Bay, trying to think of an excuse for being so late.

When the Yokohama dockside came into view, Kimitake glimpsed his father anxiously pacing the loading dock where cargo was being hoisted aboard a steamship of the Nippon Yusen Kaisha Line.

"Ah, there you are!" His father's voice rose up in a threatening tone as he rushed to Kimitake's braking car. "Why are you so late?"

"An accident blocked the highway," Kimitake lied with a sheepish grin.

The cargo master stepped between father and son. "I have a schedule to keep, Hosokawa-*san*. Pull this car over there under the crane!"

Kimitake did as he was told. Heat rippled off the Alfa Romeo's chassis. His father's reward had been given without love, and Kimitake bitterly walked away from the car while a porter unloaded the trunk, then quickly wheeled Kimi's hand luggage toward the customs area. The dockmaster's crew worked quickly, hitching the Alfa's undercarriage to the overhead crane for the lift aboard ship. "Well, I guess this is it," Kimitake said. "Sorry to have missed Angela's bon boyage party, Father."

"Never mind about that. Hurry along now, Kimitake. Your trunks have already been taken aboard." Briskly they walked to the boarding gate. "I've deposited funds with the ship's purser for you to draw against. The Old Colony Trust Company in Boston will dispense your monthly allowance—a more than adequate sum to cover your needs, Kimitake. But the bank manager won't extend advances, so budget yourself wisely." The baron reached inside his jacket pocket for an envelope. "Present these papers of identification to the bank on your arrival."

"Yes, Father."

Baron Hosokawa withheld the envelope, sniffing his son's breath. "You've been drinking."

"Just a farewell toast with my friends."

"You're well rid of that lot," the baron said, handing Kimitake the envelope. He glared at the young men who were just getting out of the roadster. Having this difficult son in America, so far removed from his stern hand, worried the baron.

"At Harvard, a young man is judged by the company he keeps. You'll profit from the influence of more studious companions than those rascals." He nodded toward Kimitake's friends, who were smiling cheerfully. "I expect you to behave as a gentleman and a scholar," he stated with firmness, while the boy's downcast look tugged at his heart. Even with all Kimitake's faults, he was an only son and heir. The baron softened his stance, thinking he had been wrong not to bring Shizue to say good-bye to her brother. Seeing Max for so short a time would have done no harm. "The ship sails in a few minutes. Go say good-bye to your friends."

White vapors rose from the main stack's whistle, blasting an all-ashore as Kimitake rushed to join Sasajima and the others for a hasty round of handshakes and slaps on the back. Ever the poor scholar, he had leaned heavily on these friends to help raise his grade average. Harvard's admission requirements were stiff, and Baron Hosokawa's generous endowments to the university over the years had been a deciding factor in his son's acceptance. Now Kimitake watched his friends sauntering off to join the dockside crowd of well-wishers who already had their handker-chiefs pulled out, ready to wave when the ship sailed.

The baron took his son by the shoulders. "Your sister sends her love and wishes of good luck," he said, startled as Kimitake embraced him and burst into tears. "What's this?"

"Father, don't send me away. I'll never make it through Harvard, no matter how hard I try. I'll fail you—I just know it." He held on to his father tightly. "Won't you let me stay here and earn my degree? Please, Father."

"Control yourself." Tadashi might have been alarmed by this display of weakness if not for the memory of his own trepidations as a youth bidding his father good-bye on this very dock. Tears hung at the corners of his eyes as he stood the boy at arm's length and said quietly, "Sending you so far away from me isn't easy. Fathering a boy isn't an easy duty. Many years ago I stood here like you, feeling sad to leave home. Bear in mind that you're a Hosokawa. Your grandfather was the first of our line to distinguish himself at Harvard. Follow his worthy example. Apply yourself, and our bloodline will do the rest. Yes, you've been a source of disappointment in the past, but blood always tells in the end. Take a firm grip on achieving your goals and let's speak no more of failure." With difficulty the baron regained his composure. "Stand up to what's expected of you like a man, Kimitake. Learn discipline and curb your boyish excesses. I expect only glowing reports on your progress at the university. Work hard and you'll return to me with honors."

Kimitake sullenly wiped his downcast eyes. "I'll do my best."

"See that you do. And don't mistake the distance between us as a free rein to do as you please. Bear in mind that falling back into your lazy ways won't go unpunished. Now, better hurry aboard." Baron Hosokawa's voice was raised against the blasting whistle. "Good luck, son." The baron shook his son's hand.

For a moment, Kimitake had felt close to his father. Then his father had begun lecturing him, dismissing any further pleas for understanding. Kimitake felt abandoned until he spotted a friendly face. "Max!" he cried, taking the ship's boarding stairs two at a time.

"We thought you'd miss the boat," said Max, their year apart melting away as they shook hands.

Kimitake accepted warm embraces from both Angela and Douglas. Then, as Angela stood talking to him, he observed Douglas Napier holding Max in a long parting embrace. Kimitake felt envious of the love that existed between this father and his son.

"I can't imagine why I'm so tearful," Angela said with a quivering smile, kissing first Kimitake, then her son good-bye. "Max, you're a grown man, but still my baby. I'll worry about you. Take care." She used her lace handkerchief to wipe lipstick off his face. "I hope your father and I will be able to visit you in Boston over summer vacation."

"You boys take care now," said Douglas. "Cable when you dock at San Francisco," he called back, going down the stairs beside his wife, who opened a small parasol to shield herself from the sun.

Douglas turned to Angela. "It looks as if the boys will have smooth sailing weather. Well, once I get things moving forward here, we'll be on our way to Paris."

"Tadashi looks so sad," Angela observed, tilting her parasol to one side as dock workers rushed to remove the boarding ramp. "I was rather expecting that young man to be on hand to see Max off. Is that who you're looking for in the crowd?"

"No, just remembering another sailing from here," Douglas told his wife. Indeed, it *was* Paul's face he had hoped to see here. Despite what Max had said, he counted on the friendship between his sons to bring Paul to the dock. But the crowd was too dense for him to continue the search. Everyone began waving their white handkerchiefs as the ship left its berth.

Douglas walked Angela over to Tadashi, and the three of them stood, fighting tears, as they waved good-bye to their sons.

Angela hugged her husband's arm and said, "It seems only yesterday that I was pregnant with our son, arriving in Japan for the first time and being helped off the ship by you. You were already the doting father, careful of every step I took. And, Tadashi, you were here on the dock with your lovely wife to greet us with flowers."

"All in the past, Angela," Tadashi said, and began to walk away. The Yokohama dock held too many memories. His son was now outward bound on a voyage that would return him home in honor or in shame. Perhaps blood could not be entirely trusted to determine the worth of a man, he thought, and prayed to the gods of his ancestors, placing Kimitake's future in their hands.

Douglas looked at the dispersing crowd. Suddenly, he saw Paul, standing just outside the customs gate. Their eyes met, then his older son quickly turned away.

"Wait here, Angela," Douglas said. "I'll get the car." He hurried off before she could object. "Paul! Son!"

Paul's shoulders stiffened at the sound of his father's voice. His first impulse was to stop and confront Douglas, but every fiber in his body resisted the urge to acknowledge his need for contact, and Paul ducked inside his waiting taxi. "Tokyo, and hurry!"

As the taxi pulled away, Douglas felt the baron's hand on his arm. "Don't tell me it's all in the past, Tadashi," he said bitterly. "Don't say a thing until you know what it is to be punished by a son. God help you, if your actions ever expose you to the pain of being turned away by either of your children."

Aboard ship, Kimitake surveyed the weathered first-class deck and scuffed one shoe across the sea-bleached planks. "Fourteen days aboard this tub. Don't suppose there's much diversion except for the bar. What's our cabin like?"

"Nothing luxurious but comfortable enough," said Max.

"I can see you're not too thrilled about Harvard either."

Elbows planted on the deck rail, Max nodded absently. "Resigned to it."

Kimitake sighed heavily. "I wish I could say the same."

As the ship slowly moved through the waters of Yokohama Bay, a gloominess set in between the friends. As their loved ones disappeared into a blur of fluttering white handkerchiefs, the two boys stood a silent watch until Japan vanished behind unbroken miles of wrinkling sea.

On a warm September day some three weeks later, Max and Kimitake stepped off the train at Boston. They strode behind redcaps, who wheeled their massive assortment of luggage from the station house. Kimitake's Alfa Romeo had traveled there by flatcar and was now arriving at the curbside. At the same time the driver of a van sent from the boys' Cambridge dormitory introduced himself and took on their luggage.

"My treat, Max," Kimitake insisted, and overtipped the redcaps.

Max watched his brash young friend with misgivings. During the voyage Kimitake had been a depressing companion. His idea of a good time was to get high at the ship's bar and roll dice with the stewards in their off hours. When Max attempted to drag him away, he would laugh and say "Don't paw me. Why not be a sport and join in?" Despite all his efforts, Max had failed to establish anything more than a superficial rapport with his boyhood friend. After the ship docked at San Francisco, Kimitake sank into moody despair and at last confessed to his fears of not living up to his father's expectations. That confession had broken the ice, and as they took the train across country together, it led to a sympathetic renewal of the bond they had sealed in blood in a Tokyo schoolyard.

"Got other errands to run. You boys find your own way over into Cambridge," the van driver said in a nasal New England accent. He handed Max a street map.

Kimitake drove them on a short tour of Boston. The city harbor, its tall buildings, its quaint winding lanes, were bathed in autumn sunlight and made a pleasant first impression on both young men. Then, as they crossed the Lars Anderson Bridge, Max viewed Harvard's clean-lined Georgian colonial architecture rising through stately elms along the gently sloping banks of the Charles River. The air was crisp, and leaves blew down the irregular brick sidewalks of Cambridge as they neared Randolph Hall.

Kimitake slowed the car, getting into a long line of vehicles dispatching other new arrivals to their freshman dormitory, which looked to him like an ivy-walled bastion under assault. "Well, Max, this is it." He slouched behind the wheel and tugged his hat brim low. "Not the grim dungeon I imagined, but nothing like home."

Max shared the feeling. Confronted with his father's old dormitory, his exile became a hard reality. "Let's check in," he said.

Randolph Hall's corridors were clogged with other incoming fresh-men, and boys were lined up at the battery of reception desks manned by the housemaster's harried staff. Max and Kimitake jockeyed for places in what seemed to be the fastest-moving line. The clamor of voices reverberated against the vaulted ceilings and bare wood floors. Finally, Max and Kimitake reached the head of the line, where they shouted their names to be heard.

"Misters Napier and Hosokawa," a young man shouted back. He bent over the papers on his desk. "Room four D, gentlemen. Bullock! Two boys for your floor here!"

The young man being shouted at calmly stepped forward to introduce himself. "Avery Bullock. Welcome to Harvard, gentlemen. Harvard *a yokoso irasshaimashita*," he said, and bowed, amused by Max and Kimitake's surprise. "Japanese is my first language. My parents are Episcopalian missionaries posted in Osaka. I was born and raised there. It's good to see two faces from home." Avery Bullock smiled. "This way. It's some climb, but the view from there is worth the inconvenience. I'll have your luggage brought up once the traffic allows."

Max's depression lifted as they followed Avery Bullock up the congested stairs. "I never hoped to find another American here with my background."

"Oh, you'll soon discover these ivy halls are a melting pot, Mr. Napier. The world washes up on the shores along the Charles River." Immersed in the upwardly spiraling whirlwind of freshmen, and Negro houseboys hauling their possessions up the stairs, Avery talked above it all. He was a graduate student, earning his master's in Oriental languages. A scholarship paid his tuition, but not his room and board. His staff job and tutoring helped pay for his other expenses. "But money is always tight," he finished, rather winded as he opened the door to their fourth-floor room. "After you, gentlemen. Your home for the freshman year. Not so bad, eh?"

Kimitake groaned as he poked his head through the doorway. "Are you sure there hasn't been some mistake?"

"The same quarters your fathers shared, Hosokawa-*san*. Reserved for you at the baron's request. His name must carry some weight," Avery Bullock commented without the slightest trace of being impressed by that fact. "Half a dozen fathers who roomed here wanted these four walls for their sons. Alumni nostalgia. The middle-aged longing to recapture those golden years of yore. They'll visit here from time to time and sit at their old study desks with a drink in hand and a tear in their eye."

Past and present converged as Max crossed the threshold into a narrow high-ceilinged room furnished with the bare essentials: beds set against opposite walls, twin study desks, one overstuffed mohair easy chair, and a matching beige sofa placed before an age-blackened stone hearth. Touching a varnished desktop, Max pictured his father seated there writing Natsu. That night he would sit there writing to Shizue.

"House rules are there on your desks," Avery Bullock cheerfully pointed out. "The bathroom plumbing wheezes and knocks like hell. Randolph is one of the older freshman dorms, but it has a somewhat rustic charm. The kitchen is being renovated—behind schedule, so you'll have to eat out for a month or so. I can recommend some nearby eateries guaranteed not to give you the shits. In fact, why not have dinner with me tonight? Dutch treat, of course. It's been four years since I've been home to Japan. You two can bring me up-to-date on things there, and I'll fill you in about the Harvard life as fair exchange."

"Yes, I'd like that," said Max.

Kimitake took a sober turn on the polished hardwood floors. "I'll go along. If only to find out what a guy does for fun around here. Or is having a good time against the rules?" he asked Avery Bullock.

Max took inventory of the trim young man wearing a worn Harris tweed jacket. His wavy hair was a coppery red, and he looked more like a freshman than a graduate student, despite the thin red mustache across his upper lip.

Avery Bullock dug his briar pipe into a tobacco pouch, packed the bowl, and pulled on its stem with a quietly thoughtful manner. "Harvard allows its students a good deal of personal freedom," he told Kimitake. "A boy could muddle through his years here, satisfied with being a C man, unnoticed from the day he arrives until commencement. Or, he can apply himself, taking on additional studies in order to obtain high honors at graduation. The choice is entirely up to you."

Kimitake fell back, groaning, across one bed. "I'll settle for just passing through, thanks all the same."

"As you will, Mr. Hosokawa. Well, work to be done. My room's just up the hall. I'll see you there"—he consulted his wristwatch—"shall we say at six, Mr. Napier?"

"Max."

"Max it is."

Avery smiled at Max disarmingly, his intense blue eyes reflecting a maturity beyond his years. Looking into them, Max felt as though he had known Avery Bullock all his life.

It was the beginning of a friendship that would one day help see Max through his darkest hours.

BOOK THREE
SAMURAI
AUTUMN

1937

Time oozed from my pores,
Drinking tea
I tasted the seven seas.

I saw in the mist formed
Around me
The fatal chrysanthemum, myself.

Its scent choked, and as I
Rose, squaring
My shoulders, the earth collapsed.

SHINKICHI TAKAHASHI

CHAPTER 18

Paul had expected Shizue to be wearing one of those tailored private school uniforms copied from the West. Instead as the train came to a stop, she appeared on the Kyoto Station House platform clad in a white wool dress. Cut high at the throat, its black leather piping accented her womanly curves as she glided regally through the crowd, obviously impatient for a glimpse of him.

Paul nervously ran a comb through his hair before leaving his seat at the window. His second-class sleeping car berth had been comfortable enough, but his disquieting fears over this visit had caused him to have a restless night on the eight-hour journey to Kyoto. His heavy workload at *Nippon Shimbun* had kept him from going to Kyoto sooner. He and Shizue had exchanged letters, and he had felt quite safe expressing himself in words at a distance. Now he was very nervous about setting foot off the train. Hideo Tamura had given him a substantial raise in salary, and Paul's expensive suit and the leather briefcase he carried were brand new. They were symbols of his status as a journalist and were meant to bolster his ego as well as to impress her.

Although Shizue had never seen Max's half brother until that moment, she knew instantly he was the tall young man who stepped off the train. "Paul, over here!"

Hearing her speak his name rendered Paul helpless to do more than stand there on the platform. Nothing could have prepared him for her ebullient welcome. As she rushed toward him, her face was radiant and smiling. Her arms went up around his neck, and she brushed his cheek with her lips. Her sweet scent laid claim to his senses. Through all his lonely years, he had known only the warmth of Natsu's maternal embraces. This was a vibrant young woman who awakened his manhood, and he experienced some weakness in his knees before she stepped back.

"Oh, how often I've thought of this very moment," Shizue said, searching out his handsome face. So like Max and yet so very different from him, she observed. "I hardly slept a wink just counting the hours, and now you're really here. Was it a pleasant journey?"

Swallowed up in the depths of her eyes, Paul could only nod.

"I'm so excited." Shizue attributed Paul's awkward silence to shyness with women. His letters spoke for a confident and bold young man, but Max had told her that his brother was not an easy person to know. "We've the whole day to ourselves. Thanks to my friend, I've managed to escape the clutches of our school chaperones. Chizuko is a dear. Her family lives in Kyoto, and those ugly old matrons at school believe I'm spending my Sunday with them," she explained brightly, then laughed.

Paul had difficulty finding his voice. "Is your school that strict?"

"Oh, very." Shizue made a grim face. "They hover over us like hawks guarding the nest. But why stand here talking when it's such a glorious morning."

"The newspaper worked me overtime," he said, awkwardly lifting his briefcase off the platform. "I barely had time to pack a few essentials before I ran to catch the midnight train."

"It's such a long way to come just for the day." Shizue took his arm and smiled. "Now you must let me show you my Kyoto, Paul. All the beautiful places that I've come to love."

"I'm entirely in your hands." He was dazzled by her nearness. As he walked beside her, his cheeks were flushed.

"See what a perfectly glorious October day it is!" Shizue exclaimed as they exited the station house. "We're in luck. That's our motor bus. Hurry!"

They found seats together on the crowded bus, and Shizue momentarily rested her head against his shoulder and sighed contentedly. Her sudden intimacy overwhelmed him. While announcing the sights along their way, she frequently pressed his arm and hand. It was her way of communicating affection between her words, he observed. When they alighted from the bus, Paul felt as though he were floating along beside her on a cloud.

Kyoto was the ancient capital of Japan. There the successive emperors came to be crowned, and the nation drew pride from that city's legendary shrines and temples. But Paul saw only Shizue's radiance as she guided him through the cool green gardens and past aristocratic palaces and majestic villas. She led him beside the mossy banks of streams, where they skipped pebbles across the rippling waters. Then quietly, she described a bygone age when young noblemen and their ladies had glided together in their boats toward dusk with plum blossoms floating in the wine cups they sipped from. Her words wove a romantic fantasy in which Paul could picture the lovers of another era reflected in the gently flowing streams, exchanging kisses while their boats sailed silently on beneath the delicately bowed cherry trees.

"*Aisu-kuriimu! Chokoreito, banira aisu-kuriimu!*" the ice cream vendor cried, pedaling his colorfully painted wagon down a winding park lane strewn with autumn leaves.

Paul called to him, and the vendor served them chocolate ice cream in tiny cones spun of brown sugar. Watching Shizue daintily lick the confection, Paul was like a schoolboy filled with the simple wonder of his first crush. He blushed when Shizue caught him staring, but she let the incident pass without a word, and they strolled on together, often in silence, listening to the dry crunch of leaves underfoot.

The hours they spent together slipped away as quickly as the white sails of gossamer clouds billowing overhead across an autumn sky. Paul felt blessed by a serenity he had never known before. They rested in a garden teahouse that preserved the essence of Kyoto's romantic past. Shizue poured them dark green tea, and Paul was mesmerized by love, unable to take his eyes off her while she spoke of growing up with Max. Shizue's memories added poignant dimension to what Max had told him. Suddenly, Shizue grew pensive, and he saw himself obscured from her vision, completely overshadowed by the love she felt for his half brother. A love born in the summers of their lives. A love he could never hope to win.

He had flown too high. Like Icarus, he had flapped his wings of wax too near the sun, and all at once he was falling back to earth, unseen, eclipsed by Max's shadow. Shizue Hosokawa had haunted his thoughts for months. Being with her had far exceeded his wildest dreams. But it had been a mistake to visit her, he thought. He had known that all along. And now he sat close to her but was ignored because of her reveries of Max.

Paul was devastated by the feeling of unrequited love. As the iron temple bells tolled the sunset hour, he nervously lit a cigarette. Finally, Shizue glanced up at him through the haze of exhaled smoke. "You've been far away with Max," he said.

She nodded dreamily. "Sorry for drifting. It's so peaceful here." She pouted as she faced the Japanese garden, which reflected the sunset's glow. "Where has the day gone? Time is such a cheat. Waiting for your visit, it simply dragged on. Paul, being with you makes me feel so much closer to Max. I've received only one letter since he arrived at Harvard. The mail takes forever. Each day, I miss him more. Each morning, I watch for the postman, desperate for the touch of Max's words."

"He gave me something for you."

"He did?" Shizue looked at him expectantly.

"Yes, Max asked me to deliver this in person. I can't imagine how it slipped my mind," he lied, opening his briefcase and taking out the small package he had forgotten to deliver because he had been so lost to love.

Paul watched the sadness lift from Shizue's face as she unwrapped Max's gift and broke the wax seal off a rice-paper envelope containing the gift card. She read his brother's words of love more than once, turning the card over with tremulous hands, heaving sigh after sigh. Then she caressed the small gift box made of bamboo reeds, childlike in her wish to prolong the moment of revealing its surprise. When she finally took off the lid, she squealed with delight.

"Oh, Max," she whispered, both hands pressed to her cheeks, far too moved by the beauty of the amulet to touch it yet. Then, after she examined the *omamori* front and back, she took the ends of its chain and slowly unraveled the glittering links until the amulet hung suspended, the fabulous bird's copper feathers seeming to catch fire with the late afternoon light. To Shizue, Max's gift was an affirmation of hope for their future that spoke more eloquently than the words in his love note.

Suddenly, she was aware of Paul's presence. "Oh, thank you, Paul. Isn't it just perfect? Have you ever seen anything quite so beautiful?" She gave him no chance to speak. "Max had it blessed as an *omamori* to protect me against harm in my journey through life. And I gave him nothing as a keepsake. How thoughtless of me. This wonderful surprise takes my breath away!"

Paul managed to smile. "Max told me it was something special."

"He wanted you to put his *omamori* around my neck in his place," she said, holding it out to him. "His note said, 'Let Paul's eyes be like my eyes on you wearing this next to your heart.' You've become so important to him. Important to us both. Would you, please?"

"If it pleases you."

Shizue gathered up her shoulder-length hair, and to Paul, her eyes were swirling novas of light mirroring the *omamori* as he placed the chain gently around her throat. She sighed, fingering the fluted links of antique gold, and imagined that Max was bending close, fastening the chain.

"There. I've done my duty to you both," Paul said, his voice sharpened by his contained anger. Playing a role in the giving of this lover's keepsake was a wounding experience. But Shizue, unaware of his feelings, let her hair fall loose around the gold chain, her tresses brushing against Paul's retreating hands as her eyes lowered to the *omamori* that hung against the nubby wool of her high collar.

"Dear Paul, you can't know how much this means to me." As Shizue fingered the charm meant to be worn next to her skin, the pealing of iron bells reminded her of the hour. "Oh, I wish Tokyo weren't so far away. Your visit was too short."

"It can't be helped." He stood back, a look of pain on his face. But Max's gift dazzled Shizue too much to notice anything else around her. "My train leaves soon. We really should be going."

She tucked the gift wrappings and Max's note inside her shoulder bag as keepsakes of that afternoon. "There's something in the park I want to show you before you go," she announced. "Come along."

Shizue guided him along the paths of Maruyama Park's sloping grounds. In the distance stood Mount Higashiyama, whose verdure-clad silhouette rose against an incredibly vibrant sky. The sunset painted everything in a vermilion glow as Paul lost himself to the majesty of his surroundings, moved as never before by what nature's hand had wrought. Through Shizue he saw the beauty of a world that had always been clouded with bitterness.

Paul broke the silence. "Where are you taking me?"

"We're here! My wishing tree." Shizue halted before an old cherry tree and bowed. The sturdy trunk writhed up from gnarled roots that crawled along the earth like serpents with their heads buried deep in time. "For more than four hundred years this tree has never failed to keep its promises," she told Paul, leading him under its canopy of outstretched limbs. "Each spring these branches burst to life in a splendid new cloak of blossoms, and thousands come here to admire its charms. When it's Night Cherry at Gion, my old friend's spring finery will be set ablaze with lights, and I'll visit him again to make a birthday wish."

She posed there wishfully, her face lit by the sky's vermilion glow. Paul ached to hold her in his arms. "Did you often visit here with Max?"

"Only in my thoughts," she replied. "You've made today more special for me than any birthday. From now on this will be our special place. Here, Paul, take my hand and make a wish."

He joined hands with her and wished for the impossible. Shizue's eyes were shut tightly, and he yearned for a kiss to end the torment of being near her like this. But then she opened her eyes.

"Now it's official. I've made it so by wishing something special for you, Paul," she said, taken aback by the way he was staring at her.

"You take such delight in everything," Paul told her, smiling.

"Is that all you were thinking?"

Before answering, he looked away from her. "Yes. That and how special today was for me as well. It's easy to see why Max is so in love. If not for him, I might easily fall in love with you myself." A forced laugh stuck in his throat. "I promised to look after his girl. I never told Max this, but his friendship helped me through some difficult times. I'm glad he sent me here to deliver his gift. I need you as a friend, Shizue."

"Oh, Paul, I haven't the words to express how very dear you've become to me." Shizue grasped both his hands. "I want us to be the very best of friends. I want to confide things to you that I couldn't possibly tell anyone else. There's something about you that makes me feel you'll be my most trusted friend."

"Whatever I am is owed to my mother," he replied somberly. "I don't think I'll ever get over her death."

"How awful it must be for you." Shizue's eyes filled with tears. "Oh, I'm going to cry." She fumbled with the catch of her shoulder bag. "I didn't want any sadness to spoil our first day together. Oh, I can't get to my handkerchief."

"Here, take mine."

"What must you think of me," she sniffled, dabbing her eyes with his pocket handkerchief.

"There, now. My mother wouldn't want to be remembered with sadness." Paul hugged her gently. With his arms around Shizue, he felt complete, no longer the half-caste but a pure-blooded Japanese. The illusion dissolved as she stepped away and returned his handkerchief.

"I understand now why Max looks up to you so." Shizue looked up at him, smiling once again. "I feel as if I've known you forever."

Just then Paul saw that she did love him. But as a bridge to Max. That day he had helped bridge the oceans between two lovers. He would be alone in the world without them and he felt inextricably bound to serve their needs.

The park lampposts flickered on at dusk, and a chill breeze swayed the branches of Shizue's wishing tree. Paul noticed the tiny copper cherry blossoms in the *omamori* she wore. The cherry blossom was a recurring theme in his life, he reflected. His mother's cotton print uniform, the pink neon sign that had lit his bedroom window at night, and now this old tree that was swayed by the chill breath of approaching winter. "Thank you for making this our special place," he said.

It was dark when they left Maruyama Park by taxi for Shizue's boarding school. The dashboard radio crackled and buzzed. Car radios were relatively new to Japan, and the driver grumbled under his breath, fiddling with its knobs.

"Can't you get the NHK any better?" Paul asked him.

"Bad reception so near Mount Higashiyama."

". . . superior strike force of Japanese bombers . . . Chinese on the run . . . " The evening news broadcast from Tokyo faded in and out. Frustrated by the interference, Paul strained forward to listen.

Shizue had known about this intense side of his nature through Paul's letters and through telephone conversations with Max before he had sailed. But now Paul was like another person, coldly obsessed with the war. All at once the radio reception cleared. Shizue covered her ears against the newscaster celebrating Japanese victories in China. Chiang Kai-shek's first line of defense in China had just been broken with the fall of Paoting, and his forces were retreating. Soon the roads into Shanghai and Nanking would lie wide open to Nippon's victorious armies. Finally, the news broadcast ended with a recording of "*Kimigayo*," the national anthem, and Shizue uncovered her ears.

"Long live his majesty the emperor," the taxi driver cried patriotically, then sounded his horn.

Paul dropped back in the seat beside Shizue, stern-faced, his jaw muscles tense. "I'm tired of being chained to a desk in Tokyo miles from the action in China. I'd give anything to be there in the thick of the fighting, dispatching reports to my newspaper. It's the chance of a lifetime, and I won't be cheated of it."

Shizue's eyes opened wide with alarm. "Paul, you can't be serious."

"My future lies in being assigned to cover this war," he answered evenly, touched by her concern. "*Nippon Shimbun*'s publisher has taken a personal interest in my career. It's only a matter of time before his prejudice is set aside and he recognizes me as the best man for the job."

"Your ambition frightens me." She prayed that the war would end quickly. "Please, let's not talk about this awful subject." Before Paul could say anything else, Shizue asked, "When can you visit again?"

"Hard to say," he hedged.

"But you will come again," she said pleadingly.

"Yes, of course."

The taxi lurched to a stop. Paul escorted her to the school gates, and Shizue was stunned when he held her there in a long, fierce embrace. "Until next Sunday," he told her, then broke away and raced to the waiting taxi before she could speak a word in reply.

En route to Kyoto Station, Paul inhaled her lingering fragrance on the handkerchief Shizue had returned to him. Her sweet scent brought the day rushing back through his mind. He knew he could never be more than a servant of love. But without Shizue's radiance warming the empty seat beside him, Paul experienced a shuddering ache. Next Sunday and all his Sundays after that would belong to her. His heart cried out to accept her love on any terms.

"Damn you, Max," he cursed aloud. "Goddamn you for letting Shizue into my life. I don't belong in your world, and now I'm damned for loving you both."

On through the fall and into the winter of 1937, Paul Yoseido became a regular passenger on the midnight train to Kyoto. The Sundays he spent with Shizue kindled his love to a feverish pitch. Then, without warning, the house of cards he had built of their precious hours together collapsed.

While they were returning to the boarding school one dank wintry night, Shizue held him outside its gates to make a shocking confession. She wept as she had on the first day they met, and told him about the marriage agreement. It threatened a loss, Paul thought, that neither brother could endure.

"I promise not to breathe a word of this in my letters to Max," Paul said, and gave Shizue his handkerchief to dry her eyes. He could not bring himself to destroy her tearfully stated belief that Jiro Mitsudara would discover the courage to object to the match. And Paul reeled against yet another blow.

"My father is coming to Kyoto," Shizue told him with difficulty. "Our weaving mill here is being retooled to manufacture parachutes, and he'll be here for months."

Paul knew that her father was ignorant of these clandestine meetings. Although he bore Paul no malice, the baron would view the friendship with Natsu's son as improper for his daughter's station and as a negative influence; he would forbid her friendship to continue.

Hosokawa-Napier, Limited's, fortunes and Paul's ambitions were now forged together with the smoking cannons of war. His mentor, Hideo Tamura, steadily gained ground on his behalf with *Nippon*

Shimbun's publisher, and it seemed a certainty that the post of war correspondent would shortly be his.

That December evening, wrapped in the cold mist that caused the iron schoolyard gates to weep, Paul realized he might be sent into the roaring jaws of war without seeing Shizue again. She had helped to fill the void created by his mother's death. Not a day had gone by without his missing some loving touch his mother had provided, such as always making sure he had a clean handkerchief in his pocket. Now Shizue returned his handkerchief. Her anguished expression, as she looked up at Paul, caused him to realize that she shared his fears. They embraced, both of them aware that it might be for the last time.

"We'll see each other in Tokyo," Shizue told him. "Father will bring me there to celebrate the new year with Jiro."

It was painful for Paul to hear Jiro's name, and the cadet became a new object of hatred. As Jiro's wife, Shizue would no longer be able to share her world with him.

From that night on, Paul steeled himself to survive the icy solitude he had known in the past. He was nothing but a name on stacks of newspapers, read by the crowds in Kyoto Station. The power of his words fired the Japanese people. But it was a fire without smoke. He passed among them invisibly, a Eurasian snubbed by everyone but the sleeping car porters who all knew him as Akira Yoseido, journalist. His growing celebrity rated him the best first-class accommodations, and he had tipped the porters generously, able to purchase their attentiveness and friendly smiles with the monetary rewards of his talents.

Paul would not ride that train again. China would be his next destination and his destiny. Thousands of miles from Shizue, he might find salvation or encounter his damnation. In either case, war would be his crucible and his ultimate escape from the past.

CHAPTER 19

The expressionless eyes of Major General Richard Dietrich scanned the gray winter skies over Germany. On the rise behind him, the driver seated in his command car kept the motor running, its hum and the cadenced squeals of the windshield wipers invading the tense quiet of an isolated countryside training ground sixty miles west of Berlin. Well below the rise lay open meadowland, whose frozen earth had been carved up into deep tracks by German tanks. The surrounding woods showed the scars of artillery practice. Trees were half-blown away, their charred trunks like jutting black spikes set against the silently falling snow.

Douglas Napier grew impatient with the general's silence, and his breath fogged the air as he voiced his thoughts. "The jump should be postponed until more favorable weather, Herr General." His objection was not well received.

"Battles are not always fought under the most ideal conditions, Herr Napier," the short, wiry general sounded back. Hearing a faintly audible drone, he raised his field glasses and regarded the overcast sky.

Heinz Karlstadt, shifting anxiously beside Douglas, wore a prayerful look. Their German competitor's contract with the Luftwaffe did not expire until after the coming new year. But the month before, in November, 1937, the new Karlstadt combat parachutes had been successfully deployed in large-scale army maneuvers, and glowing reports of that impressive showing had prompted Field Marshal Hermann Göring to have his elite air force parachutists put them to the test. General Dietrich was personally entrusted with staging today's maneuver. In the last war, he had flown with the fabled Richthofen Circus under Göring's command, and the two ex-air aces were close friends.

Nothing could yet be seen of the approaching Luftwaffe squadron. The jump had been delayed by fog that closed Stendal's military airfield until midafternoon. When the fog had lifted, Dietrich ordered his troops aboard their waiting planes. Douglas faced the general's car parked just a few yards away. The squadron leader could be reached over its radio, but Major General Dietrich seemed to ignore the deteriorating weather.

A ghostly formation of Fokker transport planes soared into view through the clouds, their swastika-painted tail sections and the German cross insignia on their fuselages blurred in the smoky gray ceiling.

"Soon we shall know if your parachutes outclass those supplied to us by the Gessler Works." General Dietrich's words were spoken in a voice as expressionless as his pale blue eyes. "Army infantry positioned in the woods will act as the enemy. Their weapons and those of our airborne assault force are loaded with blank cartridges. However, the strategy for victory remains the same. The paratroopers must land as close to the target attack point as possible. Every precious yard they land short of the target is ground they must cover under enemy crossfire." Anticipating the jump, he widened his stance, stretching the hem of his black leather trench coat taut.

Douglas and Heinz took hold of their hat brims as wind suddenly ripped the curtaining snow. A dozen flares attached to small parachutes were being dropped by the squadron's scout plane. Tendrils of bright crimson smoke drew squiggly patterns over the windswept target area. The flares would help the pilots make adjustments for wind speed and drift.

Douglas estimated its velocity at perhaps ten knots as it gusted steadily from the east. Thank God, no crosswind as yet, he thought, looking at Heinz, who shared his fears. Wind was an unpredictable element and added to the hazards of the jump. Both men turned to look at General Dietrich; they hoped he would call it off.

Dietrich mocked their looks of concern by giving them a superior smile. "My orders will not be countermanded, *meine Herren*. Paratroopers of General Göring's regiment are expected to display an unusually strong fighting spirit. To cancel the jump would be an insult to them."

"But, Herr General, this is a test of our parachutes, not of regimental honor," Douglas responded strongly. "If the wind increases or a crosswind develops, a number of men could be badly injured."

"Landing injuries are commonplace." The general slapped his gloved hands together for warmth. "It may interest you to know that my son, Captain Dietrich, will lead the jump. I expect no less of him than I do of the other brave sons who serve their fatherland today." He clicked the heels of his spit-polished black boots together and raised one hand to silence any further protest.

Douglas was hard pressed to keep still while Dietrich placed honor above the lives of his own son and other young men who would soon plunge into this menacing sky. The squadron of planes reduced air speed, their wings vanishing among the heavy clouds that showered snow on the frozen ground. In the mounting tension, Douglas envisioned paratroopers standing up, hooking their static lines to the planes' anchor lines. German paratroopers with Japanese silk harnessed to their backs were now responding to the "make ready" command. Men trained at the nearby

Stendal Parachute Academy wore streamlined steel helmets and the Luftwaffe's pale green and gray winter jump suits, padded to insulate them against the cold. Boys not much older than Max were now positioning themselves at the open door hatches, their feet spread wide on the ledges, both hands stretched back, gripping the metal rails at either side of the icy fuselages.

Douglas's breath frosted the air in short bursts that were carried off by the howling wind as the first man dove spread-eagled into space, free-falling through the snow. One after another the paratroopers plunged in an arc while Douglas counted off the critical stages of their fall. Fifty feet, sixty, and the silk canopies gradually unfurled well out behind them. Would the canopies open or be collapsed by this infernal wind? Seventy feet, eighty, and for one split second the shapes of falling men were suspended horizontal with the earth, suspended between life and death until the shroud lines reeling out behind them suddenly jerked taut. Douglas threw up his arms with a cry of relief as canopy after canopy blossomed to break the paratroopers' falls. Silk shrouds weaved and stitched on his sophisticated machines kept the first jump wave afloat, allowing them to drift down at some twenty feet per second. It would be a dangerous landing on the frozen ground.

German soldiers who acted as the enemy infantry opened fire from their machine-gun nests in the surrounding woods, tracer shells spitting crossing fingers of colored light across the landing site, where the first assault wave was touching down.

"Your parachutes appear to be functioning well even with these winds," General Dietrich crisply informed Douglas and Heinz, pleased by what he observed. "An excellent drop pattern. I see no one drifting far off target. This had been a problem with our present equipment. Once the men are free of their chutes, every second must be made to count."

General Dietrich placed one boot up on a large rock, then put an elbow on his thigh to steady his field glasses. Douglas was chilled by his toothy grin, seeing him as a leather-skinned gargoyle.

The white silk shrouds continued blossoming overhead, one following after another, peeling off beneath the squadron's tail sections to seed the air like milkweed blowing free of its pods. Douglas knotted his hands together, feeling responsible for the lives of the boys who were maneuvering their harness riggings to turn themselves downwind. It was imperative that they landed falling forward, away from their chutes, on their hands and knees. From what he could see, there were no airborne collisions, but a number of men were landing badly. The strong gusts of wind forced them backward, and they became entangled in the webs of their shroud lines and were dragged across the ground flat on their backs. Douglas saw the men struggling to get at the gravity knives they carried in the thigh pockets of their jump suits. But many of them were hopelessly ensnared in the tough silk lines of their billowing chutes. Only a handful of men managed to cut themselves free. Others were too badly injured to attempt freeing themselves and continued being dragged off by the wind.

When the final jump wave had landed, Douglas counted more than thirty casualties. Heinz Karlstadt pounded him on the shoulder and shouted, "*Wunderbar.*" He saw only the victory of the hundreds who were safely free of their chutes and had mustered into action as an orderly combat team on the frozen battlefield below. For Douglas, however, the injured boys all wore the face of his younger son, and he saw only those crippled by the fall. He shivered, feeling personally accountable for the pain they endured. Their more fortunate comrades began flanking out wide in platoons, leaving the injured behind and firing their rifles as they swept out against the enemy-held positions in the woods. No one had been killed, and Douglas silently gave thanks for that.

Armed with mortar and light machine guns to support their forward positions, the airborne strike force soon broke through the enemy lines. That day they fought with blank cartridges, but the echoing claps of gunfire and the smell of gunpowder carried on the wind made Douglas queasy with the thought of another day, when these same paratroopers might be armed with loaded weapons from Hitler's deadly arsenal. The enemy in this war game was surrendering, the men marching single file from the woods with hands clasped together on their heads. Before long, armored halftracks appeared, churning across the open ground, manned by officers who had served as battle referees. Medics riding with them were dropped off to attend the injured paratroopers, and the halftracks sent white flags up their antenna poles to signal an end to the maneuver.

"Look, Douglas! Our parachutes have won the day!" Heinz was charged with an enthusiasm that kept him grinning despite his partner's sickly white face. "Are you not feeling well?"

"Just a little tired, Heinz." Douglas's eyes were riveted on the medics rushing across the landing site. "I've seen enough for one day," he said, turning his back to the cheering paratroopers, mere boys who had bravely risked their limbs to profit Hosokawa-Napier, Limited.

"Are you pleased, Herr General?" Heinz asked.

"Yes, it would appear the army has not exaggerated the technical superiority of your parachutes," General Dietrich answered thoughtfully, kicking snow off his boots. "However, a good deal rests with what can't be judged by observers on the ground. My son will join us shortly to render his expert opinion. We shall wait for him out of this cold." He walked briskly to his car, and Douglas and Heinz followed.

The command car offered a stuffy warmth. Douglas sat there, removed from the conversation. Since returning to Germany, he had numbly gone through the motions of meeting his business obligations, while haunted by vivid memories of Natsu. Heinz and General Dietrich lit cigarettes and reminisced about the Great War, comparing today's modern battle to the trench warfare both men had fought while serving their fatherland. Time had sweetened their memories and created a wistful camaraderie between soldiers. It was broken when Captain Manfred Dietrich opened the car door, letting in an arctic blast of air.

The captain fired off a salute. "Reporting as ordered, Herr General!"

"My son, Manfred," the general said stiffly. "So, you have my permission to join us, Herr Captain. Quickly, and close the door! Take us to the jump school, Presser," he ordered his driver.

Douglas noted the cold formality between father and son. "Pretty rough out there, Captain," Douglas said, as Captain Dietrich seated himself in the leather jumpseat facing his father. He peeled off his gloves to accept a cigarette offered from the general's gold case, which was embossed with the German eagle and swastika. Manfred Dietrich was young for a captain, twenty-five at most, Douglas thought. "Things must have looked a lot worse from where you stood."

"A most difficult jump," he answered Douglas evenly. The cigarette dangling unlit from his lips, General Dietrich's son removed his steel helmet and the *Ohren Schutzer*, a knitted wool toque that had protected his ears in the subzero stratosphere. "Leaving the plane, these winds struck me like a solid wall. When the chute opened, its force bruised my ribs," he said. He ran a hand through his tangled brown hair before unbuttoning the front of his padded winter jump smock. Underneath he wore the Luftwaffe starched white dress shirt and slim black necktie. "But paratroopers must conquer their fear of the elements and concentrate their thoughts on defeating the enemy who waits on the ground."

"Manfred has seen combat in Spain serving with Generalissimo Franco's airborne Condor Legion," General Dietrich boasted, given to a moment of fatherly pride.

"*Ja*, I have had that honor." Captain Dietrich leaned forward to accept a light from the general. "I was among the fifty Germans who volunteered to fight in Spain." Taking a long drag on the cigarette, he eased back, encouraged by his father's thin smile to speak of his experience. "It was the Führer's wish that we Germans learn from parachuting under actual combat conditions. I fought in over a dozen missions with my brave comrades there, and each one taught us hard lessons. Those who did not learn so well were killed." With his fingers he brushed a crescent-shaped scar on his forehead. "Of the fifty who volunteered, only thirty of us returned to Germany with our valuable knowledge, and this led to the formation of the Stendal Parachute Academy. Those who jumped with me today have mastered their training. But schools cannot season a fighting man. For this he must face a real enemy, *meine Herren*." His tone hardened. Elbows planted on his thighs, he studied the faces of the business partners, recognizing some quality in Heinz Karlstadt's eyes that was lacking in the American, who had obviously never served his country in war. "To jump into the crossfire of real bullets is the ultimate test of a paratrooper's courage, his training, and the equipment he is given to jump with." He addressed his remarks to Heinz. "Sacrificing good men because of faulty parachutes is a waste."

"Herr Karlstadt and I are determined to improve the safety of our equipment," Douglas responded earnestly. "We'd welcome any suggestions that you learned from your combat experience. It could spare other men the injuries we witnessed today."

"This will require some thought," the captain said, stony-faced. "Herr Napier, was it? Your German is excellent for an American."

"Don't like Americans much, Captain?" Douglas fenced off the left-handed compliment with a laugh.

"Germany and America were once enemies and may well be again."

"You were ordered here to render an opinion on parachutes, not politics, Herr Captain Dietrich," his father reminded him sharply. "So, we are waiting to hear your comments." The general flicked his black leather gloves brusquely across his lap. "And bear in mind the future of the Reich is not served by your personal feelings."

The young captain's sheepish grin reminded Douglas of how Kimitake looked when he felt the steel of his father's displeasure. Japan seemed a million miles away as Captain Dietrich launched into a description of the jump. Douglas's attention wandered off to Natsu. Before leaving Tokyo he had arranged to have flowers placed at her grave every day, as homage to an undying love. The car skidded on a patch of ice, and Captain Dietrich's brash young voice invaded Douglas's solitude, forcing him to give attention to the business of war.

"After my shroud burst open, I was like an eagle riding the wind." Captain Dietrich rose partway up in his seat, swaying airily to demonstrate his courageous descent. "Then the winds shifted." He breathed in sharply, both arms lifting to clench imaginary shroud lines. "Even pulling on the lines with all my strength, I was being carried off target into the woods. I will not land properly, I thought. I will be smashed against the treetops. And then the parachute responded to my efforts. The Gessler parachutes have little maneuverability," he continued. "They resist the air currents, often taking their own course no matter how one fights to control one's glide path over the target area. But this parachute suddenly gave the control over to me. It tamed the winds. Never before have I experienced such command. I was the master of my descent, like a pilot at the stick of his plane, and not some dead weight falling to earth without power. With this new parachute answering my commands, I chose a spot nearest the target attack point. And there I landed, ready to take charge of the men who had followed my lead."

The captain sat back. "There are no words to describe the thrill I felt today. Something earthbound men must experience for themselves to understand. I very much like this Karlstadt parachute," he announced, laughing as he slapped his thighs. "It is far superior to any equipment I have ever used. After today, I am eager for more jumps with this parachute. My men are equally enthusiastic. Regiment General Göring must not be outclassed by the army airborne, Herr General. Of course, it is for you to decide." Captain Dietrich picked his steel helmet off the floor and drew his shoulders back at attention as the car lurched to a stop. "My barracks. Does the Herr General wish to be present at the debriefing?"

General Dietrich shook his head. "I shall expect a thorough report on your men. Leave out no detail of their experience in the jump. That is all, Herr Captain. Heil Hitler." His forearm went up in the Nazi salute. It was returned by his son, who then got out of the car.

The general peered outside at icicles dangling from the parachute academy's barbed wire fences, then turned to Heinz as the car door closed against the chill. "My son's report is a necessary formality. Another file to swell the air ministry's record vaults. I am favorably impressed, but there is much to discuss before I speak with Hermann Göring in Berlin," he told Heinz. "You and Herr Napier will dine with me here this evening."

Heinz eagerly accepted for them both. "I must contact my wife. She has concert tickets for this evening, Herr General." At the mention of his wife, he received a chilling look from the general. "Furtwangler conducts the Berlin Philharmonic."

"How unfortunate our business together must keep you from enjoying the Führer's favorite maestro." General Dietrich pulled on his gloves, flexing his fingers to achieve a snug fit. "Please, convey my regrets to Frau Karlstadt when you telephone her from my hotel suite."

Heinz was uncomfortable with the general's churlish manner. The Nazi high command were well aware of Inge's Jewish ancestry, but so far that fact had been passed over, as if it did not exist. "Our wives will be disappointed, but we can rely on their good dispositions to forgive us." He laughed nervously. The general's pale blue eyes were expressionless. "As a youth, I hunted deer in these woods," Heinz said, just to fill the silence.

General Dietrich's hotel suite had the cozy look of an alpine ski lodge. Heinz telephoned Berlin and talked to Inge before he passed the receiver to Douglas. "Inge is putting your wife on the line."

"Angela? I'm sorry about this evening's concert, but it can't be helped," Douglas said.

The brittleness in Angela's voice carried a reminder of their quarrel the previous night, when she had bitterly accused him of failing to live up to his promises. During their brief autumn holiday in Paris, Angela had seemed desperate to recapture the romance of their early years together. He had genuinely hoped to rebuild their marriage, but physical desire could not be forced upon him, and all his good intentions were marred by dismal failures. The night before, Angela's tears had moved him to plead for a patience and understanding he had no right to expect of her. Douglas ran a hand across his face, torn by feelings of inadequacy while hearing the smoldering discontent in his wife's voice.

"Any mail from Max?" he asked.

"Yes," she answered in a wounded tone. "Addressed to you, so I haven't opened it." Not the first such letter mailed from Harvard. Her voice broke. "I'm resigned to how our son always turns to you, sharing his most private thoughts. But I'm far from being resigned to the tired old routine between us. All day, I've tried to shake the depression caused by last night's scene."

Douglas cleared his throat. "I can't speak freely now."

"Spare yourself the effort, darling." Angela sighed wearily. "Well, I suppose Inge and I will just have to spend the evening without the pleasure of our husbands' company. Business first," she added tartly.

"Enjoy yourselves." Douglas lowered the receiver as General Dietrich called him to the dining table placed near a stone hearth in which glowed a warm, crackling fire.

Feigning a smile, Douglas seated himself in one straight-backed wooden chair, whose arms were carved with boars' heads. The führer's power-crazed eyes gazed down from an official photograph mounted over the fireplace. Compelled to spend the evening breaking bread with one of the devil's high-ranking generals, Douglas saw himself and Heinz as pawns in a deadly game of chess. General Dietrich frequently looked up at his master's portrait, while Heinz engaged him in an outwardly affable conversation. Two Germans who stood at opposite poles regarding Hitler's Mephistophelian dream of a Reich to last for a thousand years relaxed, puffing on cigarettes as Dubonnet aperitifs were served by an orderly.

Major General Dietrich had done his homework, and the relaxed conversation ended abruptly. For what seemed hours, he conducted a grueling interrogation that explored every facet of the Karlstadt Parachute Works, from its manufacturing process to the morale of its employees. Finally, dinner was wheeled to the table. Venison, potato pancakes, and a tart red cabbage were served with a dry white Rhineland wine.

Douglas let Heinz do most of the talking. His German friend was gifted with a dramatic flare. Heinz periodically removed his monocle, wagged it to underscore his words, and then slowly raised it to his eye, regarding General Dietrich as if heaven and earth rested on his cryptic remarks.

As the fire burned low, Dietrich's orderly poured wine into their crystal goblets, and Douglas shared his partner's surprise over what the general confided.

"Göring plans eventually to unify all the führer's paratroopers into one mighty airborne arm under the Luftwaffe's command," Dietrich said, just as the telephone rang and his orderly hurried to answer it. "Such a reorganization has many advantages, the standardization of equipment

and of training procedures, for example." He turned toward the telephone, annoyed by the interruption. His orderly snapped to attention and
held out the receiver. "Who is it, Kuntze?"

"Berlin, Herr General. Field Marshal Göring."

"I shall take it in the adjoining bedroom." General Dietrich excused
himself from the table. The general left the bedroom door open, and
Douglas and Heinz heard him say, "*Ja*, Hermann, I know how eager you
are for word of today's exercise. All is good here. *Ja*, the Karlstadt
parachute makes our present equipment obsolete." Then the orderly
closed the bedroom door quietly.

Heinz leaned across the table to address Douglas in a confidential
whisper. "When the Luftwaffe absorbs the army paratroopers, our
equipment will set the new standard. I can see Gessler now, pounding his
head with both fists to curse us. Soon we will have the parachute market
all to ourselves."

"If Göring decides in our favor." Douglas impatiently checked his
watch, recalling a time when winning at business had sent a rush of
adrenaline through his veins. That evening he experienced only the
weariness of having to perform until his obligations to Heinz and Tadashi
were written off the ledger. Even if they were awarded this contract, it
would be years until the interest on Lord Mitsudara's bank note was paid
in full. "The lion's share or bankruptcy, Heinz."

"It is not like you to be so negative, my friend. Everything favors
us."

"Strudel, *meine Herren*?"

Heinz sniffed the pastry offered on the orderly's serving tray and
uttered a sigh of surrender. "Inge would not allow me this self-indulgence.
But since no one is looking . . ." He chuckled and patted his bulging
middle while Douglas waved off the pastry tray. "*Ach*, how I admire your
willpower. But you carry this dieting too far, Douglas. You looked
healthier with more meat on your bones."

Douglas sipped his wine quietly. He had come to lean more heavily
on the Karlstadts, whose companionship helped ease the tension between
him and Angela. He realized how difficult it was for the couple not to pry
for explanations.

Living so closely together in the Karlstadt mansion was a mixed
blessing. It grew harder for both him and Angela to guard their privacy
while being watched with so much concern. But, Douglas realized, they
might not have survived the past months if they had taken a place of their
own in Berlin. Heinz and Inge kept things light and gay, entertaining them
with frequent parties and the welcome visits of other guests belonging to
the continental social set who had become their friends during summers
spent abroad. All this distraction prescribed by the Karlstadts was a
sensitive effort to cure whatever ailed their friends. Angela did bubble
with some of her old effervescence at times, but his melancholy only

became more oppressive in the manufactured fun. Driving to Stendal that morning, Heinz had made a rather awkward stab at trying to draw Douglas out and now sat back watching him, concerned by his friend's haggard look.

General Dietrich marched into the sitting room. "Göring has awarded the contract to you," he announced, wearing a pleased smile as he locked both hands behind his back. "The papers will be executed after Colonel Beck's ordnance staff inspects your manufacturing facilities. Usual procedure before the procurement of all Luftwaffe equipment." The general turned to the orderly. "Kuntze, pour more wine for our guests, then leave us."

Heinz stood from the table and clicked his heels. "I am honored to be of service to the fatherland, Herr General."

The general was no longer smiling. He paced until the door closed behind his orderly. "How is it you have not joined the Nazi party, Herr Karlstadt?" Taken aback, Heinz was speechless. "You meant to join, of course," the general continued in a condescending tone. "But like so many other good Germans, you have put it off. Now you will correct this oversight. It is Hermann Göring's wish that you do so quickly, as proof of your loyalty to the führer."

"My loyalty to Deutschland was proved in the trenches at Verdun, with the military honors I earned there," Heinz replied tersely. "Perhaps the field marshal should be reminded of my war record."

"These are different times," the general interrupted him. "We are building a new order in Germany, and our Führer leads us out of the defeatist past. The führer is Deutschland," he said strongly, pointing at Hitler's photograph, "and your loyalty must not be left in question."

"Forgive me, Herr General Dietrich, but I do not feel it necessary to carry the Nazi party card as proof that I am a loyal German."

"I fail to understand such obstinacy." Dietrich threw open his jacket and stood rocking, hands on hips. "Can it be possible that you are unaware of those in the high command who object to your business with the Reich while you have a Jewess for a wife? They question why you have not had this marriage annulled. They dispute your allegiance to a Jew and feel you are not to be trusted with a position of so much importance. Field Marshal Göring wants these voices silenced."

His hand trembling, Heinz removed his monocle. "Nothing has been said. It never crossed my mind that Frau Karlstadt would become the cause of such an unjust dispute."

"Awarding you this contract makes your Jewish wife an issue that can no longer be tolerated in silence." Dietrich's expression was menacing. "Take your head out of the sand and see what is taking place around you, Herr Karlstadt. Your marriage to a Jewess is an embarrassment that will be dragged out at the conference table when Field Marshal Göring announces his choice of your parachute over that of the Gessler Works."

"But my wife is an exception. Inge is first a German. A loyal German, raised as a Christian, and a Jew only on the paper of her birth certificate," Heinz insisted.

"In the eyes of German law, she is a Jew. But our führer makes certain allowances." General Dietrich surprised Heinz by giving him a friendly pat on the shoulder. "One Jew more or less is of no importance to him. Göring will simply grin at your detractors and show them proof of your loyalty to the new order. Frau Karlstadt will continue to enjoy her privileged status as the wife of a Nazi party member who performs a great service for the Reich. *Ach*, one would think you were being asked to face the firing squad." The general sighed. "Naturally, it is assumed that you fully support the cause of national socialism. So? Do we have an understanding?"

Douglas suffered his distaste in silence. This was something Heinz must decide alone. Join the Nazi party or sacrifice the contract? The question hung on a painful look exchanged between partners, and then Heinz's stance crumbled.

"I have a stubborn streak, General." Fixing the monocle in his eye, Heinz swallowed hard before capitulating in a choked voice. "Field Marshal Göring can rest assured that his wish will be carried out immediately."

"Good. Congratulations, *meine Herren*." Displaying a thin smile, General Dietrich lifted his wineglass from the table. "The Karlstadt parachute and German superiority in the air. Heil Hitler!"

It was a heel-clicking toast Heinz felt compelled to return. "Heil Hitler." Speaking these words soured the wine for Heinz.

"*Prosit*," Douglas chimed in. He was not obligated to toast the führer or swear allegiance to the Reich. But when General Dietrich shook hands with both men after seeing them to the door, Douglas felt as if his fingers had been pricked for blood to add his signature to the devil's contract.

Army trucks barreled along the autobahn's snowplowed lanes stretching toward Berlin. As Heinz drove his Mercedes-Benz, he gave voice to his festering concerns. "Perhaps my head has been buried in the sand," he told Douglas. "My blood boiled while I shamefully denied Inge's race with false rationalizations. I have turned my eyes away from the notices on shop windows urging people not to buy from Jewish merchants and those posted outside restaurants that proclaim 'no dogs or Jews served here.' I had not allowed myself to believe Inge would be threatened by this tidal wave of anti-Semitism." Heinz punched in the dashboard cigarette lighter. "Tomorrow I soil my honor by swearing an oath to that megalomaniac Hitler. Without the Luftwaffe contract, we are finished. But my actions are also dictated by concern for Inge's position." The lighter popped out, and he touched its glowing red eye to his cigarette. "These are dangerous times for the fatherland. Even with the party card in my wallet, I wonder if the Nazis can be trusted to keep their word."

"General Dietrich's ugly manner gave me the shivers. His claim that your service to Hitler would gloss over the Jewish question doesn't sit well with me," said Douglas, fearing German anti-Semitism might touch the lives of his friends with more serious repercussions if they remained here. "After tonight, I'm damn uneasy doing business with Hitler's boys."

Heinz laughed, flicking his cigarette against the ashtray. "We are like old maids peering under their beds for imagined prowlers. That wolf of a general was only testing his power over me, Douglas. The Führer can never purge Germany of all the Jews. His Jew-baiting distracts the people from the real problems facing his Reich. Soon they will tire of blaming everything on the Jews and demand more of Hitler than speeches filled with promises." Heinz switched on the car radio, and his hand moved in time to the strains of Beethoven's "Eroica" Symphony broadcast from Berlin. "There beats the noble German heart. I ask you, Douglas, what can be feared in a country that has produced Beethoven?"

Angela Napier had not planned to unburden herself on Inge Karlstadt. But that night, sitting and drinking glasses of crème de menthe in the posh Berlin restaurant where they had dined alone together, she had suddenly told Inge the whole story of her husband's infidelity. Inge listened quietly.

Speaking of this was painful for Angela. When she had finished, Inge was silent, and Angela laced her fingers together and regarded her best friend. "I've shocked you, Inge. Good Lord, I'm shocked at myself for telling all this, even to you. I've expected too much of our friendship. The most you can do is to say kind words, and that won't solve a thing or make the problem go away. I should never have spoken so openly."

"But this is what good friends are for. To listen with compassion and offer their understanding." Inge, her huge blue eyes full of sympathy, leaned across the table and touched Angela's ice cold hands. "These many weeks, I have been torn with worry. Heinz as well. We sensed an anguish in you and Douglas that kept us at a distance. Now I will not placate you with hollow words. If I cannot take away even the smallest portion of your anguish, then I am unworthy of your trust and affection. Ach, but emotions confuse my thoughts." Inge rested back in her chair. Her luxurious golden hair was parted down the middle and combed out straight like shimmering curtains framing her high cheekbones. She took a strand of hair and began twisting it. "My heart is heavy for what you must have suffered, Angela. But I think of all the good times we shared with you and Douglas over the years and ask myself how this can be if he had never loved you. I am sad for this Japanese woman who cheated you of so much. It would serve no purpose to deny that Douglas also loved her, but it was not meant to be. He chose you as his wife because you were right for each other. Yes, over the years I've seen the pride he takes in you and how he flourished with you at his side, how you laughed together. Husbands are often guilty of taking their wives for granted. Love is not always spoken between two people, but surely you must have felt loved. Perhaps your pride comes in the way of trusting what you have felt with him before you learned of his unfaithfulness," she said softly, moved by the tears welling up in Angela's eyes. "Do not think so little of yourself. It was brave of you to grant Douglas another chance. Courageous and right, Angela. Men often do not know their own hearts. Stand by him and he will come to recognize how blind he has been in the past."

"Oh, if only I could believe that were true." Angela twisted nervously against her chair, made uncomfortable by the stares of two young German officers dining alone at the adjacent table. "I so admire your outgoingness and your warmth. You have a gift for making those around you feel cherished and special. Yet I feel so alone. You've never had reason to doubt Heinz's love," she said rather jealously. Her sable coat was draped across the chair back and she drew the fur around the shoulders of her low-cut evening dress. "Please don't think me crass for saying this, but I've always been envious of what you have with Heinz."

"And I envy you for having a child to love. Max has become very dear to me. The house seems empty now that he is studying in America." Inge's confession brought an uneasy silence. Angela knew how much Inge had longed to have a child.

"Angela, we both have much to be grateful for. There is no place for envy between us. Come, we are already too late for the concert, but I shall take you to some gay cabaret. It is just the thing for chasing away our blues." Her earthy laugh invited bolder stares from the two officers. "Tomcats on the prowl," she whispered. "We are too old for them, but the candlelight flatters us." Determined to cheer her friend, she laughed again, and their male admirers rose to bow as the two women left the restaurant.

The Karlstadt limousine sat waiting at the curb.

"I couldn't possibly enjoy a cabaret," Angela said. "All that smoke and noise."

Inge turned up her fur collar. "We shall walk for a time before returning home, Fleischer."

Her uniformed chauffeur touched his cap. "*Ja,* Frau Karlstadt." Fleischer had served the couple many years. He was of peasant stock, tall and brawny, with hands like a blacksmith. There was little clearance for his head when he took the wheel to cruise slowly behind the ladies.

Berlin's Kurfurstendamm was a spacious commercial avenue brightly lit with decorations for the approaching Christmas season, and many stores remained open for business. The two women of wealth bundled in their sable coats and hats turned heads among the less fortunate Berliners who strolled beneath a light snowfall. The window of a toy shop caught Inge's fancy. Watching the mechanical clowns and acrobats, she thought of what Christmas would be like if she had a child.

When she turned from the display, she saw that Angela had wandered off on the street. As Inge hurried after her, she heard a loud crashing sound. There was a sudden explosion of shattering glass. Inge saw her friend step back from danger not a moment too soon as a shower of broken glass flew out across the pavement directly in Angela's path.

Someone had smashed the window of a jewelry store. Inge reached her friend and gripped Angela's arm while a crowd pressed in front of them. A man was being dragged from the shop into the street. He was trapped within a circle of angry men shouting insults.

"Judensau!"

"You have picked our pockets long enough, Jewish pig."

Through the crowd Inge could see the Jewish shopkeeper. He was held by the arms while his attackers took turns beating him with their fists. Angela pleaded with Inge to come away, but Inge stood rooted to the spot, shocked and horrified. Not far up the street a policeman used his call box to report the incident, then folded his arms across his chest and allowed the beating to continue.

The crowd watched mutely as the elderly man collapsed at the feet of those who had attacked him, his black skullcap dislodged when his head struck the pavement. His ashen face was covered with blood, and the twisted frames of his blood-splattered glasses dangled crookedly off one ear. Weakly, he reached out his hand in search of help, but people simply stepped back. His cries barely frosted the air before his hand grew still.

One of his attackers picked the shopkeeper's skullcap off the ground and waved it at the torn remnants of a notice pasted on the smashed window glass. "Don't buy from Jews," he addressed the onlookers. "Any German who gives his trade to bloodsucking Jewish pigs commits a crime against the state!" The man wore a Hitler mustache and his eyes were frantic with hate as he shouted, "Wipe out all Jewish businesses! Their wealth belongs to the German people, and it must be returned to us! Germany for the Germans!" Several people cheered his words.

Angela was brushed aside by a woman who screamed, "Filthy Jew," and bent over the unconscious shopkeeper to spit on his face. "That for you, Itzak!" That Jewish name was a widely used Nazi insult. The shrieking woman began viciously kicking the unconscious man until blood came bubbling from his nostrils.

"Oh, my God, she will kill him!" Inge cried, and rushed forward to seize the woman by her hair. "Ignorant animal! This poor man has done nothing!"

"Filthy Jew lover!" the woman screamed.

"*Ja*, I am also a Jew and proud of it!" Inge answered, pulling hard on the woman's hair and dragging her around in circles. Inge screamed for the policeman, who now broke into a run.

Many of the onlookers shouted anti-Semitic slogans, and Angela watched, horrified, fearing for her friend's safety. Suddenly, a tall figure charged through the crowd and lifted Inge up in his arms.

"Fleischer! Thank God," Angela exclaimed. "Hurry, we must get her into the car."

"Stand clear, all of you," the chauffeur said to the crowd that stood in the path of the parked limousine.

Inge fought his strong arms. "Nazi thugs! Murderers!" she screamed. "I am a Jew and I demand justice!"

Just then the policeman appeared to block Fleischer's path. "Halt! Release this troublemaker. The Jewess is under arrest!"

"Jewess, you say?" Fleischer stared him down and laughed. "Frau Karlstadt is not a Jew."

"Do not be fooled by him, officer," screeched the woman Inge had assaulted. She wore a shabby winter coat and began clawing at Inge's sable. "I deserve these warm furs, Jewess bitch! Give them to me!"

Inge burst into tears and pushed away the woman's clawing hands.

"For the last time, you are ordered to surrender this Jewess to me!" The policeman put his back against the limousine door, threatening Fleischer with the blunt end of his nightstick.

"And I tell you that Frau Karlstadt is not a Jew!" Fleischer tightened his hold on Inge, his craggy face set stubbornly as he talked fast. "All this is in her head, officer. She is a little crazy and under the doctor's care. Her husband is someone of great importance. Arrest his wife and your mistake will not go unpunished."

"Let us take my friend home, officer," said Angela, reaching out for the limousine door handle. "Our husbands do important business with the Reich. My friend became hysterical witnessing this violence." Her German dialect was that of the ruling class, and she arched her eyebrows and gave the policeman a challenging stare. "Look at Frau Karlstadt's face more closely, and you will see that she is not a Jew."

"I am a Jew," Inge sobbed, as the policeman shoved his nightstick under her chin to take a closer look.

To the policeman, Inge had a strong Aryan face, very like the Rhine maidens pictured on propaganda posters, working for the führer's cause. Her head was covered, but he could see her blond hair, which hung to her shoulders from beneath her fur hat. "Your husband should keep you off the streets," he hissed, prodding the ends of Inge's straight blond hair with his nightstick. "Take her home," he told Fleischer, then faced off the agitated crowd pressing around him. "Stand back! She is only a sick woman, not a Jew!"

The wailing sirens of arriving German police vans dispersed the crowd. Angela quickly took shelter inside the limousine, but before Fleischer could pass Inge to the seat beside her, a woman reached between them and snatched Inge's sable hat.

"You don't fool me! Go in rags, Jewess bitch," the woman cried, and ducked away under the policeman's outstretched arms.

Strands of Inge's golden hair fell across her eyes as she shook her head and cried, "No! I will not allow this. This did not happen." She pounded her fists on the limousine door, which Fleischer had quickly closed, and watched her fur hat vanish on the head of the woman whose hair she had pulled. Unclenching her fists, she saw threads of brown hair stuck to her palms, and she sobbed, rubbing them clean against her furs. "I must be dreaming. This awful thing could not have happened."

Angela tried comforting her friend with an embrace. "Oh, please calm yourself. It's over now and you're safe."

"No one is safe while those thugs roam the streets unpunished." Inge tore free and rolled down her window. Those who had given the jeweler a beating were now grabbing merchandise from the smashed window, while the German police ignored them and, instead, halted people in the dispersing crowd to check their papers. "Are you blind?" shouted Inge, leaning out the window to point an accusing finger at the looters. "Punish those thugs who take the law into their own hands!"

"Quiet her, Frau Napier," Fleischer called urgently from behind the wheel. He could not get the motor started. "Gestapo," he said, as unmarked black sedans arrived at the scene. "You must quiet Frau Karlstadt, or all of us will be arrested."

Inge fought Angela's efforts. "Animals! An old man lies there bleeding! How can you stand there and not call for an ambulance?" Her wild-eyed screams gained the attention of several Gestapo agents. Just then, the motor responded to Fleischer's efforts, and the limousine lurched off, sending Inge from the window.

"Turn the car back, Fleischer. We must go back and give testimony against those thugs."

"It would do no good, Frau Karlstadt," he said, swerving the limousine to pass the traffic ahead. "What took place was the Gestapo's doing, or they would not be there. Let us hope that policeman does not think to give them your name. The Gestapo do as they please. It would mean trouble even for someone of your importance, Frau Karlstadt."

"Heinz, what have I done?" Inge fell back in the seat and covered her face. "My anger might bring harm to us both. I must learn to hold my tongue. Ja, best not to draw attention to my Jewish blood. That is a bitter fact I have learned tonight. One cannot reason with the Nazi mentality. All this hatred burns like a fever in their eyes."

Fleischer sighed heavily. "You will forgive me for what I told that policeman. He and the others are the crazy ones, Frau Karlstadt. The way he treated you, I could have broken him in half with these." The limousine swerved as his powerful hands left the wheel.

"Dear Fleischer, you have a heart of gold. Thank you for rescuing me."

"I can never repay the many kindnesses you have shown my family and me. I will let no one threaten you with harm," he said in a choked voice. He lifted his broad shoulders as emotion kept him from saying more.

Angela turned to Inge. "I can't get it out of my head how everyone just stood by and watched."

"Fear, Angela. Many were afraid to help that poor man. Like us, they were shocked that such a terrifying thing could take place before their eyes."

"That policeman on duty could have stopped it. He and the others who arrived seemed so indifferent."

Inge took Angela's shivering hand in hers. "The German people are shocked and silent, but never indifferent," she assured her. The limousine now drove along a quiet residential street, leaving the jewelry store on the Kurfurstendamm and the threat of the Gestapo behind them. "See how pure the snow is. How still and peaceful, as though nothing had happened," Inge mused, rolling up the frosted window glass. "You must promise me not to speak of this to Heinz. You as well, Fleischer. God only knows what a mountain of worries he would build for himself." She smiled at Angela, forgetting her own fears in an attempt to calm her friend. "There is much love in the world to balance the hatreds being preached. Indifference is to be feared. But Germany can never be turned into a godless state, where human life means nothing. Fleischer is right. The Gestapo was behind this horrid demonstration, and the police were under orders not to interfere."

"Obeying such an inhuman order makes it all the more horrifying," Angela said quietly, hugging her arms around herself. "I used to think Germany was so civilized. But watching that dreadful woman steal your hat, I felt like the inmate of a madhouse."

"*Ach*, my hat." Inge ran her fingers through her hair. "It was a gift from Heinz. How will I explain losing it? The wind. *Ja*, the wind carried it away."

CHAPTER 20

A crystalline winter light tinted the snow along the pavement of the Ginza in shades of pearl-gray and blue. Paul kicked slush off his newly issued army boots and stared up past the Cherry Blossom Kissaten's neon sign to the familiar apartment windows above. This was the first time he had worn his tailor-made khaki uniform since being appointed *Nippon Shimbun*'s war correspondent in China. Only the press insignia on his cap distinguished him from a regular infantry office, and he felt rather vain and important as he entered the tea shop's once forbidden street door.

"Paul!" Yoko exclaimed in surprise, putting her coarse red hands to her face. Then she rushed over to embrace him. "Why do you wear this uniform?"

"My sailing orders for China came through at last. I'm leaving in a few hours."

"So little warning." Smiling sadly, Yoko touched the brass buttons of his army greatcoat. "How handsome you look."

"I can't stay long," Paul said. Returning to the tea shop always evoked painful memories, and he wanted to cut his visit short. But Yoko seated him at a corner table, then hurried off for tea and cakes. He lit a cigarette and listened to the male customers who discussed the latest war news. Nanking had fallen to Japan early in December, 1937. Now its occupation had stretched into the new year, while Japanese troops systematically raped and plundered the city. Their field commanders had disobeyed general orders for an honorable occupation and had staged a bloodbath to terrify the Chinese into negotiating an early peace. However, their tactics seemed only to harden Chiang Kai-Shek's determination to fight off the invaders.

"All Chinese are the enemy. Soldiers and civilians alike," one stern-faced man insisted loudly. He sat at one end of the long table that served as a forum for the tea shop. "These chinks refuse to admit they are beaten," he told them. "If the rape of Nanking doesn't bring them to their knees, we should burn it and other Chinese cities to the ground."

"And what of Japanese honor?" His detractor, seated at the opposite end of the table, rose up, brandishing that morning's *Nippon Shimbun*. "More eyewitness accounts from Nanking speak of Japanese soldiers chasing down women and children, killing everything that moves in the streets. Even dogs and cats. Can anything justify this shameful exhibition against the honor and glory of Japan?"

"Ah, these reports can't be trusted," another man interjected, frowning as he displayed the front page of a rival Tokyo newspaper. "Here they claim the situation is exaggerated. Only our fighting men there know what is taking place."

Paul snuffed his cigarette in the ashtray, thinking how poor communications were between Nanking and Tokyo. As a result, reports of Japanese atrocities were vague and often contradictory. Noticing Yoko's brow crease with worry, Paul was reminded that Toru's outfit was with the occupation forces there. As she served him tea, Paul asked, "Still no letter from Toru?"

"No, and I shudder each time a soldier enters my shop, afraid he will be the army's official messenger." Her voice trembled as she said, "Only the other day, I was in Mrs. Kubo's bakery shop when the messenger came to announce the death of her son. I will never forget his words. 'Please accept this notice, comforted by the knowledge that your son died for his imperial majesty, the emperor.' Mrs. Kubo swooned in my arms." Yoko hugged herself, rocking as if cradling a baby in her arms. "Months without any word from Toru. Now you are going to war, and I must live in fear for you both."

"Don't make yourself sick with worry. Toru's a born samurai. Tough as nails and trained to survive." Paul attempted to reassure her, mindful of the time, while Yoko fingered the silver in her hair and reminisced about the past. He pictured Natsu weaving gracefully among the tables, hiding her weariness behind a charming smile. Oh, God how he missed the comfort of those loving arms. "I really have to go," he blurted out with an abruptness that startled Yoko. "Some unfinished business," he explained, rising and buttoning his coat.

Yoko reached out and embraced him. As a child he had clung to Natsu's cherry-blossom-print kimono that smelled of the same tea shop scents. Gently he pried himself free of her arms and of the memories she conjured up. "I won't have much time for letter writing."

"Your stories in the newspaper will tell me you are safe." Yoko pressed his hand. "Natsu would have been so proud. So very proud. May the gods protect you," she said, then stood at the open street door waving good-bye.

From the storefront loudspeakers of a music shop, a phonograph record was playing. "What joy!" a woman's voice sang. "My child has been called to be a warrior for the emperor." The new song glorifying war brought smiles to the faces of passersby.

Paul looked back across the pavement where he and Toru had played soldier together as boys. He saw Yoko wiping the tears from her eyes and closing the tea shop's door. His step lightened, as if the weight of the past had come rolling off his shoulders. His uniform was like a magic cloak blinding everyone's eyes to his mixed blood. In spirit he was already on the high seas bound for China.

He stopped at the corner mailbox to post the last of his letters to Max from Japan. Over the months he had written vividly of the time he spent with Shizue in Kyoto. He was sure that his love for her could easily be read between the lines, but this had eluded Max, whose correspondence expressed only gratitude for the letters that enabled him to see Shizue through Paul's eyes. His brother's dreary accounts of life at Harvard were not fair exchange, for what he was enduring while serving as a link between lovers.

Shizue had celebrated the new year in Tokyo as Lord Mitsudara's houseguest. Business kept Baron Hosokawa at the Kyoto weaving mill, and she had managed to see Paul every day. He nearly cracked under the strain of being so near her again, but he did not want their good-byes prolonged, and he had used the sudden nature of his departure as an excuse, arranging for Shizue to be at Ueno Station just in time to see him off.

As Paul hailed a taxi, he heard the record again. "What joy! My child has been called to be a warrior for the emperor." Japan was selling war in China with jingles much like those used to sell tooth powder and cigarettes, he thought.

As the taxi passed *Nippon Shimbun*'s offices, Paul thought about the publisher. He had not condescended to personally wish his half-caste war correspondent good luck. But the assignment was all that really mattered, Paul told himself. His mentor, Tamura-*san*, had been tearful when Paul cleared out his desk drawers that morning, but his newsroom colleagues had snubbed him. They were jealous but glad to be rid of him. At last the call to war offered Paul escape, although, as he drove to his farewell with Shizue, he wondered if even war could rid him of the tortures of unrequited love.

It was customary at the beginning of the new year to visit Tokyo's Asakusa Kwannon and buy *daruma* dolls at the outdoor stalls near its famed Buddhist temple. Shizue, shopping there with Yufugawo, had been unable so far to choose a favorite among the thousands on display. It was an ancient belief that the Buddhist saint, Dharma, had held a meditative position for nine years, and the brightly colored pâpier-maché dolls were shaped after his meditative pose. They varied in size and design, except for their eyes, which were white sockets without pupils. When Shizue had achieved her goals for the coming year, she would draw in the rest of the eyes to celebrate her *engi*, her good fortune.

"Okigari-Kosobi. The little priest who rises up," Shizue said to Yufugawo, pushing one roly-poly doll back against the vendor's table. Its weighted bottom caused it to bob upright again. A *daruma* was symbolic of the final success one's struggle would bring, and it could not be knocked down. Shizue kept a treasured collection of them on the family god shelf. They represented her childhood years, and all had their eyes painted in as witness to the achievement of personal goals. That day Shizue saw them as a charming custom she had suddenly outgrown.

"This one resembles my O-nami." Amused, Yufugawo pushed back a very large *daruma* that was painted a bright red and gold, with black eyebrows shaped like butterfly wings. She laughed. "He rises up quivering, just like that great oaf if I catch him napping when there are chores to be done. I will buy it for him to bring about a successful spring silk harvest."

While Yufugawo haggled with the stall vendor over a price, Shizue gazed at the long sloping rooftops of Kwannon Temple. It was there a priest had blessed her *omamori*, and she scanned the nearby shops, wondering which one Max had entered to purchase the precious keepsake that she wore around her neck. The incantation inscribed on its gold setting might safeguard her against bodily harm, but that afternoon she felt the need for spiritual protection against the terrible fear of losing Paul in the war. Now Yufugawo linked arms with her, and they moved on through the teeming streets beyond Asakusa, where Japanese flags were hung from almost every shop and the neighboring houses as a display of support for the bloodshed in China.

"It isn't fair," Shizue said, trying to speak above the blare of bugles sounding on the street ahead. "First Max and Kimitake, and now Paul. Everyone is being sent far away from me."

"*Sayonara* is never easy, child."

A parading army delegation slowed traffic to a crawl. These delegations had become a common sight in Tokyo. Inducting a young man into the service of his emperor was always a ceremonial occasion, and now soldiers were marching to escort some draftee to his new home at an army barracks. At least fifty of them marched four abreast, stepping to the buglers' martial beat. To the front and rear of the buglers, men carried silk flags of the rising sun and cotton banners that proclaimed the honors that would be bestowed on the new recruit, due to his service to the emperor.

Suddenly, Shizue and Yufugawo found themselves trapped in the patriotic crowd. Shizue anxiously searched for an opening but could find none. Paul's train would be leaving shortly, and she was forced to stand there watching another young man being claimed by war.

The solemn-faced young man stepped from his house, dressed in his finest clothes. As his family gathered outside to wish him well, Shizue wondered how they could all be smiling. Should he fail in his duty to the emperor, a note from his commanding officer would inform his parents that he had lost face. If he did not shame himself in training, then he would be sent into war with the twisted obligation to lay down his life. Paul was spared that horrid obligation, Shizue thought, but the dangers he would be exposed to were no less real.

Two sergeants came forward, flanked by a standard bearer.

"I will come back victorious!" the new recruit pledged to them.

"Congratulations! Best of luck!" his family and his neighbors shouted, as they waved paper stick flags. *"Banzai! Banzai!"* they cried, and the young man marched toward the column under escort of the sergeants in command.

Young soldiers already groomed for war had lost their looks of innocence. Shizue met their hardened eyes, then looked away, horrified. Not a soldier bore arms. There should be guns and drums to wake those around her to the savagery of war, she thought. Instead, they marched to heralding bugles and carried only flags and patriotic banners as they once again fell into step.

Men too old for conscription stood at attention saluting, while others like them cried *"banzai!"* and strutted off behind the parading column.

Yufugawo tugged on Shizue's arm. "See his poor wife there," she said sadly, pointing. "A child bride and her newborn infant left behind to weep, while those foolish old men play samurai."

Shizue nodded in agreement. The new recruit's abandoned wife wore the true face of war, and Shizue felt a shiver run through her.

Just then she spotted a taxi and waved it down. "Ueno Station. And please hurry," she instructed the driver, as she and Yufugawo got in. Snuggling against Yufugawo for warmth, Shizue said, "I'm so frightened for Paul. This war in China is an obsession, nothing more to him than a means for advancing his ambitions. I don't think he's allowed himself to consider that he might be killed or maimed. I've wanted to argue against him going, but he's so determined and sure of himself. Besides, I haven't the right to hold him here even if he could be reasoned with. Oh, I don't know how to say good-bye knowing I may never see Paul again."

"Say it bravely, little one. Send him off untroubled by your womanly fears." Yufugawo smoothed Shizue's furrowed brow. "You are grown into a woman now, and Natsu's son has need of your smiles, not your tears."

There were precious few minutes left for good-byes when Shizue ran beneath the vaulting skylight roofs of Ueno Station. Paul spotted her coming through the crowd on the platform. She looked particularly ravishing today, he thought, bundled in a white sealskin coat, her sealskin hat like a white cream puff that she held in place with one gloved hand. She came to a stop and caught her breath.

"What do you think of my uniform?" he asked, giving her a brisk salute.

"Most becoming on you." Shizue avoided his eyes. "I expected your train would be swarming with soldiers."

"The regiment I've been attached to got their sailing orders days ago." Paul dug an envelope from his greatcoat pocket. "Here's my official address. We'll be on the move, but your letters will catch up with me—or so I've been told from on high."

Shizue's hand lingered on his before taking the envelope. Each time she touched him, he died a little for wanting her. "Give me one of your pretty smiles."

Max had asked that of her before they were torn apart, and she did her best to please his smiling brother. "This assignment is what you wanted most, I know. At our cherry tree on that first day in Kyoto, I wished you'd receive your heart's desire. But I just can't bear to let you go." All her best efforts gave way to tears, and she put her arms around his neck. "Come back safely to me."

Paul held her tightly. Fearing these might well be the last moments of time on earth between them, he wanted to shout his love. But the conductor's whistle blew, and the train made a jerking start, snapping him back to his senses. "Don't wrinkle that lovely face over me. I'll return safely and with honor," he promised with all the bravura he could muster.

It was an echo of what the new recruit had pledged, and it caused Shizue to tremble. With Paul's departure, a phase in her life was ending. She felt strengthened for having known Natsu's son. In him she had glimpsed the children she hoped one day to bear for Max. The way would be hard for them as well, she thought, but it would be paved with love, and they would rise above the scorn of Japanese society just as Paul had. She brushed his cheek with a kiss. "You'll always be in my thoughts and in my prayers."

His arms shuddered as he released her. Then he turned and swung aboard the slow-moving train. Paul stood between cars waving. Smiling bravely now, Shizue used her handkerchief to wave good-bye as Paul vanished from sight beneath slanting shafts of winter sunlight.

Much later that night and well out at sea, Paul stretched his legs on deck. Outward bound for China, he experienced a surge of anticipation. There was no moon, but every so often he could see the bobbing, flickering lights of the Japanese convoy far off in the blackness.

"A reassuring sight."

Startled by the voice, Paul faced the shadowy presence standing beside him at the rail and nodded. "My first time at sea."

"Sick, or just too stirred up to sleep?"

"Stirred up is putting it mildly."

His companion laughed, then bowed. "Lieutenant Ono."

Paul returned the bow. "Akira Yoseido, correspondent for *Nippon Shimbun*."

"Really?" There was a smile in his tone. "This *is* an honor. I've been an avid reader of yours. Cigarette?"

"Yes."

Lieutenant Ono shook two cigarettes from the pack. "So, it's to be my first time in combat as well," he said, searching his greatcoat pockets for a light. "Before long our guts will be tested under fire. I don't envy you marching with only a pen in your hand."

Paul felt an easy camaraderie with the lieutenant. "I must admit to a little queasiness on that score."

"The roll of the ship." Lieutenant Ono laughed. Flicking his lighter, he cupped it between his gloved hands. His pleasant young face was visible for the first time as he lit up.

"Whatever, I'm keened up to a razor's edge." Paul bent to light his cigarette. "Thanks." He stood up, exhaling smoke. The lieutenant continued to allow the lighter flame to glow. His eyes frosted over. The friendship struck between two men standing in the darkness was terminated with an arrogant, point-blank stare.

Paul stared back evenly asking, "Is Tokyo home?"

"*Hai.*" Lieutenant Ono extinguished the flame. "The night holds a nasty chill. Please excuse my rudeness, Yoseido, but my blood freezes. Good night."

"Lieutenant," Paul bowed politely. His important post changed nothing. For a moment he had allowed himself to believe otherwise, and had just been "reminded" of his place. He threw his cigarette into the sea. China would be a clean slate, he thought. Cut free of the stifling past, he had only himself to think of now.

CHAPTER 21

As an army cadet, Jiro Mitsudara had been totally out of place. Earning his army commission had been the most distasteful experience he had endured as part of his *giri*, or "duty." For an ordinary Japanese, *giri* could be defined as one's social obligations, but for the lord's only son, it carried far greater burdens. This was a young man, with the soul of a poet, forced to conform to the strict mold of his warrior ancestors and expected to assume the oppressive responsibilities of being heir to his father's industrial empire. Now he was twenty-two. He had exchanged his army uniform for the stylish clothes worn by his university classmates, but he continued to feel the painful clash between his aesthetic nature and his duty to serve the dictates of the Mitsudara bloodline.

Soon after Jiro entered the University of Tokyo, this disparity became even more obvious. Among his fellow cadets at the military academy, he had been known as a sensitive misfit. Earning his commission had been like serving out a prison term at hard labor. Earning his degree in letters, however, was one obligation the lord's son could embrace totally as a labor of love. He had found his natural element among those of like minds, and the soft qualities ill-suited to a samurai were openly nurtured in the university's great halls of learning. Applauded by his professors, he was like some magically flowering tree, attracting an admiring swarm of new friends who recognized his special gifts. He became drunk on the ambrosia of expressing his long-suppressed feelings.

With the approach of spring, the expanding conflict in China kept his father away on business. Lady Mitsudara scowlingly observed her grandson's flighty behavior. Accomplishment in letters was expected of the well-rounded samurai, but Jiro was filling their household with his dilettante friends and, she thought, wallowing in an excess of feelings. He had forsaken the sword, and there was absolutely no place for the weakness of such an imbalance in the heir to their family throne. Lady Mitsudara reported all this to the lord, insisting he return home soon to correct her grandson's appalling behavior.

At her boarding school in Kyoto, Shizue prayed that Jiro would never come back down to earth. He telephoned her frequently, made giddy by the adoration of his newfound friends to whom he referred as "kindred spirits." He now realized what joy it would be to pattern his life after the ideals of eighteenth-century Japanese poets and painters, who had rejected the financial evils of professionalism. Jiro wanted only to be *bunjin*—a man of letters. "A man of uncompromising devotion to serve beauty. A man who serves no other master," he told her over the telephone from Tokyo.

Shizue grew more hopeful as his self-confidence soared higher with each successive phone call. Near the time of her seventeeth birthday, Jiro paid a surprise visit to her school. After charming her away from the clutches of the dormitory matrons, he took her for a ride in his hired car. The charm he had shown the matrons disappeared, and he grew tense and silent.

"What brought you all the way here from Tokyo?" she asked uneasily, and watched his face tighten as he drove. "Tell me why you're so gloomy. When we last spoke over the phone, you were so happy and sure of yourself."

Jiro pulled to the curb and slumped forward, massaging his temples. "My grandmother summoned my father home from business to give me a lecture. Scholastically, my record at the university pleases him. But he disapproves of my social life and considers the friends I've made a bad influence. He accused them of turning me into a thin-skinned dilettante with his head in the clouds. He accused me of living in a fool's paradise, and I've been ordered to spend this coming summer vacation toughening up on maneuvers with my army reserve unit." Jiro groaned. "I feel as if my head's splitting apart. I was just beginning to gain some confidence about determining my own future. But after the browbeating I took from father, my resolve was turned to mush." He paused. "A funny thing, courage. When my father stood up from behind his desk and told me my obligations, I felt the courage to defy him growing inside me, but I just sat there, the submissive son.

"You don't know how much I wanted to look my father in the eye and say no to everything. No, I won't honor this marriage agreement; no, I won't sit chained behind a desk of your greedy empire; no, I won't have anything to do with the factories, the steelworks, or the Mitsudara Bank— everything you prize over me." Jiro held the wheel so tightly his knuckles showed white. "That's what I wanted to tell Father. But I gave in to fear and sat there like a mute."

Shizue felt a painful stab of defeat. "Jiro, you mustn't give in to fear again. I realize how hard it is for you to speak your feelings. But it's only a matter of learning to say no. You'll find your voice."

With his slender fingers, Jiro stroked her hair while he confessed, "I choked on that simple word. I've spent so many nights wrestling with the problem of my submissiveness. Well, maybe it isn't useless to hope. After laying down the law, my father returned to Nagasaki on business. I was on my way there today, determined to have my say. But I got only this far. I couldn't see it through and stopped here at your school." He smiled at her. "It's the closest I've ever come to standing up to him. A victory of sorts. I'm trying my best to release us both, Shizue. Even though my grandmother reports everything to my father, I'm going to keep the house filled with my friends because being with them strengthens my resolve. Perhaps the next time he tries to give me orders, I'll find the voice to shout, No!" Jiro lowered his eyes. "But speaking out doesn't carry any guarantees. If nothing comes of it, promise you won't hate me."

"Oh, Jiro, how could I? You've grown so much braver. Just keep thinking of what you stand to gain. You have the spirit in you to make an exciting and beautiful life on your own terms." Shizue was mindful of how often she had spoken those same thoughts, but that balmy spring afternoon in Kyoto, she pressed her hand across the *omamori* concealed beneath the blouse of her school uniform and took heart. Jiro's faltering step toward freeing them both might be a turning point. When they parted, Shizue rewarded him with an affectionate hug. "Thank you for making the effort. You'll face up to him, I know."

That spring of 1938, the Kyoto cherry trees bloomed early, and Shizue was unable to wait until her seventeenth birthday to open Max's present when it arrived by special delivery mail. It was an exquisite leather book of Shakespeare's love sonnets, and Max had pressed wildflowers between the pages. She could feel the warm touch of his hand through those first flowers of spring, which he had picked in some distant American field. The petals still retained their bright colors and had stained the tissue-thin paper. She was moved to tears by Max's words of love, which he had written on the flyleaf. As Shizue read the sonnets, she could hear Max's voice reciting them for her alone. Feeling this day was really her birthday, she decided she must visit the old cherry tree in Maruyama Park to make a wish.

When the sun set, it would be Night Cherry, and lovers holding hands were gathering around the blossoming tree as Shizue arrived, chaperoned by one of the school matrons and carrying her expensive new camera. With the approach of dusk, Shizue closed her eyes and made a wish. But a single wish could not encompass her heart's desire for all the men in her life. Max, Paul, Kimitake—they were so very far away, she thought, opening her eyes and regarding the tree. When she last visited there with Paul, her wishing tree's slumbering branches had been bare. Now they had awakened to celebrate another spring and were heavily laden with pink-white velvet petals that seemed to glow brightly against the evening sky.

Shizue instructed the chaperone on how to use her camera, then stepped away, responding to the woman's suggestions for where to pose so the cherry blossoms would frame her face.

"Oh, please don't snap the picture just yet," Shizue said. Max had never seen her wearing the *omamori*, and she brought the charm out from under her blouse, fussing with its gold chain. "There. Can you see this through the lens? It's very important. I want this picture to be perfect."

"Relax, dear girl. You are too pretty to take a bad picture," the woman assured her. She was the nicest of the school matrons, and she shifted with the camera left then right until satisfied with her charge's pose. "Smile now."

Shizue's face lit with a smile. Her likeness was captured for Max in America and for his half brother somewhere on the battlefields of China.

That night Shizue returned to her dormitory room and sat thinking about the men in her life. Max was doing well at Harvard, but Kimitake was barely making the grade, and her father had angrily spoken of traveling there to deal with him personally.

As for Paul, she was plagued by fears over the dangers he faced. To date, she had received just two short letters written on the eve of battles. Their tattered envelopes spoke for the great distances they had traveled. Each day she watched the newspapers for the war stories he filed. At least they were proof that he was still alive and unharmed.

There was comfort to be found in words, and after undressing and putting on a nightgown, Shizue sat in bed writing letters that would accompany the snapshots. Before leaving the park, she had plucked some blossoms from her wishing tree. Now she pressed them between the pages of the letters. A tiny bit of home that spoke for the passing spring that she could not share with her loved ones.

Thoughts of Max drew her to the open window. It was a splendid starry night. Before long the celestial pinwheel would turn the Milky Way around to yet another festive evening of Tanabata. She wished she could set it spinning faster. But then she would suddenly come of age. Only Jiro held the power to alter her future.

"He *must* find his courage," Shizue said aloud. Imagining herself in Max's arms, she stared up into the bright canopy of stars. Even half a world apart, they shared the same heaven, and no power on earth could ever take away their love. Clasping his keepsake, she fixed her mind on its fabulous bird and sent her heart winging across the oceans to Max with a message of hope. As a woman she could do no more.

CHAPTER 22

War knew no season. The smoking guns and the miles upon miles of burning Chinese villages and hamlets had choked the skies with an overhang of murky umber clouds. The spring rains came, but they fell to earth without promise. Gunpowder had seeded those clouds, and it was a sulfuric rain that turned the dead land to mud. Land burned to its roots reeked of gunpowder sulfur, saltpeter, and charcoal, and of the slaughtered peasants left to rot along the muddy country roads.

That day Paul felt as if his eyes had been scarred from bearing witness to another victory taken without honor. Now the conquering Japanese war machine was again on the march. The regimental field commander, Colonel Fukushima, had invited Paul to ride beside him in the comfort of his staff car. His orders had just put another village to the torch. The colonel considered burning villages the most efficient means of marking his forward advance, and in the months ahead, his methods were destined to be adopted as the Japanese Imperial Army's ruthlessly executed "extermination strategy."

"Ah, these miserable villages begin to look all alike," he told Paul. "Even in this rain they burn with a foul smell. But as Japan's battle zones expand, it becomes essential that our front-line positions be easily determined at a glance." His musk aftershave cologne mingled unpleasantly with the roadside stench as he leaned closer to ask Paul, "Was there any mention of my name in the story you dispatched with our hospital vans?"

"The colonel knows his name appears frequently in my dispatches to *Nippon Shimbun*." Paul's reply caused the man to smile. "You were especially prominent in my account of this brilliantly fought engagement," Paul added, and Colonel Fukushima smiled even more broadly, revealing his gold-capped front teeth.

The relationship between Paul and the oily, dandified field commander was not always so pleasant. Paul had grown to despise Colonel Fukushima, who looked upon war as an art.

The colonel reclined, brushing his thin eyebrows with a pinky finger. His army superiors in Tokyo were now in complete control of the nation's war policy. Paul still found it incomprehensible that the Diet would surrender its powers. And yet the Japanese parliament had done exactly that just months ago by passing the army's mobilization law. Under the patriotic guise of insuring the national defense, this law had given the army what amounted to dictatorial powers over the nation as a whole, to gear Japan's people and industry toward an efficient war economy. Since March, 1938, the nation's fate was given over to the twisted mentality personified by the ruthless exterminator seated beside Paul.

He watched the colonel swat a fly into a smudge across the window glass. "Flies and maggots," snarled the colonel. "War breeds a disgusting menu."

Paul averted his eyes from the carnage. Earlier that year, the sadistic rape of Nanking had left hundreds of thousands slaughtered, like these peasants rotting on the roadside. Chinese civilians were the defenseless victims of this undeclared war. In Nanking's aftermath, Prime Minister Konoye, justifiably horrified, had sought to end the ever-expanding war. What the press continued to refer to as the "China incident" might have reached some peaceful conclusion earlier that year, but Chiang Kai-shek refused to negotiate with Tokyo, and the moment for peace had been lost.

China was too vast ever to be conquered, Paul thought. Her poorly equipped Nationalist forces could only retreat from the mighty Japanese juggernaut. But Chiang Kai-shek was drawing the enemy deeper inland, away from the sea and the cargo ships that fed the enemy armies. For a moment Paul looked back at the convoy of supply trucks. An army traveled on its stomach. Japanese supply lines were already stretched thin, and Colonel Fukushima had taken the crops harvested from the villagers' fields before they were put to the torch.

While Paul sat listening in the ominous quiet, marching men and armored vehicles climbed the primitive dirt road leading away from the still smoldering valley hamlet where not a living thing had been left behind to feel the spring rain. The villagers who had fled their homes to escape death faced only starvation when they returned from the neighboring hills. Even their household pets lay slaughtered amid the ruins. But Colonel Fukushima had spared the lives of some thirty villagers, all old men and old women. They had been spared to serve as human land-mine detectors and were being marched at gunpoint slowly down the road some yards ahead of the steadily advancing troops.

To Paul, sanity lay in forgetfulness, and he fought not to remember how many other Japanese victories he had witnessed that had been taken without honor, taken with barbaric atrocities. Not the slightest mention of these horrors was dispatched to Tokyo in his heroic accounts of Japanese conquests. The stories themselves, Paul reflected, were best forgotten. It was the only way he could survive.

Somehow he had learned to eat and sleep with the roar of guns, but he could not tolerate breathing war's foul stench. And this stillness that always followed the battle forced him to remember, to think of the peasants who were marching just ahead, human mine detectors testing for death. Old men, because the young had been cut down defending their wives against rape. Old women, because the young were promptly slaughtered after satisfying the bestial appetites of Colonel Fukushima's troops.

Paul wiped the sweat from his face with a handkerchief. "The humidity," he said, noting the colonel's rather amused scrutiny.

Colonel Fukushima chuckled. "War nerves, Yoseido-*san*. You should take a woman." He put a cigarette in the carved ivory holder that had been taken from some wealthy Chinese merchant's home. He lit up, enjoying the cigarette, feeling nothing whatsoever for the old men and women who served his inhuman purpose on the road ahead. "I urge you to relax a little and share the prerogative every Japanese soldier takes for granted. You are unlikely to contract a social disease, Yoseido-*san*. The Chinese women keep themselves clean. They bathe and are faithful to their husbands."

Paul mopped his perspiring brow. He wanted to scream out against the merciless butcher beside him who so calmly discussed rape. And then the ominous quiet was shattered. Explosions rattled the car windows. The earth trembled. Everything along the road came to an abrupt standstill. And then it was quieter than before.

"Sniveling chinks!" Colonel Fukushima threw open his car door. "Rather than stand their ground and fight, they plant mines. I had suspected this. I could feel it in my bones."

Waves of nausea drove Paul into the open air after him. Perhaps no one had been killed, he thought, gasping for breath as he looked at the sharply curving road ahead. A coolie hat in flames was cartwheeling downhill. Something small lay smoking just off the road, and one old man hobbled toward where the blast had thrown it, loudly crying a woman's name. Then repeating gunfire rang out. The old man rebounded as if hammered against a stone wall. Gunfire spun him around, nearly cutting him in half with its force before uniting his corpse with the smoldering remains of his wife.

"Get up there and order those idiots not to fire again," Colonel Fukushima shouted at a staff officer, who was standing beside his truck. "Find out how many others were lost. There may be more mines than we have peasants left to sniff them out. Fan the survivors out so they can do the most good. Make every chink count!"

Paul reached dizzily for the open car door. Supported by it, he vomited that morning's breakfast. In the past he had always crawled into hiding like a sick dog before vomiting over the horrors around him. But the odor of human flesh burning kept him retching there for all to see.

"Hah, you ugly *ainoko* mongrel!" Colonel Fukushima ranted. "Sniveling half-caste! Son of a Japanese whore!" He kicked away the car door that supported Paul and then stood aside to avoid being contaminated while Paul fell forward heaving, on his hands and knees. "Better find your stomach, mongrel son of Japan. If you want to continue marching with me, then better take your testicles firmly in hand and show some courage!"

The colonel sniffed the air. "Mori!" he barked at his driver. "Fetch my cologne. Ah, I should have known better. Mixed blood always tells under fire. Hah, I had begun to think you more of a man, Yoseido. Mongrel that you are, I had begun to think of you as one of us. Well, pull yourself together, journalist. Soon we'll be on the march again."

Had Paul the courage, he would have seized the colonel's ceremonial sword from its ornamental sheath and driven its blade through his puffed-out chest. Instead, he merely wiped his mouth and struggled to his feet.

The sword's cherry blossom design was a traditional symbol of military valor. Cherry Blossom Kissaten. Shizue's cherry tree at Kyoto. A haunting symbol of his life, now worn on the samurai sword fingered by a colonel of the Imperial Army, whose absolute authority had Private Mori hopping to like a rabbit.

"As you ordered, Fukushima *Taisadono*," the private addressed his superior respectfully. He bowed and handed him the silver flask he had taken from the leather kit bag stored on the front seat.

Looking down the road, Paul watched foot soldiers standing at ease. The land mines had granted them a rest break, and they lit cigarettes and conversed about home. After the battle their thoughts were always turned away from war. Each carried reminders of Japan in his wallet. Photographs of families, wives, and lovers, and their letters, which often took months to receive. Paul knew that many of them had been raised in rural hamlets much like the ones they now pillaged and burned. Many had grandparents much like the old ones who would soon again be marched to their deaths. But these young men failed to see any resemblance. They saw only the enemy and now stood at ease, smoking cigarettes and talking of home.

Colonel Fukushima slapped his drooping jowls with cologne, rubbed the scent into his hands, then laughed. "I lost my temper, Yoseido-*san*." His tone was conciliatory. "Surely you've been called such names before. These chink mines. Ah," he groaned, and swiveled, observing the officer dispatched to carry out his orders, "let their peasants pay. They'll be shot even if there are no other mines to do the job. Let the wide scar we burn across China speak for us, and she'll surrender soon enough. It's only a matter of time until that pompous ass Chiang realizes we mean business."

Colonel Fukushima had just dishonored him, Paul thought angrily, and yet the arrogant bastard was incapable of apology. His stories had made this glowering monster a hero. All these months he had courted power, licking the boots of this butcher, only to have it made clear that he was merely being tolerated. Paul stood at attention.

"I serve my emperor as a true Japanese! There are other commands where my services might be better appreciated." The stench of vomit on Paul's breath overwhelmed Fukushima, who waved the scented fingers of one hand under his nostrils. "There are other field commanders who will show more respect for my position and my honor."

Nervously, because his men were all around, the colonel took Paul by the arm and walked them away, conversing through a saccharine smile. "You are a journalist, not a soldier. I should not have dishonored you for behaving as you did, Yoseido-*san*. Accept my apology."

Paul wanted more than a sugar-coated apology offered in private. "I've shared the fate of every soldier here," he said, raising his voice to be overheard by the men. "These are my weapons, Fukushima *Taisadono*"— he pounded the dusty canvas shoulder bag containing his writing tools— "my words, which celebrate your exploits and feed the people's belief that we're fighting a holy war. *Ainoko!* Half-caste mongrel! Only filthy names, Colonel. I'm no less a Japanese than you or any man here!"

"We'll think no more of it." Displaying his gold-toothed grin, the colonel said in a loud voice, "No man in my command has reason to question your honor, Yoseido-*san*. Every man here will forget what he *may* have overheard. That is an order," he announced, then lowered his voice to a conciliatory hush for Paul's ears alone. "I lost my temper. Now let's end this embarrassing exchange. Your services have placed me in line for promotion. When they make me general, ask anything and it will be yours."

Paul chose to see the colonel's extended hand as capitulation, and he gripped it firmly, startled by its limpness.

Then the colonel ordered the troops to resume marching. Spaced out so each life would count the most, the old peasants resumed their death march. "The men show signs of battle fatigue," the colonel said. "Before long we will join forces with units in occupied territory to the northeast," he confided, as he and Paul walked toward his car. "My nerves could use a few days rest as well. Take a woman, Yoseido-*san*. At the next village, pick yourself a young one. The younger the better. Who knows, with any luck she'll be a virgin."

Paul endured his grating laughter. "I'll march with the men," he said when they reached the car. He thought of the colonel's limp hand extended to him as a peace offering. Not the strong hand of a man who commanded the mighty killing machine that stretched down the road ahead, but the limp hand of a man whose power was taken from terrified old men and women following after one another in a line, their heads bowed. Rather than sweat beside Fukushima, listening for the next explosions, Paul sought escape in the companionship of the young men he had come to know intimately between battles.

"Join us here, Yoseido-*san*," familiar voices called out, and he fell in step beside those he had written about, the common infantrymen who accepted him as someone of importance. They wanted to know if what had been rumored about a rest leave was true. "Yes, we'll all have a chance to unwind." His words spread through the ranks quickly. "The colonel didn't say when it would be, but it should be soon."

Paul listened to the men talk of home. "Oh, did your honorable family enjoy my story, Private Tajima? And yours, Private Isa? No need to thank me," he said, laughing. "You're the real heroes in this war. It's only right that your names should be mentioned with honor." Paul chatted on, stepping through the ranks. His human interest stories about Japan's brave fighting sons had become very popular, and the men's attention always flattered him. Marching with the soldiers, he felt he was more in his element than riding in Colonel Fukushima's staff car.

For the moment, these homesick young men became the friends he never had in childhood, and their detachment from the war served to numb his senses. No one spoke of the previous battle or of dead and wounded comrades, or of the peasants marching at gunpoint somewhere ahead. Paul gave no thought to the brutality these young men were capable of while acting under orders. "You've shown me your girlfriend's photograph so often, the sun has faded her into an old man, Private Hasumi." His joke triggered waves of laughter, and other soldiers called out good-humored barbs.

"It's not the sun, Yoseido-*san*," another private sang out. "This girl Hasumi pines for was born with the face of an old man. Put her homely face back in your pocket, where it belongs."

"Blind dogs! *You* should be so lucky!" Hasumi yelled back, shaking his fist.

"Better unlucky than cursed, Hasumi!" cried someone in the ranks ahead.

Private Hasumi grudgingly dismissed them all with a shrug, then turned his lovelorn eyes on Paul. "Show us the girl who waits for you, Yoseido-*san*."

Paul kept Shizue's letter folded inside his wallet pocket. "No photograph can do her justice," he boasted, letting her most recent photo be passed down the line among those who believed that she was his. "Seventeen in April, when this picture was taken," he told them, reminded by the dated letter in his hand that one month had passed since then. She had already graduated from finishing school, and her next letter would be mailed from Kyushu. Max had also been sent a copy of this photograph. As Shizue's likeness evoked the troops' glowing compliments, Paul imagined his half brother showing it off to his friends at Harvard and accepting their praise with a more honest delight.

"My sister resembles your girl. See, Yoseido-*san*."

Paul saw no resemblance whatever in the pretty girl smiling through the dusty celluloid protector of a soldier's wallet, but he nodded politely as Shizue's photograph was passed back to him.

Shizue had written of visiting their special place to pose for this birthday picture beside her wishing tree. Time had matured her loveliness. And yet, framed by the cherry blossoms, her wistful expression was still that of the starry-eyed young girl who believed in the power of wishes to come true.

Raindrops wet her paper image, and Paul quickly put the photograph away. The top sergeant's gruff command to "make way" forced Paul back among the obediently parting ranks. An armored vehicle, with machine-gun muzzles protruding from it, was being sent up front. "What's the trouble, *sōchō?*"

"Colonel's orders, Yoseido-*san*," said the sergeant. "If there were any other mines, we would have encountered them by now, and these chinks slow us down."

As Paul marched on, rumbling thunder muffled the machine-gun fire as the Chinese prisoners were shot down in order to save time for the Japanese conquerors.

The soldier beside Paul spoke as though the stuttering bursts did not exist. "My grandmother considered it an honor to knit socks for you, Yoseido-*san*," he said. "With any luck they'll be waiting for us in the mail."

His eyes riveted straight ahead, Paul swallowed hard and marched on, past the bodies of the dead. A Japanese grandmother had knitted him socks, and he knew her face from this young private's family photograph. This man, who had only moments ago seen some resemblance between Shizue and his sister, was incapable of recognizing how the Chinese grandmothers just cut down bore the slightest resemblance to his own grandmother. Paul knew it would do no good to point this out.

"How thoughtful of your grandmother," he said instead, grateful for the wind that swept away the stench of death. Nothing stirred beyond the steadily advancing column. No human or animal. Not so much as a bird in flight to break the ominously dirty sky. Until they reached another village, death could take a holiday.

Men of Harvard's ROTC were mustered for roll call along Sever Quadrangle. It was a breezy spring day, and Max tightened the chin strap of his wide-brimmed peaked field hat while calling out the company roster. "Parisi! Reardon! Simon!"

"Yo!" the last man sounded off.

Max came sharply about face. "All present and accounted for, sir!"

Reserve Lieutenant Avery Bullock returned his salute. "Fall out and let's get rolling. On the double," he ordered, loudly clapping his hands.

Across the quadrangle, other companies were falling out to board the waiting convoys of army trucks. Max spotted Kimitake heading toward him through the crowd, and his heart sank; Kimitake wore a pained look of urgency that Max knew all too well. Max had one foot up on the running board of the truck he was assigned to drive, when Kimitake grabbed his arm and pulled him around. "If it's money, the answer is no," Max said shortly.

"You've got to bail me out. This is the last time. I swear it."

Max ruefully shook his head. "I shouldn't be such a soft touch. But, all right," he said, reaching for his wallet. "On one condition. Promise me you'll use this weekend to study for finals. I'm carrying too heavy a load to help you again."

"It's a deal."

Max saw through the mock-serious expression. Kimitake's low grades had placed him on the brink of expulsion, and Baron Hosokawa's letters ordering his son to toe the mark had resulted in only temporary spurts of discipline. "Look, this time I really mean it. Your ass is on the line." Kimitake nodded. "Okay. How much?"

"Five hundred. A run of bad luck," he added with a sheepish smile.

"I don't carry that kind of money."

"Write me a check."

"My checkbook's at the dorm."

"Make it snappy!" Avery Bullock called from the truck's cab. He had witnessed this tiresome scene before. "That's an order, Max," he said to get his friend off the hook.

Max climbed behind the wheel, impatient with Kimitake as he jumped on the running board. "It'll have to wait until I return from bivouac Monday morning."

"I'll settle for what's in your wallet."

"No way. And don't count on that five hundred dollars to borrow against."

"Have a heart," Kimitake pleaded.

"Maybe empty pockets will force you to take some responsibility for yourself," Max countered angrily, and started the truck.

"Thanks for nothing!" Kimitake jumped down from the running board.

"You should've drawn the line months ago," Avery Bullock said, as Kimitake walked away. Removing his hat, Avery regarded Max through heavy-lidded eyes. "Three good nights sleep in the fresh country air. I should pay the army for the privilege, rather than the other way around."

Max watched Kimitake cross the quadrangle, head down, hands deep inside the pockets of his blue blazer. The two had steadily drifted apart, and Max regretted the lost connection. "I shouldn't have been so hard on him," he told Avery.

"A hopeless cause, Max."

"Maybe so, but I can't help feeling that I failed him in some way."

"Stop feeling guilty. All year, I've watched you work double duty doing your own work and helping him, but I've never once heard him say thanks. Kimitake let himself down." Avery ran one hand through his coppery-red hair, then stretched out low in the seat, arms folded across his chest, and closed his eyes.

Good old Ave, thought Max, always taking things in stride. Always in need of sleep because of the many jobs he juggled to pay his way in the world, but never complaining. An uncomplicated soul, whose friendship had lifted Max from depression time and again. He had joined ROTC at Avery Bullock's urging. Over the past year, Max had found that its training program offered a good way of letting off steam, and it had proved a source of new friends. He looked forward to these outings.

As he followed the convoy, he allowed his thoughts to wander beyond the peaceful tree-lined Cambridge streets. Without fail, Shizue's letters included newspaper clippings of Paul's battlefield reports. His stirring accounts of Japanese soldiers ennobled in combat against a ruthless Chinese enemy described quite a different war from that reported by the pro-Chinese American press. There was nothing to speak for his brother's state of mind in the two slim letters Shizue had received from the battlefield, and with each new story filed by Paul, he, too, breathed a sigh of relief knowing his brother was alive and well.

Shizue had written him that there was much bitterness at home since Roosevelt had joined the League of Nations in censuring Japanese aggression. Roosevelt placed American interests in China above the goodwill that was being rebuilt between the United States and Japan, lumping the Japanese together with Nazis and Fascists. Max felt that the American position was dangerous at a time when cooperation and peaceful solutions should be sought. Destined for a rather gentlemanly country weekend playing soldier, he wondered if he might someday be called upon to serve this nation of his ancestors in a broader conflict that was building force on the distant shores of Southeast Asia and a troubled Europe.

Kevin Moriarty loomed up menacingly from behind the bar as Kimitake swaggered into the roadhouse and asked for a drink. "Word's out you're a deadbeat," Moriarty announced. "Money talks, lad, and you're into me heavy."

Kimitake squirmed. All the roadhouses he frequented outside of Boston had cut off his credit, and Moriarty's was his last hope. "No reason to get upset. Haven't I always made good on allowance day?"

"And when's that exactly?"

"When my bank opens Monday morning."

"Is that a fact now?" Moriarty arched over the bar and flicked Kimitake's jacket lapel with one large hand. "I takes a gentleman at his word. Enjoy yourself." His deep-set eyes narrowed, and he used both hands to tighten the knot in Kimitake's necktie. "But don't get no ideas about stiffin' me, boy-o. Harvard's just a short ways down the road."

Kimitake experienced a fearful sinking sensation. His father had cabled the bank to cut his monthly allowance to a paltry sum, and his other impatient creditors had issued similar warnings. Settling down at a table, he nursed a bottle of bourbon, attempting to drown his desperation. His excesses had caught up with him. It would take a miracle for him to pass the finals. Without Max's help he was certain to flunk out, and that meant returning home in disgrace to face a punishment he dared not contemplate.

A girl approached him. "Want some company, Kimi?"

The pretty platinum blonde was new there. Tall and slender, she somewhat resembled Jean Harlow. Kimitake invited her to sit. "How is it you know my name?"

"The other girls say you're fun. I ain't never been with an Oriental man. It kinda interests me"—her shoulders lifted, and she giggled—"if you know what I mean."

Kimitake laughed and poured them both a drink, thinking how much Max had missed by being faithful to Shizue. "And for what? Father won't ever give in. What a fool!" he angrily thought out loud.

The girl's heavily mascaraed eyelashes flapped. "Beg pardon?"

"None of your business!" All at once Kimitake felt contempt for himself. If only he had heeded Max's advice and not allowed his studies to slide so far behind. "Nothing you'd understand," he added gruffly. "What's your name?"

"Act nice and I'll tell you." She pursed her cupid-bow lips, and played coyly with her dry, bleached hair.

He rose and bowed. "*Sumimasen*. My apologies for having offended the lovely lady."

"Gee, the way you talk gives me goose bumps." She hugged herself and giggled. "I guess it's true what the girls say—that you're royalty. Or somethin' like royalty."

"Somethin' like royalty, yes." His cruel imitation mocked her ignorance. That she was charmed rather than hurt made him laugh. He found her more appealing than the other bleached blondes and garish redheads who did not advertise themselves as prostitutes, yet made full use of the rooms above for "favors." Kimitake knew that Moriarty got his fair cut, and his regular girls sat at tables in twos and threes, just out for a good time, should the local police drop by. "There's something sweet about you," he said flatteringly.

"Lucy," she cooed, lifting the hem of her skirt while crossing her legs.

The bar began filling with the usual Friday night crowd. The piano player hammered out an upbeat dance tune. Kimitake pulled back the girl's chair, then led her to the dance floor. He was light on his feet, and she followed him well. But his desperation was not so easily danced away.

"I like you, Kimi. Really like you."

"Shut up and dance!"

"Sure, honey. Don't get mad."

A drawn canvas window shade flapped in the morning light. Kimitake woke with a vague recollection of climbing the stairs to this room. Stretching out one arm, he hit an empty whiskey bottle on the night table, and it toppled to the floor. The girl he had slept with was standing, fully clothed, her back to Kimitake, and she spun around, startled. He saw that she was clutching his wallet. Springing from bed, he slapped her hard across the face. She was out to rob him, Kimitake thought, slapping her hard again.

She screamed and fell back against the wall, covering her face. "Goddamn Jap! I only wanted what was comin' to me."

Kimitake seized her by the shoulders. "In my country I'm nobility, a samurai—treated with respect!"

"Well, this ain't your country," she sobbed. "You're just another john, and you owe me."

He released her and picked his wallet off the floor. After opening it, he began to laugh.

"What's so funny?"

Kimitake only shook his head. A few wrinkled dollar bills were all he had. "Sorry for hitting you," he told the girl, all at once sobered by this reminder of the troubles he had gone there to forget. "See Moriarty. My credit's good with him."

"This'll cost you extra," she sniffled, examining her face in the dresser mirror.

In the cold light of day, she seemed coarse and older, Kimitake thought. Striking her was a cowardly act, and it only added to his depression.

After she left, Kimitake dressed quickly and went downstairs. The deserted roadhouse reeked of stale cigarette smoke and beer. As Kimitake pushed open its door, he decided not to return there again. Moriarty and his other creditors would make trouble for him. He had nothing more to lose, he thought, so he might just as well go out with a bang. He drove to Randolph Hall, where he cleared his littered study desk. After hastily packing a suitcase, he bid adieu to the dormitory's ivy-covered walls.

Kimitake swung the suitcase into the front seat of his Alfa Romeo. Some Japanese students walked his way. His countrymen at Harvard were a studious, no-nonsense bunch who considered him an embarrassment, and they ignored him as he pulled from the curb. Everyone expected too much of him, he thought angrily. If only his father had listened to reason. Harvard's academic demands were more than he could handle. His failure there was inevitable. And he had never liked Boston; it was a provincial bore. He had heard a lot about the razzle-dazzle action to be found in New York. He decided to sell the car to finance one last adventure.

As it happened, an Alfa Romeo was not easy to unload. Toward evening, Kimitake was running out of gas and hope.

"Too rich for my blood."

"I'm willing to take a loss," Kimitake told the operator of a used car lot, the last of many who had given him the same frustrating headshake. "Something's come up and I need the cash. Make me an offer."

"Times are lean, pal." Chewing on a burned-out cigar stub, he circled the car, itemizing its minor dents and scratches. "Not much market for used cars of this class. The rich like theirs mint condition off the ship." He opened the hood and called his mechanic over. "If Carl gives her the okay, maybe we can talk a deal."

Kimitake shifted on his feet impatiently while the mechanic gave the engine a going-over. At last he nodded. "Well, how much?"

The owner thoughtfully tipped back his hat. "Fifteen hundred."

"It's worth five times that!"

"Two thousand, cash. Take it or leave it, pal," the owner said flatly, gesturing with the chewed end of his cigar.

Kimitake glanced around the lot, deliberating how much of a fling two thousand dollars could buy. "Throw in that Mercury Zephyr and it's a deal."

"Huh-uh." The man pointed down the line to an old black coupe. "But I'll throw in the Ford over there."

Kimitake knew he didn't have a choice, so he took it. As he suspected, the engine started knocking soon after he drove from the lot. But gas was cheap in America, and it saved him the train fare. The car might bring a hundred or so when sold at his destination. Now he needed to unwind.

He looked the legal age, and the liquor store clerk bagged a fifth of rye, then gave him directions to New York City. The car radio worked until he lost sight of the Boston skyline at nightfall. "Yessir, that's my baby. Nosir, I don't mean maybe. Yessir, that's my baby now." A hot swing band conjured up images of what awaited him on the Great White Way as he swigged rye and relaxed behind the wheel.

It began to drizzle. The windshield wiper made a squealing arc to the right, then stalled in place humming before it arced left across the rain-streaked glass. Fog closed in to further hinder his ability to see. At last he realized he must have taken a wrong turn some miles back. He was on a narrow country road, and there were no lights or markers visible in the rolling fog ahead.

Before he could turn the car around, something red and shiny shot across the headlight beams. In pulsating flashes he glimpsed a bicycle jackknifing off his fender in one direction, its rider tumbling away in another. Kimitake slammed on the brakes so hard that his head struck the windshield. He blacked out for a second and had difficulty focusing his eyes as he opened the car door and stumbled outside. A boy was sprawled out crookedly in the oncoming lane. His mangled bicycle lay to the side of the road, its front wheel still spinning. Kimitake dizzily took hold of the dented right fender, which was smeared with blood. The boy lay deathly still within the cone of light thrown by his headlight beams. This road and what he could see of the dirt crossroad the boy had shot out from were deserted.

No one had witnessed the accident, Kimitake thought. The rain was washing all visible evidence of his crime away. There must be hundreds of dented fenders on the highway to New York. He decided to run. Then the boy made a sound and stirred slightly.

His legs shaky, Kimitake moved toward the boy. Shock and the whiskey made everything fuzzy. He knelt over the figure. Twelve or thirteen at the most. The boy coughed, and blood trickled down one corner of his mouth.

Left lying on the road in the fog, Kimitake thought, another car might run him over. Hitting him had been an accident, but to leave him there would be like murder. Blood soaked through the boy's clothing as Kimitake gently lifted him in his arms. The boy was limp as a rag doll.

Kimitake rested him across the backseat of the car. How would the law punish him if this boy should die? He swallowed two long slugs from the whiskey bottle just to quiet his badly shaking hands. Then he hurled the bottle out the car window. Drunk—yes, he was a little drunk, and that would be held against him. But it was an accident. Let the boy live; let him live and not be crippled were his thoughts as he drove off, peering urgently through the fog for some sign of life. The taillights of a slow-moving truck came into view. Kimitake leaned on his horn and continued blinking his headlights after passing it. Sticking one arm outside the window, he motioned toward the side of the road. The driver got the message and pulled off the road behind him.

Kimitake leaned out the car door and shouted, "This is an emergency."

The heavyset man in overalls broke into a run when he got out of his truck. "Mother of God," he exclaimed, seeing the boy.

"An accident. I've got to get him to the nearest hospital."

The man smelled alcohol on Kimitake's breath. "That's a nasty bump on your head. Are you up to driving?"

Kimitake fingered the lump above his eye and nodded.

"Follow me!"

When Max returned from bivouac Monday morning, there was a letter in his numbered pigeonhole at Randolph Hall. Each airmail envelope from Germany seemed to carry more official rubber stamps, he observed, as he tore through the wreathed swastikas and eagles while Avery Bullock drew on his pipe.

"Ever wonder how America and Germany came to share the same predatory bird as their official seal?" he queried. "Good news?"

"Hard to read with that smoke in my eyes, Ave."

Avery fanned the air between them with his own mail. "A man should have at least one vice to spare himself the pitfalls of human perfection, my saintly friend."

Max shrugged the remark off. He was more singleminded than saintly in his determination not to wait four years to return home to claim Shizue as his bride. He stood at the top of his freshman class, and his faculty adviser had laid out a stiff curriculum that would qualify him for an early graduation if he continued his studies over the summer term. In his letter Douglas wrote that he supported Max's goal and added a cheering note. "My dad's coming here for the summer."

"A shame I won't get to meet him." Avery had opened the two letters he had received, and he held them up in one hand. "Good news and bad. The hoped-for opening in Harvard's language department has failed to materialize. However, my application has been accepted by Stanford. A junior professorship to commence with their summer term."

"California." Max tried to sound pleased. "Hell, Ave, that's great news."

Avery gave Max one of his disarming smiles. "Buck up. We'll keep in touch."

"Napier," the housemaster's owlish assistant called to Max. "Mr. Belknap wants you in his office right away!"

"About what?" asked Max.

"Some trouble your roommate's gotten himself into," he said.

Kimitake looked godawful, Max thought as he watched him restlessly pacing the narrow confines of his cell in Boston's old county jailhouse. A police guard slid back the iron bars of the cell door to let Max through, then shut and locked it behind him. Kimitake faced the rectangular barred window set high on the far wall, refusing to meet Max's eyes.

"Why, Kimi?"

"I thought I had all the right answers," he said hoarsely. His silk shirt-sleeves were rolled to the elbows, and his muscular neck glistened with perspiration. Dropping his head into both hands, Kimitake said, "After what happened—well, there's no excuse for the mess I've made of things. Does my father know?"

"The dean's office cabled him yesterday. Harvard's appointing a team of their top lawyers. You'll have the best defense money can buy."

"And the boy?"

"Still on the critical list after extensive surgery."

"I'm scared. No punishment could be worse than having that boy's death on my conscience."

Max was stunned into silence as the reality of Kimitake's crime took hold. If the boy died, he would be charged with manslaughter. There were no sheets on the lumpy cot, and the police had taken the precaution of confiscating Kimitake's necktie, belt, and shoelaces to discourage any thoughts of suicide.

"It's partly my fault," Max said at last.

Kimitake ran his hands through his thick black hair. "No, Max. You covered for me since we were children. We're men now"—his voice cracked when Max touched his shoulder—"responsible for our own actions."

There was no way Max could have foreseen this catastrophe or the disastrous consequences that were destined to follow in its wake. Kimitake tearfully turned around, and they clasped each other like long lost brothers.

CHAPTER 23

Since dawn, Shizue had ridden her chestnut gelding hard and fast across the hills, hoping to dispel her anxiety. Finally, she urged him home, praying that there would be mail or another cable from America. Only word of her brother could offer relief. O-nami ran up to take the reins while she dismounted. "Has there been news of Kimi?" she asked, viewing his woebegone expression with alarm.

"*Hai*, another cable was received by your father very late in the night. I learned of this only when the baron summoned me to his study this morning." O-nami heaved a ponderous sigh. "But it was not in my power to lighten his burden, and he sits there still, alone with his torment over Ichiban's disgrace." Tears welled up in his small, childlike eyes. "Ah, I cannot bring myself to speak of the dreadful grief that might have befallen this household. Your father has need of you, little one. Go to him."

Shizue rushed away, not bothering to exchange her riding boots for the straw slippers placed outside the castle doors. Hardly three weeks had passed since her father had received the shocking news of Kimitake's arrest. Cable service provided the fastest communications link between Boston and Japan, and in the shorthand language of cables, her brother's fate seemed to hinge entirely on the survival of the boy he had run down. With a sense of foreboding, she rapped at the closed study door. "Father?"

Her father appeared at the door, a cadaverous figure, and Shizue gasped. "Papa, what happened to your hands?"

"Come in, Shizue," he said in a hoarse voice. The windows were shuttered against the day, and Shizue fell back stunned. It was as if a whirlwind had swept through the room. The display cases were shattered, their priceless antiquities scattered everywhere among shards of broken glass. Swords, suits of armor, archery bows, quivers and their arrows, and the silk flags the Hosokawa clan had carried into battle lay heaped in a shambles on the floor. Nothing remained on the walls. The atmosphere was still drenched with the baron's unleashed fury, and his hands were lacerated and stained with clotted blood. The boy had died, she thought, but could not find the voice to ask if it were so.

Before speaking again, the baron closed his study door against the servants. When he turned to his daughter, there was perspiration on his sunken face. His black silk kimono was partly open down the front and the white silk of his undergarment was stained with blood. "Twice in the night I considered my seppuku," he told Shizue, his eyes roaming the debris as he moved slowly through the broken glass. Transfixed by some object lying among the battle flags, he bowed and lifted a *wakizashi*. This was the dagger used to commit ritual suicide. With one swift stroke, he withdrew its oiled blade, then sent the sheath ringing to the floor.

"After drafting a new will disowning your brother, twice my life was weighed against this cutting edge. But each time I thought—no, live for Shizue. Your son has brought you disgrace. You have failed *him* as a father, but not Shizue. She will redeem you by honoring her obligations, and there is yet some face left you through her. So, I chose life."

Shizue felt choked for air. Her fiercely proud samurai father had surely waged a terrible battle with his blind worship of tradition. She ran to throw open the shuttered windows. The fresh light of day would dispel what the night had put there, she thought. But as daylight flooded the room, her father, still holding the *wakizashi*, shielded his eyes with his arms. Sunlight glistened off the sharp blade, and Shizue's voice trembled as she said, "It was an accident, Father. Even if the boy has died . . ."

"The boy will live," he said. "He's expected to make a full recovery from his injuries."

Jolted by his words, she burst into hysterical laughter and stood shaking her head. Her father remained silent and unchanged. Gripping the *wakizashi*'s pommel, he stared grimly down the length of the blade as though his life still hung in its balance. "*Ogisan*, we should be grateful the boy's life was spared."

Baron Hosokawa righted a toppled chair. His black silk kimono rippled around his ankles as he sat down. Resting the dagger across his lap, he spoke in a pained voice. "Kimitake's disgrace hasn't been wiped away by this turn of events. I suffered with my grief, thinking the charges against him might be dropped if the boy should live. After all, this was his first offense, and your brother didn't run from his crime. But last night's cable from his lawyers forced me to recognize that his guilt was never in question. No, only the matter of its degree in the eyes of the law. On his lawyers' advice, he'll plead guilty and place himself at the mercy of the court—waiving his right to a trial by jury. A Boston judge will pass sentence on him. The lawyers believe he'll show Kimitake leniency."

"Then he won't be sent to prison," she responded, her voice joyful with relief.

"There's hope he'll be released with nothing more than a sharp reprimand. At the very least, his student visa is certain to be revoked. I might have bought him a second chance at Harvard despite his poor grades. But now, dismissal from America and expulsion from Harvard."

He faced the lighted windows and shed tears. "Kimitake's personal disgrace is mine to share. By choosing life, I must bear his shame, and the burden of his guilt now seems too great in the light of day."

Shizue knelt at his feet. "Don't punish yourself needlessly. You haven't failed Kimitake as a father. He's made mistakes, I know, but think how terrified he must have been when his car struck down that poor boy. Imagine the courage it took for him to place the boy's life above the punishment he'd face."

The baron sighed heavily. "Yes, in that respect he did act like a Hosokawa."

She had come close to losing her father, and he never seemed more precious to her than now, bowed low in the chair and vulnerable to her comforting words. "Promise you'll never think of taking your own life again. I want you with me always, *ogisan*. I want to bring you comfort in your old age." She brightened and rested her cheek against his knee. "I want to sit here with my aged papa-*san* and talk on and on about his grandchildren and his great-grandchildren, until his gray old head nods into sleep. Then I'll stay quietly beside you like this, remembering how it was when I was a happy child."

He blinked down into her shining eyes and smiled. "Nothing would please me more than to grow old and spoiled by your sweet attentions."

"Be forgiving, *ogisan*. What Kimitake's been through is punishment enough. Give him your love and understanding, and he'll become a source of pride."

Feeling her father's leg muscles grow taut, Shizue raised her head. A sudden wildness in her father's eyes held her silent while he lifted the *wakizashi* from his lap and dangled its blade menacingly between his legs, slowing moving the weapon like a pendulum. Then he faced away, speaking to her in a distant voice.

"You and Kimitake are my life. A father's *giri* can be hard, Shizue. I hold that no man has honor if he fails in his duty to his children—a sense of duty greater than what is owed to the land and my emperor."

She remained kneeling there as her father rose from the chair. She watched him slowly bend to lift the *wakizashi*'s sheath off the floor. With one movement he put the blade into the sheath. As he crossed to the shattered display case near the windows, his posture was that of a samurai hardened in battle. He returned the *wakizashi* to its proper shelf, then bowed reverently. When he turned to face her, his eyes had grown calm.

"Join me at your mother's shrine in the garden," he invited softly. "You've truly blossomed into a woman. More like her in every way. Perhaps there's some truth in what you've said. Sumie's loving spirit will help guide my heart. Come." His bloodied hands reached down to her. "How cold you are."

"I was afraid for you, Papa."

"Forget what you saw here, Shizue." The baron drew her up against him. "This wasn't meant for your eyes. Put it from your mind and come into the garden."

Shizue wanted to erase the incident, but even with the sunshine warming the garden path, she was suddenly grimly aware that her loving father might not hesitate taking his own life the next time his children failed to honor their duty.

Tadashi Hosokawa knelt before his wife's stone statue, and Shizue knelt beside him, trembling like a leaf. Silently she petitioned Sumie's spirit to enter her father's heart, to instill the understanding he had given his children while she lived. But the mossy stone and the green grass around it grew suddenly black. Just summer clouds sailing across the sun, and yet Shizue saw the shadow as an inkblot spilling out across the land, chasing her mother's benign *kami* spirit away.

CHAPTER 24

Paul watched Colonel Fukushima's staff car swerving off in the deep mud, where a woman lay dead, one arm stretched out to her blank-faced child. The five-year-old boy squatted in a muddy rain puddle and stared out at Paul through unseeing eyes. He had witnessed his mother being raped by a long line of soldiers and then executed with their bayonets. Her husband, suspected of aiding the Chinese Communist Eighth Route Army, had been strung up on a wooden ladder. His Japanese torturers had rubbed benzine on his back and then repeatedly set fire to it until the flesh was charred black. As Paul joined the marching ranks, the man was still alive, and his agonized cries followed them.

After an uneventful march through what Colonel Fukushima had so haughtily referred to as "Japan's private hunting preserve," a surprise attack by Communist guerrillas had cost him casualties. It had been merely a token force, but no prisoners had survived for questioning, and this Chinese farmer had been tortured for information about Mao Tse-tung's troop movements, information he could not possibly give.

Paul heard the innocent farmer's scream, begging for the shots that at last ended his suffering. He had lost count of the days since the regimental field commander had promised the war-weary troops a rest leave. The sulfuric rain seeded with gunpowder had been their constant companion as Chinese blood washed away in rivers of muddy water. Now an armored vehicle splashed alongside their marching column, and a sergeant shouted the long-awaited announcement that brought waves of cheers up and down the ranks.

"A day's march and we take our leave," he shouted. "The road ahead is clear of chinks! We rest for a week or more!"

In his battle-scarred mind, Paul still heard the agonized cries of the Chinese farmer and he gave in to tears. The rain blew across his face to mask his emotional overflow. One week or more, the sergeant shouted out down the line, as Paul used his coat sleeve to wipe away his tears.

The young men he marched with had become savages, Paul thought. With each battle he had watched them come to enjoy inflicting pain on the

Chinese and to smile at the enemy's cries of suffering. Some of the men had not heard the order to "fall in." Paul saw them in the fields moving like vultures over the bodies of Mao Tse-tung's fallen soldiers. They searched for anything of value, picking the pockets of the dead, tearing open their bloodied jackets, and ripping the red five-pointed stars from the Communists' caps as souvenirs of the kill. At last they responded to the top sergeant's shouted command and quickly stuffed their pockets with the loot while they ran to the road, where they wiped blood off their hands before falling in step with the marching column.

Paul began to dread the prolonged silence that would only allow him to think and remember. The rain tapered off to a misty spray, but Paul still smelled and heard the crackling of burning human flesh and saw the blank eyes of an orphaned child who faced starvation while the conqueror rested between battles.

Swaying in the dank breezes, kerosene lanterns illuminated the crumbling walls and gates of a Chinese village. Other Japanese troops on rest leave crowded the village square. Greeting the new arrivals with shouts of *"banzai!"* they roamed through Colonel Fukushima's weary ranks to search for faces from home and barracks comrades they had trained with.

Paul squeezed free of the boisterous herds and sloshed across the square on wet, aching feet, anxious to find out where he would be housed. "Correspondent," he addressed the billeting officer who was seated at a table that had been raised off the mud on wooden planks. Lanterns held down a map of the village, and the grouchy lieutenant hunched over it, biting his lip before deciding that this *ainoko* correspondent belonged at some inn with the noncommissioned officers. His finger pointed uphill to a dilapidated structure whose uneven patchwork of windows spilled light across the sloping tile roofs below.

"Every man here looks after himself," the lieutenant informed Paul, and handed him a card entitling him to draw the generous food rations accorded Japanese sergeants.

Long waiting lines discouraged Paul's appetite. The surrounding farms had been sacked, and part of the village square served as a supply depot. Large stables, originally built to house the pack animals of trade caravans, now housed livestock and truckloads of crops. Paul judged that this village had once flourished as a way station for merchants who journeyed along China's ancient trade routes and now served its conquerors in much the same capacity.

Time not war had ravaged the dwellings that wound steeply uphill out of the village square. Electricity was unknown here, and the unpaved street was dark except for the yellowish patchy light of oil lamps flickering at open windows overhead. As Paul climbed, he heard men's laughter and that of the women entertaining them in brothels set up for Japan's combat-weary heroes. Chinese women trading sex for food were heard moaning to please their new masters. Every nation had its sluts and harlots, and whether real or manufactured, their cries of pleasure excited him.

Still a virgin, his physical needs were those of any healthy young man, but Shizue was the only woman he desired. "Never with prostitutes," Paul said to himself aloud for strength, as he hurried past the brothels. Oh, for the soft touch of a woman. How he longed to feel some gentleness and experience emotions other than the numbness caused by war.

The inn's walls were badly cracked, and its tile roof sagged and let in the rain. Paul entered the barnlike main room, which was thick with cigarette smoke. An assortment of pots and pans and tin cans placed around the warped floorboards caught dripping rainwater, the plops drowned in the clamor raised by men clustered together on straw mattresses and blankets that had been spread wherever there was dry space. Japanese sergeants were gambling and bartering over the spoils of war: jewelry, watches, carved jade—small mountains of loot that had replaced money as their coin of exchange for scarce items such as soap and cigarettes.

Made fat sharing his conquerors' rations, the innkeeper waddled a zigzag course toward the new guest, while his wife labored in the open kitchen ordering her elderly women servants about in a screeching voice. First the innkeeper bowed. Then his beady eyes judged Paul not to be another sergeant bearing valuable food rations, nor even a Japanese, and his manner grew terse at best.

"As you see, I have no room. No more room, sir," he insisted, and gestured at the noisy crowd.

"Make the room!" Paul fired back, brushing him aside angrily. "There's a dry place in that corner. Bring a clean mattress and prepare me a bath!"

The innkeeper waddled behind him, calling, "Please, sir—what manner of soldier are you?" Paul did not respond. "These others will not welcome his presence," he said aloud to himself. "There will be trouble. There will be fighting." Just then Paul treaded on a blanket displaying one sergeant's looted goods.

"Clumsy idiot!" the sergeant bellowed at the top of his voice.

Paul sailed his field pack away and raised his fists, prepared to fight the burly sergeant who was rising up before him. "No—it can't be! Toru!"

"Bastard that you are, I could kiss that ugly face!" Toru roared while lifting him off the floor in an embrace. "I knew this day would come! How I've waited for this day, my famous journalist." Laughing, he held Paul close. "Mother has written me of your fame and sent newspaper clippings."

This reunion could not have come at a greater time of need, thought Paul, until Yoko's son stood him away, and he saw how greatly the sympathetic face had changed. Toru's open laughter rang true to memory, but the kind soul Paul had known seemed to have disappeared behind empty eyes.

"What a fine uniform. Worthy of an officer!"

"And you, a *sōchō*—first sergeant," Paul observed, tapping his insignia of rank. "How long have you been on leave? How long before you march again?"

"Sitting on our behinds for nearly a week. My outfit marches at dawn. But we have tonight!" Toru put an arm around Paul's shoulders. "Everyone hear me and know this is my friend, Akira Yoseido, Japan's most famous correspondent." His boastful voice caused a crowd to gather. "Know we are like brothers, so show him respect or you'll answer to me!"

"Toru exaggerates my importance," Paul said, uncomfortable with his friend's touch. There was something different about Toru that made his skin crawl. "I'm just one of many who serve Nippon's cause."

"Modesty doesn't become you. Enjoy your celebrity status. Sakai Gōchō, bundle my valuables and watch after them," Toru ordered a junior-grade sergeant, then knelt to rummage inside his knapsack. "I have carried something very special these many months. A rare wine from Nanking for us to toast our good fortunes," he told Paul. "Two bastards who have made good. Do you remember our pact with fate? Ah so, here, you see what a fine wine this is. In this place they serve a swill that only passes for wine."

The ceramic bottle decorated with plum blossoms was displayed with a grand flourish that evoked "ahhs." Another first sergeant thrust out two hands heavy with looted rings, his forearms laden with watches and bracelets, asking Toru to name his price. "Not for sale even if you cut both arms off in the bargain," he said, laughing. "Innkeeper! Bring cups for the wine and serve us supper in your family quarters. My famous friend and I want privacy."

"I had not known your importance. Accept my humble apologies, honored sir," the innkeeper said, bowing. Then he stood rubbing his hands together. "Naturally, you were too exhausted from the march here to draw your rations," he said. "If you would allow me to perform the task for you . . ."

Toru shoved him away. "Fat chink pig! You and that mountain of a wife eat more of our rations than you serve. Thief! Hurry and obey me, or I'll skewer that fat belly with my bayonet!"

Yoko's son had always been tough, but he had never been a bully. Suddenly, Paul recognized in Toru the same savagery that had taken possession of the young fighting men he was marching with. Now he felt estranged from the man who had been his best friend. As he walked with him to the family quarters, he wondered if it was possible for them to reminisce over old times.

The innkeeper's kitchen table was lit by a hanging lantern that gave off a warm glow, and yet Paul sat across from Toru feeling chilled. Throughout dinner there had been little for him to say. Toasting their good fortunes repeatedly, Toru did all the talking, and his vivid descriptions of the destruction of Nanking destroyed Paul's appetite for the food Yoko's son gobbled up between words. He finished both their meals, while relishing the opportunity to share with Paul his accounts of women and children hunted down like wild game, their blood spilling like rainwater into the city gutters.

Toru insisted that it was the conquering samurai's right to take Chinese women, describing how he had done so in a Nanking street after throwing a woman down on the pavement. "It was merciful to kill her afterward," he said, filling their cups. They had drunk the special bottle of wine, and Paul had confiscated another bottle from the innkeeper's pantry shelf. "That first time I did hesitate killing the woman." He paused, remembering. A little drunk, he rose up from his chair to light his cigarette with the lantern flame. After dragging on his cigarette, Toru said, "But not since then, and there have been many others."

For an instant Paul thought he glimpsed a flicker of conscience before Toru's eyes went dark. The lantern swayed as his friend sat down. "Merciful?" he questioned.

"Yes, merciful," Toru answered, grinning. "My lieutenant came across me there in the street buttoning up, while the woman at my feet carried on, squealing like a stuck pig. Oh, how she wailed." His head went back to mimic the woman's suffering, and then he laughed and leaned forward to drink more wine, which dribbled down his chin as he tilted the cup to his mouth.

"'Kill her,' my lieutenant ordered me. 'She'll more than likely take her own life, rather than live with her shock and disgrace,' he said. 'Besides, left to roam the city, she can only spread disease to your comrades before someone else kills her or she starves.'"

Toru paused, wiping his lips with his hand, and then dragging on his cigarette. "There was blood on his sword from some killing he had done, and he wiped and oiled the blade so it would make a clean job of it. 'Apply the coup de grâce, and remember this lesson, *sōchō*,' my lieutenant ordered, and handed me his sword to end the woman's misery. And that I did!" His cup rattled down hard against the table.

"Ah, to be an officer and carry such a sword." Toru slumped back, shaking his head. "Not that my authority is any less absolute than a commissioned officer's, mind you. Believe me, my friend, I'm a harsher master to serve under because of all the badgering my own superiors take out on us noncoms. When I first reached China, they promoted me to junior sergeant. Before this war I lived in the garrison like a prince. And now I live almost as well here in the field. But to become an officer." He uttered a vexed sigh. "That ambition seems beyond my reach, old friend. But the gods have truly smiled on you. You've realized your ambitions. Tell me, how does it feel to laugh down the throats of those who once called you dirty names?"

Paul leaned across the table, staring at Toru, trying to find some remaining vestige of the boy who had defended him when they were children together. With that young man, he had always been able to express his feelings, and he desperately needed an outlet for them now. But the old Toru had vanished. This Toru was a hardened butcher of women; he had lost his sense of humanity. Yet, he sat grinning at Paul, unable to see himself for what he was. That blindness was a tragedy, Paul told himself. Yes, Toru disgusted him, but he also felt sadness over the loss of his friend.

While listening to Toru's tales of rape and murder, Paul had gotten very drunk. Looking into his old friend's eyes, he saw something of himself mirrored in their empty gaze. Just then it pained him to realize that war had changed him as well. He, too, had been drained by its horrors, but at least he still had a conscience. He thought of the irony in this meeting between old friends, recalling when they had talked of this very moment coming to pass. Paul still shared one thing in common with Yoko's son, which had been a joke between them both as children and as men. Now he kicked back his chair and dizzily rose up to salute their ungodly good fortunes. "Bastard to bastard, we've got the world by the tail." The sarcasm in Paul's voice was wasted on Toru, as he took hold of the table for support, knocking over the empty wine bottles.

Toru laughed so hard it brought tears to his eyes. "I hope you've learned to handle your women better than your wine," he told Paul.

The teasing voice and helping hands seemed those of the old Toru, guiding his drunken friend outside for a sobering walk in the night air. The wine helped blot out war's ugly face, and Shizue haunted Paul's thoughts as the two men walked the grassy rise above a stream that rushed downhill behind the inn.

Suddenly Toru halted. Glaring up at that night's dinner slop being heaved into the stream to be flushed away, he cursed the kitchen help for almost striking them with the garbage they were tossing from the windows above.

"Private Iwata!" Toru's anger shifted to a lone figure who stood a few feet away, exhaling smoke. "The enemy could be out there thinking to take us by surprise," he yelled at the private caught sneaking a forbidden smoke while on guard duty.

The terrified soldier hastily flicked the cigarette into the darkness and shouldered his rifle, which was leaning against a tree, then prepared for his sergeant's chewing-out. But Toru was not looking at him; he had heard a distinct metallic rattling sound in the tall grass near the stream's edge.

Toru unholstered his service pistol and whispered, "Iwata, get upstream to cut off whoever's hiding there. I'll cover the downstream banks. Shoot anything that moves." Private Iwata hurrried away.

Considering it unsafe to leave his drunken friend behind, alone and unarmed, Toru said, "Keep quiet and stay close to me."

The soft earth gave way underfoot as Paul followed Toru down to the stream. Rain had caused it to overflow, and the two men crept low along the slippery banks. Suddenly, Toru reached out his hand to halt Paul. Someone was on the run, splashing through the stream toward them. Paul heard rattling metal and Private Iwata splashing in the water not far behind his prey. Toru cocked his pistol. Then rifle fire exploded in short bursts.

"Hell!" Private Iwata called out. "Only a woman, Sergeant," he called, identifying the dead body. "And there are more like her, hiding here to catch the kitchen slop with their tin pails! Fast as rats," he shouted over the screams and splashing feet of women now escaping death farther upstream. "I've lost sight of them, *sōchō*!"

"Get back to your post! Damn, there might have been some pretty faces in the ones who got away," grumbled Toru, holstering his pistol. "If there are any pretty young girls left in this village of worn-out prostitutes, they keep well hidden from us."

Suddenly cold sober, Paul glimpsed a woman's corpse floating downstream, swept away with her conquerors' dinner slop. Both men heard a frightened whimper. Toru froze and peered into the darkness. Lanterns strung outside the inn cast just enough light for a telltale glint of metal to act as a beacon in the willowy grass.

Toru charged toward it. "What have we here?" he questioned, reaching down and dragging up a girl from her hiding place. Her tin pail spilled garbage across his canvas puttees as she tried to kick Toru. "Strike a match and let's have a look at this spirited wench."

Toru forced her head back by the hair as Paul's unsteady hand held the match flame up to her terrified face. The girl, perhaps Shizue's age, was quite beautiful. Hunger had not as yet conquered her healthy blush. Her unbound breasts heaved beneath her flimsy cotton dress.

"Why not let her go?" Paul pleaded as the match burned out.

Toru laughed. "Don't be a fool."

Paul could hear Private Iwata, standing somewhere above, answering the questions of those his rifle fire had brought running from the inn. Toru clamped his hand across the girl's mouth and warned her not to make a sound. Paul realized that nothing he might say could stop Toru from having his way with the trembling girl. Any sound might be overheard by Toru's comrades, who would then rush down to fight over her. They would all take turns having this young beauty. And so Paul waited in silence, watching Toru. Breathing hard, Toru kept his hand on the girl's mouth, until he at last ran out of patience waiting for his comrades to return to the inn.

For once, Paul was not powerless to act against the vile atrocity of rape. Toru was forcing the young girl down under him, on the spilled slop of her tin pail, promising her death if she fought him or screamed. Toru panted like a dog in heat, cursing her narrow skirt and ripping the black cotton to bare her legs, which she rigidly held together.

Paul heard the voices of the other soldiers trailing off as they entered the inn, but he could still hear Private Iwata pacing on guard directly above. Knowing that a loud struggle would bring the private running,

Paul searched the ground for a rock. Nothing but pebbles and the girl's dinner pail. Nothing heavy enough to strike a blow that would knock Toru out.

Toru feverishly pulled his swollen member from his pants. He knelt, prying the girl's legs apart, then rubbed his erect penis along the inside of her quivering thighs. "Feel this on you, bitch." He groaned in pleasure. "What silky loins. What thighs on this chink slut." His breathing came faster. Finding his pistol holster an annoyance, he unbuckled it and dropped it where he knelt.

Preparing to enter the girl, Toru was oblivious to Paul's hand inching the pistol from its holster. But the girl's eyes went to Paul, and she watched him slowly withdraw the weapon. It lay so close that he risked instant discovery if she screamed. Just as Toru brutally wrenched her thighs wider apart, Paul freed the pistol from its holster. Gripping it, he struck the back of Toru's head. There was a dull crack, and Toru collapsed forward across the girl. Involuntarily she screamed, but the sound was muffled by Toru's chest pinned against her face.

Paul knew that another, louder scream would alert the guard on duty, and he quickly whispered in Chinese, "Don't scream again. I mean you no harm. You must trust me. All Japanese aren't monsters. Let me help you."

His reassurances, spoken in fluent Chinese, kept the girl lying there quietly while Paul flipped Toru onto his back. Paul was grateful to see that Toru was alive, but knowing what he might be capable of when he regained consciousness caused Paul to take hold of the shocked girl's hands and quickly pull her up.

That night fate granted Paul an opportunity to ennoble himself. In the North everyone spoke Mandarin, a dialect Paul had learned when he was at the university, and the girl trusted his hushed promises of food, medicine, whatever she and her family needed. "Do you know a safe way home?"

The girl nodded. Her cold hand firmly holding his, she quietly guided Paul downstream. Shortly they crossed a wooden bridge, then hurried along a deserted maze of back alleyways. Long-tailed rats foraged among the rusting garbage cans. Paul kicked them away with his boots.

Some drunken soldiers weaved to a brothel on the street ahead, and he pulled the girl back into the shadows. She was barefoot but made no sound as a rat nipped at her ankle, drawing blood. When the way had cleared, she guided him to fields of thistle growing near the village walls.

Her soft voice broke the tense silence between them. "I am called Hsi-Ling," she said. "When you struck the match, I saw you were not like the others. I saw kindness in your face." Her hand was now soft and pliant, warming in his as she led him outside the village through a narrow opening in the wall.

No longer afraid to speak her gratitude, she told Paul of her widowed mother and grandparents. They had all gone into hiding while their humble farm was sacked. The Japanese conqueror had even slaughtered their precious water buffalo for meat. Without this beast of burden, they could no longer work the land, so they existed off scraps she ventured out each night to obtain. "As youngest and strongest, it is my duty. But often I return home with an empty pail. Mother and the old ones waste away," Hsi-Ling said sadly, and pointed to a dirt path wending up the blackened foothills. "They wait for my return not far from here."

Looking around, Paul felt that it was safe to leave her there while he returned to the village for what he had promised her. "Hsi-Ling," he said softly, "I want you to wait here for me. I'm going back to get food for you and your family."

Hsi-Ling nodded, her eyes shining with gratitude. "Yes, I will hide here by the wall."

After arranging a whistle signal so that Hsi-Ling would know of his return, Paul noted the wall's location and headed back, memorizing landmarks en route.

Food poured from the steaming kitchen on a flood of trays balanced by perspiring Chinese who were serving Colonel Fukushima's gluttonous demands. Lodged at the finest village inn, he and his staff feasted on the food taken from the villagers. Paul had come there to beg favors.

"Join me, Yoseido-*san*," the colonel said. "I was just about to send for you." He turned to one of the servants and ordered, "Bring a chair for my friend."

As he returned with the chair, the servant stumbled over the colonel's outstretched boots and bowed low, fearing the colonel's anger. However, Fukushima was too satiated to do more than belch.

Wiping his greasy fingers with the napkin tucked into his jacket collar, he regarded Paul drunkenly as Paul spoke of finding some girl. "So, you've taken a woman," he commented between mouthfuls of food. "Young—pretty . . . ?" He clacked his chopsticks at a servant and demanded wine be poured. "Well, speak up, journalist."

"Yes, very pleasing. But the little slut could please me more if she weren't so weak from hunger. My food rations aren't enough to satisfy her appetite, Fukushima *Taisadono*."

"Hah, feed the wench and she may bite off more than your hand." Staring down the table, Colonel Fukushima laughed with his staff, then suddenly began choking. He tore the napkin away, opening his jacket collar as he coughed. Violently he pushed away the wine cup a servant placed to his lips. Finally, he coughed up the obstruction. His face a mottled red, he sprawled back in the chair breathing heavily but normally. He fingered his new gold collar patches, each with a five-pointed silver star and grinned at Paul's look of surprise. "Yes," he said. "Official confirmation from Tokyo greeted my arrival. General now, Yoseido-*san*. *Rikugun chujo*, with new orders that send me to Shanghai."

The fresh memory of that morning's atrocities made it difficult for Paul to rise and salute this butcher he now addressed as "*kattsuka*." A general was a shogun, and *kattsuka* was the most honorable and respectful way to address him. "My congratulations," he said. "I'm confident the newly commissioned general's distinguished service will bring about many victories in the months ahead."

"Yes, my collar may grow other stars before our two paths cross again." General Fukushima laughed broadly, displaying his gold-capped front teeth. "At ease, Yoseido-*san*. While the arena of military politics beckons me to a staff position in Shanghai, there are new vistas in China for you as well. Your publisher has asked that I reassign you. At dawn you march with Major Ikeda. His batallion will be among the vanguard in our long push across China. Their exploits should provide grist for your talented pen. Hagiwara Sosha, give our journalist the dispatch we received by special courier."

The general's adjutant stood up and handed Paul an envelope. "No other mail has reached us here as yet," he told Paul.

Before reading the dispatch, Paul fortified himself with several swallows of wine, thinking that Toru's outfit also marched at dawn. The official dispatch, signed by *Nippon Shimbun*'s publisher, authorized his reassignment to report on more intensive front-line action. The Japanese people were growing jaded, it read, and numbness was setting in on the home front. The publisher wanted the public's daily rations of war spiced up. Paul's stories were now syndicated in newspapers throughout Japan, and the publisher had even written a few lines praising him for a job well done. Appalled that his gruesome accounts could induce numbness, Paul crushed the dispatch into a tight ball. But he was resigned to meet whatever fate held in store with the dawn.

Made drowsy by the feast, General Fukushima savored a cigarette and invited Paul to take what he wanted from the well-stocked kitchen. "I will personally see to it that Major Ikeda treats you with proper respect, Akira." The general chuckled. "I feel justified in being so familiar with you on the eve of my promotion. Yes, we've had our differences, but should you ever have need of my position, remember me as a man who honors his debts."

"I won't forget serving under you, *Rikugun chujo*." The irony of that statement escaped the drunken general's notice. Yawning, he wished the journalist good luck. Paul shook the new shogun's limp hand. He hoped he would never be forced to call upon him to collect that debt.

In his eagerness to leave Hsi-Ling's family well provided for, Paul could not carry everything the kitchen servants had sacked, and the inquisitive servant who helped carry the supplies was sure a woman was behind the conqueror's charity. He also knew that her whereabouts could fetch a handsome price.

"Is she very pretty, honorable master?" he asked, winded from his burden and hard pressed to keep up the fast pace. "She must be, or you would not rush to her waiting arms. Has she young sisters? If not, is her mother still desirable to men?"

Just within sight of the cracked village wall, Paul halted. "Idiot! You forget your place. Drop your sacks here and go!"

"But honorable master, how will you manage alone? The nearest farms are some distance, Ah," he cackled, his eyes searching the dark field of thistles, "the girl hides somewhere waiting to help carry your generous gifts."

Paul wrenched the sacks from his stubborn grip, then sent the man flying away by the seat of his pants. "Run and don't look back unless you want a beating!" he shouted. Some of the Chinese, Paul reflected, were little better than their conquerors. The man now fleeing was eager to sell out a young girl for profit.

Paul was able to carry everything through the opening in the village wall. His whistles brought Hsi-Ling to him. Her pretty eyes grew large, and she giggled with delight, awed by the bulging sacks of food, which she quickly helped him carry up the winding footpath. While joy lightened her step, Paul trudged behind, emotionally and physically drained.

Fear held those inside the shuttered farmhouse prisoners. A woman's tremulous voice sought confirmation that it was her daughter rapping on the bolted door. "*Aiyee,*" the woman shrieked, seeing her daughter's torn dress and the conqueror standing there beside her. Low-burning oil lamps illuminated the girl's aged grandparents. The family stood huddled together in disbelief as Hsi-Ling breathlessly told her story.

Suddenly there were smiles, bows, and expressions of gratitude for their Japanese guest. Soon happy conversation livened the shabbily furnished family room. Everyone bustled around the kitchen hearth, which had not been lit for cooking in some time. While emptying the sacks of rice, canned goods, pork, fresh vegetables, and tea, they implored Paul to dine with them and stay the night. The thought of Toru billeted at the village inn nursing his anger was the deciding factor in Paul's accepting their warm hospitality. By morning his injured friend might be less volatile. Hungry now, Paul felt at home with these warm and friendly people.

He had lived in his clothes for many days, and Hsi-Ling sensed his discomfort. She drew well water and boiled it to fill the metal bathtub that sat in one corner of the family room. Paul undressed behind a free-standing screen. His clothes that he had draped across it were taken away by unseen hands while he stretched out soaking in the bath, the cooking scent and homey family chitchat lulling him into a peaceful state. He hovered just on the threshold of sleep, when Hsi-Ling appeared before him, not the least embarrassed by his nakedness.

She had washed at the well and changed. Her long black hair was twined up into lustrous swirls held with silver combs, and she wore a charming, high-collared dress of red silk. She confided that it had been her wedding dress.

"I was a bride of only one month when my husband was killed. This was his dressing gown," she said, laying the folded garment across a chair. "I beat the dust from your uniform and have washed your undergarments to be dried at the hearth. Are you pleased?" she asked, bowing, then setting straw slippers by the tub. "Hsi-Ling wishes only to please the kind Japanese soldier who spared her disgrace and has brought great joy to this humble household. Tell me how you are called."

Without thinking, he gave his Christian name, "Paul," and she repeated it in a warm, husky-toned voice reminiscent of Shizue's. Her beauty suddenly aroused his desires, and before he could cover his erection, it buoyed up near the bathwater's surface. She saw it, then faced away with a giggle. Hsi-Ling had made it quite clear that he need only ask, and for that night she would willingly be his woman in gratitude for his kindness. He felt he must resist accepting such a payment, but as she disappeared on the other side of the paper-paneled screen, the imagined pleasures his mind conjured up had Paul stepping from the tub still painfully erect.

Her husband's silk dressing gown was tight across his chest. Its sleeves and skirt hem were much too short on him, and the straw slippers cramped his toes. Hsi-Ling was tall and long-legged. Surely her husband could not have been so tiny, he thought. When he at last came around the screen, he stood awkwardly before his politely amused hosts.

Seeing Paul in her husband's dressing gown caused Hsi-Ling to grow sad. She sat him at the family table in the place of honor, and as she served him, her eyes caressed the cloth she had sewn for her wedding night, wistfully remembering love.

Much later, after they had cleaned their bowls, the old ones spoke of their hardships so that the gods, if they overheard, would not think them too fortunate.

"We are a poor family," bemoaned the grandfather, "visited by misfortune. An old man and his old woman, with only their widowed daughter and her newly widowed woman-child to look after them." His lament whistled through his missing teeth. "Once the cock's crow wakened our humble household. Now the conqueror has silenced his welcome voice and taken our hens, taken even our beast of burden for food, and the land turns to dust."

"This night we fill our stomachs, but what of tomorrow?" the grandmother, who was all bones, lamented. She rocked in her chair while staring into the embers in the kitchen hearth. "So many tomorrows and no end to our misfortunes in sight. Oh, we will surely die. Surely we will starve."

"Yes, for tonight we do not cry ourselves to sleep. But what of tomorrow?" The mother woefully lifted her voice, taking inventory of what had not been eaten. Hunger had robbed her of beauty. Through pinched eyes, she estimated the days until Hsi-Ling must venture out again with her tin pail. "The conqueror's lusting hands have torn Hsi-Ling's dress, and it cannot be mended for lack of thread. My widowed child wears her wedding dress because she has no other."

"Woe," the grandfather cried, dipping a bony finger into his empty bowl. "What have we done to be visited by such misfortune?" Then, satisfied the gods had heard enough, he rose to bow.

"Our honored guest will forgive this old man's observation, but he does not seem like a soldier. He wears a uniform, yet he carried no weapon into this humble house. He shows this poor family kindness, yet he has asked for nothing in return. Puzzling. Most puzzling."

"Your eyes are wise, Honorable Grandfather," Paul replied, distracted when Hsi-Ling's arm brushed across his shoulder as she helped clear the table. He inhaled her flowery fragrance. "I am a correspondent, Grandfather," he explained, while Hsi-Ling moved with a natural grace that continued to distract his thoughts. "I write stories of this war for the Japanese people at home, who are not like their soldiers. I know a single act of kindness isn't enough to prove my words. Those in power have twisted our soldiers' minds and poisoned their hearts. But my people are not so different from yours, and there are many who share my wish for peace between us."

"War is war," the grandfather said sharply. "A soldier is a soldier. Forgive an old man, but you speak in circles, and the hearth burns low." He was impatient to be asked for something in return, lest Paul's charity disgrace his household.

Paul ran one hand back through his hair and smiled. "You owe me nothing in return. Your hospitality has given me more than I gave you."

The old man decided to take matters into his own hands. He turned to Hsi-Ling. "Granddaughter," he said sternly, "our honored guest sleeps in my bedchamber. See that his night is made comfortable." His granddaughter bowed obediently. The matter was settled, and he rose from the table, giving Paul a toothless grin. "May your night be a happy one."

Throughout dinner Hsi-Ling had read the desire burning in Paul's eyes, and for him to deny what the old man had also clearly seen there would be hypocrisy. Any protest would be futile, when the old man was so relieved to have at least one remaining treasure to bestow on their shy provider. Paul bowed. "You are much too generous."

"Old woman. Daughter." The grandfather's clapping hands ordered them away. "His eyes are odd. Mixed blood," he said under his breath, while leaving Hsi-Ling and Paul alone.

"Mind your tongue, old man," the grandmother scolded him, and a door squealed shut.

"The old one meant no disrespect. They are handsome eyes, Paul," Hsi-Ling said.

Being alone with her, Paul's heart violently protested against his words. "I bowed only to please him. Sleep is all I desire, and I must wake before the dawn."

Hsi-Ling suffered an injured smile, then turned and stoked the hearth. She took his undergarments from a basket and shook them out, then hung them to dry. She told him that she had emptied his uniform pockets before beating the dust out of it and had seen the beautiful girl's picture he carried in his wallet.

"I am not unattractive to your eyes," she said, turning around to face him when he remained silent. "Let me please you. Is it faithfulness to a wife that holds you prisoner? Is the beautiful girl in the picture your wife?"

Paul could easily have lied, but he shook his head. As Hsi-Ling rushed to close the space between them, he knew it was mutual desire rather than obligation that drew this ravishing creature into his arms. Her kiss melted all his resistance, a kiss unlike any Shizue had ever given him, and he was completely lost, drowning in a stormy sea of sensations. Finally to know the yielding mouth of a woman made his flesh ache in anticipation. Then Hsi-Ling breathed his name in her low, husky voice. Sensations both sublime and terrifyingly new assaulted him as she lit their way with an oil lamp, gliding tall beside him.

About to have his first experience as a man, Paul's single thought was that love must somehow play a part. He could not end his virginity like some beast in the field. Hsi-Ling was very desirable, but she was not his heart's desire, and the carnal act must not lack beauty, he told himself, imagining that she was Shizue closing the bedchamber door. After she set down the lamp, Hsi-Ling began disrobing. The silk fell down around her smooth shoulders to reveal perfect breasts. They were like ripe fruits cupped by warm shadows. Slowly she let the silk dress fall down along hips and thighs that were soft yet firm. Gracefully she stepped free of the dress. One by one she removed the silver combs. Then, tossing her head, she allowed her long hair to fall free to her waist. Her lustrous hair was set aglow in the lamplight, which also silhouetted her lithe, willowy figure. Crossing to him, she invited his touch.

Quickly she undressed him. Then Paul lifted her up in his arms and lay her down on the straw mattress. He shut reality out, and a glorious fantasy overtook him. Hsi-Ling became Shizue writhing beneath him, caressing him, speaking his name. This was Shizue rocking the earth. Only she could wobble the earth off its axis, spinning it faster and faster until a shuddering explosion hurled them both far into the cosmos.

"Shizue—Shizue." He gasped her name again and again while hurling far beyond all sight and sound into the black velvet heavens of his delirious fantasy.

Nestled against his lover's bosom, Paul was overcome by sleep, as if his body had surrendered to an overdose of an opiate. He had spent a lifetime tensed to defend himself against harm, but for that night his muscles came unknotted, turned to jelly while in his dreams Shizue caressed him and he breathed the delicate perfume of her skin. During the night he stirred, calling her name aloud. Then a flood of warmth enveloped him, and he touched the woman beside him in the same way as a child imagined touching the clouds that sailed past his outstretched fingertips.

Whose voice was this? Paul wondered. His eyes fought against opening. Someone was shaking him awake to the rude reality of a straw mattress, and he fought to hold on to his dreams of indescribable beauty. Then he saw a shuttered window leaking the harsh light of daybreak.

"You said you must wake before the dawn." Hsi-Ling quickly dressed, then went to fetch his clothes, which she had left hanging by the kitchen hearth.

Paul sat up, rubbing his eyes, wanting to escape this ugly war. But a beautiful Chinese peasant girl returned with his uniform. "I have to report at sunrise," he announced, rising and reaching for his clothes. "Orders."

"Then we must hurry," she said quietly, and began helping him dress.

Through a blue-gray mist, Hsi-Ling led him silently along the footpath to a hill overlooking the village walls. "Were you pleased? Will you come again, Paul?" she asked in a small, quivering voice.

"No, my outfit's marching out."

Tearful at his reply, she embraced him and gave him a tender kiss. "You have made me feel like a woman once again. The girl in your wallet is fortunate to have the love of such a kind man. Shizue. You called her name in the night, but it was I who stroked your hair and lulled you back to sleep."

Paul returned her kiss guiltily. "Hsi-Ling, take your family and leave this place. There's enough food to get you somewhere safe, where the war can't touch you."

"The old ones would not survive such a long journey," she answered, warming his cheek with a sigh of resignation. "My place is here with them, Paul." She moved away from him. "May the gods protect you. Good-bye."

"Sayonara." How frail and vulnerable Hsi-Ling appeared waving good-bye, he thought. A doomed figure clad in her silk wedding dress, she evaporated behind him in the predawn mist. She had given him tenderness in return for his heartfelt need to prove all Japanese were not monsters. But suddenly he felt lacerated in the aftermath of his single night of love. His remembered ecstasy had been purchased with a fantasy. His initiation into manhood was a cruel cheat, a shattering testimony to the fact that no woman but Shizue could exist for him.

Dawn tinted the village square a mustard yellow. Paul reported to Major Ikeda, whom he instantly disliked. His fat head seemed to grow straight out of his narrow shoulders. Paul regarded him as a toady martinet as he boasted in a wheezy voice of the discipline and the battalion esprit of his infantry troops. As Paul watched the major's troops, he was shocked to see Toru, striding angrily past the men under his command, inspecting them. Toru, a bandage showing under his field cap, made an about-face to salute his lieutenant. Then he saw Paul and stared daggers at him. Fate had assigned them to serve together. Paul felt a sinking sensation in his gut.

"None of my seasoned men fear an honorable death. Yes, I can promise you'll soon see some real fighting, Yoseido-*san*," Major Ikeda continued. "There's an old Chinese proverb. The winner becomes king, the loser a bandit. Chiang is the bandit in this war, a bandit generalissimo we'll soon run off the map," he assured Paul with a sneer. "General Fukushima has instructed me to give you a free rein. It honors my command—"

He broke off, and the sunlight reflected by his glasses flashed in the direction in which Paul was looking. Ikeda saw Toru glaring at the correspondent. "That sergeant appears to hold some grievance against you."

"We had an argument over a woman," Paul said. "Nothing serious, we're old friends," he added uncertainly, wondering if any friendship remained to soften Toru's murderous countenance.

"Go and settle the matter, Yoseido-*san*. Left festering, these petty quarrels undercut our esprit." Major Ikeda stood rigid, waiting to be obeyed.

So that anything said would not be heard by his ranks, Toru met Paul halfway. Overnight the mud had dried, and whirls of dust danced around the tense space between the two men. Toru grimaced while feeling behind his head. "Did you wish me dead? All night my head ached, and I thought, can my old friend have struck this blow?"

Paul bravely tried to smile. "Sorry, but I knew such a thick skull would never crack. Bastard to bastard, I wanted the girl for myself— before you could spoil her for me." He gave the only explanation Toru might buy, and it made him wince. "I got carried away."

Holding his head, Toru played to his ranks. "Ohhh! Ahhh! How you carved my skull, damned bastard! But one chink bitch isn't worth our friendship. Later you'll tell me how she was." He winked at Paul and pounded his shoulders. "Now walk with me so everyone can see we remain friends, or some night you might find a bayonet between your ribs. In place! Back in ranks there! Yoseido-*san* and I are like brothers. We fight, we make up. He'll write stories about us for the newspapers. Your families will read your names and be proud," he addressed them sternly. "Let him know us man for man, brave samurai."

Paul heard new names being called out and tried to attach them to new faces. But they were all really one nameless face poisoned by war and no different from those he had come to know serving with another merciless juggernaut exactly like this. The order was given to march out, and the village square grew hazy with rising yellow clouds of dust.

When they were well on the road, Toru washed his mouth with water from his canteen and spit. The columns ahead trailed ever-present dust. The sun's glare hurt his eyes and he squinted as he asked Paul, "Why the long face? I'm the one with the bump on his head. But still friends. Still like brothers, *hai*?"

"Brothers," he answered with hollow laughter. Toru's vacant eyes increased his depression. "Your samurai are really tough, are they, Toru?"

"First platoon into any fight and last ones out."

"Then I'll make it my platoon," Paul decided grimly.

Toru threw a friendly punch. "Good! Stick close by me, and I'll look after you, just as I did when we were boys together. Me fighting at your side again."

Paul marched the dusty road beside Toru, ever more painfully aware of his complicity in advancing the war. Its evils had forever tainted both men, and it struck him as divine justice that he and Yoko's son should challenge death together in combat.

"Do you ever think about dying?" Paul asked, looking at this seasoned killer who seemed to care for nothing but the greater glory of Japan.

Toru regarded him somberly for a beat. "Did I think about being born? Death is the same, my friend. It happens," he said, and tapped his shouldered rifle. "In battle this is my woman. I sleep and I eat with her muzzle always at my right side." He stroked the Arisaka's tapered wood barrel housing. "When I lift her sights to my eye, let the enemy worry about losing his life. Often I've had some chink stare back at me as if he had seen himself in a mirror. He knows better, yet fear for his own life plays tricks with his eyes, and he hesitates pulling the trigger. I squeeze mine, and before he falls, there is a look." Toru's widened eyes expressed disbelief. "Can this be me bleeding and about to die? But I saw myself standing just there in the trees, the enemy thinks."

Toru paused to wipe the grit off his forehead with his sleeve and to tug his cap brim lower against the sun's glare. "China," he spat. "Even the sky here is filled with shit. A word of advice, my friend. Best not to think. Always go into battle prepared to die, and chances are good you'll live to fight again."

Paul wondered if he had the courage to meet death. Toru smelled of the oil he had used to ream the blackened steel of his rifle muzzle's bore. Those blunt fingers caressed the metal skin as they had caressed Hsi-Ling's thighs.

Paul's shoulders went back as he experienced a rare moment of pride. He had acted bravely the night before. In retrospect, that night had held moments of beauty for him. He had made Hsi-Ling feel like a woman again, and she had made him feel like a man for the first time. Though Shizue had been his fantasy, her lovely Chinese counterpart was poignantly real and vulnerable. Her soft bosom had lulled Paul back to sleep while he called Shizue's name. She had shown him only sweetness. In another time and place, their meeting might have led to freeing him from the bondage of an unrequited love.

Soon Hsi-Ling would return to the stream behind the village inn to gather slop to feed the old ones. He wished fate had never thrown them together. The Chinese people would no longer wear anonymous faces.

Paul squinted up at the Japanese bombers roaring overhead. He knew the flight crews were supplied with his father's parachutes. Merely a safety device, he thought. There were no Japanese paratroops as yet, and so far the payloads had been dropped mostly on major cities. The bombers' presence in China's vast interior was an unusual sight to the infantry troops, who craned their necks, gaping with surprise as the lead plane's bomb bay doors opened. The bomb racks were empty. The plane swooped low, banking to tip its wings. The squadron leader was celebrating a successful run over some distant target area.

Taking Chinese cities and gaining control of the major roads and railway lines had been Japan's strategy for victory when the war first began. But their wily enemy was like a magnet drawing them ever deeper into a vast arena the Japanese knew only through maps, and poor ones at that. The Chinese knew the hills and mountains like the backs of their hands. Thus, they enjoyed an advantage over their enemy, and for days now, Chiang's retreating armies had lured them into a steady advance.

While serving with Colonel Fukushima, Paul had seen few armored vehicles in use; horses pulled the Imperial Army's heavy artillery through the Chinese mud. But now he was seeing a more modern, mechanized Japanese fighting force. Tractors pulled an artillery company's cannons across the rugged terrain, and clanking tanks were responsible for the tornado of acrid dust that swirled up along a steep dirt grading, which had been made wider by the corps of engineers.

Japanese ground troops and arms were being massed for some large-scale offensive. Thinking about it, Paul felt the skin crawl on the back of his neck. He was aware that his next encounter with the enemy could be more than a day's fight against an undermanned and poorly equipped Chinese force such as those Colonel Fukushima had so easily driven back. Toru sniffed at the dust-laden air as though it carried the fiery stench of some larger clash than even he had so far experienced.

By nightfall their batallion made camp with other units. Up and down the lines of resting troops, Paul watched cigarettes being lit. Their embers glowed like a thousand amber eyes peering into the pitch-black night.

Earlier that day Paul had dispatched only human interest stories of the men seated around him. Communication with the army's rear guard was provided by messengers, and his routine story had been carried away by one of them. *Nippon Shimbun*'s bloodthirsty publisher would just have to wait, Paul thought, watching Toru pace before him.

Even when they were boys, Yoko's son had been restless for the action of war games they had played together in the Tokyo streets. Now he was a seasoned warrior who craved the type of action that fed his unnatural appetite for the kill. Toru sat down, and Paul watched Toru's blunt-fingered hands caressing the rifle he rested on the ground between his legs. He seemed to be lost in a wildly crazy dream of glory that caused Paul to lament over the distance between them.

For one solid, unnerving week, Major Ikeda's batallion pushed on from campground to campground while the Chinese forces remained an unseen presence. Paul felt sure they were out there, waiting somewhere on the far horizon and treading in the footsteps of Japan's advancing columns to cut off the possibility of retreat. Toru strongly sensed that, too, his eyes growing keener and ever more alert for the slightest clue to the enemy positions. But no ray of sunlight glinted off the Chinese artillery to give them away, and no flickering glimpse of Chinese campfires showed in the night.

The next evening, after yet another long day's march, Toru ordered his platoon to halt. He squatted and lifted something off the ground. It was the crushed butt of a Chinese cigarette. One sniff told him that; and the tobacco that he rubbed between his fingers was still fresh. Usually the enemy ground his cigarette remains well into the dirt, but someone had been careless. Toru ordered his platoon to search the area.

"Tank tracks," the platoon corporal sang out, and Major Ikeda hurried across the rocky ground to investigate.

"Ah, these chinks used brush to wipe away their trail," he decried loudly, then scanned the surrounding hills through his field glasses. "Not a trace! Sergeant, double the guard tonight. Our enemy is closer at hand than was last reported."

Toru saluted him. "Well, it seems we are finally to break with this marching and see action," he told Paul.

Conferring with his staff, Major Ikeda wiped his face with a handkerchief. Perhaps no man serving under him feared an honorable death, but Paul observed the same was not true of the major, who blustered and shouted to cover his bad case of nerves.

Night closed in quickly around them as they made camp in a nest of hills. Toru looked upon darkness as a soldier's friend. Some brave Chinese might risk death to stab a guard or two, but this was a war best fought in broad daylight, and Toru stretched out comfortably on the grassy earth beside Paul. He was asleep the moment his eyes closed, but Paul remained awake, wide-eyed and tense. There were no cooking fires that night and lighting cigarettes was forbidden. Desperate for a smoke to calm his jittery nerves, Paul got up and paced with the guards on duty, asking about their families.

He did not know it then, but these boyish-faced soldiers he was talking to would soon be killed. As the night slowly lifted with a dim ribbon of light rising behind a wavy seascape of mountains, Chinese artillery squads dug in there were being mustered to their cannons. The heat generated from them would equal that of the now rising sun. Each man was stripped to his waist, tensed for the order to commence fire.

Paul had finally gone to sleep for a few hours. Now he stretched his arms and yawned as birds flapped their wings in lazy formations against the brightening sky. Some sixth sense always swept the sky of birds just before a battle, and Paul greeted the sight with a relieved smile. Thumps resonated like distant thunder. He mistook the sound for thunderclouds rolling in across the far side of the mountain. Instead, the air began to whistle, and he instinctively went down for cover while Chinese howitzers pounded the slumbering Japanese encampments.

It was the prelude to an ambitious Chinese counteroffensive, and its shocking roar jolted the Japanese troops awake. No one's shouts could be heard, and Paul felt himself being pulled up by Toru. He started back across the shuddering earth for the canvas shoulder bag in which he kept his writing tools, but Toru caught hold of him, forcing Paul to go with him. Their batallion was in a state of total chaos. All around them troops were fleeing the deafening rain of exploding shells, tripping over their dead, and falling into the newly opened mouths of smoking craters. A bugler toppled headlong directly in Paul's path. Toru's platoon trampled over the man's bloody bugle, whose call for retreat had died with the savagely hammering waves of Chinese shells.

The hunter became the hunted. Chinese infantry were charging out of the smoke, and Paul ran for his life unarmed, taking cover with Toru's platoon, who fired on the enemy. They were far outnumbered and would soon be overrun. Toru's lieutenant glimpsed a fissure in the rocks at their backs, and Paul retreated for it while the Chinese artillery barrage relentlessly shook the earth under his feet. The remnants of other platoons were driven back to join forces with them.

Toru's lieutenant unsheathed his ceremonial sword, swinging it high in the air to substitute for his shouted orders, which could not be heard. Its gleaming blade sent the men forward, and they fanned out behind trees rooted in sandy soil. Paul scrambled after Toru for cover. The opening in the rocks seemed miles away; reaching it would mean fighting for every inch of ground. Chinese bullets splintered the bark of some fallen trees only a split-second after Paul flattened himself in Toru's shadow.

Hours had passed since the Chinese assault had scattered the Japanese forces across a smoking landscape. The fighting had gone hard for both sides, but Paul came through it without a scratch. Toru now commanded the survivors of his platoon, who were cut off from their lines and being pursued by Chinese infantry. The enemy had forced them to retreat inside a cramped rock cave, which opened at the bottom of a deep ravine. High in the rocks above them stood a ridge. Toru's lieutenant was badly wounded and stayed behind with the other wounded men to guard the entrance to the ravine. Their rifle fire would buy time for the advancing column now being led by Toru, who was acting under orders to secure that ridge and make a stand. But he knew the enemy might already have possession of it, so he led the advance cautiously.

Dusty soldiers of Japan moved low to the ground, one then another darting through a scattered maze of boulders that covered their treacherous uphill ascent on the dried riverbed at the base of the ravine. There was no turning back, no way out but up, and so they climbed for the sky.

Paul took his turn darting between boulders, stalked by the enemy. Suddenly they heard the crackling roar of Chinese mortar fire, followed by sporadic rifle shots. Then a deadly silence spoke for their wounded comrades who had been killed at the entrance to the ravine. Toru signaled his men to climb faster.

"The Chinese wouldn't be snapping at our heels if they held the ridge," Toru shouted. "Ours for the taking!"

They climbed higher, their ascent slowed by the increasing steepness of the riverbed, whose rock walls closed in around them. The ravine abruptly narrowed, and blinding sunlight webbed the ridge some forty feet above the place where Toru halted his men. Erosion had formed a wide footpath that the enemy could easily scale after them, and Toru ordered the way up to be booby-trapped with hand grenades.

Paul climbed the footpath just behind Toru, who grimly shared his observations as they cleared the top of the ridge. "Not to my liking," he snarled, taking it all in.

Paul and Toru could see Chinese soldiers climbing up the rocky riverbed some distance below. Nothing but open sky lay at Toru's back on the flat anvil of earth they had just reached. There was no safe cover near the top of the footpath for his men to hide. They might lie down flat there and pick the enemy off when he got within range of their rifles, but the Chinese carried mortars, and Toru's men would be easy targets. His eyes swept around the ridge to a point where it turned. There, a snaking rock formation offered excellent cover.

"We're far outnumbered and don't stand a chance," said Paul.

"You're wrong, my friend." Toru laughed and lit a cigarette, passing it to Paul as he said, "Relax. We have those rocks there to hide behind. The chinks can't see them from below. Those dogs will have to come up the way we did, and there's no cover for them. They'll have to come at us across yards of open ground, and by that time the midday sun will be in their eyes. Hurry, let's see if there's another way down from here." He snatched the cigarette from Paul's unsteady hand, dragging on it as they walked to the rock formation. The ridge dropped off into space just a few yards behind it.

"Bad luck," Toru said, when they halted on the ledge to an abyss.

Paul looked down, then stepped away, dizzied by the precipitous drop. Toru sailed a stone into the abyss and watched it vanish down a sheer face of cliff. This was the only other way down, and from their vantage point nothing could be seen of what they might encounter if they attempted the descent.

"Little or nothing for a man to hold on to," Toru said grimly. "We could all break our necks. No wonder the chinks pursued us here."

"Yes, it's a perfect observation post," Paul said, holding his field cap against the strong updraft of wind.

The battle arena unfolded far below. With a wireless the Chinese could report on it all. Smoke drifted in dense clouds that partially obscured the armored forces pushing across the rolling foothills below. If it was the Chinese offensive still pushing the Japanese lines back toward the mountain range. They were done for, thought Paul.

"Ours!" Toru announced as the wind shifted, lifting the smoke of battle. "Our lines have regrouped! They're routing the Chinese. Soon victory will be ours!" By now, his men had all reached the top and gathered around him. "Reinforcements will soon be here to deal with those dogs snapping at our heels."

Paul saw them too. Japanese infantry marched behind light tanks and were slowly gaining ground, but it could be hours before the enemy was routed. "Toru, maybe the Chinese won't come after us once they realize how many dead it'll cost them."

"Wishful thinking, my friend. In this war life is cheap. Ours and theirs." Toru addressed the remnants of his crack platoon. "Our lieutenant's last order was to hold this ridge. As you all can see, attempting to retreat down that cliff promises us only a dishonorable death. So, take cover in those rocks and let the enemy come!"

One private stuck his rifle high in the air and cried, "*Hai, sōchō,* we will give them a fight to remember."

The dizzying heights caused Paul to decide against attempting a descent down the sheer face of the cliff alone. He hurried to take cover among the rocks. The abyss lay just behind him. Ahead lay yards of open ground and the flat ledge above the footpath they had just scaled. Paul listened to the men sing out an ammunition count. Twenty men strung left and right against how many Chinese? The time had come for Paul to fight, to prove he was a true Japanese, and when a pistol was slapped into his hand, he felt the chill of death.

"Nambu type 1904, eight millimeter automatic pistol," Toru said. He instructed Paul in its use. "It's their life or yours, so don't think twice before squeezing the trigger. Remember the game of courage we played as boys in the Tokyo graveyards? *Shibete,*" he said, prodding Paul's memory. "Remember daring each other to walk through the graveyard at night? Well," he added, and laughed, "the old belief is true. Fear comes to a man when his testicles shrink. Reach down inside your pants and stretch your testicles out as we did for courage then. Stretch them out or die a coward."

Shibete, a foolish child's game, Paul thought. Still, he sought the roots of his courage as he had then. But these were not imagined graveyard ghosts he heard climbing the dried riverbed just below. Suddenly, death whistled on the air. Mortar shells hammered across the ridge. Their impact shook the earth, and Paul hugged the ground, shielding his head. If he was about to die, then his last thoughts should be of Shizue. Yet, he was unable to think of anything but death, for two men near him lay blown apart. Then it was quiet. Paul knew the enemy could not see their position from below, so the shelling had been scattered. Toru wondered aloud if the Chinese might also be low on firepower. His casualties were quickly stripped of ammunition, their rifles emptied, and the bullets divided among the living.

Paul coughed up dirt. Taking terrified breaths, he gripped the pistol with both hands, supporting its barrel in a rock crevice, and pointed it at the ledge of the ridge not twenty yards away. He could hear the unsuspecting Chinese climbing. And then their boots tripped the wired booby traps planted on the ascent path. Exploding grenades spewed grit high into the air. Sunlight burned against Paul's neck while he watched Toru's lips move as he counted the explosions. Five in all before the air cleared.

Toru grinned, pleased by the outcries that told him this first line of defense had claimed a heavy toll. "Any second now," he whispered, and signaled an alert. He knew the enemy was inching along, feeling for wires.

Peaked tan caps with the blue-and-white Nationalist sun emblems showed above the flat rock ledge. Then Paul saw the faces of young Chinese soldiers, one after another squinting into the sun's ruthless glare. Toru's command to open fire blew their faces away. But more of them appeared, blasted away again, and still they came, Chinese following Chinese until the enemy grew into a wave crawling along the open ground without cover. Like soldier ants advancing through the jungles, they laid down their lives by drawing the enemy fire, causing the enemy to use up its ammunition to pave the way for a cresting wave of new reinforcements, who swarmed over the corpses.

Paul found his finger squeezing the pistol trigger. *Click-click.* The empty sound was repeated by the rifles left and right of him. Had he killed anyone? Paul wondered. Bodies littered the ridge, and now only silence greeted the squinting Chinese who still swarmed over its rim. They hugged the earth uncertainly, motionless as their dead, listening for the Japanese fire that never came.

Left and right Toru's men soberly fixed bayonets. It was a clearly identifiable sound that reached the enemy's ears.

"Hold your fire." The Chinese lieutenant's command preceded his appearance. Sweat rolled down his scowling face as he issued another command, and his troops rose up like sapling trees lining the rocky rim. "There will be no surrender terms! No Japanese prisoners taken here today!" The Chinese lieutenant looked out across his dead while he offered his hated enemy an honorable death. "My men will meet your bayonets where they stand," he called out. "Come to us or die as cowards. Come to us or join your ancestors in disgrace. I give you five minutes to choose your fate!" Confident his enemy needed no further encouragement, the Chinese lieutenant glanced at his wristwatch, then unholstered his German Luger and stood with its muzzle relaxed against the side of one leg. "When you are ready, defeated sons of Japan!"

"We will come, Chinese pigs!" Toru thrust a dead man's rifle into Paul's hands, his steely smile inviting Paul to use the bayonet blade. "To my eyes you have always been a Japanese. Now we die together side by side as brothers and as samurai," said Toru.

Paul detected a fleeting spark of emotion in Toru's eyes, but it was snuffed out by fanaticism as he turned to prepare his men for death. "When you charge these dogs, burst your lungs with our cry. Fall with our brave battle cry on your dying breath!" He slashed the calloused side of one palm with his bayonet. "Let them taste my blood with this steel!"

"Oh, what joy, my son has been called to be a warrior for his emperor"; the words of a war song droned through Paul's mind. Toru dusted his uniform and straightened his field cap. Every man there followed his example. Then they stood tall, each man alone with his imminent death. Except for Paul, who watched Toru fill his lungs with air as a diver would who was about to plunge into the deep. Desperately wanting life, Paul quickly went down and hugged the rocks as the others all charged away, their lungs bursting with cries of *"Wah! Wah!"*

Honorable death was a delusion, Paul thought. As yet no one could have seen the spineless serpent he made of himself, slithering across the earth toward the rim of the ridge. He heard Toru greeting death, crying *"Wah! Wah!"* That singular voice of his boyhood lifted itself above all the others and then was extinguished in a burst of Chinese fire.

The dizzying heights gave Paul pause. He could be killed descending this preciptously twisting cliff, but his only escape lay downward. Paul carefully lowered himself into the windy abyss. His chin scraped against the cliff wall, and he used both hands to take hold of crevices in the rock, his feet searching urgently for safe footholds. He tried not to think of the danger from his enemy on the ridge and dared not look up beyond the shallow crevices that he tested first with one hand, then the other. Inching downward with heartstopping uncertainty, he breathlessly explored the crumbling rock. One error in judgment, he knew, could spell sudden death.

What if the cliff ended in open space where its curving wall shot out of sight? Suppose he did touch bottom only to find the retreating Chinese dug in there? Torn by fears, he had no choice but to continue the descent. Jagged rocks shredded his trousers, cutting his knees and skinning his hands. The wind ripped off his cap, blowing it down into the void. Wildly his feet searched for a toehold as the cliff steepened. Finding none, he panicked. The sun beating down on him made him even more dizzy than the chasm yawning below.

Suddenly rock exploded to bits just inches above his head. From the ridge far above, the Chinese had spotted him. He felt what seemed like a red-hot poker enter his shoulder. His predators did not trust his death to the gods. Only empty space yawned beneath his kicking feet. The pain in his shoulder was forcing him to let go. He screamed, feeling another bullet rip through the flesh of his leg. He began to fall, scraping along blurred rock, then sliding off the edge of the world as the sharply twisting cliff wall ran out. Chinese riflemen could no longer see him as he fell screaming, his eyes shut tight to meet death.

Then all at once something miraculous and soft broke his fall. His body began slowly rolling downhill. Finally, he stopped rolling, caught in the arms of leafy branches that bowed under his weight and then buoyed him up on his back.

For a time he must have lost consciousness. Natsu had often spoken of the resurrection and the light. Now his eyes blinked open as if he might have been Lazarus rising from the blackness of his tomb. He looked around and saw that a field of shrubs was growing along the sloping embankment beneath the cliff wall. Those sturdy green anchors crisscrossing downhill had spared his life. He gazed up at the curving rock formation that rose to the jutting ridge high overhead. Even if Chinese riflemen there could see him now, he was no longer within range of their bullets. But suddenly he was aware of pain. Touching his right shoulder, he felt blood drenching his hand. Excruciating pain shuddered through his right leg. He managed to reach one hand down to his torn, blood-soaked trouser leg. The second Chinese bullet had shattered the bone. He could feel it protruding through his broken skin.

Paul saw no sign of the enemy, only Japanese infantry still advancing across the high ground below. He was losing a great deal of blood and knew he could bleed to death before help came. The vista spun dizzily. He struggled not to lose consciousness again. Thoughts of Shizue and home were powerful forces that instilled strength enough for him to stand up. Terrible pain shot through his wounded leg. Using the shrubs as support, he began a painful, hobbling descent.

Perhaps a thousand Japanese and Chinese had lost their lives on the ground stretching out beyond the ridge. There were no shrubs to support him, and Paul went down, crawling until his hand made contact with a Japanese soldier's rifle. Coming this far had cost him blood. He thirstily drank from the fallen man's canteen and poured the rest over his head, then took the dead soldier's cap to shield himself against the sun's blistering heat.

With the rifle as his crutch, Paul hobbled off through the rippling curtains of heat, losing precious drops of life with each agonizing step. The faint clanking of Japanese tanks urged him on. Alone in a wasteland of corpses, he left a trail of blood behind him.

CHAPTER 25

Shizue quickly walked along the corridors of a military hospital in Nagasaki, thinking how that summer had been marked by homecomings. Her brother had returned from America in disgrace and now Paul had come back a hero wounded in combat. But at least he was safely home. Her prayers for him had been answered, and yet she felt terribly unsettled as she entered his hospital room to find him napping in a wheelchair near the window.

For a time Shizue studied the handsome face made gaunt by war. "Paul." Twice she softly spoke his name before his eyes fluttered open as if awakening to a dream.

"Shizue—is it really you?"

Eagerly, she put her arms around him, pressing down on his wounded shoulder. But there was such heady pleasure in his painful awakening that Paul endured her embrace with scarcely a whimper. The morphine was wearing off, however, and when Shizue drew away, she questioned his pained look.

"Oh, I didn't think," she said. "Your shoulder."

Paul smiled. "Not so bad, really. It's this leg." He tapped the pajama leg elevated in the foot strut of the wheelchair. "Shattered bone. They're operating on it again in a few weeks. How did you know I was here?"

"From the newspapers. You won't lose it?" she asked, her worried gaze going to his leg.

"No. Let me see you." Paul wheeled back, and she turned the small circle his hand asked of her. She was like a fresh breeze, he thought, clad in a frilly teal blue silk dress with pale pink piping on its ruffled blouse and sleeves. Breathing deeply, he inhaled her unforgettable fragrance. Smiling prettily, Shizue fussed with the small veil of her matching juliet cap, and for the moment her radiance banished China from his thoughts.

"There's so much I want to know," she said. "Your letters were so vague. I forced myself to read all your stories about this horrid war, but nothing in them put me in touch with your true feelings." Shizue gently pressed his hand. "Now you must tell me how China really was for you."

Shizue drew up the white wooden hospital chair and sat facing him expectantly, hands folded in her lap. Paul looked at her, and for one haunting instant Hsi-Ling's face supplanted hers, and all that China had been came rushing back at him. Part of him had died on the ridge with Toru's platoon. Massaging his eyes, Paul saw the faces of the soldiers hardened for the death charge and could not bring himself to satisfy her innocent request. "Perhaps someday I'll be able to speak of it. But not now."

"I didn't think. Please forgive me. You've come home, and nothing else matters."

Pain caused spasms in Paul's shattered right leg, and he gathered his robe across his thigh. "Just a twinge. The army surgeons here are tops. Soon they'll have it patched together almost as good as new," he said, smiling away her concern.

"I feel at such a loss for words. The newspaper reports didn't say how badly wounded you were. When I read in the paper the other day that you had been shipped here, I telephoned immediately, but they said you were recuperating from surgery." Shizue nervously removed her short white cotton gloves. "Waiting is the worst part of being a woman. When you recover, will they send you back to China?"

"This leg will keep me out of action for good." He reached for a cigarette in the pocket of his robe. "I've been offered a rather important post in the Ministry of Communications once I'm up and around, but I haven't decided as yet." The match trembled as he struck it. "War nerves. It'll pass in a few seconds."

"Here, let me." Appalled, Shizue took the matchbook from his violently trembling hands and managed to light the cigarette that quivered between his lips. "There must be something I can do to help. A glass of water?"

Paul shook his head. Circumstances had made him seem a hero. Major Ikeda's troops had found him lying beyond the ridge soon after he had dropped there unconscious. The soldier's rifle he had used as his crutch was still clutched in his hand. "Cut off from our main lines, Yoseido, Akira, journalist, fought bravely alongside the heroic Japanese dead, where he was found, twice wounded in the service of His Majesty the Emperor," the army citation had read. This undeserved commendation had boosted his career immeasurably. There was bitterness and irony in Paul's acceptance of the circumstances that had made him a hero of the ugly war. Everyone now treated him with respect, Paul thought. The pretty nurses found him attractive, and they pampered him. Other women now saw him differently. But his commendation had no effect on how Shizue saw him. She was only glad to have him home. Her large eyes still looked at him in the same way, watching over him with an outpouring of sisterly love. Paul knew he could never hope for more than this, but he also knew there could never be another woman for him. That painful truth had been revealed to him by one fantasy night of love in the arms of a Chinese peasant girl.

Shizue broke the silence between them. "Do you have these attacks often?"

"Now, Shizue, don't wrinkle your pretty face over me. No more war nerves." Paul held out steady hands as proof and half-laughed. "I'm eager to hear all about you," he said, turning the wheelchair to face the serene Pacific sky unmarred by the sulfuric clouds of war. The weary father confessor to Shizue's secret heart, he could only selflessly give to love. Dragging on the cigarette, he wiped moisture off his upper lip and listened while she spoke of Kimitake's disgrace and her father's courtship with seppuku.

"If you want my opinion, your father's incapable of living up to the demands he makes on others."

"You're wrong, Paul. If not for me he would have taken his own life," she said, hurt by his coldly stated reply. "I haven't seen Kimitake since he returned weeks ago. Father's been here with him all this time, while I was kept at home. Now I've been summoned to Nagasaki without a word of explanation. Yufugawo is waiting in a taxi. I should have gone directly to Father's office at the weaving mill, but I simply had to see you first."

"Maybe it has to do with your brother's punishment," Paul answered hoarsely. "Or perhaps Jiro objected to the wedding match, and you've been spared."

"Oh, how I've wished for that. But I don't see how Jiro could have spoken with his father. He's still on training maneuvers with his reserve unit. I tried telephoning, but he was in the field."

"I'm afraid you count too heavily on wishes, Shizue." As Paul spun the wheelchair around, he suddenly felt dizzy. Intense pain caused him to turn pale and robbed him of his voice. Shizue quickly rang for the nurse.

"I didn't want to speak of my problems." She held his hand and cradled his head against her breasts. "Paul, dearest Paul, I can't begin to imagine what you've suffered." Two nurses rushed in and ordered her to leave. Reluctantly, she stood up and let go of his hand. "I must go now."

"No, stay with me. I'm chilled to the bone, Shizue. Don't leave," Paul begged. "Don't let go of me."

"Can't I stay, just for a little while?" she implored the nurses.

"Sorry, but you must leave him to us."

"To us," the second nurse chimed in tersely.

Shizue kissed his fevered brow. "When will I see you again?"

Paul glanced up at her despondent, searching eyes but could not speak. Then Shizue vanished, and he surrendered to the cool bed linen, welcoming the jab of morphine.

His mother, he thought groggily, had once been numbed insensate by the same drug, which drained all his strength away, along with his pain. "Mother!" he cried out to her in his suffering, his hands groping for her healing touch. But a stranger's hands eased him back against the pillows, and Paul closed his eyes, drifting and alone as even China became a fading episode he might have only imagined.

A dynasty had begun on this gray factory street where Hosokawa-Napier, Limited's, old iron gates stood open once again. Shizue heard the sledgehammer roar pounding within the weathered brick walls. Machines throbbed more loudly still as she entered the mill's great cavern, where silk being woven into parachutes billowed out and down the long assembly lines of monstrous looms. They created an inferno. Not since her mother's death had she visited the oppressive mill.

The source of her wealth thundered inside the sturdy fortress walls she had been summoned to without explanation. As a child, mother and daughter would hold their ears while they ran along the passageway toward the vaultlike metal door, as she and Yufugawo did together now. Shizue remembered herself as a little girl unable to reach the bell button. Her mother had always lifted her up so that she could press it. Today Shizue hesitated a moment, then rang it, as Yufugawo regarded her woefully. Then an office clerk ushered them inside, quickly shutting the thick metal door. Suddenly there was silence.

Employees jumped up from their desks, bowing and asking if Shizue remembered them after all these years. She was quite taken by surprise to recall so vividly each man's beaming face. "Unno-*san*, you always gave me chocolates. And you, Azechi-*san*, would sit me on your knee telling wonderful fairy tales," she said, hugging the elderly office manager who had spoiled her most of all.

"True stories, young lady," he corrected her. "Tales of brave samurai. I'll inform the baron that you've arrived."

Surrounded by beaming faces from the past, Shizue saw herself in that innocent time of childhood. While she was being spoiled by the office workers, her mother would visit the baron's private office alone. Then his cheery voice over the intercom would call for her to join them, and she would hurry inside, where he always had some wonderful surprise awaiting her. It had been a loving time.

"Have my daughter come in alone," her father's voice now sounded over the intercom.

All at once the beaming faces grew old before her eyes, mirthless. Her father's voice had sounded so stern, Shizue thought, as she walked alone down the hall to the short flight of stairs that led to her father's private office on the floor above. Each step caused the old wooden stairs to groan. A young soldier appeared on the top landing.

"Kimitake?" she gasped in shock. "What have you done?"

"Father's doing. Officer's training academy to earn my commission and redeem my honor. I passed the requirements with flying colors," he boasted and grinned. "Who knows, there may be some hope for me yet."

Having just left Paul, she could not accept the finality of her brother's punishment. But there he stood in uniform, and Shizue shuddered as she embraced him. "How could Father do this to you? I begged him to show you love and understanding."

There was pain in Kimitake's handsome face as he let her go. "You've enjoyed all his love," he said softly. The door to his father's office stood open just behind him and he did not want to be overheard. "Maybe I've always failed to live up to Father's expectations because I needed his punishment. It's the only time he shows the least sign of caring for me. Maybe there's love in being punished." He spoke as if this revelation had just come to him. "There's always a moment when I glimpse something like love melting the ice in his eyes, but when I've reached out to take hold of that, he's always pushed me away. Except for this once, Shizue. I put him through hell, and it wasn't easy for him to give me another chance." There was a long, emotion-filled moment of silence. "When I swore I wouldn't fail him again, Father took me in his arms and wept."

Shizue clasped her brother's smooth, strong hand, thinking the war would not drag on forever. By the time he finished his military training, it might be over, and he would not be forced to serve. "I suppose there's nothing I can do but accept Father's will."

Tadashi called for her. "Shizue."

"You'd better go in," said Kimitake.

"Aren't you coming with me?"

"He wants to speak with you alone. We'll talk later. My train doesn't leave until after dinner." Kimitake gave her an affectionate hug, then walked away, down the groaning stairs.

The office seemed smaller than Shizue remembered it. Her father was seated at his desk silhouetted against a broad octagonal window, the leaded glass panes radiating outward from its center like a giant spiderweb. She started across the room anticipating his warm embrace, but she felt chilled by the expression on his face. He motioned for her to sit.

Although her father poured water from the decanter, he never drank from it. "I thought it best Kimitake spoke for himself," he said wearily. "Everything I decide is in the best interests of my children, and I'll say no more on the painful subject of his punishment. This has been a trying time for me, Shizue. Reason for much soul searching."

It hurt Shizue to look at him as he rose slowly from his desk. His haggard face expressed a paternal sentimentality, a longing for the past. She followed his gaze to the wall behind her, turning in the chair to see her mother's portrait hanging there. Sumie smiled benignly, one arm twined around the waist of her little girl.

"I can remember posing in the garden for what seemed hours on end," Shizue said, warmed by the memory.

"You were only four. A constant source of joy to us both." Smiling wistfully, he moved toward her and stretched out his hands, inviting her to rush into his embrace. "Sadly, one can't hold back time. There comes a day in every father's life when he must give up his children."

As he held her tightly, Shizue said, "*Ogisan*, how hard it must be for you to send Kimitake into the army. We've both outgrown childhood, but you'll always be our dear papa. Kimitake desperately wants to please you," she said, startled when he abruptly released her and stalked away.

Suddenly she felt isolated. "Are you having second thoughts about his punishment?" Even before asking this, she had a dreadful premonition something else was the cause of his unrest.

"Lord Mitsudara was taken to the hospital some days ago complaining of chest pains. It was diagnosed as a mild heart attack—a warning to slow down that threw quite a scare into him. He's getting on in years and after this"—Baron Hosokawa faced his daughter and uttered a heavy sigh—"well, I can understand the anxiety that prompted him to approach me on the terms of our marriage agreement."

Shizue took a faltering step forward. "Approached you to ask what, Father?" Instinctively her hands touched the *omamori* beneath her dress.

"Lord Mitsudara wants to spend what years may be left him experiencing the joys of his grandsons and heirs, secure in the knowledge that his bloodline will be continued," he told her quietly. Well aware she had not yet given up her dream of love, the baron smiled, his voice warm and understanding. "Shizue, I've watched you cling to Max's letters, fighting the painful process of letting him go, as if this marriage agreement didn't exist. Perhaps I should have forbidden you to correspond with him. Once Max knew you were pledged to Jiro, I'd counted on his resigning himself to it, rather than encouraging your false hopes." Baron Hosokawa shook his head sadly. "Now that you've graduated from school, the lord sees no reason to wait until you come of age next spring. It's his feeling you're mature enough to accept the responsibilities of a wife and mother. I hesitate giving my little girl away. But she's a young woman now, and so I've agreed to this early union. Max and his parents are obligated to attend, and the wedding will take place soon after they arrive. I've cabled America, advising them to book immediate transportation home."

"No, it can't be true." His words made Shizue reel. "Max doesn't know about the marriage pledge. I couldn't bring myself to tell him, Papa." The floor seemed to rock violently beneath her feet, and she reached up one hand to the rays of sunlight flooding through the window as if to anchor herself. "I kept this awful thing to myself—hoping today would never come," she confessed in a gasping voice. "I wanted Max spared the agony of living without hope."

"It grieves me to learn that you've used deceit, Shizue. Now I understand the meaning of this charm Max gave you. Did you think the gold chain you wear constantly escaped my notice?" Her father took the fluted chain between his fingers. "No, I chose to spare your feelings by saying nothing. Yufugawo told me his gift was merely a token of friendship. You were wrong to lead the boy on. Now he'll be shocked and hurt, but the harm you've done Max can't be undone," he said quietly, and let go of the chain.

Rather than admonish her further, he said sympathetically, "It wounds me to shatter your illusions. But the traditions of our ancestors must rule over my heart. If this makes me appear cruel in your eyes, bear in mind that I know no other way and I believe that time will prove me right. It's my firm belief you'll discover love and happiness with Jiro."

Where was her voice? Shizue wanted to scream, but no sound escaped her trembling lips. This could not be happening! she thought. But her father hovered over her, speaking in a relentlessly loving tone.

"Before the wedding, I'll grant you time alone with Max," he said. "Time enough in which to express your feelings. It's difficult for a young man in love to accept our ways even though he was raised to respect them. He'll challenge your obligations, Shizue, and only you can help him understand it's best for you both. Make your peace with Douglas's son. After all, you'll still be friends. One day he will also find happiness with someone of his own race. Someday your children will play together, and you'll thank me for the wisdom that spared you both so much grief."

Shizue burst into tears and fell into her father's arms. She had just lost her gamble, and now she could only weep helplessly against his shoulder while he stroked her hair, saying that she would always be his little girl. Her heart cried out to be set free, but she could only weep. He had no need to voice threats of what loss of face it would bring him if she failed to honor this agreement. Her deepest emotions were still those of his dutiful little girl. Loving him imprisoned her. In her mind's eye, she could see the *wakizashi* gripped in his bloodied hands. She suddenly felt on fire, engulfed in a fever of despair that made her shiver.

The intercom buzzed.

"Lord Mitsudara is on the telephone, Baron," the office manager said.

Tadashi looked at his daughter.

"Have him wait. Shizue, are you all right?"

Shizue did not answer. Wordlessly she drifted across her father's office like a sleepwalker. Time had been her hope, time in which Jiro would find his courage to save her from a fate worse than death. Now she was drained of all hope. Max's keepsake had failed her, wishes and prayers to the gods had failed her, and suddenly she was drained of all belief in *kami* presences guarding over her. The priest's incantation engraved on her talisman was meaningless, and no unseen powers existed to protect her against harm. To her eyes the office door seemed miles away. Dizzily she reached out for it, then felt herself falling into a well of darkness.

* * *

Some miles north of Tokyo, Jiro Mitsudara approached his father's waiting limousine. He was anxious to learn the reason for his father's unexpected visit to his army training camp. He had just been called away from war maneuvers and carried his kit bag. It was filled mostly with books, whose covers poked jagged edges in the canvas. Among them were notebooks of the poetry he had written to preserve his sanity. After his intoxicating taste of academic life, being forced back into the military straitjacket even for a short term of duty was an abrasive experience that only heightened his longing to become his own master. Now he faced his lord and father, who reclined in the limousine chewing on an unlit cigar.

Following Lord Mitsudara's mild heart attack, the doctors had forbidden him to smoke. Jiro had expected his father to be pale and somewhat weakened. Instead, the lord was irascible as ever. "You're looking remarkably well, Father."

"The strong constitution of our bloodline. Well, get in," he ordered gruffly. "Business calls me away. We'll talk en route to the airport. You're excused from training maneuvers. Yamaguchi has already put your belongings in the trunk. Drive on," he told the chauffeur, who bowed and closed the door.

"Might I ask what occasions this unexpected reprieve?" Jiro started to light up a cigarette, but his father slapped it from his hand.

"Don't smoke in my presence!" Scowling, he regarded Jiro's buffed fingernails. "Your spotless appearance doesn't speak well for a soldier just called in from the field."

Jiro swallowed hard. "I'm not required to crawl on the ground like a common trainee," he said, startled by the authority in his voice.

"Perhaps not," the lord allowed tartly, and consulted his wristwatch. "Drive faster, Yamaguchi," he barked through the gold-plated speaker tube, then slapped it back on the hook. "Doctors and their orders. They forbid a man everything. But one can't properly conduct business from a sickbed, and I feel fit enough to resume my duties. Production has fallen off during my absence, Jiro. A shortage of scrap metal from America—or so our plant managers claim. I've called a meeting and want you there at my side to see how these affairs are handled. It's time you began to show an interest in more than your studies at the university. You'll marry Shizue next month. Now that you'll be settling down as a husband, it's my wish that you set your mind to having children and learning to handle the reins of power."

Shocked speechless, Jiro pulled off his field cap and crushed it with sweaty hands. "But Shizue's not of age. She's only a child" was all he could manage to say. He recalled his grandmother's displeasure over Shizue's behavior at the garden party that had honored his graduation from the military academy. "I feel sure Grandmother would agree the girl's far too immature. Given another year . . ."

"Don't waste my time! Shizue is now a young woman. Your grandmother concurs with my decision that you wed the girl promptly and bless our household with heirs. Marriage and motherhood will wean her to maturity soon enough and provide the stabilizing influence you so sorely need."

His father's explosion was like another slap across the hand. Jiro nervously toyed with his platinum cigarette lighter, cringing under his father's icy glare. Although his thoughts were focused on the encouragement Shizue had given him to speak for himself, his voice failed him once again. "Has Shizue been told?"

"Yes. Tadashi announced our plans only this morning. I've spoken with him over the telephone and was assured that his daughter is prepared to meet her obligation."

"Excuse me, Father, but I don't welcome your decision," Jiro advanced meekly. Picturing Shizue's devastation, he wanted to be bold but was restrained by fear. "I'd counted on another year of bachelorhood—at least that to prepare myself for the duties of a husband. After all, I didn't have much opportunity for play while I was earning my army commission. I do wish you'd reconsider. Attending the university is one obligation I've enjoyed."

"Too much so!" The lord rolled the unlit cigar between his thumb and forefinger. "Ah, I've had enough of doctors and their orders. Give me your lighter."

"No." Jiro could not believe he had spoken that word. His father's eyes flashed. "Smoking is bad for your heart, Father," Jiro said with feigned concern.

The lord snatched the lighter from his hand. "I'll be the judge of what's best for me *and* for my son. Your obligations are a matter of honor. Personal preferences must take second place to the realities, Jiro. Our ancestors may have looked down their noses at handling money, but we live in a different world, and indulging your feelings ill suits the responsibilities you'll one day inherit." Angrily he flicked the lighter again and again until its wick caught fire.

Jiro realized that it was his father's weak heart that was plunging him into the slavery of siring heirs and attending dull business meetings. Suddenly, he found his voice. "Die with a cigar in your hand if you want," he said strongly, "but I will not marry Shizue." His father's mouth dropped open in astonishment. Jiro fell back, stunned by his moment of courage and incapable of saying more.

"What? Did I hear you object to my choice of a wife?" Lord Mitsudara lowered the cigar, racked by a choking cough that brought tears to his eyes. Then for a long moment he stared at his son incredulously. "Answer me!"

"Yes—I mean to say, no. It isn't Shizue I object to." Jiro folded his arms tightly across his waist and began to rock back and forth, something he had done as a boy when fearing his father's wrath.

"You try my patience, Jiro. If you have something on your mind, then speak out."

Jiro sat upright. Perhaps his meek effort at courage was doomed from the start, he thought, but he struggled to breathe fire into its dying ember. "I'm not capable of filling your shoes, Father. I'm not cut out to be a businessman. I'm not your firstborn son, only his survivor, and I can never take his place. You've always discouraged the best in me, but the world also has need of men dedicated to the spiritual aspects of life. The world can exist without the ugliness of your factories, but not without beauty."

His father laughed. "There is an ugly side to everything. If one looks closely one can always find flaws. The machinery in my factories possesses a beauty you'll soon learn to appreciate, Jiro. Your eyes are so dazzled by the superficial that you fail to see the true nature of things. As a Mitsudara, it's only natural you should have an appreciation for beauty. Yet you look in the mirror and see only a poet, while I can see beneath your weak exterior to our bloodline, which imbues you with more strength than you give yourself credit for." Breathing cigar smoke, he patted Jiro's thigh and laughed once more. "Today you've shown some spirit. But I'll hear no more foolishness about shirking your duties," he warned. "As a husband, you'll have no time to waste with that flighty university crowd who've kept your head in the clouds. I have high hopes for the children of your marriage with Shizue. Sire me a sturdy grandson. Ah, your brother was a lion cub who growled and pulled my hair. What a pity he died so young."

"Yes, a pity." Jiro also grieved the death of that firstborn son, but for quite selfish reasons.

The limousine sped along the outer perimeters of Jiro's military training grounds. Through the roadside trees, he could glimpse other young men being honed to kill the Chinese enemy, dark stick figures participating in the maneuvers from which his father had spared him. They charged the peaceful Japanese countryside with fixed bayonets. Next month Jiro's infantry reserve would be activated to face real bullets in China. A number of cadets who had graduated from the academy with him were already serving there as front-line officers.

Jiro was relieved that his sworn obligation to fight for his emperor was deferred at least for another year while he earned his degree. The press claimed Japan was winning this war. But he wondered how much longer the conflict might rage.

Sweat blackened the chest and shoulders of Jiro's tailormade khaki uniform. His father's eyes lingered over the young lieutenant, crediting him with the strong spine of a samurai. Handed his cigarette lighter, Jiro Mitsudara was invited to smoke if he wished, and the flame shot up trembling in his hands.

*   *   *

Shizue returned home to Kyushu, still weak from the fever that had consumed her over several days and nights. The doctors could not diagnose its cause, but Shizue knew it was a broken heart and felt a scar where her dreams had been torn away. There was not enough time for her to reach Max by letter. The Napiers had already sailed from America. Her tearstained letter begging Max's forgiveness and his understanding had been posted to Tokyo.

Night after sleepless night, she lay across her bed sobbing uncontrollably. She walked through the days of waiting in a numbing state of grief. O-nami and Yufugawo's attempts to console her only brought on more fits of weeping.

Shizue was dreading her reunion with Max. She had promised him the future, and he would fight to hold her to that now impossible promise. She could no longer bring herself to wear the *omamori*. Just touching the keepsake caused her unendurable sadness. Yet, time and again she was drawn to its resting place in the bamboo reed gift box. The fabulous bird Hōō's copper plumage seemed to glow more brightly from months of contact against her skin. Its delicately etched feathers and the copper cherry blossoms remained untarnished by some mysterious process of the artisan's skill. To look upon the charm's sparkling beauty, one might believe again in the power of wishes to come true, that the gods would somehow intervene and lovers would not be parted forever. But Shizue found no comfort in such wishful imaginings.

In her unbearable sorrow, she turned to Paul over the telephone. He was still confined to the Nagasaki army hospital, mending from yet another operation on his shattered leg. Hearing the pain in his voice while he offered her compassion only made Shizue feel guilty for demanding so much of him.

In her anguish, Shizue decided that someday Max must find love with another woman. Placing his happiness above all else was the supreme indication of her love; this alone would make her lot in life bearable. Every day she sat before the household *kami-dana*, petitioning the gods to heal Max's broken heart and grant her the strength to make her peace with losing him.

The first day of August was chosen by Lord Mitsudara's astrologer as a lucky date for the wedding. Gifts of clothing, fish, and seaweed were exchanged between her and Jiro. This custom of *yuino* made their betrothal final and binding. An elderly cousin of the lord's served in the customary role of middleman for the approaching nuptials. Shizue had no contact with the bridegroom except over the telephone. She might have hated Jiro if not for the emotion-choked confession of his weak effort to challenge his father's decision.

"We can't escape, Shizue. Any effort was doomed to failure," Jiro had told her in a tremulous voice.

Shizue had been left shaken by the knowledge that both of them lacked the courage to determine their own lives. But Jiro's loss was not so great as hers.

The father who had always loved and spoiled his daughter now observed her anguish. He cradled her head against his chest, yet revealed not the slightest glint of remorse. Believing himself in the right, he remained unyielding.

On the eve of Max's arrival home, Shizue was shocked out of her numbing grief by her reflection in the bedroom mirror. She pulled her hair back from her high cheekbones, thinking the thin, sorrow-ravaged face could not possibly be hers, thinking of the added pain it would cause Max if he saw her like this. Suddenly, she realized it was in her power to grant him so very much more than the total devastation of being confronted only with her anguish and her empty words.

She rushed to take the *omamori* from its box and fastened the antique gold chain around her neck. Now her hands slowly traced it as it fell between her breasts. She thought of Max's firm, masculine touch caressing her as she recalled their last carefree summer together.

Shizue threw out her arms and spun around the room. She could not give Max a lifetime together, but tomorrow she could give him a few precious hours—moments that must equal an eternity between them.

CHAPTER 26

From the air the Hosokawa meadowlands looked like a deep green sea of grassy waves parted by the concrete airstrip. It was the first time Max had seen that ugly scar, which defaced the eastern meadow within view of the castle rooftops. He watched O-nami mounted on horseback, riding out to greet him alone. Max's plane made a bumpy landing, taxiing past oil drums and gas pumps. The pilot cut its engines. Max was the only passenger, and he quickly opened the door and stepped off the plane.

"Ichiban!" O-nami rushed across the airstrip, his white cotton tunic flapping in the wind. As Max came toward him, O-nami regarded the strapping figure of a full-grown man. After rubbing his eyes he looked again and roared with laughter. "What a sight you are! *Okaerinasai!*"

Max was moved to tears as he recalled all the summers he had been welcomed home by O-nami's strong embrace. They hugged each other, then O-nami stood Max away, hands on Max's shoulders. Douglas's son no longer had to look up to him. O-nami squared off one flattened hand between their foreheads, then raised it to slap the topknot that still gave him the edge. They both laughed, but their laughter quickly died.

It was not a joyous occasion, and O-nami shook his head, his eyes growing moist as he said, "Much is changed since we last stood together, Ichiban. Shizue waits for you where the kerria bloom. She said you would know the place." Max nodded. "Your horse is over there," O-nami said, pointing to where he had left Mercury grazing just off the concrete runway.

Max's whistle brought the chestnut gelding he had raised from a spring foal cantering over, and he stroked its head, reminded of the night two years before when he had ridden the Hosokawa lands, storing up memories of his last summer with Shizue. Her choice of a meeting place came as a surprise. He was not dressed for riding. The midday sun blazed down from a clear sky, and he discarded his suit coat and unbuttoned his silk shirt to the waist.

"Tell me what it's been like for Shizue."

O-nami's chest sagged as he sighed despairingly. "No words can describe her suffering. Until this very morning she walked in a daze, with the look of the dying on her face. Your homecoming lifted her veil of sorrow. 'Time is precious,' Shizue told me. 'Do not keep Max to yourself for very long,' she made me promise. She was even smiling when she rode from the stables. She loves you, Ichiban," he said, resting both hands on Max's shoulders. "But Shizue cannot choose between you and her father. She must wed the lord's son. Two hearts must be broken, or the baron will suffer a grievous loss of face. Your eyes are fired with determination, but this obligation is not something a man can fight."

"Well, I didn't come here to surrender. Wish me luck." Smiling now, Max quickly mounted and spurred Mercury for the nearby woods. He was given hope. Shizue had experienced some drastic change of heart, which accounted for her uplifted spirits that morning. His thoughts swept back to Boston, where Baron Hosokawa had cabled the shocking news of her pledge to Jiro Mitsudara. Max's parents had been with him at the time. Revisiting the scene of their passionate courtship had drawn them closer, and it seemed their shaky marriage would survive.

Then the baron's wedding announcement reached across the ocean to strike at them through Max. On the voyage to Japan, Angela Napier had watched helplessly while Douglas attempted to console their son, reliving all the anguish of his own youthful loss. Max had not seen his father so stricken since the time of Natsu's death.

Their ship had docked only the night before, and Shizue's letter waiting for Max at home had read like a eulogy to the death of their dreams. Her words were like a page torn from the tragic love story of the past. Shizue had sent him to America with lies, and when he telephoned her from Tokyo that night, she had wept, barely able to speak through her tears. She could not be reached by his pleading words. Finally, he grew angry, shouting demands, warning her that he would not be responsible for his actions if she sacrificed herself to her father's honor.

"Oh, I'm so frightened and confused," Shizue had sobbed on the line. "I can't bear the anger in your voice. Now that you've come home, I can't bear the short distance between us. Tomorrow we'll be together again. The wedding is only a few days off, but we still have tomorrow, my darling."

Before Max could respond, she had broken the connection. He telephoned Kyushu again, but Shizue refused to come to the phone. Then Douglas took the receiver and attempted to reason with the baron; Angela had her say as well, but their efforts had been in vain. Max was touched to have both his parents rally around him, but he knew this was his fight, so he had traveled to Kyushu alone.

Once he held Shizue in his arms, the wedding would never take place, he told himself now, galloping Mercury through splintering shafts of sunlight that were suddenly extinguished beneath a dense overhang of branches. The horse carried him from the wood's velvet shadows into the sunlit explosion of tall bamboo, a forest of leafy stalks combed low by the mountain breezes.

Here the valley floor softly unfolded, twisting hill bent upon twisting hill. Max navigated the steep path sprinkled with moss-covered boulders, his ears keened to the faintly gushing sound of the waterfall. Where the path vanished in a lush orchard of flowering trees, Shizue had tied a length of gold ribbon to mark the way to the hidden place they had discovered that summer when their love was new. He remembered choosing that golden ribbon to adorn his gift, and now it streamed on the breeze with a message of renewed hope. Shizue wanted that keepsake to speak for her change of heart, he reasoned. Loving him had proved stronger than her sworn obligations. And yet he hesitated placing so much faith on a bit of ribbon. Shizue's state of mind the evening before caused him to feel uncertain. Steeling himself for a fight, he was determined to bring her to her senses in the single afternoon Baron Hosokawa had so confidently granted them.

Shizue had prepared herself for love, bathing in the crystal pool fed by water spilling down from the waterfall high among the rocks above her. There was a hushed atmosphere in this place sheltered from the world by an extravagance of foliage. A whispering breeze stirred the leaves of trees whose branches gentled the heat of the sun. That day the kerria had bloomed as if on command, yellow roses of rare beauty, whose intoxicating fragrance enveloped her as she gathered their petals in a basket. She took straw mats from her saddle and rolled them out on the ground, then showered them with rose petals.

Sensing Max's approach, Shizue quickly knelt beside the pool, decorating her hair with a garland of wildflowers. After bathing, she had put on a simple cotton *yukata*. Alerted by the sounds of snapping twigs, she looked up, facing the cathedrallike archway formed by two willowy trees and saw Max coming toward her.

Shizue loved the way the sunlight turned his hair to golden flax. As he rushed toward her, she remained kneeling before him, smiling. The grim determination on his face was not surprising, she thought. The night before, over the telephone, everything had been said, her final tears shed. Now, she wore her lover's *omamori* nestled between her breasts, which were exposed to Max as she bowed low. The straw mats perfumed with rose petals spoke for her heart's desire. Slowly, she glanced up to see the grimness lifting from his face. But his eyes showed pained confusion, and she desperately wanted them to shine only with love.

"Shizue. I want—"

"No, Max," she quickly said, "don't put words between us again. Just hold me and I'm yours for always."

Max knelt and cupped her exquisite face. Another empty year, another century spent apart. But they had returned to their hidden oasis, and she had prepared the ground for love. Surely there was no longer any reason to fight.

Max felt in the presence of an unfolding miracle. As he held Shizue close, nothing else mattered. Electrified by Shizue's touch, nothing existed beyond the reality of this serene world. Unquestioning, he kissed her smiling lips, her silken cheeks, her lustrous hair scented by the garland of summer wildflowers.

Her robe fell down around Shizue's shoulders, and Max kissed the stiffening nipples of her breasts while she ran her fingers through his hair. Both felt touched by magic.

Soon they were lost to sensation, innocent in their nakedness but unafraid, each searching touch bringing some fresh awakening leading them deeper into a glorious awareness. The place where the kerria bloomed became an Eden for young lovers. Joined together on their perfumed bed of yellow rose petals, Shizue and Max celebrated a ritual communion rooted in the beginnings of time.

Lovers flowed together as twin streams uniting. In one long and incandescent moment, they touched upon eternity. The most glorious experience of their existence left them shuddering, urgently holding on to each other, convinced they were the first humans on earth to experience this sublime ecstasy, until the last rippling shockwaves had spent themselves.

Then Shizue and Max nestled together quietly. The dark imminence of her marriage to Jiro was swept from consciousness. The ecstasy they shared created a sanctuary, a safe harbor isolated from a hostile world. Exhausted, bathed in a tingling afterglow, they both surrendered to sleep.

Shizue dreamed of an unending field of yellow roses, whose vines climbed the castle walls and wove their thorny tendrils across the tiered rooftops, sealing off every door, every window except one. The window of her bedroom stood open wide to the garden, framed by the soft yellow petals. The atmosphere was so heavy with their perfume, Shizue could hardly breathe.

Max embraced her protectively. The garden below them was a dense wilderness of roses, and she grew frightened at the sight of her father, wielding the long sword of a samurai, hacking the thorny vines that barred his entrance to the castle. Baron Hosokawa wore the armor of his ancestors, and the lead gray skirt of scales draping down from his horned helmet swayed while the thorny overgrowth resisted his mightiest blows. He shouted war cries and intensified his assault, swinging his long blade with such a force that it snapped in half. One razor-sharp length of blade twirled high in the air, and he fell back to shield his face against the falling steel, which struck sparks across the heavy armor of his breastplates. The helmet toppled from his head as he glared up at Shizue's bedroom window, helpless to enter the castle and part her from Max.

"It's no use, Papa," she called to him, laughing in her dream. "You can't fight the gods. Oh, please, give us your blessings."

"I seem to have no choice." Her father threw down his blunted sword, then shook his head and smiled. "How can I deny my little girl, when the gods have opened my eyes. Take your happiness, Shizue."

In her dream Shizue watched the day turn into night, the sky exploding with fireworks that showered yellow rosebuds over the garden where she stood, dressed as a bride, beside Max. Her father came toward her, blessing their union. Then his outstretched arms grew transparent, and his voice faded away as her eyelids fluttered open to the daylight.

Gray rain clouds were gathering in the real sky overhead. The wishful dream had left her vision blurred, but the dank breeze cleared it. Max lay beside her sleeping soundly, and his nakedness stirred her back to reality. How long had they lain there asleep together? How much precious time was left them? Shizue wondered. She was about to wake him but then stopped. She did not want to confront the grim reality of their fate.

Rose petals clung to her skin as she sat up, careful not to wake him. She felt so completely different. Gazing down at Max's nakedness, she thought him marvelously beautiful and trembled as though once more experiencing the ecstasy of holding part of him inside her. The sensations were still so fresh, so deeply etched within her being that she ached with happiness, while at the same time she was chilled by the realization that she would never again know such rapture. Having experienced the fulfillment their love could bring, to live with the memory of that day, seemed the cruelest stroke of all. Still, it would shine for them throughout all the dark, loveless years ahead, like a bright star in the heavens. The pain of being forever lost to each other might dim with time, leaving only the beauty they had known here to be remembered.

Max stirred lazily, and she covered her face. Oh, this joyous union was certain to mislead him, she thought. He might waken soon, and she had nothing more to give of herself but anguished words. Kneeling over Max, she was unable to tear herself away, grateful for his deep sleep, which allowed her a few precious moments of silent adoration. Her fingertips passed over his lean, muscular frame, inches short of waking him with her touch. How she burned to hold him close against her breasts. At that moment, she understood the suffering Natsu had endured.

Max was jarred from sleep by a hissing rain that drenched the straw mats, beading up on a single yellow rose that Shizue had left in her place. "Shizue!" he shouted, but his shout went unanswered. "Shizue!" he called again. How could she abandon him?

Max's only thought was to take chase. Racing from the sanctuary, he seized the reins of his horse. As he started to mount, he felt the stirrup's hard edge against his bare foot. Shocked, he realized he was naked, and he lowered himself to the ground. Suddenly, he saw Shizue's surrender not as a victory over tradition, but as a crushing defeat for their love. Her virginity had been a gift of farewell. She had given him the most precious thing she could, and yet even that bravely defiant act of love had not instilled her with courage enough to free herself from bondage.

Max stroked the gelding's rain-slicked coat, calming it before he returned to the sheltered oasis where rain was floating the bed of rose petals away, removing the traces of his one afternoon of love. Shizue had kept his words from coming between them, and now he realized nothing he might have said could have won him more than their shared moments of ecstasy. Then he saw the gold chain of the *omamori* twined around the stem of a single yellow rose. She had left it there while he slept peacefully, believing their happiness was secured. Shizue was lost to him. The keepsake was her way of saying good-bye.

Thorns pricked his fingers as he unwound the fluted links of antique gold, yellow as the petals of the wild rose. The rain clouds lifted slowly, and birds fluttered their dewy wings, taking to the air. He stared at the *omamori*'s mystical bird poised as if about to join the others in flight. Angrily he flung the charm to the ground, grinding it under his heel. A talisman against harm! A symbol of hope! What a fool he had been to place any faith in cold metal blessed by a priest.

All around him the kerria drooped their yellow heads, bowing under the weight of rainwater. Max bowed with them, heavy with tears. The beauty he had known here while in Shizue's arms was already passing into a cherished memory. Perhaps the gods had witnessed their communion, he thought, which had been like a silent exchange of vows wedding their souls for all eternity. A Japanese would take Shizue as his bride, but she would be his in name only.

Max bent for the *omamori*, plucking it from the wet earth and rubbing its surface clean. Shizue had worn his symbol of hope next to her skin for all those lonely months, and the *omamori* seemed to emit a warm glow. Fastening it around his neck, Max felt warmed, as if by the kiss of her soft lips. She must have intended him to wear it as a keepsake of their communion in this place where the kerria bloomed. He could not endure the thought of her belonging to another man. As he dressed, the *omamori* swung loosely on its gold chain, sparkling like a dying star somewhere far out in space.

Max retreated in defeat. Suddenly he felt angry with the vulnerable boy who had been deceived by Shizue's sweet surrender. He rode back along the same path, the solitude pressing in around him, his mount's loping gait echoing in this fertile valley, which had once been his home. He whipped his horse into a furious gallop through the tall meadow grasses to the spot where O-nami stood alone on the airstrip. He dismounted and stroked Mercury's head, wondering if they would ever ride those lands together again.

O-nami took Max by the shoulders. There was no need to speak. He and Yufugawo would attend the wedding in Tokyo, and so this was not good-bye. The two men walked together toward the plane.

Looking up, Max saw the castle. Slanting rays of sunlight struck the windows. Max could not see Shizue through the glare, but he strongly sensed her watching him. He pictured her looking out her bedroom window, a prisoner of her obligations, clutching a handkerchief as she wept.

Boarding the plane, he squinted back across the airstrip, thinking he had lost the battle but not the war. That decisive conflict was yet to be fought when Shizue stood before the Shinto priests with Jiro Mitsudara at her side.

As his plane climbed away through the clouds, he decided to honor his obligations and attend the wedding. He looked down on an unbroken floor of gray clouds. Kyushu was shuttering her windows to the rain, he thought, her warm heart hidden from the sunshine beneath that gray umbrella of clouds.

Max drifted with the sensation of flight, until Nagasaki came into view below. Getting up, he entered the cockpit. "How long will it take you to refuel here?" he asked the pilot.

"Maybe one hour, Napier-*san*."

Lacy white clouds skimmed the Urakami Hills, where Paul was convalescing at the military hospital. The Japanese press had made him a heroic figure. Max knew that his brother had dipped his pen into the bloody crucible of war to advance his own ambitions, but he could not judge him for seizing his moment of glory. One afternoon in Shizue's arms had altered his own view of the world. He could not begin to imagine what one year of war in China had done to his brother.

His plane was landing in Nagasaki as if by some grand design, leading him to renew his brotherly bonds with Paul.

While the plane was being refueled, Max took a taxi to the military hospital. An orderly escorted him to Akira Yoseido's room. Max hesitated outside the closed door. He had ambivalent feelings about visiting Paul while so overwhelmed by emotions that were perhaps better left unconfessed.

Paul did not hear Max enter. He was seated in his wheelchair reading the afternoon paper. Another correspondent had replaced him in China, and the gruesomeness of the man's poorly written story caused Paul to fling the paper across the room. Then he saw his half brother standing there. "Max!"

Instantly, tears welled up in both their eyes. Max rushed forward to embrace his brother, giving no thought to Paul's wounded shoulder. When Shizue had visited Paul, her arms had brought the same pleasure, which made it possible for him to endure the pain. Max's grasp was stronger, however, and Paul finally cried out.

"Sorry," Max said, releasing him. "I'm just so damn glad to see you again."

"You've given my morale a boost," Paul said with a smile. "This is a depressing place. A dull routine of needles and sponge baths. Well, I should be out of here before very long. Sit down."

He knew what had brought Max back to Japan. As his half brother settled down in a wooden chair, Paul watched his face grow dark. "You've been with Shizue. Do you want to talk about it?" he asked with difficulty.

Max nodded. He felt he should be asking Paul about his wounds, about China, but his brother appeared anxious to hear what he had to say. Max thanked God for Paul's safe return. "I need a moment to collect my thoughts," he said, then got up and walked to the window. It was beginning to rain. In the past he had always turned to his father, he thought, but today he had reached the crossroads of his manhood. Paul's eyes searched him out as if recognizing that fact, still the older brother whom Max looked up to. After taking a deep breath, he decided to unburden himself man to man.

Shizue's wedding day was suddenly upon her, and she numbly went through the motions of dressing all in white, the Japanese color of mourning. The bride's white traveling attire was symbolic of a ceremony that would usher Shizue from the house of her father. Yufugawo sniffled, fussing over her like a doting mother. Very soon Shizue was to leave the happy place of her childhood, and she felt chilled as Yufugawo placed on her head the large white bridal hat Sumie had worn. It was shaped like a boat whose bow extended away from her forehead, drawing a dark mask across Shizue's eyes. Yufugawo had coiffed Shizue's lustrous, raven hair into a swirling crown at the back of her head, where it poked through a small opening in the hat.

Symbolically, the hat was designed to conceal the bride's horns of jealousy over rivals for her groom. But there was no jealousy without love, Shizue thought. For now the white silk hat was unadorned. Before the ceremony it would be decorated with tiny brushes made of flax, and with red flowers, a color of importance. In accordance with tradition, the Shinto wedding would take place at the home of the groom's father. Arriving there, the bride would quickly change into a splendid bridal kimono provided by the groom.

Soon Shizue's fate would be sealed, and as she prepared to meet it, nothing could lift the grief she felt sweeping over her life.

"I have never seen you look more beautiful," said Yufugawo, standing back to dry her eyes. "My little Shizue, a bride," she sniffed, twisting her handkerchief as she fought back tears. "Today I am losing a daughter. But after all your weeping, it warms my heart to see the rosy blush returned to your cheeks."

"This isn't the blush of a happy bride." Shizue hugged the woman tightly. "Yufugawo, you can't know the depths of my despair." Though she had willed herself cold inside, her discipline failed to dim the outward glow of her secret communion with Max. In the days since then, she had floated on air, indulging her fantasies of escaping the reality of her wedding day.

She took a final turn around her bedroom, touching the friendly objects she must leave behind. Just then an elderly couple appeared at her door. Seeing them, Shizue felt a sinking sensation.

"Shizue. It is time for us to go," the husband announced in a croaking voice.

"Yes, time to go," his wife weakly echoed. Shizue's father was already in Tokyo, and Lord Mitsudara's private plane had brought the cousin who acted as the middleman for this arranged marriage. He and his wife were the bride's official escorts. They bowed stiffly. He had a parrot's beak of a nose; his wife wore the pinched face of a woman who had lived too long without love.

Shizue's face grew flushed. She leaned the back of one hand across her moist brow, feeling short of breath and faint. In a daze she was led away, past the vacant room Max had occupied all the summers of their lives, past her soldier-brother's vacated quarters, and the spacious bedchamber where her mother had died so very long ago. She paused there beside Yufugawo, looking in at Sumie's ebony vanity chest, the combs and brushes, the pillows her mother once had knelt on when grooming herself before the oval mirror that her husband still kept draped with a white shroud. As a little girl Shizue had thought her mother's reflection was preserved under this cloth. She recalled sneaking inside to lift it from the mirror and how disappointed she had been to see only a sad-faced child weeping for her mother. Had Sumie lived, Shizue thought, she might have intervened to spare her daughter.

One last time Shizue entered the bedchamber to uncover the shrouded mirror as she had years before. "Mother?" she gasped, shocked to see her mother's reflection. But it was her own face. She had grown into her mother's image and wore her bridal hat. Shizue imagined Sumie kneeling on those pillows for the very first time as the baron's wife, preparing to give herself to love.

"We have no time to waste," said the lord's cousin, impatiently snapping open the lid of his pocket watch. "Hurry, or our plane won't arrive on schedule."

With trembling hands Shizue lowered the cloth across her reflection. At that moment she wished the gods would strike her dead. Yes, her death would be easier for Max to bear than losing her to Jiro. Slowly Shizue resumed her march through the familiar corridors. How she hated the envoys from the Mitsudara household, whose presence would not let her forget that beastly mansion filled with ticking clocks. She could almost hear them all chiming the hours of her slavery. In that house she would grow old and sexless like these two bent-shouldered vultures attired in black silk kimonos, so afraid of the lord's wrath if his wedding schedule was not met to the second.

The Hosokawa servants had grouped together to wish Shizue good fortune. Brooms lined the wall behind their bowing figures. The castle would be swept clean once she set foot outside its open doors, where bonfires were being lit. Those were ceremonies symbolic of the ancient purification rites, which followed after the removal of the dead. Somehow she found the strength to bid each servant good-bye, then stepped into the bright sunshine, taking hold of Yufugawo's hand for reassurance. Shizue was experiencing a death of sorts: she was dressed in the color of mourning to signify that she would die to her own family, that she would be bound to her husband's household until death freed her to leave it as a corpse. The castle doors remained open, but the way back was sealed off in dusty clouds caused by the servants' swishing brooms.

Shizue hesitated, feeling faint.

"Are you all right?" the old woman asked, coming forward to take Shizue's arm.

"I'm fine," Shizue assured the elderly couple, rejecting their possessive touch. Even so, they grasped both her arms, forcing Yufugawo to step back, and pushed Shizue forward along the path, worrying over the time already lost, whining at each other over the unpredictable nature of the weather between Kyushu and Tokyo. Shizue felt manacled between the couple. She was being torn away from all she held dear—even Yufugawo, who hurried behind them.

Ordinarily, the bride was escorted to her new home at nightfall. But due to the distance between Kyushu and Tokyo, Shizue was being uprooted in the merciless light of day. There was no mountain breeze to fan the stagnant air. The bonfires crackled loudly, and she smelled her ancestral lands burning in the smoke of their black minarets.

Shizue struggled to think only of her glorious afternoon of love, but the rosy glow of its ecstasy had drained from her cheeks, and they were cold now. Suddenly, she felt a sharp pain in her chest. "Oh, please, let me go," she pleaded, too dizzy and weak to break the couple's grip on her arms.

Yufugawo rushed to her defense, crying, "Stand away from the poor child and let her breathe! Have you no sense?" She pushed the lord's cousins aside, and they glared at her, regarding her as a servant who had forgotten her place. "There, my baby. I will protect you from these strangers," she said, fanning Shizue's pale face. "You will sit with me on the airplane, and I will not leave your side again until you stand before the priests for *san-san ku-do*."

"Keep to your place, meddling woman," the lord's cousin snarled. "We are in charge here."

"*Hai*, whatever you have been to Shizue is in the past," his wife pointed out. "She now belongs to us."

*   *   *

Dressed in the traditional kimonos called for by his gold-embossed wedding invitation, the Napiers arrived at Lord Mitsudara's house. It was a stifling hot evening in Tokyo, and though the servants had removed the glass doors opening to the garden, there was no relief from the closeness. The wedding guests solemnly filed inside a sprawling room in which the wedding would take place. It was heavy with the scent of flower arrangements.

Angela Napier twisted the diamond rings on her wedding finger round and round. Douglas pressed his son's arm while Max, who was wearing the *omamori* next to his heart, silently prayed that Shizue would refuse to marry Jiro at the last moment. After they had consummated their love, he could not imagine Shizue throwing it all away.

When Max had visited Paul at the military hospital two days earlier, he had told his brother about Shizue's sweet surrender, unaware of the envy, pain, and sadness Paul felt at hearing Max's confession. Paul had not supported Max's belief that if he attended the wedding, Shizue's resolve to see it through would crumble.

Max still clung to hope. As she sat at the front of the room, near the Shinto priests who were officiating at the ceremony, she was beyond the reach of his words, but he knew she was acutely aware of his eyes watching her from the hushed congregation of guests gathered around the marriage altar.

The bride and groom were seated in meditative poses, purifying their minds and hearts to petition the favor of the gods. Max had only seen Jiro Mitsudara once before, the day he had glimpsed him seated with Shizue in his father's limousine as they entered the gates to this very house. Tonight the lord's son looked like a handsome prince in a black silk kimono stamped in five places with the Mitsudara crest. Underneath the kimono he was wearing the broad black-and-white-striped divided skirt worn on ceremonial occasions.

All at once Jiro's soft dark eyes broke from meditation to single out Max. They stared at each other. Max had never felt hatred until that moment. This weak young nobleman held the power to spare Baron Hosokawa's honor by objecting to the match, Max thought. Jiro had given Shizue reason to hope, reason to keep their marriage pledge a secret. Her letter waiting for Max on his return to Japan had mentioned Jiro's weak attempt to spare them both. Now the bridegroom looked away.

The head priest's incantations brought Shizue and Jiro slowly to their feet. Max grew taut bearing witness to the ancient rites, his eyes riveted on Shizue, who stood under a glaring canopy of electric lights. He knew her tortured thoughts. Every fiber of Max's body was primed for some sign that she was weakening under the strain and would be shocked to her senses. But each moment of the priest's incantations drew her farther away from his arms.

Shizue inclined her head submissively, her downcast eyes fixed and unseeing, shadowed by her large bridal hat. Her pale hands were limply joined together below the pleats of her embroidered obi, and she seemed weighed down by the gold threading through the silk of her bridal kimono. The bright red tassel of a small knife hung from the silk folds crossing her breasts. This knife was to be used in seppuku if Shizue dishonored her husband. It was customary for the bride to wear this symbol of Bushido, and Max could feel the awful force that the red tassel exerted on Shizue as it swayed with the quickness of her breathing. The sheathed blade was tucked beneath the silk folds in the same spot where she had once worn his *omamori* as a symbol of hope, and that observation inflamed Max.

He wet his lips, thinking the battle was not as yet lost. In the Shinto ceremony no vows would be spoken, no rings would be exchanged. The bride and groom would sip rice wine from three cups of different sizes, each touching their lips to them nine times as a symbolic offering to the *kami* in the Shinto wedding pledge of *san-san ku-do*. Only then would their marriage bond be sealed for all time.

Shizue unfolded her pale hands and reached out for the cup that the priest handed her. As a guest in her husband's house, the bride drank first, and Max felt his muscles coiling like steel strings. At any moment he expected her to cry out no! But she lifted the first cup unsteadily, touching it to her lips the required three times. When she passed it to the groom, he barely touched the rim with his lips, as if his duty were a formality he wished to be done with.

Jiro perspired, and his eyelids blinked nervously as he waited for the second cup to be passed from Shizue's trembling lips to his. It was not customary to drink the wine, but this time Jiro drained the cup dry. Shizue appeared on the verge of cracking under the strain. As she took hold of the third and last cup, her body swayed. Brides were expected to be nervous, and the head priest leaned forward, whispering encouragement while the cup remained inches short of touching her lips.

Jiro anxiously clenched the fingers of one hand around a small white pom-pom looped with braided ropes of white silk. He seemed about to tear off this symbol of his manhood that decorated his chest. And then, her hands shaking, Shizue sealed their marriage vows by drinking from the cup. She passed the third cup to Jiro, then jerked away her hands as if they were burned. Max could swear he heard her whimpering like a small child.

The wedding guests all clapped their hands. Suddenly the room grew loud with overlapping voices. A beaming Lord Mitsudara shook hands with the bride's father. Baron Hosokawa had just given away his most precious possession, and tears hung at the corners of his eyes as he searched for Max across the sea of smiling faces.

Tadashi Hosokawa had been like a second father to Max during the summers of his parents' travels abroad, but he shivered at this samurai's look of sympathy. The warm feelings of his boyhood had been snuffed out by the cold wind of Japanese tradition. Max damned him with an icy glare.

Servants were moving through the garden now, lighting colorful silk lanterns with flaming tapers, while more servants circulated among the guests balancing trays of chilled French champagne. The guests lit cigarettes and cigars, fogging the air with smoke. And in the middle of it all, Shizue posed beside her new husband, circled by well-wishers: the arrogant elders of the Mitsudara household mingling with the bride's family and that of Japan's elite. Max suffered their raucous laughter and felt sick with hate. He watched Shizue for some sign that would jolt him awake from his nightmare. Bodies pressed in around him as champagne glasses were lifted high to toast the newlyweds with cries of *banzai*!

An opening cleared in the expanse of milling people, and at last Shizue's gaze sought Max out, her eyes filled with pain. She searched his face for a spark of forgiveness. She belonged to Jiro now.

Even in her despair she was radiant. Max thought of all they would never share together and felt an awesome gulf open between them as he punished Shizue with empty eyes. In the most wrenching moment of his life, he turned his back on her gorgeous face, mortally wounded by the pity for him he saw there. He shoved through the noisy tide of Japanese, who were all dressed as he was in the traditional silk kimono. He felt smothered by the touch of Hosokawa silk. He cursed the symbol of his wealth, cursed the Napier generations bound by those slender threads and a covenant that had inflicted too much pain for him ever to be the same again. He walked faster, wanting to be alone beyond all sight and sound of the world. Shizue was dead to him now, and he could only mourn the finality of his loss.

"Thank God, it's over," Angela said, pressing a lace handkerchief to her throat. "I felt about to suffocate. Why we came all this distance just to bear witness to this awful event, I'll never know. Really, Douglas, it would have been easier on Max if we'd simply cabled our regrets. Just look at him, rushing off alone. I'm so afraid of what he might do in such a state of mind." She waved off a servant's tray. "I'm in need of something stronger than champagne. Bring me a brandy. Make that a double with lots of ice. Oh, this awful heat. If only it would rain."

"Weddings are trying events," Douglas said, watching their son walk away, down the long corridor of ticking antique clocks.

Angela smoothed her auburn hair, which she had swept up in the Japanese fashion to complement her stunning kimono. The work of many seamstresses, it had been a gift to her from Shizue's mother, and she had worn it at festivals in the gardens in Kyushu. Remembrances of those times saddened her. "Now that we've met our obligation, there's no reason to stay in Japan. There's nothing here for Max but memories. We should take him far away. Perhaps a cruise of the Greek isles. Why not cable our friends abroad? Niki and Jean-Claude's yacht is anchored at Nice." The Henris were such fun to be with, she thought, picturing their charming town house, where she and Douglas had been entertained on holidays in Paris. "Their daughter is quite lovely," Angela continued. "Just Max's age. We mustn't let him go under in this dismal place."

"It isn't the sort of thing a man can run away from." Douglas tenderly reached out to touch his wife's cheek. "You mean well, I know. But we can't do more than back off and respect Max's need for privacy. He's no longer a boy, Angela; we can't make decisions for him. Considering all that's happened, I don't think he'll return to Harvard in the fall. He'd face too much loneliness there. But whatever Max decides, we've got to back him up. He has to work this out in his own time and in his own way."

"You're perfectly right, darling. The choices must be his."

Angela clasped his hand and smiled. His gentleness brought a lump to her throat. Perhaps the wedding had rekindled her husband's memories of Natsu, but she had stood by him without complaint, heeding Inge Karlstadt's advice that her patience would be rewarded. Tonight she felt the promise of that in Douglas's gentle caress. "In a cruel way, this has set Max free," she said. "The dynasty that's controlled our lives no longer has any hold on our son, darling. I'll support his decisions in every way I can. Perhaps he'll be happier building a life on his own terms."

Douglas sipped from his champagne glass. That morning he had visited Natsu's grave to find it altered by time, the earth carpeted with grass and flowering plants, and shaded by the saplings he had instructed the cemetery gardener to plant one year ago. While kneeling there, he had felt some release from his guilt. But the wedding had made him realize that the past would always carry a sting. His attention shifted to Shizue, besieged by a flowing stream of guests. He was amazed by her stamina. Of course, the poise she maintained was an act of love for her father; hysteria would cause the baron loss of face. Douglas grew angry with his friend for demanding such a personal sacrifice.

Baron Hosokawa's honor had been preserved, Douglas thought bitterly. He himself was honor-bound to fulfill his business obligations, and so their dynasty had not fallen. But that night his son had felt the hard lash of Tadashi's blind worship of tradition. His friend must have known that he could not wound Max without also wounding his father. So far as Douglas was concerned, it was a premeditated blow, which destroyed the mutual respect between men of East and West. A mortal blow to their friendship.

Tadashi motioned with his arm for the Napiers to join him beside the newlyweds.

"Let's go home, Angela," Douglas told his wife angrily. "Damned if

I'll live and let live, after what Tadashi's done. Damned if I'll march over there to offer congratulations, just for the sake of appearances."

Angela rose to the occasion. "Douglas, please set your personal feelings aside and think of Shizue. We mustn't abandon the girl just when she needs friends around her most."

Watching his wife stride off with a smile painted on her face, Douglas felt proud of her for following the dictates of her heart. He watched her hug Shizue and saw that both Angela and the girl were in tears.

Moved by his deep affection for Shizue, he crossed the room and reached out to her. She trembled when he brought her close. He whispered, "Whatever comes of this, never forget that you have friends. Turn to us if . . ." He did not finish the thought. Shizue's marriage could not be dissolved on any grounds.

The groom tensely jerked a bow, and Douglas silently returned it, wincing as Angela wished the newlyweds good luck for them both.

"You look rather faint, Shizue," Lady Mitsudara observed after the Napiers had stood aside. Her fluttering fan caused particles of white face powder to float around her austere face like a cloud. "A wife's first duty is a healthy constitution. You should take a bowl of herb soup before retiring, to ward off the approach of any illness."

"Only a new bride's faintness of heart and the heat, Mother." Lord Mitsudara laughed and wagged the cigar he enjoyed despite his doctor's warnings. "It's time they were escorted to the bridal chamber, Cousins."

Following a day and night of trial, Shizue's worst ordeal was yet to come. The parrot-beaked cousin bowed with his pinch-faced wife and motioned the newlyweds to follow them. Only that morning they had torn Shizue away from home, and now it was time for the middleman to escort her to the bridal chamber. Shizue began the slow march with Jiro, staring at the faces of those she loved: Max's parents, the ever-tearful Yufugawo, O-nami, who looked distraught as she passed, and Kimitake, who tugged at the high collar of his uniform, fighting back tears. They all grieved for her, while the father who had forced his will upon her stared wistfully into space as if remembering his own wedding night. He had given his son to the army, Shizue thought, and his daughter to his lord. Before sealing the marriage vow, Shizue had wanted to defy him. Now she could only pity him, a man blinded by tradition, who would be left alone with his honor to wander through the castle's vacant rooms. Set free of his domination over her life but forever made a slave to tradition, Shizue followed her elderly jailers, haunted by the remembrance of Max's eyes emptied of love.

The furnishings of the bridal chamber were traditional Japanese. No expense had been spared to create an ambience of understated luxury. Flower arrangements and jasmine incense delicately scented the air. Immediately on entering with the cousins, Jiro was handed a wine cup. The Shinto pledge of *san-san ku-do* was repeated. Shizue was no longer a guest in her husband's house, and this time Jiro drank first as her lord and master.

When the doors were slid shut by the bowing cousins, Shizue felt a stifling sense of entrapment. Although she had willed herself into a state of numbness, she could not bear it if Jiro imposed his husbandly rights on her. But they were man and wife; nothing she might say or do could alter that fact. What happened between them that night would determine their lifetime together, and she faced Jiro, resigned to making the best of things.

He smiled and took a cigarette from his platinum case. "I had prepared something in the nature of a speech, but"—he laughed nervously, tapping the cigarette on the lid—"now it seems so studiously cut-and-dried. To be perfectly honest, I'm rather afraid of you. Surprised?"

"Shocked," she answered after a moment.

"After all, you aren't one of those docile cows Father might have chosen to bear him heirs." Jiro lit up. "Look, why not take that boxy wedding hat off your pretty head and get comfortable? Then we'll sit and talk like friends. We are still friends?"

Shizue answered with a nod, and he appeared relieved. While she removed her bridal hat and the tortoiseshell combs that held her hairdo in place, Jiro wearily dropped to a seat on one of the twin *futons* and patted the downy bedding at the foot of the other. She felt unthreatened by their intimacy as he relaxed back contentedly with his cigarette. Sitting, she fluffed out her shoulder-length hair and enjoyed a rare moment of peace. There was safety in words, but for now she cherished the silence. Finally, she felt able to breathe again.

"Shizue, please don't be so sad." Jiro reached out and touched her, and Shizue jumped. "It's only me—Jiro, not your lord and master. I doubt any man could be that to you. What a sorry pair we are. The young husband sitting with his fearful child bride on their conjugal beds, knowing what's expected of them but not sure how to begin." The cigarette burned down to his fingers, and he put it out in an onyx ashtray. "Suddenly we're expected to behave as lovers in a marriage neither of us wanted." Jiro's eyes thoughtfully searched her out. "Poor Shizue. All your dreams of finding love have just gone up in smoke. Take heart. I won't add to the injury. I wouldn't hurt you for the world. Perhaps we'll never find love together, but in time we may find happiness as friends who respect each other's feelings. I won't destroy the fondness between us by forcing myself on you. I'm prepared to wait for your consent."

"Jiro." Reaching for his hand, Shizue began to cry. "Kind and gentle Jiro. You deserve so much more than I can ever give you. To you, love is only a word." She gripped his hand tightly. "You don't know the happiness I've lost. There are so many things you don't know." She quickly looked away, her feelings for Max left unspoken. Ahead lay the desolate years as Jiro's wife and the mother of his children. That night his kindness had spared her, but she could not withhold her sexual consent indefinitely. "It's been such a trial," she said, bravely smiling at him through her tears. "I suppose all brides cry on their wedding night. It's hard for a young girl to part with her dreams. Thank you for understanding that."

Jiro returned her smile, and she tenderly clasped both his hands. "Mr. and Mrs. Jiro Mitsudara. None of this seems real to me. I've always hated this dreary household. Cousins, aunts, your grandmother—old women with sour faces, watching my every move. And now that I'm your wife they'll be at me constantly, dictating everything I do. They'll chain me here until I conform and grow to look like one of them."

Jiro firmly shook his head. "I won't permit it. In this matter I do have some say. When school resumes in fall, we'll have a grand time." His eyes brightened, and there was a cheerfulness in his mellow baritone voice as he said, "My university friends are stimulating company. We'll attend parties, dances. You'll meet other young women with minds of their own. You won't be chained here, Shizue. I'll see to it that you're free to come and go as you please."

Free to go where? Shizue wondered. To endless parties with her husband's friends? To the fashionable Tokyo shops? To Hibiya Park, where she had sent Max away to America with promises she had failed to keep? And what of Max? What must it be like for him left alone, imagining her in Jiro's arms?

"What will become of us?" She quietly voiced her fears for them both, closing her eyes to the night and to the gentle husband, who sighed patiently.

"Take all the time you need, Shizue," he said. "Both of us are entitled to a period of adjustment. We're in charge of what takes place behind the closed doors of our bridal chamber. Let's make a pact. Friends, to become lovers when it suits them, and duty be damned."

"Yes, friends," Shizue agreed, joining hands with her grinning roommate. In one respect the gods had shown her kindness. The man she was forced to marry was both kind and sensitive. He had spared her for another night of sweet dreams of Max in the place where the kerria bloomed. Yawning, he placed a record on the phonograph. A romantic Chopin étude drifted through the speaker as he dragged his downy *futon* into an adjoining room to grant her privacy. The music brought tears to her eyes.

"Sweet dreams," said Jiro, closing the shoji between rooms.

Dreams of love awaited Shizue, but only a door of thin white paper panels stood between her and the husband she did not love. His shadow moving behind the paper was real, while Max was just the smoke of memories, drifting from the incense holders, perfuming the air to conjure remembrances of a bed showered with rose petals. That night, Shizue wept on the lonely pillows of her marriage bed.

CHAPTER 27

Sweet and gentle Jiro. Shizue turned up her coat collar to the brisk October night, while her husband purchased the late editions at a newsstall. The heat of the year had finally ended, and Japan was entering the autumn season of *ko-haru*, the Little Spring, with balmy days of clear blue skies. Soon the maple trees would "put on their damask robes," Jiro had told her in one of his poetic moods.

For almost two months they had lived as brother and sister before she at last consented to perform her wifely duties, moved by how Jiro suffered under pressure from Lord Mitsudara to give him heirs. He had entered her bed for the first time like a small boy cuddling against his mother. A boy masquerading as a man had spent himself prematurely and had been ashamed. But she could not have felt more even if he had proved a more able lover. She held herself inviolate, in communion with Max, while in some strange way extending to Jiro a tenderness bordering on love in their quiet moments before sleep came. Yes, life was bearable, she supposed. The days seemed to fly by. Social gatherings with Jiro's intellectual friends. Weekly luncheons with Paul, who had not received a single letter from his brother since Max had returned to Berlin with his parents, shortly after the wedding. It was as if the earth had swallowed him up, and she anguished over the state of mind that had driven him to Germany, when he abhorred it so.

"Jiro! Don't forget the debate Friday night," called a friend, as the newlyweds left the Tokyo apartment house where the newlyweds had attended a party.

"We're counting on your clever tongue to trounce those ultra-Nationalist boors!" another young man yelled from up the street. "An end to war! Peace with Chiang at any price!"

Jiro belonged to the university debating society and was among the growing number of students who opposed the war as immoral and unjust. That night he ignored his friends. "Here, Shizue, take these."

He kept one newspaper, then thrust the others into Shizue's gloved hands. "This horrible war has become an obsession," she said.

"Can't turn your back on it," he answered soberly, reading *Nippon Shimbun* under a streetlamp as his father's limousine braked to the curb. "Staggering casualties. It appears Hankow and Wuchang will fall to us before the month is out," he said. "But the Chinese are making us pay heavily for every advance, using what they call 'magnetic warfare.'" Ducking inside the limousine after Shizue, he flicked on the overhead light and continued. "Our advancing troops are attracted to a strategic point, then slaughtered in encirclements and flanking attacks. Chiang is trading space for time. Building up strength."

Jiro's brow creased as he turned to the back page and began reading the casualty lists. One finger smeared the ink as he traced the columns of names. "Tanaka, Togo, Lieutenant. Killed. . . ." Jiro's voice trailed off and his head jerked back. "He was in my graduating class at the military academy. You met him once—at the party given in my honor. Three of my classmates already slaughtered. How many others must fall before Japan comes to its senses? Neither side can hope to win this war."

Shizue shivered as she vaguely recalled the young cadet. "Your classmates' deaths. Is that why you've been having these nightmares?" He avoided her eyes. "It might help if you talked about them, Jiro. I've never seen you so on edge," she prodded, "so moody and withdrawn, even from your friends."

Jiro lifted the newspapers off her lap. "My friends are all talk," he stated hoarsely. "To them, China is a jigsaw puzzle shape on the map. Four hundred million people and their suffering, crawling across it like so many ants. I've lost my stomach for debating politics while men like Tanaka are losing their lives." Jiro retreated into silence.

Most of the members of the Mitsudara household were alseep when Shizue and Jiro arrived at the mansion. "The lord wishes to see you in his study," the servant informed them, taking their hats and coats.

Lord Mitsudara was signing documents placed on his desk by the owlish-looking aide. "Urgent business matters. I'm leaving Tokyo within the hour." He glanced up at his aide. "Is this the last of it?"

"*Hai, Kōshaku-sama.*"

Shizue nervously clasped her hands together. The lord peeled off his reading glasses, looking from her to Jiro as his aide left the room.

Shizue had great trouble hiding her intense dislike for the lord. "Will you be gone long?" she forced herself to ask politely.

"A week or more." Sighing, he placed his glasses beside a round silver tray of pill vials. "The doctors keep at me to slow down. But I've an empire to run. One day it will pass on to Jiro and your sons. Assuming that my son has done his duty, you should have been with child by now. Excuse my indelicacy, Shizue, but we must get at the cause of this unfortunate delay. I've scheduled an appointment for you with a specialist in these matters."

"Perhaps Jiro should be examined as well," she suggested curtly, and watched the lord's eyes bulge.

"If there is a fault, it lies with the woman," he blustered. "Always with the woman." Lord Mitsudara experienced some shortness of breath. "A succession of firstborn sons runs through our bloodline." He poured water from a decanter and held one hand across his heart as he drank. "A healthy young woman like you should have no difficulty conceiving Jiro's child. If there is some minor deficiency, I'm confident the specialist will set things right. Now, I have other matters to attend to."

Jiro wished his father a pleasant journey and was dismissed with a brusque wag of the lord's hand.

In the rooms that served as their private apartment, Shizue dressed for bed while Jiro paced, lighting cigarette after cigarette. She believed it was her destiny to bear his children in time, and she would have them to love. But she knew that it was war, not fathering a child, that preyed on Jiro's mind. His distress seemed to involve something more than the deaths of his classmates. His recurring nightmares kept him pacing to avoid sleep.

That night she tossed and turned, plagued by thoughts of Max. When she woke to the gray October dawn, Jiro's bed was empty. Its sheets and pillows were soaked with sweat, cold to her touch.

"Jiro?"

The sitting room doors stood open to the garden. Jiro sat shivering on a stone bench, barefooted, his pajama top soaked with perspiration. She rushed toward him but was halted by the terror in his eyes.

"It was so real. Please"—his voice shook, as did his hands, which reached out to take her around the waist—"don't ask me to explain. Just hold me and the nightmare will fade away."

Holding Jiro, Shizue felt chilled to the bone. At last he quieted, and she coaxed him inside the house.

That afternoon she met him as usual between classes. They picnicked on the university promenade, and Jiro smiled and apologized for acting like a frightened child. But a dark undercurrent of fear swelled across the week that followed. Each night Shizue watched Jiro fight sleep more desperately until he was overcome finally by exhaustion. Then his cries would jar her awake, and she would find him thrashing in a cold sweat. And always it was the same: the terror in his eyes when they snapped open, a terror so real that he pushed her away angrily, refusing to speak of it no matter how she implored him. And in the mornings he played the radio loudly, anxious for the latest war news while he searched the newspaper casualty lists for familiar names.

While Lord Mitsudara remained away on business, Shizue visited the specialist several times. Potted flowers lined the windowsills, and she stared outside at the yellowing leaves in Hibiya Park, her thoughts adrift as he pronounced her fit for motherhood. She was told to follow the guidelines in the pamphlet he handed her. The doctor questioned her look of fatigue. When she confessed to not sleeping well, he wrote her a prescription for sleeping pills.

It was windy when she left the doctor's office. Shizue turned her coat collar up, and observed how many soldiers there were in the streets. More of them every day. She had arranged to meet Paul at the Cherry Blossom Kissaten and was terribly disappointed not to find him there.

"He telephoned," Yoko said, leading her to the corner table. "An important meeting keeps him away."

Once Paul had avoided the tea shop and the woman who had been his mother's dearest friend. But his experience in China had drawn him back to the memories there, and Shizue met him for lunch each week at the shop. Yoko brought them tea and cakes, then sat quietly, her sad eyes roaming the shop; she was alone with the past. Shizue usually had little to say to Yoko, but the warm, homey atmosphere of the shop always helped calm her nerves. While Yoko poured them tea, she often spoke of Natsu, and Shizue felt a special bond with her at those moments.

That afternoon, seated under the painted silk lanterns, Shizue watched the tea maids dressed in their cherry blossom print kimonos and felt the warm presence of the mother Paul had shown her in a faded photograph taken long ago. Now she, too, had lost her bid for happiness, and she sat, near tears, at the very table where lovers of the past had once held hands.

Shizue was brought back to the present by the startled expression on Yoko's face. "Yoko, what's wrong?"

"That soldier," she gasped, rising partway off her chair. "He's so like my son. Oh, for a moment I thought it was Toru. No, my son was killed in China. But this young man is like his ghost."

The tall, rather fierce-looking soldier took a seat. He caught Shizue staring, and she abruptly turned to Yoko, who looked grief-stricken. "Paul has talked about how they grew up like brothers."

"*Hai, hai,*" she said, drawing a handkerchief from the pink folds of her obi. "Brothers, *hai.* I thank the gods Natsu's son was spared. But my only child was laid to rest beside his comrades. Their plain wooden coffins were draped with silk flags, which were taken up and folded while mothers stood around the open graves weeping. 'You should be proud. Your sons died heroes,' an officer said." As she rocked in the chair, her eyes filled with tears. She knew nothing of the atrocities committed by her son. Paul had never spoken of their encounter in China. Natsu's son had spared Yoko that as an act of kindness, which allowed the woman to remember only the goodness in Toru. "If I had other sons, I would not sacrifice them to a hero's death. I would hide them in the basement, Shizue. I would keep them safe until this storm passed over their lives." Yoko slowly pushed herself up from the chair. "I must see to it that this young soldier has my best cakes. The ones Toru used to love."

Shizue marveled at how Yoko gathered strength, lavishing affection on a soldier who resembled her dead son. It was a depressing visit, and Shizue left the tea shop feeling drained. If only Paul had been there to help cheer her up. She took a taxi home and absently thumbed through the doctor's pamphlet. When her taxi arrived, she saw a black sedan pulling away from the gates, an army sergeant at the wheel.

Jiro was standing just inside the open front door, his eyes wide with shock. He held both arms rigidly at his sides, as though he had been struck a blow. A document held together by a khaki spine was clenched in the fingers of one trembling hand, a manila envelope in the other.

Shizue quickly left the taxi and hurried to the door.

"It's happened," Jiro said in a choked whisper. "My commission has been activated. A critical shortage of trained officers. I'm under orders to report in ten days." He let the orders drop to the floor. "I knew it. I knew that I was living on borrowed time."

Terror entered his eyes. The same cold terror put there by his night-mares, Shizue observed, rendered speechless while Jiro turned and ran. She told herself there was some mistake, that the lord was too powerful for this to happen. Stooping, she picked up the orders, needing to read them with her own eyes before accepting what Jiro had said. Her hands shook. There was no mistake! Her husband's infantry regiment would sail for China in ten days. Folding his orders, Shizue moved down a corridor toward the sound of Jiro's voice.

"Tell the lord it's urgent. Yes, I'll hold." Seated in his father's study, Jiro nervously moved the telephone back and forth across the desk. "Father will use his influence," he told Shizue. "Yes, he must. The orders can be rescinded."

She dropped into a chair, stunned by this unexpected turn of events, and leaned forward expectantly as Jiro told his father what had happened. Lord Mitsudara's voice buzzed over the receiver, but Shizue could not hear what he was saying.

"Oh." Jiro's face collapsed, and he was silent, biting down hard on his lower lip. "Is there nothing you can do?" he questioned frantically. "I know you don't control the army—but your influential friends could have me reassigned to some noncombatant post. Adjutant to some general . . ." Jiro covered his eyes with one hand. "I see. Yes, Father, I quite understand the loss of face it must have caused you to request such a post." After cradling the receiver, Jiro remained hunched over the desk.

"Father's been pulling strings since General Hoshi alerted him this morning," Jiro said at last. "It's hit him hard. He's afraid I might be killed before providing him with heirs. He's done everything in his power to keep me from serving on the front lines, but the army won't budge, and I'm going to die, just like in my dream. The same dream over and over. Now I have only to close my eyes to see it all happening." He was breathing hard.

"First the sudden roar of artillery shells bursting all around us. The Chinese have led us into a trap, and we're scattered, crawling on our bellies with no place to take cover. We're caught inside a horseshoe sweep of hills. Machine guns nested in them are cutting men down as I shout an order to retreat. I crawl away, the earth shuddering beneath me, and suddenly I'm covered with blood—someone near me has been hit. His corpse stares up at me from a smoldering crater, and I'm covered with the stench of death."

Jiro's words came faster, his voice choked by the horror he brought to life. "All at once the shelling is well behind me. But a wave of Chinese infantry is on the march ahead. Somehow I've made it to a crevice in the rocks and I squeeze inside the safety of a narrow chamber. Room enough to hide until the battle ends. And then I see him. My executioner." Slowly he looked at Shizue, who was poised on the edge of her chair, speechless. "As real to me as you are now. A Chinese soldier stands on the rocks above. So close I could reach up and touch his boots with my hand. His back is to me, a rifle lowered in his hands as I unholster my revolver and take aim. But I can't pull the trigger. Even as he senses the danger and turns, I can't take his life. It's the face of a young boy—no malice in it, only terror. For a split-second he's too terrified to raise his rifle. It's this boy's life or mine, but I fall back against the jagged rocks paralyzed, the revolver aimed to kill but frozen in my hand. The boy takes aim with his rifle. It misfires and he clears the chamber quickly. I can't find the voice to scream as his rifle misfires again—jammed. Now he acts unthinkingly. He leaps down at me and thrusts the long steel of his bayonet up into my chest. I feel his breath on my face—and the convulsive pain as his bayonet is withdrawn. Then I drop away silently, fixed in the eyes of my executioner. While I lay dying, he unbuckles my ceremonial sword. A souvenir and proof of the kill. 'Coward. Why didn't you shoot?' he asks, a grin on his boyish face. That face—or one like it—is waiting for me in China."

While listening, Shizue had nervously creased the folded orders into a sharp edge with her fingernails. "It's a dream, Jiro. Only a horrible dream."

"No," he answered flatly, wiping the sweat from his forehead, "it's a window on my future. Read the casualty lists. Front-line infantry lieutenants are fair game, Shizue. The bravest may survive, but I'm a coward. I'll run under fire. I'll run straight into the arms of a Chinese soldier. My finger will freeze on the trigger. . . ."

Shizue's heart pounded in her ears. Jiro looked at her with staring eyes that pleaded for help. "We'll tell the army I'm expecting your child."

"Are you?"

"The doctor said I'm fit. We do have ten days."

"Children won't exempt me from duty. You know that."

She was grasping at straws. Jiro was so convinced he would be killed. The orders she held in her hands could make her a widow. His death would set her free—but how could she entertain such a ghastly thought, even for a moment?

Suddenly she stood and fled the room. Wishing Jiro had never told her his nightmare, she left the house and walked for hours. But Shizue found no escape among the uniforms, flags, and newspapers with their headlines that shouted war. She tried reaching Paul at the Ministry of Communications, but the operator there said he had been called away on official business and would be gone for several days.

When she returned home at nightfall, she noticed that a change had come over Jiro. Outwardly calm, smoking a cigarette, he sat renumbering the squares of a calendar with his pen. The cork board mounted near his desk had been swept clean, the notes pertaining to his studies dumped in the wastebasket.

"Your father telephoned. Word reached him via mine. He sounded strained." Jiro neatly ripped off the October calendar page and tacked it and his army orders on the cork board. "So much for day one."

She watched his fountain pen draw a wobbly X. Then its point jabbed the calendar square numbered ten, and a tear of black ink bled down from where the point had punctured the paper. "I brought sleeping pills. The doctor prescribed them for me, but—"

Jiro snatched the vial from her hand, shook out two pills, and swallowed them.

In the early morning hours, Shizue tossed on the ragged edge of a terrifying dream. She saw the Chinese soldier lunging with his bayonet— she was a helpless witness to Jiro's death as he silently dropped away just at her feet. The dream was still vivid when she woke. She looked over at Jiro. While he lay beside her in a drugged sleep, she had taken on his nightmare.

The day began as usual. Coming out of her shower, Shizue saw that the maids had left breakfast trays and the morning paper. Jiro was playing the radio loudly. Winding a towel around her wet hair, she felt pushed to the breaking point as Radio Tokyo vibrated through the room.

Abruptly, Jiro silenced the newscaster's voice. "I can't listen to more!" He bowed, like a rag doll over the radio. "If only I weren't such a coward."

"Wanting life doesn't make you a coward, Jiro."

"Perhaps you're right," he said, turning around. "I'm terrified of death. But do I want life desperately enough to find the courage not to report for duty?"

"Desertion?" she asked in a small voice.

Jiro wet his lips. "Since the orders came, I've thought of nothing else. Thousands of Japanese already killed. Hundreds of thousands wounded. Japan can't afford to wage this costly war much longer. Prison or the death penalty if I'm caught before it's ended. But I'd rather take my chances with a firing squad than face certain death in China."

He stood there, running both hands nervously through his hair. He was on the verge of tears. "I must be losing my mind even to consider such a thing. Where could I hide? How would I live? It wouldn't be safe to show my face on the streets, and no one would harbor a deserter. My only way out, but I can't take it without help. Even if I found the courage."

"I've courage enough for us both."

"What are you saying?"

As he came toward her, fragile and questioning, Shizue was possessed by a single thought. "I won't let you be killed in this senseless war." She recalled what Yoko had said just the other day, while mourning the loss of her son. "We'll find a safe place to hide until the storm passes."

"Drag you down into disgrace with me?"

"I'm your wife. It's my duty to stand by you." Jiro stared at her incredulously. "Stop thinking of me as only a woman," Shizue said. "Let me be your strength." She reached out for him. "We're not all alone. I know someone who will help us."

"Please," Jiro begged, covering his ears against hearing more, "I need time to think—time to decide. But time is running out." He began pacing, taut with indecision. Suddenly he stopped and faced her. "A hopeless cause if we don't begin planning for it now. Are you sure? Have you courage enough to sustain us both?"

He saw a flash of uncertainty as he searched her eyes, but she said, "Yes. Oh, trust me, Jiro," and embraced him tightly.

"Then it's decided."

As Jiro clung to her, Shizue felt strengthened in her resolve. Tradition had made Jiro her husband, and now she held his life in her hands. For the first time she was not utterly helpless to defy the forces of tradition. Jiro must not be claimed by this war. Paul would understand, she thought, all at once besieged by Jiro's questions. She lied, telling him that she had known Douglas Napier's illegitimate son since childhood. "It was a well-kept family secret," she said. "I'll go to Paul the instant he returns."

Jiro barely nodded. "We'll need money."

"I can pawn the jewelry mother left me, and there's your art collection."

She followed Jiro into the adjoining room, where he seated himself at the desk and listed their assets. He paused long enough to take down his orders from the cork board and deposit them in a drawer. The calendar page was left tacked there, nine days remaining until he was to report. Flight was his new obsession. The wheels had been set into motion. He sighed deeply as though a great weight had been lifted from his shoulders.

Paul leaned heavily on his cane, anxiously pacing the platform at Ueno Station. Every now and again he broke stride, one hand going down to massage the tendons of his bad leg. His nightmares of China were real, and his scarred leg, pieced together by the army surgeons, ached in the dampness as he waited with last-minute instructions for Jiro Mitsudara's escape. The Osaka-bound train was already taking on passengers as he saw Shizue hurrying through the crowd with her husband. Paul met them halfway.

"What kept you?"

"We had a devil of a time leaving the house," Jiro said breathlessly, dropping their luggage on the platform. "My father—"

"Lord Mitsudara suddenly argued against our plans to spend these last few days alone together in the country," Shizue interrupted.

Paul handed her an envelope. "Directions to your house. My bank draft to Osaka cleared this morning, and the rent's paid up for the year. Everything was arranged in your new names. From now on you're Mr. and Mrs. Yoshiro Mizutani. You'll arrive before daybreak, so there's little chance of being seen by the neighbors. Later on, if they ask questions about your husband, say he's a disabled veteran, too ill to leave the house. You'll find a key in the gate lamp. Use what time is left to stock up on food. It's Jiro they'll be searching for, but the authorities might circulate your description as well over the first few weeks, so it's best to keep off the streets."

"How will I know when it's safe to go out?"

"I'll keep you posted through the mail," Paul answered wearily.

"I'll never be able to repay you," said Jiro.

"Good luck." Paul shook Jiro's clammy hand, noting that his eyes were already those of a fugitive, darting everywhere as he quickly boarded with the luggage.

"There's still time to reconsider," Paul told Shizue.

"Dearest Paul"—her lips brushed across his cheek—"you mustn't be afraid for me. What I'm doing is right."

"Better get on the train."

"*Sayonara.*"

Paul managed a smile. She was ravishing even wiping tears from the corners of her eyes, he thought. Her voice was husky with emotion as she thanked him. Not so very long ago, she had stood on this same platform seeing him off to war. There was a slim possibility the war would end before their luck ran out, and no one could foretell what punishment Jiro might receive in its aftermath.

Shizue waved from their compartment window, her eyes fiery with determination. She had cast herself in the role of Jiro's savior, and Paul knew she would have acted without him had he refused to help. So he had bought them time, he thought. He would bring them money when the need arose. They were running from a nightmare, but he wondered if they might be exchanging that nightmare for a living hell.

God only knew how Max would react when he learned of this. As he limped away, Paul reflected on his unanswered letters to Germany. He had been hurt by his brother's silence. Life had scarred Max, and he had crawled inside a hole to lick his wounds. Well, Paul thought, this news would bring him out of hiding. But Max might figure out that Shizue had turned to him for help. Suddenly, Paul's mind churned with thoughts of his brother's returning home, demanding answers that could place them all in jeopardy.

There were a number of army officers aboard the second-class sleeper car. Jiro's posture was rigid as he sat, his hands clutching the leather briefcase in his lap. Shizue had not seen him pack it.

"Books," he told her shortly, "and a few things of value we might pawn." Jiro's hands tensed around the briefcase handle.

A young lieutenant negotiating the aisle was thrown against him as the car listed to one side. The soldier apologized. "Not your fault," Jiro said, avoiding the soldier's eyes. Then he turned to Shizue. "His face looked familiar," he whispered.

Shizue glanced back at the lieutenant, who was taking his seat. "You're mistaken. Please, Jiro, won't you try and relax. No one's looking for us yet." She pried the briefcase from his grip, surprised to find it so heavy. "Perhaps it would help if you tried reading."

Jiro's hand went down on hers before Shizue could open the clasp. "Reading won't help," he said, holding her hand firmly. "I keep thinking of Father—what the loss of face will do to him. Yours will be spared the shame. It's my dishonor, my disgrace, not yours. I'm the coward, and somehow I've got to learn to live with that." His gaze lowered on the briefcase. "Sleep is what I need. Did you bring the pills?"

"Yes, in my purse."

The only other passenger on the bus that Shizue and Jiro boarded near Osaka Central early the next morning was an old woman. She was carrying a package wrapped in newspapers and tied in string, and she toyed with the string, quietly talking to herself. Osaka was a sprawling metropolis of canals and bridges. Some of the bridges were quite beautiful, Shizue observed, stifling a yawn as Jiro pressed her arm.

The sleeping pills had left Jiro groggy, so when it was their stop, Shizue lightened Jiro's burden by carrying one suitcase. Their footsteps echoed hollowly in the gray dawn. Silver lightning illuminated the overcast sky, and the Japanese thunder god beat loudly on his ring of drums, but the rain never came. Industrial smokestacks rose behind block after block of wooden houses squatted low together.

Paul had said that their faces would be lost among Osaka's three million inhabitants, and he had probably been right, Shizue thought. But this working-class neighborhood was a shocking comedown from the luxury they had known.

"This can't be the right address," Shizue said when they stopped in front of a small, rundown row house. There was no mistake. It was the right street, and the house number Paul had given them was clearly visible on the gate of a high wooden fence. Shizue heaved a deep breath for courage and said, "It might not be so dreadful on the inside."

Jiro fumbled for the key that had been left in the gatepost. "Be quiet or you'll wake the neighbors," he whispered while he unlocked the door.

When the front door closed behind them, Shizue confronted an arrangement of tiny, squalid rooms. Kitchen, bath, bedrooms. The floorboards, carpeted in tatami nearly worn through in spots, groaned with their steps. The cheap furnishings were nicked and soiled, and panes were missing from the shoji between rooms. She saw how depressed Jiro was, but he said nothing. The back door opened onto a small yard overgrown with weeds. Beyond its fence was an alleyway facing houses exactly like theirs. A dog barked. A baby cried. The neighborhood was waking.

Faced with Jiro's depressing silence, Shizue put her back to the door and smiled bravely. "It's really not so bad," she said. "I'll brighten up the place. You'll see."

"We can't throw money away on decorations. I'll be safe here. That's all that matters."

Both were jarred by the ring of a neighbor's alarm clock. A woman's voice, then a man's, sounded through the thin walls between houses. "Don't prod me, woman. Go put the kettle on."

"These walls have ears," Jiro whispered, suddenly holding her close.

This oppressive place had tested their resolve, Shizue thought. Now there was no turning back. For better or worse, they were there to stay.

Aromas drifting in from the next-door neighbor's kitchen reminded Shizue that her first priority was to stock up on food. She went to a bedroom and unpacked the cheap, unstylish clothing Paul had selected for her. She was bred to the tender touch of silk and satins, but the dress she put on was of a coarse material, worn by women of lowly station. "Oh, no," she wailed when she saw the shabbily dressed woman in the mirror. She saw herself as plain, even ugly. Paul had said she must not draw attention to herself and that she should blend in with the crowd in this working-class neighborhood. But her vanity was not so easily set aside. Standing in front of the cracked bedroom mirror, she suffered a momentary loss of pride.

The house was suddenly shaken by a symphony of blasting factory whistles. It did no good to hold her ears. At last their screams died, and Shizue listened to the roar of voices outside—workers who sounded like an army on the march.

Jiro sat in the kitchen counting their money. He seemed oblivious to the roar and gave her appearance only a cursory glance. "How much will you need?" he asked.

A panic swept through her. What did food cost? She had never shopped for groceries before. How far was it to the marketplace, and what would she do if the neighbors saw her? She lifted twenty yen from the table. "This should do for the first trip."

"Don't forget cigarettes," he said, crumbling an empty pack as she put on the coat Paul had bought for her, "and the newspaper. I don't want to lose all contact with the outside world."

Shizue turned before he could see her tears. Everything had always been done for her by servants, but now she must learn how to cook and to clean. She could not help wishing that she were anywhere but in this clamoring city filled with strangers. Leaving by the alleyway gate, she never felt so alone.

"Ah, so, the new tenant."

"*Hai.*" Shizue's heart seemed to stop as she frantically searched her memory for her new name while a squat little woman set a garbage can on the ground. "I am Mrs. Mizutani." Shizue introduced herself and bowed.

"Mrs. Takada. How do you do?" The next-door neighbor bowed politely. "We did not hear you arrive."

"It was late in the night. My husband is still asleep."

"Tuesdays they collect the garbage." Mrs. Takada made a sour face and massaged her back with her stubby little hands. "A wonder we have any, with prices as they are. Are you going to the market?"

"Yes. It was so crowded in the street," Shizue explained nervously.

"I often take the alleyway. There is a shortcut."

The woman held Shizue there, giving directions to the market, warning her to avoid certain greengrocers' stalls. "In a new house there is much work. I should not have kept you here talking," she said. "Husbands are always hungriest when they awake. Have a good day."

Shizue thanked the woman for helping her, then quickly started away.

Other neighbors were setting out their garbage cans along the alley she had taken to avoid being seen. Keeping her head low, she fought the impulse to run past their curious faces. The street ahead teemed with bicycles. Shizue felt displaced and struggled to recall Mrs. Takada's directions to the marketplace. Her thin woolen coat let in the chill October wind, and she wished for the comforts of home. Saving Jiro would require more courage than she had thought.

CHAPTER 28

In Berlin a stern-faced portrait of Adolf Hitler peered over the ticket clerk's shoulder as Max angrily slapped his gloves against the counter. "My passage on the November tenth departure was confirmed. Everything is in order. Swastika stamps and all!"

"As I told you over the telephone, there has been an unfortunate mistake." The clerk lowered the railway ticket in his manicured hands. "There is nothing available on the Trans-Siberian route until the first of next year, Herr Napier. I can only apologize for the inconvenience."

"See here," Douglas Napier intervened. "Issuing that ticket constitutes a binding contract. Who's your superior?"

"I am the manager here." Clearing his throat, the man opened the cash drawer, took out an envelope, and extended it with a precise nod of his head. "Your refund, *meine Herren*. Of course, we will notify you in the event of a cancellation."

Douglas pushed through the street door behind his son. "Come on, let's have lunch. Fritz's is just around the corner. Things won't look so bleak over a good stein of beer."

Fritz's was an unpretentious restaurant tucked away on a cobblestone street near the fire-gutted remains of the Reichstag. A waiter served them dark Bavarian beer in huge, fancifully sculpted ceramic steins, and Max quietly drained his down to its foamy glass bottom. "I can't accept what Paul wrote me as the truth," he blurted out, fishing the letter from his pocket. It had arrived only that morning. Two thin pages of Japanese characters penned in dark blue ink. Earlier, Douglas had received a cable from the baron telling them that Shizue and Jiro had disappeared, but Paul's letter was the first to reach them with any explanation. "I had hoped my refusal to assist Shizue would dissuade her," Max read aloud. "She stands little chance of being prosecuted if they're found. Small consolation for what you must be going through, I know. But, Max, there is nothing either of us can do but wait." He looked up at Douglas, seated across from him. "Paul's right, dammit. Even if he is lying about refusing to help

Shizue and Jiro and I forced the truth out of him, I still couldn't do anything."

"I'm afraid so," Douglas said. "Shizue's taken this all on herself. Unless you're prepared to risk exposing Jiro and implicating Paul in his desertion, you'll just have to ride it out."

"I suppose I should be grateful for Paul's letter. But knowing what prompted Shizue's actions doesn't make it any easier, Dad. Why couldn't she leave well enough alone?" Max tore the letter into pieces and left them scattered across the tablecloth. He stood up. "I'm not hungry, Dad. If you don't mind, I'd rather be alone." Before Douglas could say a word, Max was heading toward the restaurant's revolving door.

Douglas rose, about to follow his son, then sat down again, deciding to stay and dine alone. He had not questioned Max's motives for returning to Germany, but he was aware that Max had spent most of his time since their arrival in Berlin alone, grieving over his loss and oblivious to everything around him. Then Tadashi's succinct cable, announcing the disappearance of the newlyweds, followed by this letter from Paul had stirred him back to life. Douglas glanced down at its torn pieces, which Max had scattered on the tablecloth, and lost his appetite. These brotherly ties offered a painful link to Natsu's son and the guilt-ridden past.

Berlin was a grim study in black and white. The pasty-white faces of the pedestrians moved against the dark stone fronts of its buildings. Max wandered the city aimlessly, his thoughts at odds with his emotions. Here and there a burst of crimson seemed to jump out from the stone, as the Nazi flags with their black swastikas writhed snakelike in the wintry breeze.

"Max!"

Someone's hand came down on his shoulder, and Max turned. "Fleischer."

"Sorry to have startled you. I called several times." The Karlstadts' uniformed chauffeur grinned broadly. "An anniversary gift for the happy couple," he said, tapping the parcel nestled under one large arm. "Ja, tonight there will be a feast and champagne in the kitchen. Frau Karlstadt always sees to that."

"I'd forgotten their anniversary party was tonight." Fleischer was like one of the family, and Max walked beside him, thinking affectionately of the Karlstadts.

Suddenly Fleischer pulled Max back from the curb. Hitler Youth, carrying paste pots, brushes, and rolls of paper, climbed down from a truck that had just screeched to a stop. At least a dozen boys dressed in tan uniforms hurried along the street, slapping up notices.

Max approached one swastika-decorated billboard, puzzled by what he read. "Who's vom Rath?"

Fleischer's deep-set eyes rolled. "Have you not read the newspapers?"

"I've had other things on my mind."

"*Ach*, the Nazis have had nothing else on their minds since the man was assassinated in Paris two days ago. Shot by a seventeen-year-old Jew. Vom Rath was only a minor official in the German Embassy there," he told Max. "Not even a party member. Now this propaganda tells everyone he was a hero to the Nazi cause. Herr Dr. Goebbels is using the assassination to stir up trouble."

Fleischer pointed at the Hitler Youth, running to board their truck. "Look how they rush to spread this cry for spontaneous demonstrations against the Jews. Come, I will drive us home."

The limousine glided beneath the Brandenburg Gate, headed west. Max settled back with the newspaper that was on the rear seat. "Deutschland Mourns," the headline exclaimed in bold German typeface. There were photographs of Ernst vom Rath's funeral bier in Paris, and of Herschel Feibel Grynzspan, his Jewish assassin, a rather handsome, dark-haired youth of seventeen with soft, steady eyes that showed no hatred or remorse. The civilized world seemed not to care about the fate of German Jewry, and this boy had taken it upon himself to rock the foundations of their indifference.

Shizue was not so different from vom Rath's determined assassin, he mused, pressing his fingers against his eyes. Grynzspan hoped to alter the course of human events by taking a life; Shizue sought to stem the tide by saving one.

"I have never seen so many black shirts in the streets," Fleischer observed darkly, as he braked for a strutting gang of Waffen S.S. troopers.

Max cranked the window down and heard the raucous laughter of black-shirted Nazis. For some reason the S.S. were making themselves highly visible. Clusters of Heinrich Himmler's thugs halted outside the entrances to Jewish-owned stores, frightening off customers with their icy stares before moving on. Max felt as though he were waking from a long sleep. He had been so overwhelmed with self-pity that he had paid no attention to what was going on around him. Suddenly he could see nothing else. He had Fleischer stop the limousine at a news stall.

"*Japana Zeitung?*"

The news stall operator responded to Max's request for a Japanese newspaper. "One moment." The newsstand attracted an international clientele, who frequented Cafe Freidiger just across the street. Max impatiently beat his hands together as the proprietor looked over his racks. "*Japana Zeitung* arrived only today, *mein Herr*," he said, passing it over the counter.

Max returned to the limousine without waiting for his change. He rested back in the seat while Fleischer drove them home. This edition of *Asahi Gurafu*, two weeks old and shipped via the Trans-Siberian route, was little more than a propaganda sheet edited for foreign consumption.

Max scanned the pages but found no mention of Jiro Mitsudara's desertion. It was pointless to have wanted some further confirmation of the facts, he thought bitterly, looking out the window at linden trees along the wide street as they neared the Karlstadts'.

Fleischer braked the limousine and sounded its horn. The Karlstadt coat of arms dignified the graceful iron gates, which were opened by a servant. Gardeners tended flower beds and pruned hedges along the driveway, monklike in their tireless devotion. There was no sense of the abrasive city beyond the high garden walls. French windows and curving balconies spared the grandiose mansion from coldness. The Karlstadts resided there in cloistered elegance. After twelve years of marriage, Heinz and Inge fawned over each other like young lovers. That night the driveway would be lined with limousines, thought Max, rankled by the prospect of spending the evening straitjacketed inside a tuxedo. However fond he was of the Karlstadts, he was definitely not in a festive mood.

"Thought you could do with a pick-me-up." Douglas entered his son's room with a whiskey glass in each hand.

Stuffing his starched white shirttails inside his tuxedo trousers, Max turned from the dresser. "Sure," he said, taking the glass. He was not used to hard liquor and coughed when he took the first swallow. "A man should have at least one vice," he said, still coughing. "I quote a friend at Harvard, where I distinguished myself as a priss-assed saint. Nose to the grindstone"—another swallow brought tears to his eyes—"saving myself for love. Well, no more. Shizue's put me through hell. I don't want any part of love and the pain it brings. Why should I give a damn about anyone but myself?"

"Max, I've tried not to be a meddling father."

"Thanks!" Max walked over to the dresser and emptied the contents of a leather box. Cuff links and shirt studs rattled out across the dresser top. "Sorry, Dad. You've been great."

Douglas put an arm around his son's sagging shoulders. "Listen, I'm the last person to be handing out advice on how to live your life. But don't let this destroy you. In some crazy, mixed-up way, everything could resolve itself for the better." A Dresden clock on the mantelpiece chimed the hour. "Better join your mother downstairs. Inge's planned quite an evening. Friends from Paris and Rome. Far from just another evening dominated by the boorish Hun. Given half a chance, you might enjoy yourself."

Max heard limousines arriving, punctually at the stroke of eight. He reached out and touched his glass to Douglas's. "To what can never be," he said, "for you, for me—and we mustn't neglect to toast the Führer for picking up the tab. *Sieg heil!*"

As his father opened the door and left the room, Max heard high-pitched laughter rising from the foyer below. He chose onyx studs set in platinum and matching cuff links. Doing up his shirt front, he paused, fingering the gold chain around his neck. The gold setting of the *omamori* was scarred where his heel had crushed it into the ground. At the height of his sorrow, Max had wanted to bury this lovers' keepsake. Even now, he felt its pull uniting him with Shizue. He could not hold her accountable for all his sufferings.

Finally, Max was ready. He went downstairs and confronted the group gathered in the main salon, where a pianist was sitting at the keyboard of the concert grand, playing quiet music as background for their conversations.

"There you are!" Inge Karlstadt swept forward to capture both his hands. "I had given you up for lost."

"Happy anniversary." Max kissed her cheek lightly.

"See what Heinz gave me," Inge said, showing off an emerald necklace.

"It's a knockout," Max said. "I'm embarrassed. I meant to get you something, but—"

"Max, *liebling,* your presence is gift enough. Come, meet our guests."

Perhaps it was the whiskey that altered his dreary view of things. He knew the Karlstadts' German friends and was relieved to see that their eligible daughters had been left at home. Inge led him along, shifting effortlessly into French and Italian.

"*Sì,* Il Duce owes everything to his chin," Count Frascotti resumed after being introduced, then stuck out the chin of his lean, hook-nosed face to the amusement of those around him. "Lacking this boulder that punctuates his speeches, he would not be taken seriously. I hold to the theory that the masses are swayed more by a man's bone structure than by his brains."

"And the Führer?" Max said, laughing. "What's his beauty secret?"

"High cheekbones. The thirsting jowls of a lion," Count Frascotti intoned theatrically. "The lusting eyes of a demon. But"—he lifted his shoulders and hands—"the Führer owes everything to the mustache that conceals a rather weak upper lip. Lacking this camouflage, he would appear a rather comical figure."

"Really, Count Frascotti," someone said over the laughter. "As a guest in my country, you owe our Führer proper respect."

The count offered a flowery bow. "*Scusi,* Herr Stossel. When in Rome . . . " He threw up both hands and gave a droll laugh. "*Prego,* we are all friends here. One should maintain his sense of humor about these would-be Caesars."

"Otto, it is a harmless jest," Heinz Karlstadt said, adjusting his monocle.

Herr Stossel regarded his host. "These Italians and their flair for the ridiculous," he huffed.

Dinner was served in the banquet room, which opened off the main salon. Strings now augmented the piano, and the guests were serenaded with Schubert and Mozart selections as they dined under crystal chandeliers. Max sat beside Count Frascotti, who described his vineyards in Siena. Max observed his parents' spirited conversation with a French couple, Jean-Claude and Niki Henri. In the midst of all this opulence his parents seemed a perfect match, he thought. Servants kept his wineglass filled, and his thoughts grew cloudy. The Mozart gave way to a lilting waltz, and Heinz sped around the table, bringing Inge to her feet with a kiss. He began dancing her around the room.

Everyone applauded the waltzing couple. "Speech, speech!" they all said, clapping in unison.

Inge's earthy laughter terminated abruptly.

"Serve her this!" a gruff male voice shouted from the kitchen. Then there was a resounding crash.

A moment later, everyone's eyes went to the butler, Heydrich, who entered the dining room through the pantry doors. He had been supervising the kitchen staff and appeared flustered.

"What is it, Heydrich?"

"Some difficulty with the temporary help, Herr Karlstadt," the butler said, stiffly tugging at his vest.

Heinz drew the man aside, and they conversed in whispers. "*Ach,*" he groaned, "discharge that clumsy idiot and have the chef prepare something else for dessert."

"One moment, Heydrich."

"Frau Karlstadt?"

"Our guests deserve some explanation."

"*Liebling,* why not leave well enough alone?" Heinz implored.

"No," Inge said adamantly. "We all heard this kitchen servant's words. The man refused to serve me because I am a Jew. Is that not so?"

Heydrich brought his heels together. "*Ja,* that is the talk among the kitchen help, Madam."

"I see. You are excused." Inge stared out across the table. "Never has there been such an incident in my home."

"Appalling," said Count Frascotti.

"*Ach,* servants," Herr Stossel put in. "Forever gossiping behind our backs. Look to the source, dear lady. I am not an anti-Semite, but there are Jews—and there are Jews." His palms balanced like scales, one going up, the other down. "You cannot expect the lower-class mentality to distinguish between them."

"What a gloomy lot." Angela Napier clanged on her wineglass. "Heinz, we were about to have a speech."

Inge's eyes misted over while Heinz took her in his arms. "I love you more than on that first day, when you captured my heart." Heinz turned to the guests. "After all these years, Inge has only to smile, and my pulse races like a schoolboy's. She is my wife, my lover, the friend whose arms have comforted me at times of distress. Her love is everything; she gives meaning to my life. All these worldly possessions would be nothing without my adorable Ingelein at my side." Heinz cupped her face between his hands. "You are even more beautiful than on our wedding day. I kiss you now as I did then."

As the Karlstadts embraced, Max fought back tears.

"Heinz, I'm so happy." Inge sighed. "I wonder if we have a right to so much happiness."

"Forgive me," Max said, standing. "Inge, Heinz—sorry, too much wine."

Inge called after him, "Max!" When he did not respond, she turned to her guests. "He does not look well."

"*Aria, signora*. Fresh air will clear the young man's head," Count Frascotti assured her.

The servants barely had enough time to hand Max his white silk evening scarf and drape his topcoat across his shoulders. He was drowning in emotions and quickly got behind the wheel of an open-topped Mercedes. The garage staff had just oiled its leather seats, and the canvas top was left folded back, exposing Max to the biting cold as he sped from the garage. Servants rushed to open the gates to him.

His face was flushed hot. Instead of sobering him, the cold wind made him choke. He swerved, made dizzy by the car's momentum. Suddenly, he saw a bright light on the quiet residential street ahead. Police waved for him to stop. Max braked, shielding his eyes against the glare of a spotlight, while two figures walked menacingly toward him.

One policeman gruffly knocked the hand from his face, then grinned. Max's Aryan features pleased him. "On your way, handsome," he ordered. "Quickly."

Max gripped the wheel, shaken by what he saw as the spotlight of the squad car was extinguished. Other police cars were parked outside a town house that was being vandalized. The star of David had been painted across the front door in yellow paint. Broken furniture littered the sidewalk, and helmeted police wielding axes moved behind the smashed-out windows, hacking everything within sight. There was an eerie madness to the scene that riveted him to the seat. What had become of those who lived there?

"Get going! Quickly!" ordered the police, who marched away, laughing.

Max floored the accelerator. What he had witnessed was simply too irrational for him to comprehend. Then he recalled the Hitler Youth posting notices that called for spontaneous demonstrations against the Jews. At that moment a convoy of padlocked police vans roared past an intersection, where he stopped. He glanced at the dashboard clock. Not quite ten, but the streets were strangely empty. Driving on, he had a gut feeling that Jews were padlocked inside the police vans.

Something had chased away the nightlife. Nearing the business district, he saw that beer halls and cabarets were shuttered. Only a handful of passengers rode a passing trolley, and there was not a taxi in view. Max turned the corner. "Jesus," he cried aloud, jamming on the brakes.

The long thoroughfare ahead was a shimmering sea of broken glass. Up and down the length of it, shattered store windows gaped like shocked, open mouths. Kline, Bromberg, Lowenstein; he read the brass names embedded in the stone above the stores as he cruised slowly, oblivious to the crunch of glass under his tires. A mob had obviously passed that way, hurling bricks and rocks. Fewer than a dozen stores had been spared the barrage. By some odd reckoning, he seemed to be following directly in the wake of an ongoing storm that devastated only the storefront windows of Jewish businesses.

Something caught fire on the horizon. Max glimpsed an orangy glow, then smoke and flames. Although he was not a Jew, he felt threatened by the savagery at work on this November night, and he altered his course for home.

Finally, he reached streets untouched by the storm. But the car wobbled, now bumping along on a flat tire that forced him to the curb. Glass must have punctured it, he thought. Max hurriedly freed the spare, then tensed as he heard a howling sound.

Suddenly a mob of Nazi troopers burst into view. Beating clubs against their hands, they formed a solid wall, spearheading a procession of torchlit trucks. Phalanxes of troopers armed with bricks rode in open trucks that advanced steadily up the street. Over and over the men chanted, "Jews must die! Jews must die!" This barbaric juggernaut was after blood. Some of the marchers halted to point at Max. He feared they might use their clubs first and ask questions later. A gang suddenly broke from the pack, and he ran.

His lungs ached as he ran down street after street until his would-be attackers gave up the chase. When he at last fell heaving against an iron fence, the air he breathed reeked of smoke. The chase had led him into a neighborhood of apartment houses. He saw flames breaking through the roof of a synagogue on the corner not far from where he stood. A *Schutzstaffeln* officer exchanged the *Sieg heil* with a sergeant, while squads dressed in black uniforms hurried out of the synagogue they had just put to the torch. As flames rose up behind the smashed-out windows, Max saw Nazi troopers, the police, and the S.S. board their waiting trucks in an orderly fashion. How many other well-organized barbaric acts were taking place? Max wondered. To his horror, an elderly man was being dragged through the synagogue's cellar gate.

"See what I found hiding in the cellar!" a hulking corporal shouted.

The gray-bearded Jew cried, "Oy, oy, oy!" He was dwarfed by the hulking corporal pulling him into the street. The old man, wearing a prayer shawl under his button-down sweater, flinched as his captor tore off his black skull cap and sailed it away with a laugh. "I am only the *shammes* here," he pleaded.

"I have no time to waste on minnows," an S.S. sergeant riding on the running board of one slow-moving truck announced. "Give the old Jew a few good whacks, then join us up ahead at number twenty, where more important Jews are in for a surprise!"

Max was enraged at the sight of the laughing thug tormenting the helpless old man. The S.S. trucks had rolled off, evening the odds, and Max sprinted toward the flaming synagogue. "*Hör auf!* Stop it, damn you!"

The S.S. corporal turned abruptly. "What's this?"

Max hit the corporal squarely in the face with a karate blow. The corporal, dazed but still on his feet, charged, swinging his fists. Max pivoted, seizing the arm coming at him and converting its thrust into a lever that flipped his adversary to the pavement. The man's head bounced, then he rolled limp to one side. Feeling exhilarated, Max stood, looking down at him.

"*Gut! Oy Gutenyu!*" the old Jew wailed, holding his bruised face. He was pinned against the cellar gate, his sweater caught in its sharp spokes. "*Riboyne Shel O'lem,*" he wailed over and over as Max freed him.

"Are you badly hurt? *Ich verstehe Sie nicht,*" Max said communicating in German. "I don't understand your language."

"*Goyisher,*" he muttered, smiling weakly. "*Danke schön.* Thank God for you, kind *mensch. Oy, gevalt.*" Gasping. The old man toppled forward, clutching his side. "*Meine Rippen.*"

Max caught him around the waist. "Do you live nearby?"

"In the synagogue."

"Do you have friends in the neighborhood?" Max asked him urgently. "Someone who'd give you shelter?"

"*Ja,* everyone is Jewish here."

The S.S. corporal stirred with a groan. Flaming embers rained down through the thickening smoke. "It'll be faster if I carry you," Max decided, gently lifting the old man.

He heard shouts from down the street and saw at least three black-uniformed soldiers jumping from a braking truck. They must have witnessed his assault, he thought. But it had taken time to alert the truck's driver, so Max enjoyed a healthy lead.

The old man clung to his neck like a child, pleading, "*Mensh, geh' veg.* Leave me. Save yourself."

"You there! Halt!" His pursuers' shouts grew nearer.

Max realized he could not outrun them. Already his arms were tiring, and there were nothing but apartment houses up the street ahead. He slowed long enough to glance over his shoulder. The burning synagogue had put a smoke screen between him and the S.S. men as he darted inside the vestibule of an apartment house. The inner door was locked, but after setting the old man down, Max began frantically pushing the buttons of a number of apartments.

"Why doesn't someone answer with the buzzer?" Max hollered, frantically pressing the buttons.

"*Oy*, they are afraid. I was sweeping the shul when suddenly there was this terrible crash at the window." Painfully unbuttoning his sweater, the old Jew covered his bald head with the prayer shawl he wore underneath it, then kissed its fringed end. "God's will be done." He began to pray in Hebrew.

Max did not understand his muttered words or the man's beliefs, which allowed him to pray calmly in that moment of crisis. The S.S. men would have slowed down by now, he reasoned, perhaps splitting up to search the entrances of the other buildings in the block. He might get away if he made a run for it. But he could not abandon the injured old man. Max wound his silk scarf around one hand, then punched through a glass door pane and reached inside to flip the latch. He scooped the old man into his arms.

"Someone help!" he yelled up the hallway stairs. There was no response. He rushed to an apartment door on the first landing. "One of your people has been hurt!" In frustration he kicked the locked door. "Tell them who you are, old man!"

"The *shammes*—Chaim," the old man called out. "Help us!"

A voice echoed down the stairwell. "Chaim? Who is that with you? No matter, bring him up!"

"No time!" Max addressed men in skullcaps who gathered at the railing several flights above. "It'll mean trouble for you if I'm found here!"

"Leave him on the landing!"

"*Schutzstaffel. Oy, oy, oy,*" the old Jew's wails and alarmed voices jabbering in Yiddish followed Max as he returned to the vestibule.

The outer doors were solid wood. Max braced himself there, listening to the S.S. wolves sniffing at his trail in this ghetto of terrified Jews. He had every reason to be terrified as well. Tonight there was no law in the streets of Berlin, he thought, realizing that he might be killed. His right hand was cut and bleeding through the white silk scarf. He tied it securely around his knuckles as a bandage. Taking a deep breath for courage, he plunged into the open, shocked to see two S.S. officers facing him directly across the street.

Max bolted away. A third figure in black took chase and suddenly grounded him with a choke hold. Max called upon every trick he knew, but he could not break this brute's hold. "Those who consort with Jews are traitors to the people," his captor hissed, easing up on the choke hold only slightly while a second S.S. officer twisted Max's arms behind his back. His struggling only increased their painful holds.

"What do we do with this Jew-lover?" Their husky leader asked, grabbing Max by the hair. "Or maybe there is some Jewish blood in you, *ja?*"

Max glared at the ferocious face, refusing to show his fear. Wearing a sardonic grin, the S.S. officer cuffed his chin playfully, then swiftly drove a knee into Max's groin. The choke hold prevented him from crying out. Pain shot through him as he absorbed the murderous blows to his groin and kidneys. His legs gave way, but the men kept him from falling, taking turns hitting him. While he spun in a fiery whirlwind of bloodred armbands, a huge man vaulted from out of the shadows.

The giant grabbed two S.S. men around their necks and banged their skulls together until they dropped unconscious at his feet. Max painfully slipped to the cold ground, his vision swimming. The S.S. officer who had released him now dangled in the giant's arms, and was sent headfirst against the lamppost with a dull thud.

"We must leave here. These *graubyon* will not sleep for very long," a friendly voice warned him.

Ham-sized hands reached down for Max. It pained him to speak, but he asked, "Where did you come from?"

"The house you brought old Chaim to. Here, put your arm around my shoulders."

Max looked up into the piercing blue eyes of a good-looking young man of about twenty. "If it hadn't been for you, they might have killed me."

"You helped a Jew. Why?"

"I helped an old man."

Emotion choked the soft-spoken voice. *"Haimisher mensh.* On such a night, it is difficult keeping to one's faith."

For a long moment Max stood warmed by this gentle giant's embrace, experiencing a kinship born out of violence. Then, coughing smoke, they backtracked up an alley to the loud clangs of fire engines. Max did not question their destination. The pain took his breath away, and he noticed little about the building they entered. They rose in an elevator to an apartment on the top floor.

"The rabbi will take us in," he told Max, ringing the bell. "It is Avrum Rothstein, Rabbi."

Max leaned heavily against his guide. The scarf had unraveled from his cut hand and trailed to his feet. Max watched Avrum kiss a mezuzah nailed to the doorframe before they stepped inside.

Everything was foreign to him. Photographs of robed, bearded men hung along the entrance hall, and Avrum was conversing with the rabbi in a language Max had not heard until that night. In the spacious parlor lit by candles, a small congregation of men wearing silk prayer shawls and black skullcaps stared at Max through sad, wary eyes. Behind them, a wide bay of windows glowed red. The burning synagogue could be glimpsed far down the street below. Sparks from its flames threatened the surrounding rooftops. The fire brigade's clanging arrival had come too late. Their hoses merely contained the blaze, and even at this distance the parlor reeked of smoke.

Avrum rested Max down in an overstuffed chair and he began to tremble, more from shock than the pain. Everyone seemed to be talking at once. The rabbi poured him a glass of dark red wine. Its sweetness had a soothing effect. The ache in his kidneys subsided, and he fingered his bruised throat, assuring the rabbi it was not necessary for Avrum to risk bringing the Jewish doctor there. Women with covered heads clustered hesitantly just inside the doorway of a connecting room.

Max had assisted a helpless old man, not a Jew. He knew little about Judaism or Jews, but now these sad-eyed faces were all around him, nodding as the rabbi insisted that he stay the night. "Thanks for your kindness, but it's safer for you if I go. I'll telephone my father to send a car."

Gravely shaking his head, the rabbi laid his hands on Max's shoulders. "It is not safe for your people to come here while these hoodlums roam our streets. We are under siege. For hours my telephone has been ringing. Prominent members of my congregation have been arrested. The jeweler, Bromberg, and his family were just taken by the police. Their possessions, their home, were put to the torch not far from where our synagogue still burns. By morning Temple Beth Sholom will lie in ruins. God willing, this pogrom will not outlive the night."

The men weaved back and forth, uttering some prayer from their open books that the rabbi knew by heart. Eyes closed, he weaved, too, sounding an "amen" with his flock.

Then he saw Max attempting to rise. "Please, young man, it is best for everyone that you stay." He smiled, stroking his wavy brown beard. "A son reflects the goodness of his father. I will set his mind to rest over the telephone."

Max conceded out of sheer exhaustion, doubtful anyone at the Karlstadts' knew what was taking place. When the telephone was handed to him, it was dead.

"We will try again later. You will have my son's room. He is at the yeshiva," the rabbi said, as Avrum helped Max to his feet. "The rabbinical college in Cologne. My daughter will see to your hand. Rachela."

A dainty wisp of a girl parted from the group of women segregated from the parlor, where their men stood davening in whispered voices. Max leaned heavily on Avrum. As they walked from the parlor, he sensed a spiritual unity among the silk-draped figures, whose drone was not so unlike the guttural drone of Shinto priests performing their ageless rites. Fate had swept him into the presence of an ancient culture, he thought, perhaps no less bound to their traditions than the Japanese.

"Avrum!" Rachel covered her mouth, giggling as his large head struck the bedroom doorway. "If you want to help, fill the basin with hot water. And do be careful not to spill it." She turned to Max. "He is so clumsy. Let me take your coat."

Max pulled off his bow tie and slowly reclined against the bed pillows. He noticed how Avrum blushed. Obviously he was in love. Rachel's eyes made him awkward as he lifted the empty basin. He narrowly avoided another bump on the head as he went out the door.

Rachel sat down on a chair beside the bed. "You have good hands," she told Max, gently rolling back one of his sleeves. He smiled at her. She was a dark-haired beauty with exotic brown eyes that reminded him of Shizue. Her creamy complexion blended with the lace scarf that framed her oval face. Lowering her eyes, she examined his injured hand.

Avrum entered the room, spilling the water from the basin he had filled. Rachel looked up at him and laughed, then pressed his arm lovingly. They gazed into one another's eyes, innocent of being watched. The terror was momentarily forgotten.

Avrum obviously adored Rachel, Max thought. For weeks he had existed apart from the world, empty of beliefs and closed to the feelings that flowered inside him once again. The girl's delicate hands were like velvet as she gently washed his cuts, but they suddenly trembled at the sound of the doorbell.

"Only the Levys," said Avrum, glancing into the hall.

Just then, Max pictured Shizue crouched somewhere in hiding with Jiro, fearful of the slightest sound outside their door while she waited for the war in China to end. He had never felt closer to her than now, trapped among these persecuted Jews waiting for dawn to end their nightmare. "Ouch, that hurts."

Rachel placed his injured hand across her cheek. "Bits of glass. They must come out. Trust me not to hurt you too much."

"My name is Max." He returned her smile, wincing as she cleaned the deep gash on the back of his right hand. A jagged scar would be a permanent reminder of *Kristallnacht*.

Rachel's mother appeared, a plump little woman bringing kosher wine and pastries. *"Essen, essen,"* the rabbi's wife encouraged Max quietly. "It will help you sleep." She crossed to lift a nightshirt from the dresser drawer, then all at once dropped her face against it sobbing. *"Oy,* my son, my Yussel. Are these attacks happening in Cologne? Has the yeshiva been destroyed as well?"

"Mama, calm yourself. Why would they harm anyone at the yeshiva?"

"Rachel, you are too young to understand," her mother wept. "Your poor *tateh* is worried half to death. But the rabbi does not show this, or his broken heart. His shul is gone. The work of a lifetime—gone! *Mechuleh.*"

Avrum made a fist and punched the wall. "We should fight, not pray. What good has prayer ever done?"

"God forgive you. *Oy,"* the rabbi's wife moaned, tears streaming down her anguished face. "Are things not bad enough already? Bite your tongue, Avrum. The rabbi would have a fit if he heard such talk in his house. What must our guest think of us?" She dried her tears and fussed over Max, speaking Yiddish in a motherly tone of voice.

There were prunes in the tart pastry he sampled. Drowsily Max sipped wine from a cut-glass goblet, as Rachel continued to attend to his hand. Suddenly, he felt the sting of iodine on the cut.

Rachel quickly bandaged Max's hand, then gave it a gentle pat and said, "So, it is finished." She turned to Avrum. "This bed will not hold the both of you. Avrum, you must sleep on the floor. Good night."

"Such *edelkeit*, my Rachel. Sweetness," Avrum defined for Max, red as a beet from her parting touch. "How is it with you? In pain, Max, *ja*. Give that hand a rest. *Ach*, those S.S.," he said, bending over to remove Max's shirt studs. "What a pleasure to crack open their thick heads. Our leaders tell us not to protest, not to resist. That will only make things worse for the Jews, they all say. Pacifists." His soft voice hardened. "Pulling tallithim up over our heads in prayer will not end the persecution. How can a man keep his self-respect and his dignity if he does not stand and fight? I speak with you not as a Jew, but as a fellow German. Off with your shirt."

It cheered Avrum to see him as a German, and Max only nodded, painfully shifting his weight on the bed.

"This object you wear around your neck. It is religious?"

"A keepsake," Max said, then gasped as a pain shot through him when he raised his arms so that Avrum could slip off his undershirt.

"*Gevalt!* Such welts."

"Not a pretty sight," Max agreed.

"*Ach*, to have survived such a beating. You are made of bricks, my friend. Ice may help the swelling."

Left alone, Max rested his eyes. In the room beyond, he heard Jews taking solace from prayer. God willing, this terror would not outlive the night, the rabbi had said. But gazing down at the ugly welts across his midsection, he wondered if *Kristallnacht* was only a prelude to more terrible events.

He touched the *omamori*. Was it chance or some unseen power that had guided Avrum Rothstein to him? He had worn the *omamori* only as a keepsake. But the priest had blessed it in the names of ancient Japanese deities. Silently Max called upon them to watch over Shizue and protect her from harm. It was a small though comforting gesture. For once in her life, Shizue had not wanted to be so helpless, and that night he, too, had tasted the exhilaration of lashing out against forces seemingly beyond his control. Now he understood. Paul would cable him when and if Shizue and Jiro were found.

Max's thoughts wandered. He imagined how frantic his parents would be when he did not return home. With the phone dead, there was no way to spare them the worry. Tomorrow they and the Karlstadts would share his painful experience. He hoped that might alert them to the dangers of continuing to do business with Hitler. Now he wanted sleep.

*   *   *

Three days after *Kristallnacht* Max approached the charred ruins of Temple Beth Sholom, where men from the congregation were sifting through the ashes. "That's the rabbi," he told Inge. "I'll introduce you."

Inge Karlstadt took his arm and whispered, "No, I was wrong to come." She drew Max behind a stone pillar that was still standing at the entranceway. "Be a dear. Give the rabbi this and say it is from someone who cares." Inside the envelope she pressed into his hands were twenty thousand marks. "I will wait with Fleischer in the car."

Flames had carved out an opening to the sky in the blackened roof of the synagogue, and Max crossed under it. "Rabbi."

The rabbi looked up, not recognizing Max. "What do you want of us?"

"Your wife said I'd find you here." The rabbi squinted up at Max again, then wiped soot from his glasses with one sleeve and smiled.

"The young man who sought refuge with us on that awful night," he said, briefly turning to the men around him. The rabbi sighed, shaking his head. "The streets here are still not safe for Jews, Max. Look what they have done."

"I have a gift for you, Rabbi. To help rebuild the synagogue," Max said, handing him the envelope.

The rabbi seemed perplexed and weighed the offering for a moment. Everyone gathered around him as he opened the envelope. *"Ai-yi-yil"* Hands reached out to support the rabbi, and he sat on a mound of rubble. "From where does this mitzvah come to us?"

"A friend of mine. Someone who cares."

"May both your names be inscribed in the book. *Sholem aleichim.*"

Max turned away in a sudden gust of wind that clouded the ruins with ash and cinders. Outside, Jews fearfully hurried past Fleischer, who stood beside the waiting limousine in his black uniform, which resembled that worn by the S.S. Fleischer opened the door, and Max got in.

"Cinders," Max told Inge, as he wiped the tears from his eyes. She sighed, aware it was not only cinders that made him cry. "Your gift meant a great deal to them," he said.

"Money is not enough. But perhaps the worst is over. Now that the world has expressed its outrage and concern, perhaps Hitler has learned he can no longer do as he pleases with the Jews. Then she brightened. *"Ach,* Max, enough sadness for one day. Cafe Geiger, Fleischer. We shall have lunch and get a little tipsy together."

Max was silent as they rode, noting the boarded storefront windows. *Kristallnacht* had swept across Germany. Tens of thousands of Jews had been arrested, hundreds of synagogues, Jewish shops, and homes destroyed, store windows smashed in every city. The insurance companies cried that it would bankrupt them to make good on all the damages.

At that moment Max realized that he needed to do something more purposeful than get tipsy at lunch.

Douglas Napier was shocked when his son visited the Karlstadt Parachute Works one morning and announced that he wanted to learn the business.

"The idleness is driving me nuts," Max said. "It's time I earned my keep, Dad."

"There was a time when I looked forward to us working as a team. But knowing how you feel about our dealings with Hitler . . ." Douglas broke off the thought. As he smiled, the years were lifted from his face, and he tousled Max's hair. "Hell, whatever made you decide, it's a damn sight better than sitting around doing nothing. Of course you'll draw a salary. Let's say two hundred a week for openers."

"Fine. When do I start?"

"Right now. I'll show you around and introduce you to the staff."

In the year since Max had last visited, the parachute works had grown into an awesome complex of modern structures. This was his father's element; here he was in command. Proud of his creations, Douglas conducted his son through the din of intricate machinery operated by German assembly-line workers clad in white smocks. Men with push-brooms were constantly on the move, keeping the floors spit-polish clean. The production of a single parachute involved far more than Max imagined. But it was his father he watched; Douglas seemed to thrive in the cold, antiseptic environment. And yet Max detected an undercurrent of dissatisfaction. More than once his father's eyes glazed over as though his involvement lacked meaning.

The same man whose talented hands had fashioned jack-in-the-boxes for a child now looked out on his inventions that might one day flood the skies over Europe with trained killers—paratroopers sworn to serve a megalomaniac. Yes, Max thought, here Douglas was in full command, but not in control of what use Hitler would make of the parachutes rolling off the assembly lines.

Hundreds of German women clad all in white packed each silk parachute by hand. They knew a soldier's life hung in the balance with each chute they packed. Perhaps, Max thought, they realized that their own sons might plunge into the fuming atmosphere of battle to serve the fatherland. The women never looked up from the silk. Even when the lunch whistles screamed, a number of them continued to work as though to rest were a sign of weakness.

Covering Heinz Karlstadt's facilities used up the morning. Then father and son rode to the roof in the outdoor work elevator of another mammoth building under construction. A howling wind blew across the car as it rose through the scaffolding. Max held on to his hat and looked down at a panoramic view of the facility.

"By January our new heavy-cargo chutes will go into production here." Douglas spoke over the wind.

"Impressive, Dad." Frighteningly so, Max thought.

The car jerked to a stop, but Douglas held Max on the elevator to make a confession. "Listen, being a party to this troubles my conscience. When it all began, I put business before politics. With everything that's happened since then, I might have given it all up. But there's Heinz and the baron to think of. Our loan from Lord Mitsudara has got to be repaid next year."

Douglas turned his collar up and viewed the windswept scene below. "Standing up here cuts a man down to size. It was my idea to grab a piece of the war industry pie. Going in, it seemed a smart move—actually, the only move open to us. Now it's become a monumental burden, and it's too late for backing out, Max. If the machinery ground to a halt, we'd be bankrupt."

Max's shoulders lifted on a sigh. "Damned if we do and damned if we don't. Is that what you're trying to say?"

"Yes. Hitler can't be stopped. These parachutes are just one weapon in his arsenal. If we don't supply them, the Gessler Works will." Douglas searched for understanding, although he knew he was rationalizing. "Look, I engineered this venture. Like it or not, I've got to bail everyone out of debt. Poor Heinz is the one really caught in the middle, between his loyalty to the fatherland and assisting the Führer's ambitions. *Kristallnacht* threw quite a scare into him."

"That night still gives me the shudders," said Max, painfully moving the fingers of his still-bandaged hand. His ribs remained still tender from the beating he had taken. "It's beyond me how the Karlstadts keep looking the other way. Germany's like a cage of wild beasts, Dad. I don't even want to think what these thugs will do the next time Hitler sets them loose in the streets. There may be worse things in store for us than bankruptcy."

"I've shared similar concerns with Heinz," Douglas said. "But this vicious attack has backfired on Hitler, and it could spell the finish to his persecution of the Jews."

"An alarm's been sounded, and we should all take the warning more seriously," Max countered strongly.

"Walking out on my responsibilities here isn't a solution, Max. Fear can send you running from one problem straight into the jaws of another. Shizue must be discovering the truth in that. Oh, her efforts are noble enough, but her own strength can't make up for what's lacking in Jiro. We both know the tragedy of losing the women we loved. But in the final analysis, we have only ourselves." Douglas firmly gripped the elevator control handle, and his voice shook with emotion. "Natsu's death left something inside me walled up so tight, if not for the work, I'd choke on it. Work isn't a cure-all, but it helps—even under these strained circumstances."

"I'm prepared to give it a try."

"Good having you aboard. We'll make a fine team." Douglas smiled, and then his eyes turned inward, reflecting on the events that had made Germany his home for so long. As the elevator car began descending, he saw an anthill of German workers being called in from the yard by screaming whistles. He knew none of their faces; he felt no real sense of ownership in the Karlstadt Parachute Works. Suddenly he longed for the Nagasaki weaving mill and the Urakami Hills, where he had flown his kite as a boy.

The elevator touched bottom. Douglas put an arm around his son's shoulder and walked him away. "I want us to work closely together, Max. I'll have a desk brought into my office for you."

"All right." Max said nothing of his true motives. His father was a man who stood at cross purposes with his troubled conscience and the obligations forced upon him by a code of honor that was perhaps no less binding than the baron's. Those closest to Max had been corrupted by wealth, and he doubted any of them could settle for a less privileged and luxurious existence. Until that very day, Max had lived off the profits while refusing to soil his hands. He was aware that his contributions to the business would be small, but they would eventually earn him the right to have a say. If he hoped to influence Douglas and Heinz, working alongside them seemed the only way to bring the awesome complex of machinery to a grinding halt before it was too late.

So, Max remained in Berlin toiling in the gusty roar of his father's machines. It soon became apparent that Douglas and Heinz were mired in a quicksand of personal loyalties and financial considerations, which sucked them down ever further from the light of reason into the darkness cast by Hitler's ominously rising shadow. Perhaps nothing short of war could open their eyes. Still, Max took a firm foothold in their turf, prodding their consciences whenever the opportunity arose.

Paul wrote him that the search for Jiro Mitsudara was being conducted quietly, without any fanfare in the Japanese press. Japan was at war, and if there were others like Jiro who had refused to serve their emperor, the army had chosen not to publicize the scandalous facts. While Lord Mitsudara suffered the disgrace in relative privacy, posters and handbills bearing his son's official army photo were being widely circulated. Shizue's complicity was relegated to several lines of fine print. As the weeks wore on, it seemed that the odds favored Shizue's cause, and Max resigned himself to a long vigil. He had but one consolation: if his brother had played a role, the feelings he expressed in the letters they exchanged would be passed on to Shizue.

All that December the Japanese battled for ground in southern

Kwangsi. The war was being fought to a stalemate. Despite their heavy losses, neither side showed signs of weakening, and Max saw no end to the bloody conflict that kept Shizue in hiding. Each day, he would return home from the parachute works exhausted, at odds with having betrayed his principles and questioning the value of his commitment there. Yuletide brought a letter from the baron, who finally broke his silence and reached out to Douglas, confessing his anguish and his loneliness. But he was inured to the pain his blind worship of tradition had caused Shizue. The blame was placed squarely on Lord Mitsudara's shoulders for having failed his son as a father.

"Shizue could not have turned to me without betraying her husband," the baron wrote. "She shared in that coward's disgrace only by virtue of her obligation to stand by him, the dutiful wife, and my daughter will be exonerated once this tragic affair has run its course."

Max was tempted to return to Japan, if only to confront Baron Hosokawa's smugness with the truth. His father sent no reply. For Douglas it was business as usual, while the door to friendship with the baron remained closed.

The new year passed uneventfully, and 1939 was ushered in to the toots of paper horns and a gaudy rain of confetti streamers unleashed by Angela and Douglas and the Karlstadts. To Max's eyes it was a desperate burst of gaiety.

Then Inge sat at the piano and they all joined arms, gathered around her in their silly party hats, to sing "Auld Lang Syne." Afterward there were wet eyes, hugs, and kisses. On the surface, it was just another sentimental New Year's Eve, but at its heart was a disquieting awareness of time and tide. *Kristallnacht* had not passed from memory. The previous year, Hitler had annexed Austria and the Sudentenland. Great Britain's capitulation to his demands at Munich gave him a free hand to gobble up more territory for the Reich, and now the Führer sat hungrily eyeing Czechoslovakia. Max did not join in a toast to their good fortune. While everyone's thoughts were turned away from what the coming year might hold in store, he could already feel the darkness touching all their lives.

Since Hitler had first come to power, Germany's artistic community had fled in droves. Now, in the first months of 1939, the Nazi vise was closing tighter, squashing all enemies of the Reich. Germans of conscience from every walk of life and of many religious beliefs fled under the blackening clouds of Nazi persecution. Existing concentration camps were enlarged and new ones built on the fringes of sharp-spired towns and beyond the somber stone walls of medieval hamlets. Friends and neighbors vanished without a trace. Those who dared question the disappearances often vanished themselves. Max watched on as people looked over their shoulders, conversing in hushed whispers or afraid to speak at all. Strangers were avoided. Friends were mistrusted, and one carefully chose one's words when in their company. On the streets,

Gestapo, Nazi troopers, and S.S. smothered Germany's laughter, while the masses who had once so gaily celebrated Hitler's triumphs now walked silent and trembling among these presences of evil.

When Max decided to revisit Temple Beth Sholom, he found the synagogue still in ruins, vandalized with painted swastikas and anti-Semitic slogans. He went to Avrum Rothstein's apartment house. The nameplate had been removed from the family mailbox, and no one responded to the buzzer. The same was true at the rabbi's apartment house, where a Star of David had been slashed in yellow paint on the door.

Max buzzed for the janitor. A bearded face peered guardedly at him through a crack in the opening door. Max said that he was a friend of the rabbi's. The elderly Jew responded to his questions with sadly rolling eyes. A German contractor had taken the congregation's money but failed to do the work, he said. When the rabbi complained, the contractor laughed in his face—the man never intended to rebuild the synagogue. Jews had no rights, and the German authorities would respond to their charges with more violence. The rabbi had been offered another shul near Essen. Avrum Rothstein's father was Beth Sholom's cantor, and his family had moved there as well.

Standing outside, Max looked up and down the street. Painted yellow stars and black swastikas glared out at him from the doors of a Berlin ghetto. There were many Jewish ghettos like it in Germany. He imagined the ghetto near Essen looked much the same, the doors of its apartment houses also scarred with the painted symbols of a hatred that Avrum, Rachel, and their parents could not have escaped. As he walked away, his heart heavy, he thought of their sympathetic faces. He was never going to see his Jewish friends again.

Two other events jarred Max that dreary day in March: Hitler's virtually bloodless occupation of Czechoslovakia and Paul's letter announcing that Lord Mitsudara had suffered a crippling stroke.

CHAPTER 29

With the new year in Japan began the annual cycle of the blossoms: in February the plum; the peach and pear in March; and now it was early April. Soon, Shizue reflected, as she left the house to go shopping, it would be her eighteenth birthday and another Night Cherry at Kyoto. That day Osaka was bathed in spring sunlight. Instead of going directly to the market, she wandered off beneath the budding cherry trees, losing all track of time. Hours passed in daydreams before she returned to her senses and hurried off to do the marketing.

When she finally left the marketplace, the handles of her net shopping bag tore loose, and she had to carry the bag in her arms. It grew heavy and Shizue quickened her step on the canal bridge walkway. Jiro would be pacing their squalid quarters fearing she had met with some peril. He hated it when she went out to shop for more than his cigarettes and the daily paper. Nearing home, she saw police circulating handbills. She was startled as one of the policemen loomed up directly in her path.

"Keep an eye out for this man. Any information leading to his capture will bring a handsome reward."

Jiro's photograph was on the handbill he stuffed inside her shopping bag. Shizue covered her panic with a forced smile. She had hoped the authorities would give up the search, but after six long months, it was being intensified. She noticed that handbills had been tacked to the wooden fences leading toward the open gate where her next-door neighbor stood sweeping the sidewalk.

"*Konnichi-wa.*" Mrs. Takada folded her small hands around the broom handle. "And how is your ailing husband today?"

"No better, no worse," she answered. Except for these chance encounters, Mrs. Takada kept to herself. Thanks to her, the other neighbors believed that Jiro was a disabled veteran, confined to his bed. "But the army doctors said that his care would require patience," Shizue added. "I live in hope that his condition will improve in time."

The woman sighed heavily. "A terrible burden for one so young. Have you seen these notices?"

"Yes."

"When I think what your brave husband has given for our emperor, my blood boils at the news of this traitor. No punishment is too great for such a coward. If I see his face around here, I will beat him over the head with this," Mrs. Takada exclaimed in a shrill voice, raising her broom, "and scream until it brings the police!"

"Forgive me, but my husband worries so, and I'm very late." Shizue rushed through her front gate.

Hardly any daylight entered the dismal house. Cooking odors, stale cigarette smoke, and a musty smell given off by its furnishings held sway no matter how much she scrubbed and cleaned, and the thin walls forced them to speak in hushed voices. "Jiro, I'm back," she called to him softly.

Crossing the threshold, she tripped on a ragged tatami. Shizue fell to her knees, and the groceries spilled out across the floor.

"Where have you been? Just look at this mess!"

Jiro glared down at her, one foot on the policeman's handbill.

How could she have been so careless? He must be kept from seeing it. Gathering up the groceries, she said, "I'm sorry, but it was such a beautiful day. I selfishly took a little time for myself. Don't be cross with me, Jiro," Shizue pleaded, her upturned eyes filled with remorse. "Say I'm forgiven."

He angrily shook his head. "What gives you the right to enjoy the outdoors, while I'm confined to this rat trap," he snapped. "I wouldn't be rotting away here, if not for you. Don't ever do anything like that again."

Hardly a day went by without Jiro accusing her of being responsible for his torment. Rather than adjust to their harsh circumstances, he fought them ever more bitterly. His sweetness and gentleness had disappeared, and he treated Shizue like a servant, finding fault with everything she did. She could not begrudge him the need to release his pent-up emotions on her. She had promised to have courage enough to sustain them both. Since the newspaper reports of his father's stroke, however, it was as though a time bomb were ticking away inside him, and she feared the handbill under his foot would trigger an explosion. "Here's your newspaper," she said. "Why not relax while I fix dinner?"

The loud screams of factory whistles sent the newspaper flying from Jiro's hand, and he reeled back, holding his ears. "These infernal whistles are driving me mad," he shouted over them.

Shizue reached for the handbill.

"What's that?"

"Only some advertisement." Before she could crumple it up, Jiro took her by the wrist.

"Give it to me!"

As he looked at it, she watched the blood drain from his face. The screaming whistles mercifully trailed off, and Jiro crossed to sit at the kitchen table. With unsteady hands, he slipped on his reading glasses. Jiro's official army photograph, which had been used on the flyer, was several years old. The months of confinement had given him a gaunt, sickly look, and one would have to look twice before recognizing him as the confident young cadet lieutenant on the handbill. Shizue had described the posters circulated by the authorities, but the handbill was his first terrible contact with their search. For the first time, he saw the word *deserter* printed in bold type. His lips trembled as he read the charges against him. Then, stunned, he lifted his eyes to her.

"Where did you get this?"

"I don't remember."

"I can see you're lying. Where?" Jiro demanded.

"Near the canal bridge. A policeman forced one on me." Shizue hugged herself, avoiding his eyes. "If not for Mrs. Takada stopping to question me, I never would have brought it into the house. I wanted to spare you from—"

Jiro cut her off with a pained laugh. "Spare me? The police are practically at our front door. For all we know, they could be making a house-to-house search. Your precious Paul said they'd never think of looking for us here. So much for him and all your talk about them giving up the search."

"There's no reason for the police to suspect we're in the neighborhood. They're just passing out handbills. It's a coincidence—only that." She went to him only to be pushed away. From the moment they set foot inside this house, sex between them had ceased to exist. It was his fear that she might become pregnant, Jiro said. Yet for months they had not embraced, even to comfort each other as friends.

"Jiro, we're safe. Oh, why must you go on torturing yourself? Nothing I do seems to please you. I've tried so hard, but you shut me out. I want to be strong, but your struggle weakens me."

Jiro buried his face in his hands, and she wondered how much longer they could live this way, isolated from the world and from each other. Shizue ran to her room in tears, threw herself across the bed, and wept. At that moment she wished Max would return home to find her, break down the door, and carry her away in his arms.

A phone booth down the street was her only link with the two men she loved. Paul had read her all Max's letters over the telephone lines from Tokyo. Once a week, she was warmed by his voice. On her birthday she would speak to him again. Perhaps he had received another letter from Max.

Drying her eyes, Shizue glimpsed her reflection in the cracked mirror. Her hands were coarse and red. Her hair had grown to well below her shoulders, and she wore it combed back and twisted into a severe bun. So sorrowful and defeated, she observed. Once she had taken such pride in her appearance. She stood up tall and plucked the pins from her hair, deciding it would help lift her spirits and Jiro's if she made herself pretty for dinner.

When she entered the kitchen, Jiro was still seated at the table. On it were his scrapbooks and glue jars. Bent over the newspaper, he did not even bother to comment on her appearance. "No news of father's condition," he said.

There had been none in weeks. Shizue's smile faded as he resumed cutting out the latest war news. As always, he cut slowly, carefully, and she had grown to detest the unnerving sound of the blades inching through the paper. China and its dead filled the pages of those cheap scrapbooks. Another of Jiro's classmates had been killed in action. Jiro neatly snipped his name from the casualty lists, and laid the clipping on the table to be glued into the book. Her husband never spoke of them, but their faces haunted his nights. He never slept for more than a few hours at a time. In the hour between darkness and the dawn, she would wake to hear him pacing the floor.

"The butcher had pork today," she told him. Just for a moment, with her scented hair brushed out and the smooth touch of satin against her skin, she had felt like a woman again. Now she wearily slipped on an apron. The dress she had traveled in belonged to the past. Sighing, she rolled up its blousy sleeves and began slicing pork and vegetables at the chopping block.

All their days were the same. At breakfast and dinner, Mr. Takada loudly played his radio. They could not afford to buy one, and Jiro looked forward to eavesdropping on the news broadcasts. That night he gobbled down his food, then stood and moved closer to the wall between the neighboring houses. Shizue pinched her cheeks for color and sank at his feet, desperate for some human contact, a kind word. "Jiro . . ."

"Be still."

"Ah, this war," Mr. Takada complained after silencing his radio. "Same, same, woman. We kill three of them for every one of us, but still no end in sight. How many victories before we crush those chink dogs?"

"Lower your voice," Mrs. Takada pleaded. "Give some thought to our neighbors. Mrs. Mizutani's husband is—"

"Speak up, woman. You know working in the factory these many years has dulled my hearing."

"Mr. Mizutani fought bravely in this war and should be given some consideration."

"So you say. So the neighbors say. But who has seen the man? Look here. I found this handbill tacked to our fence." Mr. Takada's voice dropped to a barely audible hum.

Shizue tensed, and Jiro's eyes were wild as he put his ear against the wall.

"Foolish old man—what are you saying?"

"Then tell me why they never speak in there. Not a word," Mr. Takada challenged.

"It's no business of yours. That sweet young thing has enough to burden her. Don't be a troublemaker. Read your newspaper and keep your suspicions to yourself."

Jiro began pacing frantically. Shizue feared he was about to break apart. Then he let out a long wail. "There's canned fruit, darling. Peaches—your favorite," she announced loudly, hoping to cover his cry. "Oh, you're in pain."

The Takadas grew quiet. Jiro began to perspire; he realized they were listening. Suddenly he heard the front gate squealing on its hinges. He took hold of Shizue with his icy hands as someone knocked at the door.

"Mrs. Mizutani?" Mrs. Takada inquired. When there was no answer, she knocked again. "I must speak with you."

"Yes—coming. Jiro, I can't refuse to answer the door. Go to your room," she whispered, fighting hysteria as he held her there. "Jiro, you're hurting me."

Blinking, Jiro released her and stared at his hands as if they were covered with dirt. "I've become a beast."

He rushed away. The shoji to his room rattled shut, and Shizue took a deep breath before opening the door. "I would have come sooner, but I was tending to my husband."

"I thought I heard him cry out." Mrs. Takada returned her bow. "These old houses keep no secrets. I'm so ashamed for my husband's words. He is blessed with too much imagination. Please, accept this. Custard made with fresh milk and eggs. It will help make your honorable husband strong." Holding the covered bowl, she bowed until it was accepted. "My, what a fine dress."

Shizue had given no thought to her appearance. "A gift on my wedding day. Tonight is our anniversary."

"Omedetō." Mrs. Takada offered congratulations, while her eyes narrowly took in what could be seen of the kitchen table set for two. "He left his bed?"

"Just for dinner. But it proved too much for him." Shizue managed a smile, then bowed to thank the woman. "When may I return the bowl?"

"Any time will do," Mrs. Takada answered, and turned toward the gate.

Shizue was about to close the door, when the woman abruptly faced around. Massaging the small of her back, she gave Shizue a questioning look but then sighed. "Tomorrow it will rain," she said. "Hai, my aching bones never lie. Good night."

"Good night." Another second and Shizue might have cracked under the strain. She put her back against the door and was confronted by Jiro's terror-stricken face. He lit a cigarette. Mrs. Takada posed no threat, but her husband did. There was no escape from here, nowhere else they could go, and they stood apart, both thinking the same thing: the next knock at their door could be the police.

Shizue set the custard bowl on the table and was shaken by Jiro's urgent embrace.

"I've reached the breaking point," he said, holding her tightly in his arms. "Everything is working against us. In time I'll be found, or be driven into the open by madness and hunted down like an animal. I've treated you like my jailer. In your place I'd walk away from here and never look back. If I were any kind of a man, I'd order you to go."

"I'd never abandon you."

"I'm the cause of father's stroke, and if he dies . . ." Jiro made a shivering sound and released her.

"You aren't thinking clearly."

"It's useless pretending that the war will end. Even with your hope and strength to lean on, I feared it was hopeless from the start. I knew it might end this way. The ultimate disgrace of a court-martial. The firing squad. A coward's death, Shizue. If I weren't such a coward, I'd walk out the door and be done with it. But I can't even do that for myself. Perhaps our neighbor will do it for me."

"Oh, Jiro," she said softly. He regarded her vacantly, through fixed, staring eyes. There was nothing she could say that had not already been said. He had lost all hope, while hers now hung on a slender thread.

That night was the longest of Shizue's life. She washed the dishes and swept the kitchen floor. The house was as clean as it would ever be, but she moved from room to room dusting the shabby furniture. She even did the laundry, mindlessly bending over her scrub board until she was overcome by exhaustion.

Jiro switched off the lamp as she passed his room to hers. An illustrated calender hung on a nail by her bedside. April cherry blossoms framed two lovers who embraced near a mountain waterfall, evoking memories of the place where the kerria bloomed. Drowsily, she wrapped herself in the bittersweet memory of her union with Max. She often recaptured their ecstasy in her dreams, but that night she could not sleep. The house creaked and moaned on its rotting timbers. Mice scratched and scurried between its walls. Finally, the first faint light touched the windowpanes. Jiro was safe for another day, she thought.

She was on the threshold of sleep, when some sound caused her to sit up in bed. Then she heard it again, an awful gasping sound that rose and fell. It was coming from Jiro's room.

She hurried there. Shocked and horrified, Shizue took hold of the doorframe for support. Jiro knelt on a pillow, both hands gripping the handle of the *wakizashi* he had plunged into his abdomen only brief seconds before.

As she watched, he painfully withdrew its blade. He recoiled. His head snapped back. His mouth opened wide, and the dagger seemed to jump from his grasp before he toppled to the floor, half doubled over, clutching his side. Blood oozed between his fingers and glistened red on the *wakizashi*'s razor-sharp blade, which came to rest near his violently jerking legs.

Shizue screamed. "No, Jiro! No, no!"

Even with him lying there, her dazed mind wanted to deny the horrible reality of his act. She saw the *wakizashi*'s ornamental scabbard. One corner of the worn tatami had been rolled back, revealing several loose floorboards under which Jiro had kept the dagger hidden from her. She realized that Jiro had carried it in his briefcase that night on the train, had contemplated his seppuku even then.

Dropping beside him, she cradled his head in her lap. "Why?" she sobbed. His hair was soaked with sweat. Jiro's facial muscles twitched, and she could feel his pain shuddering through her while his contorted mouth struggled to form the words.

"The right thing. The only way out—but I failed. I lived as a coward. Don't let me die as one. You're strong. Samurai. You know what must be done." His words came in short, tremulous bursts, his voice barely a whisper. "Help me to die like a man. You owe me that much. You can't refuse me, Shizue. My life is over." Beads of sweat stung his eyes, and his torso convulsed. "I'm no longer afraid of death, but I haven't the strength to finish the task. Find your courage. Help put an end to my shame and suffering. Grant me peace. The *wakizashi*—quickly. Don't let me be found like this."

Mrs. Takada pounded on their front door. Shizue was unable to move or answer the woman's hysterical shouts.

A thick pool of blood widened across the tatami. Jiro's bloody hands reached out for the dagger that lay just beyond his reach. Writhing, he unleashed an agonized cry for help as his robe fell open to expose his naked flesh.

Shizue saw the wound. It was a mortal but shameful wound. At the moment of truth his courage had faltered. Nearly twelve inches of cold steel had penetrated deep inside his intestines, but he had failed to apply the coup de grâce. A braver samurai would have disemboweled himself with a sure, swift stroke, ripping through his abdominal wall from side to side. Now this kind and gentle young man lay bleeding in her arms, and only her hand could grant him an honorable death. The throbbing veins in his neck stood out like purple worms about to burst their skins. With each tortured breath he heaved, more blood gushed from his open wound.

Outside, Mr. Takada was arguing with his wife. "Get back into the house, woman. I am telephoning for the police," Shizue heard him say.

Shizue's horror, her revulsion, gave way to a numbing calm. She saw herself as split in two. The real Shizue was incapable of performing such a gruesome task and turned her tear-streaked face away, while her samurai counterpart dragged Jiro to the bed and sat him upright against it. Nothing could save him. How he died was all that mattered now. How to accomplish what he asked of her was all she could think of as, with an unreasoning sense of purpose, she spread his legs apart, then knelt between them, holding the *wakizashi*. Jiro's tongue rolled out heavily across his lips. He barely had strength enough to grip the silk-braided handle, and her fingers locked tightly around his hands, sticky to the touch.

Jiro gasped, "Now, Shizue. Release me now."

If she hesitated at all, it was only long enough to position the point of the blade in contact with his open wound. Bowing slowly from the waist, her weight supplied the initial thrust. She looked deep into his eyes, feeling Jiro's hot breath on her face as the slashing movement of the blade caused them to sway closely together in a final embrace.

He uttered a faint gurgling sound. Then death brought peace to his sensitive eyes, and Shizue saw Jiro as he once had been, teasing her with one of his charming smiles. His corpse slumped forward, then listed sideways. She had released him from shame, but what of her own shame? She had failed Jiro, and the hands still locked around the *wakizashi* were the hands of his executioner.

Rain tapped softly against the roof. Shizue heard voices, but they were unreal to her and far away. She felt no sense of time or place. Her duty as a samurai was clear. Double suicide would be the ultimate indication of the role she had played in leading Jiro to this tragic end. Even while his death grip seemed to fight her for possession of the *wakizashi*, she did not question using its blade to seal her fate.

When the instrument of his death slithered free, she bowed low and rested the *wakizashi* across her palms. As she prepared to join her ancestors, there was no fear, no sense of self. But then, in that moment when the steel edge met with her throat, something inside her fought for life.

Still, Shizue ran the blade across her throat. Her blood mingled with Jiro's, and she gagged, expecting death to claim her. Instead, her lungs filled with air. She had only broken her skin. She stared down at the *wakizashi* as she lowered it in her trembling hands. An involuntary reflex broke her grip on the dagger, sending it to the floor. She placed both hands up to a thin cut across her throat, and mindlessly she began to rock. Someone was making an awful racket at the door.

Much later, she would recall admitting the police, their black boots and oilskin slickers dripping water on the worn tatami as she answered their questions in a cold, steady voice. "My husband has killed himself."

The cherry trees were in full bloom, their branches bowing along the Buddhist temple grounds; Shizue, wearing a white mourning veil and accompanied by her father, faltered on the path that led away from Jiro's grave. While he was laid to rest beside his ancestors, she had shed no tears.

In the week since his seppuku, she felt as though she had lived a life-time. Her bandaged throat was sore but healing, and everyone had attributed her aborted suicide attempt to hysteria. As Jiro's grieving widow, the authorities had treated her with sympathy and respect. Everyone had drawn his own conclusion. Confessing the truth would have disgraced her father and stripped Jiro of his honorable death, so Shizue had taken refuge in silence.

Before leaving Osaka, she had endured the rigors of an army inquest, then put her signature to a document that had satisfied everyone's needs but her own. Now Shizue clung to her father's arm, stricken by the realization that she could never speak out.

A uniformed nurse stood behind Lord Mitsudara's wheelchair. One side of his body had been paralyzed. His right eye was frozen shut, the mouth twisted in a permanently lopsided grin. He said something to Shizue, who looked questioningly at the nurse.

The woman interpreted the lord's badly slurred speech. "Lord Mitsudara asks if you are ill."

"No—a little dizzy." The lord's good eye searched her face with an unmistakable glint of hope. Shizue knew what he was thinking and shook her head. There would be no grandson and heir to bind her to his household. After the traditional mourning period had been observed, she would be set free.

The courage of her convictions had extracted a hideous cost. It had all been for nothing, she thought, watching Lord Mitsudara being wheeled through the cemetery gate. Her unsparing silence was the final irony. Even if she dared to voice the truth, it would change nothing. Lady Mitsudara and the family elders swooped past her to board the waiting limousines.

"Go on without me, Father. I'll stay here for a while."

"If you wish." The baron gently lifted her veil. The little girl he had given into marriage was now a widow. "To think I nearly lost you."

Shizue lowered her eyes, tolerating his kiss. Perhaps she would never again love him with all her heart. Smiling sadly, she turned from the departing motorcade and followed a solemn procession of Buddhist monks who marched to their meditation. A hilltop pagoda rose up amid the splendor of cherry blossoms, and the air she breathed was heavy with their scent.

She was startled by Paul's appearance on the road ahead. "Paul!" Shizue ran, tearfully pulling back her widow's veil. "Oh, Paul, I've been so alone." She embraced him, sobbing. "Jiro's gone, and I'm to blame. Oh, what have I done?"

"Thank God, you're alive." He dropped his cane to the ground, freeing both hands to caress her. "There, it's over now. Nothing short of a miracle could have saved Jiro. He belongs to the past. You've suffered enough as it is, Shizue. Think of the future."

"The future," she repeated dully.

"Yes. You and Max."

Suddenly her eyes grew dry. As if she had just completed a long journey from darkness into the light, she blinked up at Paul's strong face and felt alive again. "I want to see him so badly. Those final days in hiding with Jiro, I was guilty of wanting Max to rush home and rescue me."

"We've exchanged several cables. Max is leaving Germany on the first available transportation."

"Yes, let him come quickly. Once he holds me, this will be only a bad dream." Just then Shizue was stricken by a vision of her husband, writhing in a pool of blood. She saw his blood on her hands and heard him cry out to be released. Jiro was not yet cold in his grave, she thought, reliving his death all over again. How could she think of being with Max so soon?

"No, I mustn't give in to desperation," she said. "I need time. The memories are still too fresh, Paul. I still hurt from my failure to spare Jiro. In time the memories will fade—they must."

Shizue slipped free of his arms, and Paul teetered like a broken tin soldier. "My cane."

She stooped for the cane and quickly placed it into his groping hand. "Please, cable Max to wait. Say that I'll write him explaining everything. He'll understand why I can't possibly see him yet. I need time to heal. Jiro was my friend. Now I'm his widow, and in spite of everything, I owe it to his memory to respect the mourning period, to grieve him as the sensitive young man who made it possible for me to endure a marriage neither of us wanted. I led him to disgrace, Paul. He chose to die with honor by his own hand. Thirteen months will seem an eternity, but not to mourn him would be the ultimate disgrace."

Shizue wrung her hands, overwhelmed with the memory of how she had clasped them over Jiro's hands, giving strength to one sweeping stroke of the *wakizashi*'s blade. "It was horrible. I never imagined he planned to take his life—and it happened without warning. I heard him cry out. I watched him topple to the floor. In the end, I was his only hope."

"There's something you haven't told me."

His hurt look tempted Shizue to unburden her soul. "Paul, I've been such a burden to you," she said. "I've turned to you so often, confessing every little thing and expecting you somehow to make it right." Brushing Paul's cheek with a kiss, she gave thanks for his tireless devotion. "Perhaps one day I'll turn to you again. But not in the same way. Not as the spoiled child. How you've put up with me, I'll never know." She looked up at him. "For now, I just want you to stay with me, Paul. Being near you, I feel safe."

Paul walked beside her to the pagoda's shaded gardens. Seated in the quiet beauty there, he recalled their first day at Kyoto. The ice cream vendor. Her wishing tree. Today the cherry trees were in bloom, and their white blossoms fringed with pink reminded him that she had just turned eighteen. "What are you thinking?"

Shizue hesitated. "I can't stop thinking of how Jiro's death has paved the way to my happiness with Max. My life is just beginning." She sighed, gazing up at the cherry blossoms. "It's a new beginning for us both. But I'm not yet ready to accept it."

"I'll cable Max this afternoon," Paul replied. He knew he had been a source of comfort to her. Shizue's rock. But after she observed the mourning period, Max would replace him. Paul was chilled by the prospect of being reduced to a lesser role. He reached down to massage his bad leg. It ached constantly; it gave him no peace. "You've never been a burden to me, Shizue. Don't take this all on yourself. I'm only as far away as the telephone."

"Dear Paul. If only you could find someone to love."

He managed to smile and rose beside her, sadly aware that tragedy had brought a new maturity to the woman he had vowed to protect. Shizue leaned on his arm, her touch like a kiss, her weight always a blessing, although it burdened his step.

Had she loved him, Shizue could not have grieved for Jiro more. She continued to reside in his father's house, occupying the rooms they had shared together as husband and wife. Her days were passed there alone, as she painfully retraced the events that had shaped her determination to act as Jiro's savior. At night she was visited by phantoms and woke to the sound of him tossing beside her in a cold sweat.

The disposal of his personal belongings fell to her. Emptying his desk, she came across a portfolio of his poems. Touched by their loveliness, she wept. His last poem was dated several days before they had taken flight. He had not finished that melancholy song of death. She read it over and over, seeing his head cradled in her lap, hearing him gasp to be released. While gathering together his army uniforms, she mourned the loss of a sensitive soul consigned to the mortal shell of a noble samurai.

Jiro had believed that one's fate was determined at birth, Shizue mused one afternoon while seated before her mirror. Time had healed the wound at her throat, but a hairline scar would never allow Shizue to forget that her Bushido had almost laid claim to her as well.

Gradually she became reconciled to her lot. The Mitsudara household regarded her as an unwanted guest. A number of Jiro's university friends came to pay their respects, and Shizue served tea, tight-lipped and aloof while they coldly discussed the war. Her father telephoned often from Nagasaki, but he had little to say. Her emotions were no longer those of his dutiful little girl. She was a widow, a young woman with a past. Her beauty and breeding might lure a few worthy suitors, but their parents would surely turn Baron Hosokawa down if he tried to arrange another match.

Max's letters sustained her, for they exuded an infectious optimism. He foresaw no obstacles to their happiness when he returned. How she longed for the day when she could cast off her mourning clothes. Sweet thoughts of being in Max's arms intruded on her grief.

Summer colored Lord Mitsudara's driveway with flowers, and

Shizue was swept back into the current of life, half-running to meet the postman at the gate. She eagerly sifted the mail for German stamps, crestfallen when there was nothing from Max. Only a letter from Kimitake. Her brother was coming to Tokyo. An overnight stay, he wrote, giving the name of his hotel.

The lobby of the Yashima Hotel was crowded with people taking shelter from the early evening rain. Kimitake stood head and shoulders above them. As Shizue entered beneath the doorman's umbrella, he rushed to her. "Little sister. I've missed you like hell." His deep voice broke, and he awkwardly removed his cap. "So much to say. You're changed. But you're still my gorgeous kid sister. Not glad to see me?"

Shizue hugged him. "It's your uniform." She had imagined Jiro standing there, dressed for war. "Kimi, I know you visited father on leave, but all he would tell me over the telephone was that you've been reassigned."

"That's right. Imperial Guards Division," he boasted.

"Based where?"

"All in good time." Kimitake put his arm around Shizue's slender waist. "First dinner. The rain shows no sign of letting up. I'll have the doorman get us a taxi."

At dinner Kimitake made no mention of his assignment. Shizue, happy to be with him and enjoying reminiscing about their childhood, did not question his evasiveness.

Kimitake made no effort to conceal his vanity. He was all too aware of his attractiveness as the waitresses flirted with him. His officer's uniform had been scrupulously tailored to hug his muscular frame, and Shizue observed how aware he was of his smooth, strong hands. He seemed to derive a sensual pleasure from everything they touched.

After dinner, the two strolled arm in arm, splashing through puddles under a cloudy night sky. "Wait, Kimitake," Shizue said, tugging at his arm. "Don't step on the moon's reflection. It's bad luck."

"Women and their silly superstitions." With a rather devilish laugh, he struck the puddled reflection with his boot. "Come along, there's a dance hall just across the bridge."

"Kimi, I can't go dancing dressed like this."

"Sorry. We were having such a good time, I'd forgotten you were in mourning. Jiro's seppuku. Well, I won't dredge it up by asking a lot of stupid questions. Poor kid." His gaze drifted off to the glittering city lights, and he was silent. Finally he said, "I'm no good with words. Maybe I should have let Father break the news. I'm shipping out for China in the morning."

Shizue gasped. Now she knew why he had been so evasive about his assignment. Cars rumbled across Nihonbashi Bridge as she grasped a cast-iron railing for support. "Will you fight?"

"Oh, yes. I'll stand up against the best of them."

"Jiro would have run under fire. He would have been killed. I know it, I know it." Shizue had difficulty focusing her eyes. Just for a moment, this became the canal bridge at Osaka she had crossed almost every day. Then Kimitake held her close, and she took heart. "Jiro said only the bravest would survive. I'd give anything to keep you safe at home. But since you must go, then fight, Kimi. Fight bravely and live."

"You sound a little like Father."

"How is he taking this?"

"Soberly. Not so much pleased as proud that I've been called to serve our emperor." It began to drizzle. Kimitake took her arm and set a brisk pace. "If father had any other feelings, he didn't show them. He just rattled off my obligations, as usual."

Guiding her down the rain-slickened bridge stairs, he said, "Mind your step," then continued. "Why upset you with the details? Except for a hint of tears when we said good-bye, you'd think I was boarding the train for summer vacation at the seashore. There's no pleasing him, Shizue. Earning my commission wasn't enough. Now he's asking for my blood. Damn!"

"What do you mean? Tell me."

A brilliant thunderclap muffled her brother's reply. On the street below, the awning of a building gave them shelter from the heavy downpour, and Kimitake avoided her eyes.

"You're pale as a ghost," Shizue said.

"Am I? Too much sake."

"My innocence died with Jiro. I'm years older." Shizue laced her fingers together and paused, watching the rain. "Trust me, Kimi. I won't go to pieces."

"All right." He shook the water off his cap, then cleared his throat. "To make it short, Father expects me to do more than fight hard and well. Just getting through this damn war won't satisfy him. As an officer and a samurai, it's my duty to set a heroic example for the men serving under me, he said. He expects me to emerge decorated for valor. Anything less would be 'an admission of cowardice.' Father's very words. Hell, Shizue, I'm no coward. But a hero . . ."

"Father hasn't the right to demand that of you."

"Perhaps not." He smiled. "Listen, don't get lines on that pretty face worrying over me. A man doesn't decide to become a hero. It's just something that happens—spur of the moment." Kimitake stretched and sighed. "We've both been hurt by Father's impossible demands. He's always in the right. I doubt if anything will ever shake his beliefs, but even he can't tamper with fate."

A soldier swung toward them on crutches. Shizue stiffened as he halted, peering at Kimitake through sheets of rain. One empty trouser leg was pinned above the knee, and his khaki uniform was drenched. He managed a wobbly salute.

"Take shelter with us," Shizue told him.

"Yes. At ease, Corporal."

"Thank you very much, Lieutenant, sir."

The corporal wiped his eyes with a sleeve. Balanced on his crutches, he lit a cigarette, holding it between two nicotine-stained fingers while Kimitake's friendly manner encouraged him to speak about the action he had seen.

Shizue pitied him. The corporal's slight voice lacked emotion, and her brother leaned on his every word. She tried listening only to the rain, wishing it would stop. Kimitake's hands were clenched into fists. Now and then his eyes sought her out, and she considered how desperately he wanted their father's love. No one could foretell what might happen in combat. Perhaps their father could not tamper with fate, but he had planted a seed for heroism in Kimitake, and that frightened her. "Is Tokyo your home, Corporal?" she asked.

Jarred from his morbid remembrances, the corporal displayed a yellow-toothed grin. "I am from Hokkaido, miss. Before the war, I worked in the coal mines there with my father and older brothers. The army promises me a wooden leg. They sent my father a letter, and he wrote back words of pride, saying that we will work together again side by side. But I think not. The mine is a hard life, even for someone with two good legs." He looked down sorrowfully at his pinned trouser leg. "I wake at night with a tingling in my missing toes and wonder where they have gone to. Maybe some Chinese soldier wears my dead toes around his neck. They fight like savages. But I have upset you. Forgive me for not recognizing you are in mourning."

"Yes—for my husband."

The corporal did his best to bow. "What is the loss of a leg to the loss of a husband? My deepest condolences."

The rain had stopped. Shizue looked away as Kimitake returned the corporal's salute, wishing him good luck. The chance encounter had cast a pall of gloom over them both. Her brother walked along, brooding and silent until they neared a gaudy neon sign. The rhythmic beat of a swing band filtered into the street through a dance hall's revolving doors. Suddenly, Kimitake swept her up and glided to the music.

"I had no idea you were such a marvelous dancer."

"Nothing like dancing your cares away with a pretty girl." He laughed. "There's a lot you don't know about me, little sister. After all, we haven't spent much time alone together in years."

At dinner Shizue had noticed the waitresses flirting with her brother. He was right; there *were* many things she did not know about him. "I must confess," she said, "it came as a surprise to discover how terribly attractive my brother is to women. Have you broken many hearts?"

"None that I know of. Life's too unpredictable to be taken seriously.

We have only the moment, Shizue. After tonight, there won't be much chance for fun. Hell, that's some band."

Dancing had made her brother lighthearted and happy. Now he slouched, jealously watching young couples entering the dance hall. "Let's go inside," she said.

"Are you sure?"

"Yes." She smiled prettily, cheered by his boyish enthusiasm. "I don't care what people think. Let them stare. We'll live for the moment and have wonderful memories of tonight."

With each dance Shizue clung to her brother more tightly. Other sad farewells entered her thoughts as the mirrored globe above them slowly turned the night away. Then, all too soon, their last dance ended. It was well after midnight.

Kimitake whistled as they walked down the quiet street toward his hotel. "I'm dead on my feet," he said, yawning. "Little sister's turned out to be quite a lady. Well, as the song says, thanks for the memories."

As Kimitake kissed Shizue, she had to fight back tears. His train left at dawn, so this was good-bye. "Kimitake. Oh, I'm so angry with myself. There's no reason to cry," she sniffled, dropping her forehead against his chest. "When you come back from this terrible war, we'll go dancing again."

"That's a date."

"Promise to write."

"Sure thing. Now give me a smile. I want to remember you that way."

Kimitake saw her to a taxi. *"Sayonara."*

Looking out the window, she waved good-bye, forcing herself to smile brightly. In the months ahead, Shizue would remember that final glimpse of her brother's tall figure striding off beneath the thundering clouds and pray for his safe return home.

BOOK FOUR
THE UPHEAVAL
WINTER

1940

The universe is forever falling apart—
No need to push the button,
It collapses at a finger's touch:
Why, it barely hangs on the tail of a sparrow's eye.

SHINKICHI TAKAHASHI

CHAPTER 30

Snow fell from an angry German sky. Whipped into a frenzy by icy winds, it blew around Max as he neared the test hangar. His father had been closeted inside for hours, laboring over the birth of some new parachute. Flashing red lights signaled that the wind tunnel was in use. That explained why no one had answered the telephone.

Max used his fist to open the iced-over latch of a metal cabinet that hung to one side of the hangar's steel outer door. To protect his hearing, he donned a bulky padded leather headset before entering. As he rushed inside, a canvas curtain absorbed the wintry blast.

Douglas Napier had been hovering over the engineers seated at an illuminated control panel. He jumped when Max tapped him on the shoulder. He faced away from a giant parachute tethered behind the wind tunnel's safety glass window.

Because of the noise, the engineers communicated with slate boards. Max seized one and wrote: "Heinz phoned. Urgent we return home at once. He didn't say why!"

Douglas shook his head, then quickly erased the message and scrawled, "Take charge, Anton," and passed the slate to his chief engineer. Heinz Karlstadt was not given to panic, he thought, as he raced off beside his son across the wide expanse of concrete and steel to an adjoining garage where the Mercedes was parked.

For some time, they followed a slow-moving plow truck. Max flexed his fingers on the steering wheel and cursed the delay. "Why would Heinz refuse to explain over the phone?"

His father shrugged, eyes fixed on the truck ahead.

Max glanced out the window. Hitler Youth had turned their schoolyard into fortresses of snow and crouched behind the battlements hurling snowballs. Just boys playing soldier. But many of them would soon be old enough to fight, Max observed.

Germany was now at war. In September, 1939, Hitler's surprise blitzkrieg had brought Poland to its knees. Great Britain and France had declared war against the Third Reich, while America remained neutral.

Germany's paratroopers had not seen combat in the taking of Poland, and Douglas's conscience was salved by the rationalization that this was not his war.

Because of spiraling production costs, their German profits had fallen short of expectations. Only two thirds of Lord Mitsudara's loan could be repaid on time, and Tadashi had asked for an extension. The lord, confined to his bed, had surrendered his powers to a board of directors, who were applying pressure for the remainder of Hosokawa-Napier, Limited's, debt to be paid.

Douglas opened his briefcase, nervously shifting through the latest production figures, which almost edged the business ledger from red to black. Nearly six months had passed without any decisive action by either Great Britain or France. So far they seemed content with blockading Germany by sea. This had cut off shipments of raw silk from Japan, but enough raw materials were stockpiled in the Karlstadt warehouses to last for years. Hitler tolerated the blockade. The next move was his, and Douglas believed it would come from the air, when the spring thaw opened the skies to the Luftwaffe.

Max agreed with his father, and he intended to leave for Japan before the lid blew. Shizue's period of mourning would end in May. A few short months, he thought. As he drove along the broad avenue of linden trees, he saw something that caused him to grow tense. "Gestapo?"

"Hold yourself in check, son," Douglas warned. Gestapo agents climbed from a black sedan parked outside the gates to the Karlstadt mansion. Three men blocked access to the driveway, while two others approached the stopped Mercedes.

Max cranked the window open. "Good afternoon," he said.

The stout, jowly Gestapo agent in charge slapped his gloved hands together for warmth. *"Guten tag."* He peered menacingly at Max and Douglas. Then his gaze shifted to the agent under his command. "This is Herr Napier and his son Max. You will not detain them or Frau Napier, unless given cause. Pass them through." Without a word of explanation he marched off stiffly.

One did not ask questions of the Gestapo, and Max stepped on the gas pedal, accelerating past the dark figures who now stood aside from the gates.

"Jesus, Dad. What's behind all this?" he asked, looking toward the house. The household servants, heads bowed, bundled against the cold, filed down the driveway, moving like a funeral procession. Only the butler lifted his head to stare back grimly at Max. Then that once friendly face took on a smug arrogance as he raised his arm in the *"Sieg heil"* gesture.

Max parked at the steps to the front door and hurried from the car with his father. Douglas narrowly avoided a spill on the icy steps in his haste to learn why the mansion was under siege by the Gestapo, who were checking the servants' papers before allowing them to pass outside the high garden walls.

"Everyone has been given the weekend, Herr Napier," Fleischer informed him at the front door. Then the liveried chauffeur whispered, "It is not safe to talk here. Some are still about. Please, go into the study."

In the study, Heinz Karlstadt stood with his back to a crackling fire in the fireplace. His wife and Angela were snuggled together in a deep leather sofa. Both women's eyes were red from crying.

"Heinz, what the devil is going on?"

"First close the door, Douglas."

As Heinz began to speak, Inge pressed a handkerchief against her mouth, her other hand kneading the plush fox fur throw draped across her lap.

"Inge is accused of consorting with a group of political undesirables who have been circulating anti-Nazi literature. Of course, she knew nothing about their activities. *Ja*, she is sympathetic to their cause, but she would never jeopardize all we have together. Courage, *Liebling*." Heinz stilled Inge's hand and tucked the fur throw around her shivering legs.

"It was an innocent friendship, Douglas. The Gestapo has no real evidence against her. Inge frequently visited Frau Muller, and the Gestapo had been watching the house for months. Now there have been arrests. Gestapo barged into our home with her name on a list of the guilty parties. They are being sent to concentration camps. Inge as well, even though she has denied these charges under questioning and refused to sign their false confession. If not for my position, they would have taken her away this morning. The Gestapo is granting me the privilege of another forty-eight hours with my wife. A period of adjustment, meant to soften the blow."

"Good God," said Douglas.

Still wearing his hat and overcoat, Max dropped into a high, wing-back chair. "I don't understand. How can Inge be found guilty without a trial?"

"Dear Max. I am a Jew. What more is there to understand?" With great effort, Inge straightened up and asked for a cigarette. Angela fumbled with the cigarette box, a bundle of nerves as she lit one and handed it to her friend.

"Thank you. Even now I find it hard to accept that this awful thing has happened," Inge said, taking dainty puffs while her gaze shifted from Max to his father. "Frau Muller is a sweet old lady. She was my governess. Like a mother to me. Through the years, once a week we sat together over tea. Often, her elderly friends were gathered there. The minister of her church and his wife. Dr. Hanauer, who cared for me as a child. No one ever spoke of politics. *Ach*, I shall miss those afternoons. I am afraid for Frau Muller and her friends. The concentration camp. Who knows what takes place there."

"Be afraid for yourself." Heinz's voice took on a hard edge. "Forgive me, Ingelein. But we have already examined the situation from all sides, and time grows short. So long as there is breath in my body, I will not surrender you. There is yet much to be decided, after Douglas hears my plan."

Fleischer knocked, then entered to announce the house was empty of servants. "Good riddance. They would surely have given us away. Sit down, Fleischer."

"See here," Max exclaimed in a commanding voice reminiscent of his father's in times of stress, "you've served the Führer well. Why not just pick up that phone and petition some higher-ups on Inge's behalf?" Heinz regarded him as though he had said something incredibly stupid. Still Max persisted. "Hermann Göring, for openers."

"Easy, son. The Gestapo wouldn't act before going through the chain of command. Isn't that so, Heinz?"

"*Ja.*" He sighed. "The Gestapo is thorough. No one is willing to stick his nose into their hornet's nest on behalf of a Jewess, even though she is my wife. So, they hope to smooth things over by giving me certain privileges."

Taking his gold watch from his vest pocket, Heinz snapped open the lid as its tinkling bell chimed the hour. "On Sunday morning I will have the privilege of driving Inge to the Ravensbrück Concentration Camp for Women. It is not far from Berlin, and I am to enjoy certain—unspecified—visitation rights. The Gestapo major who interrogated Inge was specific on one point only. She will be confined to Ravensbrück indefinitely." He snapped his watch shut.

"As I looked into Major Kuh's eyes, I knew that she would never leave its gates. She will be left to rot there like the other poor souls damned to Hitler's camps. Or worse. As God is my witness, Douglas, today I have stared into the eyes of death and seen his hand reaching out for Inge. Four hours already gone." Heinz's eyes filled with tears. He had bowed to Nazi authority, and this treachery was his reward.

Max could hear his wristwatch ticking in the heavy silence. Inge was pale with fear. Mascara smudged around her blue eyes gave her a deathly look, and Max experienced a sinking sensation low in his gut, with the memory of the beating he had taken from the S.S. "We'll get you out of Germany," Max said. "At Ravensbrück you'd be at the mercy of those thugs, and they're capable of anything."

Douglas gritted his teeth and nodded. "Right, Max. We can't let her be taken there. Did you think I'd give a damn about protecting our investments here, when Inge is being taken away?"

Seeing his son's look of surprise, Douglas confessed, "Yes, my track record isn't exactly something to be proud of. You saw what was happening, but I was too busy putting financial considerations first and trying to do right by everyone concerned. Suddenly this has become my war, and it isn't the time for hindsight. If there's some way out, let's have it, Heinz."

Inge sat quite still, Angela clinging to her hand protectively, while Heinz placed his monocle in his eye. "Escape for Inge rests with deceiving those on watch at our gate," he began. "Inge and Angela will exchange places. Inge will dye her hair, and with the proper hat, she will be able to pass as Angela. Seated in the limousine between you and Max, Inge will easily pass as your wife. The Gestapo will have no reason to suspect otherwise. She will keep a handkerchief to her eyes, having become ill over her friend's misfortune. The Netherlands is the only safe border you can reach within the time allowed us. Once aboard the train, Inge will keep to the compartment. At the border crossing, she will be in the rest room, the door slightly ajar. 'I am so sick,' she will moan. 'Something my wife ate,' you will tell the border guards. Angela's American passport will satisfy them. We must be open about your sudden travel plans. Fleischer will see to that when he goes for your tickets."

Fleischer turned from stoking the fire. "I will tell the men on watch that Herr Napier is taking his family on a short holiday because they are so upset. Especially Frau Napier." His expression grew pained. "Then I will say, 'Such tears over that Jewish pig.'" He looked sadly to Inge. "It hurts me to speak these words."

"They will be remembered when you are questioned," Heinz assured him. He unfolded a train schedule across the study desk. "Travel by day is far too dangerous, for there is only a local train. There are many stops where police are likely to board for routine identity checks. So, you must take the Schnellzug, which departs from Berlin at ten tomorrow night. Assuming it is on schedule, you will be safely out of Germany at nine-thirty on Sunday morning."

Max threw off his hat and coat. "Okay," he said, "I'm sold on the chances for getting Inge out. But what about you and my mother?"

"We wait here until you have telephoned that Inge is safely across. En Schede is the first scheduled stop. If our deception is exposed before then, the Gestapo will alert their agents at the border. However, I am not expected to leave for Ravensbrück until ten. When I drive from here, those standing watch will glimpse a blond woman seated beside me sobbing, her face pressed against my shoulder. Their car will follow my lead and will be completely taken by surprise as we near the American Embassy and I quickly pull into its courtyard. We pass there en route to the autobahn." Removing his monocle, Heinz pinched the bridge of his nose. "Technically we are on American soil, and Angela is spared any trouble with the Gestapo," he advanced in a strained voice. "Your government must protect her rights as an American citizen. Once we have explained the true circumstances, your officials must act on her behalf. There is no question of her safety. Some diplomatic back-and-forth—then Angela will be given a new passport and safe passage from Germany."

"Fine," Douglas said shortly. "But you're too important to Hitler's war machine for the United States to stick its neck out by granting you asylum."

"No, my friend. I am a member of the Nazi party. As Max said, I have served the Führer well. And the Karlstadt Works—my value to him there far outweighs the nature of my crime. So, my heart ruled over obeying the Gestapo's orders. So, I have given the Nazis one less Jew to worry about. They will punish me with a sharp reprimand. A slap on the wrist, Douglas, nothing more."

Heinz rested both hands on his friend's shoulders. "Trust my judgment. Take Inge to our good friends in Paris. This means you can never return to Germany. But the Nazi pact with Japan protects your investment, Douglas. Your share of the profits will be released to Baron Hosokawa. While I go to the plant each day, acting the role of a loyal Nazi, the outstanding debt is soon repaid, and the Gestapo no longer watches me so closely. When it can be arranged, I slip across the border into Switzerland, and Inge will join me there. *Ja*, there we can begin a new life together."

"Christ, I'd feel a damn sight easier if so much weren't left to chance," Douglas said. It sounded too simple. Too easy. He didn't trust it, but he could think of no alternate plan.

Smiling at her husband, Angela twined a lock of auburn hair around her finger. "Well, I'm not the least bit worried, darling. Inge is the only one in any real danger."

Inge embraced her. "I pray that is so. You are all so wonderful." Rising from the sofa, she went to embrace Fleischer, then Douglas, and lastly Max. "Bless you. I would never have asked this for myself. But Heinz has decided."

Max felt the shiver that ran through her. The afternoon light was fading, and he switched on the desk lamp, toying with the long fringe of its silk shade. "We're losing time, Dad. Unless you have a better way out—"

"I wish to hell I did." Douglas interrupted. "If the baron were here, his code of honor wouldn't permit him to abandon Inge. And I'm prepared to accept the responsibility for forfeiting our business interests, if it comes to that."

He turned to Heinz. "You may be punished with nothing but a slap on the wrist, but suppose the Nazis don't buy your act of loyalty?" Douglas challenged him. "You could be trapped here long after we're gone, working a bad debt off the account books. You're gambling too much on the Gestapo relaxing their watch on you."

Heinz shook his head and chuckled. "Credit me with more brains than those apes dressed up as men. During the Great War, I was taken prisoner and escaped my captors under more difficult circumstances than these. The Gestapo has its hands full watching so many suspected enemies of the Führer. Suspicion runs high even among their own ranks. In the war I was a fox who left the hounds sniffing after false trails, bumping noses while I crept across France to our German lines and drank schnapps with my comrades." He stood at attention, displaying his Prussian pride with a tight-lipped grin. "Experience, Douglas. In this matter you must defer to me as your superior officer. My strategy is sound. By keeping our heads and staying strictly to the schedule, Inge's escape will be assured. My own escape will follow within the year—made easier because I travel alone. No well-meaning friends to slow me down with their unwarranted fears. Doubt only endangers us. The first step toward victory is taken with a decision to act quickly."

"Maybe so, but I'd like to hold out for more time to think."

Angry with himself, Douglas paced, desperate to come up with some less risky escape plan. But his usually fertile brain was barren of ideas. He scanned the impatient, trusting faces of his wife and son; Inge seemed incapable of independent judgment; and Fleischer calmly stoked the fire. He was outnumbered by those who refused to see any possibility of failure. Grudgingly, he threw up both hands. "Heinz, you're a persuasive devil. All right, I'll gamble on your experience for survival. Enough time wasted on doubts. What next?"

"I suppose someone should go to the chemist's," said Angela. "Good Lord, I've never allowed the beautician to use more than a mild henna rinse on my hair. I have such sensitive hair. I'm afraid bleaching it to Inge's color may damage it beyond repair. Good Lord"—she laughed nervously—"how awfully vain and silly of me."

Max was packing a suitcase when Heinz Karlstadt quietly entered the bedroom. He smelled of cologne and wore a red velvet smoking jacket with an ascot. Their eyes met as Heinz drew on his cigarette with the tranquil expression of a man fresh from the arms of love.

"I have a favor to ask," he said. "Another hour or so and you will be on the train. Then it is in God's hands. Should anything happen to me, give Inge this. I know you can be trusted to keep it a secret between us."

Inge urgently called his name. "Now I must go to her." He removed a sealed envelope from his jacket pocket and left it on the dresser.

All that day Max had observed everyone moving around him as if in a fog. Husbands and their wives were suddenly ending a way of life they might never know again. Max pocketed the envelope. An unfinished letter to Shizue lay beside his moroccan-bound calendar on the writing desk, and he jotted a final notation under the day: 23 February 1940. Burning our bridges. Pointless to think beyond tonight!

Douglas found his wife seated before the vanity mirror, fussing over her bleached hair.

"I look positively washed out," she complained. "Is that drink for me?"

"One martini, very dry."

"How thoughtful, darling." Angela took a sip. "Mmm, just right. I've been in such a blue mood."

"Me too. Fleischer's bringing the car around."

Wincing, she put the frosty glass to her temple. "My passport's there on the bed." The night before, Douglas had made love to her. Recently sex between them had been good, and over the past year, he had shown her a new tenderness; complimenting her attire, holding her closer when they danced, and even surprising her with expensive gifts at times when she felt most neglected by his business demands. Douglas treated her as a young bride, and she glimpsed no trace of effort to make her doubt the sincerity of his attentiveness. It seemed that patience had rewarded her with some small measure of his love. Not since they were first married had she felt so happily in love with him and full of hope for the years to come. But soon Douglas would be leaving Germany without her. She had utmost confidence in Heinz's plan, and yet this night of parting held a threat. "All at once I'm feeling a little scared, darling."

"Nothing to be ashamed of. I'm very proud of you." He lifted the glass from Angela's hand, set it on the vanity, and kissed her long and passionately.

Flinging her arms around his neck, Angela kissed him back with an intensity that brought tears into her cool green eyes.

Max knocked on the door. "Ready to go, Dad."

Douglas opened the door and nodded, still rather dazed by his wife's kiss. Angela pulled herself together and descended the marble staircase, gripping her son's arm. The Karlstadts clung to each other, speaking in hushed voices. Inge wore a large black hat, its wide brim pulled down front and back. Dark hair made her even more striking, Angela thought, as Inge turned around to accept her hug.

Fleischer poked his head inside the front door. "As we thought. The Gestapo have left their car and are watching from the gate."

"Well, this is it," said Douglas, pulling on his gloves. "Wish us luck. Inge, take my arm and remember to keep your head down."

Max was to exit first. Inge would be seated between him and Douglas in the limousine.

"Wait." She suddenly rushed to Heinz. "*Schatzken*, what is there for me without you?"

"Have faith, my love. Cling to life. This is not good-bye. Be brave, and in no time at all we will be together again." Heinz stood her away, then kissed her pale hands. "Now, go. Take her, Douglas."

"See you in Paris," Angela managed to say in a tense voice. Her husband, her son, her dearest friend vanished behind the closing door, and she went to pieces as Heinz urged her toward the parlor. Its bay windows could be glimpsed from the gate, and as planned, she sat down at the piano. "Oh, Heinz."

"Keep your back to me and play."

She had not touched the piano in years. While Heinz drew open the curtains, she mindlessly struggled through a sad refrain.

"They are being stopped just outside the gate," Heinz announced, and Angela felt as though her hands were frozen to the keyboard. "You must keep playing," he told her urgently.

Inge buried her eyes in a handkerchief as Gestapo flanked the limousine. One agent pounded on Douglas's window, and his comrade ordered Fleischer to unlock the trunk.

"Security check, Herr Napier. Your papers. Quickly."

Douglas stared him down. They had not anticipated a passport check, and he made no move to reach inside his overcoat. "See here, you've no right to detain us. My wife's been under a terrible emotional strain. She's quite ill, and we have a train to catch. If we miss it, Reichsmarschall Göring will hear of this."

The agent smacked his lips. "You are a friend of the Reichsmarschall's?"

"We supply the parachutes for his Luftwaffe," Max answered. Inge sobbed more loudly, and he feared she was about to panic. "There, Mother, we'll soon be on the train," he said, bringing her close.

"Only luggage," the second agent said.

Slamming the trunk lid, Fleischer looked toward the mansion. "Did you expect to find that Jewess hiding inside?"

His laughter directed both Gestapo agents to the brightly lit parlor window. They watched Heinz cross to his wife, who was seated at the piano playing. He took her by the shoulders, and they kissed. It was a thoroughly convincing performance.

"Go on with you."

"About time!" Douglas bristled and rolled his window up. After they were safely away from the mansion, he pressed Inge's hand. Her eyelids fluttered, and her fragile smile tugged at his heart. Something was unwinding inside him. In the midst of this chaos, he seemed to be shedding the old wrinkled skin of guilt. Failing Natsu had been his cross. Now Inge Karlstadt offered him some measure of salvation.

At the Berlin station, Nazi flags decorated the gray stone columns where Fleischer braked the limousine. There were always Gestapo on watch at the station, and Inge could not risk drawing suspicion to herself by embracing the chauffeur good-bye. As porters advanced inside with their luggage, Fleischer clicked his heels. A chauffeur merely opened and closed doors; he would tell the Gestapo that he had been deceived as well.

"Auf wiedersehen, Fleischer." Inge kept her face lowered, holding down the brim of her large black hat as Douglas anchored her against him. The platform was ablaze with light, and she felt threatened by the crowd.

Finally, they were on the train, but an S.S. colonel momentarily blocked the passageway outside their first-class compartment. Even when he stood aside, Inge felt choked. Even after Max had closed the door and drawn the window shades, she did not feel safe.

Their express train departed punctually at ten. One hour out of Berlin, it steamed through a driving rain, which turned the previous day's snowfall into slush. A white-haired porter served them brandies and gave Inge a long-stemmed hothouse tulip in a fluted vase. Touching its petals, Inge recalled visits to Holland in happier days.

"The Zuider Zee. The quaint little towns and windmills turning their patchwork arms along the green canals," she remembered aloud, then laughed softly. "There was an inn. May wine. Violins. And a fat little waiter who kept tripping over his feet, the chair legs, everything in his path. That funny little man. How he made us laugh."

The porter knocked and entered to make up their berths. Germany shot past the windows, black as hell. At last Inge succumbed to an exhausted sleep. Max shared the adjoining compartment with his father. During the night, they woke at every stop, checking the timetable, alert for the unexpected.

"Shake loose, son!"

Max rose up squinty-eyed. It was daylight. The window was partially sheeted with ice. Looking through a clear spot, he saw the platform sign. "Osnabruck?" he asked. "Why are we stopping here?"

Douglas buzzed for the porter and checked his watch. "Seven-fifteen. Come!" He responded to a knock at the door. "What's going on?"

The porter's shoulders lifted. "There must be some trouble on the tracks, *mein Herr*. We should soon know how long the train will be delayed."

"Tell me the minute you hear anything."

"I'll go see what I can find out," Max said, reaching for his clothes.

"Stay put. The train could get moving again at any minute." Douglas cracked open the door between compartments. "Inge's dead to the world. Best not to wake her until we know the score."

Ten minutes elapsed before the porter returned. There had been a derailment in the night. "The tracks might be cleared within the hour," he informed.

"Of all the rotten luck," Max said, and his father nodded. "But things could be worse, Dad. Heinz doesn't have to leave the house until ten. Even with the delay, we'll be out of Germany by then."

"Trust you to look at the bright side." Douglas scanned the train schedule wearily. "Barring any other unforeseen delays, it's still going to be a very close call. Heinz may have to buy us time. How much time depends on when the tracks are cleared. In any event, he should be alerted."

From a pay booth in the Osnabruck station, Douglas telephoned Berlin. It was the first of two calls he would place to Heinz on that fateful

Sunday morning. Before the tracks had been cleared, well over an hour had stretched between calls, and now the express train was priming to roll.

"You've got to stall for time, Heinz. We'll be across at eleven-twenty."

Heinz absorbed the news calmly. Douglas's voice was charged with urgency. Angela paced nearby, and Heinz did not want a hysterical woman on his hands. "Do not worry. It can be accomplished without endangering our plans. How is Inge?"

"Frayed, but holding her own."

Heinz passed the receiver to Angela. "Darling, I just wanted to hear your voice."

"There's a lot riding on this, so keep your head. Hell, the goddamn train's leaving without me!"

As she surrendered the buzzing receiver, Heinz captured both her hands and kissed them. "My dear Angela, everything now rests with you," he said. "Any delay in leaving here will bring the Gestapo to our door. So we must keep them satisfied for the eighty minutes it will take before Inge's train crosses the border, and this can be accomplished only by taking the road to Ravensbrück."

Angela took a deep breath. "But they'll arrest me. I have no passport. They'll put me behind barbed wire in Inge's place," she said, pulling away. "With my hair like this . . ."

"Please, calm yourself. You may pass for Inge while in the car, but once the Gestapo have a closer look, they will know very well who you are. As an American neutral, they cannot hold you for long. But I would never subject you to that unpleasantness. Once Inge is out of danger, somehow I will lose their car and get you to the American Embassy as we had planned."

"Somehow." Struck by the dreadful uncertainty of that word, her eyes riveted on Heinz, who removed his gold watch from his vest pocket. Its tiny mechanism chimed the half hour. Just thirty minutes remained in the security of this grand house, Angela thought, and there was no turning back. She had already made her decision by exchanging places with Inge. What was the possibility of her arrest weighed against the safety of her dearest friend? Yes, Inge must escape.

The morning sun lay hidden behind rolling gray clouds, and there was a dank chill to the air. Angela wore a sable coat, and her straight dyed-yellow hair trailed down from a plump fur hat. Heinz started the Mercedes, and she nestled beside him, turning her face against his shoulder as they approached the gates.

"I can feel their eyes on me." Angela shivered.

The Gestapo remained in the warmth of their black sedan. Heinz was shocked to see the major who had interrogated his wife seated up front with the driver. Cigarette smoke curlicued around his face. His dark eyes narrowed on Angela, and Heinz could only imagine what the major had planned for Inge after she was surrendered at Ravensbrück.

The sedan followed, remaining a safe distance behind on the icy streets. Heinz kept Major Kuh's presence to himself, shuddering with the thought of Angela being at the mercy of that beast if they were arrested. He lit a cigarette to calm his nerves. A convoy of Wehrmacht trucks roared up Kaiser Wilhelmstrasse, past churchgoers, who waved and gave the "*Sieg heil*". Even on Sunday, Berlin was at war.

"Some music to help relax us," Heinz said, tuning in the morning concert.

To the accompaniment of Bach performed on the harpsichord, Angela watched U.S. Marines salute a motorcade of limousines entering the American Embassy courtyard. The Stars and Stripes had never looked so good to her, and unthinkingly she reached across for the wheel, causing the car to swerve toward the courtyard drive. Suddenly she sat up straight and put both hands to her face. "Good Lord, I don't know what came over me."

Heinz checked the rearview mirror. The Gestapo car sped up, then slowed as he regained control and drove on. "It could have been the ice. No harm done." The sedan followed closer now. "Keep your face from the mirror," he warned. Major Kuh appeared agitated, his hand drumming the dashboard as he pulled on a cigarette. "It is not far to the autobahn. Trust me and do not lose your nerve again."

She sank low in the seat, quietly hugging herself. Radio Berlin announced the time. "Ten forty five." In little over half an hour Inge would be safe. Angela tried thinking only of her. The morning concert resumed, and "Tales of the Vienna Woods" gaily measured the distance as they neared the autobahn turnoff.

Heinz stiffened. "They want us to pull over!" The sedan's headlights flashed on and off, and the major pointed at the curb ahead. "That accursed Major Kuh suspects we are up to something. Perhaps he thinks we hope to escape together on the autobahn."

"Major Kuh? Oh, it's all my fault." Covering her face, she prayed Inge might yet escape. "If only I hadn't panicked."

"*Ach*, who knows what goes on in the mind of a man like that! Unless we obey, he will force us over." Heinz steered for the curb. Then, as the Gestapo car slowed to park behind him, he shouted, "Brace yourself, Angela!" Flooring the accelerator, he shot away.

Luck was with him. No other cars were waiting at the turnoff, and he ran the stop sign and took the concrete grading that fed the autobahn. Traffic was light, mostly trailer trucks and military vehicles rolling cautiously on the patchy ice. The black sedan flashed across his rearview mirror as it sped out of the turnoff. It was gaining fast. "Good," he cried.

"The major would not waste his time chasing after us if he suspected you were not my wife."

Angela braced herself with both hands on the dashboard. "Heinz! My God, what are you doing?"

"Giving them a chase until the train has—"

Heinz never finished the thought. Changing lanes to pass a slow-moving bus, his foot pumped the brakes too late. The Mercedes careened on a glistening ribbon of ice and spun dizzily over the divider directly in the path of an oncoming truck. Angela felt some terrifying force wrench her off the seat. Her screams were lost in a deafening crash.

She lived for one instant longer. Then her head and torso were propelled outward through a fissuring membrane of glass. Sequined in glass, her body slumped back through the ruptured windshield, jostled as the wreckage was dragged to a hissing stop by the crippled truck.

The Gestapo sedan careened as it braked to avoid striking other vehicles in its path, and the other drivers all swerved to avoid the wreckage. A series of collisions took place and almost blocked the icy highway before the Gestapo car narrowly passed by them.

Major Kuh looked out his rear window at the chain of accidents. There was a concrete divider to separate traffic both leaving and entering Berlin. The major lit a cigarette and relaxed. "Drive carefully, Betz," he told his driver. "If our prey has not been killed, their injuries will keep them where they are. At the next exit we will drive back to the scene of the accident."

Feeling secure with his decision, Kuh enjoyed his smoke. It was some minutes before his sedan had doubled back along the autobahn. He saw police there setting up flares and directing traffic around the debris.

When Major Kuh got out of his car, police saluted him. The entire front end of Herr Karlstadt's Mercedes had been squashed, its doors buckled from the impact and hammered shut. "Such a mess," he hissed, leaning in through the shattered windshield.

Heinz lay across the wheel, pinned against it with his bleeding head turned to Angela. By some miracle he was still alive, but he could not move or feel his legs, and the major was a fuzzy blur.

Major Kuh snarled, "God, what a fool you are." Angrily he peered in at the woman. Her bloodied head was bowed to him, and suddenly he took her by the hair. The roots were dark. The Jewess had been a natural blond. Raising the lacerated face, he looked into Angela Napier's cool green eyes, which mocked him in death. "Your wife will never leave Germany. I promise you that!"

Heinz coughed up blood. The last sound he heard was the faint tinkle of his gold pocket watch chiming the half hour. Eleven-thirty. By the grace of God, Inge was beyond harm.

*　*　*

Inge Karlstadt sipped coffee from a bone china cup. The dining car buzzed with cheerful voices, while the first of many windmills turned lazily against the flattening horizon. The lowlands sprawled outside her window, drained of color in the curtaining snow. Holland and safety were pale realities without Heinz. They had never been apart for even a day. Max and his father sat across the table, smiling confidently. Her beloved Heinz was a resourceful man. Somehow he had bought her time, and all was well. But crossing the border at Rheine, she had felt a stabbing pain that took her breath away.

"My two handsome men." She reached her hands across the table to Douglas and Max. "After all we have been through, I want to share your confidence. But I need more than your words to quiet my fears. Can you understand?"

Douglas nodded. "When we stop at En Schede, I'll telephone the American Embassy. Then you can talk to Angela. She can put your fears to rest."

Max gazed dreamily out the window. Until then his destiny had been shaped by other people's lives and their loves. Now, in his twenty-first year, he had finally become his own man. All that Germany had been lay far behind him, and his thoughts turned to Shizue and home.

CHAPTER 31

"Come in, Mr. Napier." Ian Caldwell rose from his desk at the American Embassy in Paris. "Frau Karlstadt. Max. Sorry to call you out on such a rainy evening. Excuse the chill, but our antiquated heating system has gone on strike again." Suave, graying at the temples, he rubbed both hands together and chuckled nervously. "Yes—well, I quite understand what a trial this waiting has been for you all." Turning from his visitors, Caldwell viewed the lights of Paris diffused through a misty rain. "But since France declared war on Germany some months ago, communications between the two countries have been limited to diplomatic channels. As friends of both France and Great Britain, our diplomatic ties with Nazi Germany are strained at best. Acting on your behalf hasn't been easy, despite America's neutrality of the moment."

Douglas Napier sat down, then looked at the aggrieved faces of Inge and his son. Two weeks before, they had come here to inquire about Angela and Heinz. A few days later, the shocking news of their deaths on the autobahn had been dispatched to Paris from the American Embassy in Berlin. Knowing that Heinz had needed to play for time, both Douglas and Max had been forced to accept the reality of that tragic news.

"I'm resigned to the deaths of our loved ones, Mr. Caldwell." Douglas addressed him hoarsely, and Caldwell turned away from the window. "But fully accepting this tragedy demands some hard evidence. Something more than the words of a Nazi report of the accident in which my wife and Heinz were killed. What have you done to obtain documented proof?"

"The ambassador hasn't been idle," Caldwell said, his gaze fixed on Douglas. "Just a short while ago, Berlin's response to his latest inquiries arrived in our diplomatic pouch. I'm sorry to say, there can no longer be any question about the deaths of Heinz Karlstadt and your wife. I have here a copy of the police file. Death certificates, photographs taken at the scene of the accident. Morgue shots."

Only Inge had clung to a shred of hope, telling herself that the Nazis were tormenting her with lies, that Heinz and Angela had not died. Now she stared mutely at the file being handed to Douglas, thinking those were false papers. These past two weeks, Max had suffered the blow of his mother's death, sharing his grief with Douglas. His father opened the file, and Max bent over Douglas's shoulder and recoiled, stunned by gruesome photographs of the wrecked car, the bodies of his mother and Heinz laid out in the Berlin morgue. As Douglas numbly bowed his head, the photographs slipped through his fingers. It was then that Inge saw the faces of the dead. Clutching the photographs, she went down on her knees.

"I want to die," she sobbed. "Merciful God, strike me dead."

Douglas lifted Inge to her feet and gently pried the photographs from her hands. Their grim reality had destroyed the hope she had lived on, he thought, and perhaps destroyed her will to go on without Heinz. He watched Inge's eyes grow suddenly empty as she looked down at her wedding ring. "Is there someplace she can lie down?"

"Certainly. My secretary will see after her."

Inge inhaled sharply. *"Nein."* She sat twisting the gold diamond-studded wedding band Heinz had placed on her finger next to the flawless blue-white diamond engagement ring. The band would not come off. "Now and for always," she said softly to herself, voicing its inscription.

Ian Caldwell settled behind his desk with an air of detachment. "You have my sympathies. However, in the eyes of German law, you are the guilty parties. The Nazis disclaim any responsibility for the unfortunate accident."

"They're guilty as sin!" Max flared, slapping the police file. "The least you can do is have the bodies released to us, so we can give my mother and Heinz a decent burial. Or have those thugs already disposed of them?"

"They had no wish to punish the dead," Caldwell said politely. "Both victims were given a proper Christian burial. Here are copies of their grave registration certificates. The German obsession with record-keeping." He smiled as he passed them across the desk. "As you can see, they were laid to rest together in consecrated ground. As things stand, Frau Karlstadt has no valid claim on her husband's remains. However, I can request that your wife's body be exhumed—"

"No, leave her in peace." Douglas pressed his son's arm. "I doubt the Nazis would agree to such a request," he said quietly. "Your mother's beyond harm now. I feel she'd want to remain at rest beside her friend."

Max nodded. "Viewing mother's body would have made it easier to mourn her," he said, then folded his hands and tried to picture Angela as he had last seen her, standing in the Karlstadt mansion fussing with her bleached hair.

"There was another document in today's pouch that requires your attention, Mr. Napier," said Caldwell. "The Nazis seem anxious to settle the matter of your German holdings."

Douglas regarded him distractedly. "Beg pardon?"

"Study the document and let me know if I can be of further assistance." Drawing a deep breath, Caldwell buzzed for his secretary.

"Now, I realize this isn't the time to discuss Frau Karlstadt's status. However, the French are an intolerant bunch. As a Jewish refugee with no visible means of support, even your well-connected friends can't shelter her indefinitely. And since she's under your protective wing, I'd suggest you find a way to smuggle her into Portugal or Switzerland. No telling when this may become an all-out war. We're advising U.S. citizens to leave Europe."

Ian Caldwell looked up as his secretary opened the door. "Miss Walden, transfer these papers into one of our official envelopes. We can't have Mr. Napier leave us carrying the Nazi eagle and swastika through the Paris streets."

"Your meeting with the ambassador, sir," the pert young woman reminded him, adjusting the wool sweater that was draped around her shoulders.

"Spare us the droll humor, Mr. Caldwell," Max said angrily. "We're not going anywhere without Inge. We're all the family she has. Dad?"

Douglas shook himself alert. "Yes, we're a family now." He touched Inge's hand, but she was in a place apart, and he looked at his son. "Our roots are still in Japan. Japan is our home, Mr. Caldwell. She'll need authorization to travel with us. How do we go about obtaining the necessary papers?"

"Sorry, but I can't help you in that department. If she was a blood relation, you could sponsor her emigration to the United States. But even then it would take months of paperwork." Caldwell's secretary buzzed him on the intercom. "Tell the ambassador I'm on my way. Listen," he said, gathering up some file folders, "the ports are crowded with hundreds of Jewish refugees. Germans, Poles, you name it. A damn sad state of affairs, Mr. Napier. We won't take them in. Great Britain won't take them in. Quite frankly, the world fears the flood and has closed its doors to the Jews. Things can only get worse. Anyone who's taken the trouble to read *Mein Kampf* knows that Hitler would like nothing better than to sweep them all off the map. Now, I must run. Don't forget your envelope."

Max rode from the embassy in a taxi with his father and Inge. Since arriving in Paris, they had been houseguests of the Henris, whose friendship with both the Napiers and the Karlstadts stretched back for years. Max had met the French couple once before, at the Karlstadts' anniversary party. Jean-Claude owned banks, a stable of racehorses, and chateaus in Provence and Nice. His attractive wife, Niki, was a vigorous supporter of the arts, and her coterie of bohemian friends were in the habit of dropping by unannounced, paintings and manuscripts under their arms.

As they rode, images of *Kristallnacht* flashed through Max's mind: a burning synagogue; streets littered with broken glass; the howling mob of torchlit Nazi troopers. That night of terror for Germany's Jews had served as a warning of things to come. Now Inge was stranded in an indifferent world, her freedom purchased at the cost of two lives.

Paris would not give her shelter for very long. Max worried over Inge's future as he viewed the glittering cafes along the Champs Elysées, the Arc de Triomphe straddling the congested thoroughfare of honking taxis and pretty women cuddled beside their lovers under black silk umbrellas. To his eyes, Paris was a playground for those who seemed immune to the deadly contagion of war.

When they arrived at their destination, the taxi driver wished them a good evening. As they got out, a servant sprang from the imposing town house to shelter them with his umbrella. Max smelled cognac on the man's breath, which accounted for his cluminess and his robust laughter as he stumbled across the threshold.

As they entered the town house, Inge held her ears against the servant's laughter. She began trembling like a leaf. The Henris appeared in the foyer, dressed for dinner, and Inge reached out to them, uttering their names in a choked voice. "Jean-Claude, Niki." Then her legs began to give way.

If not for Jean-Claude's quickness, she would have struck the floor. He was a powerfully built man, and he carried Inge to a magnificent bedroom filled with freshly cut flowers. Niki and Max rushed along behind him with Douglas, who related what had taken place at the embassy. Both the Henris had come to accept the deaths of their friends, but they supported Inge's hopes with silent understanding. Now her collapse brought the couple to tears as Jean-Claude rested her across the bed.

"Shattering for her to be faced with the truth in such an awful manner," Niki said, opening a dresser drawer for a handkerchief to dry her eyes. "I was just a little hopeful that this was only a Nazi lie. But now that all doubt has been removed, I feel the sense of loss even more keenly."

"I feel rage, Douglas. And sorrow for all of you." Jean-Claude said huskily, massaging Inge's hands. "It is Jean-Claude, Inge. You are among friends. Niki, telephone for the doctor."

Niki's jaw was set with determination as she crossed to the bedside telephone. "I am taking Inge to Nice. Sunshine and the sea air will do her more good than the doctor." She turned to her husband. "We must not let her sink into despair."

Inge stirred at the sound of distant voices. She fought the light, wanting only to slip away into that quiet void with her grief.

The Henris exercised an aristocratic restraint over their emotions. Soon the doctor arrived. After he had assured everyone concerned that Frau Karlstadt was in good health, Niki quietly closed the door on her sleeping friend and embraced Douglas. "I have not spoken of this before. But you and Angela had so much together," she said. "How will you manage without her?"

"I have Max. Inge's lost everything, and she's my responsibility. Europe isn't safe for her. I'm taking her to Japan."

Standing beside his wife, Jean-Claude said, "*Oui*, she is in no frame of mind to be making decisions for herself. Your concern is justified, Douglas. We must take action. Might I suggest we discuss the matter over dinner."

There were always extra place settings at the Henri dinner table, and one of Niki's friends arrived before the first bottle of wine had been poured. Maurice Guillaume was introduced as a poet and the publisher of a small literary journal. He was a scrawny little man in his fifties, with a prominent nose. Tufts of unkempt gray hair poked every which way on his balding dome, and his thick eyeglasses were perched high on his head like a tiara. Monsieur Guillaume had come there to eat. "Conversation is bad for the digestion," he announced in a scratchy voice, tucking the napkin around his frayed shirt collar. "Go on without me. I am an exceptional listener."

Max had no appetite. His mother, Heinz, their grisly morgue shots, haunted him. In death, Angela Napier had taken on a stature she had not enjoyed while alive.

Douglas addressed the problem of Inge's passage to Japan. More than once his voice choked up, and he stared off vacantly. Monsieur Guillaume interrupted his meal, prying for information about Inge's escape and the business dealings of Hosokawa-Napier, Limited, in Japan. He grew increasingly excited, then pensive, and finally pushed his plate away.

Max wrote him off as an eccentric, and was rather amused when he produced a tattered notebook and the nub of a pencil from his jacket pockets. He lowered his glasses from his forehead to his keen brown eyes. Bent over the notebook talking to himself, Guillaume filled several pages before Niki announced that brandy would be served in the drawing room.

Monsieur Guillaume startled everyone by crying out, "There is a maniac on the loose, and his name is Adolf Hitler!" He slapped the notebook shut and pushed himself up from the table. "Forgive me, Niki, but I have other business. Monsieur Napier, we may be of assistance to one another, but it cannot be discussed here. I will contact you in a few days time."

"Can he be taken seriously?" Max asked after Maurice Guillaume had left.

"Do not be misled by his outward appearance," Niki told Max. "Guillaume is a leader in the Zionist movement. Their ambition is to establish a Jewish homeland in Palestine. I have never seen him so stirred up."

"Let us hope he is not all wind," Jean-Claude commented dryly.

An onslaught of visitors followed in Guillaume's wake, and Max retreated to his upstairs room. Since arriving in Paris two weeks ago, he had kept Paul informed by cable. That was now his only link with Shizue.

Mail between France and Japan was shipped by sea, and that took forever. He sat drafting another cable. Having to set the day's events down in simple language focused them into an equation; two women had exchanged places and fates.

He opened his calendar, where he had kept the sealed envelope Heinz had given him. He had not been able to bring himself to pass it on to Inge while she still clung to hope, and Douglas had agreed. Now this final contact with her husband might bring Inge solace in her grief, thought Max.

"Feast your eyes on this!" Douglas suddenly charged through the door to his son's room, red in the face and brandishing the documents Caldwell had given him at the embassy. "The Nazis are offering a small fortune in exchange for my shares in the Karlstadt holdings and a buy-out of the German patent rights for our parachute. We retain Japanese patent rights. I expected Hitler to confiscate the lot, but the close ties with Japan have forced him to observe the legalities. The bastard wants my signature, there on the dotted line." His finger angrily jabbed the document. "It's more than enough to wipe the slate clean of debt. But the Nazis can damn well stand on their heads before I accept a penny of their blood money."

"Just tear it up, Dad."

"That won't solve anything. A copy's been sent to Japan for Tadashi's signature, and this letter promises to make trouble for us with the Japanese government if we don't agree. Caldwell made it clear what we're up against." He settled on the edge of the bed and said grimly, "America's relations with Japan are strained at best. The Nazis could back up their threat. Jeopardize our residency there. As if we didn't have enough on our hands."

The documents were like a long swastika-decorated arm reaching out for them, and Max paced to the window, half-expecting to see Nazi flags strung along the tree-lined Paris boulevard. Instead, hansom cabs lured young couples to a romantic ride in the park and gendarmes in capes strolled along saluting the passersby.

"May I come in?" Inge swayed precariously at the open door.

"You shouldn't be out of bed."

"I woke in the darkness," she told Douglas, "cold and alone." Her natural hair color had begun to grow out, and she pushed the dyed auburn tresses back from her face, drifting across the room in an ankle-length satin peignoir that showed off her voluptuous figure. "I am numb. I have no more tears."

"I have something for you," Max said quietly. "This is from Heinz." Inge went limp, shaking her head as though the envelope in his hand did not exist. "I was to give you this if anything happened to him. Perhaps I was wrong keeping it until now." He handed it to her.

Inge sat down in an overstuffed lounge and opened the letter. "*Ach, Heinz—my Schatzken.*"

Douglas motioned his son from the room. "You did the right thing," he whispered. "Heinz's letter couldn't have meant more to her than it does now."

Misty-eyed, Max's gaze roamed the mirrored corridor, which seemed to stretch into infinity. "We're a long way from home. I wouldn't count on Monsieur Guillaume's help. Caldwell is only an undersecretary. I say we go straight to the ambassador."

Douglas agreed, and early the next morning they were given a brief audience with Ambassador Taylor. What he had to say was a disappointing reprise of what Caldwell had told them. He was sympathetic but hamstrung by the law. And so they waited for Monsieur Guillaume to call.

The French concierge wore a navy blue beret low across his ears. He frowned suspiciously at the well-dressed Americans. "Monsieur Guillaume? Number five."

In a cobblestone courtyard, cats lazed in the April sun and others prowled the worn stairs of the dingy apartment house on the Left Bank. Max shared his father's anxiety as they climbed to number five. Maurice Guillaume's name was etched in the tarnished brass doorplate. Rust had eaten through the painted tin mezuzah nailed above the bell. Max rang and the door opened.

"Good of you to come," Maurice Guillaume said. "I would have contacted you sooner, but these things take time." He warily scanned the stairwell. "Hurry inside. No mystery, just a healthy distrust of my neighbors. One can't be too careful."

His apartment was one enormous room. Books crowded the walls, and even with the French doors open to a small balcony, it reeked of aging paper. Guillaume gestured at two shabby chairs upholstered in faded green mohair, then leaned against a massive antique desk of the Napoleonic era. Bending down, he lifted the tabby cat that emerged from beneath the desk's ornate legs.

"First, I must ask some questions," he said, stroking the cat. "Are you a friend of the Jews, or is Frau Karlstadt merely an isolated case of compassion?"

"We're not bigots, Guillaume," Douglas answered shortly. "I'm appalled by what's happening to your people."

"Since *Kristallnacht*, my feelings for the Jews run deeper than that," Max said.

"So I see." Guillaume rewarded Max's youthful earnestness with a twinkling smile. "And Inge Karlstadt. How is she coping with the loss of her husband and your mother?"

"Not very well."

"She's plagued by guilt and feels their lives were wasted for her," Douglas said. "How else can she feel?"

The cat tried to break away, and Guillaume set him down. "Independent creatures without a care in the world. He tolerates my company in return for a tasty morsel of fish and a saucer of cream." He chuckled. "At night he is a fierce gladiator, fighting off the rodents at our door. Often I find him perched on the bookshelf menacing this caricature of Hitler."

Standing on tiptoe, he brought down a framed drawing: Hitler crouched on all fours, a fang-toothed, mustachioed rat in dress uniform. "The devil. The Antichrist. Rocks were hurled through my office windows after I published this likeness in my journal. There are legions of Frenchmen who would welcome the Führer in Paris. They see him as another Napoleon, who will bring unity and order to a fractured Europe. We are in the calm before the storm, *messieurs*."

Douglas passed the drawing to his son. "I don't need a lecture on the evils of Hitler. Can you help us or not?"

"When we first met, I said that we might be of assistance to each other. Your business in Japan struck me as the answer to a prayer. I've been in contact with many people, here and in London." Guillaume spoke excellent English, pausing occasionally to sniff the air in search of a word. "Apocalypse is near at hand. A lucky few have fled Poland with stories of Nazi brutality. Jews are being rounded up into overcrowded ghettos and forced to serve in slave-labor gangs. Mankind has stepped backward in time. Your wife and friend were early casualties of the mounting storm, while one Jew escaped Hitler's clutches. What I propose will give some meaning to their deaths and a renewed sense of purpose to Frau Karlstadt's life. You are in a unique position to help save others like her. Men, women, children, trapped in the same web. I won't bargain with Frau Karlstadt's passage to Japan. Once you've heard me out, the choice is yours."

"All right, let's have it," Douglas said.

Sitting on the edge of his chair, Max sensed that the course of his destiny was about to be altered by this restless little man who circled around his desk.

Guillaume picked up a typewritten list of names, which he displayed with an angry flourish. "As we speak, these Jewish refugees wait in Marseille for some ship that will smuggle them into Palestine. Few ships get through. The British keep a close watch on all ships sailing from European ports. Their gunboats cruise the shipping lanes, and these people are likely to be turned back at sea. Often they are discovered within sight of the homeland. Many are without funds. It's difficult to find ships that will take the risks, and buying off their captains doesn't come cheap. But how can you set a price on human life?"

"If it's money you need . . ."

"*Oui.*" Maurice Guillaume nodded, and emotion caused his scratchy voice to deepen. "Money and something more. I belong to an organization that has been assembled to assist these helpless victims. We receive some financial aid through the World Jewish Congress and members of the Zionist movement. Private donations account for the rest. At present, our network is small, and the number of refugees we are dealing with is merely a trickle. But when Hitler marches again, their numbers will increase. Unfortunately, we can't guarantee their safe passage to Palestine or elsewhere. As I've said, ships sailing from European ports are suspect. However, ships sailing from Japan to the West are not, and you can buy their captains."

Douglas looked at him, incredulous. "What possible use can that be to your people here?"

"Ah." Guillaume chuckled and raised his thick eyeglasses up across the top of his balding head. "Rendezvous at sea, Monsieur. The ships you buy for us in Japan meet with ours somewhere in safe waters and take on their precious cargoes. From there, Palestine and other shores lie open to them. It can be done—and without any personal risks. After all, a man of industry such as yourself deals in shipping as a matter of course. I've worked everything out to the smallest detail." Excitedly, he pressed a gray folio into Douglas's hands.

Father and son exchanged wary looks. Inge's escape had seemed to involve no personal risk. Now, neither man jumped to accept Guillaume's proposal.

"Don't rush to a decision," he implored. "Take time to think it over. Discuss things with Frau Karlstadt. God moves in mysterious ways, my friends." He paused and looked down, his eyes filled with tears. "Salvaging even one cargo of doomed souls would be a blessing."

Douglas nodded. "You did say no strings were attached to Inge's passage."

"Arranged. Go to this address," said Guillaume, fishing a business card from his vest pocket. "The card will identify you to Monsieur Breillat. His work is expensive. Fifteen thousand American dollars will buy her the papers of a Swiss national." His shoulders lifted. "It's the best I can do. With these she can obtain a tourist visa, but her stay in Japan would be limited. However, there is a better way open to you."

"What?"

"Marry her, Monsieur. As your wife, she becomes an American citizen with an American passport. No questions asked."

After leaving Guillaume, father and son wandered past the Left Bank bookstalls and into a sidewalk cafe, where Douglas ordered them Pernods. A marriage of convenience seemed the perfect solution. That is, if Inge would agree.

While Douglas studied the folio, Max stretched out both legs and tipped his pale face to the spring sunshine. With Guillaume's proposal, a purpose had emerged out of the chaos, and he saw no way they could refuse. The homeless waiting at Marseille were not strangers to him: he saw them as Rachel, Avrum Rothstein, and their families. One day the faces of his Jewish friends might surface among the needy, only to be turned back at sea.

Douglas seemed impressed by what he read. "Guess we're in for it, Max," he said, putting the papers back in the folio. "Ironic. I tried to redeem myself through your mother. When she took me back, my efforts to undo the harm I caused her were a dismal failure. But our last months together, I tried my damnedest to please her. I'd like to believe that I brought Angela some happiness." Douglas paused, staring out across the Seine. "Even so, it wasn't nearly enough to make restitution for all those empty years. Now her death has granted me the chance to earn some self-esteem."

Max did not comment on his father's painfully stated admissions. Fate had given them both an opportunity to serve a larger cause than themselves. He picked up the folio and took out the papers. Rather than dwell on the past, Max's thoughts were on the present.

Guillaume had drawn a tidy little map. One sweeping line marked the sea-lane from Japan. Their ships would enter the Mediterranean via the Suez Canal. Dotted lines indicated the ships sailing from Lisbon, Marseille, and Naples. Three European ports were within easy reach of a rendezvous point near Crete, where the human cargos would be transferred under cover of nightfall. Time factors, how Douglas would communicate with Guillaume's European network, and the logistics of their operation were all neatly laid out. Max put everything back in the folio, finished the last warm dregs of Pernod, and said, "Well, he's got my vote. I guess the next step is to put this to Inge."

The afternoon sun streamed through the tall French windows in Niki and Jean-Claude Henri's town house, the warm light touching Inge's golden hair as she sat at the piano. Most of the temporary dye had washed out, and the remaining traces of Angela's color were hidden among the folds of a soft bun.

As she played, Douglas quietly lowered himself into the sofa, unseen. He was touched by the familiar melody she played. Beethoven's "Moonlight Sonata" had been a favorite of her husband's, and the resonating notes evoked evenings in the Karlstadt mansion, with Heinz seated near his wife at the piano, his dark eyes glistening with love. That afternoon, though, the romance of Beethoven's sonata was lost in the dirge Inge made of its notes. Her fingers ponderously marched across the keyboard like mourners at a funeral procession, until she abruptly stopped playing, removing her hands from the keys as if stung with pain.

Douglas cleared his throat and watched her grip the piano bench. "You play beautifully, Inge," he said, unable to think of some more appropriate response. She turned and regarded him vacantly, her eyes heavy with tears.

In an effort to make contact with her, he said, "Max and I spent the afternoon with one of Niki's friends. Maurice Guillaume. He's a Jew, active in the Zionist movement. He's offered us help."

"Politics," Inge said in a choked voice. "Politics killed my Heinz. The Jews are lost. Zionism is talk—only talk."

"No, there's more to it than that."

"You think so? Can you really think the world cares what happens to the Jews?" she challenged him. Before he could answer, Inge attacked the piano, furiously hammering out the notes of Chopin's "Polonaise." "This is hopeless talk of justice set to music," she cried over the thundering chords. "No one will give the Jews a homeland. Justice is only a word! Words will not bring Heinz back to life. I should have died with him—not Angela!"

Douglas went to the piano bench and forcefully took hold of her arms. "Stop crippling yourself with guilt and let me help you. Let me help us both find some meaning in all this sorrow." Inge's head fell back against his body, and she made a whimpering sound. "Please, hear me out. I've watched you waste away on grief long enough. Now there's a chance for us to do something more than feel sorry for ourselves. We can't bring back the dead, Inge. But we can help save the living."

"I am not a hysterical woman." Inge looked up at him with searching eyes. "*Ja*, once in Berlin I lost control of my senses. The Gestapo was beating a Jewish merchant, and no one came to his defense. Indifferent— even the police were indifferent. Angela saw what I had refused to see. If only . . ."

"You're safe from the Gestapo here," Douglas broke in. "But you're not welcome in France or any country in Europe. It's dangerous for all of us to remain here. Come to Japan with me, Inge. We can be useful to the Jews by returning there. Maurice Guillaume proposed a plan." He grew silent as the butler appeared, wheeling a tea cart.

"Madame Henri thought you might like tea in the garden."

"Dear Niki. So thoughtful and patient with me." Inge sighed and stood. Taking Douglas's arm, she managed a faint smile as they entered the sun-filled garden. "All these lovely spring flowers. Our garden in Berlin must also be coming to life." She sat under the bright yellow table parasol. "Heinz would sit there with me at breakfast, crumbling up some toast for the birds," she reminisced, crumbling one of the tea cakes served by the butler to feed the birds alighting at her feet. "Being with Heinz gave meaning to simple moments like these." She met Douglas's eyes. "You said that this man Guillaume might help us give some meaning to his death?"

"Yes." Douglas did not trust speaking in the butler's presence.

While he hesitated, Inge regarded Douglas. They had loved each other as friends, and now he offered her a special comfort. A good deal of his grief over Angela's loss was built on the happy times the two couples had shared together over the years. Yes, he missed Angela dearly—Inge could see that, and she silently mourned the loss of her best friend. Her husband's and Angela's witty comments had brought laughter to moments spent in the garden at Berlin, and in this Paris garden, where the two couples had sat together when visiting the Henris.

The butler asked if there would be anything else they required.

"No, just close the garden doors." Douglas watched the butler leave. "It's safe for us to talk now," he told Inge.

The smile faded from Inge's face as she stirred her tea and listened to Douglas tell her of Maurice Guillaume's plan. When he had finished, she sat reflecting for a moment before speaking. "Money. To save so many we must have a great sum of money." She raised her eyes to Douglas's smiling face. "I want to believe this man's friends can do all you say. But with the ports watched so closely, how can they get Jews safely aboard the ships we will buy in Japan? How can they land the people safely in Palestine?"

"Money isn't a problem. And Guillaume will satisfy all your questions when you meet." There was a strong wind, and Douglas stood to collapse the parasol. Then it began to rain. He and Inge ran inside the house to the music room. For the first time in weeks, she laughed, and then tears joined with the raindrops on her beautiful face.

"Heinz wouldn't want you to suffer like this," Douglas said.

Inge embraced him. "Thank you for holding out something for me to believe in again. How selfish I have been, giving no thought to your own grief. Angela was my dearest friend, and I owe her husband more than the self-pity that has kept me from helping to ease your pain, from sharing in your great loss. Can you ever forgive me?"

"Nothing to forgive," Douglas answered evenly, holding her and thinking of the two women who had shared his life, both of them so tragically lost. "Our losses have cut us in half, Inge. I know what it is to feel there's no reason for going on. I know what it is to crawl before learning how to walk again." He did not know that Angela had told Inge of his infidelity, but something in her look told him that she knew, and her understanding smile brought them closer. "Angela meant so much more to me than I realized while she was alive," he confessed.

"Yes, you went well together, Douglas. We are fortunate at least to have the consolation of our memories," Inge said. She felt comforted by his strong arms. Angela's confession to her was a sacred trust, she decided, never to be spoken of. "I also must learn to walk again and grow strong like you."

"Then you'll come to Japan?"

"Ja, to work with you and Max." Inge dried her tears and paced, looking out the windows sheeted with rain. "But I have no papers. No passport." She spun around. "Can Monsieur Guillaume help with this as well?"

"No. There's only one way open to us, Inge, and that is for us to get married." Douglas observed her shock at his candor. He saw no reason to bring up Guillaume's offer of forged papers, which offered only a temporary solution to the problem. "For the sake of convenience," he added rather awkwardly. "It's only a marriage on paper. A legality to obtain your U.S. citizenship and your right to become a resident with me in Japan. The practical solution."

"Practical but dreadful," she said, twisting her diamond wedding band. "The good we can do is too important for me to think how this will look to your Japanese friends so soon after Angela's death. But to live as husband and wife in the house you once shared—to falsely swear holy marriage vows is a sin before God."

"Your feelings are understandable, but it won't be a church wedding. Just a civil ceremony. Cut-and-dried," Douglas reassured her, trying unsuccessfully to smile away her objections.

"No, I will not betray Heinz's memory by living a lie."

"Inge, we have no other choice. To refuse would betray the dead. We've both led complacent lives, Inge. Now we can't pick and choose what suits us. Under the circumstances, our marriage is a small sacrifice to make."

Inge sank to the piano bench and nodded slowly. "You are right. What we once had is no more. I cling to the diamonds Heinz placed on my finger, but without him they are cold glass and better sacrificed to our cause. While people are in need, I can no longer afford to place sentimental value on worldly goods. If exchanging vows with you before God is a sin, then so be it."

Douglas brushed her lips with his, kissing her as a friend. It was a heartfelt gesture that struck a new accord between two survivors. They held each other, feeling in the presence of the nameless souls whose destinies would be joined with theirs in an unspoken pact.

From that afternoon on, a whirlwind of activity paved the way for their mission in Japan. Maurice Guillaume's cause had given Inge new life, and Max, Douglas, and Inge met frequently at his Left Bank apartment. Inge had taken to his cat, and that day she cradled the tabby like an infant, her eyes touched with fire as Guillaume gave them a final briefing. The cat purred contentedly, and Inge smiled at Douglas. Soon she would become his wife, but in name only. He had signed the Nazi documents, and she thought it ironic that Hilter's blood money would buy back the lives of many Jews.

"Now, a last bit of good news to mark your departure." Guillaume stood at his desk and poured cream into a saucer, which he placed on the floor. "Our Lisbon agents have found just the right man for you in Tokyo. His name is Teofilo Aquida. A communications clerk at the Portuguese consulate. Jewish on his mother's side, which is in our favor. Also, he's poorly paid. I'm sure you'll have no difficulty purchasing his services. Since we've already bought one of his trusted counterparts in Lisbon, all communications between us can be sent over the diplomatic wire in code."

Beaming, he took the cat from Inge and placed him before the saucer.

"Drink, *mon petit chou*," he encouraged his pet. But the animal turned away to rub up against Inge's legs. "*Oui*, it's sad to see our friends go. He will miss you, dear lady."

Inge opened her purse. "My husband left me well provided for. He lived in fear for me and quietly took measures to insure our future if it became necessary to flee Germany. Over the years he managed to smuggle funds out of the country. It amounts to quite a large sum, deposited in a numbered Swiss bank account. I learned of this only through a letter he had given Max before we parted. These papers will give you access to his funds. Take them, Maurice. Perhaps my fears are unjustified, but we face a long journey, and your work here must continue. Each life you buy avenges the dead."

His round brown eyes grew moist as he bowed to kiss her hand. "Then I humbly accept your gift in the names of the dead, Madame. At sundown, I will visit the synagogue and say Kaddish for them."

She quietly thanked Guillaume, suddenly ashamed of her ignorance. Raised in the Christian faith, she had no idea how to pray as a Jew. But for the word *Jude* stamped on a German birth certificate, she might have lived out her days with Heinz, and Inge experienced a moment of cold rage.

Douglas consulted his watch. "We're running late."

"Godspeed, my friends," said Guillaume, embracing each of them in turn. "Business calls me away in the morning. You'll be contacted at Lisbon and given the code book and full particulars on Senhor Aquida."

Before their taxi swung away, Max observed the pragmatic little Jew watering the geraniums on his balcony, faced out across the Seine as if he could see Palestine within reach of its narrow banks. Inge and his father avoided eye contact. The impending marriage ceremony was causing them both uneasiness. That afternoon, Inge had exchanged her widow's black for a handsome tweed suit, and she fussed nervously with the short veil of a businesslike, gray felt hat. As they neared the Paris city hall, Douglas slid the black mourning band off his arm and stuffed it in one pocket.

"What kept you?" Niki and Jean-Claude Henri's voices overlapped as Douglas, Max, and Inge got out of the cab.

"The mayor is about to leave," Niki panted, urging everyone inside. They hurried down the vaulted hallway to the mayor's office.

"*Merde,*" grumbled Jean-Claude. "That pompous ass would not be sitting where he is if not for me." There had been a mountain of red tape attached to arranging the marriage. Due to Jean-Claude's powerful connections, the legal process had been speeded up.

"No reason to be nervous," he told Douglas, handing over two gold wedding bands as they stood outside the door to the mayor's office. "Only a formality. Ready, then?"

It was as Douglas had predicted, a cut-and-dried civil ceremony. The portly mayor examined his fingernails while his sallow-faced clerk rattled off words printed on a soiled blue card. Tears ran down Inge's cheeks as the rings were exchanged. The pen quivered in her hand as she signed her half of the innumerable papers. Max and the Henris signed as witnesses. The mayor thumped on his desk, then exercised his privilege to kiss the bride. This marriage of convenience had stirred up ghosts, and everyone departed in a funereal silence.

Three days later, the second Mrs. Douglas Napier boarded an Air France plane at Orly for Lisbon. U.S. passports did not require the bearer's religion, and she was identified only as Inge Napier. She suffered a disabling loss of identity. Waving back at Niki and Jean-Claude, she fought to retain hold of her previous existence. But even these two dear friends now belonged to the past, and she wept against Douglas's shoulder until Paris dissolved into the clouds.

Lisbon twinkled in a black velvet night, warmer than Max had expected, and he shed his wool jacket. Lit by spots, the *Yankee Clipper* ebbed on its moorings with the rising tide. Pan American's huge transoceanic sea plane was being readied for flight. It was the only commercial aircraft providing service from Europe to America. By morning Max would have crossed the Atlantic and would land on the shores of New Jersey. From there another flight would take him across America to San Francisco, where the *China Clipper* was moored, and that sea plane would span the Pacific to home in little under sixty hours.

Max anxiously searched the busy dock. Lisbon was a hotbed of intrigue. Since landing there, he'd had the feeling they were being watched, but Guillaume's agents had yet to establish contact. "If they don't act soon, we'll miss the flight."

"Keep your voice down," his father cautioned, as the passengers were called to the boarding gate.

Just then, an olive-skinned porter trailed along the boarding line with a tan briefcase in hand. "Senhor Nap*eer*! You are Doog-a-loss Nap*eer*?" he inquired, reading from the name tag chained to its handle. "This was forgotten by you in the customs shed." Their eyes met, and the young man displayed a toothy grin. "Is important, no?"

"Yes, very." Douglas feigned great relief. "Thanks," he said, accepting ownership of the leather briefcase he had never seen before. "Here's something for your trouble."

"Good voyage, Senhor."

During the exchange, Max experienced a surge of adrenaline. Guillaume's agent pocketed the tip and moved off without so much as a backward glance.

A boisterous group of Germans shoved through the boarding line, identifying themselves to the chief steward as members of the diplomatic corps and demanding to be put aboard the flight. Passage was at a premium.

"Waiting lists for every flight," the chief steward explained. After some heated discussion, he called the captain over to settle the dispute.

"Our two countries extend a common diplomatic courtesy, Herr Captain," the uniformed Wehrmacht major loudly interrupted him. "We enjoy priority over civilians, and six of them must give up their seats to us."

"Very well." The captain stepped forward to explain the situation and asked for volunteers. There were none. "Sorry, folks, but you'll have to wait for the next flight," he said, counting off the first six people in line.

Douglas brought Inge close. "Not on your life. The ambassador in Paris arranged for our passage, and I'm not about to give an inch to these rude servants of the Reich. Do I make myself clear?"

"You do." The captain frowned and tugged on his flight cap. "Don't care for their manner either, but they've got me over a barrel. How many in your party?"

"Three."

"Go aboard, sir."

Inge shivered with contempt. She yearned to lash out at her husband's murderers, but Douglas kept her well in tow and whisked them aboard.

"We can't afford to make a scene," Douglas warned her, as the Germans marched to their seats directly across the aisle. "You'll see more of their kind in Tokyo. Think of the work ahead."

"*Ja*, I will try."

Max let himself go with the sensation of flight as the transoceanic plane lifted into the air. Stars shone overhead, and as the plane tilted one silvery wing, Max could see the edge of the shoreline. Then Europe's colored lights were snuffed out by the darkness at sea. Max closed his eyes. Without Shizue, he had been incomplete, only half a man. In a flight of fancy, he imagined himself already home. In his dreams somewhere over the North Atlantic, Shizue rushed toward him, all desire, and there were no longer any wars to run from.

CHAPTER 32

"Max! It's good to have you back." Paul hugged his brother. He had been drinking, and he slung one arm around Max's shoulders, then escorted him into his spacious Tokyo apartment. "Celebrating your return. But drinking alone is a downer. I'm a little soggy around the edges." He laughed and waved his cane in the direction of the living room. "How do you like my new apartment?"

Uncomfortable, Max surveyed the luxurious appointments, then turned back to Paul. His brother had changed. He was thinner in the face, and his hazel eyes were restive and full of pain. But he seemed stronger, surer of himself, and comfortable with his hard-earned importance. "Quite a layout. Any servants?"

"Just the houseboy. His day off." Paul limped behind an elaborately carved ebony bar. A shock of white now streaked his dark brown hair, and worry lines creased his brow. "Mixed blood, like me. We're the perfect couple. What'll you have? Name your poison, prodigal brother. I'm well stocked. Some mighty important people drop by to bend elbows with this clever *ainoko*. Odd, how a few well-chosen words can eradicate the racial barrier. Smudge the filthy line is closer to the truth."

"I could use a Scotch. It's hard coming down to earth after all those days in the air." His plane had touched down barely an hour ago. From the air he had observed the changing face of Tokyo. The city had been constructing facilities to host the 1940 Olympic Games. But war in Europe had forced everything to a halt. Max had seen the weeds overtaking the shells of housing for athletes and the barren field of the stadium. Grim evidence that the world was no longer at peace.

"Here's your whiskey. Now let's drink a proper toast. To Shizue. To your happiness."

"And to yours, Paul."

He slumped over the bar, making circles with his glass. "I've given up on pipe dreams. We're older now. Bumped around by life and, hopefully, wiser. When you telephoned from the airport, I thought—God, how narrow the world has become. Time and place, squeezed into a nutshell.

But here I am, waxing philosophical when you came here for more than a look at my ugly puss."

Feeling comfortable now, Max patted his brother's arm and smiled. "Listen, I intend to make a nuisance of myself, so be warned. I know Shizue wanted everything about our reunion to be perfect. Now, tell me what she's planned before I go stark raving mad."

Paul freshened his drink. Once again, Shizue had turned to him—perhaps for the last time. As he spoke, melancholy settled in. "All things considered, Tokyo holds too much conflict for you both. I suggested somewhere with room to breathe. The spas at Beppu seemed the perfect choice for a young widow to recuperate following her long months of mourning. Yufugawo traveled there with her. Hey, don't get angry. Only a ploy to keep Baron Hosokawa from barging in. You can't bypass her father just like that," he flared, snapping his fingers. "Like it or not, he's still in the picture."

"How much in the picture?"

"Goddammit, Max, I'm not her lover. That's for you to find out."

Max nodded. "Love brings out the best and the worst in a man. I deserve a swift kick in the behind."

"Bend over and I'll gladly oblige. I've still got one good leg to do the job."

Brothers squared off across the bar, then broke into laughter, joined glasses, and drank. Paul had located a cottage nestled in the hills of Beppu. "No telephones or neighbors to intrude," he said. "Shizue's there now, feathering the nest. She'll be waiting for you at the door, day after tomorrow."

Max sighed heavily. "Thanks doesn't cover all you've done. You're right about life bumping us around. I can still feel the bruises."

"Have another drink and fill me in on things. Your cables left a lot of gaps."

Whiskey loosened his tongue and mellowed his temperament as Max fleshed out the events between Inge's escape and their pact with Guillaume. Paul was shocked. Just a bit tipsy and in need of fresh air, he suggested they go for a walk. Outside Max noticed a work crew pulling down a lamppost. Riding through Tokyo, he had seen other crews similar to this one. "What's going on?"

"Scrap drive," Paul answered, listing on his cane. "Emergency measures. Fighting China has bled us dry. Bridge railings, even the radiators from some hotels, dumped into the melting pot for guns and planes. A systematic rape. Where it'll stop, nobody knows."

With his free hand, he took Max by the arm as they walked on. "So, your father's married a Jew. Given her his name and his home. If only he had done as much for my mother," he said bitterly. "At last he's found his balls, but it comes too late. As for your illegal trafficking in human souls, be on guard, Max. This is a hostile climate for Americans. Japan is committed to winning in China. Scrap metal, oil—the U.S. of A. is the primary supplier of the critical resources we need, and Roosevelt is slowly tightening the screws on our war effort."

It was a calm May afternoon. Paul talked of war, and Max's eyes roamed the familiar street crowded with Japanese soldiers on furlough. The mood here was not so very different from Berlin, he reflected. Just ahead, men clamored around a newsstand. The skies over Europe had cleared, and Hitler had pushed across the borders into Holland, Belgium, and Luxembourg. Word of this had reached Max five days before. Now he stood beside his brother reading a headline: "Rotterdam Surrenders." A German wire service had provided an account of the battle. The victory had been won by Hitler's paratroopers, who had captured vital bridges before the Dutch could destroy them.

"If Belgium falls, Hitler's armored columns will storm into France. You didn't get out any too soon," Paul commented ruefully.

Max felt sick to the stomach. For the first time, his father's parachutes had been put to use. He felt as though he himself had taken a direct hand in enslaving a free nation. All through dinner with Paul, he could not shake his depression.

When he taxied home later that evening, he found that the Napier mansion had fallen into disrepair. Morita had stayed on as caretaker. But he was now past seventy and had grown very forgetful. He greeted Max's arrival with sad, hollow eyes that expressed confusion. "Is your mother not with you?" he asked, peering out the front door for signs of Angela. "I have waited all this day for her return. But your father brings another woman into the house and says she is now the *okusama*."

"Morita, what's keeping you with those bathtowels?" Douglas called from the stairs. "There, under your arm," he pointed out impatiently. "Take them up to Mrs. Napier."

Shaking his head, Morita shuffled across the foyer.

Douglas came down the stairs and said to Max, "I've explained things a dozen times, but it just doesn't register. How's Paul?"

"Different. Nothing's quite the same, Dad."

"I know."

For a time, the two men sat talking in the library. His brother was the main subject, and Max was quite candid about Paul's feelings. Douglas made no mention of it, but returning home had brought on a wave of nostalgia for the past—unhappy though it was. Angela's old clothes hung in the upstairs closets, her perfume bottles were arranged on the bedroom vanity, and strands of her hair were twined among the bristles of a tarnished silver brush. His wife was still very much present in this house she had so hated. Inge had felt that, too, and saw herself as a usurper.

"Tadashi telephoned from Nagasaki," said Douglas. "The Japanese were impressed by Hitler's use of airborne troops in the taking of Holland. It's created a sudden demand for our parachutes. The Imperial Navy awarded us a huge contract. Germany is sending jump school cadre to train the Japanese recruits. Continuing to do business here is a necessary evil, Max." Douglas pitted a smile against his son's sad expression. "Stop carrying the world on your shoulders. Go to Shizue. I'll handle the business while you're away."

With a weary nod, Max bid him good night.

Had Max stayed longer, Douglas thought, he might have lost control and voiced his torment over the closeness between his sons. But he had no right to intrude, despite the anguish it caused him to be excluded. Sliding open a desk drawer, he removed the snapshots Natsu had taken of their growing son over the years. Suddenly angry, he threw them across the desk. Did Paul intend to punish him forever?

Beppu appeared to be on fire. Viewed from the ricksha Max had hired, minarets of white steam billowed up from all corners in this picturesque city of hot springs and boiling ponds. An endless source of scalding water gushed from the geothermal cauldron beneath its surface. The climate was mild, however, the sea air invigorating, as the ricksha coolie pulled Max up steeply winding paths lined with quaint inns. Two stone lanterns marked a narrow footpath. Steam rose out of the treetops on the hill above, and in the breeze a red ribbon danced. Shizue had tied it there to point the way.

"Stop here!" Max got out of the ricksha and quickly paid his fare.

Tears filled Max's eyes as he climbed for that dancing red finger. Lush foliage shaded the hilltop. Max shifted his suitcase from one hand to the other as he followed other red ribbons down a grassy incline toward the sound of wind bells. He was surprised and delighted as he entered a small clearing. At the center of the clearing there was a natural rock pool of steaming water. Shizue had transformed this place as a labor of love. Garlands of flowers were draped from the branches of the trees that surrounded the pool. Near it, on the smooth stones, Shizue had artfully arranged food and drink on bamboo trays, and she had laid out straw slippers and a blue cotton *yukata* for him to wear. There was a note folded under a single yellow rose.

"Dearest Max, I'm desperate to rush into your arms. But after all the waiting, our long journey has ended, and there's no longer any need to rush. My darling, my love, hold back this precious moment. Refresh yourself. I'm yours, and soon we'll be together for always."

Although drunk with desire, he was helpless to resist the lure of Shizue's unhurried world and stripped off his city clothes. Wind bells sang all around him, a cool tinkling symphony that freed his mind of troubled thoughts as he bathed in the steaming pool. His cares drifted away on the misty white vapors, and his muscles slowly relaxed. Shizue was right not to rush this moment, he thought, as he savored the delicate sensations of the atmosphere she had created for him.

After drying off, he put on the blue cotton *yukata* and sat down on a straw mat. The teapot was cozied in a straw basket. He poured some tea; it was rich and hot. The sushi melted in his mouth: the delicacy of *tai* fish, eel, and squid pulled from Beppu Bay. He felt Shizue's presence in these loving gifts that made his homecoming a reality. Shizue had anticipated the tensions he carried with him from Tokyo, and Max emerged a new man.

As he left the clearing, he could not see the cottage, but a moss-covered stone path beckoned him on, and he walked slowly along it.

First, he glimpsed the gently sloping tile roof, then the charming wooden footbridge that spanned a break in the volcanic rocks. He did not see the cottage itself—only Shizue, kneeling and sliding open its doors, her violet robe caught by a solitary ray of sunlight. There was a dreaminess in her smiling repose. Her raven hair was unadorned, her skin smooth as silk, her sensuous mouth that of a full-grown woman.

"Max." Her voice played on the stillness. "*O-kaeri-nasai*—welcome home."

Stones scattered as he hastened across the footbridge, and birds were flushed from the cottage roof. There was magic at work here. So much sadness had been attached to their love. They had lived on the ecstasy of a single afternoon, and now their feelings overflowed as they kissed.

Passions ran deep for them both. Simply holding each other was breathlessly exciting; the torrent of feelings was overwhelming. There at the door to the cottage they urgently undressed each other, lost in their desire to reclaim the remembered ecstasy that had sustained them during their long separation.

At last joined together, there was tenderness in the passion that engulfed them. With every sense heightened, they journeyed as if buoyed on the swiftly moving current of a never-ending stream. They kissed, sharing the same breath. And finally both cried out, proclaiming their love, releasing it from bondage with a shuddering of their loins.

Now the rapture of fulfillment swept over their trembling bodies, and they clung together listening to the sounds of nature, sharing the pulse of its rhythms, watching the sunlight twinkle in leafy branches overhead until the air grew cool. Speaking only with the love in his eyes, Max lifted Shizue in his arms and carried her inside the cottage.

All that day and night they never strayed from the warm lap of the cottage. Shizue had brightened its cozy rooms with flower arrangements. The bedchamber lay open to a pretty Japanese garden and the sea. Here the lovers filled the quiet with their sighs, discovering one another all over again. Their remembered ecstasy had been only a prelude, one shining moment before parting. Here there would be no good-byes. Here the hour glass cracked, and each time they joined together was like the very first time, charged with an intensity that left them weak. They stood in awe of each other, their expressions serious. Love was not to be taken lightly. But the utter seriousness they had brought to it soon gave way to laughter and play. Like kittens, they rolled together, pawing each other's hair. Shizue tickled Max and led him into a chase, which ended when he captured her in a passionate embrace. This was the joyful side of love—to play as children without a care in the world.

At daybreak they woke together, a man and a woman whose bodies lazily stirred to life with pleasant aches.

"Good morning." Shizue rolled on top of Max and ruffled his hair. "What are you thinking?"

He laughed and said, "I'm hungry. I could eat a tree."

"Oh, really? Then I'll get the ax and cut you down one. Nothing's too good for my lord and master." Giggling, she straddled him with her knees and pinned down his arms. "First, tell me that you love me. Say it!"

"Still the tomboy." Max groaned and pretended helplessness. "I love you. Now, how about that tree?"

"Oh, Max, I'm so happy. So gloriously happy I could cry. But that would spoil everything," she decided, freeing him after a kiss on the nose.

She rose and put on her *yukata*, then looked down at him. "You're far too handsome. One day I'll turn wrinkled and gray, and you'll still be attractive to women." Shizue closed the *yukata* across her breasts and frowned. "Will you love me then, or throw me away like an old shoe?"

Max sat up cross-legged on the bed. "It's hard to picture you wrinkled and gray—but I'll give it some thought and let you know." He winked, and she laughed.

"Get dressed," she said. "We'll breakfast in the garden. I found a stable nearby where we can hire horses. They say it's a wonderful ride to the sea." Beaming now, she handed Max his *yukata*, then flitted away to fix breakfast.

The kitchen was a cheerful, sunny place, and she hummed, planning a number of things for them to do in the days ahead. Yufugawo was registered at a hotel in the city and would handle her father if he telephoned there.

Max surprised her from behind. "God, that smells good," he said, squeezing her slender waist. "But first, I could use a shave."

His cheek was rough against hers. "Let me do it for you, darling."

"Since when do you know how to shave a man?"

She smiled prettily. "I'm willing to learn."

"Not on my face, thanks all the same."

"You're right. I'd leave you in an awful mess. Full of cuts and nicks." It was a lie. Toward the end she had shaved Jiro when his trembling hand could not steady the razor. She had learned to cook and clean for him. Until the end, she had been his friend and his nurse. Finally, she had been his strength on the instrument of his self-destruction. But what had passed between them was better left unconfessed. "Max, I love your fuzzy cheeks. All pink underneath like the boy I once knew."

"Maybe I should chuck the razor and grow a beard."

"Oh, no, it would make you look stern and—well, fatherly."

"Stern and fatherly, huh?" His expression grew thoughtful.

The subject of her father was inevitable. "Dearest, I'm no longer bound to his will," she said, covering his face with kisses. "He'll fight me, I know. But after being together like this, I'm prepared to marry you without his blessings. Please, don't say more. We have days and days to plan our future."

Max took her chin in his hand and looked down at her, seeking traces of the wishful girl. But maturity, love, and an inner strength were mirrored in the depths of her eyes, and he had no reason on earth to doubt her sincerity. "Give me one of your beautiful smiles, and it's a bargain."

Breakfast consisted of fish with eggs, rice, and pickled beans. Max devoured every morsel Shizue placed before him in the garden. A maid was supplied with the cottage. Amiko, a pretty girl of eighteen, shyly bowed and collected the dishes. Max inquired about her family, and her eyes lifted. Amiko blushed as he smiled. Suddenly Shizue felt jealous of her—and all other women. She flung her arms around Max in a blatant display of ownership and then laughed at herself, vowing never to be so foolish again.

Amiko did the shopping, so they had no reason to venture into the crowded city. Without telephones, radios, and newspapers, it was easy to turn their backs on the world. Afternoons they rode to the seaside at Ibusuki, where they laid claim to a sheltered cove. A half moon of white sandy beach was their private domain, except when an occasional fisherman cast his net. They often picnicked there, shaded by a parasol. Max had rented a sailboat, and afterward the two would swim the calm breakwaters to where it lay anchored. The coastline abounded with interesting places to be explored: crystal blue sanctuaries, where rainbow-colored fish ate out of their hands, and rocky bluffs, which they climbed to spectacular views of the sea and mountains beyond. Often they sailed until sunset, then weighed anchor to make love beneath the burning vermilion sky. Max grew bronze, even between his toes, and his hair was bleached to a silvery-blond. Shizue took great delight massaging him with oil, memorizing every detail of his muscular body. A delirious languor set in. There was so much splendor in the present that they spent little time speaking of the future. Neither of them counted the sunsets.

One morning they were having breakfast in the garden as usual, when Amiko presented them with a message from the rental agent.

Her teacup froze in midair, and Shizue's mouth dropped. "But it can't be three weeks."

"Three weeks tomorrow," Max said, balling up the note. "He wants to know if we'd like to extend our stay."

"Oh, yes, this is too sudden. Amiko, tell him we'll take the cottage for another week. Hurry on, before he rents it to someone else."

Amiko bowed, answering in her small girlish voice, "*Hai*, I will go like the wind."

"I think we should discuss this." Max ran both hands through his hair and faced the sea. "I'm tempted to be selfish, but I've neglected my obligations in Tokyo long enough. We've only touched on what we can have together. It's time we got on with our lives. I want you as my wife, and your father won't be any easier to deal with in another week. I say, let the feathers fly and have done with it."

"You're right, Max." Shizue grasped his sun-bronzed hands and placed them on the hairline scar etched across her throat. "Once I thought I had nothing more to live for. Now I've never felt so alive. These past days have been like make-believe. Oh, Max, I want to give you children. I want to feel your child growing inside me."

"Slow down. I'd like to have you all to myself for a while."

That last afternoon they took the sailboat out. The sea grew choppy and dangerous. Knowing that a storm was brewing, Max turned for port. Shizue huddled beside him at the tiller while he talked about helping the Jews. To Shizue, the Jews were as alien and remote as the bearded race of Ainos who inhabited the Japanese island of Yezo. Although she was anxious to know what progress his father and Inge had made, she secretly worried over Max's involvement. She vaguely recalled meeting Inge Karlstadt at the Napier mansion years ago when the business of parachutes had first separated her from Max. Perhaps in time she would become friends with her. But Angela Napier was part of her earliest memories, and Douglas's new wife could never replace her in Shizue's heart.

"Damn, we're in for it," Max shouted above the howling wind. It began to rain.

Swells washed over the sides of the sailboat as Shizue moved aft to drag hats and oil slickers from a wooden chest. "Can we make it to port?"

"With any luck. Scared?"

"No. It's rather exciting and romantic, riding out the storm with your arm around me."

They laughed as they put on their rain slickers, then snuggled together. The storm was short-lived. As they approached the dock at Ibusuki, sunlight broke through the clouds, and dockhands ran out to catch their lines. Until that day Max and Shizue had moved slowly, mindless of the world at large. Now they both felt jarred by the clamor of this seaside resort a few miles south of Beppu. They had not set foot here since hiring out the boat weeks ago, and it was crowded with tourists.

"*Konnichi-wa*. We're returning boat number seven."

The rental office clerk peered up at Max from his newspaper, then left it on the counter while he went to fetch their records. Max lifted the paper and began reading. Belgium had surrendered. Hitler's tanks had stormed across its borders into France, bypassing the Maginot Line and crippling the French forces.

"If France falls, it'll halt Guillaume's efforts there," Max worried aloud.

Plunged back into a war-torn world, Shizue scoured the paper for mention of her brother's regiment. China had taken a backseat to Hitler's latest triumph. No news was good news, she thought, taking Max by the hand. "There's been no letter from Kimitake in months."

"He never was one for putting pen to paper."

At day's end they returned to the cottage. The doors stood open, and they heard someone inside snoring. Yufugawo dozed in a chair, her plump arms folded across her bosom. Shizue murmured her name, and the woman made a gurgling noise, then blinked and questioned the hour.

"Where have you been, child? Max—ah," she groaned, struggling to her feet. "I have soaked in Beppu until this old skin almost fell off my bones. And still I ache. Ah, the climb here proved too much for me."

Max tenderly kissed one rouged cheek. "What brings you here?"

"The baron telephoned." Her face sagged. "Kimitake has been wounded in action."

Shizue drew in a sharp breath. "How badly wounded?"

"The army cable did not say. Your father is trying to find out more. I told him you were in the mud baths. That was hours ago. By this time he may have telephoned the hotel again."

Kimitake was alive. Shizue could think of nothing else while rickshas carried them downhill toward Beppu's steaming landscape. There were messages waiting for her at the hotel desk.

Max stood watch outside a lobby phone booth, while Shizue called her father. She wept, one palm flattened against the glass door pane as her father conveyed what he had learned. Finally, she cradled the receiver and emerged, her lower lip trembling as she found her voice.

"He fought in some awful battle. It was days before the Japanese dead and wounded could be reached. He's being cared for at a field hospital. His condition is listed as critical, but that report is a week old. Communications with the front lines are poor, and there's nothing to do but wait. Oh, Max, for all we know Kimitake may be dead." She clung to him, crying. It went without saying that the clash of wills with her father must wait.

Shizue looked up at Max and smiled bravely. "Before Kimi sailed, we danced the night away. We made a date to go dancing again when he returned. So, you see, he can't be dead."

For another night the cottage sheltered them. The unknown had cast a shadow over its cheerful rooms, but the power and the beauty of their love sustained them. In the morning, Amiko bid them good-bye. It was not a sorrowful parting. What they had shared here was only the beginning, Shizue thought. She and Max turned back to look at the cottage one last time. It was as though a marker had been placed between the pages of a book, and would remain there until they returned.

CHAPTER 33

A nurse entered the overcrowded waiting room, blotting her sweaty brow as she wearily scanned the expectant faces. After weeks on end without any word, the army had cabled that Kimitake was out of danger and had recovered from his wounds well enough to be shipped home. But there was no mention of the extent of his injuries. He had received two citations for heroism, which had made the baron very proud.

"The family of Hosokawa, Kimitake, Lieutenant," the nurse said. "Dr. Onogi will see you now."

"An insufferable wait. Someone should repair that ceiling fan," Baron Hosokawa complained as he rose from his chair. "Why can't I go directly to my son?"

"Hospital rules, Hosokawa-*san*."

Shizue held on to her father's arm. There had been no such rule the summer she had visited Paul at this same army hospital in Nagasaki. As they followed the nurse down the sweltering corridors, Shizue averted her eyes from the bandaged young men confined to their wheelchairs and from others who hobbled along like the old on canes and wooden crutches. She had an aversion to the antiseptic smells of hospitals and doctors' offices. Only then did she realize why: she associated those smells with her mother's illness. The sensory connection made her queasy. "The air is so close—I can hardly breathe."

"*Hai*, we have run out of space and beds," the nurse commented with a wilted look.

Dr. Onogi stood haloed in bluish light, studying X rays clipped to the light boxes mounted on his office wall. When the nurse announced Shizue and her father, the doctor switched the light box off.

"Onogi, chief of surgery. Please, sit down. I prefer to stand. Force of habit. Will you have a cigarette? No? A filthy addiction, but I find it relaxing after the operating room." His tone was conciliatory.

A tall, lanky man in his early fifties, Dr. Onogi had kind eyes that put his visitors at ease. Before speaking again, he lit a cigarette. "I'll come straight to the point. Lieutenant Hosokawa is making excellent progress.

The young heal quickly. However"—he gestured at the X rays—"there are wounds that can't be mended through surgical procedures. When your son arrived at the field hospital, gangrene had already set in. Emergency measures were taken to save his life, and he has suffered through a great ordeal."

"He's been crippled." Shizue grasped the chair arms for support. The unlit X rays were dark splotches against the white wall, and they seemed to swim before her eyes as Dr. Onogi nodded yes.

Baron Hosokawa opened his shirt collar and seemed to gasp for breath. "Why was the truth kept from me?"

"Cases of this nature are better dealt with in person, Hosokawa-*san*. There's more involved than the loss of a limb."

"Where's my brother? I must go to him."

"All in good time. Don't think me cold and clinical, but it's my duty to prepare you for what's in store. The wrong response could do your brother irreparable harm."

Shizue watched the surgeon's hands lock together, and she fought hysteria. Was Kimitake horribly disfigured? Her father asked for water. His face perspired heavily and his hand shook with the glass. She dug her perfumed handkerchief from her purse, holding it to her nostrils to ward off the antiseptic smells. "Is it my brother's face?"

"Miraculously, that was spared injury, except for minor powder burns. The same holds true for his vital organs." The dropping sun was in their eyes, and Dr. Onogi slanted the blinds. "There was some damage to his spleen and kidneys, but they seem to be repairing nicely. Lieutenant Hosokawa's body was riddled with shrapnel. It's a wonder he survived. Had our forces only reached his unit sooner, the multiple amputations might not have been necessary or so extreme in their nature." Dr. Onogi faced the light boxes on his office wall, speaking as he flicked their switches. "I can assure you, everything humanly possible was done to save his limbs. But the damage to them threatened Lieutenant Hosokawa's life. The amputations were crucial to his survival. I felt these X rays would help prepare you for the shock."

Shizue stammered. "No. Oh, no—what have you cut away?" Her handkerchief fluttered to the floor at her feet as the fluorescent tubes blinked on, and she saw the trunk of a man stripped of all its limbs. "This is all a horrible mistake. Another soldier was shipped here in Kimitake's place. Don't look, Papa."

Her father pushed up from his chair, wide-eyed and pointing a trembling finger at the surgeon. "Butcher," he accused in a hoarse voice. "You've taken my son's arms?" The X-ray film sparkled. What little remained of a man's arms and legs was clearly defined—like the stumps of branches sawed from a tree. And yet Baron Hosokawa dragged himself across the floor toward the hideous sight, refusing to accept what he saw. "Surely you haven't taken both legs. Surely not both arms. My son.

Kimitake. No arms, no legs?" Cramming both hands deep inside his jacket pockets, the baron hung his head and sobbed.

"I realize how painful this is for you," said Dr. Onogi, "but there's no way I can soften the blow." Placing his back to the bluish light, he approached Shizue. "This isn't a case of mistaken identity. Such cases are rare. The loss of all one's limbs is usually fatal. Your brother fought for his life as bravely as he fought on the battlefield."

Detached from her father and the gray X ray images, Shizue could find no tears. "We must go to him, Papa."

In her mind's eye she saw Kimitake as whole, a handsome young officer striding off on his long legs beneath the rumbling Tokyo sky of yesteryear. "Doctor, I can't bear to wait any longer. My brother's come home to us, and I'm not afraid. But I don't know what's expected of me. I might hurt him with a look or by saying the wrong things. It's love he needs, not pity. Please, tell me what to do."

"You're a very courageous young woman." Dr. Onogi pressed her arm. "I find it difficult to convey such tragic news. Death is often easier to announce. Your brother fears you may turn away from him in disgust. My only advice is to follow your heart. Remember that your son is a hero," he said to the baron. "The true measure of a man isn't found in his arms and legs, Hosokawa-san. Our skills can do no more for him here. Soon your son will be strong enough to be cared for at home. He's endured much physical pain. Now only you can help him come to terms with his disabilities. You both must set your own needs aside. Before he accepts life as he is, you may even wish him dead."

Shizue covered her mouth. "How can you say such a thing?"

All at once her father's tearful eyes caught fire. "We are samurai, Onogi-san. No sacrifice is too great for the victor. Once I've embraced my son, he'll come around soon enough."

"I'm afraid I can't permit that, Hosokawa-san. He refuses to see anyone but his sister. He's refused to have any contact with you."

The baron dropped back, stunned. "But he can't refuse to see his own father."

"Whatever his reasons, the lieutenant was most adamant. I was forced to sedate him. Perhaps he will open up to your daughter. The fact that he will see her is a positive sign. There are other men in our isolation ward who have turned their entire families away."

Grim-faced, Dr. Onogi flexed his fingers as the hospital public address system called him to surgery. "So, Baron, the first sacrifice is being asked of you. Fail this test and your son could very well slam the door in your face for good." He smiled slightly, and his tone softened. "Be patient. My nurse will attend to Shizue. You're welcome to wait here."

The baron seized his daughter's wrist and said, "I've always tried to do what's best for my children. Tell Kimitake I'll do anything he asks of me." He was alarmed when Shizue bitterly pulled free.

How she despised him for holding to that awful lie, she thought. As she walked down the hallway, she discovered that the maimed were no longer so horrible to look upon. Even those confined to wheelchairs still had arms to propel themselves up and down the polished corridors.

There was no relief from the oppressive heat. The hospital room doors had been jammed open for ventilation, and Shizue saw other families who had been reunited with their loved ones laughing and weeping for joy. She envied them as she followed the nurse through two swinging doors. Suddenly she felt paralyzed as they stopped before a locked metal door on which was a sign: Isolation Ward; Staff Only. "Why is the door kept locked?" she asked the nurse.

"Our other patients would be depressed if they were exposed to these severe cases. But mostly it's to shield them from unwanted visitors and guard against the possibility that they might do injury to themselves."

A white-haired orderly responded to the bell.

"Lieutenant Hosokawa's sister," whispered the nurse. "You may keep your handkerchief, but leave your purse with him. It's the rule."

The windowless corridors were dark and empty. White muslin screens stood at the open doors to rooms that reeked of urine, feces, and a sickly sweet odor that Shizue could not identify. She felt she was being watched. Here and there shadowy figures loomed behind the screens, prisoners of their deformities, and they were watching her in the suffocating silence. Kimitake did not belong here with those faceless phantoms, isolated even from one another, she told herself. She fought to hold the image of her brother as he once was.

The nurse halted, wheeling aside the screen at the threshold of a narrow room, and Shizue froze there, faint of spirit and faint of heart. A ceiling fan droned overhead. Mosquito netting was draped around the bed, and light from a window set high on the opposite wall illuminated the solitary presence trapped inside. Kimitake lay flat on his back, helpless as a butterfly caught in a net.

"Lieutenant, your sister is here."

"Shizue?"

It was the same voice. The same handsome face struggled up from the pillows while she cried out, "Kimitake," and parted the netting, kissing him, holding him, sharing his tears. While the moment lasted, she was mercifully blinded to his missing limbs. Then his armless torso writhed in her embrace. Two bandaged stubs dangled just inches below his broad shoulders. Perspiration had soaked through the sleeveless white hospital smock, and he looked away, whimpering in pain.

"Too much pressure on my legs. Rest me down."

Shizue glanced speechlessly at the empty sheet. His long legs had been amputated well above both knees and the fat stubs were swathed in surgical dressings that gave off a sickly sweet odor. "Don't look away. Kimi, it doesn't matter. I don't love you any less. Here, let me," she said without thinking, using her perfumed handkerchief to wipe the sweat from his brow. "How can they expect you to get well in this dreadful place? Those dressings should be changed. You should be bathed—rubbed down with alcohol and have fresh linen on the bed. I'll speak with the doctor."

"No. I won't let the nurses touch me. I can't stand their cold hands or their looks of disgust. I prefer to lie here in my own filth."

Kimitake wet his parched lips, his eyes shifting to the door. "This is an asylum for freaks. Everyone speaks in whispers. At night the screams of the other damned souls keep me awake. When I arrived, another bed was here. The man in it was only a voice. Half his face had been shot off. The surgeons had left him with one good arm, and while we spoke he smoked through a hole in the bandages. After months of confinement, he had decided to kill himself. His mother smuggled in a vial of poison." His head thrashed against the pillows. "I watched him drink it and said nothing. I watched him die a peaceful death. And I was glad for him. If I rot here much longer, I'll be asking that of you, Shizue."

Shizue recoiled with the memory of Jiro begging her to be released. "You mustn't think of death."

"Then take care of me. Be my hands." Kimitake flinched, ashamed of his utter helplessness, as a housefly crawled across his pleading face. "Help me grow strong so I can go home."

"Yes, I'll watch over you. We'll have you home in no time." Shizue captured the fly in one hand. With this simple act, her task had begun. She made no mention of her father, nor did he. But she could not help blaming him for this tragedy. He had ordered her brother to return a hero. As she brushed the hair from Kimitake's forehead, his narrowed eyes seemed to read her angry thoughts. "Now, don't worry," she said. "I'm sure Dr. Onogi won't object. But you must let the nurses tend your wounds so I can watch them and learn."

"Little sister, you're wonderful." His eyes filled with tears. "If only I could hold you. Damn," Kimitake cried, violently rocking back and forth. "I'd trade half my face for that dead man's good arm. What good is a face to a freak like me?"

The mournful wails of other men echoed in the corridor. Shizue had clenched her hand around the fly, and it rolled dead off her fingers as she attempted to quiet Kimitake. But he would not be comforted.

Hearing his outburst, a nurse, followed by an orderly, entered the room. The nurse prepared a hypodermic syringe, while a muscular orderly lifted Kimitake like an infant, placed him flat on his stomach, and exposed his bare buttocks for the needle. Shizue watched the nurse sedate her brother with a crude jab of the needle. He groaned, and urine streamed out against the sheet.

The nurse shook her head in disgust. "Well, it can't be helped. Sometimes he has no control. He'll sleep now. The orderly will clean up this mess."

"You see what I am?" Kimitake asked, his eyelids drooping. "If you don't come again, I'll understand."

Shizue could only smile. This brief encounter had spared her nothing. Quietly withdrawing from his bedside, she thought about what he had become. For the rest of his days he would be totally dependent on those who loved him—particularly on her, since he had shut out their father. Although she was prepared to sacrifice herself to Kimitake's needs, she felt a great sadness over how this would affect the future she had planned with Max.

Baron Hosokawa did not return on the plane that bore Shizue and his son home. All those weeks spent caring for Kimitake in the hospital isolation ward had been a nightmare for them both. Day by day he grew more demanding of his sister and ever more difficult to please. The military hospital had made no effort to offer its patients more than bed and board and the privacy in which to hide their gruesome infirmities from their families and neighbors.

A nation that applauded heroism had turned away from these repulsive proofs of the heavy tolls of war. People still liked to wave their paper stick flags as sons were marched from home to serve the emperor. Yet, in the isolation ward, Shizue had watched those same patriots shudder at the sight of loved ones returned home, brave samurai returned to them as lepers. Wives and parents cut their visits short. From the window of her brother's hospital room, Shizue had watched them rush away down the street, haunted by the memory of loved ones better off kept out of sight, imprisoned behind the isolation ward's locked door.

At last Shizue had escaped that nightmare world of groans issuing through the sickening-smelling hospital corridors. But while flying home with Kimitake, she found his foul mood distressing, for it undercut her hopes that his humor would improve in the comforting surroundings of his childhood. Her brother's limbless body was beyond repair, and perhaps there was no miraculous cure for the tortured spirit housed within its violated shell. Every bump of the landing airplane brought a yelp of complaint. Kimitake shouted accusations of being neglected while Shizue remained buckled in her seat, enduring his impatience with a patient smile. What began as an act of love was slowly deteriorating into the bondage of servitude, and she foresaw no release from the role she played in his life. She held her ears against the plane's screeching wheels.

It was a sultry evening in early July, and O-nami waited alone on the airstrip. It honored him to be Kimitake's legs. Boarding the plane, he saw a cot lashed between the aisle seats. Kimitake was dressed in uniform, his empty jacket sleeves and trouser legs folded up and pinned. War had cut a man down to the size of a boy.

"Ichiban." O-nami had vowed not to weep, but tears ran down his fat cheeks as he lifted Kimitake into his massive arms. "I carried you once as a boy, and now I will carry the man."

Unsmiling and dry-eyed, Kimitake gave no reply. Shizue was anxious to get him settled in, so she was rather short with O-nami. "Oh, do please get him to the car. And don't hold him so tightly around the waist. His kidneys are still giving him trouble."

"*Hai*, gently then, Ichiban."

A wicker basket piled high with pillows sat on the rear seat of the baron's Rolls-Royce. After some grumbling, Kimitake allowed himself to be rested inside it. The short drive along the bumpy dirt road brought more yelps of complaint.

Shizue had telephoned ahead to issue instructions, so there were no servants at the door. Even Yufugawo had been barred from seeing Kimitake. In a hushed, secret ceremony, O-nami carried Kimitake to his old room. Wearily, Shizue itemized the essentials that had been brought there according to her instructions. A treatment table on wheels, bedpans, stacks of fresh linen, mosquito netting around the bed, a movable screen that concealed the shallow wooden tubs constructed for his bathing. She set down the leather cases Dr. Onogi had given her. Drugs for his pain, drugs to help him sleep, instruments to chart his bodily functions. With the proper care her brother would have a long life. But for what purpose? To what end? she wondered.

"Where are my photographs? My fencing gear?"

"You told me to have all that removed," Shizue answered patiently.

"Well, I've changed my mind. Put them back on the walls. This uniform makes my skin crawl. Get it off. But first, open the windows. Damn, I've wet myself again."

"Oh, Jiro, is there no pleasing you?"

"How dare you mistake me for that coward?"

"Forgive me. I'm simply exhausted." It went deeper than a slip of the tongue. This hero was not so very different from the coward she had sheltered from war. Just then, Shizue confronted her resentment. Kimitake was an albatross weighing her down, and she regretted having given in to his every whim. Her sacrifices were allowing him to remain in hiding. She had meant to strengthen him, but it seemed that she had only encouraged his weakness.

"Sorry for bossing you around," he said. "I've behaved like a spoiled child. Now that we're home, I promise to do better."

She took heart and unfolded a sheet across the treatment table. "Let's get you ready for bed. O-nami, I'll need your help."

His surgical dressings had been removed several days before Kimitake was discharged from the hospital. O-nami's eyes showed tenderness while Shizue rubbed down the rounded pink stumps with alcohol. As his body servant, there were no limits to the intimacy between brother and sister.

Sponging his groin and testicles often gave him an erection and evoked a pained, wistful look of remembered pleasures. She thought of the women he would never know. To function still as a man, only to lie there unloved and unspent, seemed the most cruel stroke of all. But the saltpeter Dr. Onogi had prescribed inflamed his weakened kidneys.

At last, he was dressed in a silk pajama top and was ready for bed. Shizue carefully checked the mosquito netting before she closed it around him. Then O-nami stood quietly by as she sat at the bedside reading, until her brother nodded off to sleep. Another grueling day had ended.

"Poor Ichiban. It breaks my heart."

"Hush," she whispered, motioning O-nami to enter the adjoining room, where she would sleep. While she was nursing Kimitake at the hospital, her nights had been her own. "Oh, O-nami, he didn't even want *you* to see him as he is. But I couldn't possibly manage without you."

O-nami brought her close. "And your father? What of the baron?"

"Devastated. I've tried talking with him, but he just sits and stares. Kimitake won't open up to me, and I'm caught in the silent struggle between them. Oh, tonight I could have given Kimi a hard push. But the doctor said his acceptance can't be forced."

"Cheer up, little one. Ichiban will outgrow his stubbornness." O-nami held her away and grinned. "Together we will make a man of him again. He has no reason to feel shame. All here are prepared to give him a hero's welcome. *Hai*, Ichiban will sing a different tune once we get him to poke his head out of the nest. Max should pay a visit."

"I promised to telephone him the moment we arrived."

Static on the line to Tokyo fought their voices. Shizue looked to Max for solace, while he maintained the resigned tone of a lover held at bay by forces beyond his control.

"I miss you terribly. But I can't pressure my father anymore, or he might crumble. And Kimitake takes up all my time."

"Everyone has his breaking point, Shizue," he said. "My only concern is that you'll buckle under the strain. It's too much for you to handle alone. I'll come as soon as I can get away. Kimi might agree to see me once I'm there—at least it's worth a try."

Kimitake woke and called for her. "Dearest, I must go to him. We'll talk again tomorrow. Just hearing your voice has done me a world of good. I love you."

On the first of many nights that were to follow, Shizue lit a cigarette and held it to her brother's lips. He described regaining consciousness in the gruesome confines of the hospital tent, where he had demanded to be shown his dismembered limbs. But they had gone up in smoke, cremated with those of other brave young men. He spoke of the men who had fought beside him, but said nothing about the battle that had cost him so much, nothing about what had prompted his acts of heroism. After exhaling a final drag on the cigarette, he turned his head to the open window and groaned, as if the nightmare of China had entered on the evening breeze. Then he suddenly broke into a cold sweat. Shizue comforted him until he surrendered to sleep. Kimitake was afraid to be alone in the dark, and she left one lamp burning low.

The breeze strummed the mosquito netting, and Shizue saw him as a silkworm slumbering within its safe cocoon. He would emerge in his own time.

Happy to have a few moments to herself, she went downstairs and walked outside in the garden alone with her thoughts. It was the quality and not the quantity of one's life that mattered. Ultimately, Kimitake would either accept or reject life as he was. The terms were cruel, but the choice was his, and she could only encourage him with love. Kneeling before her mother's garden shrine, she mourned his dead arms and legs, scattered as ashes across some distant Chinese outpost. Perhaps he would have been better off dead.

CHAPTER 34

Douglas Napier surveyed the rusting hull of a Greek freighter berthed at Yokohama, her lights glowing eerily in the drifting fog. Earlier that week, Max had sounded out the captain. The man drove a hard bargain, but finally they had negotiated a deal. So far, their efforts had gotten seven cargoes of refugees safely out of Europe on tramp steamers much like this one, manned by unscrupulous captains and ragtag crews. Such men were not to be trusted. Inge wore a fretful look as the ship's first officer greeted the three of them at the gangplank and welcomed them aboard. There was no one else in sight.

"The crew was given shore leave," the first officer said, scratching his curly black beard. "Captain Zaimas thought it wise to conduct our business in private. This way, please, lady and gentlemens." His wrinkled uniform bagged at the knees, and he swaggered rather drunkenly as he led the way to the captain's cabin. "I see you have brought the gems."

Douglas tightened his grip on the briefcase. "If you expect trouble with the crew, our deal is off."

"Merely a precaution, Mr. Napier. Captain Zaimas does not wish to divide the spoils among his greedy men. Once at sea, he is master and they must obey. There will be no trouble."

Max did not care for the explanation, but deferred to his father's guarded silence.

As they entered the captain's cabin, a worn record hissed on the turntable of a windup Victrola. Captain Zaimas moved his head with the bouzouki music as he bent over charts on his desk. He spoke no English, or at least pretended not to, and his first mate acted as interpreter.

"The captain invites you to sit at his table."

"Tell him we want to check his sailing papers," Douglas snapped.

Captain Zaimas made a long face, then mumbled something in Greek before handing them over. He considered himself a ladies' man, and he winked at Inge, who averted her eyes. Seated at the table, he uncorked a bottle of ouzo with his teeth and drank from it. His papers were in order, but Douglas distrusted his grin, so he kept the briefcase well in hand.

"Something does not please you?" the first mate inquired.

"That's right. I don't like the crew being left to chance. Money talks louder than authority. The other captains we've dealt with have paid off their men."

As his first officer began to translate this into Greek, Captain Zaimas rubbed his unshaven face and said irritably, "Enough, Stavros, I will speak for myself. You are surprised, yes?" He glanced around the table and laughed. "Bargaining through Stavros has its advantages, but my English is better than his, and I want no misunderstanding. If you wish to 'buy' my crew, then it will cost you more. Say, one thousand American dollars for each man. Cash for them, the gems and pearls for me, as previously agreed. Half payable in advance, the rest after your cargo has been safely delivered."

Douglas needed this ship, and her ouzo-swigging skipper knew that. Only ships flying neutral flags were protected in the offshore waters of a war-torn Europe. France had fallen months ago, in June. Intoxicated by Hitler's victories, the Japanese military had decided to strike out into Southeast Asia to seize the oil fields and the resources denied Japan by America's embargo on strategic materials. Ever fewer merchant ships plied the trade routes into Yokohama Bay. Douglas was forced to compromise. "All right, Captain. But I want a guarantee the money won't go into your own pocket."

"Oh, Mr. Napier, you twist a knife in my heart." Captain Zaimas banged down the wine bottle and uttered a wounded sound. "I am not a thief." He put both hands up, gesturing theatrically as he leaned back in his chair. "A little of a liar, maybe. A little of a cheat. But one must use cunning when dealing with scum like my crew. You are people of quality, and maybe we do business again."

"Maybe. In any event, my son will be present when you inform the crew and pay them off."

"As you wish." Leaning across the table, Captain Zaimas rubbed his hands together. "Now, to the gems. In these times, money is often not worth the paper it is printed on. Stavros, fix your expert eye on these."

Over the months, Max had learned a great deal about gems and precious metals. The other sea captains had also demanded something more stable than currency for their services. Converting large sums of money into precious gems, Japanese pearls, and solid gold without inviting suspicion was a difficult task. What his father spread on the table had been purchased piece by piece from reputable dealers in numerous cities. Law required the dealers to keep records, so the Napiers had decided not to visit the same shop twice. Douglas and Inge operated best as a married couple and Max traveled alone, retracing their steps in the guise of a wealthy American tourist with money to burn. Now he watched the first officer place a jeweler's loupe into one eye, then use tweezers to lift a square-cut ruby up to the light. Slowly he turned it. Captain Zaimas swilled wine, and Stavros continued to lift gems off the black velvet cloth to determine that they were genuine. Finally, he tested the strings of perfectly matched pearls by chewing on them. Stavros smiled. "There are good fakes on the market, but these are genuine, Captain."

"Hah, I think you are even more cunning than me." He laughed broadly. "Lock them in the safe. Now, Mr. Napier, to complete our business. The ship I am to rendezvous with. Where does she sail from and under what flag? How many Jews will I be taking on?"

"I don't have that information. It could sail from any one of several European ports still open to my people. Ships are in short supply for them as well. Your estimated time of arrival in Mediterranean waters will determine the port they choose, and circumstances will determine the number of refugees who can safely be assembled there."

Douglas slid a large manila envelope across the table. "You'll rendezvous at night at these grid coordinates. There's also a code book. The other ship will establish radio contact with you in code. Afterward, maintain strict radio silence until you're well away. Keep the passengers below decks and don't lose your nerve if you encounter any British gunboats. Your cargo is Japanese silk destined for Palestine. So far, the operation has gone off without a hitch. Any questions?"

Captain Zaimas looked inside the envelope and shrugged. "What becomes of the silk?"

"Our agents at Haifa will sign for it," Max said evenly. "They'll know if you lived up to the bargain."

"Hah, I like this young man. No monkey business while he is around. We shall seal the bargain with a drink. Stavros, bring glasses and a fresh bottle."

Inge thought the captain a swine and stared daggers at him when he fired off another of his lecherous winks. "We have important business elsewhere, Captain. Our people are waiting to be notified of your arrival time."

"Yes, my wife is right."

"I envy you such a woman." Stepping to the chart table, Captain Zaimas used his navigation instruments and plotted his course. "With favorable seas, I would say thirty-two days. Add one more for the unforeseen. Midnight, of the new year, 1941."

The approaching new year had come upon them suddenly, and Inge sat shivering in the sleek gray Duesenberg as it left the harbor with Max at the wheel. Soon Heinz would have been dead for a year. Her vision of the world had changed. Her life now revolved around Douglas, Max, and their mission for the Jews. Each effort had brought the three closer together. Max was the son she had never had. And Douglas, well, she could no longer deny the mutual attraction that had grown between old friends. For years she had loved and respected Angela's husband as a friend. Heinz had dearly loved him as well, and they had been the two most important men in her life, both of them strong, virile, and disarmingly attractive. Inge recalled how both wives had flirted with their opposite spouses, flattered by their attentions, taking fun in that innocent repartee, which had added spice to their friendship as couples. Now she had been widowed nearly one year while living as Douglas Napier's wife in name only. But his constant presence had provided more than a source of comfort; she was beginning to feel like a woman again, guiltily so. Only her conscience prevented her from reaching out as a woman to the handsome man who rode beside her in the backseat. Douglas appeared to fear crossing the threshold from friend to lover as well, she observed. But it went beyond a purely physical need, and both were weakening.

"There's Aquida." Max braked to pick up the man who was pacing for warmth at a bus stop on the outskirts of Tokyo.

"You are late." Everything about Teofilo Aquida was tiny except for his ears, which stuck out like pitcher handles, bright red from the cold. "Ah, my bones they are frozen. You have the sheep?"

Max nodded, amused by his accent and the habitual twitching of his tiny rabbit's nose. Aquida's position at the Portuguese consulate was the key to their operations. The communications clerk brought out his pocket notebook, then jotted down the information he would wire to Lisbon. Not a wrinkle showed on his elfin face, but his tiny hands were prematurely aged. A nervous man, he lived in fear of being found out and took great precautions against their being seen together.

"I have received another message from Lisbon." Aquida's squeaky voice trailed off as he paused to blow his nose. "Maurice Guillaume was among those sent to Palestine in the last shipment. Safely landed two days ago. He was in ill health, and your people decided he would benefit from the warm climate. Senhor Guillaume thought you would like to know this was so."

Inge took Douglas's hand. Their friend had escaped from occupied France and was safe. One friend among the nameless many. "Thank God, Douglas. We must have Captain Zaimas carry a letter to him." Aware that she was grasping Douglas's hand, she quickly withdrew her touch.

"Where are we?" Aquida peered anxiously through the windshield, attempting to get his bearings in the dimly lit Tokyo streets. The critical need for scrap metal had systematically denuded the streets of lampposts. Harumidori Avenue was marked by lights on the Imperial Palace and the Diet on a small hill above. "Stop now, please," he told Max. "From here, I take the tram. Quickly, the money. I must be at my post in the next half hour."

The quixotic little man did not bother to count what was handed him in an envelope. Coattails blowing in the wind, Teofilo Aquida held on to his soft felt hat and vanished aboard the tram car.

Max drove back to the mansion. It had been refurbished, but white paint slapped on its Victorian exterior and on the dark mahogany paneling within had failed to brighten the old girl up, Douglas reflected. And none of the old social crowd, Angela's crowd, had come to call on Douglas Napier's Jewish bride.

At the door, Morita absently took Inge's sable coat. "Will Madame require anything before retiring?"

"Just tea, Morita. In my room." Inge stifled a yawn. "Perhaps our letter to Guillaume can wait until morning."

Douglas smiled. "Sure, go on up."

Observing how she and his father quietly desired each other, Max felt gripped by despair over the course his own life had taken. Kimitake had remained behind closed doors, an immovable object who bound Shizue to him with promised hope. By her accounts, the once demanding tyrant had gradually become a sweet, purring kitten, who lavished her with affection as payment for her servitude, and the turnabout had nurtured her hopes for his resurrection. Meanwhile, Baron Hosokawa had broken under the yoke of being exiled from his son. He had abandoned the business and had drifted into seclusion, leaving Douglas and Max to run it.

On rare occasions when Max could visit Shizue, the baron pretended to look the other way. After all, she was a young widow without suitors, shackled to his dismembered son perhaps for life. He was powerless now. A sad, tormented shell of a man. "Do as you please," his silent withdrawal seemed to convey.

Max had found it impossible to make love to Shizue with her brother lying helpless in the adjoining room, able to hear their every sound and likely to call for her at any moment. She could not stray beyond the sound of Kimitake's voice, so her movements were restricted to the garden below his windows.

Only once did Kimitake allow Max to see him. Their encounter had made Kimitake violently ill, and he sank into a deep depression for weeks afterward. The heart-wrenching shock of that single meeting had left its mark on Max as well. Shizue's brother was above reproach. Max knew that Kimitake clung to life by virtue of his sister's patient, loving hands. Still he would let no one else minister to him, and while Max railed silently against the devotion that made Shizue refuse even to consider leaving her brother to other help, he had not the heart to take Kimitake to task for coming between them.

"Guess I'll turn in, son," Douglas said, bringing Max back to the present. "Busy day ahead."

"This may be way off base, Dad," Max said, climbing the stairs with him, "but for some time now, I've noticed that you've been circling Inge like some lovestruck kid afraid to make his move."

Douglas raised his eyebrows and half-laughed. "Is that a fact?"

"I think she's waiting for a little encouragement. Dad, why deprive yourselves?"

"Max, following in Heinz's footsteps isn't all that easy."

Max decided not to pursue the subject. "I just wanted you to know how I felt."

"Appreciated," Douglas said, affectionately mussing his son's hair. He had not done that for years, and the gesture struck an emotional chord in them both. "I'm not sure if it's love. We go back a long way, and my feelings are confused." He had been trying to get up the nerve to broach the subject with Inge.

Turning, he saw an elderly maid carrying a tea service tray upstairs. "I'll take this in to my wife."

After the maid gave her tray to Douglas, he looked down the hall to the master bedroom he had once shared with Angela Napier. It was now Inge's room. He reflected on how thoroughly Inge had changed its atmosphere, making it into a lacy boudoir that resembled the room in Berlin she and Heinz had shared.

Max put a hand on his father's shoulder and smiled. "Well, good night, Dad."

"Good night—and thanks."

As his father carried the tea tray to Inge's door, Max silently wished him luck, then turned away.

Inge was surprised to see Douglas at the threshold of her room. Both stood there awkwardly for a moment.

"Mind if I come in?" asked Douglas. "If you're too tired for company . . ."

"*Nein.*"

Now that he had taken the initiative, Douglas was at a loss for words. He placed the tray on the small table where Inge often sat alone drinking her bedtime tea. She was in the process of removing her makeup. Her long, thick hair was held back with a ribbon, and she had cold cream on the fingers of one hand. She wiped it off with cotton while he poured them tea.

Not exactly a romantic beginning, Douglas thought, sitting down with her at the table. Intimate friends were thrown off balance as potential lovers. As he passed the sugar, his hand lightly brushed hers.

"You're a very beautiful woman."

Inge ran a painted fingernail across her full lower lip and sighed. "How hard it is to exist on memories. But they cannot be erased, *Schatzken. Ach*, what have I said?" Heinz alone was her *Schatzken*. Yet, she had addressed this man so endearingly and wanted to be embraced by him, to feel his mouth pressed on hers. Instead, she rose from the table abruptly, struggling with those feelings while Douglas came forward to take her in his arms. "*Nein*—no, Douglas, this is wrong," she pleaded, trembling against him.

"Inge, I've fallen in love with you," he confessed, caressing her cheek with his lips. "I never thought I'd feel this way about anyone again."

"I as well. But it hurts to feel as I do," she murmured, running her hands through his hair. "Have we the right to this happiness?"

"Yes, we can't give up everything to the dead."

"Kiss me then." Inge sighed and abandoned herself to love. Douglas's kiss was so painfully sweet. To know the love of a man once again swept her guilty thoughts away, and she lost herself as he caressed her. She wore nothing under her robe and he gently removed it from her bare shoulders. *"Schatzken."*

Douglas kissed her breasts, breathing in the fragrance of her skin. Slowly lifting his face, he saw the desire shining in Inge's eyes. For the briefest moment the two just stood holding hands, until they were overpowered by feelings. Then, exchanging kisses, they lay down together across the bed.

Coupled there on the smooth satin bedsheets, they discovered their love was like a slow-burning flame. It was different from the loves each had known and lost. Maturity and experience brought a tender compassion to their sharing, and they were set free of the inhibitions that had once separated them.

Inge whispered, *"Schatzken*—my *Schatzken*,*"* and cleaved to Douglas's strong arms as his force was spent.

"My darling Inge." He smiled and pressed his lips to her golden hair. Ended were his empty nights. Holding this woman, he felt the years lifting from him. "Now we're man and wife," he told Inge, planting kisses on her smooth brow.

Inge lay against the pillow smiling at her husband. There in the bedroom that had belonged to her dearest friend, they had consummated their wedding vows. In that moment, Angela's presence seemed to depart from the house; that friendly haunting no longer inhabited the shadows. "Douglas, I sense that our happiness is known—and forgiven."

He nodded, watching tears well in Inge's eyes. Both their thoughts turned to those who were lost. Although their memories of the dead remained, that evening Douglas and Inge ceased to live with ghosts.

Max had sat alone in his room trying to distract his thoughts from Douglas and Inge by reading the evening papers. Finally, he peered down the hall and watched a sliver of light go out behind the door to Inge's room. Two lonely people had been given a second chance for happiness, he thought. He was pleased but envious.

Despite the late hour, he decided to telephone Shizue. As he lifted the receiver, he heard a clicking sound. When he lifted it again, he heard the same distinctive sound. He realized the line was tapped. Perhaps all American residents had been placed under suspicion.

Although the street outside his window appeared to be deserted, he wanted to know for sure if the house was being watched. The best way to find out was to take the car and drive to the main part of the city, he thought. If he was not being followed, it would be safe for him to visit Paul's apartment to talk about this.

To Max's great relief, no car followed his when he drove to Tokyo. Roused from sleep, Paul was in a foul mood.

"If the authorities have tapped your phone, it's probably because of your business with the military," he told Max, as he fixed drinks at the bar. He was feeling depressed over his lonely existence. Sleep had not come easily, and his brother's intrusion made him short-tempered. "Quite frankly, you've damn near outlived your welcome in Japan. I'm advising you to give up your clandestine activities and put yourself first for once. Shizue needs a firm hand, or she's likely to waste her life away nursing Kimitake."

"If you saw him, you wouldn't be so callous," Max answered strongly.

"I've seen worse things in China. Sure, I got off light. Just a bum leg. Aches like hell in this weather." Wincing, Paul limped around the bar on his cane. "To be honest, position isn't everything I'd hoped for. But maybe it's given me a swelled head." He worked up a smile, aware of being just a little arrogant and insensitive in his advice. "Listen, Max, what's done is done. I feel sorry as hell for Kimitake, but two wrongs don't make a right. His demands are unfair to you both. Eventually, he'll have to let Shizue go and face up to his disabilities. Sink or swim on his own. I'm not being cruel," he added softly. "He deserves everyone's sympathy. But Shizue's babying him only encourages him to keep feeding off her."

"He can't be pushed into accepting how he is, Paul. She's doing what she believes is right."

"Forgive me, but I'm reminded of how she risked everything for Jiro." Paul stared into his whiskey tumbler. "One of life's bitterest ironies. We can't solve someone else's problems. Well, maybe time will nudge Kimitake from his inertia, as Shizue believes."

Max set his whiskey on the bar untouched. "I'm not prepared to wait indefinitely. Hell, I'd lose my mind if not for the work we're doing. But even its rewards don't begin to compensate for living without her."

"I've got an early morning appointment," Paul responded shortly. "If there's nothing else you'd like to get off your chest, then let's call it a night." His brother's self-pity had touched a nerve, and he was anxious to end the visit. "Think over what I said about putting yourself first for once. Sure, things look bleak just now, but you're no use to Shizue locked behind bars. The authorities may not stop at tapping your phone."

"Appreciated." Max put on his hat and turned down the brim. He walked over to the door, opened it cautiously, then peered out at the deserted hallway. "Confidentially, I'm kind of enjoying the excitement."

"Don't let it bite you." Paul could not help being amused as his brother slunk away like a spy in movies. The levity was short-lived, however. He regarded the luxurious quarters he had purchased at the cost of his leg and his ideals. Those of importance he often entertained were just acquaintances, fair-weather friends, hangers-on to his rising star. Max was his only real friend. By day Paul lost himself in work. At night there was nothing to fill the void. Shizue constantly haunted his thoughts. He knew that Kimitake was dragging her down with him, but her voice always cheerily responded to his frequent phone calls. Natsu had also endured great hardships wearing a pretty smile, he thought, never once complaining of her lot. He could not think of one woman without thinking of the other.

Paul yawned, feeling grateful for the two women who had shaped his life by giving him a special kind of love. Loving Shizue no longer pained him quite as much. Perhaps he was growing mellow with the years. His mother had never tired of saying it was better to give than to receive, and perhaps he had benefited from the truth in that, he mused, smiling to himself. He rested his cane on the chair beside the bed no woman had shared. "Love must enter into it," he remembered telling his friend Toru a lifetime ago, before China and one night spent in Hsi-Ling's arms, before his escape from an honorable death on a rocky abyss.

He had bargained his soul for the trappings of power. His love for Shizue now shone as the only pure, selfless thing in his life that might earn him a pardon from hell.

As the first weeks and months of 1941 swept past, Kimitake remained intractable. His unseen presence reigned over the household. Everyone spoke of the baron's son in reverent whispers, as if he were no longer a mortal man but some heroic deity they were forbidden to look upon. In truth, his handsome face had taken on a benign, scholarly countenance. The once poor scholar now turned his mind to philosophy and the religious mysticisms embraced by East and West.

Shizue saw his obsessive quest for knowledge as a positive sign of recovery. She would tirelessly read to him until her voice grew hoarse, then O-nami would assume the chore of struggling on through the difficult pages. One day in the early spring, Kimitake asked her to send for a Zen master to instruct him. He had chosen a way to follow, but the path he sought could not be found in books.

At last he had opened his door to the outside world. Only a crack, to admit the pious old monk wearing long black robes, but in the days that followed the holy man's arrival, Shizue watched her brother blossom. Kimitake was reaching out from within, she thought. His health steadily improved. He no longer called for her in the night shaken by dreams of China and asking to have a cigarette held to his lips. He spoke to her of worlds beyond the flesh, and his waking hours were spent in deep meditation, seeking satori. Propped up against a mountain of bed pillows, his torso wrapped in a brightly colored silk robe, he looked like a *daruma* doll that would insure good fortune.

The master was delighted with his young disciple's progress. For one month he had neglected his flock at the monastery, and tears sparkled in his wise old eyes when they said good-byes.

Kimitake had learned to smile again. A rather solemn, private smile, but returning it, Shizue felt herself in the presence of a miracle. However, while Kimitake's spiritual consciousness had soared, the baron wallowed in a spiritless abyss, and Shizue feared for his state of mind. Often she would see him in the garden, standing under his son's window, waiting for Kimitake's edict to be lifted so that he might enter and find peace.

On the morning of her twentieth birthday, she woke to blossoming cherry trees in the garden. This had always been a season of renewed hope, a time for wishes. But the hours passed uneventfully. Only Max remembered her birthday. His voice on the line from the port at Kobe sounded tired and strained. Business there had caused him to cancel the visit they had planned. Their future together seemed more distant than ever.

Peasants toiled in the mulberry orchards and the tall sericulture houses, singing to lighten their burden. As in centuries past, the silkworm moths spun another spring harvest. Hosokawa–Napier, Limited, grew rich on the tides of war. From her window Shizue watched cargo planes buzz over the rooftops, transporting the raw silk harvests to the weaving mills.

Summer waned into autumn, but the miraculous recovery she had hoped for failed to materialize. Even when Kimitake was not meditating, he existed on some ethereal plateau out of touch with reality. Shaving him, changing his sheets, washing his bedpan—all the endless drudgery—finally got the better of her, and she broke down one day and wept.

"Don't cry, Shizue. I realize you can't go on like this. Giving, waiting, living on hope. You belong to Max, and it's time I let go."

Kimitake had given voice to what she was afraid to say, and she embraced him protectively. "No, I won't abandon you."

"A nurse can take over your chores. I've come to an acceptance of sorts. Don't ask me to explain, because it can't be put into words. Now, dry your pretty eyes and sit here beside me. Come on, let's have a smile," he encouraged in a cheerful tone of voice.

"Kimi, I don't know whether to laugh or cry," she sniffled. "This is all so sudden."

"Not really. I've been on the verge of a breakthrough for months. Your tears gave me a gentle shove in the right direction. How people respond to me no longer matters."

"Then you'll see Father?"

"Yes, but only on my terms. He's always been a dark cloud overshadowing our lives, demanding that we live up to the code of the samurai. We've both paid dearly to preserve his honor. But his own Bushido has never been put to the test."

The subject caused him discomfort. Lowering his eyes, Kimitake asked for a cigarette, then quickly changed his mind. "After the fighting, I used to hold one between my fingers like a stick of incense to mask the stench. Now tobacco smells like death. Let's talk about you and Max. Of course, you'll get married. Have you approached Father?"

"I couldn't possibly, while you—"

"Then leave it to me. Please," he implored, shifting the stump of one arm as though it still had a hand to touch hers. "I won't allow him to spoil your happiness. You'll have his blessings. I've nothing left to give you but this. Father can visit tonight, after my bath. I want to be dressed in uniform. Have him bring my decorations. Now, I'd like to meditate."

Ecstatic, Shizue hugged and kissed him. "Oh, I'm speechless. I don't know what to say."

Kimitake smiled. That solemn, private smile of his gave Shizue pause. However, she was far too happy to question if things were truly as they seemed.

Tadashi Hosokawa sat alone in his study, distractedly leafing through the account ledgers. Managing the land had fallen entirely on O-nami's shoulders, but his old friend had no head for figures and this was Tadashi's single concession to the business. Shizue entered without knocking, and he glanced up at her beaming face, stunned by her announcement.

"Kimitake has recovered. He'll see you tonight."

The edict had been lifted with a suddenness that made him tremble. *Tonight*, he thought, somewhat quieted by the soft, womanly arms now circling his neck. Since the day of Jiro's burial, his daughter had extended to him only a portion of the love he once enjoyed, and this was a rare moment he wished to prolong. But she slipped away. "Must you go?"

"Kimi might be calling for me. Oh, I nearly forgot. He wants you to bring his decorations."

As the study door closed, Tadashi surveyed the antiquities preserved behind glass. Years ago his son had shamed him, and he had courted seppuku. Now Kimitake had redeemed himself. The ceremonial sword he had worn in combat rested in a glass case with the war medal, minted from the bronze of captured enemy guns. There was even a letter from the emperor awarding Kimitake the Order of the Kite for exceptional military valor.

As the caretaker of these objects, Tadashi had suffered from his son's rejection. During the long, lonely nights, more than once he had stealthily approached the room where his son lay sleeping. Each time, however, conscience stopped him from crossing the threshold to steal a look. Paralyzed by remorse, he would stand with one hand frozen on the door, his heart pounding loudly enough to wake the dead, convinced that Kimitake sensed his presence there before he fled.

After unlocking the cabinet, the baron lifted his son's bronze medal from its satin-lined case. The lowering afternoon sun glinted on suits of armor, silk battle flags, bows and arrows, and on the swords his warrior ancestors had made their souls. His ancestors had engaged in hand-to-hand combat. Brave samurai wielding swords, standing eye to eye while searching for a point of entry—the better man finding it first. And when it was done and the victor's blade withdrawn, the vanquished lay at his feet, and there was a sense of release. He had fought well and honorably. It was something he could tell his grandchildren with pride.

But there were no more warring clans whose exploits would be celebrated in poetry and song. The time of warrior heroes had vanished, and their weapons held no meaning for him now. His ancestor worship seemed misplaced in a world where impersonal killing tools had blown his son apart. According to the citations, Kimitake had breached the enemy lines against insurmountable odds. He had singlehandedly taken out Chinese tanks and a machine-gun nest. He had led his men in the taking of some strategic hill, only to be caught in a hellfire of enemy shells. He and many of the young men serving under him were maimed; others had been killed. And for what? Some gutted Chinese hill that had changed hands with the enemy many times before.

Tears streaming down his face, the baron clenched the bit of ribbon and bronze that Kimitake had been awarded for meritorious service to country and emperor. What right had he to order his son to return a hero from such a senseless and dishonorable war? Bushido had blinded his mind to the truth. When evening came he would see what remained of his handsome young son, who had posed in uniform, smiling for the photograph Tadashi kept on his study desk.

At twilight O-nami fussed over Kimitake's uniform. His fat fingers got in the way of the collar buttonholes. "Hold still, Ichiban."

"And let you strangle me."

Shizue could not help laughing. "Here, I'll do that. Go tell Father we're ready."

"I want to be alone with him," Kimitake told her. "What I have to say is private. Between men. Father and son. No eavesdropping from the next room. Promise, or I won't go through with it."

"You look so stern," she said, concerned.

"I'm confident of reaching him at last." He smiled. "Trust me, little sister. I've forgiven him."

As Shizue kissed his furrowed brow, she saw her brother as a heroic figure. She could not entirely forgive their father, and Kimitake's courage made her ashamed. "I'm so proud to be your sister. But, oh, Kimi"—she sighed, fondling the cloth of his empty sleeves—"I wonder if *ogisan* can ever forgive himself."

"That will be found through the sense of honor he prizes so highly. Enough questions. How do I look? Bring the mirror."

Holding the hand mirror out before him, she wistfully recalled the night when they had danced beneath the make-believe stars projected by a mirrored globe. An orb of reflected light now moved across his sober face, then down along the pinned-up sleeves and trouser legs of the khaki uniform. Perhaps he, too, was thinking of that rainy night and of the one-legged soldier on crutches who had taken shelter with them.

Kimitake nodded approval and then withdrew into a meditative silence.

"I'll wait in the garden," Shizue said. As she left the room, she saw her father standing down the hall, clutching Kimitake's decorations.

"Shizue, I'm afraid. Tell me what to do."

"Your love is all he's ever wanted," she said quietly. "Be gentle with him and things will take their course." Her father numbly moved on as she turned away and went downstairs. After draping a wool shawl around her shoulders, she entered the garden.

O-nami walked with her, reminiscing about the past while Shizue's thoughts were focused on the future. That evening the bounce had returned to her friend's step, and his graying topknot was like a silver ball floating through the moonbeams until his head collided with some low-hanging branches.

"These trees should be pruned," he huffed indignantly. He no longer saw things so well, but vanity prevented him from wearing glasses. "You seem chilled, little one," he said, squinting down at Shizue.

"Yes," she lied to spare his feelings. He could not see her well enough to know that her shivering had nothing to do with the evening air. Dear O-nami was growing old, and the observation saddened Shizue.

He put one arm around her shoulders to help guide him along the shadowy path, and though they walked beyond sight of the castle, she still felt bound to the confines of her brother's room. She might be set free on the outcome of this evening, she reflected, although trusting Kimitake's care to the hands of a nurse would not be easy.

Crossing a footbridge, Shizue gazed down at the reflection of the autumn moon in the rippling waters of a stream, remembering that rainy night before her brother went to war, how his long legs had stepped through puddled reflections of the moon while his cocky laughter dismissed her superstition that it might bring him bad luck. She recalled again the one-legged soldier who had hobbled out of the rain to speak, unknowingly, of the horrors awaiting Kimitake.

"Perhaps the gods warn us of things to come, only we're helpless to alter destiny even if we recognized their signs," she said to O-nami.

He nodded grimly. "*Hai*, as I have always said, these things are decided in advance."

"If so, then all our efforts are in vain. We're like the bubbles floating in this stream, dashed on the rocks put in their path, then bubbling up again full of hope where the water calms and it seems nothing else stands in the way." With both hands folded under her chin, Shizue watched leaf boats being carried downstream. "Kimi is able to forgive Father. But I can't bring myself to make that gesture." She sighed. "Time hasn't mended my feelings, and it hurts me not to feel the same about Papa. Love is such a fragile thing."

O-nami yawned and rubbed his eyes. "The hour grows late. Your father does not know how to care for Ichiban and he may have need of us."

"Oh, I shouldn't have stayed out so long." Shizue took hold of O-nami's arm, anxiously quickening her step on the path. It was yet some distance to the castle, and Kimitake might be calling for her.

Suddenly she stopped. She heard someone sobbing. They were near her mother's garden shrine, and in the moonlight she glimpsed her father embracing Sumie's statue, searching its stone face. His hands were trembling violently. Kimitake had not been honest with her, she thought. Instead of offering forgiveness, he must have lashed out against their father.

She left O-nami alone, to stumble in the darkness, and ran, fearing the consequences of that night. "Papa, you're not entirely to blame, no matter what was said."

"I weep for joy, Shizue." The baron sank to his knees and bowed low to kiss the earth at the feet of the statue. Tears choked his voice, but he seemed to draw strength from Shizue's presence beside him. "As your mother is my witness, these are tears of joy," he said, cupping her face between two ice-cold hands.

"Don't be alarmed. Seeing your brother as he is turned my blood to ice. But he's forgiven me. Yes, tonight I've found the son I never knew. I cannot tell you what passed between us, Shizue. Just know that we both found peace. Your brother seemed so at peace. His eyes grew heavy, as they did when he was a child, and I left him sleeping peacefully there in his room."

The baron lifted his eyes to a shining square of window light visible through the branches. "The bed was empty where my son's limbs should be," he addressed himself, his voice barely above a whisper. "His words made me weep. But as I wept, his missing arms reached out for me. I swear I could feel them embracing me. I swear Kimitake's legs were strong and true, lifting him from the bed to stand firmly behind his words. All these years he wanted me to love him, but I turned away. When he had the arms to reach out to me, I pushed them away. Now my love comes too late."

"Oh, Papa, you mustn't think that." Shizue clasped her hands on his and smiled. "Nothing I've done has helped Kimi to do more than hold on to life. At last he's opened the door to you, and now he can begin to live again."

"To live as he is?" Her father covered both his eyes. His despairing groan seemed to issue from the depths of his soul. "Your brother is noble and courageous. A credit to our bloodline. More of a man than I."

"Your words make me afraid."

"Hush, my daughter." Tadashi seemed to be listening to something. "I thought I heard your mother's voice calling me on the breeze. But she's only the ghost of an old dream. Shadow without substance. Stone and rings of moss on the stone to number each year of her passing." The dank mountain breezes fanned his jet black hair into streamers as he bowed quietly in thought before speaking again.

"I didn't mean to frighten you. Nothing can undo the suffering I've brought to both my children. I came to your brother prepared to suffer for my failures as a father. But Kimitake helped me look inside myself." His sunken eyes were glazed over, while his mouth struggled to form a smile. "What I saw there was more punishing than anything he might have said in anger. Then he spoke of your unhappiness, Shizue. My little girl. There's still hope for me in granting you what I've denied by my blindness. Once again I must give my precious treasure away in marriage. But this time to the man she loves. It's not too late for your happiness. Marry Douglas's son with my blessings."

"Do you really mean it, Papa?"

"Yes, my blessings on you both."

Shizue's hands pressed across her throbbing heart while her father's simple words, spoken quietly, made the air around her sing. He caressed her hair, then somberly rose to his feet and quietly returned to the house.

As she watched him walk away, Shizue knew that her father was emotionally drained from the grim reality of seeing his son's deformity for the first time. Tonight he would seek refuge in the solitude of his study. Shizue told herself that in time he would caress those scarred stumps, soft as the skin of an infant.

Somehow Kimitake had touched the depths of their father's soul and obtained this blessing for her union with Max. Miracles were not to be questioned, and she gave thanks to the gods, feeling blessed by her mother's spirit. Perhaps it was only the moonbeams casting light and shadows across the statue's large stone eyes, but there seemed to be a warm smile on Sumie's face. Just then, O-nami's voice startled her.

"I felt it was not my place to intrude and listened from the bushes," he said. "Did my ears hear the baron give you his blessings to marry Ichiban?"

"Yes, isn't it wonderful! Come, help me undress Kimi for bed."

Shizue could not help laughing while he groped through the darkness with widened eyes. "Here, better take my hand, or you'll stumble over your vanity. It's silly to be so proud. You'd look distinguished wearing glasses."

"Ah, spectacles are for the elderly to push up and down their wrinkled noses," O-nami insisted before grudgingly accepting her hand. "My sight is keen enough by daylight. Even in this darkness I see the happy glow on your face, little one. Now we will become a family again. The laughter of your children will lift the sadness from our household." He lifted Shizue off her feet and spun her through the castle doors. "I will teach them how to ride and fence, and teach them manners when they do mischief."

"I can't wait to tell Max the news. But first we must think of Kimi." She hurried to his room. For the first time since Kimitake's return home, the door stood open. Her brother was sound asleep, and Shizue entered on tiptoe, motioning for O-nami to be quiet.

The baron's visit had brought a peaceful slumber Kimitake had not known in months, and Shizue stifled the need to hug him tightly. "I'll call you if he wakes later in the night," she whispered to O-nami, as she gently unbuttoned Kimitake's high-collared officer's jacket to make him comfortable. Their father had pinned the bronze medal to his chest, and its satin-lined case rested on the night table, along with his citations for valor. That night a ceremony had taken place between father and son, the significance of which eluded Shizue. Her brother's handsome face was turned in profile against the pillows, and she observed sweat forming across his brow. The room was cool. His night sweats had ended months ago, but this reunion, she thought, must have kindled painful memories. What father and son felt for each other had lain dormant until that night. Both men faced a difficult adjustment, Shizue told herself, quietly closing the door to her adjoining room.

Overcome by tears, she lifted the receiver to telephone Max. All the weary nights she had sat in this room with only the sound of Max's voice to hold against her ear, all the loneliness she had felt was suddenly behind her.

The telephone rang in Tokyo. Breathing deeply, she wiped the last tears that rolled down her cheeks. Morita answered the phone in his rasping voice, and she spoke loudly to penetrate his old ears. She was devastated when he told her the Napiers were not at home.

"Traveling on business, Hosokawa-san," the butler informed her. "I do not know when they will return."

Shizue hung up quickly, afraid her emotions might lead to some slip of the tongue. Max had told her that the Napier phone was tapped; he always called her from pay phones. He must be on another mission of mercy for the Jews, she thought. Its danger threatened their future on this starry night of miracles.

There she was, cut off from the sound of Max's voice while bursting to share the news of her freedom. And so Paul became the first to know. His voice sounded happy for her, but Shizue sensed a tension on the line between them, as if something were being withheld. He ended the conversation abruptly, saying that important guests were arriving at his Tokyo apartment. She was left feeling that her wedding announcement was an anticlimactic event. However, the contact with Paul did bring a measure of reality to her dreamy condition, and warm thoughts of his many kindnesses took her to the dresser drawer filled with keepsakes: the locked diaries, Max's love letters, the snapshots they had exchanged, and the box made of bamboo reeds, which had held his gift of the *omamori*. It seemed a lifetime ago when Paul had fastened the gold chain around her neck in Max's place. Now Max wore the *omamori* that she had returned to him as a gesture of farewell when it had seemed their journeys through life would separate them forever.

She would not sleep that night. Shizue threw open her bedroom window. The gardens had been painted by autumn. Under the moon, leaves showered to earth like a golden rain. She thought of her wishing tree and the showering cherry blossoms of each passing spring when she had wished for this very moment. Once more her father would give her away in marriage, but she would not leave home dressed all in white, the color of mourning. The wedding would take place here, among those she loved. But on what day? After all the waiting, even a few days more would seem an eternity before she stood beside Max as his bride.

CHAPTER 35

Max and Shizue were married on a crisp November afternoon in the garden, with only the immediate family in attendance. The bride wore a long-sleeved dress of teal blue crepe de chine and a stylish turban hat of the same material. The groom wore a dark blue suit with a yellow rosebud pinned to his lapel. It and the bouquet of yellow roses carried by the bride were symbolic of their first communion taken in the place where the kerria bloomed.

They had decided on a Buddhist ceremony. The traditional Shinto ritual would have pleased Baron Hosokawa more, but Shizue felt there was too much sorrow and misfortune attached to the wedding pledge of *san-san ku-do*, which had placed Jiro's life in her hands. Shizue now bowed her head to the fragrant rosebuds while the vows she shared with Max in secrecy years before were made binding in the name of the Amida Buddha, a shining deity of pure love.

Max faced his bride, feeling bathed in the dazzling aura of her radiance. Holding her hand, he wondered if other men came to the marriage altar burning with such love. He grew impatient with the priest's long-winded incantations, but he was fond of the old man. As a boy, Max had worshipped with the Hosokawa family at his hilltop temple overlooking their ancestral shrine. The elderly Shinto priest's cold eyes had always looked upon Max as a foreigner, while this Buddhist priest smiled warmly, making no distinction between the races. He saw only a man and woman joined before him in love.

"Amida is light and life and love," the old priest said to the couple informally. He spread his wrinkled hands out in a benediction. "Your vows emanate from Buddha's love, and he is connected to you through them, demanding only your faith. One's karma may bring times of struggle between good and evil, the loss of riches and the hunger of poverty. Place no value on these transitory hindrances. Faith alone retains its value. Faith alone is pure and absolute. Amida is the pure light of love, and now you are one, joined with him in the universe shared by all beings. Let his joy shine upon you both."

O-nami loudly clapped his hands to acknowledge the *kami* presence, and although the ceremony was not a Shinto rite, everyone observed that custom.

While Shizue smiled radiantly at Max, Douglas Napier sought Inge's hand, and she smiled at him tearfully. This moment belonged to the newlyweds, who sealed their vows in a long, sweet kiss. But Kimitake could not be ignored. He was seated in a wheelchair, held upright by a leather strap buckled around his waist. As those around him clapped hands, he glanced down at the empty sleeves of his officer's uniform. Baron Hosokawa stood rigidly at one side of his chair, O-nami on the other, patting Yufugawo's shoulder as she sobbed into her handkerchief. An undercurrent of pathos clouded the occasion for everyone but the newlyweds.

Shizue rushed to award Kimitake the honor of kissing the bride first. "Happy now?" he asked, twisting against the wheelchair as if he still had arms to embrace his sister.

"Ecstatic!" Her smile lavished him with affection before she was pulled away from him by Yufugawo, who tearfully embraced her. "Please, don't carry on so," Shizue said, smiling, "or you'll make me cry as well."

Inge felt out of place and stood back, watching the effusive exchange between the newlyweds and members of the household. She had yet to feel at home in Japan. The mountainous surroundings evoked memories of Switzerland, of climbs there with Heinz. The life she had left behind her seemed so far removed from where she stood today, as a witness to the marriage of Angela's son. But she had come to celebrate a happy event, and her sadness melted with a smile.

Douglas embraced Tadashi with a masculine hug, moved to renew their lifelong friendship. Angela's son and Shizue linked arms, beaming at each other worshipfully as Inge fondly embraced them both. "I could not be happier for you. Max, such a handsome groom. And, Shizue, such a beautiful bride. I know we will become good friends."

"Yes, I feel that too," said Shizue. Force of habit caused her to shift her gaze to Kimitake. "Excuse me, my brother doesn't look well."

"It's only the excitement," Kimitake told those who gathered around his wheelchair. He was having difficulty breathing. "Being strapped in this bed on wheels will take some getting used to, little sister."

"Are you sure it's only that?" Shizue asked, seeing his pained smile.

Before he could answer, the garden was ripped by strong winds, and servants carrying champagne glasses and hors d'oeuvres were turned back in the storm of autumn leaves and twigs. The wedding party was forced indoors, where Max bent over Kimitake, thinking he would loosen the strap around his waist a notch. But Shizue stilled his hands.

"She's right, Max. Any looser and I'd fall like Humpty Dumpty," he said with a grin. "Listen, you two, I wouldn't have missed this event for anything, but I've overdone it for my first day out. Don't interrupt the festivities on my account. Father and the nurse will get me comfortable and to bed."

"Yes, you need rest," said the baron, dutifully taking charge of his son's wheelchair. "I won't be long."

"Papa, do be careful carrying him up the stairs." Shizue wrung her hands, finding it infinitely more difficult to let go than she had thought. Her father had taken over O-nami's chores, and Kimitake seemed delighted with the arrangement. He was so eager to set her free, employing one of the first nurses they had interviewed. Aki was a homely, bucktoothed matron of fifty, with a kind disposition and gentle hands. Even so, Shizue had barely been given time to instruct the woman. "Max, would you mind very much if I went up to Kimi?"

"It'll cost you a kiss, Mrs. Napier."

Hearing Max call her that brought her a sudden thrill. "Oh, I adore you," she said, throwing both arms around his neck. Max lifted her in his arms and they kissed. Shizue felt delirious with joy as he spun her around the room, then gently set her feet on the floor and kissed her once again.

"A toast to Ichiban and his new bride!" O-nami raised his champagne glass to the rafters. "May all their days be filled with health, happiness, and good fortune. *Banzai! Banzai! Banzai!*"

Mr. and Mrs. Max Napier acknowledged the moist eyes and smiling faces with bows. Then Douglas came forward and put champagne glasses in their hands while the servants applauded, free for the evening to step out of their places and become part of the family that their ancestors had served for generations. The elders among them appeared rather uncomfortable with this marriage that broke with tradition, but the young were not in the least restrained, and everyone seemed to be talking at once.

Shizue felt tugs on her lifeline to Kimitake. But others' hands must serve him now, she thought. Her new place was with Max, and it was wrong for her to hold on. From that day on, her brother would be nourished by other loved ones. At the moment what she desired most was to have Max all to herself. But O-nami, who was rather drunk, took Max aside for a sentimental discussion.

Shizue turned to Inge, whose maternal instincts had found expression through Angela Napier's son. "There was so much to do, I haven't had a chance to welcome you properly," she told her. "No one's even welcomed you into the family since you arrived in Japan. This is your home now, and you mustn't feel like a stranger."

"Shizue, how sweet of you to think of me."

The two Mrs. Napiers hugged, then began chatting comfortably, searching each other out for similarities in their markedly different backgrounds. Inge looked over at Douglas, and Shizue observed the love in her eyes. Shizue thought Inge was very brave to have trusted her heart again, opening it to the vulnerability of loving another man. As if reading her thoughts, Inge clasped Shizue's hands in a gesture of friendship between women who had both known tragedy but were unafraid to love.

Max approached his father, watching him run a finger around the rim of his champagne glass. "What's on your mind, Dad?"

"Natsu. Paul. How things might have been," he answered, without breaking his reflective mood.

"I'm hurt by Paul's refusal to attend the wedding," said Max. "Nothing either Shizue or I said would change his mind."

"Maybe it's just as well he didn't come. I'd hoped he might use the occasion as an excuse for testing his feelings about me after so many years. But this is your day, Max, not the time for opening old wounds."

Tadashi entered the room, wiping one hand across his face before accepting the glass of champagne O-nami handed to him. The light-hearted atmosphere grew hushed, and all eyes looked to him, anticipating some fatherly address to the bride.

"My heart is too full for words," he began, and cleared his throat. "Shizue, you already have my blessings. You've been a constant source of joy to me. Now I happily pass you from my care to Douglas's son. Your future rests with Max. Always remember this as a day that brought great joy to me and to your brother. Always look back on this day for the brightness it held." The baron's voice faltered, and wind rattling the garden doors filled the emotion-charged silence. "Yes, my heart is too full for words," he said softly, then steadily raised his glass. "I stand before you for my courageous son, who asked me to toast this union in his place. May it prosper with happy children."

His reference to Kimitake left a heavy silence over the gathering until O-nami rose to the occasion. *"Banzai!"* he cried, one arm jerking up and down like a bandmaster leading everyone in the cry. "Ah, this bubbly juice creeps up on a man unannounced." He groaned and rolled his eyes. "But what a rosy feeling it brings down into my toes." Laughing, he helped himself to another glass. "Is there to be a feast, or must these newlyweds go hungry? Yufugawo, go and speak with the cook!"

Max steadied his friend. "You shouldn't drink so much on an empty stomach," he advised.

"Hah, this mountain of a stomach is never empty," said Yufugawo, fondly rubbing her husband's belly.

Shizue laughed, but the sober tone of her father's wedding toast echoed in her mind with an unsettling ring. "Father, is something wrong? You are happy for us?"

"What have I done to warrant such a question?" he asked in a wounded tone.

"Nothing, really."

His shoulders relaxed. "Well, then, let the feast commence. Max, take charge of your bride. I do believe she's feeling rather skittish."

"Not in the least," Shizue demurred, and then laughed. To make love as Max's wife excited her, and she hugged his arm, lost to the desire she saw in his smiling blue eyes. "Oh, wait everyone! Where did I put my bridal bouquet?"

"Here it is!"

A young servant girl rushed to hand Shizue the small bouquet of yellow roses. According to her wishes, the servants' daughters of marriageable age had acted as her bridesmaids, and she asked them all to gather around her. "It's customary in the West for the bride to toss away her bouquet, and the girl who catches it will be the next to wed her heart's desire." She closed her eyes before tossing her bouquet up in the air.

"Oh, it's to be me!"

The girl who caught Shizue's bouquet crushed its petals to her bosom, dreamy-eyed and hopeful amid the flock of giggling future brides. This lovely girl of eighteen had hovered near Kimitake's room attentively over the months, eager to help Shizue by performing the most menial chores. Kimitake pretended to ignore her, but every now and then his eyes would go to her longingly while she blushed as if seeing only his handsome face, smiling as if blinded to his missing limbs. How it had grieved Shizue to watch her brother desiring this sweet, generous girl, aware that she could never be moved even by pity to grant him some moments of womanly tenderness.

As they entered the dining hall, his empty wheelchair in the corridor reminded everyone of his absence. Shizue realized he had wished to spare himself and everyone the awkwardness of being fed by his nurse. Yet, he remained the center of attention in their thoughts as the wedding party seated themselves on pillows at the low wooden tables laden with food.

Douglas glanced around the family table, counting the years and the missing faces. Weighty concerns over the future of their dynasty had brought him here alone two days earlier, but the baron had been reclusive, spending long hours with Kimitake and withdrawing to the privacy of his study whenever Douglas attempted more than superficial conversation. He reasoned that his friend's mind was occupied by similar concerns over the future, but that Tadashi did not wish to share his feelings as yet.

Douglas let others carry the dinner conversation. He noted the urgent looks exchanged between Shizue and his son. Youthful exuberance made them wild to be alone, so they were oblivious to what took place around them until the baron suddenly asked for their attention.

Douglas listened intently to the fears Tadashi now voiced over how current world events affected their lives. All trade between Japan and America had ceased. Roosevelt had frozen Japanese assets in the United States, and his increased support of Great Britain in the war against Hitler had eroded America's diplomatic ties with Japan to an alarming degree.

"This is a critical situation, Douglas, and our children must know my thoughts. Roosevelt is playing a dangerous game. I'm worried about which way Japan will jump if America enters the fight with Great Britain. Now that Shizue is part of your family, she may face internment as well if our two countries should go to war." Baron Hosokawa laid down his chopsticks and gave the newlyweds a fatherly smile. "Kimitake shares my feelings. War isn't a certainty, but just to be on the safe side you must go to America and begin your lives together there."

"Yes, I've already given serious thought to our position here," Douglas said, relieved to have the subject finally open to discussion.

Inge was ill at ease. Early warning signals in Japan could not be ignored; too many people had done that in Germany.

The baron knew nothing about their refugee work, and Douglas chose to leave it at that. "Our welcome has worn thin. Nothing's been said, but the military is making it damn tough for me to do business. Extra paperwork to do. Unannounced inspections of the weaving mills. Impossible demands to increase production quotas. Even unfounded complaints of faulty parachutes. Their harassment is clearly aimed at forcing me to pull up stakes here. But that's more easily said than done."

The baron's nod and lowering eyes conveyed his sorrow. "All these months I've unfairly left you to carry the full burden, Douglas. If negotiations break down, war could follow quickly. Drastic measures are necessary to free us both of this dirty business. We should begin to settle our affairs tonight."

Inge fluttered her napkin. "*Ach*, business and romance do not mix. The bride and groom wish to be alone." She aimed her remark at Shizue, then sighed. "My *Schatzkens*, so very young and so very much in love. Max, take your bride away before these men smother you both with their serious words."

Max quickly rose from the table and took Shizue by the hand. "Good night. *Oyasumi nasai*," he said, bowing with her.

She giggled as he dragged her upstairs. "My, what a forceful husband you are."

"Your old room or mine, Mrs. Napier?"

"Mine. Say it again."

"What?"

"My new name, silly."

"As it's done in the West, Mrs. Napier," said Max, lifting Shizue in his arms at her bedroom door. "The blushing bride carried across the threshold and taken with a kiss."

"All these months of wanting you," Shizue responded, smiling as with one foot she sent the door shut behind them.

O-nami fell back from the wedding feast table, flat on the floor, patting his huge belly with satisfied groans. Yufugawo laughed and prodded him to leave for bed. He had overindulged since the bride and groom fled hours before. Getting to his feet was a difficult maneuver that amused the baron and Douglas. But O-nami's comical withdrawal offered only momentary relief from their depression.

Inge, realizing that her presence was an intrusion, bid her husband good night with a kiss as Tadashi observed the couple's loving exchange through glistening eyes. Shizue's marriage to Max had broken the covenant he once held sacred; now a dynasty must be dissolved. This was a solemn occasion for lifelong friends, who silently studied each other's aging faces. The wistfulness of times remembered led them into the cool night air.

Only a thin sliver of moon showed in the clear starry sky. A dank breeze scattered fallen leaves across their path and made a sighing sound through the shedding branches overhead. In these fragrant gardens Douglas Napier had first seen Natsu, sitting with other pretty young girls under the old tree he had climbed as a boy. Tonight another woman shared his love. Douglas had no taste for business on such a night as this, filled with echoes from the past. The future promised healthy grandchildren, but they might never run at play, filling these gardens with laughter as their grandfathers and their parents had. Grandchildren of mixed blood would grow up as Americans, and the dissolution of a dynasty, which had begun with the wedding, was an unavoidable reality.

The two old friends walked in silence. Douglas's thoughts turned to the black metal box containing the legal documents of their partnership. It had been passed down to their heirs by Fujio Hosokawa and Andrew Napier. "Have you ever wondered why our grandfathers' wills kept the papers of their agreement under lock and key?"

The baron shrugged. "I never considered the papers of very much importance to our partnership," he answered distantly. "I never thought we'd reach the point when it would be necessary to go through them."

"Neither of us did." Soon the silk threads binding the lives of two families in Japan would be cut, Douglas told himself. But transplanting the Napier roots in American soil could not sever three generations of personal ties with those firmly rooted to this ageless valley on Kyushu. "Max and Shizue looked so happy. It's been a day to remember, Tadashi. But I suppose we can't put off opening that box."

The baron sighed. "Tonight carries a heavy burden."

Douglas glimpsed his torment as they passed under Kimitake's windows, where a brass bell had recently been installed. Shizue's worry over the care her brother would receive when left in the hands of a stranger had prompted Douglas to devise an alarm system of brass bells through- out the castle. Simply by pressing a small pillow within easy reach of his head, Kimitake could trigger an electric switch to summon help. The system would free his nurse from the rigors of constant duty, which his sister had so tirelessly performed. Whenever time permitted, Douglas worked over his drawing board devising a mechanical arm for Kimitake. No such prosthesis as yet existed for the many amputees of Japan's war in Asia. Useless dummy arms and legs were issued for cosmetic purposes, to fill out empty sleeves and trouser legs. Douglas had set himself a difficult challenge, and his compassionate labor of love might soon grant Kimitake some freedom of movement. "I've made steady progress with the mechanical arm and hand," he told the baron, somewhat cheered by that fact. "Quite an engineering problem, but in time I'll have it licked. Then Kimitake can do a lot for himself and not feel so dependent on others."

Tadashi responded in a hoarse, weary voice. "Who can say what time will bring? Witnessing the happiness of our two children, I wished to the gods these last years could be relived. Nothing can make my son whole again. I'm grateful for your efforts, Douglas, but no feat of engineering skill can replace his blood and bone. His stumps are like an infant's skin to my touch. When I help the nurse undress him for bed, my eyes are scarred by the sight, and I take his pain upon myself. Had I known the horrors my decisions would bring about . . ." Overcome with emotion, he gripped Douglas's shoulders and wept. "It's over for us, old friend. We may not be together again after tonight. I've given Shizue into your care and that of your son. Watch over my little girl. Guard her well."

Mightier forces than the destiny that had linked together these men of different races were now wrenching them apart. As Douglas embraced his friend, he realized that he had played out the role assigned to him as a boy, while the baron remained trapped in a suit of armor built of his teachings. Douglas worried over the cause of his weeping. "What a gloomy soothsayer. This is only a practical arrangement," he insisted. "Hell, Tadashi, it'll take more than a war to do us in."

"Age makes one sentimental." Once more the proud samurai, he returned Douglas's manly hug and stood back, smiling. "It wasn't my intention to bring an end to things on such a mournful note. I'd prefer to think only of the good years we shared. That going our separate ways won't set us permanently apart. Now to business."

The moment they entered the study, the baron grew despondent. Surrounded by totems of honor and heroism, the mundane concerns of setting a price on Hosokawa-Napier, Limited's, joint holdings seemed of little consequence, a formality that had no bearing on his and Douglas's deep emotional bonds.

The baron took down the dust-encrusted metal box from a high shelf, where it had rested, undisturbed, for so long. He sent a servant to bring oil for the rusty lock. Before that night, no member of either family had been permitted to delve into the contents of this black box. Documents defining the legal parameters of their partnership had gone untouched since that night in 1871, when Andrew Napier and Fujio Hosokawa had sat down together across a table in humbler quarters once occupied by the castle servants. After their grandfathers had visited the Shinto shrine to petition the gods for a successful business venture, a celebration had been held in the gardens just outside these study windows. Then paper lanterns had illuminated the fire-blackened ruins of Fujio's ancestral castle.

The Hosokawa castle now stood on the ashes of past misfortune, restored with the wealth of a partnership the founding fathers of the dynasty had known would outlive them. On that long-ago night, their signatures had determined the lives of future generations. Andrew Napier had fashioned the handsome box to hold their agreement. Neither man foresaw a time when their inheritors would need to unlock its contents. Fujio had been honored by his American partner's gift, which made the Hosokawa family its guardians. The box had been willed to their heirs with the stipulation that it was to remain locked, that it would be opened only if circumstances forced the pact between families to be broken—as it had on the night of a marriage that mixed their blood.

Before this evening the existence of those documents had been unimportant to Douglas. Until now, even the baron had no cause to think of their grandfathers' motive for locking away the exact nature of the agreement. After all, everyone felt secure. The wealth was always equally divided between families, and the duties inherited by each succeeding generation were carried out unquestioningly.

Now Baron Hosokawa squeezed oil into the rusty lock and inserted the old key. Seventy years had passed since Baron Fujio had locked this black lacquered box. On its lid, the name of the firm, Hosokawa-Napier, Limited, had appeared for the very first time, etched in gold leaf by Andrew's talented hands. As Japanese, the Hosokawa name was placed first, but joined to that of the Napier family by a fancy scrollwork hyphen and printed in flowery English letters of equal size and importance. Finally, the lid groaned open. A musty smell rushed out from the airless vacuum, where the past had been preserved.

One by one the red sealing wax of yellowing documents was broken, a dozen in all. The brittle pages inked with tiny Japanese characters were hard to read. Douglas and Tadashi grew weary of trying to decipher the words and interpret the technicalities of old Japanese law. After many hours of scrutiny, both men gave up.

The baron summoned his aged secretary from sleep. Akihiri crouched behind his small desk in one corner of the study. Bowing over the documents with a magnifying glass, he mumbled to himself, scanning down the lines of fine print. The old man's legal background soon shed light on the confusing wordage.

Douglas poured snifters of brandy, then he and the baron reclined in their chairs, warming the crystal glasses between their hands while Akihiri untied the legal knots strand by strand.

"Your confusion is quite understandable, gentlemen. At the time of this agreement, the codes of Japanese law were like wheels within wheels." The old man leaned back, massaging his eyes. "These documents refer to the treaty signed in 1858, which applied to all foreigners in Japan. The partnership entered into between your grandfathers rests on this, and limits were imposed on Andrew Napier's side of the partnership." Akihiri's bony shoulders poked up through the black cloth of his robe as he scrunched down over the written words again. He mumbled to himself for a time. "Ah, here I have found the most important clause," he announced in a rasping voice. "Worded, I might say, in a confusing fashion. To paraphrase"—he cleared his throat—"Andrew Napier was recognized as a partner in the firm of Hosokawa-Napier, Limited. But as a foreigner, he was not permitted to purchase land. And so, the land on which your mills now stand was purchased by your grandfather, Baron. *Hai*, that land is yours, and no part of its ownership is attached to Napier-*san*'s holdings in the firm. No, the terms of this agreement had been governed by a point of Japanese law that made the Hosokawa family the primary partner in your firm."

Douglas Napier rose to his feet, stunned. "But it can't be true!"

"I am afraid your grandfather could only make the best of this bargain, Napier-*san*. There is a further clarification of your division of ownership," said Akihiri. Once again he bent over the documents, murmuring for a time under his breath before raising his head to address Douglas Napier's shock.

"It pains me to inform you of this—but you have no recourse under Japanese law. Your grandfathers had agreed to abide by the terms set forth in these documents. Under no circumstance could either partner seek to amend them. As men of honor, they bound themselves and all their heirs to uphold what had been decided with their signatures in 1871. That agreement is still legal and binding today. The baron has sole ownership of the firm's land. Napier-*san* owns his shares of stock in that firm, but there is no land attached to him in these documents. Our courts will favor the baron in any litigation arising from the dissolution of this partnership. And in accordance with these terms, it is for the baron and the baron alone to decide the worth of Napier-*san*'s interest in the mills."

While Baron Hosokawa gaped at his friend in disbelief, Douglas took hold of the desk for support. According to the agreement, he actually owned nothing in Japan! He stood there reeling. The truth was incomprehensible, unfathomable, and his mind refused to accept it. Their dynasty was held together by the sweat of its male heirs, and its continuation rested solely on that, not the actual division of its real property. But he had every reason to believe that the division was fair and equitable. Then Akihiri's unraveling of these legal documents disclaimed any equality between partners of East and West. Now Douglas saw things for what they were, and the blow rendered him speechless.

Wearily, Akihiri peered through the lens of his magnifying glass. "The legal technicalities set forth here are cut-and-dried, Baron," he said. "They merely support what I have already explained. You might have difficulty understanding the language it is written in. However, I feel it my duty to read this to you both."

Baron Hosokawa nodded. "Read it then."

Douglas bowed his head as Akihiri spelled out the legal technicalities exposing an ugly conspiracy that had been kept under lock and key until that night. Much of it was repetition, the litany of Japanese lawyers who had wanted nothing left to chance.

Behind their words lay the untold story of a dynasty. In Andrew Napier's time, the distrustful Japanese had forbidden him to own land, so he had sought a Japanese partner as a matter of necessity. He had come there to build a dynasty whose permanent claim on Japanese soil had demanded concessions. Knowing the truth—that in fact they owned nothing at all except on the sufferance of the Hosokawas—Andrew's heirs might not have dutifully followed in his footsteps, and so both grand-fathers had conspired to keep the facts locked from sight.

In silence Douglas watched Akihiri's wrinkled hands turn over the yellowing pieces of paper that stripped him of his worth, his identity, and all that he had sacrificed himself to. His identity had been a fabrication, his grandfather's way of ruling over his heirs for a lifetime and from beyond the grave.

Passing one hand across his eyes, Douglas thought of his life spent fulfilling the obligations to serve a dynasty built on falsehoods, of the countless hours he had spent designing and developing machines to further the dynasty's interests.

"If only I'd known!" he shouted, seizing the metal box. He flung it hard against the floor, wanting to crush its metal shell as he had been crushed. But the box rattled hollowly. He could not avenge himself against ghosts.

The baron touched Douglas's arm. "Douglas, it's not in our power to right the wrongs of the dead," he said quietly. "This agreement struck between our grandfathers belongs to the time they lived in. They expected us to break with their pact only if there were bad blood between our families. That isn't the case. The law may favor me, but I refuse to honor such bitter terms. No, it's for us to dissolve the dynasty as we see fit. For us to decide what's fair. I know how you must feel. But does it really matter now?"

"Yes, it matters," said Douglas, as he lifted the box off the floor. "The emptiness matters. The suffering this caused will always matter to me, Tadashi. What might have been if not for the deceptions can't be written off or dealt with fairly."

Baron Hosokawa's sigh showed an understanding that went beyond words. "I want nothing more to do with war, Douglas. For me the dissolution of our partnership boils down to a cold accounting of our tangible assets—to be sold and divided fairly." That would not heal his friend's scars, but he had nothing else to offer. "Akihiri, is there anything else in those papers for us to be concerned about?"

His secretary coughed, wiping spittle from his thin lips with a handkerchief before answering. "No, Baron, the terms of dissolution are yours to decide. But there is one other matter which deals with the Napier family's private holdings. Their house in Tokyo. Shall I read it to you?"

Douglas nodded vacantly and sank in the chair across from his friend. Placing the empty black box between them, he listened as Akihiri dryly informed him that even the soil on which the Napier mansion stood had only been leased, for the term of ninety-one years, and was renewable upon the discretion of the Japanese trust company that held its deed. The mansion could be rented to others, but Douglas could not sell it outright.

Douglas shook his head at the irony of the situation. Angela had loathed that cavernous mausoleum built to house the heirs of his grandfather's American dynasty who were obliged to live there according to Andrew's will. Suddenly he found that his ancestral home was not even his to sell. He was left empty-handed; he had nothing to show for the years devoted to an industry that had drained his life's blood. "What a travesty," he told the baron, and emptied his brandy glass.

Baron Hosokawa refilled their glasses. "For tonight we can't do more than estimate the firm's present market value. But I insist on a fair accounting down to the last brick, Douglas. The firm's land as well, Akihiri. Give us some estimate of it all. I want everything divided equally between us."

"That won't change anything," said Douglas, grappling with his grandfather's ultimate lie. Seventy years of servitude in the mills, all the suffering of unhappy sons and their unloved wives—all that had amounted to nothing but the bricks and mortar of their Tokyo mansion and one half of the weaving mills' brick walls in Nagasaki and Kyoto. Structures anchored in Japanese soil could not be sawed in half and uprooted. In the final analysis, the Napier family had been transients, outsiders permitted to reside in a civilization bound to tradition and inured against change.

Douglas was alone with his thoughts, unable to share them with Tadashi. As he sat there, shock eventually gave way to a numb resignation. Anger bowed to the realities. Daylight touched the study windows, and he felt stirred by the subtle nuances of change taking place inside him. He watched his years in Japan being summed up in the loud clacking of the wooden balls of Akihiri's abacus. Only a thorough study of the company books in Tokyo would reveal his net worth as a partner in Hosokawa-Napier, Limited; but that night he was forced to confront his personal worth as a man who had invested his best years toiling in a foreign land.

The chair groaned as Akihiri rose to hand Baron Hosokawa his figures. "My estimate is based on last year's business accounting," he said.

"It's something to go on. Once the business is sold, Douglas, you'll receive a draft good for your equal share to be paid by an American bank."

Douglas muttered under his breath, "Just so much paper, Tadashi." He closed the lid of the empty box and felt a shiver. Refusing to accept his fair share of the firm's monetary worth would be a useless protest against the architects of a cruel deception. "Well, perhaps these funds can serve some useful purpose." In America it might assist the cause of Jewish refugees, he mused. He was resourceful, but he would need funds to rebuild his life and he had loved ones to think about. "I won't be leaving Japan empty-handed. Max, Shizue, and Inge are my family now. They're my fortune." Douglas brightened, turning from the past to what lay ahead. "I'm reminded of what you once told me about wealth not being enough in itself."

"Yes—our true wealth is the love of our children," the baron replied. "Some things can't be bought."

"It is dawn, Baron," Akihiri said loudly, to gain the attention of his employer, who sat staring off into space. "Is there more you require of me?"

"Dawn, already." Baron Hosokawa wiped both hands across his face. "Yes, I have something to dictate," he told the bleary-eyed old man, and then wearily got to his feet, pacing while he dictated a letter of agreement between partners. It was a simple statement in which his friend was granted the equal division of property he justly deserved. "So, this frees us of the terms set forth in our grandfathers' documents once and for all. Akihiri, I want you to act as witness to our signatures."

"*Hai*, Baron." His secretary blew on the wet ink, then set the letter down on Tadashi's desk. "What I have taken down here is legal and binding. I can foresee no difficulties arising from the sale."

After Baron Hosokawa and Douglas had signed the agreement, Akihiri was sent back to his bed, and the two men lapsed into silence. Only a single sheet of white paper lay on the desk between them to speak for everything three generations had built up and now had torn down. So much importance attached to the preservation of their dynasty, which had begun with the signatures of its founding fathers on stacks of papers and ended with their inheritors' signatures on a letter of dissolution.

"How will you fill the time?" Douglas asked.

"With my son. What time the gods allow me belongs to Kimitake."

"You're too young to remain idle."

"I never found any joy in our business," Tadashi confessed, and brushed their letter of agreement aside. "All I really cared about were the workers and their families. Now others will be given that position of trust. I'd appreciate it if you saw to the business details. After you've studied the company books, we can place Hosokawa-Napier, Limited, on the auction block. With the fortune being earned from our parachute contracts, no doubt we'll have our choice of buyers."

"I'll handle the paperwork. But the sale could take a month or so to clear legal channels." Douglas recalled standing beside his friend at the closing of their Nagasaki mill as they locked the old iron gates. "Despite everything, selling out to strangers doesn't go down easily."

"Still, it must be done as quickly as possible. Before you sail, my government may decide to retaliate against Roosevelt's seizure of Japanese assets in America by seizing your assets. However, the transaction can be arranged here through the bank branch of some other neutral country to prevent Japan from stopping payment on the draft when you reach America." Baron Hosokawa's gaze drifted to the glass case where Kimitake's medal and citations had been restored to their places of honor. "Japanese casualties in China and elsewhere in Asia are mounting at an alarming rate. I'd like to silence the mills for good, but my government wouldn't permit them to be shut down. So, let the spoils of war go to the highest bidder and good riddance."

"I should have trusted my intuitions about Hitler," Douglas said, feeling remorse.

"All that's behind us now. Over and done with."

"You still have these lands. When the world comes to its senses, Japanese silk will find a peacetime market in the West again." Douglas worked up a smile, hoping to lift his friend's depression. But the grimness of the moment closed in around them both. "Silk is in my blood, Tadashi, the devotion of a lifetime. Leaving here won't rid me of its pull. Japan is my home, and its people will always be my brothers." He interlocked his fingers tightly as he reflected on the looms that still served Hitler's cause, the assembly lines that could not be stopped from serving Japan at war. "From what I've read, synthetics are coming into their own. Before long, nylon parachutes may replace those made of silk."

"In the hands of the gods," said the baron.

"Things look bleak right now, but our friendship never rested on those documents. As friends and partners we made a damn good team," Douglas said forcefully, desperate to salvage something from the debris of their shattered illusions.

"You were always the mover, Douglas. I merely hung on your coattails, never soiling my hands. As for the silk, it's in my blood as well." Baron Hosokawa rubbed his arms. "The dawns here break with a chill no matter the season. These lands where we harvested the silk have an existence of their own. My ancestors and I were just caretakers."

He bowed over the black metal box, running his fingers across the names of their two families. The years were only dust on his fingertips, yet the letters etched in gold leaf on its lid mocked time's passage by taking on a fresh shine. "Our children made it all worthwhile. My daughter and your son's children will erase this hyphen that stood between us, that divided the races like a two-edged knife," he said. "So many wounds inflicted by tarnished ideals handed down from father to son. Perhaps if you hadn't been stopped from marrying Natsu . . ." Tadashi sighed heavily and left the thought unfinished. He stood and walked to the window. "Soon you'll be leaving Paul behind. He's been in my thoughts. Especially so tonight. Is the door still barred against you?"

"Yes." Leaving Paul without so much as a good-bye now preyed on Douglas's mind. Squinting into the first light of daybreak, he wondered if Natsu's son would seek him out before he sailed. "Forcing myself on him is a painful last measure," he said aloud. "But if Paul doesn't make the effort, then I'll go to him. Even if he continues to be cold to me, I must see him again."

"I've learned what it is to be turned away by my own son. But in his case, that rebuke was justified. Paul has yet to learn that we only punish ourselves by denying the love we feel for others. He's won a private war against bigotry and now enjoys a distinguished position. I was taught that blood would tell, that mixed blood watered down the spirit of a man. Ah, old beliefs die hard. More than bloodlines determine the true worth of men. I've come to recognize my absurdity too late." Silent for a time, the baron massaged his eyes. "But there's hope for Shizue's children. That hope gives me peace."

"You're keeping something from me." Douglas crossed to his friend and put his hand on Tadashi's shoulder. "We know each other too well for keeping secrets. Tell me what's burdening you."

"Remorse. Regrets." Tears clouded his eyes. "Releasing the ghosts from that old box was a trial. I've retraced a lifetime in the span of a few hours. Tonight's been hard for us both. We've done what was expected of us, now let's put things to rest."

"All right," said Douglas, uneasy with his friend's reassuring smile. At that very moment the two men had never been closer, and he thought back over their personal travails, their failures, their small victories. Through it all they had respected each other's privacy, leaving much that passed between them unsaid.

Stretching, Douglas felt the weight of his years. "I feel hamstrung by it all. Too much so to think of sleep. Let's stretch our legs."

Mist was rising from the valley floor as they crossed the footbridge to Sumie's garden shrine. In his heart, Tadashi felt sure that his wife would have blessed their daughter's union to Max. He lit the stone oil lanterns and knelt, paying homage to her memory while the flames shot sparks through the chill morning air.

Douglas paid his respects to Sumie by kneeling beside his friend. The ground under his knees was wet with dew. He thought of Angela laid to rest in German soil. While sunlight dispelled the misty white vapors of night, Douglas was besieged by vivid images of that last night in Berlin, when Angela had kissed him with all the passion of a woman deeply in love. He had stood there rather dazed, her lipstick smeared across his mouth while his wife's eyes shouted her love and her fear of never seeing him again. Everyone close to Angela must have seen how she had loved him, and it was a deeply painful illumination.

You blind fool, he thought. Sumie Hosokawa's eyes of stone seemed to offer him forgiveness.

The sudden clanging of brass bells startled both men. Baron Hosokawa rushed toward the castle, where the hero stripped of his limbs had triggered Douglas's newly installed alarm system. Kimitake had closed an electrical circuit by applying pressure to the small pillow within easy reach of his head.

Tadashi's son could have called for his nurse asleep in the adjoining bedroom, Douglas thought, but it seemed he was testing his father's love. Douglas saw no reason to panic and walked to the castle with a slow, measured step, reflecting on what his life had been up until now. A dynasty had been dissolved, but what tests of love and devotion yet awaited its survivors, he wondered in the dawn of a new day.

Suddenly, the valley grew quiet. Tadashi had reached his son's room to silence the clanging alarm bells. Looking up at the castle, Douglas noted the newlyweds' shuttered windows. He doubted that any sound could invade their ecstasy. The triumph of his son's marriage to Shizue now swept over him like a fresh wind, carrying off the vestigial dust of Andrew Napier's bitter legacy. Thoughts of becoming a grandfather lit Douglas's face with a smile.

The household had been awakened. On the way to his bedroom, Douglas passed yawning servants. When he opened his bedroom door, he found Inge wide awake, seated upright in bed with the telephone in her hand.

"Aquida has telephoned from Tokyo," she whispered, cradling the receiver. "Another ship is needed."

Later that morning, in the bed where Shizue had so often dreamed of love, Mr. and Mrs. Maxwell Napier woke playfully snuggling under the covers and groaning in unison, "Oh, no," when someone knocked at their door.

"Be quiet and maybe they'll go away," Max whispered in Shizue's ear, then kissed it and the locks of hair trailing down her cheek.

"Max! I've got to have a word with you," Douglas called from outside.

"I'll be right there, Dad!" Yawning, Max swung his long legs from the bed and stood over Shizue, naked. He stretched his muscular frame. "What's behind that silly grin on your face?"

"A woman doesn't tell all her secrets," she answered coyly. Douglas rapped loudly on the door, and she flopped a pillow across her face. "Oh, see what he wants and come back to bed."

"Jesus, what a mess." Max laughed as he dug for his trousers in the mass of tangled clothing they had left scattered around the bed. He stepped into them on his way to the door. To his surprise his father was dressed for traveling and carried a briefcase.

"Sorry to disturb you, but it's important. I was up all night with Tadashi. We're leaving Japan very soon, and there's a lot of work to be done before our affairs are settled." He spoke quickly, not troubling Max with the details and checking the hall to make sure no servants were moving about. "Lisbon wired for another ship. Inge and I are flying home to meet with Aquida."

"I'll start packing."

"We can manage without your help." Douglas observed the afterglow of love in his son's sleepy eyes. "It could be our last mission. You're entitled to sit this one out. Stay here and enjoy the honeymoon."

Max scratched his head and yawned. "When would we leave Japan?"

"Sometime next month is a fair guess."

"Be extra careful, Dad."

Douglas nodded. "We're old pros at the game. Now put this mission from your mind and go to your wife."

Max nodded, closed the door, and returned to Shizue. "Such a long face," Shizue commented. "I overheard what was said. Dearest Max, I'll miss everyone here as well. But we have each other now, and home is wherever we can be together."

The honeymoon had been a glorious, carefree time, blending the summers of their childhood with the autumn of their maturing love. Shizue had wanted the honeymoon never to end. November slipped away quickly, and now she nestled beside Max on one dreary winter day, bound for the Napier mansion in a taxi. Early that morning she had sadly bid good-bye to her loved ones, knowing she might not see them again for years. Kimitake had looked so shattered after her parting embrace. Her father had smiled tearfully, waving until her plane soared across the blue rooftops into a sunny sky. Her last view of home remained fixed in her mind, the valley shining like an emerald, the mountain peaks surrounding it streaked with gold. She seemed forever to be saying good-bye.

Now, in Tokyo, Max helped her from the taxi. The sky grew ever murkier, and the gray clouds were ominously dense, like billowing black curtains blocking out light and warmth.

The Napier family was preparing to sail for America. Hosokawa-Napier, Limited, had been sold to a *zaibatsu*, and the dynasty was a thing of the past. The Napier mansion took on a stark gray, abandoned look, as though its inhabitants were already far out at sea. A new generation would be born across the deep Pacific waters, and Shizue worried about those she must leave on Japanese shores. Her gaze went up to the mansion's gabled rooftop, where birds flapped their wings against the churning gray clouds. She and Jiro had begun their ordeal in Osaka on just such a day as this. Much as she tried, she could not forget that episode in her life, and the dreariness it evoked made her cling tightly to the security of Max's arm as they entered the house.

Morita squinted at the young woman who had returned home with Max. "You are Shizue, the baron's daughter now all grown-up," he remembered, pleased as he took their coats. "I welcome the young bride to our household. She is very pretty," he told Max. "As was your mother when I first greeted her at this very door. Ah, I have sadly neglected my duties. Now there will be parties again. *Hai*, the silver must be polished."

Neither one had the heart to remind him that the house would soon be closed for good.

Shizue peeled off her gloves, relieved to see a fire burning in the sitting room hearth. Inge and Douglas entered the room, arm in arm. "We would have met your plane, only Douglas had business at the American consulate."

"Shizue's passport," he said. "She'll have to put in an appearance there tomorrow."

"Come, let's sit by the fire."

The doorbell rang. "Morita," Douglas called out loudly. "Doorbell."

Half-turned toward the staircase with two suitcases in hand, Morita rolled his eyes. "No need to shout, *dannasama*."

"Oh, I'll get it myself," Douglas grumbled, crossing to open the front door.

"Senhor Napier, quickly let me in," Teofilo Aquida said, looking over his shoulder nervously.

Douglas had terminated their association after the last ship had sailed two weeks earlier. "What are you doing here?"

"An urgent message from Lisbon. Since I could not trust your telephone, and our usual means of contact is no more . . ."

"Not here," Douglas cautioned, steering the tiny man away from the hallway and into the sitting room. Morita was hard of hearing, but there were other servants in the house, so Douglas closed the sitting room doors. "Now you can speak freely. This is my daughter-in-law, Shizue."

"Charmed." Hat in hand, Teofilo Aquida bowed from the waist. "The situation in Europe grows very bad. This time many Jews, and your people have pleaded that you buy for them two more ships. This long time I have risked much, but not only for the money. No, it is something owed the memory of my Jewish mother." Aquida crossed himself. "God rest her soul."

Douglas shook his head. "Two ships. That's a tall order. It could mean changing our travel plans, but I don't see how we can refuse. Inge? Max?"

"*Ja*, we must do what we can," Inge answered.

"Agreed. That is, if Shizue has no objections," said Max.

Shizue hesitated, putting her arms around Max before speaking. "Just for once I'd like to be selfish and say no—we've given enough to others and our happiness must come first. Even realizing how important this is to you. But knowing all you've been through, I couldn't selfishly turn my back on people whose lives are in jeopardy."

Max rewarded her with a kiss. "That's my sweetheart."

"Then you are decided?" Aquida opened his coat to the crackling hearth. "If so, I will notify Lisbon tonight."

"Yes, it's decided," Shizue answered for them all. As much as she wanted to embrace their cause, the dangers involved made her uneasy. "Father will be upset if we change our travel plans. He's so anxious for us to leave Japan."

"There's no reason for any anxiety," Douglas said. "I'd be worried if Japan withdrew its envoys from Washington, but war's unlikely while they're still engaged in talks. Has your father changed his mind about coming here to see us off?"

"No, the journey would be a trial for Kimi, and father won't leave him." Shizue sighed. "Well, I should telephone home that we've arrived safely."

"Shizue, it's important that your father believe everything here is going smoothly," Douglas told her. "His anxiety could pose a real problem, and I don't want him implicated in our affairs. As I've said, getting two merchant ships safely out of Japanese ports is a tall order, and we can't be too careful."

"Yes, I understand the need for secrecy."

"Good. When you call home, remember the police are listening in, so think before you speak."

Douglas shifted his attention to Aquida. "Don't risk coming here again. We'll operate as in the past, and I won't contact you again until we've something definite to wire Lisbon."

"Finding those ships is the first order of business," said Max, opening the afternoon paper to the shipping news while his father ushered Aquida from the house.

Inge put an arm around Shizue's shoulders. "Our men have work to do. Let me help you unpack, and we shall talk of other things."

"Yes, I'd like that."

Morita stood in the upstairs hallway with a lost look on his wrinkled face. He stared at Shizue through watery eyes, then cocked his head and pulled on one fleshy earlobe as if to remind himself of something. "Your luggage is in Max-*san*'s room. I have lit a fire in the hearth." He bowed and moved on with a halting, stoop-shouldered gait.

"That poor old man," Inge whispered, watching him pause to dust the hall table with one sleeve and straighten the painting hung above it. "Douglas has arranged a generous pension for him. But this is the only home Morita has ever known, and I think he will not live for very long without its familiar things around him.

"*Ach*, it is torment to leave one's home," she said, walking with Shizue into Max's childhood room. "Part of me remains in the Berlin house I shared so many years with Heinz. In dreams, I often walk through its rooms touching the things we bought together. The memories remain intact, Shizue. How I wonder what has become of that once cheerful house, set among the linden trees."

As Shizue picked up the telephone receiver to call her father, her heart was also full of home. She had only just left Kyushu that morning, after placing flowers at her mother's garden shrine.

Her father answered the phone. "I already miss you and Kimi terribly," Shizue told him, filling the long silences on the other end with talk of the gloomy weather and the flight. When Kimitake was put on the line, she strained to be cheerful, but he was almost as silent as her father had been and seemed anxious to end the conversation.

When she cradled the receiver, Inge asked if all was well. "My brother sounded under great stress. He's being well cared for, but I can't help feeling Kimi's lost without me. And my father hardly spoke a word."

"You look tired. Why not rest before dinner?"

"I was a little sick to my stomach this morning. Emotions," she said. Inge left, and Shizue reclined on the bed. The fire blazing in the marble hearth cast warm shadows across the framed Japanese prints of quiet forest scenes and rocky waterfalls. She imagined Max lying here through the long winters of his youth, longing for another summer in Kyushu. As they prepared to leave for America, she could already feel the distance grow vast between these two Japanese homes, which had once linked the generations of their dynasty.

Soon Max entered to lie quietly beside her. She touched his hair, his smooth brow, and determined chin. "I love the prickly feeling of your beard. Tell me about America. I know everything you didn't like when you were at Harvard, but you've never told me what you *did* like."

"Well, it's a big country with miles and miles of open space. Not so overcrowded like here. I liked the people, and Boston. The pace is different from Japan. Hectic but exciting, as if everyone were trying to cram a lifetime into their hours between work, home, family, and friends. It's a jazzy place." Max swung his hips on the bed and snapped his fingers. "Americans know how to have fun. They laugh easily, they're informal, and they make friends faster than the Japanese. There's rich and poor, but no one's stuck in the class of his birth. It's a place where dreams can come true if you're willing to work for them."

"My, I'm very surprised." Shizue propped herself up in bed on one elbow. "How different America sounds from the grim place you described in your letters."

"I was suffering too much without you to have any objectivity, Shizue. Now my observations could be exaggerated. But I don't think so. I think you'll like America. I'm sure it'll like you, and I'm looking forward to returning there with you as my wife."

Shizue bent to kiss him on the mouth. "Oh, Max, if only everyone we love could share in that experience."

Max hummed, not really listening. He was thinking about his final mission for the Jews. "All those people in Europe flooding to the sea and we can't save more than a handful," he mused aloud. "Who makes the choice? If there are gods, how do they decide who lives and who dies?"

"Dearest, please don't be so morbid. It gives me the chills."

"I've got just the cure for that, Mrs. Napier." He rolled on top of her just as Morita passed outside their door chiming the dinner hour.

Shizue whispered, "Don't stop, Max. No one will miss us."

"Not hungry?"

"Only for you, my sweetheart. Only to be held by you."

In the flurry of activity that had followed Teofilo Aquida's visit, Shizue participated as an observer and kept her uneasiness hidden from Max behind a smile. When they found time to visit Paul at his Tokyo apartment, he was packing to leave on sudden business for the Ministry of Communications.

"My houseboy's day off. Sorry I won't be here when you sail," Paul told his brother, who helped him close an overstuffed suitcase. Brooding over the couple's imminent departure, he uttered dark warnings against pursuing their final mission for the Jews.

Max assured him that luck was with them. Two merchant ships had already been found. A Turkish freighter moored at Kobe was scheduled to sail the evening of December seventh, and the second ship moored at Yokohama would leave port on the following morning. She was American-owned, manned by a U.S. skipper and crew but registered in neutral Panama. Sailing under the Panamanian flag, she was still free to trade with Japan and would not be suspect in Mediterranean waters. Negotiations had gone smoothly. It was now the third of December, and all that remained was to convert cash into precious gems and pearls to pay off the ships' captains.

"I'm going to miss you two lovebirds," Paul said. "But with the increased likelihood of war, you're better off in America. So, finish this refugee business quickly and watch your step." A car horn sounded on the street below. "That's for me." Leaning heavily on his cane, he swung one suitcase from the bed. "I'd appreciate some help getting these bags down to my car."

Wind whipped the flags that were displayed up and down this Tokyo street like sheets hung out to dry. Paul's ministry staff car waited at the curb, where Max and Shizue said their good-byes. As the three of them hugged one another, Max realized the futility of asking his brother to bridge the chasm of the past to his father before their departure from Japan. He thought it wrong for Douglas to have waited in the hope that Paul would come to him. For quite different reasons, neither man was able to give an inch.

"Dearest Paul, you'll always be in my thoughts," said Shizue.

Paul managed to grin reassuringly. "Don't fret over me. I'm used to looking after myself. Be happy, you two."

"We'll expect to hear from you in letters," said Max as Paul got into the car.

The most important chapters of their lives were linked to Natsu's son, and Shizue used her handkerchief to wave at him, then pressed it across her eyes when Paul turned away from the rear window. If there were war between Japan and America, she realized they would be cut off completely from those they were leaving behind.

The winter evening closed in quickly as they hurried away to an appointment with Douglas. Shizue clung to Max's arm, thinking of home and of the dark warnings Paul had voiced. Her father and Kimitake shared similar fears of an approaching war and anxiously counted the days until her sailing. The night before, they had telephoned her at the Napier mansion, and she had found it difficult to be in good spirits, to pretend everything was normal, afraid of making some slip while the police listened in.

"There's pain attached to this prolonged farewell," her father had said to her on the phone the night before, his voice cracking with emotion. "What can I tell my little girl that hasn't already been said? You mustn't dwell on us. You've Max to look after now. Enjoy your happiness."

Then there was silence. "Papa?" Shizue had asked. Kimitake's voice echoed rather distantly over the line in place of the baron. "Is everything there all right?"

"I gave father and the nurse a bad afternoon," Kimitake had confided. "These kidneys. A minor flare-up, little sister. I'm fine now."

"Promise you'll take your pills and have Father telephone Dr. Onogi at the least sign of complications. Promise," she had insisted when he gave no reply.

"Cross my heart, if I could," Kimitake had laughed painfully as he spoke. "Honestly, Shizue, you've got to let go and stop worrying about me. It was hard saying good-bye, especially hard on Father. What's the situation there? No change of plans? You are still sailing on the seventh?"

"Yes, we'll definitely be leaving on schedule." Shizue had done her best to sound convincing. She knew the mission might cause a delay, but she had wanted to put Kimitake's anxieties to rest, and she knew her father had been listening in with the receiver held to his son's ear. "You're right, it doesn't help to worry. Perhaps it's selfish of me to keep at you on the phone."

"We'd both find it easier to adjust if you didn't call again before you sail," Kimitake had told her in a pleading voice. "Father's unable to speak. Good luck from us both, Shizue. Have a safe journey. Never forget how much we both love you," he said emotionally, and the line clicked dead.

Although Max assured her they were not being watched, Shizue jumped at shadows on the dimly lit street facing Hosokawa–Napier, Limited's, Tokyo offices. The night watchman admitted them, his wheezing cough echoing after their footsteps down the empty corridors. Douglas was in his private office, where he had worked most of that day preparing for a takeover by the firm's new owners. He stood at the open safe, clearing out the records of their refugee operations.

"Looks like there's enough cash on hand," he told Max, as he shifted the bundled money and the files to his desk. "Let's get to work."

Inge sat wrapped in her furs as she counted the money. The radiators had been confiscated for the accelerating scrap drive. Even Buddhist temple bells were being donated to Japan's smelting pots. Shizue paced to keep warm, distracted by private concerns, her breath frosting the air.

Max and his father pored over records of gem dealers they had done business with over the months. They could not risk retracing their steps. Their sources for gems in Tokyo had been exhausted, and they drew up lists from register books of other dealers throughout Japan. Much depended on the availability of the precious gems they sought, and dealers did not make such disclosures over the telephone. Train schedules were checked. Many of the cities they would visit were not served by Japan's commercial airlines. The country's roads were poor and trains would get them between cities faster.

"We'll split the workload to save time," Douglas announced, gathering up all their records and packing them inside two leather briefcases. "Inge and I will handle the transaction at Kobe. Max and Shizue, the one at Yokohama. This could put off our departure. But no point changing plans until we see how things turn out."

He stretched and patted his breast pocket. "I've got the bank draft for our share of the sale. It became final this morning. Hold on to your steamship tickets. This war scare has made it difficult to book passage. If we finish close to the wire, don't return home. We may have to run for the dock carrying only what's in our pockets, and we'll meet aboard. No detours. Understand?"

"We'll be there." Max flipped the desk calendar to December 7, 1941, a Sunday. His father had jotted down their departure time and pier number under the large red numeral, and Max ripped that page from the binder rings, noting how the pencil had left an impression under the large red figure 8. "I'll take this along as a reminder," he said, never suspecting that Japan's fate and their destinies stared him squarely in the eye.

Nothing of a personal nature remained on Douglas's desk except one silver-framed photograph of himself, Angela, and their son, taken when Max was only a baby. He picked up the small oval-shaped family portrait. The happily beaming father had not yet learned that he had another son, he thought. "Have you seen your brother?"

Max nodded. "Paul's been sent away on business and won't be returning before we sail."

"I see." Douglas looked sadly at Inge, who had witnessed his struggle against reopening old wounds by forcing himself on Natsu's son. His stomach churned over missing the opportunity to embrace Paul and perhaps to break down the barrier between them. "I've only myself to blame."

He rested the old family portrait facedown on his desk; it belonged to the past. He needed no keepsake to remind him of Angela, just as he had not needed to take a keepsake of Natsu from the apartment they had shared. It seemed he would never redeem himself in Paul's eyes. But he had regained his self-esteem through the work represented by the briefcases filled with records of his mission for Europe's Jews. He had not failed them, or Inge in her hour of need. Max stood before him embracing

Shizue. Douglas hoped their children would grow up in America without being scarred by racism.

Snapping the briefcases shut, he sent one across the desk to Max. "I'm proud to have you as a son. Proud and grateful. Well, I never thought I'd miss this office. But now that it's time to leave . . ."

Soberly Douglas Napier viewed the mahogany paneled office he had occupied for the better part of a lifetime. From behind this impressive desk, he reflected, three generations of Napiers had shared rule over a dynasty that was no more. Although a great deal of pain and sorrow had been attached to his tenure as the last generation to serve the silk dynasty, he knew that the business of silk would always be in his blood.

Douglas took hold of Inge's hand and found it trembling. "It's cold here like Berlin," he observed, looking at the ripped floorboards where the radiators had once stood. "There's no turning back. We've done all we can, Inge. In America, we'll break free of the past."

Inge clasped the collar of the sable coat she had worn when fleeing the Gestapo. "Perhaps we can somehow continue our work there."

Douglas smiled. "Right now, we've got a timetable to meet." He ushered Inge from his office, never looking back as his son closed the door. He and Max were the last Napiers to walk those corridors. As he bid the old watchman good night, Douglas felt a lump in his throat. The last employee of a dynasty rattled his keys in the lock, sounding the end of an era as the Napiers walked away.

On the street they passed a news stall, where men stood jangling bells strapped around their waists, shouting, "*Gowai!* Extra!"

Max bought the extra edition of *Nippon Shimbun*. "U.S. Leaders Dogmatic in Their Policy for Japan. But Japan Will Increase Efforts to Reach an Understanding," the headline proclaimed. As his father drove them home, Max read the lead article aloud. It spoke of Japan's adamant stance against withdrawing from territory that Japanese troops had fought and died for in Indochina, China, and Manchuria. Japan had paid too dearly in those wars to compromise its views to the United States. It seemed the feeling among Japan's leaders was sharply divided. Some felt the talks were a useless exercise; others held out hope of room for further negotiations.

"At least, Japan's negotiating in good faith," Max commented. Only the emperor's emissaries in Washington knew if that was so. Still, everyone rested a little easier that chilly night of December 3, 1941.

Morita was confused during the family's brief stop at the Napier mansion, where they hurriedly packed for separate journeys aboard trains leaving Tokyo within the hour.

Max and Shizue departed first, speeding off in Angela's bright red Bugatti as Douglas quickly emptied the briefcase of records across his study desk. He would have burned the incriminating documents himself if not for Inge sounding the horn of the Duesenberg and the mantelpiece clock chiming the hour nearing train time.

Morita hovered nearby, wasted by age and pensioned off to live out his days in comfort, but alone. He had been like a member of the family and Douglas felt the need to embrace him. The old eyes searched him out, failing to understand what lay behind this emotional display as Inge sounded the car horn more urgently.

"I will attend to the house in your absence," said Morita, handing him his hat.

"Burn all these papers in the fireplace. Do it at once, Morita, before you forget!" Douglas spoke loudly to be sure the old man heard him. "It's most important that you don't forget!" he shouted again as he went out the door.

"*Hai, dannasama.*" Morita bowed low as his master drove away. Left there alone, he returned to the study. As he tidied up the study desk, he talked to himself. "Important papers left in my care." The papers he had been told to burn were now neatly stored inside the desk drawers.

"Ah, so, everything in its proper place. They think me old and forgetful. They bring new wives into this house, but none will sit with me over tea as the previous *okusama* once did. Now they all rush away and say nothing of when they will return. Unfair to an old man. Unfair," he rasped to himself, forgetting to switch off the lamp and shuffling to his ground-floor quarters behind the kitchen.

The cook had been dismissed, as had the many servants he once commanded like a well-trained army. "*Hai,* Angela Napier is no more. How very sad. But the baron's daughter will soon bring children into the household. I must prepare the nursery and clean the attic playroom. Tomorrow." Morita yawned. The attic stairs were hard to climb, and by the next morning he would forget his comforting thoughts of Napier grandchildren.

CHAPTER 36

The Japanese gem merchant smoothed his moustache with a long fingernail and impatiently eyed the wall clock. It was Sunday, and he had just sat down to supper in the apartment above his shop when the rich American rang his bell. "You will not find two stones of such quality elsewhere, that I can guarantee. My price is a fair one, Napier-*san*."

"All right. I've no time to bargain over a few yen." Max glanced up at Shizue's weary face. Since leaving Tokyo, they had found no time to rest. They had slept aboard trains while hunting down the precious stones collected inside his briefcase. Dealers in Kyoto, Osaka, and elsewhere had thrown up their hands, bemoaning the depressed market for gems. Only a few had anything of real value, and Max was forced to rely on one dealer sending him to another before he had gathered enough stones to pay off the American captain, whose freighter sailed from Yokohama soon after dawn the next day, the eighth of December. His last stop was this gem dealer in Nagoya, whose shop windows grew dark with the approach of evening.

His father and Inge had also been hindered in gathering payment for the Turkish captain, whose freighter was moored at Kobe. She sailed at midnight, and Douglas had just six hours to complete his part of this mission, which had forestalled their own departure from Japan. That morning the passenger ship to America had sailed without them.

Shizue massaged the nape of her husband's neck. "You're so tense, Max."

"Oh, that feels good. I'd give anything to check into some hotel for the night." Max clicked the latch of his briefcase wearily as the merchant inked the transaction into his registry book with a pointy-tipped bamboo brush. "Please, hurry. We've a train to catch."

"Your papers of ownership and the reciept, Napier-*san*. Madame. *Konban-wa*. Pleasant journey," said the merchant, as Max and Shizue hurried out of the shop.

Finding a taxi was no problem. Nagoya's once busy port had harbored ships from every corner of the globe. Now the docks and streets were quiet. Rickshas dotted the curbstones waiting for tourists who never came. As they rode past them, Shizue's heart went out to the sallow-faced coolies who squatted playing go to help pass the time, while others stared vacantly into the night, shielding their eyes from the taxi headlights. She was exhausted by days of traveling. Revisiting industrial Osaka, with its belching smokestacks and screaming factory whistles, had been a grim experience, a jolting reminder of Jiro and the costly warfare still raging in China and Southeast Asia. Her husband did not think beyond the success of this mission. Her country and America continued their negotiations, and Max saw no reason to be alarmed about the ship they had missed. Yet she clung to his arm, wishing they had sailed that day.

"It's as if everyone is holding his breath, expecting a time bomb to explode," she said to Max as he helped her from the taxi outside Nagoya Station. "Oh, I should have telephoned home. Father will think we've already sailed. Is there time before our train leaves?"

"About twenty minutes." Max handed her some coins and decided to place a call to the Tor Hotel in Kobe, where his parents planned to spend the night. Mr. and Mrs. Napier had registered a short time ago, the desk clerk informed him, but they were out.

Douglas had left a cleverly worded message for his son conveying that all was going well and the Turkish captain would be paid off on time. Max left a message in reply. "Say that my business will be completed on schedule as well," he told the clerk, relieved to know his father's half of their mission was under control. By midnight he would arrive in Yokohama with payment for the second ship's captain, and it would sail for Mediterranean waters as scheduled on Monday morning.

Max joined his wife at another pay phone. "Trouble getting through?" he asked, setting the briefcase of valuables between his legs.

"The number's been ringing and ringing." Shizue twisted around, anxiously pulling the receiver cord. "Why doesn't anyone answer? Oh, finally." She sighed. "Hello? Who is this?" A woman's voice was garbled by static on the line, and she faintly heard the clanging sound of brass bells. Her brother must have triggered Douglas's alarm system. "This is Shizue! Speak up so I can hear you."

"Shizue—but you have sailed."

She recognized the voice of Kimitake's nurse, Aki. The woman began to sob. Why was this woman on the line, Shizue wondered, ignoring the alarm bells and sobbing so hysterically it was impossible to understand a word she said? "Aki, what's wrong? Put my father on the line!"

"No—no, I cannot. He is with your brother and—"

"Oh, this static. Why are you weeping? Go and bring Yufugawo to the phone! Tell her my sailing was delayed!" Shizue jiggled the hook frantically as Aki's sobbing voice was lost in static. Only the clanging alarm bells rose above the static on the line that was still connected to home.

"Max, something's happened to Kimi. I know it has."

"Don't jump to conclusions," he said, seeing the fear in her eyes. She trembled as his arms tightened around her waist. He, too, was able to hear the clanging bells filtering through the static of the receiver pressed to her ear.

"Yufugawo, what's wrong?" Shizue cried out in response to the woman's familiar voice. "Please, speak louder!"

"Oh, child, no one expected to hear your voice again!" Just then the line grew quiet, and in that moment Yufugawo's hysterically spoken words registered a shocking blow. "Kimitake is dead. Dead in seppuku by your father's hand."

"No, it can't be true!" If not for Max's arms, Shizue would have collapsed. Tears rolled down her cheeks as she listened to Yufugawo's wailing voice repeating that Kimitake was dead. Suddenly the brass bells stopped clanging. Yufugawo screamed, then loudly screamed again and again as if witnessing a horrible sight.

Loud static cut off Shizue's fragile link with home. For what seemed an eternity, she trembled speechlessly against Max until the noise on the line abruptly ended and Yufugawo was heard screaming her husband's name. "O-nami—hold the baron here! Ah, he has lost his mind."

"Yufugawo, don't leave the phone!" Shizue cried, running one hand through her hair. She choked on tears. Then she heard O-nami shouting something at his wife, who must have laid down the receiver. Overlapping voices sounded distantly over the buzzing connection. A long silence followed, and Shizue thought she might faint. "Oh, why doesn't she come back to the phone?"

"Ah—ah, my heart," Yufugawo said, speaking into the receiver again. She gasped for breath, her words interspersed between heaving breaths of air. "Ah, Shizue, what grief the gods have visited upon us."

"No, tell me Kimi isn't dead!"

"Child, did you not hear me scream the truth? Kimitake deceived us all. He wished to die, and the alarm bells rang and rang while the baron sat locked inside your brother's room—until only a moment ago, when he appeared covered with blood, the *wakizashi* still in his hand." Yufugawo spoke in a monotone that reflected the shock of what she had witnessed. "I tried to tell him that you had not sailed, that you were on the telephone. But your father was deaf to my words. Now he has gone to his study with O-nami. I ran after them, but they have bolted the doors to the corridor."

"Go pound on the doors. Call to Father and plead with him to speak to me. Tell Papa he must live for me."

"He will not hear me, child! Oh, return here quickly. The baron surely means to kill himself. My husband is bound by duty to assist his seppuku, and only you can stop his hand from using the blade. Hurry home to us before it is too late!"

As Yufugawo's plea traveled across the miles of hissing telephone cables, Shizue heard a distinct click.

"Father—is that you on the line?" Baron Hosokawa had picked up the study extension phone; she could just hear his labored breathing on the open line between them. "*Ogisan*, please speak to me. Don't do this horrible thing. I'm coming home to you, and you must wait for me." The hissing sound grew louder, but Shizue strongly felt her father's presence still on the line. "Papa, you spared your life for me once before. I beg of you to wait . . ." The line sputtered and died. She jiggled the receiver hook.

"Operator, I've been cut off! This is an emergency. Oh, you must reconnect me quickly!"

"I am sorry, but there is some trouble on the lines to Kyushu," the operator told her.

"How long before you can put me through again?"

"I can't say."

Shizue lowered the receiver in her ice cold hand and placed it on its hook. Her father was not in his right mind, and she could accomplish nothing over the telephone. Max held her more tightly. Words were useless to express their shock and profound sense of loss. Shizue wanted to deny Kimitake's death, but Yufugawo's horrified screams had told the truth. Kimitake was dead, truly dead in seppuku by her father's hand, and she could not wish him back to life.

"Max, I must go home." She dug her fingers into Max's arms, calling upon that same reservoir of inner strength that had sustained her while hiding Jiro. "I failed Jiro, and now I've failed Kimitake," she said. "But Father mustn't die. I know I can reason with him in person. Oh, Max, help me reach home in time to save Papa from himself."

Max took her chin in hand and nodded grimly, numbed by the shock of Kimitake's seppuku. "We'll find a plane," he decided, unable to share in her belief that the baron could be prevented from following his son, even if Shizue did reach home in time to plead for his life. But the utter desperation in her eyes held Max silent.

The operator connected Max with an air charter service located on the outskirts of Nagoya. Luckily they were open for business on Sunday, and a plane was available.

He rushed Shizue there by taxi, torn between allegiance to his wife and that owed hundreds of Jews whose lives rested with the ship's captain waiting to be paid at Yokohama. As they rode, he gave voice to the hardest decision of his life. "Sweetheart, I can't go with you. Much as I want to stand by you now, I've got to finish this mission, or I couldn't live with myself."

"Of course, you mustn't abandon those unfortunate people. For a moment I forgot about everything but poor Kimi and Father." Shizue's eyes glassed over, and she leaned her head against his chest. "Oh, I can't think. My mind's a blank."

"Let me do the thinking for you," said Max, caressing her hair.

"Just for once, I believed my actions had accomplished something."

"Stop blaming yourself for failures," he told Shizue quietly. The army surgeons' knives had only forestalled the battlefield death of a hero.

How badly Kimitake must have wanted to die, Max thought, remembering a night long ago when boyhood friends had fought a kendo match to let off steam. He could see Kimitake's room cluttered with weapons, his athletic friend stripped to the waist and rippling the muscles of his strong arms. And hanging on the black felt mannequin standing in one corner, he could see Baron Hosokawa's gift of samurai armor scaled down to fit a small boy, already being groomed to die for his Bushido.

Shivering with the memory of two boys who had joined their blood in a Tokyo schoolyard, Max felt as if his own limbs had been cut away by Kimitake's death. "The suicide pact Kimi made with your father was behind their anxiety to have us leave for America today," he said. "You couldn't be Jiro's courage or Kimi's arms and legs. Your brother chose not to exist as he was. There's only so much anyone can do for another person, sweetheart. Even love has its limitations."

"Oh, Max, just hold me. I feel so safe close against you like this."

Max kissed her perfumed hair. "I'll make sure you get to Kyushu safely. You'll be home in a matter of hours. Whatever happens after that, we'll see it through together. When we leave Japan isn't important now."

The taxi bumped along an unpaved road to the charter service airfield. The air service shipped freight, not passengers, and the grounds were overgrown with weeds. "Watch your step," Max cautioned when they got out of the taxi. He put his arm around Shizue as they hurried along the warped wooden walkway to the aircraft hangar.

Sunday had been bright and warm for December, and the evening sky was clear overhead. Max exchanged bows with Mr. Akanuma, the lean, thirtyish pilot in charge, and insisted on inspecting his twin-engine plane, which was being serviced by the hangar crew. It was designed for carrying cargo, and Shizue would have to ride beside Akanuma at the controls. He pointed out its safety features.

"The reserve tanks can land me at your destination without refueling, Napier-san. My radio will keep me posted on the latest conditions over Kyushu. If the weather is bad, I will land at the nearest airfield and wait until it lifts." Akanuma smiled pleasantly to remove the worry from his client's face.

"See that you do." Max poked his head inside the clean, shiny cockpit. "I'm trusting you to get my wife home safe and sound. Bad weather could be what interrupted telephone service there."

"Easily checked with the central weather bureau." Akanuma used the hangar phone, and announced a grim weather forecast. "There are strong gusting winds and the possibility of rainstorms later this evening. We must take off at once, Napier-san."

Max used the phone to do some checking of his own and learned that strong winds had disrupted telephone service to Kyushu's agricultural heartland. It was a condition not uncommon to that mountainous region. In the event of storms, work crews dispatched to the area would be hindered in making repairs on the lines strung down Kyushu's precipitous slopes. "Shizue, you could be caught over the mountains in this bad weather, or be grounded by it overnight. I don't suppose it would do any good if I begged you not to go."

"Oh, Max, I'm torn as well." Mechanics wheeled the plane to the airstrip, and shivers went up her spine. "I don't want to leave you, but there isn't any choice."

The pilot handed Max a fleece-lined leather flight jacket and a floppy-eared leather cap. "Your wife will be warmer in these."

"Thanks. Better hurry and get into these," Max said, attempting to lighten the moment by smiling. Shizue exchanged her tailored wool coat for the flight jacket. Its sleeves came down around her hands, and its bottom nearly reached to her knees. "You look like a little Eskimo." Max rolled back the sleeves, then gathered the fronts together and started zipping the jacket up.

"Now, promise me you'll behave if the weather turns bad. No back-talk to the pilot. I want you to have this." Opening his shirt collar, he reached back to unfasten the gold chain of the *omamori* he had worn for so long. "This charm's seen me through some very dangerous situations. I've come to have faith in the priest's blessing, and you're not getting on that plane without it. There," he said, fastening the chain around her neck tenderly. "Think of it as part of me going with you."

"Now I don't feel quite so alone." Wearing the *omamori* next to her heart once again was comforting. But fears for them both caused her to look up at Max, her eyes heavy with tears. "Dearest, promise me you'll be careful. Pray with me for Father's life and promise me we won't be separated for very long."

"I promise."

"Napier-*san*, we are ready for takeoff," the pilot called from across the airstrip.

Max insisted that Shizue put on the flight cap. "I don't want you catching cold. When my job's finished at Yokohama, I'll fly home to join you. We won't be separated for even twenty-four hours. Hold to that thought, my little Eskimo." Tugging down the fleecy earflaps, he kissed her quickly. "Love me?"

"Oh, yes, more than ever." She clung to him. "But why this grief in exchange for our happiness?"

"Come on, chin up. With luck you'll soon be home."

Akanuma stood near the plane, waving at Max to hurry. It was dangerous enough landing in strong winds, and the prospect of storms made Max shaky about entrusting Shizue's life to the grinning pilot. He was also concerned that she might use both money and tears to bribe the pilot into taking risks.

As they crossed the airstrip, he suddenly took hold of her tightly and said, "Don't gamble with our lives, Shizue. We've earned our happiness.

More than earned the right to be together, and no amount of grief can cheat us of that."

"In my heart I know you're right. But it doesn't help, my dearest. Tonight it doesn't spare me a thing."

The noise from the plane's engines made it impossible to say more. Their lips met in a lingering kiss, and then Max boosted her aboard.

The plane taxied away, and Shizue saw Max waving with his hat, his blond hair blown back from his forehead, a cheerful smile on his face. She could not imagine life without him now. As Max was swallowed up by the night, Shizue unzipped her flight jacket to clasp his *omamori*.

Her thoughts turned to home. She was sure Yufugawo's hysteria would have given way to reason. Shizue imagined her standing in the garden under the study windows, pleading for the baron to listen to her. O-nami was closed up with her father. He could be very persuasive. If the baron could not be reached through words, O-nami might use his muscles to buy her time. But would his loyalty permit that? She prayed that just this once, O-nami's code of honor would be set aside. He must keep her father talking. He must keep the instrument of death from her father. Let the gods not bring this rain, she prayed. Let the thunder god be satisfied with beating loudly on his ring of drums while storm clouds passed over the valley, only rumbling in the distance as the plane landed in time for her to save her father from himself.

Max caught himself nodding off and jerked upright in his seat aboard the moving train. Bleary-eyed, he squinted into the rising sun. It was now six-fifteen. Arranging Shizue's flight had left him stranded in Nagoya Station until just after midnight. On Sundays the Chuo Main Line ran fewer trains, which had cost him an extra hour of travel time to Yokohama. Before boarding the train, he had tried contacting his father by telephone, but Douglas and Inge had not yet returned to their Kobe hotel room, and he reasoned they had waited near the dock for visible proof that the Turkish captain's freighter would sail as promised. He had left no message with the hotel desk clerk. Shizue's situation and Kimitake's death could be related only by speaking to his father personally. But none of the train's scheduled stops had allowed time enough for Max to get to a phone.

Now his train screeched to a halt at Yokohama. With the war effort in Japan at full swing, the workday began early. Monday morning commuters crowded the platform as Max got off the train. He hurried past the public phones. He knew that telephone service to Kyushu was not expected to be restored before noon. The *Star of Panama* sailed in less than an hour, and contacting his father would have to wait. He hailed a taxi. "Pier thirty-two. Get me there in twenty minutes, and I'll make it worth your while."

The driver wrinkled his nose. "No room in the streets this morning, *danna*. But I will do my best."

Anxiously drumming on his briefcase, Max looked out the window and observed a number of trucks with loudspeakers mounted on their cabs cruising the busy streets. It was an unusual sight. The taxi driver tuned his radio to NHK. A musical interlude preceded the seven o'clock news broadcast from Tokyo, and Max glanced at his wristwatch, thinking that Japan could set its clocks by Morio Tateno's sonorous voice announcing the latest war news from the Asian and European fronts. For now, recorded music filled in the time as Max worried about his wife. While stranded in Nagoya Station, he had kept in touch with the central weather bureau. Storms had pelted the Hosokawa valley. Max could only pray the pilot had kept his promise to land elsewhere until the bad weather lifted. If so, Shizue would not reach home before sometime that morning.

Max was overcome with fatigue. He grew itchy to complete his business with the *Star of Panama*'s captain so he could contact Douglas, then hire a plane that would wing him to Shizue's side. He did not cling to any hope that the baron would still be alive, and he thought about his grief-stricken wife arriving at the scene of two suicides. O-nami and Yufugawo's comforting presences were no substitute for the arms of her husband. The deaths could not have been foreseen or prevented, but without him there to lean on, Shizue might take the blame upon herself.

Ritual suicide had written a bloody epitaph to their dynasty. The dead now bound their loved ones to Japan until their bodies were laid to rest. Shizue's ancestral valley was calling them back, jealously holding them in its grip. It seemed they were not meant to leave Japan.

"Drop me here at the gates," he instructed the taxi driver.

Brilliant sunshine touched the pier rooftops. It was twenty minutes to seven. He shook himself alert, paid the driver, then hurried beneath screaming gulls, who floated on the mild offshore breeze. The *Star of Panama* was not in her berth at the dock. Max looked out to sea, shocked as he glimpsed the freighter leaving port. Why had she sailed ahead of schedule? Why had her captain not waited for his payoff?

For an instant Max just stood there, flabbergasted, the briefcase heavy in his hand. Then he took action, springing for a pilot launch moored at the dock's end. He jumped aboard and charged past the scowling crew. Her white-haired skipper stood in the wheelhouse, drinking coffee. Voices squawked over his ship-to-shore radio as he hungrily eyed the yen Max took from his wallet. "Cast off immediately! I'll explain after you're under way."

While the captain spurred his crew, the *Star of Panama* approached the last marker buoy before entering the mouth of Yokohama Bay. She had not yet built up a full head of steam. Max was certain the launch would overtake her, and he shouted urgently to the skipper. "Radio ahead. Tell them Napier-*san* requests permission to come aboard!" His actions invited suspicion, but no questions were asked. When permission to board was granted, his relief was tempered with anger.

Captain James of the *Star of Panama* had slowed his engines in open sea, and the pilot launch heaved to alongside, taking on lines cast down by the freighter's crew. Rocked by swells, the launch stood fast, prepared to wait while Max did business.

Max climbed the rope ladder that was sent down to him, winded as he reached the top, where two sailors helped him aboard.

"Napier, hopping mad, are you?" Captain James posed on the bridge above deck, hands on hips, a pipe jutting from his mouth. "Well, step lively, lad. I don't like the lay of things in these shores," he said, while Max joined him on the bridge. "That's why I gave the order to sail. Damn radio's been jabbering away like hell since before dawn. Couldn't make any sense of it, even though I speak a fair amount of Japanese. Some goddamn Jap navy code is my guess. Sounds like half the Imperial fleet's out there somewhere, and I don't like the feel of things. Quiet now. Too goddamn quiet. Not a peep. The safety of my ship and crew come first. I thought twice before slowing to take you on."

The bridge telephone jangled loudly as Max shouted, "I've got everything here."

"Get to it then. Sooner I'm clear of these waters the better."

"Radio room, sir."

Captain James thrust out one hand for the receiver. "Pipe it in over the loudspeakers. Newscast from Tokyo due any second now. Could be the usual propaganda rubbish, then again not."

Chewing on his pipe, he settled in a leather swivel chair that commanded a view of the deck and the launch, which was steadily being towed out to sea. "Won't bother checking the goods," he told Max. "Just give me the rendezvous coordinates, and I'll put you off."

"We *now* present you *urgent news!*" announced Morio Tateno. The Japanese newscaster's familiar voice struck Max's ears like a shockwave. It had thundered across the ship's loudspeakers as if Tateno had been waiting for hours to address the nation. Now Max could hear the man pausing to catch his breath. When he spoke again, his voice was pitched down a tone. "Here is the news. The army and navy divisions of Imperial headquarters jointly announced at six o'clock this morning, December eighth, that the Imperial Army and Navy forces have begun hostilities against the American and British forces in the Pacific at dawn today."

Captain James's eyes opened wide in shock. His American crew gathered together, unable to understand a word of what was broadcast. Pearl Harbor bombed in a surprise attack! The Malay Peninsula attacked by a second Japanese strike force!

Max looked at the shocked faces of the Japanese crew, which had mustered on the launch below him. Japan's calculated acts of aggression were inconceivable to him. As the newscast ended and martial music drummed on the loudspeakers, Max rubbed his eyes, stunned by the hideous news.

Suddenly the Japanese captain of the launch started applauding, and his crew joined in to celebrate Japan's first victory over America. A new war had begun.

Captain James took over the loudspeakers abruptly, explaining to his men what the Japanese newscaster had announced. At first they just stared at one another mutely. Then one craggy-faced sailor bolted to the rail.

"Filthy Japs!" he yelled, heaving a swab bucket overboard. Captain James shouted for order, but his crew went wild, bombarding the launch with everything they could lay their hands on. Enemies now, the Japanese cursed them back, dodging what was thrown while they cast off.

Max fought his way to the rail too late. His hat blew away and floated on the launch's bubbling wake. Those aboard her shook their fists. His Japanese brothers now saw him as the enemy.

Max grew frantic. Miles of icy water stretched between him and Japan. He might freeze to death attempting to swim the distance to shore. The *Star of Panama* was picking up speed, and he ran for the bridge.

"Now hear this!" Captain James addressed his crew over the loudspeakers. "This means you, Mr. Napier. You're my responsibility now. Keep him off the bridge until I've finished!"

As the crew closed in around him, Max assumed a defensive stance, punching the first man who came within range of his angry fists. "My wife's back there!" he shouted, hitting another sailor before both his arms were seized from behind. "Captain, I demand that you put me ashore!"

"Be sensible and make the best of it, man," he responded shortly. "When the U.S. declares war on Japan, that Panama flag dancing over our heads won't be worth shit. Panama's sure to come in with us. No choice but to make a run for it. Now hear this! I'm setting course for the States. We'll steer clear of Hawaii. There's Jap subs to worry about, but taking our chances with a torpedo's a damn sight better than surrendering ourselves to the Japs without a fight. With God on our side, I'm giving odds that we get through in one piece. Every man here can serve his country better at home than locked in some Jap prison camp ashore. Now, hats off. A minute of prayer wouldn't hurt."

Max was set free, and Captain James and the crew bowed their heads. News of Pearl Harbor had whipped them into a patriotic frenzy. They prayed for a safe voyage, to their loved ones who waited on American soil.

But Max's place was with Shizue, his father, Inge—to share whatever fate held in store for them here. War or not, he could never fight the Japanese. In the silence, he backed toward a lifeboat. Its winch motor set up an awful clatter as he started it. One of the rope pulleys had rusted, and the lifeboat sharply inclined bow-first over the rushing sea. It had been a vain effort. The *Star of Panama* now cruised under a full head of steam, and the lifeboat would only have capsized on impact. Max bitterly stalked away. He had to get word to Shizue.

The radio operator cracked his chewing gum, immersed in a *Superman* comic book. "Radio silence. Captain's orders."

Max commandeered his message pad and the pencil stuck behind one ear and began to write. "Get him on the phone!"

Minutes later, Captain James descended from the bridge. "Can't give away our destination, Napier. Besides, the Jap harbor master won't relay a personal message to your wife. That launch must've reported our little encounter by now." All the things Max had wanted to say were chucked in the wastebasket. "That's where anything wired from my ship'll end up," the captain continued. "No, sir, don't want to draw more attention to our presence in these waters by using the radio. Sorry. I know it's hard being cut off from your wife and folks."

Max scorned the captain's sympathy. Never before had he known such complete isolation. Ironically, his final efforts on behalf of the Jews had made him a refugee.

"Well," Captain James said, tapping the briefcase Max had carried aboard, "I can't honor our bargain, so I'll keep this lot in my safe till you dock at Frisco. You'll bunk with the first mate."

The deck pitched and rolled in the deep Pacific waters. Standing at the fantail, Max looked out across the foaming wake curving from the unbroken horizon like a desolate highway. He was traveling backward in time across the world that was now at war. In Honolulu it was still Sunday, December 7. One day had altered his destiny. His eyes burned with tears as he cursed the gods for casting him adrift.

Rain had flooded the valley's concrete airstrip, and water sprayed in all directions as the plane taxied to a stop. Shizue unbuckled her seat belt quickly. Pools of rainwater reflected the blue morning sky. The storm had lifted at dawn, and her nerves were badly frayed after being forced to wait in a Kyushu airport throughout the long night. Flying over the mountains, radio reception had been garbled, so she as yet knew nothing of the war. She dismissed the pilot, leaving his borrowed cap and flight jacket on the seat.

Surely the household had heard her plane land, she thought, but there was no sign of anyone on the muddy road. She started running. Her high-heeled shoes were soaked, and she felt exhausted. Suddenly O-nami appeared behind the wheel of the Rolls-Royce, splashing to a stop in the mud. He left the car and walked toward her. She saw how deathly ill he looked; even his lips were ashen. He placed two shivering hands on her shoulders.

"Father," she spoke in a small voice, fearing what she saw in O-nami's eyes. "Oh, tell me he's still alive. Tell me he's waiting at home."

Swallowing hard, O-nami looked at the sky. "We believed you had gone, little one. You were not to learn of this until you were safely in America." His voice was choked. "The baron has followed your brother in seppuku. Both have now joined their ancestors."

The strength drained from her legs, and O-nami took hold of her. Sheltered in O-nami's powerful arms, she felt a numbness head to toe, and her vision was blurred. "Both dead?"

"*Hai*, they made a secret pact. Kimitake wished his life to end with the setting sun. I was called upon to witness the act. To assist the baron if his strength faltered in the honorable death that could be granted Kimitake only by your father's hand. But his stroke was steady and true." O-nami's tone was flat, as if the horror he related had taken place in a dream. "The moment of your brother's death rang throughout the castle as his head rolled against the pillow switch, sounding the brass bells. Your father was deaf to the sound. He sat at the bedside for hours, mourning the dead as though in a trance. He would not allow me to disturb Kimitake's remains. Then, finally, he lifted Kimitake's head from the pillow and rocked his son in his arms.

"Yufugawo stood in the way when he walked from the room. I heard her scream that you had not yet sailed—that you were now on the telephone. But my first duty was to the baron. Once we were locked inside the study, he lifted the receiver, and the sound of your voice made him weep. I took it from his hand, but the line went dead. I could not prevent your father from using the same blade, little one. No one could. His fate was sealed with that of your brother. Once again his stroke was steady and true. They both died as they had lived. Samurai to the end."

Thunder rumbled in the distance. Despite all her praying, the gods had brought rain, and death greeted her under the sunny skies. "Take me to them." O-nami helped Shizue into the limousine. "When did Father die?" she asked weakly as he turned the car and drove back toward the castle.

"With the rising sun. We observed the tea ceremony and spent the night talking of many things. The baron drew comfort from thoughts of your happiness. He wrote down a new will, and then we prayed to the gods. He did not wish to end his life in the darkness of that stormy night. 'Tell Shizue that the future rests with her. Say I died with hope in my heart.' Your brother died with the setting sun, and your father joined him with the sunrise of a new day."

"Their spirits were joined together in the sunlight," Shizue thought aloud, wanting to take solace in her belief that those who passed on shared a spirit life alongside the living. She thought of Kimitake, afraid of being left alone in the dark as she held cigarettes to his lips through countless nights. Her temples throbbed as the castle appeared ahead, seeming to float like a mirage, the gardens weeping with last night's rain. It was an effort to speak. "What have you done with their bodies?"

"They are covered, at rest together before the household *kami-dana*, as your father wished," O-nami answered. "I have sent someone to fetch the village police. Our telephone and electricity are not working. The storm. Ah, the tears stick in my eyes. I cannot weep."

"The tears stick in my eyes as well."

"In time they will come to us, little one."

Yufugawo ran out to the limosine. "We were deceived," she wailed, at no loss for tears. "Who could have known what they planned?"

Wordlessly, Shizue got out of the car and embraced Yufugawo. Then she entered the castle. Grief-stricken servants hung their heads, unable to look at her as they filed from the room where two corpses lay covered with sheets.

Shizue knelt on the tatami between their shrouded remains. Kimitake had set her free so that he, too, might be released. Raising the shroud, she kissed his face. "Dear Kimi, you bought me happiness with lies. Where are you now?" she whispered, brushing the hair from his smooth, untroubled brow. He wore the jacket of his army uniform, its empty sleeves neatly tucked up and pinned, and she could not bring herself to look below his belt, where his life had oozed away. "Is there another world without suffering? Are you there with Father? If only I could look into your eyes, I'd know."

"His eyes were at peace when the baron closed them," O-nami told her softly. "Your father instructed me to remove the hero's medal from Ichiban's uniform. 'Keep it for Shizue's firstborn son,' he said. 'When the boy is old enough to understand, tell him what you witnessed here. Tell him that war is wrong. Tell him that his uncle and his grandfather were the last of our bloodline to honor a Bushido that must forever remain buried with them in the past. His samurai spirit will test him in many ways, but he must resist taking up the sword. The next generations must not repeat our mistakes.' These were the baron's very words, and he smiled as I repeated them so as not to forget. It was I who closed his eyes. They flickered from side to side, and then he stared up at me in awe, as though he had glimpsed the gods."

"Ogisan!" The tears came, and they wet the deep hollows of her father's sealed eyes. "Papa, I forgive you everything. Oh, why couldn't I say that while you were alive to hear me?" Shizue pressed her cheek against his cold lips, sobbing quietly, reliving all the joyful moments she had known as his little girl. "Father, what a price to set on your honor."

Then slowly, she covered his face with the white linen cloth. The Hosokawa bloodline would live on through her children.

She was now the head of the household, and its dead could not be left lying there. Already there was a strong odor of death in the room. "O-nami, we must prepare them for burial. Your testimony will be enough to satisfy the police when they arrive."

"I will attend to it, little one. Go with Yufugawo and rest."

Yufugawo had not been called upon to mother Shizue for some time, and the woman's rouged face took on strength. "No one is to blame, child. One can only mourn the loss and wonder what will become of us now."

"I know Max will telephone once the line is open. Promise to wake me when he does." Shizue felt dizzy and nauseated. But lying down in the familiar surroundings of her room, with Yufugawo's soft hands caressing her hair, she surrendered to sleep.

At the Hotel Tor in Kobe, police had taken over, going from room to room and ordering all foreigners to assemble in the lobby. The hotel doors had been sealed off. Bells rang in the street outside. After the news of Japanese hostilities was blared to the public over the loudspeakers, the newspapers had rushed out special editions, and vendors wearing bells around their waists drew noisy crowds.

As Douglas and Inge waited in the lobby, he encouraged her not to panic. But the dark-suited Japanese policemen reminded her of S.S. officers and stirred up old fears. The other foreigners registered at the hotel kept to themselves. All foreign passports had been confiscated and were in the process of being checked by Captain Yamashita of the police. A group of American clergymen and their wives had begun to pray for the dead and wounded at Pearl Harbor.

Captain Yamashita screeched an order for silence. "It is my duty to inform you that the royal seal has been placed on an official declaration of war against America and Great Britain. What effect this may have on the neutrality of other western governments represented here remains to be seen. So, until further notice, all of you are confined to this hotel under close house arrest. Anyone attempting to leave will be severely dealt with." He extracted two U.S. passports from the pile. "Bring these people along for questioning."

His dark-suited confederate singled out Douglas. "You and the woman, come with me!" he ordered with a chilling grin.

Inge backed away. "Why us?"

"Steady. Behave naturally, or they'll think we've got something to hide," Douglas said softly. In a louder voice, he said, "We'll get our coats from the room."

"No! Come as you are. At once."

Douglas had wanted a moment alone to prepare his wife. "Just routine. They'll probably question everyone before they decide what to do with us."

He saw his briefcase being carried by another policeman. It was obvious their room had been searched while they had been detained in the lobby. The policeman carried the briefcase out to Captain Yamashita's waiting car. Train tickets, a large sum of cash, purchase receipts for gems—its contents were bound to raise some questions, Douglas thought. He would have to account for his movements and the missing gems.

Sitting in the police car, Inge twined her arm around his, and he smiled at the men riding up front, telling his wife to "*sprech Deutsch.*"

"I am concerned for Max and Shizue," she said in German. "At least we are together. I thank God for that. Will they put us in a concentration camp?"

"Not for long. Japan can't win this war."

There were no comments from the policemen up front in response to his statement, so Douglas figured it was safe to continue speaking in German. Still, he chose his words carefully. "Bear in mind that we came here on legitimate business. The cargo of silk we shipped is a matter of record. The freighter's captain refused to accept currency, so we paid him in gems. This shipment was arranged before our firm's sale was closed. Gathering the payment took longer than we expected and delayed our departure from Japan. Just stick to that story, and we'll be fine."

"*Ja*, I understand."

"Good. Now, relax. This isn't Nazi Germany. Here you're just another American citizen. Christ only knows what questions they'll throw at us, but the police can't use force. As prisoners of war, we're protected under the rules of the Geneva Convention. The same holds true for Max. I don't know what Shizue's status will be. I'm sure her father will somehow get word to us about them when the excitement cools down."

"I have no regrets. Nothing to fear with your hand in mine." Inge took out her compact and lipstick from her handbag. She had been ordered from their room with hardly time enough to dress. "*Ach*, what a face. Perhaps I should give in to looking plain. I doubt they will allow us such simple luxuries."

Douglas was concerned about Max and Shizue. He thought about the message Max had left him early the night before. His son should have telephoned again if all had gone well. The *Star of Panama* was scheduled to sail at seven that morning, but it might have been impounded at the dock despite its flag of neutrality. If his son had also been arrested with incriminating evidence in his possession, Shizue would be implicated and questioned by the police. But he was sure that Max was smart enough to give them a similar explanation. At some point the authorities might bring them all together for questioning. Perhaps they would be allowed to remain together as a family.

He calmed himself for Inge's sake. Their car sped along streets lined with people as Prime Minister Tojo's address to the nation was carried over loudspeakers. Tojo's sober, lackluster voice echoed back on itself, and Douglas could not make much sense of it. Japan would annihilate the West. Something about a stable new order being established in East Asia. Tojo foresaw a long war. Suddenly, the car came to a stop.

"Headquarters! Out!" the driver ordered. "The woman goes with me."

Inge cried, *"Nein!"* Seized by uniformed police, she was dragged off.

Douglas quickly lost sight of her as he was pushed and shoved up a flight of stairs. "See here, I must protest this treatment—" A rubber truncheon lashed down hard across his neck and spine. His legs were kicked out from under him, and he fell forward, his face striking the metal landing.

"Idiots! Show some respect for our enemy," their superior growled.

Douglas painfully raised his head, at eye level with Captain Yamashita's black patent-leather shoe. On the street behind him, Tojo's amplified voice commended the Japanese Empire into the hands of fate. Wiping blood from his mouth, Douglas heard loudspeakers blare a martial song while the police hauled him erect.

Captain Yamashita bent for Doulgas's hat, then stood up and dusted it off. "My men were carried away. You have lived with us long enough to know that we Japanese are not savages, Napier-*san*. But I strongly advise that you cooperate to avoid any further unpleasantness."

Staring into his cold eyes, Douglas felt a pang of sadness. War had estranged him from Japan and its people. "Across the sea, corpses in the water/Across the mountain, corpses in the field. I shall die only for the emperor/I shall never look back." He listened to war celebrated in a song reverberating over the loudspeakers.

"Where has my wife been taken?"

"We ask the questions here," Captain Yamashita answered shortly.

Somewhere below ground, Inge sat alone, shivering on a wooden chair. The squalid room was bare and very damp. An unshaded light bulb glowed dimly overhead, casting her shadow across the earthen floor. Hardly any light reached the gray stone walls, and her ears rang in the silence. Before locking the iron door, the police had taken her handbag. She was terrified and thirsty, and jumped at the sound of the peephole being slid open.

"Please, a glass of water."

Her plea went unanswered. The peephole slid shut. The light bulb flickered out, then on again. These were fear tactics, she thought, steeling her nerves to fight them. Inge focused her mind on the Jews she and Douglas had saved. Cherished memories, past and present, kept her company during the long spells of pitch blackness.

She had lost all sense of time, when a dented tin cup was sent through a swivel device at the base of the door. "How much longer must I wait?"

An eye at the peephole blinked and watched her drink the water thirstily. It was tepid and acrid, but she drank it all. Setting down the empty cup, she smiled bravely as it vanished with her captor's eye. "Thank you."

The light bulb flickered out. When would they take her away for questioning? Inge wondered, thinking this was only the first of many trials she and Douglas must somehow rise above.

CHAPTER 37

Paul hammered the Yokohama dockboards with his cane. Max's photograph was several years old. He had questioned everyone who had been on the dock the morning of December 8. But nothing had come of it until now. The white-haired skipper of a pilot launch seemed to know the face. "Well, do you recognize him or not?"

"*Hai*, the American caused me a great deal of trouble, Yoseido-*san*."

"Tell me about it!" Paul generously seeded the man's hand with yen. What he learned explained why Max's name had not appeared on any of the internment lists and caused him to head for the nearest telephone to call Shizue.

War in the Pacific was just entering the new year of 1942. Once again, Shizue had turned to him for help. Since Japan's reckless attack on Pearl Harbor, however, the Ministry of Communications had kept Paul on the move, and he had returned to Tokyo only that morning when he had promised Shizue to find out what he could about her loved ones. His highly placed friends had whispered news of Douglas's and Inge's arrests, but the police were secretive about the exact charges leveled against the American couple. An investigation was under way, and Paul could not press for details without implicating himself.

Paul entered a dockside telephone booth and asked the operator to ring Kyushu.

The phone was picked up on the third ring. "*Moshi-moshi!* Major Shinoda!"

The crass, authoritarian voice on the line startled Paul. "Is this the Hasumi residence?" He made up the name, then gave a fake telephone number.

"No, the Hosokawa residence." Major Shinoda rattled off the correct number. "This line is reserved for official army business. Don't tie it up again," he said, then banged down the receiver.

Paul reconciled himself to the worst. Japanese authorities must have obtained evidence of Douglas's clandestine refugee operations. The army would not be involved unless they had a strong case. He reasoned that Shizue had been implicated by virture of her marriage to Max.

But his hands were tied until the army announced charges against her. Important men who owed him favors would prove useful then—or so Paul hoped. Lighting a cigarette nervously, he leafed through his mental account book. Ah, Fukushima, the colonel he had served in China. The man he had made a general now resided in Tokyo among the chiefs of staff. Power and its high cost took on an added dimension as he limped off to his waiting car.

"Cherry Blossom Kissaten," he instructed the chauffeur, who held open the car door. He had risen another rung up the ladder, and the ministry had issued him a comfortable limousine with a special footrest for his aching leg. "I've neglected my old friend, Yoko. Family," he mused aloud to the chauffeur, folding his kid-gloved hands across the ornate silver handle of his cane.

"Where is this *kissaten*, sir?"

"On the Ginza." Being accorded respect pleased him. His chauffeur elevated Paul's bad leg on the footrest, then covered his legs with a cashmere throw to ward off the chill. How swiftly the years had passed since he had played war on these streets with his childhood friend, Toru. Now he rode them in luxury, although his achievement was soured by loneliness, and he felt burdened by his sacrificed ideals. But position would help spare the woman he loved.

Paul had no illusions about his country emerging the victor. As in China, the Japanese would never admit defeat. He knew that a long and bitter campaign lay ahead. Perhaps his brother wearing the uniform of the victor, would return to claim the Japanese wife they both loved. Meanwhile, he was Shizue's guardian against harm, and he would not take no for an answer from those who owed him favors.

Dressed in mourning, Shizue maintained an aloof, dignified posture as she sat in front of Major Shinoda. He was like a snake, she thought, coiling up and ready to spring at her. Standing in front of her father's desk, he told her she was accused of treasonous acts.

This army prosecutor had arrived without warning. Troops had landed by plane and were searching everywhere for Max, which convinced Shizue that he was safely beyond their reach.

"You disgrace the uniform you wear by these outrageous accusations." Her cool demeanor flustered the major. "I would never betray my country."

"Ah, you try my patience. The Kobe police were fooled by the admission of your in-laws to the lesser crime of assisting European Jews. However, everything points to the fact that your husband and his parents operated here as American spies." Major Shinoda hissed the word, his hooded eyes fired with a crazed sense of purpose as he forced Douglas and Inge's signed confessions into Shizue's hands.

"These are nothing but a clever ruse to disguise the true nature of their crimes against Japan. Detailed records of this spy ring's operations and the code books used by its agents were found in our search of the Napier mansion. Under questioning, I managed to prod their servant Morita's memory, and the old man has offered more incriminating evidence that substantiates my charges. The Napiers were constantly on the move, leaving Tokyo under cover of darkness to visit our major ports and industrial cities. Their servant may be senile, but my methods encouraged him to recall that his master ordered him to burn the records before rushing off to board a train.

"I put it to you, this network of spies was paid in gems for gathering sensitive military information, which they then smuggled to the American Secret Service and to our British enemies in Mediterranean waters. Those cargoes of silk they sent to Palestine were merely a cover. I further put it to you that Baron Hosokawa discovered his partner's treachery and your complicity in it. This accounts for Hosokawa-Napier, Limited, suddenly being sold to the highest bidder. Because of the long association between your families, the baron ordered the Napiers from Japan rather than bear witness against them. The financial arrangement between them was conducted so as not to draw suspicion to their motives. But the shame and loss of face suffered by your father led to his seppuku! In shielding the Napiers, your father was disgraced. Lieutenant Hosokawa was a helpless victim of circumstances, brought to shame by his sister's betrayal of the family honor. I intend to avenge the death of a great army hero and patriot. The guilty must not go unpunished, and I will make a shambles of these false confessions by getting at the truth!"

"How dare you disgrace the memory of the dead." Shizue stared down at the signed confessions. Obviously, Douglas and Inge had been browbeaten into confessing how they had assisted the Jews. "Your twisting of the facts is preposterous, Major. I won't be intimidated by them or by threats lodged under the guise of avenging a hero's death. You know nothing of my brother's suffering. O-nami has already testified that Kimitake wished to end his life in seppuku. And that could be accomplished with honor only by my father's hand. Here's the truth, Major Shinoda!" She flung the confessions at his feet. "The Napiers have testified to the truth, and you won't get me to bear false witness against them. I promise you that."

"These are only copies, Hosokawa-san." Major Shinoda trampled the papers under his boots. "Lies. You see how easily crushed they are," he said, then stood back wearing a sinister grin. "As for your servant, his loyalty is admirable. I feel sure he was misled into believing a hero of Japan had lost the will to live."

He turned to O-nami, seated in a chair beside Shizue. "Your masters shielded you from Madame Napier's guilt. In the event of an investigation, you would have been obligated to denounce the baron's daughter and that would have left the brand of shame on the family name. Their suicides would have gone for nothing."

O-nami tugged his topknot furiously. Only Shizue's courageous front kept him from tearing the captain apart, despite the armed soldiers who guarded the study door. "Your reasoning ignores the facts, Major," he said angrily. "Baron Hosokawa's new will leaves his lands in trust for Shizue's firstborn son. That son also inherits his title. I ask you—can this be the last wish of a noble samurai, brought to seppuku by his daughter's crimes?"

"Facing death, Hosokawa-san would have forgiven her anything." Shaking his head, he glared at O-nami. "To have given such a legacy to a grandson of mixed blood only speaks for his anguished state of mind. Your stupidity is matched only by your size, servant! Hold your tongue unless you're prepared to lose it. Your mistress is guilty of treason. The baron's will and your testimony are inadmissible evidence. His lands are now requisitioned for the greater glory of Imperial Japan. By nightfall the army will have assumed command here. You have until then to gather your belongings and leave!"

Stunned by this announcement, O-nami fell back in his chair. "And the baron's daughter?"

"Accompanies me to the Urakami Prison in Nagasaki, where her husband will join us when he is found." Major Shinoda lifted his riding crop from the desk and teased Shizue's shoulder-length hair with its leather loop as he spoke.

"So, we shall soon arrive at the truth. In time we shall see which of us is the stronger, Madame Napier. You have broken with your race and with your emperor by marrying this American spy. I look forward to dealing with you both." He chuckled. "Oh, how you smile, full of defiance and spirit. But stronger wills have been broken. Even you can't hide for long beneath that cool facade, noblewoman. I am a hard master. You'll soon be broken and bowed. Ah, so, do you still insist these confessions are true?"

"I do, Major. My vindication rests there under your boots." Shizue stilled herself from flinching as he ran his riding crop across her cheek. "I am a Hosokawa and a samurai," she said. "That and my innocence are my strength."

"Breeding may prove your downfall." Major Shinoda rocked back on his heels, slapping the riding crop hard against one leg. "Guards, escort this woman to my plane. She is to take nothing with her. She is not to speak or have contact with anyone in the household. So you see, Madame Napier, the contest between us begins. Get that servant out of the way!"

Shoved aside by a rifle butt, O-nami raised his fists. But Shizue touched him and shook her hed. Ordered not to speak, she bid him good-bye with a determined smile. This was a war of wills she intended to win. O-nami called after her, saying he and Yufugawo would be nearby. Her eyes misted over. They knew no other home, no other way of life, and their souls were tied to this land.

On the day she had wed Jiro, strangers had escorted her from the castle. Then there had been a bonfire, and she had smelled the land burning in the spiraling smoke. Now soldiers marched through the gardens and the woods searching for Max. She had the strong premonition that he had left these hostile shores. But she was not alone. The *omamori* he had placed around her neck was part of him, a keepsake to be exchanged between lovers when they met again.

"My baby, my child, let me go with her," Yufugawo sobbed hysterically, restrained by the soldiers.

Shizue broke her silence. "Don't be afraid for me."

"Losing control, Madame Napier?" the major commented.

While her heart went out to Yufugawo, Shizue looked straight ahead. She knew that Major Shinoda saw her as soft and pampered, a woman easily broken by the hardships of prison. But, for Jiro, she had endured a living nightmare. For Kimitake, she had stretched her endurance to the very limits of love. She had come to accept herself as she was, Hosokawa and samurai. If the major expected her to give false testimony against Max's father and Inge, he was in for a surprise.

At nightfall, O-nami helped his wife into a horse-drawn wagon. Yufugawo wept, loudly bemoaning their fate. Many of her prized possessions had to be left behind. Soldiers watched as her husband quickly loaded the wagon with what they could carry on the train. Hundreds of troops had arrived during the day. Tents had been erected in the valley, which was now lit with the glow of campfires. "It makes no sense to waste so many soldiers tending the silkworms, when there is fighting to be done."

"They mean some other purpose for the land," said O-nami.

"The gods' curses on their heads if they harm the land," Yufugawo said.

O-nami climbed into the wagon beside his wife and took the reins. She faced backward until she could no longer see the castle walls and was stirred from her sad reveries when the wagon rocked to a stop. "What business have you here?" she asked O-nami.

"Our royal silkworms must not perish at the hands of these infidels, woman."

There were no guards stationed outside the sericulture laboratory. O-nami entered the refrigeration vaults. The finest eggs selected from the winter mating were preserved there in sealed containers. Each season a number of these were sold to other farms, shipped inside the insulated crates like the one he now carefully packed for his journey.

Baron Hosokawa had been a generous provider and invested his faithful friend's wages wisely, so O-nami would be able to draw against his account at a Nagasaki bank to purchase land. Come the spring, these bombyx mori would be hatched to continue their unbroken lineage. And for every season thereafter until this war had ended.

O-nami carried the crate back to his wagon. "The land will never die," he told Yufugawo, as he sat beside her and whipped the horse into a trot along the steep mountain road. "One day, Shizue's firstborn son will reclaim his birthright, and we will begin anew. Ah, dry your tears, old woman. Do not look back. Look ahead and think of the work to be done. We must hire a lawyer to defend Shizue. The law will find her innocent." Flickering fires on the valley floor below evoked a bygone age, when samurai warriors had camped there preparing for battle. "Here, come close under my arm and give us a kiss."

"Natsu's son, Paul. He is an important man. Perhaps he has some news of Max." Yufugawo cheered with the thought. "Perhaps he can be of help to us."

"Hah, you see what comes of a kiss." Age had put a wheeze into O-nami's laughter. "This child of love must stand by his brother's wife. No harm will come to Shizue. Trust the gods, woman. As I have always said, these things are decided in advance."

Staring down at the floor tiles being mopped by other inmates of the Urakami Prison, Shizue followed behind the buxom prison matron. It would be another degrading session presided over by Major Shinoda, she thought. As she passed the other inmates, they spat at her and screamed *"Hangyakusha!"* Branded a traitor, she had been segregated from the main cell block and confined to the security of an attic room, which was little more than a crawl space. The first day there, matrons had shaved her head and boxed her mourning clothes with the *omamori*. From time to time, she was allowed to bathe and launder the skimpy gray cotton smock they had given her to wear. She had lost weight, and the smock hung loosely off her shoulders. Hunger pains robbed her of sleep. In the mornings, she often woke feeling fuzzy and nauseated. She was fed infrequently or not at all and had learned to keep down the rancid vegetable soup purely as a matter of survival.

Rather than break her spirit, the major's methods had only strengthened her determination to resist. However, she had more than herself to think of now. Six weeks of imprisonment—at least that, she judged from the growth of her new hair on her bowed head. For two months now she had missed her period.

"Bathe and change into these," the matron ordered sharply, closing the bathhouse door behind them.

To Shizue's surprise, her own clothes had been laid out along with the *omamori*. No, this was just some cruel trick of Major Shinoda's. "You mustn't bend, you mustn't break." She talked to herself and touched the satin undergarments, which still held a faint trace of perfume. Her distrust slowly gave way to hope. Although no visitors had been allowed, those she loved must have been working in her defense, and here was the proof: cosmetics, hairbrushes, a mirror—all promising freedom. She lifted the mirror to her face, shocked to tears when she saw herself.

The matron chattered an icy warning. "Be quick about it, or there will be punishment. Important people are waiting, and I'll be held accountable if we are late."

Casting off her prison garb, Shizue dared not ask what lay in store. Her breasts had grown small. But if Max were there, he would kiss them all the same. As the bath water caressed her skin, she recalled the ecstasy of his touch and could almost hear his voice whispering that he loved her. Sponging herself, she remembered lying in his arms on their wedding night and on that last night they had together before they were parted.

When she emerged from the steaming tub, she nearly fainted. Not from memories of love. Max had given her something real to cleave to and that secret happiness made her weak.

After dressing and putting on makeup, she was taken away in a prison van. When its doors opened at their destination, Shizue recognized the Nagasaki courthouse. The shackles were removed from her wrists and ankles before she was led down a very long stretch of corridor. Iron bars stood between her and those seated on wooden benches. O-nami. Yufugawo. The private nurse who had cared for Kimitake and Dr. Onogi, chief surgeon at the army hospital. They all seemed not to know her.

Then Yufugawo ran to the bars, crying "Shizue," but she was forcefully taken through a doorway into a small room. Paul faced her there in shocked disbelief, and Shizue took hold of a chair, weaving on rubbery legs, unable to speak. Another man rose up beside Paul and ordered the prison matron to leave.

Paul rushed forward. "They won't touch you again," he promised, holding Shizue close. Her violated beauty filled him with rage. "You're all bones. Major Shinoda will pay for this. He used every dirty trick he could to stop us from getting you a fair hearing. By keeping us from seeing you until now, he hoped that we couldn't prepare an adequate defense. But I fought Shinoda with tactics of my own. The army has appointed Judge Nakao to review the evidence, and he's already heard enough testimony to justify dismissing the charges brought against you."

Helped to sit, her first concern was for Max. "My husband. Is he safe?" Her fingers tightened around Paul's hand while he related the launch skipper's story.

"Panama was quick to declare war on Japan. The freighter must have headed for America."

"I'm pregnant with his child."

"Are you sure, Napier-*san*?" asked the other man.

Paul identified the man as her lawyer. "Yuki-*san* is in charge of your defense."

The lawyer repeated his question. "Are you sure?"

"Well, I haven't seen the prison doctor," Shizue placed her hands over her stomach. "But I know it's so."

Mr. Yuki deliberated for a time, then he smiled and said, "I think this turn of events favors us. Stand for a moment, please. Yes, the major has outfoxed himself. You are a frail, sympathetic victim of circumstances. The judge must take into account the well-being of your unborn child. No matter the father. Sit, Napier-*san*, and fix your mind on the fact of your innocence. This is an informal hearing, not a trial. Major Shinoda will no doubt glare at you in an intimidating fashion, but he has no right to cross-examine you. So, keep your eyes on the judge. Speak slowly and answer his questions truthfully. Hold nothing back. Describe the treatment you received in prison. If you feel in need of tears, then let them flow. Have you a handkerchief?"

Shizue glanced down at her empty lap. "I have nothing but these clothes and a keepsake. How will I support my child?"

Paul handed her his handkerchief. "It's too much for Shizue to comprehend. She needs nourishment. A few days to gather her senses."

"After pushing so long for this hearing, any delay would weaken our defense. Judge Nakao is getting on in years and may not retain the favorable impression our witnesses have brought to bear on him."

Yuki thoughtfully adjusted his eyeglasses. "Shizue, may I address you on our position with the court?"

"Oh, yes, help me understand what's expected of me," she answered. "I don't want to lose the baby. Paul, you're so dear to me. Soon you'll be an uncle."

"First things first." Yuki planted both elbows on the table, his palms weighing the air. "The judgment could go either way. Now, reliable witnesses have testified to your character and the sacrifices you made for your brother. The judge's eyes clouded when he heard of your tireless devotion to him. The many months you spent caring for a hero speaks for your patriotism. Also, since you were confined to your brother's bedside for so long a time, it would have been impossible for you to have taken part in the intrigues suggested by Major Shinoda. Now, as to the motive for seppuku, we have Dr. Onogil's expert testimony, which supports the testimony given by your friend O-nami. Once again, the judge was moved by an account of the hospital isolation ward, where others like Lieutenant Hosokawa lost their will to live. Finally, we have the confessions of Douglas Napier and his Jewish wife. A thorough police investigation unearthed nothing whatsoever to refute these. Much to the contrary, it revealed that the Napiers were well motivated to work on behalf of the European Jews. Of course, you must renounce all claims to American citizenship by virtue of your marriage. That will prove your loyalty to Japan. And there we stand. If you are exonerated, it destroys Major Shinoda's case for treason."

"Yes, I'll do everything you say. The life of my baby comes first," said Shizue, thinking her American citizenship was worthless now. Once it would have allowed her to leave Japan with Max. Now they were separated for the duration of this war. The father of her unborn baby was considered an enemy of Japan and nothing must threaten the life she carried inside her womb. "But what punishment will the Napiers receive?" she asked the lawyer.

"Since Japan has no official policy on the Jews, I imagine they'll be detained together with the other prisoners of war."

"My influence with the army doesn't extend to them," Paul said to Shizue.

He turned to the lawyer. "Before Shizue goes in, I'd like a minute alone." Nodding, Yuki stepped into the corridor.

Paul took Shizue's hands in his. "Listen, I don't want to put an added burden on you, but Major Shinoda will raise a stink if he learns that Douglas Napier is my father. The army general who got us this hearing believes that my mother was related to your family. That Baron Hosokawa was my mentor and I felt obligated to help you by getting at the truth. That's what you'll tell Judge Nakao. Otherwise, I'll be accused of using you to bail out Douglas. Like it or not, he *is* the enemy."

"I won't forget." Shizue began to tremble. "Will you be with me?"

"In spirit only."

"Then I'm ready."

Paul had brought her this far and now she stood on her own. She thought of the child growing inside her, hungry for the nourishment that was denied it during her imprisonment. The baby she carried must not go hungry for even another day, she told herself, and called upon all the strength she could muster.

When she stepped into the corridor with Paul, she saw no one else there but the lawyer. His name escaped her. "Where are my friends?"

"Dismissed," he said, escorting her past the vacated benches. Shizue trembled at the sight of Major Shinoda in the corridor ahead. He was just entering the judge's chambers with his adjutant. "Be calm, Shizue," the lawyer said softly. "Major Shinoda has no authority within these chamber doors."

Shizue held herself with dignity. Lighting a cigarette, Paul marveled at her poise as she entered the judge's chambers. From behind she looked like a child dressed in her mother's clothes, he thought. He watched Shizue lower her shorn head in a bow, as the doors closed. Judge Nakao was sure to be swayed by such a compelling figure, Paul assured himself.

In a roundabout way he had helped his father. Their lives were inexorably intertwined, and he had no wish to see Douglas harmed. Shizue's pregnancy had a profound effect on him. Suddenly he felt even more protective, the expectant father anxiously pacing the floor with one eye on the clock. He paced back and forth, chain smoking, until at last the chamber doors sprang open wide. Major Shinoda stormed through them, trailed by his adjutant.

"Lose the battle, Major?" Paul queried gleefully.

"We'll meet again under different circumstances, *ainoko!*"

"*Happa* pig," the adjutant growled, cramming papers inside his briefcase. "You haven't heard the last of this!"

"Not a complete victory," the lawyer announced. "The army retains possession of the Hosokawa lands. However, Shizue has been awarded a small income as payment for its military use."

Shizue leaned heavily on the lawyer's arm, moving toward Paul on her last ounce of strength. She had won. She was free. But everything was spinning. And then everything turned black.

Shizue had come dangerously close to losing her baby. An ambulance had rushed her from the courthouse to a hospital. Now, several days later, she was quickly regaining strength. Flowers brightened the Nagasaki hospital room where Yufugawo and O-nami were visiting with her. Shizue sat in bed sipping a brew of milk, black molasses, raw eggs, and other ingredients prescribed by the doctor. O-nami's expression of disgust made her laugh.

"It's good for the baby," Shizue told him.

Yufugawo sniffed the dregs. "Ah, my cooking would do you both more good. A healthy mother should have meat on her bones."

"*Hai*, we must fatten you up, little one. The farm I have leased is not so grand. But the soil is rich, and there is a small grove of mulberry trees to feed our silkworms." O-nami looked out the window and sighed longingly. "Home is far away. The city is unfit for children. A boy must have room. Fresh air to make his lungs grow strong."

Shizue ran one hand over her short hair, impatient to have it reach her shoulders again. "Will it be a son?"

"Look to your bloodlines, little one. With Ichiban as the father, your firstborn will most certainly be a son. These things are decided in advance," said O-nami, and Yufugawo echoed that oft-repeated claim.

Puffing up his great chest, O-nami displayed his bulging wallet. "I'll wager all this against a girlchild."

"Wager the money for our livestock? Oaf, give it to me!"

"Stop this. Both of you are acting like children. Boy or girl, I want only what's best for my baby." Shizue's friends nodded contritely. Then Yufugawo took away her tray.

"It's hard to believe we're at war, with the sky so quiet," Shizue said to O-nami, who struck a thoughtful pose at the sunny window. "A threatening quiet," she added with a shiver. "But war or not, we mustn't abandon Max's father and his wife. Somehow we must find a way to help them."

"My very thoughts," O-nami agreed. "But we cannot expect to solve that problem in the blink of an eye."

Paul entered the room carrying flowers. He looked at the somber faces. "Maybe I should go out and come in again," he said.

"Not more flowers." Something was troubling him, Shizue observed, smiling all the same. "Oh, Paul, roses. They're lovely." She lifted one long-stemmed rose from the box. "But I'm sick of being confined to this room. I want to stretch my legs outside in the sunshine."

"The doctor says you can leave tomorrow. Won't you change your mind about coming to Tokyo?" Paul's voice stuck in his throat. "Plenty of room for you and the child in my apartment. I promise you won't be bored. I'm invited to the best parties."

"Think of your reputation. The gossip . . ."

"Hang my reputation."

"Paul, I want us all to be together, but I can't cut myself in half. Tokyo has become so ugly. Your work takes you away most of the time, and I'd go mad just sitting there alone. On the farm I can be useful until my baby arrives. I want it to know the warmth of a real home and shield it from the awfulness of war."

"Maybe it's safest for you in the country," Paul agreed reluctantly. Much as he loved her, work was his master, and he could not take care of her half as well as O-nami and Yufugawo, who offered the stability of a family unit. "I've got a bit of news. Douglas and Inge were shipped from Kobe with a bunch of other internees. Couldn't learn anything about their destination. I do know that Japan intends to make them work for their keep. Sooner or later, they'll show up on some list. Then, we'll see."

"Anything you could do would be a blessing." Shizue thought she fully understood what lay behind his tormented look. "I know how difficult it is to forgive."

"My animosity has withered over the years since Mother was laid to rest. Her grave has been neglected. Overgrown with weeds when I visited it last." He looked down at the silver handle of his cane. "I cleared the ground, but the weeds will only grow up again. War has taken priority over everything else. The Cherry Blossom Kissaten now caters to soldiers. Yoko fawns over each boy as if he were her own son. The Ginza is brasher and gaudier than before, and every day more young men are marched from their homes to the buglers' call. Yes, Tokyo isn't the place for you. When the enemy retaliates, it'll be a prime target for American bombers."

A silence followed his grim pronouncement. Shizue wondered if Max would ever see their child. Where was he now? What would this war make of him and of those she loved? It seemed as if the better part of her life had been touched by war. "What will it take to end the fighting?"

Paul had no answer. As of February, 1942, the Japanese forces seemed unstoppable. They swarmed across the Pacific like a plague of locusts, chewing up territory that the enemy would have to win back. His long-stemmed roses were a parting gift. A veritable mountain of propaganda awaited his editorial touch: speeches for the mighty, broadcast scripts for Radio Tokyo, pamphlets to inspire the troops. "I'll visit when I can," he promised. As always, parting from Shizue left him drained.

Leaving the hospital, Paul encountered a number of women who stood on street corners petitioning passersby to stop. The wives and mothers of soldiers, they held out strips of white cloth and threaded needles to other women, asking them to please add a stitch of bright red thread. Red was an auspicious color to the Japanese, and these *sennimbari*, thousand-stitch belts, would be given to their fighting men to be worn in combat. No woman could refuse to stitch another knot on the sashes, for they were believed to ward off bullets. Once blessed with stitches sewn by a thousand women, the sashes would insure that their sons and husbands would return safely from war. But Paul had seen too many Japanese dead and wounded whose waists were adorned with *sennimbari*. He frowned on the superstitious nature of his people.

"All three of my sons have been called to serve," a graying woman flanked by her two daughters hoarsely addressed the passersby. "*Mei fa tzu*. Will you not add a stitch?"

Mei fa tzu—it is fate. This popular saying borrowed from the Chinese ran through Paul's mind as he limped off. Japan was an amalgam of borrowed cultures and technologies, but its people remained unique unto themselves. War with the West had unified them as never before. Thousand-stitch belts breathed new life into their old gods. The samurai's Bushido and the ancient Shinto cult of the *kami* way had been given a renaissance. An entire nation had committed itself to victory or seppuku. Even one of the few surviving lampposts in Nagasaki had been imbued with the *kami* presence and given a voice: "I too will help destroy the Americans and the English!" its paper sign proclaimed. Laborers with *haki-machi* knotted across their brows heaved on ropes noosed around the lamppost's cast-iron filigree as bystanders applauded.

The uprooted relic spewed dust into the air, and Paul shielded his eyes. He was rudely jostled by soldiers hurrying for a tram. Balancing on his cane, he felt burned out, old before his time. The victor or the vanquished, his world would die.

BOOK FIVE
THE WAY HOME
SUMMER

1942

Even in my dreams, there is a waking.
My mind journeys far to quiet castle gardens.
The dream takes me home again.

Jolting moments of confusion shatter the invention:
The shuddering roar of cannons opens my eyes,
But I am still in a dream.

My mind has invented this war.
Swallowed whole, reality is too rude,
And so I must still be dreaming.

ANONYMOUS

As Max got out of a taxi, he was pelted by a hissing summer rain that flushed litter down the steep San Francisco hills. Blackout curtains were drawn across the windows of the sprawling town house that was his destination. The city was on air raid alert, and a helmeted civil defense warden patrolling the street halted to question him.

"Can I be of help, Lieutenant?"

"Yeah, can't find the doorbell."

The man's flashlight beam was muted by a red gel. "Right in front of your nose."

"Much obliged." Max checked the address, thinking his taxi driver must have had rabbit's eyes. "Lieutenant Napier," he told the potbellied master sergeant who answered the door. "My orders from the Western Defense Command."

The air raid warden doused his flashlight and called, "Good night, son."

"Pretty fancy quarters," Max observed, shaking the rain off his hat. "Those orders don't explain a damn thing. What gives here, Sergeant?"

"Tuttle, sir! CO will brief you. Right this way, Lieutenant." Hitching up his trousers, Sergeant Dan Tuttle conducted him to an upstairs parlor. "More paperwork," he said, handing Max's orders to his clerk-typist. "CO's got some big brass on the telephone. Could be a while, sir. Coffee?"

"Okay. Black, no sugar." Max settled into a plush velvet easy chair. People of some wealth had once occupied this elegant town house, which had been donated to the war effort. The parlor was decorated in blues and golds. Photographs of Roosevelt, Churchill, and Joseph Stalin hung on flocked wallpaper. The clerk hammered away on his Remington while the sergeant brought Max coffee in a delicate bone china cup.

The Victorian ambiance made him think of home. After docking in San Francisco, there was no way he could have escaped the draft. His year of ROTC at Harvard had put him in line to earn a commission, but he had signed up for officer candidate school only because the army promised he would serve duty in Europe. Just the day before, he had been at Fort Knox, Kentucky, assigned to Third Army Intelligence, with sailing orders for the European theater of war. Then he was suddenly called before his CO and handed new orders transferring him for special duty. The company commander could tell him nothing more. One hour later he was aboard a Pan Am flight to San Francisco. Now he was sitting in a town house drinking a brew that was more chicory than coffee. He was rather amused by Sergeant Tuttle, who chomped on a Tootsie Roll as if it were a great delicacy. Tuttle choked for a beat, swallowing hard as his CO's voice sounded over the intercom.

"Has Lieutenant Napier reported in?"

"Yessir, not five minutes ago," Tuttle said.

The mellow voice pricked Max's memory. Tucking his hat under one arm, he turned to face the adjoining doorway and snapped to attention. "Avery?"

Avery Bullock strode from the adjoining room, grinning from ear to ear. "A sight for sore eyes, you old moose!" He laughed and pumped Max's hand. The years had fleshed out his pleasant face. His coppery red hair was trimmed short, but his mustache had grown bushier. He smiled in the same disarming way Max remembered so well. "You're one lousy correspondent, Napier. No letter since 'thirty-nine. Hell, get into my office. I've got a branch water in there guaranteed to counteract Tuttle's poisonous coffee."

Max shook his head and laughed. "What a stroke of luck. Dammit, Avery, I tried getting in touch with you at Stanford . . ."

"Pulled from the academic ranks, day after Pearl. Captain's bars just like that." Avery snapped his fingers. "Not a stroke of luck, you coming here. I've had the joint services working overtime conducting a records search for someone with your background. Imagine my surprise when your file turned up on my desk. Couldn't get the old ball rolling fast enough to yank your butt through that door." He stretched and yawned. "Army's sweated my tail off, but with you on the team I expect to get some shut-eye. Well, business later. Take a load off and tell me everything. I'll fix us two long drinks."

It was as though Max were back at Harvard and no time at all had elapsed. Avery Bullock lit his briar pipe and rested his feet on the desk while Max talked nonstop. Now and then he paused to swallow some bourbon and just stare at Avery with a grin on his face. "This is swell," he must have said a dozen times or more before talking himself out.

All lines of communication between America and the Japanese enemy had been severed immediately after Roosevelt's declaration of war. The communications blackout was designed to protect the U.S. mainland, and only those on the highest government level had access to the enemy through diplomatic channels.

"If not for the tight restrictions on our national security, I might have gotten some letter through to Japan," Max told Avery. "It's going on seven months now without knowing about Shizue or my father and Inge. I tried my damnedest to get someone in command to lift the restrictions, but no such luck. They looked at me like I might be an enemy spy. Well, thanks to you, at least I got it off my chest."

"Yeah, it's hell, but we can't have Japanese spies mailing secrets across the Pacific. We're in the same boat," Avery said. "The church didn't have the foresight to recall my parents from Japan. Stuck there for the duration. I don't imagine Christian missionaries will receive preferential treatment." Avery tapped out his pipe against a fancy brass ashtray. "Dad's over sixty. Would've retired soon. It's tough not having any contact with our folks. But with security so tight, you might as well try getting a letter through to Hirohito himself."

Just then Sergeant Tuttle buzzed the intercom, announcing that Avery's car had arrived. "Button up and let's get some chow. I'll brief you on the way."

The olive-drab Ford parked outside was army issue. Its driver was a WAC private. A pretty young woman, she wore her soft brown hair gathered at the back in a net snood. "Hotel Fairmont, yessir." She responded to Avery's command with an over-the-shoulder glance and a smile directed at Max.

"Eyes front, Sally. The lieutenant's a married man."

Her shoulders dropped on a sigh. "Wouldn't you know it."

"Okay, I'll make this short and sweet," Avery said. It was no longer raining, and he cranked the window open, then pushed his hat back from his forehead to catch the breeze. "Sergeant Tuttle's appropriately dubbed our headquarters 'the little red schoolhouse.' We're putting together a special intelligence unit. Max, just about nobody knows Japan, the people, or the language like we do. I don't have to tell you about the shabby treatment our Japanese-Americans have received. Property confiscated and crammed into detention camps. Their American-born sons would be perfect material for us, but they've been barred from military service in the Pacific. So, we've got to make do with Caucasian recruits who have an ear for the Japanese language. I've already tested thousands of men. You'll help me screen the most promising candidates. Then we'll drill them until they talk Japanese in their sleep. There's also a crash course in intelligence operations mapped out by the O.S.S. General MacArthur has given us carte blanche to mold a topflight team by no later than November of this year. With you as my associate professor, I think it can be done. That's why I snatched you away from Third Army Intelligence at Fort Knox."

"Ave, I won't fire a shot at the Japanese," Max said.

"Hey, you're being asked to use your brains, not your muscle. Interrogating prisoners. Cracking codes," Avery Bullock defined. "Evaluating captured documents and helping to make value judgments on the enemy's strengths and weaknesses. Let me tell you, being at MacArthur's right arm is the quickest way home for us both, my recalcitrant friend."

The truth sank in slowly. A noncombatant post. Shizue was only two weeks away by sea. But until the war ended, she might as well be waiting on the moon. The bottom line was that he had no say in the matter. "What the hell."

Avery cuffed his arm. "That's the spirit."

Cars from the army and navy motor pools deposited passengers along the Hotel Fairmont's circular drive. Navy whites held sway over the lobby. "The fleet's in," Avery quipped, steering Max for the dining room, past couples queued up waiting to be seated. "My table, François."

The maître d' unhooked the velvet rope. "An excellent turbot this evening, Captain. And I have reserved a delicate French Chablis from our rapidly declining wine cellar."

Max took his friend by the elbow. "Ave, how can you afford this?"

"Uncle Sam picks up the tab. We've got a suite with a damn spectacular view of the bay. Anything you want, just sign for it. Two of the usual, François."

Avery Bullock clearly was enjoying this taste of the good life. His eyes roamed across the glistening parquet dance floor, where ladies clad in off-the-shoulder gowns rhumbaed with their uniformed escorts. Except for blackout curtains drawn across the tall windows, one might forget that America was at war. The rhumba beat gave way to romantic violins, and Max slipped into an introspective mood. He heard Avery's voice, but the words did not register. Then he saw the smashing brunette who had caught his friend's eye. She was seated with a middle-aged couple, and when they looked away, she gave Avery a demure smile.

"Smooth and silky," Max said.

"Early twenties, unattached, and dining with her parents," Avery surmised, and rose, straightening his tie. "I could fall in love with that face. Well, nothing ventured, nothing gained."

Max dined alone, forgotten while Avery held the petite brunette ever closer with each dance. Her dark eyes lowered in disappointment when her father came between them. Polite but firm, he displayed tickets for the opera that she was obliged to attend.

"I'm in the book," she managed to tell Avery, waving with the sequined evening bag in her hand.

Avery floated to the table. "Her name is Jennifer, but her friends call her Jen. Yep, I'm hooked. I'm sunk. Did you see the sparks flying? Damn, her perfume's all over me. Get a whiff of that."

"Ave, cool down. You only just met her."

"No time to waste on long engagements. Before the month is out, we'll be married."

On that confident note, Avery Bullock dug into his cold dinner. Max toyed with his wineglass, considering how the uncertain times made love hit fast and hard. "Better shift into neutral, or you'll strip gears before popping the question."

"Ah, the droll Napier wit. 'Course you'll be best man," he said between mouthfuls. "Meantime, we've got a job to do."

Suddenly the orchestra stopped playing. "Ladies and gentlemen, your attention please," the orchestra leader said, tapping the microphone with his baton. A hush fell over the room. "I've just been handed news. The battle for Midway Island has been won. American forces have beaten back the Japs."

America's first major victory in the Pacific brought them all to their feet applauding. Sheet music rustled on the musicians' stands. The "National Athem" began with a drum roll and the crash of cymbals.

Max had risen from the table slowly. Standing at attention, he felt compelled to salute with Avery and the other stony-faced officers around them. A number of women had tears in their eyes. Emotions ran high as people sang the words. When the last stanza had ended, no one stirred. The final crash of cymbals seemed to hang on the air, and Max experienced a tingling at the back of his neck. Not many months had passed since Japan's sneak attack had turned Pearl Harbor into a slaughterhouse, and all around Max there was a feeling that its dead had been avenged. He could not bring himself to return Avery's smile. Clearly, his friend had drawn a line between the Japanese he had been raised with as a child and the Japanese who had become his enemy. It was a distinction that eluded Max that night in June, 1942. Some navy men requested "Anchors Aweigh." Ladies dried their eyes and drifted toward the powder room to repair their makeup.

Avery signed the tab. "One step closer to victory."

One step closer to home and Shizue were Max's thoughts as he and Avery entered the sumptuous hotel suite they would share.

The telephone rang, and Avery answered it. "Right you are, Tuttle. Process and billet the lot." He turned to Max. "First bunch of recruits arrived ahead of schedule." To Tuttle, he said, "Give me a wakeup call at six. No, better make that five-thirty."

Max fingered the stubble on his face. The airline had lost his luggage somewhere en route. He would have to make do until it turned up. After stripping to his underwear, he crossed to the bathroom to use Avery's shaving things. "Shaving at bedtime gives me a head start in the morning," he said.

"Go easy on the razor blade, they're getting scarce." Avery stretched his lean body, yawned, then vanished behind the shower curtain. "Damn cold water's running warm. Hell, now I'll never get any shut-eye. Not that I've been saving it up, mind you. But Jennifer . . ." His wails alternated between pleasure and pain.

"I know the feeling." The bathroom mirror fogged up, and Max gave it a swipe with one hand. Shaving cream dribbled on his dog tags. Two slices of metal embossed with his name, rank, and serial number had taken the place of the *omamori* he had worn next to his heart through all the frustrating years he had spent apart from Shizue. He could see her now, looking like a little Eskimo as they kissed good-bye. Perhaps the charm was meant to be passed on. She would always have it to remember him by. No priests had blessed these dog tags that would identify him if he were captured or killed.

"What a sad sack. Half-shaved, half-undressed," Avery Bullock regarded his somber friend. "Might I remind you that we didn't ask for this lousy war. But no man is an island unto himself. Can't remember who penned those wise words." He finished drying himself off and wrapped the bath towel around his waist. "Listen, too much innocent blood's been spilled for us to just sit on our cans staring at our navels. Got to take sides, old pal. 'Let old acquaintance be forgot and never brought to mind.' Quote and unquote."

"Ave, you're a glib sonofabitch."

"Lovable all the same." He chuckled. "Shower's yours. Easy on the soap, it's getting scarce."

Max snapped a towel at Avery's butt. "These days everything's scarce but love. I envy you. Not the girl, just her availability."

"Maybe she's got a friend." Avery ran a comb through his wet hair while the question hovered between them unanswered. "Nah, I can see you intend to remain celibate for the duration."

"Faithful," Max corrected him. "There's never been anyone else for me and never will be."

"War might be hell. But ain't love grand."

By daylight San Francisco was picture-postcard pretty. A Red Cross flag billowed out from their headquarters, which faced Union Square. Office workers on lunch hour were sunning themselves in the park. Since Max's arrival weeks before, he and Avery had visited the agency twice without results, and that day was no different.

Mrs. Rutledge, the woman in charge, pursed her lips sadly and fluffed her tinted white hair, wishing she could offer more help. The Japanese were uncooperative, she said. Even the Swiss legation in Tokyo had been unsuccessful in obtaining information about the locations of POW camps in Southeast Asia. Some scanty lists of prisoners had been released, but hardly anything was known about them, civilians and military alike. The Red Cross would continue to lodge formal complaints. But to date, nothing whatsoever was known about those who were being held on the Japanese mainland. "One can only hope they are being treated humanely and that word of the captives will be forthcoming soon," the woman said.

Avery Bullock consulted his watch and shrugged. Max envied the man's capacity to take things in stride. Wearily Max put on sunglasses to cover his bloodshot eyes. Their little red schoolhouse was within walking distance of Union Square. Out of hundreds of candidates, seventy had passed muster. But cramming the Japanese language down their throats was only partly responsible for Max's exhaustion. Avery's whirlwind courtship had kept him up nights, curled on a sofa in the hotel lobby while the lovebirds had the suite to themselves.

The July Fourth weekend was approaching. On Saturday, Jennifer Lowell and Avery Bullock would say their "I do's," and they would motor to a seaside hideaway for the nuptial fireworks. On their return, Avery would move in with the bride's society parents. How Max longed for that blissful day so that he could get a good night's sleep.

Churches were working overtime. Avery halted them near the church steps, where well-wishers were showering rice on a navy ensign and his young bride. The newlyweds rushed to get into a prewar Lincoln Continental festooned with yards of pink-and-white crepe paper. Its canvas top was down, and the bride stood up and tossed her bouquet at the outstretched arms of her bridesmaids. Holding on to the crown of her veil, she dropped back in the seat and waved with her other hand as the car started away.

"Will you look at that!" Avery pointed to the gasoline ration sticker pasted on its windshield. "An E rating! Jesus, these two must have pull in Washington."

Max nudged him along. "You've done all right for yourself, Captain."

"Just now I'm feeling a bit jittery about tying the knot. Jen's set on having a baby—part of me for her to cuddle and love. But this war makes me think twice about burdening Jen with the added responsibility of a child. It's hard enough leaving a wife behind. November isn't all that far off, and we'll be sailing for enemy waters, Max. Right into the thick of things."

"Yeah," Max said absently. Church bells and rice thrown on a San Francisco sidewalk took him back to his own wedding day. Shizue had also set her heart on having his baby. He thought of her lying in his arms through those last nights together, and wondered if their love had conceived a child. He halted, counting their months apart on his fingers as the hopeful possibility took root. Avery questioned his dumbstruck look.

"Wishful thinking." Max half-laughed, deciding it was just a crazy notion. "If you ask me, giving Jennifer your child would help ease her burden, not add to it, Ave. Life's not a sure bet even in peacetime." He put his hands into his pants pockets. "Ah, hell, it's none of my business."

"That so? Well, after poking your nose into my business, I glimpse the error of my selfish ways." Avery laughed good-naturedly and pounded Max's shoulder. "Let there be a kid to warm sweet Jen's bosom. Maybe I'm jealous he'll steal the show while I'm off playing soldier. But ten dollars says the little darling who replaces me will be a boy."

"You're on."

"First cigar goes to you, pal. After all, you'll be footing the bill for those long weeds."

The two men laughed and shook hands.

"Well, back to school, Mr. Chips." Captain Bullock tapped his briar pipe against the lamppost, then dug its bowl inside his tobacco pouch. "Lots of tin ears yet to be tuned to Japanese pitch before this party's over."

Avery paused to light up, shielding his pipe against the wind. Max gazed down from the steep hilltop. San Francisco Bay was like a sheet of blue ice on which an aircraft carrier skated serenely out toward the Pacific. Before Christmas, he and Avery Bullock would be standing on the flight deck of a carrier much like this one, Max thought, watching gulls floating high above the bay on the sea breeze. He remembered gulls winging overhead on that day he stood trapped aboard the rolling deck of a freighter, outward bound from Yokohama Bay. Now Avery urged him to move on, and Max wondered how long the war would last, how many battles there were to be fought and won before he was reunited with his loved ones.

CHAPTER 39

The pain of giving birth brought tears into Shizue's eyes. Her child was not expected for at least another two weeks, but the labor pains had come upon her suddenly while she was helping Yufugawo fix dinner.

O-nami fought to remain calm. He knew there was no way to reach the Nagasaki hospital in time from his small farm located in the suburban countryside. It was just a short ride to the city on the local bus, but with gasoline in short supply, it now ran only twice each day. After hitching the oxen to his cart, O-nami went to fetch the village doctor, who was very old. But Dr. Kurozaki had delivered many babies in his lifetime.

Shizue lay on her bed, praying for her baby to wait just a little while longer. "I can feel its strength, Yufugawo."

"Ah, that city doctor is to blame. 'Do not panic,' he told me. 'Bring Shizue to the hospital in ten days' time, and all will go well.' That charlatan! May the gods cover him with boils if any harm comes to this child."

"Do stop whining. The pains are coming closer together," she gasped. She heard the squeal of ox-cart wheels nearing the farmhouse. "Go—tell the doctor to hurry."

One of the farmhands' wives was called in to assist. A fat moth flapped around the lamps as Dr. Kurozaki ordered the women to unshade the electric bulbs and place the lamps at either side of the bed. The woman put pillows behind Shizue's back, then lifted up the bottom of her cotton slip so the doctor could position her legs. His voice instructed her to push harder. Whatever else he may have said was lost to her. The pain was overwhelming, and she pushed harder and harder. At last the baby's perfectly formed head slid into the light.

Now there was joy in her pain. Little by little she saw her child take shape—a son, anchored to her by the umbilical cord. Max's son announced himself with a healthy cry, and Shizue drifted between wakefulness and dreams as the doctor cared for the new mother and her child with gentle hands.

"And did I not say it would be a son?" she heard O-nami shout to those gathered outside the house. "A healthy boy, perfect in every way. Ah, yes, seven pounds or more and blessed with the lungs of a warrior. Just hear how he cries. Let us welcome Shizue's firstborn son into our household. A long and prosperous life."

"Banzai, banzai, banzai!" The farmhands shouted with him. Several families who had once served her father had been given a home there, and the women celebrated the birth of Shizue's child with an old song from his ancestral lands.

Blessed is the family
Where the crane and tortoise
Dance gaily here and there.

Weakly, Shizue asked for her baby. He had stopped crying. Wrapped in a blanket, he looked so tiny. Yufugawo nestled him against her breast, and Shizue kissed his wrinkled little face. "Oh, is he truly perfect?"

The country doctor hummed. "Sound in every respect. A handsome boy. When you write his father of this, he will be proud."

Her baby yawned and briefly opened his eyes. They were dark brown. There were no flecks of the Napier blue as in Paul's eyes. His fine baby hair was dark as well. No wonder Dr. Kurozaki had assumed the father was Japanese and away at war. But her son was only minutes old. What he had inherited from Max would reveal itself in time. Yes, he was part of them both, she thought, somehow wanting to make his father known to him. She still wore the *omamori* around her neck, and she touched it to her son's doll-like hand. "This belongs to your father. Perhaps it helped you travel safely into this world and will bring him safely back to us soon."

The baby was asleep. Shizue could not take her eyes off him, exhausted as she was. "Isn't he beautiful?"

O-nami tiptoed across the room, but its floorboards groaned loudly under his weight, and Yufugawo shooed him to a standstill. "Ah, he will outgrow the cradle before long," he whispered softly. "Then I will sit him on a horse. Have you decided on a name?"

"Oh, there's no question of that. My son will do honor to Kimitake's memory by carrying on his name." With the birth of little Kimitake, her faith in the future was restored. It comforted her to believe that her brother's and father's spirits now dwelled among the *kami*, whose presence watched over her slumbering infant. Barely able to keep her eyes open, she imagined the faces of her papa and Kimitake smiling from the shadows closing around her bed in this humble farmhouse. *"Ogisan,"* she whispered, "look what a fine grandson you have. Kimi, does your namesake please you?"

Yufugawo waited until Shizue was asleep, then tenderly lifted the baby and cradled him in her plump arms. To her mind, she was his rightful grandmother. The crickets chirped a lullaby, and familiar faces hovered just outside the door, oohing and ahhing as she possessively displayed the child. His mixed blood did not show, and she thanked the gods for that. With this war upon them, a Eurasian child would face especially cruel treatment. Unable to bear children of her own, Yufugawo now rocked this precious son, named after the uncle she had cared for as her very own flesh and blood.

And so, another generation had entered the world. Shizue nursed Max's healthy son at her breasts, dreaming of the day when his father would return to share her great joy. Her neighbors in the small farm community were ignorant peasants who considered Shizue a high-born intruder, and they gossiped about the new mother's modern ways. Shizue did observe their custom of carrying little Kimitake on her back in the *obui-himo*, a cloth wrap that secured him like an Indian papoose. This freed both her hands to do the chores between nursing him.

Kimi grew more handsome with each passing month. He was a well-behaved and smiling baby, quick to learn, and his large eyes dazzled her. Japanese eyes, but imbued with Max's charming twinkle, and they would always look straight at her as though he understood every word she spoke. Shizue wanted him to learn English and spoke it to him frequently. It was the language of his father, but it was also the language of the enemy, and when she took her growing son to the village marketplace, her voice drew angry looks from the peasants. She ignored them all, going about her business with dignity and pride.

At nine months, little Kimi began to resemble his father. He had inherited Max's strong-featured face, but that made him no less a Japanese to everyone else's eyes.

Working the farm helped to keep her mind off the war, and the seasons blended one into the other, uneventful except for her son's first wobbly attempt to stand and the miracle of his tiny voice speaking his first words. Paul visited infrequently, never able to stay for long. The war years were charted by little Kimi's birthdays. In July of 1944, he was two, and Paul visited the farm bearing gifts, arriving in a car powered by a charcoal-burning engine. According to Radio Tokyo, Japan was winning the war. But he knew differently. American bombers were devastating most every major port and city. The people had given these B-29 bombers a name of respect: B-*san*. For some unknown reason, the B-*sans* had not as yet struck over Nagasaki. But one had only to visit the city to observe the inevitability of Japan's defeat. Everything was in short supply and life there was hard. Gas was available only for military vehicles. Bicycles and charcoal-burning cars were the only civilian transportation on its virtually empty streets. With their men at war, women exchanged their kimonos and dresses for man-tailored blouses and baggy pants like the *mompei* Shizue now wore to work the farm.

While mothers toiled in the Mitsudara Munitions and Arms Works, the Nagasaki steel works, the colliery, and the torpedo factory, their children had been put to work in the busy freight yards. The entire civilian population of Japan was now being trained to help defend the mainland in the event of an Allied invasion. Air raid sirens wailed throughout Japan. Here and in other major cities, underground bomb shelters were being built. Fire wardens drilled the Japanese people day and night, and ever greater sacrifices were being asked of them. All for the glory of the empire. And while Radio Tokyo announced that the real shortages were in America, long lines of Nagasaki bicyclists rolled into the countryside every Sunday, willing to barter their valuables for food.

In his new post with the National Board of Information, Paul had access to a true account of the fighting. In the summer of 1944, the tide had turned against Japan. "Rather than sue for peace, our leaders are prepared to take desperate measures," he announced grimly.

"Not another word." Shizue refused to have her son's birthday party marred by a discussion of war. Here there was an abundance of fresh food on the family table, and she forbade the loved ones gathered around little Kimi to spoil this celebration by discussing their fears. But Douglas Napier and Inge were still unaccounted for, and Max was not there to watch their giggling son playing with his handmade wooden toys. Kimi stacked spelling blocks with a seriousness that made Paul laugh. Then Shizue sat him on a wooden horse on wheels, O-nami's gift, and O-nami got down on all fours to gently push the toy animal and its rider, whinnying and snorting as they circled the kitchen floor. O-nami tired, but Kimi clung to the wooden horse's neck, wanting more. Paul took a turn, leaning over on his cane and smiling. Shizue saw that his efforts caused him pain.

After a few minutes, she intervened. "That's quite enough, Paul," she said, pressing his arm. "Kimi must learn not to take advantage of those who love him." Paul's eyes welled with tears. He tried covering them with a smile, then reached down to massage his bad leg as if it were to blame.

Shizue could not remember when she had first recognized that his love for her went beyond that of a friend. Now, as their eyes met again, she smiled with pretended innocence, understanding how deeply it would wound him to know that his secret had been found out.

Lifting Kimi from the wooden horse, she groaned and said, "You're growing too heavy to be carried on Mommy's back. Let's bring out your birthday cake."

Yufugawo lit two candles centered on a rice cake. Shizue closed her eyes and made a birthday wish for her son. She puckered her mouth, then squeezed his chubby cheeks, hoping he would mimic her and blow out the candles. But her comical face only made him giggle, so she did the honors. Shizue looked at the smiling faces of those who had once been servants in her father's castle, where birthdays had always been celebrated with the "Happy Birthday" song. It had always been sung in English, and everyone now lifted their voices to sing "Happy Birthday" to little Kimi. Everyone clapped as Kimi pulled off his colorful paper hat and gleefully waved it up and down. Afterward, he sat sleepily on Shizue's lap as everyone around her grew sentimental and began talking of home. They were interrupted by the sound of a bicyle bell jangling on the path outside their door. It was the village postman.

"Mail at this hour?" O-nami questioned him.

"Army priority. For Mr. Ikeda," he announced.

The Ikedas' young son, Sato, had recently come of age. Soberly, his father read the letter aloud, which inducted his son into the army. He was an only child, and his mother mutely bowed her head. There would be no parade with buglers to march her handsome boy away. The next day he would report to the village for transportation to his new home at an army training barracks. Sato displayed a youthful eagerness as everyone wished him well. Those who had once been her father's servants were like a family to Shizue now. The war itself was her only enemy. She could not take sides against her own people, and she gave the young man a warm hug.

But with Sato's departure, Shizue's neutrality began to fall apart. Someone close to her was joining the millions who posed a threat to Max if he had been forced to serve against Japan. Every day Sato's mother bicycled to Nagasaki, moving through the streets with needle and bright red thread, gathering a thousand stitches on the strip of white cloth her son would be given to wear in battle. Shizue could not refuse the honor of adding the final stitch to his thousand-stitch belt, and yet her hands trembled with the needle and thread. The *sennimbari* might ward off enemy bullets and insure Sato's safe return home, but he would kill other men like Max, who would never return.

In the days that followed, she shared his parents' vigil, but her prayers were for Max alone. Little Kimi was her rock. In her heart she knew that his father was still alive. She was consoled by the belief that if he were dead, she would have sensed the loss.

Paul's work kept him in Tokyo. Shizue received a box of gifts, scarce items such as soap, coffee, wheat flour, and sugar. There was a bright-colored spinning top for Kimi. "All of you are in my thoughts. Love, Paul," he had written on a plain card. While Shizue gratefully accepted Paul's selfless devotion as a necessary expression of his love for her, she wished he would find someone else to love, a woman who could give him more than her gratitude.

Each Sunday hundreds of people bicycled to O-nami's farm, holding out silk kimonos, jewelry, and family antiques. They refused to be turned away. But the soil had been overworked. The sweet potato crops did not yield enough surplus to satisfy everyone's demands, and their fruit trees had to be guarded against pillagers. Of course, there had never been a market for their silk harvests, and there were no parts to repair the antiquated refrigeration pump when it finally gave out. Lacking modern storage facilities for the eggs that were gathered after the silkworm moth's seasonal mating, O-nami had been forced to fall back on primitive sericulture methods, which were unsuccessful. At last, he woefully had to accept the demise of their royal lineage. Nothing on his small farm went to waste, and it was a sad day when the mulberry trees were cut down to provide fuel for the next winter.

Evenings were spent around the radio, listening to the "Home and Empire" broadcasts over Radio Tokyo. Shizue would rock her son to sleep, weary of the monotonous toil and the waiting. Peace seemed no closer at hand.

As the autumn of 1944 approached, Japan's critical food shortage brought thousands of city children into the countryside. The government had developed a process for converting acorns into edible food. An emergency quota had been set, and the children came in droves, carrying baskets and combing the woods to help the war effort.

One afternoon, Shizue was feeding the chickens, when a group of these hungry children appeared on the road. She ran out to stop them, offering fresh vegetables that she had hastily stuffed inside a sack and the pockets of her baggy pants. She had not forgotten her own hunger pains, and she knew that children suffered the most. But soon her pockets were empty.

Yufugawo called to her, reminding her there were mouths to feed at home. Dark thunderclouds swirled ominously overhead, and Shizue swept little Kimi into her arms. "It's only fireworks," she assured him as lightning bolts flashed across the sky.

He covered his eyes and cried, "No, Mama, no!"

"Hush now, there's nothing to be afraid of." Her son had grown so fast. It still amazed her to hear him speak. He knew so many words in both English and Japanese and often jumbled the two together. In time he would sort them out, she thought, tickling his ribs to make him laugh at the thunder. "There, you see, it's just a big noise. The thunder god is having a grand time, banging on his ring of drums."

"Big bang," he said, giggling and pointing at the clouds.

The city children had moved on, but something was stirring up clouds of dust far down the road. Shizue wondered what it could be. Only bicycles and the neighbors' ox carts traveled this dirt road. Yufugawo urged her to come inside the house, but curiosity held her there, unaware that it had begun to drizzle.

Army trucks came into view. They were part of a long convoy. Horse-drawn wagons were spaced between the trucks, and armed troops marched alongside. People rode in the uncovered wagons. There was no room to sit, and they stood crowded together. From what she could see, they were all Caucasians. Prisoners of war. The first wagon carried American soldiers, whose uniforms were soiled and tattered. She handed Kimi to Yufugawo and hurried toward the convoy, thinking Max might be among the gaunt men she had glimpsed through the dust.

She almost shouted Max's name, but a Japanese sergeant ordered her to halt, and she became aware of the danger in drawing attention to herself. "Where are they being taken?" she asked calmly.

"Prison camp."

Her smile encouraged the sergeant to break ranks with his men. Wagonloads of civilian prisoners rolled along behind him. Her pulse raced as she asked, "Is it very far?"

"Not twenty miles by the main road. But work is being done on some bridge ahead, so we've been detoured through here. And now this rain."

The men and women rode in separate wagons. Suddenly, Shizue's heart skipped a beat. She saw Inge among the prisoners, and her legs nearly gave way to the shock. Inge drew a ragged scarf over her unkempt blond hair. How she had aged! Shizue thought. It took all of Shizue's willpower not to rush across the road to her. Raindrops rolled down the sunken hollows of Inge's cheeks like tears. As the wagon passed by, she looked directly at Shizue without seeing her. Shizue's shock had registered on her face, prompting the sergeant to question what she was staring at.

"They're all so thin," Shizue told him.

"Why waste food on the enemy?"

Breathlessly, Shizue watched the wagonloads of men, hoping she might find Douglas among them. All at once she saw him. He was pressed against the wooden railing of a wagon. But she had to stare at him a few moments to convince herself that this man was Max's father. His hair had turned completely white. The collar and sleeves of his shirt had been ripped off, and a handkerchief was knotted around his thin neck. His bare arms were emaciated, and his face was gaunt. Dark pockets hung under his lifeless blue eyes. Shizue could see that he was very ill, that it was an effort for him to breathe. Then he saw her standing there, and his eyes came alive while Shizue fought back tears.

"Douglas," she mouthed silently.

The shock of seeing Shizue triggered a seizure of hacking coughs. Two sturdier men riding with him asked those in the wagon to make room, then helped Douglas off his feet. He shrank from view.

Douglas had seen her, but not Inge, whose wagon had already turned from sight down a bend in the dirt road. "At the camp—are the men kept separated from the women?" Shizue asked of the sergeant, doing all she could to appear only mildly curious.

He laughed. "But of course. Contact between the sexes is strictly forbidden. What a question! These are prisoners of war, not guests of Japan on their way to a party. Even talking between them is forbidden."

"Silly of me to have asked," Shizue demurred, thinking how awful it was for her loved ones to be imprisoned together but kept apart, never touching, never speaking. The severity of their punishment tore her heart. But she could be of no help to them now.

"Tell me your name. Maybe I'll pass this way again."

"Shizue," she answered, pretending the dust had brought tears to her eyes.

"Shizue." He grinned as he hopped on the running board of the last truck in line. "A royal name, country girl, but it suits you well. *Sayonara!*"

Left standing in the rain, she realized it would take Paul's influence to gain entrance to the prison camp not twenty miles away. She was struck numb by the impact of seeing those she loved. It was obvious they had suffered harsh treatment, and conditions at their new camp were unlikely to be better. But they were found, and her eyes filled with tears. At last there was a ray of hope. Douglas had appeared to be so ill. He must have the proper medication, and how to obtain it obsessed her thoughts. What she risked by helping prisoners of war paled to her sense of duty.

First, she must contact Paul. None of the farms had telephones, and Shizue decided against using the one at the village post office. Gossip was the last thing she could afford.

At the dinner table that night, O-nami brought out a keg of homemade sake he had been saving for an auspicious occasion. The gods had caused the detour from the main road, he insisted. Otherwise Douglas Napier and his wife would not have passed his farm.

After they had toasted their good fortune, sadness prevailed over those seated around the table. Little Kimitake was too young to understand why his mother and the others were so sad. Shizue held him close, saying he would soon meet his grandfather. His *ogisan*. That night he learned to speak a new word, while his mother thought of her brother, a long time ago, lying in the isolation ward of the army hospital some miles down the main road from there. That painful memory suddenly pointed the way to how she might assist Douglas.

Bright and early the next morning, Shizue kissed her son good-bye. She had never left him before, and he cried as she pedaled off for Nagasaki. The bicycle she rode belonged to Sato, who now fought on the battlefront. Each day his parents anxiously waited for the postman, but so far no letter had come to quiet their fears. Mail was low on the army's priority list.

The miles to Shizue's destination were mostly a downhill coast through picturesque hills. She passed other bicyclists and horse-drawn wagons, but no motor traffic. The critical fuel shortage had given birth to the saying, "A drop of gasoline equals a drop of blood." Every ounce of metal went to the war effort, and bicycles were valuable property. Without one, Shizue would be trapped on the farm, and she carefully watched the paved road, swerving around potholes to avoid damaging the tires.

Nagasaki was a small gem of a city. One could easily walk through it, and strolling under the delicate cherry blossoms in spring remained a delightful experience one could still enjoy. That August, the American B-*sans* had disturbed its peaceful skies for the very first time. However, little damage was done, and the high-flying bombers had not returned again. It seemed, Shizue thought, that this city was to be spared the ravages suffered by Tokyo and Osaka.

Nagasaki meant "long valley." But actually there were two valleys nestled side by side and divided by mountainous ridges. The shortest valley was Nagasaki's densely populated downtown section of the old city, which now lay spread out to the right of Shizue as she pedaled along a winding lane. Soon the neighboring Urakami Valley unfolded just below her to the left. It was the longest valley, and the heart of Nagasaki's heavy industry beat loudly there. Hosokawa-Napier, Limited's, first weaving mill sat in the shadow of Lord Mitsudara's munitions and arms works. Seeing their stark facades again after so long a time rekindled the past.

Despite the smokestacks belching coal dust into the air, the sheltered valley offered a serene vista. Cows grazed in a field of clover, and there were small vegetable gardens behind the houses. Larger communal gardens were neatly laid out on plots of land, which created a bucolic atmosphere that offset the industrial ugliness. But the food grown here was barely enough to sustain the lives of those who worked the gardens.

Resting for a moment, Shizue looked down at the Urakami River. She could glimpse boys in bright-colored loincloths playing Find the Bell. On the narrow upper banks, they tossed a shiny bell into the water and, on the count of three, dived to search for it. The first boy to surface with the catch in hand was the winner.

Shizue walked her bicycle along the the northwestern slope of a hill to the army hospital, whose gray stone walls evoked another time of personal trial. She leaned her bike against a telephone booth and fished coins from the pocket of her baggy trousers.

Waiting for Paul to answer in Tokyo, she observed ambulances arriving with Japanese wounded. So many to be cared for—perhaps others like Kimitake, stripped of their limbs and in need of her gentle hands to ease their sufferings. She would visit Dr. Onogi, offering to volunteer her time, and in return she would ask him to help Douglas Napier.

"I was just thinking of you." Paul's warm voice sounded on the line. "Why are you crying? Is little Kimitake sick?"

"No, he grows bigger and more like Max with each passing day. Oh, Paul, I've seen Douglas." Drying her eyes, Shizue related everything, hardly taking a breath. "Paul, we can't allow your father to die. We can't allow him to suffer without hope. He's forbidden even to speak with his wife. Think what it would mean if I could visit with them, even for a short time each week. Your important friends can get me through the prison camp gates. In spite of everything, Douglas is part of my family. He was my father's closest friend. The Hosokawa name must still carry some honor. Say it's a matter of my honor. No harm can be done by allowing me to visit him. Oh, please help me."

There was a long silence, and when Paul spoke, his voice shook with emotion. "I'll find a way to get you inside the camp. I'm still owed some favors by those in command. But the rest is up to you. None of my contacts will directly assist a POW, and if they knew he's my father, it would only make things worse." He paused. "Now, listen carefully. It's dangerous smuggling food and drugs through the prison gates. Your pass will come from a high authority, and I doubt you'll be searched. But hide things well. Once you're inside, you'll need valuables to bribe the guards to look the other way. Even then, it'll take all the charm you can muster and a good deal of luck."

"Is there anything else I should plan for?"

"I'll give it some thought and put everything down in a letter. Obtaining the pass will take time. Make use of the time to prepare yourself." Paul heaved a sigh. "Shizue, put your son's welfare first. Be careful. You're no use to anyone if they imprison you with Douglas."

"Yes, I'll be careful. Bless you, Paul."

The rest was up to her, and Shizue's mission began that very morning. Dr. Onogi was only too glad to have her as a volunteer nurse. He offered her a cup of coffee, a rare treat, and spoke of when Kimitake had lain there suffering in the isolation ward. Dr. Onogi's exhaustion showed in the pockets under his eyes. He told her that most of the wounded being brought in were far worse off than those who had fought in China. His wards were grossly overcrowded and understaffed; many of the corridors were now cramped with the beds of dying soldiers and sailors. The navy hospital some miles distant was overflowing as well. The Nagasaki Medical College could not turn out doctors fast enough, and he was incapable of handling all the surgery himself. As a matter of necessity, he had obtained the assistance of an American army surgeon captured in the Philippines.

Shizue was put to work at once, assisting the American major. Dr. Haefele had sworn an oath to save lives, and as he made his rounds, his kindly face expressed a genuine compassion for his Japanese patients.

"The men we get here won't recover enough to fight again. I like to think that some Japanese doctor who's been taken prisoner is doing the same for our boys," he confided in a friendly tone as he lit the cigarette an amputee held in his remaining hand. "Yes, boys," he repeated. "Their faces get younger by the day, Shizue. Your fluency in English is a welcome surprise. For a moment there, I could've sworn I was making rounds with an American nurse."

Shizue saw no reason to hold back. Before the day was over, she had told Dr. Haefele a good deal about herself and was just beginning to explain Douglas's situation, when Dr. Onogi approached them in the corridor. Suddenly, she decided it was unwise to trust the Japanese surgeon. "Please keep this to yourself. I don't want him to think my work here is selfishly motivated." As the American doctor nodded, she knew she had found a friend. Others at the prison camp could be desperately in need of drugs, and his sympathetic blue eyes conveyed an unspoken promise of help for his own people.

"That old war horse with Dr. Onogi is Commander Sekino, head of this hospital and all forces in Nagasaki. Watch your step around him," Dr. Haefele warned her.

Shizue took an instant dislike to the swarthy commander. He was old enough to be her father, but the leer in his eyes made her skin crawl. After Dr. Onogi introduced him to her, Shizue quickly looked away from his lascivious grin. "Excuse me, but I must go before it gets dark. My little boy. Only two and it's his first day without me."

Commander Sekino bowed. "You are like a breath of fresh air in this gloomy place. We appreciate the time you have volunteered. If I can be of service to you and your family, please don't hesitate to ask."

The day Shizue had awaited was at last a reality. Her first journey to the prison camp had begun early that morning. The twenty-mile distance seemed like a hundred in the slow-moving ox cart driven by O-nami. Finally, she glimpsed watchtowers and barbed wire fences through the trees ahead. Yufugawo took charge of Kimitake as Shizue worried over being searched at the camp gates.

Paul had sent a letter with the official papers authorizing her to visit the camp once a week. His letter explained that she would not be permitted to enter the main compound, where Douglas and Inge were interred with the other prisoners of war. There a wall of barbed wire separating the men from the women. But husband and wife would be reunited for the time of her visit with them somewhere within the camp.

Paul's letter had helped Shizue to lay plans for this mission of mercy. O-nami would play an important role in the scheme, and he grew anxious when he slowed the cart to a stop.

Their arrival was expected. Many soldiers stood on duty at the outer gates. Shizue's gaze went to the guardhouse, then to the sign above the door to the commandant's office. A search would destroy her plans. Just two of the armed guards approached her, and Shizue handed her papers down to one of them, a corporal.

"Good morning. These are members of my family," she said cheerfully. "The papers say they're permitted to visit with me."

The corporal lifted his eyebrows, impressed by the high-ranking official who had signed her pass. "Open the gates. No need to search these people," he told his comrade. "Remain in the cart and follow us. The prisoners are waiting in a building not far from here. You will have one hour alone with them."

Yufugawo's eyes rolled skyward in silent thanks to the gods. "Have they been told of our visit?"

"*Hai,* the woman nearly swooned," said the corporal, tugging at the strap of his shouldered rifle. "We gave her water, and the man as well. Guarding enemy soldiers is one thing. But these civilians." He shook his head, lowering the visor of his cap against the sun. "What have they done, I ask myself?"

Shizue felt a sense of relief. This corporal seemed sympathetic. If the other soldiers were like him, it would aid her cause. O-nami guided the ox cart just behind their escort until the corporal signaled him to halt. The cart squealed to a stop near a shabby wooden building surrounded by a high barbed-wire fence.

The soldiers who had brought Douglas and Inge there lounged on the front steps, smoking cigarettes made of chopped hay. Tobacco could be obtained only by the privileged and those who could afford the black market price. There was no cigarette paper, and the soldiers had rolled their smokes in thin pages torn from a dictionary. This was boring duty, and they spoke of the war while the camp guards who had escorted the ox cart helped the women down politely.

"You have important connections in Tokyo, Hosokawa-*san*," the sympathetic corporal told Shizue. "No doubt you have brought gifts for the prisoners."

Shizue returned his friendly smile. Everything was hidden in the cart, and it would do no good to lie. "A few small gifts, yes."

"I must warn you, that is forbidden," he said. "But my comrades and I have needs as well."

That was what Shizue had hoped he would say, and she brought to bear all her charm. "I appreciate your kindness, Corporal. It should be rewarded. My friend, O-nami, has something in payment for you all."

"Then we can do business." He laughed and turned to nod at the other soldiers on guard, who grinned back, pleased.

Little Kimi clung tightly to his mother's neck, threatened by the bleak atmosphere. "Hush, soon you'll meet your grandfather. Now, I want you to give him a great big hug. But first we must make friends with these nice young men."

O-nami motioned for the corporal to step to the back of his cart. He had taken the precautions suggested by Paul and pushed aside the bed of hay, then lifted a board that concealed a wooden trough. In it were some of the city valuables that had been bartered for food at his farm. "I have this and other items of value to be exchanged in return for small favors," he said, and dangled a gold pocket watch on its chain. "You and your comrades have only to look the other way."

"*Hai*, we can't be held accountable for what we have not seen," the corporal replied, accepting the watch as a bribe. "There seems enough here to satisfy my comrades. Now show me what you are smuggling to the prisoners. I must pass judgment on what we risk."

O-nami removed other boards to expose what lay hidden in the cart's false bottom. "As you can see, my wife prepared a meal for them. There is some medicine, soap, and these cotton jackets."

"Fresh vegetables!" After pocketing a sweet potato, the corporal lifted the lids of two dinner pails and sniffed their aromas. "Ah," he sighed, "better than we are served in the mess. When you visit next, bring us a home-cooked meal, and cigarettes."

O-nami bowed. "As you wish, Corporal."

"Can we visit the prisoners now?" Shizue asked him.

"*Hai!* Let these people go inside, then come here and choose for yourselves."

Yufugawo took charge of the dinner pails, leaving the rest to be carried by her husband. "Can they be trusted?" she whispered.

"So long as we keep them happy," O-nami said under his breath, grinning and bowing at the guards.

Shizue anxiously climbed the steps with Kimi in her arms. One guard remained on watch just outside the building door.

Douglas did not hear Shizue enter. He had not held Inge in months. Since being brought there, the two had sat together on the bare springs of a rusty cot, locked in an embrace, sharing the love denied them for so very long.

"Douglas—Inge." Emotion choked Shizue's voice as she spoke their names.

"Shizue!" Seeing her and the child, Inge began to weep.

Douglas was simply too weak for a demonstrative display. Max's son stretched out his tiny arms and said, "*Ogisan.*"

"A grandson?" he gasped, struggling for breath. "What a joy!"

Shizue wept, unable to embrace both her loved ones at once. Then O-nami entered the building with Yufugawo, and tears streamed down their shocked faces.

"Ah, Douglas," sobbed Yufugawo. "The gods have led us back to you. How you must have suffered."

O-nami came forward, wanting to embrace his old friend. But his arms were filled with gifts, and Douglas was like a twig he feared might snap in two. "We have brought food. Come, Douglas, sit here at this table. Both of you must eat."

Barely able to stand on his own, Douglas leaned on Shizue's arm while his grandson clung to his pant leg, giggling.

"Your child is so beautiful." Inge found the strength to lift Max's son and held him tightly. "All these long months without word of you— without hope. Max—what has become of him?"

"Max left Japan on the day of Pearl Harbor," Shizue told her. "Oh, there's so much to say. I don't know where to begin." She was hysterical with joy. There was not room enough at the small wooden table for everyone to sit there, nor enough chairs. "Please, have something to eat. It will give you strength. I need a moment to gather my thoughts. Then I'll tell you everything."

Seated at the table, Douglas buried his face in his hands while she related what Paul had learned about Max on the dock at Yokohama. "Safe. Both my sons are safe. Thank God."

O-nami dragged the rusty cot near the table, where Douglas at last

regained enough composure to eat the food Yufugawo set before him and
Inge. Both ate slowly, their eyes darting from face to face and welling with
tears. Shizue did her best to tell them everything of the events leading up
to that happy moment of their reunion. Little Kimi had instantly taken a
shine to his grandfather and was now curled up in Douglas's lap, yawning
drowsily.

Douglas reached across the table to take Inge's hand. In the course of a
single hour, they felt as though they had been exhumed from the grave.
"Long ago, our army interrogators told us of the baron's suicide. But until
now I'd hoped it was just another lie added to the case against us."
Learning the truth from Shizue had hit him hard, and he stared off into
space for a time. "I'll always remember your father as I last saw him, on
your wedding night. That night we dissolved our partnership and sat
together until dawn, wondering what the years had meant. My grandson
has given meaning to everything in the past. If Max is fighting in this war,
may God protect him," he said in a voice drained of breath. "I've never
been a religious man, but I've prayed a lot over these past years. I'm
deeply moved by Paul's intervention on our behalf. Tell me more about
him. Is he well? Does he still live alone? Or has he found someone? I've
prayed he would find a woman to give him love."

"No," Shizue answered sadly, "he lives alone—still lives for his work.
He's well, except for his leg. That pains him, but Paul hides it from us. He
hides most of his feelings, Douglas." She wondered if helping his father
was purely an act of Paul's love for her or if it expressed a forgiveness of
sorts. No matter, Douglas's spirits were uplifted, and she silently gave
thanks for that. "He's grown very close to Kimi. Paul gives Kimi all his
love. Whenever they're together it brings him joy, and I feel so much
closer to Max. But Paul's visits to us are rare."

"It's hard to believe I'm a grandfather. Kimi's so big and healthy."

Inge's face showed concern. "Too heavy for you, Douglas."

"Yes, but a wonderful heaviness." He passed the boy to her, mussing
Kimi's hair in the warmly affectionate way he had done to Max.

Douglas looked from Shizue to Yufugawo and O-nami. "Being with
you again is a blessing. The other prisoners aren't so fortunate. Each day is
an uphill battle against despair."

O-nami tugged on his topknot and asked, "What is it like for you
here, Douglas?"

"Lonely, old friend. We have no contact with the military prisoners.
The men are segregated from the women by a barbed wire fence strung
across the civilian compound. Every morning we're assembled for roll call
and must go through the ritual of bowing before our captors. Many of us
were forced to labor in the coal mines," he said. "I'm not the only one
whose lungs were infected by the dust. It's worse at night. The huts are
cold, the blankets thin. Sometimes we're given a few sticks of wood for
the stove. Anything you bring us will be shared. We share everything in
order to survive. Our diet is mostly soup made of kitchen slop."

Inge's stomach growled loudly. "The meal you brought us. We are not used to such a feast." Kimi put his ear against her stomach and giggled. The intimacy between them quelled her tears. "At this camp, only the strongest are put to work. The rest of us sit and wait, praying for peace. If Japan loses, those who survive will be used as hostages to bargain with at the peace table. If not for this, I think we would all be put to death."

Shizue shivered. "Let's not speak of death. I'll need blood samples from you both." The American doctor had given her explicit instructions. She drew blood samples into the hypodermic syringes she had concealed in her pockets, then took their temperatures and had them spit on glass slides that would be studied under his microscope at the hospital. Dr. Haefele had agreed with Shizue that it was unwise to trust his Japanese colleague. If approached for help, Dr. Onogi was likely to give them away, so Dr. Haefele had devised a clever scheme for borrowing from the hospital drug supplies. She kept these concerns to herself. "This is a sulfa drug to treat any general infection you might have," Shizue told Douglas and Inge. "The American doctor said that both of you are probably anemic. Until he's analyzed your blood, take these pills with the sulfa."

"Can you help the other prisoners?"

"Douglas, I'll do what I can. We've bribed the guards. They're sympathetic, but I'm afraid what we have to give them in return isn't enough for them to risk very much. I'm grateful for whatever they'll allow you to smuggle inside the main compound. We'll have to concentrate on bringing you back to health, and I'll try helping those with you who are most in need."

"We understand." Inge put one hand on Douglas's cheek. "To touch you again. How I have longed for that. Now I will live for the next visit between us, and soon you will grow strong with Shizue's help."

Shizue wanted to bundle them up in her arms and carry them safely away. "Douglas, take these cards. They're medical questionnaires printed in Japanese, but you can translate it for the others. Next week, I'll bring cards for Inge to take into the women's compound."

Her eyes went to the closed door. "Oh, there's so little time left us. Bring the jackets, O-nami. Clothing is hard to come by. It's the best I could find." She helped Douglas put on a blue cotton work jacket with pockets large enough to hold the few essentials she had smuggled in. Inge put on a similar garment. "I've laundered the jackets many times to make them look worn and old. The guards waiting outside won't search you. But can you safely get past the others guarding the compound?"

"They hardly look at us," said Inge, helping Douglas to button up his jacket. "To them we are nothing."

"Inge is right," Douglas assured her. "They've no reason to suspect anything when the guards you bribed escort us to our barracks. The jacket will keep me warm at night." He brought Shizue close. "Tell Paul how grateful I am."

"Your hour is up," announced the corporal who appeared at the door.

He was winding the stem of his new gold watch. "Clear the table well and leave nothing behind. The commandant is sure to inspect here once you have gone."

Douglas and Inge kissed before they were escorted from the building. Shizue watched them move together up a dirt path to the barbed wire gate, where husband and wife were torn apart. All too soon they were lost to sight along separate paths that crossed a field of tall brown grass.

"Will you be on duty when we visit next week?" she asked the corporal.

"I will make a point of it, Hosokawa-*san*." He smiled and helped her to board the cart, then hoisted Kimi from the ground. "A handsome boy. One day you will make a fine soldier. Here, go to your mother."

"*Arigato*. Have you children of your own?"

"Two boys, four and six years," said the corporal. "They are with their mother in Osaka. She works in a factory there, while I am left to rot in this place."

"It must be lonely for you." Shizue stroked her son's hair, thinking she had made a friend in this smiling young soldier. As he escorted them to the main gates, she knew that entering there again would not be such a trial.

"Until next week," Shizue said, waving good-bye.

"Don't forget to bring that meal you promised us, big fellow," he called to O-nami. "And cigarettes!"

"*Hai*, cigarettes!" O-nami forced himself to laugh. "Ah, I cannot wait to put this awful place on the road behind us," he complained to his wife.

The cart rolled toward freedom while Shizue looked back at the prison camp gates, tears streaming down her face. Once each week her visits would allow Douglas and Inge to share an hour together, she thought, cradling her sleepy-eyed son. "You've made *ogisan* very happy today. He loves you very much."

Yufugawo fanned herself. "Ah, I was so terrified. Now it would seem we are welcome. Poor Douglas. I thought I would faint when I saw him."

Autumn had come early. The ox cart started for home beneath a shower of yellow leaves, while Yufugawo bemoaned the fate of those imprisoned at the camp.

Shizue watched the wind scatter the leaves across the hilly road that slowed the oxen to a crawl. This primitive means of transportation had allowed her to smuggle drugs and food to her loved ones, she thought. Her mission could not continue without O-nami's ox cart and without the bicycle she rode to the hospital each day. Now she worried over the tires of her bicycle, which had already begun to wear thin. New ones were impossible to come by, even on the black market. Commander Sekino had repeated his offer to be of service. But what might he ask in return? she wondered. He eyed her like a hungry animal, popping up when she least expected him and watching her every move. Perhaps she could handle Commander Sekino with a beguiling smile.

CHAPTER 40

Port Moresby and Milne Bay. Buna and Lae. General MacArthur's forces continued to push on through the Vitiaz Strait to the Admiralties, and Max's intelligence unit had seen action with them. Hollandia and the Vogelkop became pins stuck in the battle map for Allied victory. One after another, the heavy convoys had stretched out as far as the eye could see: great battleships and aircraft carriers zigzagging stem to stern, maneuvering to avoid detection.

On nights before the battles, Max would pass among the men, who were writing what could be their last letters to loved ones at home and saying their last prayers. He had lost his innocence long ago, while having to scramble for his life as the sea exploded into roaring geysers, the ship's decks around him splintered by Japanese shelling from the air. Once ashore, his eyes no longer turned away from the American dead washed up on the bloody beaches, littered with shelled-out LSTs and amphtracks. Mop-up operations were thorough, and he had been spared a kill-or-be-killed confrontation with the enemy. But Max kept his holstered .45 clean. And as the corpses piled up steadily before his eyes, that virgin piece of metal grew heavier against his hip, testing his vow never to draw the blood of his Japanese brothers.

Morotai was to be the final springboard for MacArthur's drive across the central Pacific. Soon after dawn, Max and Avery Bullock stood aboard the general's flagship, the *Nashville*, waiting for the show to begin.

At first light the target beachheads had been obscured by clouds, but now the clouds had rolled back, and the first assault wave of landing crafts spread out from their mother ships. They were like black dots streaming comet tails of white foam. Max had not slept in forty-eight hours. The latest Japanese code had been tough to crack, but it yielded some vital last-minute information about the enemy's positions on Morotai. Now his cryptologists slept below decks, deaf to the steady whine and awesome roar of naval artillery fire. Battleships heaved on their broadsides, recoiled then heaved again under the force of their steaming cannons. Air support squadrons joined the bombardment. Dark clusters of P-51's and Thunderbolts peeled off through the black puffs of Japanese ack-ack, swooping low to plant their bombs. So far, it appeared that earlier intelligence reports had been accurate. Morotai was inadequately garrisoned. The Japanese had little to throw against them, virtually no air power at all.

The silver oak leaves of a lieutenant colonel shone on Avery Bullock's khaki lapels. Max wore captain's bars, his reward from Douglas MacArthur, who enjoyed chatting with him from time to time. They shared a knowledge and respect for the Japanese people, which had made serving under the man easier for Max to bear. Now MacArthur stood above them on the captain's bridge. He wore a gold braided cap and drooping sunglasses. A corncob pipe hung from the corner of his mouth. Someone handed him reports that had been radioed in from his initial task force, and MacArthur's somber face broke into a rare smile.

"Just look at the old man, itching to set foot on shore." Avery puffed his own corncob pipe, a present from the general. It looked rather silly in Avery's mouth, and Max regarded his friend with an amused grin. "Better get some sleep while we can."

"Too overtired to sleep."

Sergeant Tuttle waddled into view. "Word is we'll be landing before long, sir!" His expression was queasy as the ship listed in the wake of a passing aircraft carrier. Tuttle removed his helmet quickly, then heaved up over the rail.

"Don't wake the men until it's been confirmed," Max said, patting Tuttle's shoulder. The poor guy had yet to get his sea legs. Max had taken a liking to the pot-bellied sergeant. Tuttle had a knack for requisitioning the essentials, which kept their outfit running smoothly in the chaos they usually found after landing ashore. "Get down to sick bay and let the doc fix you up. Can't do without you, Sergeant."

When the order came to move out, Max scrambled down the rope netting lowered to one of a dozen LSTs. There were no tops on these steel landing crafts, and it was like stepping into a caldron. The tropical sun blazed directly overhead, and his men crouched together, some rereading the tissue-paper-thin V-mail from home, others, like Avery Bullock, pulling out wallet snapshots of their wives and kids. Avery's wife, Jen, had given birth to a baby girl, and Max responded with a sweaty grin, glancing away from the baby pictures he had seen countless times.

The naval bombardment had ended. Waves slapped against the open hull of the LST, an eerie echoing sound in the silence. Nearing shore, Sergeant Tuttle hit the wheel of the company Jeep with his fists, bellowing a groan of relief while the LST landing ramp opened to slam down in shallow water. Max and Avery got into the Jeep and were thrown back in their seats as Tuttle stepped on the gas, showering them all in his rush for dry land.

Troops of the XI Corps were engaging the enemy farther inland. Max could distinguish the peculiar burping noise made by Japanese machine guns from the sharp staccato reports of American small arms fire. They rode past Japanese dead lying among burning palm trees. The jungle was foggy with their smoking stench. A logistics officer halted the Jeep. Teary-eyed from the smoke, he had knotted a wet handkerchief around his forehead. He pointed out the safest route to an evacuated Japanese airstrip. "Temporary GHQ being set up there, Colonel."

"Taken any prisoners?" Max asked.

"You kidding? These goddamn Japs don't give up. They keep coming at you until they're cut in half or their fucking heads are blown off. Keep an eye peeled for snipers!"

His statement was not an exaggeration. Japanese clutching unpinned grenades buried themselves in the sand as human mines, who were blown to bits with their unsuspecting enemy. They burrowed into caves and were put to the torch by flamethrowers rather than face the dishonor of surrender.

Max's stomach churned. Each island taken revealed worse horrors than the one before. Wholesale suicide was becoming Japan's most effective weapon. But there would be prisoners, and he would give them cigarettes and share his memories of their motherland. His Japanese captives would either fabricate stories or refuse to speak a word. But interrogation was an art. His cleverly framed questions spared them loss of face while he got at the truth by reading their silences. Although he took no direct hand in the killing, what he learned had led others to do the dirty work for him. But often his intelligence-gathering had helped save lives on both sides, and so he learned to live with the double standard. Perhaps the prisoners taken on Morotai or the next island could tell him things that would quicken the end of this abominable massacre.

A mop-up squad was extinguishing the collapsed remains of the airstrip supply dump. Fallen coconuts in the debris exploded like popcorn. Zero fighter planes sat off the runway, torn apart by P-51's before the Japanese could get them airborne. The airstrip ended at a shady jungle cul-de-sac. Two squat wooden shacks were all that remained of the enemy camp.

"First come, first served! Let's requisition 'em, sir," Tuttle exclaimed, swerving past an infantry platoon on the march.

Suddenly shots rang out. A sniper hidden among the treetops sprayed the area, and everyone within range scattered for cover. Max leapt from the Jeep just as bullets ripped into the imprint of his sweating back, which had been left on the upholstery. He rolled behind some oil drums.

Avery hit the dirt beside him. "Got his sights set on the brass."

"Closest I've come to packing it in." Max tried to laugh. He had unholstered his .45 without realizing it and spotted the sniper's roost high in the palms near a radio shack. But his finger froze on the trigger. Sergeant Tuttle squeezed off a volley that toppled the sniper, who somersaulted, his rifle blasting away before he crashed into the dense foliage. The fall alone was enough to kill him. Max's gaze shifted to the radio shack. He could hear the tapping of the wireless key. Someone was sending a coded message. "Do you hear that, Ave?"

"Yeah, our sniper wanted to buy the operator time."

Max ran for the shack. "No grenades. I want him taken alive!" His shout came a split-second too late, and he fell to the ground, shaken by the blast. A second grenade was lobbed through the smoking door. These battle-wise troops were taking no chances. As they charged inside, their bullets swept the hut for anything left alive.

When Max entered, the Japanese operator's code book was on fire. Attempting to smother the flames, Max burned his hands. "Shit! What's that clutched in his hand?"

"Looks like a map, sir."

Max blew on his burns as he examined the crudely drawn map, which showed the way to some underground caves. The dead man was a signal corps officer, probably intelligence. "His unit must've fallen back to these caves, but you'd have to know the island to find them," he told Avery. "If his message got through, they'll know all about us. This double line could be another airstrip."

"I'll check it out. Tend to those burns."

By sundown, the area had been swept clean and tents were raised for housing. They were lit by chugging gas generators that competed with the jungle's loudening voice. Its nocturnal inhabitants had come out of hiding in the coolness of night, and mosquitoes were a constant source of annoyance. Max swatted them with his bandaged hands while dining with Avery Bullock in the officer's mess. They listened to Tokyo Rose on the radio. Her broadcasts were aimed at demoralizing the Allied troops with false claims about Japan's superior might and interviews with prisoners who bore false witness to her lies, no doubt held at gunpoint while they performed. But she was listened to more as entertainment. The propaganda was laced between phonograph records from the States. Glenn Miller, the Dorsey band, and that night the crooning tones of Carol Landis floated through the mess tent putting everyone into a wistful mood.

Oh, give me something to remember you by
When you are far away from me.
Some little something meaning love cannot die,
No matter where you chance to be.
Though I'll pray for you, night and day for you,
It will see me through like a charm
Till you're returning.

The lyrics brought Max close to Shizue, and he thought of the *omamori* he had given her to remember him by. Avery's eyes were moist, as he stared off through the smoke of his corncob pipe.

"Now I have some news for all you homesick GI's."

Tokyo Rose's silky voice mentioned the assault by the XI Corps on

Morotai, claiming they had sustained heavy losses and would be pushed back into the sea.

"Talking through your hat, Rosey," Avery sounded off. "Pushed into the sea, that's a laugh. Eleven Corps losses have been light. No small thanks to our teamwork, Max."

"Prisoners being brought in, Colonel," Sergeant Tuttle announced.

Max regarded the sergeant wearily. "What condition are they in?"

"Shot up, but ambulatory, sir." Tuttle slapped the back of his neck. "Friggin' mosquitoes. Sneak up on you like Japs and bite like hell."

"Japanese," Max corrected him irritably.

"Call 'em what you will, sir, but they're still the enemy."

About thirty Japanese marched toward the interrogation tent, noncoms patched up by the medics. They had already been searched for concealed weapons. Those who could put both hands on their heads while Tuttle emptied the contents of their pockets into manila envelopes.

Avery and Max stood at the door of the tent. "Well, Max, maybe they can tell you something about that map you found."

As Avery addressed Max, one of the prisoners stiffened. The light coming from the tent was poor, yet Max glimpsed what could have passed for a smile on a Japanese sergeant's face. The prisoner's head and one eye were bandaged, so Max could not see much of his face before he was herded with the others into a circle on the open ground, where he sat looking straight ahead.

Max settled behind his field desk in the interrogation tent, scrutinizing that sergeant's personal affects. Snapshots, wrinkled letters from home, Army ID—bits of a soldier's life and clues to his personality. Koichi Okamura was a familiar name, and the snapshots from his wallet rang bells. "Aye, these people worked for Shizue's father!"

Sergeant Okamura was the grandson of Baron Hosokawa's revered head gardener. Max recalled Koichi cutting flowers for Shizue to place at her mother's garden shrine on the day the newlyweds bid everyone goodbye.

He asked Tuttle to bring Sergeant Okamura into the tent. Wearily Koichi got to his feet. Seeing Max Napier had shocked him. He knew that Shizue and her husband had been separated because she had returned home alone to bury her dead. Then there had been an extensive army search for the American. Now he and Max were enemies, Koichi thought, stiffening as he walked inside the tent.

Warily he accepted the cigarette Max offered him along with an excited barrage of questions. Max pounded his shoulders as if the two were long-lost friends. "*Hai*, much has happened since you left Japan. But I am sworn to tell you nothing. I do not hate you, Napier-*san*. But we kill each other now," he confessed bitterly, on the verge of tears. "Why do we kill each other?"

"Because we don't know any better. Koichi, this war has nothing to do with how we feel about each other and those waiting for us to return home." Desperate to break through, Max brought out his own wallet. Unlike Avery, he rarely displayed his snapshots of Shizue. It was all he had of her, and he would save up the moments before looking at them once again in a privacy that could not be shared. One browning snapshot dated to their childhood: he and Shizue posed in the castle stables grooming their twin colts, watched over by a youthful O-nami. "Look at these, Koichi. I've known your grandfather all my life. We're family."

"*Hai*, but at war. How is a man to separate the two?"

"By remembering what came first. How it was between us all. How it will be again, when we both go home."

Koichi gazed at the snapshots taken in the gardens he had once so reverently tended beside his grandfather. This smiling captain was Shizue's husband, a member of the Hosokawa clan his family had served for generations.

"My friend." Koichi wept and embraced Max. The contact brought him closer to home as well, and suddenly he could not tell it all fast enough. Tragic news of Baron Hosokawa following his son in seppuku. Shocking news of the lands being confiscated, of Shizue's arrest, and of the Napiers being arrested in Kobe, charged wth espionage. "Shizue was quickly taken away to the Urakami Prison in Nagasaki. Of course, none of us believed those disgraceful charges that you had spied against Japan. Ah," he sighed, exhaling smoke, "but the officer sent to arrest her would not hear the truth. She was accused of helping you. Accused of treason. O-nami tried to defend her and was ordered to leave the land by nightfall. He told us that your father was forced to sign a confession to helping some unfortunate people in need far across the seas, but that this was not a crime against Japan. He and Yufugawo went to Nagasaki to be near the baron's daughter—to help free her from prison there if they could. Only the peasants who farmed the silk remained on the land. Everyone who served the household was ordered to leave at a moment's notice. Some went to live with relatives in other provinces. My own family went south to Kagoshima in hopes of finding work in the factories. I was taken into the army soon afterward, and they put a rifle in these hands that are better suited to pruning shears."

Max sat before Koichi, stunned. This was not the uplifting news of home he had hoped for, and the old gardener's grandson somberly paced the wooden floor of the tent on his split-toed jungle *tabi* shoes, unable to answer for what had happened to those he had left in Japan years before. "But you must've heard something in letters about Shizue, my dad?"

"No. My family was afraid to become involved. It shames me, but they were afraid to inquire about Shizue. They feared O-nami might have been arrested as well for attempting to help her." Koichi sank in the chair, a tear of blood running from his bandaged eye. "Since the fighting grew worse, few letters have reached me. They tell us we will win this war. But I think not." His bandaged head dropped to his chest. "I am sorry to be the bearer of such bad news," he said in a pained voice. "I have no more to tell of those waiting for our return, Max-*san*."

A numbing depression held Max silent as he considered the worst. After Pearl Harbor, the Japanese military were drunk on power and, to suit their lust for blood, they must have twisted any evidence found on Douglas when he was arrested. Max reasoned that brutal methods had been used to obtain his father's and Inge's confessions to helping Europe's Jews. But that would not carry the death penalty, and they had nothing else to confess even under torture. Espionage charges would have carried a sentence of death, but there was no real evidence to support it against them or Shizue. He breathed a little easier, feeling sure Paul must have rescued her by calling upon the important people who owed him favors. Granted a fair trail and a good defense attorney, her innocence would have been proved with the truth. The facts of her case would also have exonerated Douglas and Inge. Max clung to faith in Paul's abilities to make use of what powers he had earned and in the faith that some justice still prevailed in war-torn Japan.

Koichi groaned. "I feel there is metal in my head from one of your grenades."

"Sergeant Tuttle, have the medics see to this man again and get him something to eat." Max pressed a pack of cigarettes into Koichi's hand. "Take these."

"No, I will lose face with my comrades. Do not show that you know me, Max-*san*. Do not treat me better than them."

"All right." Had he been just another prisoner, Max would have grilled him about the map. Now he could only thank his friend by treating him as the enemy. "Dammit, Ave." He turned to his friend, who had remained quietly in the background listening for all this time. "It was better not knowing anything about home," he said.

Avery put his hand on Max's shoulder. "Buck up, it's ancient news at best. One man's version of what took place a long time ago."

"You're right. The situation could have improved since then." Max paced away and shared his reasoning. "At best, Shizue would have been exonerated in a fair trial. Or the serious charges against her might have been reduced to serving a sentence in that Nagasaki prison. At best, my dad and Inge wouldn't be punished with more than confinement in some internment camp for the duration," he decided. "Yes, I'm sure all three of them are still alive."

"That's the spirit. Trust the Japanese reverence for nobility. If Shizue's in prison, she's probably being treated better than most. Ditto for your folks, with your resourceful brother pulling the right strings." Avery soberly lit his pipe, visibly moved by thoughts of his elderly missionary parents imprisoned on mainland Japan. They had no friends in high places. "Well, let's get back to work."

Max had no presence of mind for interrogating the prisoners, and Avery did most of the work. Enough was learned to plan a daylight raid against the Japanese, who had gone underground in caves near their well-camouflaged airstrip. Sergeant Tuttle marched the prisoners away.

"I'd say what's ailing you calls for a liberal drop of the brew flown in by our accommodating C-47 pilots," Avery quipped, uncorking a whiskey bottle. "We'll drink to another beachhead fought and won. Remember that every pin on the battle map narrows the distance to home. Cheers, you old moose."

"Cheers," Max echoed half-heartedly.

The jungle was peaceful now that the killing had stopped. Attempting to drown his fears of the unknown, Max helped his army buddy polish off a fifth of Jim Beam. He got very drunk and very depressed. Staring into his mess-kit cup, he mourned the dead left buried on the Hosokawa lands Shizue had been forced to leave. As his wife, she was legally an American citizen, and now he faced the harsh reality that even found innocent of treason she would not be set free.

Max took a drunken walk alone, sick with fear of losing his family ones before the final shot was fired. Somehow he would manage to be among the first wave of troops to occupy Japan. His thoughts shot forward in time to when the countless thousands being held in Japan's prison camps would be repatriated. Listing and processing them all could take months, and finding his family would not be easy. One thing surfaced as a certainty: Shizue would not be waiting for him at home in the castle gardens.

He leaned against a palm tree and imagined Shizue's face materializing from out of the steamy jungle mist. She might still be locked up in the Nagasaki prison. Max had a terrible vision of his wife, both her hands grasping the bars of her cell, her large eyes staring into space as she wondered what had become of him.

Listening to the restless surf pounding against yet another bloody beachhead, Max struggled with the question of Paul's willingness to forgive and forget. He knew that Paul would have done his utmost to aid Shizue, but he did not know if Natsu's son would be willing to help their father.

Drunkenly, he turned back toward his tent, passing the small barbed wire compound that contained the Japanese prisoners. Since Max could not give Koichi special treatment, he had the guards pass out Lucky Strikes to everyone and showed equal concern for each man while inquiring about his wounds. His sympathy gained their trust and respect. Koichi smiled at him because the others smiled. Destiny had crossed their paths, but many battles were yet to be fought and won before the two men found their ways home.

Some weeks following the victory at Morotai, Max and his outfit were put aboard General MacArthur's flagship, cruising seas so choppy that Max felt sick. By contrast, Avery was chipper and clear-eyed, adding his pipe smoke to the already smoky briefing room as MacArthur discussed future strategy. Rather than launch an invasion against the heavily garrisoned island of Mindanao, he intended to outsmart the Japanese by bypassing it and taking the Leyte Gulf instead, thus severing the enemy's supply lines and paving his way back to the Philippines.

This vain old soldier wore his thinning hair parted low and slicked down across his narrow skull to cover what he could. On the surface he seemed superior and cold, but when he spoke of the men who would be lost in liberating the Philippines, his dark eyes softened. After the session, he held Max and Avery for a brief chat.

"You've earned another citation for a job well done, gentlemen," MacArthur informed them, looking toward the wall of battle maps decorated with colored stickpins. "Yes, losses would have been heavier if not for your fine work. Avery has told me of your chance encounter with a familiar face from home, Max. I can understand how such moving news of your wife and family must have added to your concern over them."

"Yes, sir. I can only hope our victories will soon bring this killing to an end."

"We share a personal stake in the outcome of this war." In a rare emotional display, Douglas MacArthur took Max by the shoulders. "Those we care about have not lost faith in our return. Our souls and our destinies are rooted in this hemisphere, Captain Napier. Mine in the Philippines and its noble people. Yours in Japan, where your family is waiting to be liberated from tyranny. Tyranny is the enemy of all mankind. That's what we're fighting to purge the world of, and I pray it can be accomplished without sustaining greater losses than can be endured by either side." His voice broke.

Just then an aide handed him the latest casualty totals of his fighting forces in the Pacific, and his impeccable posture sagged. "Good morning, gentlemen."

Max followed Avery's lead, feeling stressed to the breaking point over the unknown fates of his loved ones. He glanced back at the aging general, who bore the enormous responsibility of the fates of tens of thousands serving under him. He alone was responsible for deciding when and where to risk their lives next. "How can MacArthur stand up under the stress of supreme command?" Max wondered aloud.

"The old man thrives on it," said Avery. "Watching his men die is what gets him down. He keeps a running total of fatalities in his head, and every victory is a disaster so far as that's concerned."

Walking to the ward room for coffee, Max asked. "Ave, any thoughts about what you'll do after the war?"

"Pick up where I left off. Teach, have more kids. Hopefully live to a ripe old age and quietly pass on in my sleep never knowing what hit me. Asking too goddamn much of life can only lead to ulcers, disappointment, and an early grave." He judged Max's consternation with a disarming smile. "Yes, I'd like the feel of silk shirts and the wheels of fancy cars. But I wasn't born with a silver spoon in my mouth, Captain."

"Since you've stooped low enough to remind me of that, I'll suffer the insult with dignity." He saluted. "Fuck you very much, Colonel." Avery laughed, and Max yanked the corncob pipe from his hand, threatening to ditch it over the side. "Bastard, if not for you I'd be in Germany, driving up Hitler's ass with Patton."

"Don't bother thanking me for dragging you along in the right direction. Wienerschnitzel or Shizue? Can't have them both, ingrate!"

Max soberly handed back Avery's pipe, no longer amused by the friendly banter. "It's damn hard living on hope. MacArthur's push to the Philippines is a detour that'll cost us time."

"Better than being bogged down in a battle we might not win." Avery adjusted his sunglasses and struck a MacArthur-like pose with the pipe. "Tell you what. When we reach the Philippines, I'll put you in for major."

"Looking to pin chickens on your collar?"

"Hell, yes. More benefits for Jen and the kid."

"I'm too young to be a major."

"I'm too young to be a colonel. But it's a young man's war."

"Guess so," Max allowed, scratching his mosquito bites. The tropical sun had frosted his hair and eyebrows white. He contemplated growing a mustache to add some maturity to his youthful face, then observed how little it accomplished for Avery and dismissed the notion.

That day he felt far older than he looked, and he wondered how the years had changed the faces of his father, Inge, and his young bride. Suddenly he felt the need to comfort himself with the old snapshots he carried in his wallet. Its leather was cracked and stained by sweat. Avery walked on as Max stood alone at the ship's rail, gazing down at the faces preserved in brittle peeling celluloid envelopes. He could not remember when this wallet was shiny and new or if he had carried it while fleeing Germany. He could not account for how the bits of sand had found their way inside its folds or to which beachhead they belonged. Wind claimed them like grains of time. The commander-in-chief's flagship pitched and yawed in choppy seas, and the whitecaps stretched on to the unending Pacific horizon, where Kyushu's wave-battered shores remained a distant memory.

General MacArthur's timetable for victory had been stalled by the forces of nature. Rain slowed the construction of airstrips, while Max spent his twenty-fifth birthday sloshing through the rain-soaked marshes of Leyte Island. Now the long months of delay were behind him, and MacArthur had just struck at Okinawa, Japan's last stronghold of defense against an invasion of the islands and only a stone's throw from the Hosokawa ancestral lands.

For once Max's unit had not been in at the start of the show. Approaching from the air, he could see nothing of the ongoing battle. The island was sixty miles long and blanketed under murky clouds. *Angel in Blue* was splashed across the nose of his landing C-47, and ground crews waved at the gorgeous blonde painted below its cockpit. Parked along the airstrip were other transport and fighter planes that had also been personalized by their pilots and crews with catchy names and brightly colored cartoons. It was a morale booster that broke the monotonous gray-green Okinawa terrain.

Disembarking, he realized he was standing at the crossroads to home. Then a torrential downpour suddenly struck. The covered Jeep was not five yards away, but Max and Avery were soaked through before they ducked inside. "Manila was paradise compared to this."

"Yeah," Avery sullenly agreed. "Our two weeks R and R there wasn't enough to recharge the old batteries."

On this wet afternoon in April, 1945, Japan no longer had any air force left to speak of. The better part of its army and fleet had been destroyed. After Leyte, the Imperial Navy had limped off like a scraggly wolfpack, its leaders destroyed or maimed, while lesser vessels tracked the Allied scent, howling threateningly and snapping at their heels. Desperation had given birth to a new weapon—the kamikaze. Japanese pilots strapped at the controls of flying bombs had become a horrifying version of Hitler's V-2 rockets. Flying over the ships anchored in one of Okinawa's deep-water bays, Max had witnessed gun crews drilling in preparation to repel a kamikaze attack. The morning before they had come in droves, destroying thirty U.S. ships. For every suicide bomber blown to pieces, two or three others got through. Even here, somewhere in the middle of the island, everyone eyed the sky nervously.

Once again he and Avery were billeted in a tent. Sergeant Tuttle poked around inside it like a mother hen. "Leak," he pointed out cryptically and slid one cot away from the drip. "I'll get it patched. Word is, there's lots of Jap civilians hereabouts."

"Okinawans." Max unbuckled his gear. "One of the reasons we're here, Tuttle. We'd like to avoid a repeat of what happened at Saipan," he said, digging for his shaving kit. "The civilians here have been told we'll torture them to death. Okinawa is honeycombed with caves for them to hide in. Using force won't budge them, but maybe our interpreters can talk them out when the situation presents itself."

He doubted that the effort would save many lives. Attempting to reason with the terrified Japanese civilians on Saipan had met with failure. Gathered on a high cliff with the sea at their backs, three thousand had committed mass suicide. Mothers had leaped to their deaths with babies clutched in their arms. The surf below had been turned into a cemetery of floating corpses. Similar incidents had occurred on Iwo Jima. He had only read accounts of those tragedies. "There's no sense to this terror propaganda," he said. "If we're forced to storm the Japanese mainland, Christ knows how many innocent people will take their own lives."

A young shavetail lieutenant ran along the boardwalk outside their tent, shouting, "Roosevelt's dead. The President's dead!"

Avery shouted back. "Who says so?"

"AFR broadcast, sir. He died at Warm Springs, Georgia, and the Vice-President's been sworn in. CO wants everyone to fall out on the double!"

Firing off a salute, Avery stood there, stunned. "I thought the man was indestructible. This could bring the whole shebang to a halt."

Max slipped his rain parka over his head. Up and down the airstrip, companies were falling in under the pounding rain. Roosevelt had been a charismatic and inspirational figurehead, and his sudden death cast a pall over the long lines of soldiers. Rain obscured their tears while taps was played over the loudspeakers. The flag was slowly lowered to half mast. The drenched silk hung heavy and lame against the flagpole. To those fighting men, Harry Truman was an unknown entity, a stranger who still resided in Roosevelt's shadow. They fell out silently, uncertain and rather frightened, like children who had just lost their father. The clouds peeled back to let ghostly rays of sunlight stream down through the unending rain, illuminating the scene.

Although they did not know it, a turning point would soon be reached on the desert test flats at Alamogordo, New Mexico. And the man no one knew was destined to alter the course of history.

May brought more rain. The threat of typhoons hung over the campaign for Okinawa. Casualties mounted as the Japanese forces clung on tenaciously, waging a bloody fight for every yard of ground taken by the Americans. While island-hopping ever closer to Japan, Max had often monitored the NHK broadcasts on his shortwave radio. He was listening in again one dank night while sharing the burgeoning workload with Avery Bullock. A dispatcher delivered copies of the latest aerial photographs taken by raiding B-29's. Tokyo, Osaka, and Nagoya practically lay in ruins. For all Max knew, Paul, his father, and Inge had perished in the fire storms that laid waste to Japan's major cities. "Thank God, Nagasaki hasn't been chosen as a target. If only we had some info on where the POW camps are located."

Wincing, Avery set the photographs aside and lit his pipe. "Better not to know."

"I get night sweats just thinking about it."

"Well, I'll bet the emperor isn't losing any sleep. B-29's steer clear of his palace. MacArthur's right. Once it's over, Hirohito will be invaluable to us."

"Listen to this." Max turned up the volume as Radio Tokyo played a catchy little jingle set to music.

Why should we be afraid of air raids?
The big sky is protected with iron defenses.

For young and old it is a time to stand up.
We are loaded with the honor of defending the
   homeland.
Come on, enemy planes! Come on many times!

"Iron defenses? Hardly any Zeros or fuel enough to get them off the
ground. Hardly any antiaircraft guns still operational." Switching the
radio off, Max put a cigarette in his mouth and lit it. "Hell, I'm slowly
going nuts. Bring on the bombs? What a goddamn travesty."

"Here, drink this down. It'll settle your war nerves."

Their C-47's flew in a liberal supply of booze, and Max downed the
Scotch neat, then poured another two fingers to help him forget. "Ave,
sometimes I think you're not human. Just once, I'd like to see you crack
like the rest of us. What would it take to wipe that glib smile off your
face?"

"Sackcloth and ashes aren't for me. No, my saintly friend. It's
healthier to greet each day wearing a crisp uniform and a smile. Grin and
bear it, that's my motto." After helping himself from the bottle, Avery
stretched out both legs and chuckled. "If you're waiting for me to crack,
don't hold your breath."

Not since Harvard had Avery referred to Max as "saintly." "Iron
defenses, eh?" His unflappable friend nodded, yawned, and decided to call
it a night.

Night sweats kept Max tossing and turning. A buzzing noise had him
swatting at imaginary mosquitoes. Then he heard the drone of planes.
Avery heard them, too, and they both kicked through the netting around
their cots and pulled their boots on quickly. The camp was still asleep
except for a handful of groggy men searching the early morning sky. The
drone came to an abrupt stop. Visibility was hindered by ground fog
rolling in from the sea.

"There!" Max pointed to the wingtips of a Japanese light bomber
plane just breaking through the mist. The pilot had cut its engines, and it
glided in above the treetops silently with little room to spare. "The
giretsus! Five—no, six planes!"

Suddenly, the planes were zooming down over the airfield. The
giretsus were superkamikazes, whose death-defying raids utilized the
element of surprise. The Japanese had run out of bombs to drop and had
flown in low to avoid radar detection. It was a one-way trip, and the
planes were modified for the quick kill. Stripped of their landing gears,
they belly-landed on the field, not enough gas in their tanks to set them
ablaze.

Dog tags rattling against his undershirt, Max took Avery to the
ground with him as machine-gun fire strafed the camp. Only the
American soldiers standing guard duty were armed at that hour. Almost
everyone else was pinned down in his underwear. At least a dozen giretsus
were jumping down from each plane, firing while they attacked on the

run, tossing grenades and incendiaries by the basketloads. These super-kamikazes had taken an oath to kill and destroy what they could, to spread death and destruction until they themselves were killed. Twelve *giretsu*s could take the lives of seventy men or more. They fought alone, dashing helter-skelter through the airfield, leaving corpses and burning planes and tents in their wakes.

Max crawled back inside the tent with Avery. Wild shots kept them low to the floorboards just beyond the reach of their weapons. There was no cover outside, and Max finally laid hands on his holstered .45, dragged his ammo belt from the tent post nail, and draped the belt around his neck.

Avery followed suit, flipping the safety catch of his .45 nervously. "Dead ducks if we stay here. Any suggestions?"

"The motor pool's our only chance, but we can't get across the runway to it from here," Max said, peering out from the tent at what could be seen of the battle. "I say we make a run through that grove of palms directly behind out tent. It circles to the far end of the airstrip—about a football field away. With luck, we can get across to the motor pool there and take cover."

"Okay! But don't forget it's us or them. Flip off that safety and think of your own almighty ass!"

They ran from the tent, shaved by machine-gun bullets before reaching the grove of palms. Here the island was completely flat. At least a third of the camp was in flames, and in the billowing smoke, it was hard to distinguish the superkamikazes from their own soldiers. The palms caught fire, and they dodged burning embers.

"Wah! Wah!" The Japanese war cry raised goose flesh on Max's arms. He and Avery were choked by the smoke. Through the crackling trees, he glimpsed the far end of the runway. It was a no-man's land of concrete littered with the dead. But they would have to get across it to reach the motor pool, which appeared to be safe. Something moved in the foliage just ahead. Avery prepared to fire, but Max stopped him. "Could be one of our own men!"

"Don't risk your neck finding out!" Avery shouted as Max broke away for the spot. "Crazy sonofabitch!"

A bullet-riddled *giretsu* writhed on his back, pumping blood with his dying breaths. His submachine gun lay at his feet in the shrubs. He had no other weapons on him that Max could see, and he stretched up one bloody hand, a plea for help gurgling deep inside his throat.

He was only a boy. He had taken a suicide oath, and now he wanted to live, Max thought, bending over him. "I can only offer prayers to the gods."

The knife materialized as if by magic, and the Japanese drove the blade through Max's shoulder to the bone. Shock sent him to his knees. His attacker managed to pull out the blade and was just about to strike at Max again, when his head was blown away. Avery's smoking .45 splattered them both with the Japanese soldier's blood.

"Give me your good arm! Dammit Max, move it or lose it!"

Max could not see much for the blood in his eyes. His left arm and hand went numb. The .45 slithered from his fingers. Max clutched the fleshy part of his bleeding shoulder. Surprisingly, he felt little pain and was able to keep pace with Avery, listening to the now sporadic rattle of small arms fire. "I owe you my life."

"Why in God's name did you have to get stung?"

Incendiaries flared up and flames leapfrogged across the canvas backs of some parked trucks. Max pulled back with Avery.

"Wah! Wah!" Two *giretsu*s darted into view, screaming their blood-curdling war cry while emptying their last rounds into a scattering pack of unarmed soldiers who had taken cover in the motor pool. One truck's gas tank blew, hammering the kamikazes to the ground. They were seared and set ablaze by a white-hot tunnel of liquid flames.

It seemed impossible, but one of them was suddenly on his feet. Screaming the war cry, he charged at Max and Avery with both arms spread wide, a flaming cross bent on using his body for the kill.

Avery took aim, stumbling back, squeezing the trigger until his .45 clicked empty. Engulfed in flames, the body tumbled facedown within inches of his boots. "Already dead. This boy and the one back there were already dead. I didn't kill them, Max."

Max reeled, stepping in his own blood as he coaxed Avery to move along. Several armed platoons were double-timing it down the runway, fanning out to poke the dead *giretsu*s with their bayonets. Medics crouched here and there, tending to the American wounded, and fire brigades were foaming down burning debris scattered across the airfield. "Looks like it's over."

"Yeah. Medic!"

While a medic saw to Max's wound, his unflappable friend stared blankly into thin air. "Ave, you had no choice."

"Will he be laid up for long?" Avery asked the medic, sidestepping the issue.

"I'd say a couple weeks, sir."

"Lucky bastard. The Purple Heart rates you leave. But don't get any ideas. I need you here to push the paper clips."

Max felt groggy from the medic's shot. Avery laughed, but his scarred eyes dropped to the .45 he still held in one trembling hand. Circumstances had turned this mild-mannered college professor into a killer. Although he never shed a tear, Avery Bullock was not the same after that.

When the smoke had cleared, Sergeant Tuttle reported in. By the grace of God, their outfit had come through without a casualty. Max was driven to the nearby field hospital, which had also escaped damage. Army nurses ministered to the more seriously wounded, preparing them for the OR.

At last a bed was assigned Max. Even its hard mattress felt good.

Closing his eyes, Max thought of home. The shot given him by the medic and another by the doctor who had sutured his wound allowed him to sleep more soundly than he had in years. Germany's surrender registered as a dream whispered to him from afar. Then he woke to the scent of perfume and a woman's soft touch. "Shizue?"

"My name is Terry," answered the pretty nurse who was bending over him.

The scents of her makeup and the perfume she wore reminded Max of how long he had gone without the nearness of women. "Why am I so stiff?"

"You've been asleep two days, Major. Here, let me fluff up those pillows. You must be hungry."

"Was I dreaming, or did you say something about Germany surrendering?"

"Yes, this morning. Hitler is dead."

Max fought back tears. "Maybe now Japan will see the light."

"My fiancé was killed in action over there. Not a year ago."

"I'm sorry." He brought her tear-streaked face against his, wanting to comfort her. Feeling the softness of a woman's cheek once again led him to kiss her tenderly.

"For so long now, I've wanted to be held and kissed in the worst way," the nurse said.

They were just two people desperately in need of being held, thought Max, warmed by this tender moment and missing Shizue more desperately then ever. The nurse returned his smile, then looked away in tears.

"The killing will end soon," he told her quietly. "Before long, we'll all be going home."

Bedrest made him antsy. After a week of it, Max checked himself out of the hospital and went back to work, dispatching intelligence reports to Douglas MacArthur's headquarters in Manila. With the fall of the Third Reich, Japan had lost its strongest ally. But Japanese forces on Okinawa were still exacting a heavy toll. Continuous rainfall and General Ushijima's brilliant deployment of troops across the island's difficult terrain prolonged the end of the fighting.

The rain finally stopped in the first week of June. As the 96th Division launched a massive campaign for victory, Max anxiously charted their advance on the battle map. It was to be General Ushijima's last stand. Within ten days, enemy resistance on the island would cease to exist.

The way home now appeared to be clear. Max had put a circle around Nagasaki on the battle map of Japan. It was the map for a projected U.S. invasion and had been drawn up from aerial photographs that targeted the beachheads of vulnerable Japanese ports. Almost four years had passed since Shizue was taken to Urakami Prison, as Max had learned from the old gardener's grandson, Koichi, after the battle for Morotai. He had no way of knowing if she had been released from prison and transferred to some detention camp in Nagasaki or its outskirts. But he knew that she would not be found at home on her ancestral lands. When he landed on the Japanese mainland, his search for Shizue and his father would begin in Nagasaki. He was grateful the B-*sans* had not flown missions over that city as yet, and the circle he had drawn around it was his goal, something tangible he could touch with his finger.

As he looked at the map, he thought of Hosokawa-Napier, Limited's, weaving mill. Earlier in the war, Japan had made good use of paratroops. But the parachutes woven of Hosokawa silk had been redesigned and bore little resemblance to those Douglas had helped to engineer. Silk no longer played an important role in Japan's war effort, and the Japanese lacked the planes to deploy paratroops against a large-scale invasion. Max took a particle of solace in that fact.

Avery Bullock plucked at his sweat-soaked shirt while an electric fan rustled the latest intelligence reports that Sergeant Tuttle handed him. "The remnants of Ushijima's army are holed up in caves near the southern tip of the island," Avery told Max. "Could be thousands of civilians hiding out down there with him. Tank fire hasn't budged the general. By this time they've got to be awful thirsty. Well"—he sighed and angled the fan toward his face—"now it's up to us. Let's pray the Okinawans can be talked into surrendering. Tuttle, muster a detachment of our best interpreters."

"I want to be in on this, Ave."

"Okay, but first I want your word that you won't take any damn foolish risks."

Max massaged his shoulder, which had healed but was still stiff. "You've got it. I don't intend to get stung twice."

His outfit had been prepared for this well in advance. Avery helped write the mimeographed pleas for surrender that Max passed out among them. The exact locations of all the caves were not known. Max reflected on what they were up against. General Ushijima was drawing them to his underground lairs, where he was prepared to stand and fight. The general was of that elite class of samurai, who would accept nothing less than death with honor for himself and his men.

Max assigned half of his interpreters to navy boats, which would cruise around beneath the sea cliffs, where their amplified voices would hopefully reach inside the least accessible hiding places. By noon, Tuttle had managed to find enough amplification equipment to augment what was reported to be on hand at their destination. "Ready to roll, sir."

As they walked outside and boarded their Jeep, a man came running up to Max. "Major Napier, wait for me! Joe—Joe Peterson, *Life* magazine," the war correspondent introduced himself, out of breath from his run. He wore long-sleeved fatigues too heavy for the subtropical climate and his pale face was smeared with suntan lotion. Wilted by the heat, he managed to smile amiably. "Your colonel said I could hitch a ride. Might be a good story in it."

"Hop aboard, Mr. Peterson."

"Joe, and much obliged. The tools of my trade," he said, dumping a portable typewriter stored in a chewed-up leather case and an equally disreputable-looking camera bag on the rear seat beside him. "Gosh, it's hot. I suppose it takes some time to get acclimatized. Only days ago, I was picking my way through the London fog in search of a pub."

Max sized him up. Joe was in his early forties, and his alert brown eyes missed nothing that took place around him. "Did you cover much of the action?"

"Yes, yes, a little too much for the soul to bear. I left Germany near the end. After Buchenwald my heart gave out. Being on the other side of the world, I guess you haven't been exposed to the horrors uncovered at Hitler's death camps. No, even in America news of the Jewish Holocaust is being soft-pedaled by the press. They're awaiting further documentation. I suppose it's justified. Such heinous crimes against humanity are incomprehensible, Major. But you've faced enough nightmares of your own, fighting the Japanese."

"Tell me what you've seen!" Max said. He climbed in back and shifted Peterson's gear to the seat up front. "Sorry, Joe," he apologized to the startled reporter as he sat down beside him. "I didn't mean to lose control. But this is goddamn important to me. My stepmother is a German Jew. She was slated for the concentration camp at Ravensbrück, but we got her out. It's a long story."

"Gosh, let me catch my breath." Peterson removed his helmet and wiped his bald head with a handkerchief as he launched into the horrors of Buchenwald. "Operated like an efficient German factory. Assembly-line death, Major, with quotas to be met. The Jews were classified and numbered with tattoos on their forearms. Each day thousands of them at similar camps in Germany and Poland began the extermination process by marching into shower rooms. Then the airtight doors were locked by S.S. men, and the rooms became gas chambers. Lethal cyanide gas was pumped through the shower heads. Quick, efficient, a matter of minutes. After that, the corpses were carted away, the gold teeth and fillings plucked from their mouths before they were cremated. Some of the corpses were skinned. Lampshades and wallets resembling pigskin were manufactured from human hides. When Hitler realized the end was near, the extermination quotas were accelerated. But they couldn't possibly be met. Stacks upon stacks of rotting corpses were heaped on the camp yards and in mass graves that the S.S. had no time to fill in before we arrived. They also had no time to burn the records of their crimes. Buchenwald, Belsen, Auschwitz—their smokestacks blackened the sky. And yet, no German living within sight of them claims to have known what was taking place right before their eyes. I couldn't steady my camera. Even now I can't talk about it without my hands shaking. Every roll of film blurred. Even my prose was blurred. How does one speak of the unspeakable?"

In his mind's eye, Max could see it all. For a minute he was too moved to speak. Then he looked into Joe Peterson's eyes and they mirrored the horrors that still caused this man to shake. "How many thousands perished?"

"At last count, the toll was soaring into millions. I did come away with some photographs of the survivors. Living skeletons staring out through the barbed wire." He took a notebook and pencil from his fatigue pocket. "It's a lot to swallow in one sitting. Join me for a drink when we get back, and we'll exchange stories. Now, give me the rundown on these Japanese civilians."

"Mostly farmers, living hand-to-mouth. I think they'll look to the soldiers to set an example. You might say that these caves are potential death camps created by the minds of those in hiding. To the Japanese an honorable death is preferable to a dishonorable surrender."

"That doesn't leave you much of an appeal."

"I said 'preferable,' Joe. Not intractable or absolute. They've been abandoned, written off by the rulers who promised a glory they couldn't deliver. Their country has lost. No personal sacrifice can alter Japan's destiny. Surrender is just around the corner, and the Japanese people must accept its terms, endure the loss of face, and work to rebuild. Sitting down there in one of those caves, how would you decide?"

"Major Napier, you intrigue me. Where did you gain so much insight into the Japanese?"

"Some other time. Right now I'm in the business of saving lives." Max tried to turn his thoughts away from the dead millions. The thousands of Jews he had helped to save enabled him to absorb the shockwave of Buchenwald. But he could never take credit for their lives. He thought how the world press had virtually turned its back on the Jews. It was too late for his personal story to make a difference. Looking into the reporter's eyes once again, he felt vulnerable to his emotions. Too much so. Whiskey might loosen his tongue, and he decided not to have that drink with Joe Peterson.

Now the Jeep swerved and bounced over dried mud roads. The volcanic terrain was reminiscent of Kyushu. As they cleared a rise, they saw steep cliffs to the left. The East China Sea glistened far below them and they could hear amplified voices, faint and echoing off the sea walls.

"Some of our men, cruising down there in boats," Max said to Joe.

Peterson strapped on his helmet. "What are they saying?"

Max translated while a captain signaled the small convoy forward to a wavy line of American tanks. "Men of Okinawa, we have no wish to avenge ourselves on you, your wives, and your children. Soldiers of Japan, you have fought bravely. Now the fight has ended. Lay down your weapons." Max turned to the correspondent. "There could be some diehards among the soldiers, Joe, so we're asking them to strip down before coming out. It's rough terrain. We'll use these tanks to get us within earshot of the caves. Hopefully, we won't need their guns to back us up. What's the dope, Captain?" he asked, hopping from the Jeep.

"The caves are pretty well scattered over the area, sir." The tank captain spread a map across the hood. Its metal was boiling hot and leather driving gloves protected his hands. "The island's not a mile wide here. Our lines are strung out from the China Sea to the Pacific. Our tanks are making a sweeping search of every inch of ground. No telling how many caves'll be shelled by our boys before we catch up with them."

Munching on his daily ration of Tootsie Rolls, Sergeant Tuttle ordered his own men to climb onto the Sherman tanks and hook up the loudspeakers they had brought with them. After the speakers were operational, Tuttle's men got inside the tanks assigned to them. Max boarded the lead tank. Its seasoned crew was indifferent to the claustrophobia and searing heat. But Max swam in his own sweat, and Peterson looked wilted as he huddled against one corner with his camera bag.

The tanks clanked forward in an ever-widening V formation. Max lost sight of them in the periscope and tapped the crew sergeant's leather helmet, shouting to be heard. "Maintain radio contact."

"A message coming in from Seventh Infantry, sir," he shouted back, then flattened both hands against the helmet's built-in earphones. "Reports of surrendering just down the coast. Japanese soldiers and civilians. A hundred, maybe more, and still coming out. Any reply, sir?"

"Tell my men in those boats to keep up the good work!" It was too soon for rejoicing. Max heard the muffled barrage of small arms fire followed by the dull thuds of exploding grenades. The tank pitched nose first on a steep incline, mowing down sapling trees before it clanked to a halt. "What's going on?"

"Our boys, on to some Japs, sir!"

Taking over the periscope, he spotted infantry men lobbing grenades down the rocky mouth of some cave not marked on the map. "Cease fire," he ordered over the loudspeaker mounted on the tank's chassis. "This is Major Napier, GS intelligence. Lob another grenade in there and I'll have your asses! I'm going outside," he told one of the crew. "Get that hatch door open on the double. Some of those volcanic caves are like a labyrinth. But if our boys keep sending down grenades, they could kill everyone hiding inside, and some of them may be civilians."

Max had brought along a battery-operated bull horn for just such an emergency. He quickly hooked it to his pistol belt, then looked at Peterson, who was preparing to follow him up the hatch. "As you were, Joe."

"Awe, give me a break, major."

"I don't want any more corpses posing for your camera, dammit! Now stay put! That's an order!" After pulling himself up through the open hatch, Max jumped clear of the tank and skidded downhill on the crumbling earth. "Who's in command?"

"Jaffe, sir."

"Never mind the salute. There could be civilians down there." He judged the platoon lieutenant to be about his age, battle-wise and itching for the kill. "We're trying to prevent the extermination of innocent people. Don't get trigger-happy again."

"I was only following orders, Major. A couple of Japs surfaced for water, and we tracked them to the nest."

The dead soldiers lay on the ground nearby, their blood mixing with the water that dribbled from the punctured canteens tied around their waists.

Max was silent for a moment, listening. "Sounds like a baby crying." He put the bull horn to his mouth. "You won't be fired on again. You can come out."

No one below responded. Overcome by emotion, he listened to the baby's cries, then spoke slowly from the heart. "Mothers, brave soldiers, show yourselves without fear. We offer you an honorable surrender. Come into the sunlight and let us treat your wounded. Let us feed your hungry children. The gods have not brought this suffering on you. It was the will of men. Soon the emperor will lay down his sword, and you'll be needed to help rebuild a better Japan. Your deaths can serve no purpose. I beg of you to think of the future."

He thought of Shizue and the children she would one day bear him. A woman cried out, "*Hai*, we believe you. But my poor husband is wounded in the legs and can't walk!" Then she screamed.

The hollow pops of gunfire echoed back and forth in the depths below. When the sound died, a young boy ran from the cave holding a frightened little girl by the hand.

"We are only two families. The soldiers have killed themselves." His lower lip trembled as other children wearing straw mushroom hats stepped into the dusty light. They stood in a row and bowed. A Japanese farmer emerged with two wide-eyed women, one carrying her baby in a *ubui-himo*.

"Have pity," she sobbed. "Please don't let my husband die."

"We'll do all we can." Max embraced her, touching the baby's head. In that moment he felt as if Shizue had reached out to him through these terrified people.

Similar scenes occurred throughout the day. With the setting sun at his back, Max joined the division infantry lines mustered above a barren escarpment of rock, where Japanese soldiers began to file from their hiding places underground. Their lengthening shadows crisscrossed in the sun's orangy glow. On the ocean swells below Max, his men riding in navy boats could be heard still broadcasting the plea for surrender.

Stripped to their loincloths, the Japanese who had responded to it were sad, embittered men. They had been vanquished, dishonored by accepting surrender. A number of officers and their men had chosen suicide in the caves below, and some now hid their faces from the correspondent's igniting flashbulbs.

"Ease off, Joe."

"One last shot, Major." Peterson coaxed him into posing between two Sherman tanks mounted with loudspeakers. "Okay, let's have a victorious smile for your folks back home."

Unsmiling, Max blinked, temporarily blinded by the burst of light. Its afterimage floated like a second sun rising in the twilight. Maybe some of his classmates at Harvard would see his picture in *Life* magazine, he thought, as he trudged along the infantry ranks. If so, he doubted if any of them would recognize his war-weary face. Even the colonel who returned his salute saw him as old enough to wear oak leaves. "Any word on the final tally, sir?"

"About four thousand Okinawans and better than six hundred soldiers."

"Guess the next move is up to the Japanese," Max said.

"Japanese coastal defenses are weak. But what's left of the Imperial Navy might have enough kamikazes to give us one hell of a fight." The colonel spoke in a southern drawl. He removed his helmet to wipe the sweat off his balding head. "Those new *oka* cherry bombs carry enough nitro to cut a ship in half. And there're maybe five million troops garrisoned on the mainland. If it comes to a suicide charge, we could be pushed back by the sheer weight of their bodies. Being intelligence, you'd have a better overview of the situation, Major. But I've fought the Japs long enough to guess they'll go for broke."

Max nodded. Another mighty adversary was howling at Japan's gates. There was now a strong possibility of Russian intervention in the Pacific, and Japan could not sustain a second front. He rejoined his men, who were questioning the prisoners. All of them said there were no stragglers hiding in the caves. That day sanity had ruled over the madness of prolonging this war in the Pacific.

Unfortunately, Max thought, peace did not rest with these defeated soldiers on Okinawa. Would Japan surrender or commit millions to the bloodbath of an Allied invasion? That burning question tormented him as he offered the prisoners cigarettes. "Where do you hail from, soldier?" he asked one man.

The soldier drew to attention. "Tokyo, *rikugun shosa*. You speak like one of us."

Lighting the soldier's cigarette, Max conversed about their home town and things Japanese. "Don't regret having surrendered."

"But I am miserable," the soldier wailed. "How will I face my family?"

"Alive and well." Max smiled. But as he stood facing the East China Sea, he thought of the families already killed and injured by American bombs. Those very waters fed into Nagasaki Bay. Its factories now lay vulnerable to aircraft launched from flattops ready to sail at a moment's notice. He wondered when and if they might strike. He wondered if his own family would be among the missing when he set foot on Kyushu alive and well.

CHAPTER 41

Shizue was in a turmoil and nearly took a spill from her bicycle as she swerved in the path of a mangy dog. He was a pitiful sight, his ribs poking through his thin coat of hair and whimpering as he tagged along beside her. "As if I didn't have enough on my mind. Well, maybe I can find you some scraps to eat." She sighed as she pedaled for the army hospital. This was only the first day in August, but the leaves were already rusting and turning to yellow. Nature was strangely unbalanced, she thought, turning summer into autumn, after weeks of unbearable humidity and heat.

Not one week ago, Japan had been given the choice of unconditional surrender or total destruction. To Shizue, the alternative was unthinkable. But so far her country had remained silent to the Allied demands.

Through the long winter and into early spring, Douglas Napier's health had showed improvement, thanks to drugs and the fresh vegetables she had smuggled through the prison gates. Then suddenly he suffered a reversal. Without chest X rays, the American doctor could not diagnose the exact condition of his failing lungs. Tuberculosis was common among the war prisoners and Nagasaki's undernourished citizens as well. Dr. Haefele could only surmise that Douglas had contracted it some time ago and that laboring in the coal mines had accelerated the disease. In the rarefied air of some mountain sanitorium, his lesions might be arrested and eventually healed. But in the squalor and dust of prison camp, he was slowly wasting away. During her last visit, he had coughed up blood. The precious drugs she smuggled to him were all that prolonged his life, and these were in critically short supply. Dr. Haefele took ever greater risks to obtain them from the dispensary.

Shizue parked at the bicycle stand, thinking how the stray dog who followed her to the hospital kitchen's back door resembled the people of her starving nation.

The cook was irate at Shizue's request for scraps. "Surely there's something for this poor animal in the garbage," she pleaded with the unsympathetic woman. "Feed him, and I'll bring you fresh fruit from the farm."

Shaking her graying head, the cook poked inside the garbage pail with a wooden spoon. "You are too soft. Feed this mongrel and he may lead others to my door. But for fresh fruit, I will make an exception just this once, Hosokawa-*san*."

All the staff addressed her by her maiden name. "Thank you. Poor thing. I'd give him a home, but we've already taken in so many strays."

As Shizue entered the hospital corridor, one of the administration nurses called to her. Paul had telephoned. He would arrive at the farm the next morning. How she had begged him to visit his father, to drop the barrier between them before it was too late. At last he had relented. Perhaps he would find it in his heart to forgive the past. If not, just seeing his son might do Douglas more good than drugs.

She walked down the hall and saw an ambulance driver delivering a shipment of drugs to the head nurse. "Thank the gods. Our dispensary shelves are almost empty," the nurse said. She put on her glasses to check the driver's shipping manifest. "But this won't do. You've cut our requisition by half."

"All there is for now," he answered tersely, waiting for her signature. The ink bled through the coarse yellowish paper, and he blew on it. "Shortages. These days even the paper falls apart in your hands."

Shizue started for the nurses' changing room, when Commander Sekino blocked her path. "You startled me."

"I have been waiting for you, Hosokawa-*san*. Step inside my office." He stood ramrod straight, an unpleasant expression on his face as she stepped inside nervously. "Don't worry about neglecting your duties. Sit down," Commander Sekino said. He placed his back against the closing door. "Yes, you have good reason to be nervous. As you know, I'm a man of few words. Spare me any denials and feminine displays of tears. It was necessary to use certain methods on your accomplice, Dr. Haefele, in order to encourage him to tell me everything: the prison camp near your farm, your loved ones there. Discrepancies in the hospital records have puzzled me for some time, Hosokawa-*san*. But even the cleverest of thieves makes mistakes. I could have him shot and you put behind bars. Stealing drugs from our own wounded to treat the enemy is a serious offense."

"We took only what could be spared." While he grinned at her lasciviously, she bravely met his eyes, although she was terrified for Douglas and Dr. Haefele. She knew the American doctor must have been tortured to obtain his confession. If the commander intended to arrest her, then why these threats? she wondered.

As he bent over her, Shizue watched his ugly hands caress the wooden arms of her chair. Suddenly she realized that Sekino had an ulterior motive, and the thought of what he wanted from her made her shudder in revulsion. "I appeal to your sense of humanity, Commander. I look upon you as a father, who has many of our wounded to care for. But the prisoners in your camps are suffering as well. Some of them are gravely ill.

The war can't last much longer. Why not show a little mercy? In the past, you've showed me kindness—"

"Ah, yes, on several occasions you came to me asking for bicycle tires," he interrupted with a harsh laugh. "So, you look upon me as a father, easily twisted around your finger with your smile. Please, don't make the effort. A smile won't keep you out of prison or buy the lives you hold so dear."

He stood back from Shizue's chair and undressed her with his eyes. "No, it's you I want. I've hungered too long for you. Satisfy my desire and the incident will be forgotten. Dr. Haefele will resume his work here." While speaking, he had locked the door, and now he quickly crossed to draw the window blinds. "You'll be given the drugs you need. I swear it on my honor."

Shizue's skin crawled as she felt his breath against the nape of her neck. He was wild with lust, and she knew that nothing prevented him from raping her if she refused. "Let the gods and your ancestors bear witness to what you've sworn to me, Commander."

"Yes—yes, as they are my witness, I swear it to you again."

"Then take your payment and have done with it." Before Commander Sekino had removed the pins from her upswept hair, she was numb to his feverish touch. Snorting like a bull, he tore the blouse from around her shoulders, and she stared coldly at the ceiling, lifeless as a mannequin. Max was the only man she had given herself to. As with Jiro, she now held herself inviolate. Jiro had been gentle, but this aging man was a clumsy brute who forced her to the floor.

Shizue had never seen him perspire even on the hottest days. Now the sweat beaded up across his brow. She closed her eyes, shutting him out. She soaked in an imaginary tub, already purged of the commander's filth before his gasping mouth drooled across her cheek and it was over. She opened her eyes, telling herself this had never happened. "Have you finished?" she inquired impassively.

"Bitch! You've been asking for this." Commander Sekino staggered to his feet, pulling up his trousers. "Don't play high and mighty with me! The next time, I'll make you cry out and beg for more."

Shizue numbly picked her hairpins off the floor. Her thighs were wet with his semen. She would wash at the public bathhouse nearby. "You used me as a prostitute. You bargained for my body, not my soul. Tomorrow I'll visit my loved ones, and I'll take the drugs with me now." She stared back at him with nobility. She was not the slut he would have her be. For the moment, his carnal appetite had been satisfied, and she buttoned her blouse while he telephoned the dispensary to make good the promise he had sworn to her on his honor. She had bought Douglas another week of life. Perhaps the last week before Japan surrendered. If so, she would be spared from enduring this monster's brutality again.

Later, pedaling for the bathhouse, she looked down on the Urakami

Valley, still so peaceful and serene. Since May of that year the B-*sans* had bombed the city of Nagasaki three times, and yet the damage was surprisingly light. Air raid sirens were sounded mostly for drills. There were bomb shelters everywhere, but children still enjoyed a cooling swim in the river while others flew their kites near the riverbanks. Only the day before, the city was bombed, but the distant explosions merely rattled the hospital windows, and Shizue had felt relatively safe until today. Now the bruises inflicted by Commander Sekino's ugly hands caused her pain, and she stopped to rest. All at once she felt totally drained of strength.

Without warning, she began to tremble. The handlebars spun away from her grip as her violated body went into shock. Shizue crouched down, shivering in the roadside grass near the spinning wheels of her toppled bicycle, struggling to blot out the indignity of rape.

Eventually she gathered strength enough to right the bicycle. Just then she heard a loud roar in the sky as American fighter bombers skimmed over Mount Anakobo. For the very first time, carrier-borne aircraft swooped down across the quiet sky, short-range planes launched from the East China Sea divebombing so low that she could see the insignia painted on their fuselages. In an instant the planes winged across the valley bottom, discharging gray pellets that fell to earth, exploding as the aircraft zoomed off into the horizon.

While the bombs' thunder reverberated through the Urakami Hills, Shizue pedaled faster. From her lofty vantage point, she watched flames and billowing black smoke claim several buildings near the medical school complex. Was this a hit-and-run raid, or would the bombers come again? she wondered. O-nami had dug a bomb shelter under his farmhouse. The high-flying B-*sans* were slow, their engines giving advance warning, and their bombs were released only if weather conditions allowed the pilots to see the targets through the crosshairs of their bombsights. But these fighter bombers struck swiftly as lightning bolts, and the sirens near O-nami's farm would warn of their deadly approach too late. Rather than seek shelter, she altered her course for home, afraid for little Kimi. Mother love overrode her pain and shock.

People stood on the terraced hillsides mesmerized by the sudden invasion. They watched the sea as if expecting to glimpse the enemy aircraft carriers now so near their shores. Again the planes were coming, but Shizue did not look back. The countryside skies ahead were safe.

When she reached the farm, Kimi was romping with the stray dogs they had given a home to. Giggling, he hurried through the yard to welcome her. "No—don't touch Mommy. She's too dirty."

The robust three-year-old stood there sucking his thumb, puzzled by his mother's tears as Shizue ran inside the house. "They've bombed the city again. This time with fast planes swooping down like bolts of lightning. It was terrifying."

Turning from Yufugawo's outstretched arms, she felt like a leper afraid of contaminating her loved ones. "A patient at the hospital vomited all over me. I must bathe."

Here the bombs had been mistaken for distant thunder. Now the countryside was quiet. Shizue scrubbed and scoured herself raw, willing the filth from her memory with the rising steam. At nightfall, everyone in the household spread his *futon* around the bomb shelter's trapdoor, and she kept little Kimi very close to her, grateful for the innocence that allowed him to sleep without fear.

In a hushed voice, O-nami insisted it was unsafe to continue her work at the hospital. "The American carriers will bring other lightning raids, Shizue. Say that you are ill. Go only for the drugs and return home quickly."

"Yes, ill from exhaustion." Smiling drowsily, she decided to follow O-nami's advice. That would temporarily hold Commander Sekino at bay. O-nami blew out the oil lamp and whispered good night to his household.

That night Shizue longed for the safety and security of her childhood home. She recalled her bedroom in the castle, and waking in Max's arms on the morning after their wedding night. Douglas had come to the door to say they would soon be leaving Japan. She remembered sharing her husband's sadness. Then she had told Max that home was wherever they could be together. Now, with little Kimitake cuddled securely against her, Shizue felt in Max's presence. When she closed her eyes, father and son were one and the same, and for tonight a humble farmhouse was home.

Paul arrived late the next morning. His nerves were on edge and that made him short-tempered. With city after city in rubble, transportation was a mess. He spoke of American planes bombarding the rubble with leaflets appealing for the people to surrender.

"Don't lecture me on forgiveness," he snapped at Shizue. "It's enough that I came. I've run out of strings to pull. You'll have to get me through the gates dressed as a farmhand."

Shaken by how depressed and gaunt Paul was, Shizue did not intrude on his silence during the long ride by ox cart. With Kimi beside her, she guided the beasts until the camp watchtowers came into view. Then Paul took her place at the reins, and they rode toward the barbed wire gates.

"*Konnichi-wa*, Hosokawa-*san*."

"*Konnichi-wa.*" Shizue wore a cheerful smile for the friendly corporal. "O-nami wasn't feeling well today, so Akira brought me."

Paul's large straw hat shaded his eyes while the cart rolled on to the fenced-in compound Shizue had visited so often. He dreaded this confrontation with the past. His pulse quickened. His mouth grew dry and even in the heat of the sun he felt chilled to the bone.

Their soldier escort accepted Paul as a lame peasant. Paul walked with the aid of a stick instead of his silver-handled cane.

He froze outside the shabby wooden building where his father waited with the wife he had never seen. This was a far cry from Douglas's mansion in the Tokyo hills. Paul felt choked by the years of having denied his father. The words spoken to Douglas across his mother's open grave came back to haunt him. "Mother was the only link between us, and you're dead to me now, Douglas. You no longer exist. Today I'm burying you with the dead." Then he had turned away, refusing to grant his mother's final wish. As he stared at the building's peeling wooden door, he realized he had waited too long. Max and Shizue's son toddled past him, crying excitedly, *ogisan*. Paul could not help seeing himself in this child of mixed blood, so eager to receive Douglas's love. He twisted his walking stick in the dirt.

"Perhaps it's best if I go in first and tell Douglas that you're here," Shizue said.

"No, Shizue. Just hold my hand. I'm a bit wobbly."

Douglas Napier had never been a deeply religious man. While Inge placed her faith in God, he was reconciled to the fact that he was dying. He cherished the rare moments he spent with his healthy grandson. His one regret was that he would not live to see either of his sons again. "Where's Mommy?"

"With Uncle Paul. There," he squealed, pulling his grandfather to the open door. "Look see, *ogisan*."

Douglas swayed dizzily on his thin legs and ran a pale hand across his sunken eyes. "Son?"

Paul's walking stick clattered to the floor. Nothing could have prepared him for the emotional impact as he faced this hollowed-out shell of a man. Illness had reduced his father to a skeleton; there was little left of the man whose memory he had carried with him throughout the lonely years. By punishing his father, he had denied himself the need that suddenly engulfed him.

"Father, I love you." Like a child taking his first steps, Paul reached out for him with both arms. "Don't die. Please, don't die. I should have forgiven you long ago."

Douglas clung to his son, weeping for the time lost and the times they would never know. He knew his life was over. "Paul, it's all right. The senseless things we once did don't really matter in the end."

Tears ran down Paul's face. "Father. How I've longed to call you that. You've been constantly in my thoughts over the years. How could I have been so unrelenting?"

Douglas was unable to speak, and he ran his fingers over his son's face like a blind man piecing together an image in his mind.

"You shouldn't be on your feet," Paul said. "Lean on me." Taking the weight on his bad leg, he helped Douglas to sit. "I've never felt so helpless."

Shizue put the walking stick in Paul's hand. "You aren't helpless, Paul. By setting aside the past, you've made your father very happy," she told him softly, her eyes aglow with fresh hope as she saw the darkness lift from Douglas's face with his smile.

"Shizue's right," Douglas said. Reaching up, he pressed his son's arm weakly. "I want you to meet my wife." He motioned for Inge to come near. "Don't stand there apart from us. She's very dear to me, Paul. I'd like for you to be friends."

Inge's fingers trembled as she held out her hand to him. "Max's brother—yes, there is much of him in your face," she observed. "I know of your mother and of the sadness in your lives. To meet you at last—" Her voice broke off. "Forgive me, these are tears of happiness."

Paul took her hand in his. He thought Inge quite beautiful and was grateful for her presence in his father's life. "I've imagined you like this. Shizue spoke of you often."

"Now that you have come to Douglas, the ordeal is easier for him to bear," said Inge. Some color had returned to her husband's face, and her eyes shone with hope for his recovery. "But your leg. Please, sit with your father. Your presence seems to give him strength."

"I'd give him my lungs if I could," Paul said, resting himself in a chair at the table. "Father, all the times you reached out to me, only to be turned away. So much time lost between us. I can still hear Mother's last words, pleading with me to forgive you. It was the only thing she ever asked of me in a lifetime of giving."

Douglas gazed into this son's blue-flecked hazel eyes. He saw Natsu's face mirrored in them and was filled with the warm remembrance of their youthful love. "She's been given her wish, son. Don't look at me so sadly. You're the medicine I needed."

Douglas spoke to Shizue. "This time you've worked a miracle. Really, I feel better than I have in months."

More than anything, Shizue wanted to believe in miracles. "All the same, you shouldn't overtax yourself." She turned to Paul. "It tires your father to speak, Paul."

"*Ogisan*—Uncle Paul," Little Kimi tugged their pant legs, craving attention.

"Here, come to me." Inge gathered the boy into her lap. Her happy smile faded as she watched Douglas suddenly seem to shrivel up in the chair. Bringing a frayed handkerchief to his mouth, he began to cough.

Paul watched his father suffer through a seizure that racked his frail body. When it was over, he saw blood on the handkerchief, which Douglas quickly concealed in a jacket pocket.

After that Douglas could not speak much above a whisper. "Don't be alarmed. You've done me a world of good, Paul. I can't express it in words. How have things been for you? Tell me everything. After all these years, it's a joy just to hear your voice." Shizue insisted that he eat the nourishing meal she had brought while he listened to his son.

Paul talked of his career and about the critical situation faced by Japan. He desperately wanted to offer more than a grim rehashing of the facts. But his father listened with great interest and appeared anxious to know more. "The Allies are bombing us with leaflets asking for Japan's surrender. It's had some impact on the people, but the government in Tokyo has taken a stubborn posture," Paul said, his voice growing tired. "We might have negotiated an acceptable peace with the Allies if not for the ultimatum calling for unconditional surrender. Now it's a waiting game, Father." He managed to smile, including Inge as he said, "The war is in its last days. There's every reason to hope it will end any week now."

"The devastation you described makes me sad." Douglas held Inge's hand. He had forced himself to eat the meal served by Shizue. But it gave him no strength and the drugs he had swallowed with his tea now made him dizzy. "I'm concerned for you, son. Tokyo might be completely leveled before the government accepts defeat."

"It's where I have to be. I sold my ideals in China. Now I'm committed to seeing this through until the end, and I've got to return tonight." Paul consulted his watch, feeling bereft as the hour drew to a close. "Father—how easily that word comes to me now. Listen, you'll be repatriated soon and given proper medical attention. Your life is important to us all. You've got to hold on."

"I've never been a quitter, son."

His father mustered a smile, but Paul sensed this was good-bye. Douglas stood up and Paul rocked him in a fierce embrace, not wanting to let go.

A soldier leaned inside the creaking door to announce their time was up. Shizue had bribed him to allow the prisoners another few minutes here alone together, and she quickly cleared everything from the table.

"Until next week," said Inge, cheerfully hugging Kimi and Shizue. "Paul, God bless you." She touched his arm.

He found solace in her warm touch. "Bless you, for being with him. *Sayonara.*"

Shizue, then his grandson kissed Douglas good-bye. "*Sayonara,*" he whispered. Then he reached out to caress Paul's cheek in a gesture of love that held Paul at the door for one last moment between them. "God bless. When you visit your mother's grave, put flowers on it for me. I think she'll know."

Paul could only nod before he turned away.

After their loved ones had gone, Inge took her husband's arm. "This son has a good heart. I feel as if Max visited with us."

"Come, lie on the cot beside me."

"*Ach*, these hours together go so fast. It seems a lifetime between them, *Schatzken.*"

Quietly stroking Inge's hair, Douglas could not see beyond today. Her sweetness had been a source of joy, and he could not shatter their last seconds together by confessing his premonition of death. Paul's forgiveness made it easier to surrender. When he was gone, what remained in his pockets would be divided among the needy confined to his drafty barracks. A new dynasty would rise on the ashes of the old, and Inge would be part of it, along with his sons, Shizue, and Kimi. This was his legacy. "I feel a little stronger," he lied, kissing her forehead. Their time had run out. "Next week could bring peace."

"*Ja*, we must keep faith with God."

Led away down separate paths, Douglas Napier waved to his wife. A seizure caused him to stagger against the barbed wire fence, where he coughed up blood. The guard took him around the waist, feeling pity for a sickly old man. Douglas was not yet fifty. Shuffling through bright sunlight, Douglas smelled the scent of wildflowers. It led him back to his early youth, to the Hosokawa gardens, where a beautiful girl closed her fan to boldly return his smile.

Paul dusted bits of falling plaster off his lapels. Bombing had caused deep cracks in his office walls at the National Board of Information, and timbers supporting the damaged ceiling were set shaking as his neighbor in the office above crossed the floor. His desk was littered with directives issued from the press division at Imperial Headquarters. The possibility of defeat was gloomy news they wanted him to bury. Radio Tokyo broadcast that for Japan to accept unconditional surrender was unworthy of consideration and absurd. Lighting a rare cigarette, he glowered at the official statement released two days earlier. "Hiroshima was raided by a small number of American B-29's," it read. "The city incurred extremely heavy damage. The enemy used a new type of bomb. Details are still under investigation."

His secretary carefully opened the door. "Copy for your approval, Yoseido-*san*." Keeping one eye on the cracked ceiling, she approached with mincing steps. "I was informed that a follow-up story on Hiroshima is en route from headquarters."

"Finally." Paul limped to the shattered window, peering through the spaces between boards at a wasteland of twisted girders and crumbled masonry. "What kind of bomb could decimate an entire city?" His cane whacked the boards. The accursed bomb had interrupted telephone communications between Tokyo, Hiroshima, and Nagasaki. All communications were now sent via the military wireless. He had lost contact with Shizue, and she was due to visit his father again.

Paul saw an army messenger parking his bicycle on the street below. "Well, our story's arrived," he said to his secretary. "No doubt there'll be a long directive attached, ordering us to bury the gloom with the Hiroshima dead."

Slumping down in his chair, he waited as the messenger arrived at the office door and handed the official envelope to the secretary. "Move your feet, Sumako, the ceiling won't come down on your head."

Sumako opened the envelope. "No directive," she said, reading what she could before Paul snatched the story from her hands.

"Do you mind?" In his anger, he tore the cheap, coarse paper. As he pieced it together, his anger gave way to shock. Never before had so many civilians been killed or wounded. Accounts from the survivors assaulted his imagination with a chilling vision of hell. Eyewitnesses who had viewed the blast from a distance spoke of a mushrooming cloud that had eclipsed the sun over Hiroshima. He read the press division's cut-and-dried summation several times over.

Then he read it aloud to his secretary, who hovered expectantly across the desk. "The new type bomb, to which a parachute is attached, explodes with a blinding flash of light in the air, five to six hundred yards above the ground. The skin of a person on the ground exposed to the bomb explosion becomes ulcerated. War lessons to be learned from it are that burns are slight when a person is clad in white and that more tunnels should be dug for air raid shelters, since wooden buildings are often smashed flat." He pounded his fist on the desk in frustration. "What good are shelters against a bomb like this!"

Sumako responded in a quiet voice. "I think there is a trick to the American bomb. It blind's one's eyes to many other planes whose bombs—"

"Some of the military appear to agree with you! Here, read it for yourself!" Paul threw the paper at his secretary. One of the telephones on his desk was a direct line to the Imperial Headquarters press division, and Paul decided to see what other information he could obtain.

"Yoseido-*san*, here," Paul told the operator. "Put Tomita-*san* on the line."

After some delay, Tomita's crisp voice sounded over the noisy line. "Having anticipated your call, the answer is no. The Americans have issued no formal threat to use the new bomb again."

"Fill me in, off the record."

"Oh, very well. Hold on while I change phones."

Paul tucked the receiver between his chin and shoulder, tapping his last cigarette from the pack. Earlier in the war, Tomita had worked under him, and now the chief press officer rubbed elbows with the general staff. Paul's recommendation had elevated this pure-blooded Japanese to the position that should rightly have gone to him, and the oversight still hurt. "I'm waiting."

"Don't try my patience, Akira. I shouldn't be divulging more, even off the record," Tomita said in a harsh, superior tone. "My position isn't to be taken for granted. Is that understood?"

"Perfectly." The man's arrogance infuriated Paul, but he could not afford to antagonize him. "I appreciate the favor. What's the reaction over there?"

"We're all shocked by the enormous power of this new weapon. Those nearest the center of the blast were charred beyond recognition.

There is a possibility that it will be used against us again. We just received a wireless report that leaflets were found in a farmer's field on the outskirts of Nagasaki. Dropped by American planes last night. There was a printed warning to evacuate the city. A clock with dates was pictured below the message, and today's date was circled. August eighth."

Paul was struck by a thought that had him jerking the telephone cord taut. "But can't you see the significance of that date?" his voice challenged Tomita. "We bombed Pearl Harbor on December eighth, Tokyo time. The Americans are telling us that they plan to even the score today. And it seems a good guess that Nagasaki is their target."

"Mind your tone of voice, Yoseido."

"Sorry—please, hold on a minute." Paul fought to calm himself. Hiroshima had been bombed at eight-fifteen in the morning, he thought. Not many hours of daylight remained for the Americans to attempt a drop today. "They can't pinpoint their target at night," he said. "When we attacked Honolulu, our time zone put us one calendar day ahead. I think they're playing a game with us, and plan to drop the next bomb tomorrow, August ninth. Surely the general staff must recognize how urgent it is to evacuate Nagasaki."

"Yes, others have drawn the same conclusion. But there are some who've expressed doubt that the enemy possesses two of these bombs. Considering the technology involved, the Americans may not have had sufficient time to manufacture another. In either event, we lack the transportation to evacuate a city that size. No official warning will be broadcast or published. Throwing the citizens into a panic would cost many lives. All reasoning aside, this is an unsubstantiated threat. Now, I'm very busy, Akira."

"Wait! I have family in Nagasaki. Help me get a warning to them through the military wireless."

"Not a chance."

The line went dead. Paul let the receiver drop, and it spun on its cord like a top while he sat there powerless to act. He had used up his last favor, only to be cut off from Shizue at a time of impending doom. Perhaps those leaflets had been found on O-nami's farm, or that of a neighbor. Perhaps Shizue would be safe in the countryside. But what if she visited the army hospital on that day? Just sitting there would surely drive him mad. "Sumako, find out what trains are still running to Hiroshima and Nagasaki. Hurry!"

With Japan's transportation systems in a state of collapse, Paul knew it would take a miracle for him to reach Shizue before morning. Bowing his head, for the first time since his early childhood, Paul prayed to his mother's Christian God.

*   *   *

On Okinawa, nothing had been sacred to the guns of war. Max glimpsed torchlight flickering amid the shelled ruins of a Buddhist temple, where he braked his Jeep and set off alone. A black-robed priest moved through the gutted cemetery yard. Parts of it had collapsed into the sea, and he saw that other torches flickered below the jagged edge. They were carried by parishioners who were digging tombstones from the sandy beach. Dozens of tombstones had already been dragged up to the desecrated ground. Although the priest heard Max's footsteps, he remained bent over the tombstones, holding his torch, muttering the names of the dead prayerfully. Many of the stones were too fragmented to read the names chiseled on them, and his hand touched the pieces in a silent blessing.

"Forgive me for intruding, *bozu.*" Max bowed respectfully. "I saw your temple and felt the need for prayer."

"My eyes are troubled. Come nearer the light." The priest was an elderly man, but his voice was surprisingly young. He drew erect, squinting to bring the visitor into sharper focus. "I see a man all at once or not at all. You know our tongue and our ways, *rikugun shosa.*"

"And your grief, *hata sensei.*"

"*Hai,* that as well. Soon after the shells came, the earth began to slip away. We could not stem the tide, and this night more of our dead have been claimed by the sea." The wind fanned his sputtering torch as he thrust it out toward a rise of volcanic rock just above where they stood. "Their stones will be joined together in a circle there, as a monument to their spirits, at one with the sky and safe from the sea. *Hai,* even our dead have suffered. This is how the war will be remembered. But even the victor has reason to mourn. Have you come to pray for your own dead?"

Max did not know how to express his anguish. After learning that a second atomic bomb was being readied, he had driven in circles for hours. Kokura had been chosen as the primary target, Nagasaki's urban area the secondary target. The fateful decision would be determined by weather conditions. Like Hiroshima, neither city was of any strategic importance. An inhuman weapon was being dropped on his defeated homeland to demoralize a people who had been subjugated far too long ever to speak out. Japan had responded to Hiroshima with silence. And so tomorrow an even more powerful bomb would threaten his loved ones. But Max was at a loss to describe its horrors.

"It's the living I would pray for, *hata sensei.* But while I'm a party to all this killing, how can I turn to Buddha? How can I ask the favors of any god with so much blood on my hands?"

Lowering his torch, the priest gave Max an understanding smile. "You call me *hata sensei*—master—but there are no masters unless you would be a slave. Master and slave are in us all. Faith is the divine mediator. Do not be the slave of your doubts. In the sight of Buddha there is no blood on your hands. Nothing has been asked of you that has not been asked of every man in war. Turn to him, lest you turn away from yourself."

To Max the temple's ruins evoked images of the ravaged synagogue in Berlin. Charred planks had been set on rocks to serve as an altar, and the fire-charred gilded wooden image of Buddha no longer had a face. Max rested on one of the surviving pews. For some time he stared into the shadows, reconstructing Nagasaki in his mind. Its port, its factories rising up on the Urakami Valley where the breezes were perfect for flying kites. When he was a boy, the skies were always alive with fanciful kites in the shapes of birds, fish, and spiny dragons. The bomb that would be dropped tomorrow was over ten feet long, equivalent to more than 20,000 tons of TNT. At dawn the B-29's would take to the air from Tinian Island in the Marianas. Not six hours later they would be over Kyushu.

Max feared that Shizue was still in Urakami Prison, that his father and Inge might also be trapped behind its bars or the barbed wire fences of some prison camp nearby. If Nagasaki became the primary target, his loves ones would perish together. Man had stolen the fire from the heavens. And if there was a God, He would decide who would live and who would die.

BOOK SIX
OUT OF THE ASHES
AUGUST

1945

While I slept it was all over,
Everything, My eyes squashed white,
Flowed off toward dawn.

There was a noise,
Which, like all else, spread and disappeared:
There's nothing worth seeing, listening for.

When I woke, everything seemed cut off.
I was a pipe, still smoking,
Which daylight would knock empty once again.

SHINKICHI TAKAHASHI

O-nami scratched his sides and yawned. Dawn was breaking across the unclouded horizon, but he smelled rain in the offing. Yes, by midday clouds would blanket the skies. The thunder god was a wily deity, he thought, as he splashed cold water on his face at the well. Shizue had risen before him and was oiling her bicycle for her journey to the army hospital. She had not returned there in almost a week, O-nami reflected, and today she must go there again to obtain the drugs that kept Douglas Napier alive. Although no enemy planes had raided Nagasaki in the past few days, he was concerned over her safety.

One of their neighbors pedaled by on her way to the village. "Good morning," O-nami said politely.

"Good morning," the woman replied, thrusting her chin upward.

"Mind you do not run into a tree." O-nami dismissed her with a laugh. Except for such brief exchanges, the peasants remained aloof. The day before, he had encountered that woman gossiping on the road and glimpsed some leaflet before she hid it behind her back. He had been impressed by the fine quality of the paper, but he was refused a look at what it said.

"Ichiban, keep your fingers from the spokes!" He lifted Kimi away from the spinning bicycle wheels not a moment too soon. "Did you not see the boy playing here?"

"Oh, how could I be so careless?" Shizue wiped the oil off her hands. Fearful thoughts of encountering Commander Sekino had distracted her. "Give him to me. Bad boy, must you put your fingers into everything?"

"You did the same at his age," O-nami reminded her. "Curiosity is a sign of intelligence."

"Maybe so, but don't take your eyes off him while I'm gone."

Yufugawo called them to breakfast. Seated at the table, everyone gave thanks for what the land provided. O-nami was anxious for news. Newspapers were no longer delivered to the countryside. The old radio functioned intermittently, and he cursed it, pounding the cabinet. "A bomb was dropped on Hiroshima at eight-fifteen on the morning of

August sixth," the announcer said. Then static interrupted the announcer's voice, and a second voice overlapped. O-nami tried tuning it out, but the conflicting Home Broadcast from Tokyo only came in louder.

Yufugawo set down her chopsticks. "Why tell us of a bomb that was dropped three days ago?"

"Quiet, woman." Seizing the radio, O-nami shook it hard, then groaned as the radio made a sputtering noise and died. "This contraption is worthy of the junk heap. To my ear, that was not the voice of a Japanese. The enemy is broadcasting something the government does not wish us to know."

"Paul will know what it is. I'll telephone him from the city."

"This forbidden broadcast could be meant to warn us," O-nami worried aloud. "I feel a threat in the air today. Since you must go for the drugs, do it quickly. If you hear planes, take shelter where you can and wait until the sky is safe."

Shizue scooped up her child. "Mommy is sorry for being angry with you. Give her a kiss good-bye."

She had spent a restless night, and the journey into Nagasaki seemed farther than ever before.

Commander Sekino's office window faced the bicycle racks and she wanted to avoid being seen by him. Shizue pedaled to a back-street alley near the hospital and chained her bicycle to what remained of an iron gate that had been cut away during the scrap drive. After entering by the rear door, she checked up and down the corridor, hoping to find Dr. Haefele on his rounds. Some nurses gathered outside the administration office saw her.

"Hosokawa-san, feeling well enough to work again?"

"For an hour or so. Is Commander Sekino in today?"

"Not as yet," the administration nurse answered her. "Since the bombing raid last week we haven't seen very much of him. Workers were buried alive inside a shelter at the shipyards. There have been no other bombings, but every day the air raid sirens wail. They sounded again earlier this morning." She sighed. "Another false alarm."

"Yesterday the planes came again and dropped these," said another nurse, handing Shizue an oblong sheet of white paper. My little sister found this blowing around our garden."

Shizue glanced at the bold Japanese characters, stunned by the poetry of the American threat. "Back in April, Nagasaki was all flowers. August in Nagasaki there will be flame showers."

"Frightening," she said. Forgetting that the commander wasn't there, she jumped as his office door swung open. Only the cleaning woman. "Where can I find Dr. Haefele?"

"Try Ward C."

Eager to be gone, she bypassed the nurses' changing room and hurried up the stairs. Dr. Haefele approached her, walking with a slight limp. She knew that Commander Sekino had used torture to obtain his confession. But it was a shock to see that his left hand was bandaged and splints were taped to his thumb and index finger. "How awful. You shouldn't have tried to protect me."

"Oh, it was tolerable until they went to work on my hand. A surgeon and his hands are not soon parted. You're an amazing woman, Shizue. How ever did you manage Commander Sekino?" His smiling blue eyes questioned her reticence. "Modest as well."

"I begged him to show a little mercy. But I'd like to avoid pleading with him again for the drugs. The way he stares at me. Well, I thought it best to keep my distance." She averted her eyes, aware her friend had guessed the truth. "I must return to the prison camp tomorrow."

"Come with me." Taking her arm, he waited for the corridor to clear and then drew Shizue inside the linen closet. "I felt sure you'd turn up, so I went back to my old tricks." Dr. Haefele slid his good hand into a space between the linen shelves and wall. "This will have to last the week." The drugs were bundled in a knotted handkerchief. "Hide it in your pocket. Let's get out of here before someone comes." He opened the door and looked both ways. "Hurry."

"You've taken so many risks."

"Keep walking. I'll feel better once you're safely out of the building. How was Mr. Napier when you saw him last?"

"He's coughing up blood."

"The man must have an iron constitution to have lasted this long." They paused on the deserted landing, and Dr. Haefele held her as a father would. His voice broke. "I won't lie to you about his chances. The drugs are wasted on him now. We did our best for him and the other prisoners. Go home and don't expose yourself to Commander Sekino by coming here again."

She refused to see anything but peace in the days ahead and interpreted his hopelessness as a gesture meant to spare her further sacrifice. As she walked down the stairs, her heart skipped a beat. She heard Commander Sekino's voice. He was standing with his back to her, speaking with the administration nurse.

"I have an eleven o'clock meeting at the air defense chief's office. Have the paperwork brought to me immediately. Has Hosokawa-*san* returned to her duties?"

"Yes, you might find her in Ward C."

Before he turned around, Shizue just had time enough to squeeze into hiding behind some mattresses that were stacked in the hallway waiting to be cleaned. She gagged on the stench of dead soldiers as the commander strode down the corridor. Shizue realized that he had only to look more closely into the shadows to find her. She heaved a sigh of relief when someone called him to the telephone.

"Say that I'm busy inspecting the wards," he said. Under his breath

Shizue heard him murmur, "This time the slut won't mock me," as he headed toward the stairs.

Shizue listened to his footsteps vanish above, then she rushed away to exit by the hospital's rear door. It closed behind her with a bang as she ran up the street.

Commander Sekino's ugliness reawakened the memories she had fought to bury. Her breath gave out, and feeling faint, she rested against the window of a neighborhood tea shop. There was a public phone inside, and the jingling bell above the door took her back to the Cherry Blossom Kissaten. An elderly man chatted with the proprietress, who bowed, inviting Shizue to sit at the counter. "Just tea, the strongest you have. And coins for the telephone."

"So many yen?"

"I'm calling Tokyo," she told the man, and his eyes widened in surprise. "Is something wrong?"

"Have you not heard the news? Hiroshima was destroyed. Leveled in a single raid by some new-type bombs. You cannot possibly get through to Tokyo."

Shizue recalled the poetic threat of flame showers. "Are you sure the entire city was destroyed?"

"The greater part of it, yes. I am on the editorial staff of *Nagasaki Nippo*." He stood from the counter and bowed. "The air defense chief is a personal friend. Shortly, our reporters will meet with him to be briefed on the war lessons learned from the bombing of Hiroshima. He does not believe the citizens of Nagasaki will have need of them, but in my opinion, publishing the facts may help to save lives. The explosion shoots flames through the air. Then a typhoon smashes everything in its path and hurls the debris miles into the air. The enemy means to kill as many of us as he can. Our coastal artillery have no ammunition. Our gunners merely watch the sky, and today there are not many clouds to discourage the enemy planes. Forgive me, young woman. It was not my intention to frighten you. But once the B-*san*s are heard, you have only minutes in which to act. The chances for survival are greater underground. I would not stray very far from the nearest bomb shelter."

The proprietress tapped the floor with her wooden shoes. "The trapdoor to my shelter is here. Relax and enjoy your tea."

"Thank you, but I live in the country and my family will worry if I don't return home soon." Shizue quickly swallowed a cupful of dark green tea and stared at the telephone, longing for the comfort of Paul's voice. His father might go at any time. The drugs were wasted on Douglas. She had seen that clearly etched in his sallow face, and refusing to accept Dr. Haefele's prognosis would not make it otherwise.

Leaving the tea shop, her gaze wandered out to the shadows made by clouds drifting in across the Urakami Valley, where the shipyards and factories operated as usual. A rattling sound alerted her as she approached the alleyway where she had chained her bicycle to the remains of an iron fence. Someone wearing a coolie hat was striking at the padlock with a long metal object, and it broke apart from the chain. "Thief!" She rushed forward to defend her property, shouting, "You'd better run if you know what's good for you!"

"I do not run from women!"

Shizue did not see much of his face. Before she could find a jujitsu hold, the squat little man pounced on top of her, hitting her with his crowbar, and she staggered beneath the force of its blow. One side of her head felt on fire, and her eyes rolled back in her head as the thief pushed her to the ground. She raised both arms to ward off his blows, then let herself go limp. Lying there quite still, she had enough presence of mind to realize he might kill her if she moved or cried for help. He did not bother to rob her pockets. The bicycle was all he wanted, and he worked quickly. She struggled to remain conscious, praying someone would pass on the street before he could get away. But the chain she had used to anchor her bicycle clattered to the dirt, and the thief pedaled off. Dust swirled up around her, and the sky grew black as night. She heard a plane droning overhead, but her eyelids felt nailed shut, and she lost consciousness.

The plane she had heard was the American weather plane. It circled Nagasaki and reported there was little cloud cover over the secondary target area. Kokura had been obscured by smoke and haze. Now the B-29 instrument plane and its sister ship carrying an atom bomb named Fat Man were winging toward Nagasaki at an altitude of thirty thousand feet. But the favorable weather conditions were rapidly deteriorating. Clouds and haze drifted inland from the East China Sea.

When Shizue's eyes fluttered open, she had no idea how much time had elapsed. Gently she felt her head. The skin was broken just behind her ear. She managed to stand, but she was extremely dizzy. Near tears, she hugged the alley wall. Her only means of transportation was gone, and she was in no condition to make the long walk home.

As she stepped into the street, her vision blurred. Her injury needed a doctor's care. She was so dazed that she unthinkingly walked back toward the army hospital. Then she realized that Commander Sekino might still be there. He had no jurisdiction over the Nagasaki University Hospital located on the city's eastern slopes, however. She turned away and started downhill along a steep winding path, able to glimpse a field of clover near the university campus below.

There was hardly any breeze to relieve the intense heat and humidity. The overcast skies provided shade, but the air was stagnant. Quaint old houses with vegetable gardens were nestled together on the path she walked, her step made heavy by the ache in her head. The throbbing voices of cicadas usually had a calming effect on her, but that day their singing added to her discomfort. A little girl skipped gaily past her, carrying a colorful cloth bag. Then the drone of planes made Shizue look to the sky.

"B-*sans*," the little girl cried, pointing at the clouds as she began to run.

Shizue watched her trip on the path, taking a hard fall while vegetables rolled downhill from the bag she dropped. The girl, who was eight or nine at most and small for her age, was sobbing as she tried to stand. She had injured her ankle. People below them were scattering to find shelter.

"Don't cry," Shizue said, reaching down for her. "Let me help you. Is there a bomb shelter nearby?"

"Yes, at the schoolyard," she said, her voice trembling. "But it's way down there."

Terrified for them both, Shizue lifted the child into her arms, searching the cloudy sky and able to glimpse a silver dot circling out across the city in a wide arc. No air raid sirens shrieked an alarm, but the bomber's droning engines were real enough. She recalled what the man in the tea shop had said. She had minutes, perhaps only seconds in which to act. "Hold tightly around my neck and be brave."

To survive they must burrow themselves underground. There were just a few flimsy wooden houses directly off the path below. Calling forth all her strength, she followed a woman who scurried out of sight down stone steps that led to a basement.

Once inside, Shizue set the girl down and looked around. The stone walls and wooden beams appeared sturdy enough to shelter them. "We'll be safe here after the door is bolted shut," she reassured the child.

"*Hai*, this place is safe from bombs. It is the factories the B-*sans* come for." The old woman Shizue had followed squatted passively on the damp earth floor. "No need to bolt the door," she said, fingering her Buddhist prayer beads. "Leave it open for air and light."

"This time there may be flames shooting through the air." While carrying the child, Shizue had forgotten about her head injury. Now a loud-pitched ringing sounded in her ears as she quickly bolted the door. The basement grew pitch black. "It is best to stay away from the door. Give me your hand, child."

"I'm so scared. My mother sent me on an errand to fetch vegetables from her friend's garden," said the girl, holding to Shizue tightly with both her hands. "Papa is in the navy. Our house is near the river, and Mama is there with my baby brother, doing the laundry. Why are there no sirens to warn Mama of the B-*sans*?"

"There, I'm sure she heard their engines as we did and took shelter." Dizzily, she felt her way along the damp stone walls until she reached a far corner of the basement. "Come sit here with me between the timbers. I'll be your mother for now." Crouching there and listening in the intense silence, Shizue hugged the frightened girl as if she were her own.

Overcast skies spared Shizue her life. Because of them, the bombardier could not visually find the scheduled aiming point. Otherwise he would have released his payload minutes earlier. Now a B-29 was sweeping in from Nagasaki harbor, headed north and bypassing the old city in the valley to the right. The bombardier was searching for some window in the clouds while Shizue grasped her *omamori* for courage and rocked the little girl, softly singing a childhood lullaby to quiet both their fears.

At that moment, the plane was cruising high over unbroken clouds, its bomb bay doors open. Major Chuck Sweeney was critically low on fuel but determined to complete his mission even though the drop would have to be accomplished by radar. He surrendered control of the B-29 to the bombardier, whose steady hands now guided the plane to an approximate drop point. Ground zero would be the center of the Urakami Valley, only some two miles inland and within walking distance from the hillside basement where Shizue huddled with the child, and listened to the old woman muttering over her prayer beads. The plutonium device about to be detonated over the high ground would explode where its maximum force would wreak the most damage on Nagasaki's heavy industry. Aboard the instrument plane, the team of American scientists prepared to record the event as the city with its two hundred thousand people appeared on radar scopes, reduced to frosty green patches of phosphorescent light.

At exactly one minute past eleven, the spherical missile latched safely within the bomb bay doors was released. The B-29 rose, relieved of its heavy burden. Severed from the umbilical wires, the silvery projectile plummeted earthward.

Many citizens laboring in the city's longest valley had not heard or seen the B-*sans*. Those who had for the most part ignored them because no siren sounded the alarm. But others now looked to a silver dot sailing down through the clouds. Men and women blinked up at an opening parachute and glimpsed the shiny object tethered to its shroud lines. But this was only the metal canister filled with instruments to record the holocaust. More leaflets pleading for Japan's surrender, some thought, dismissing the instrument canister as no threat.

Few people actually saw the true instrument of their destruction, which was silently divebombing with its trigger primed to release the hellfires that would forever stop the clocks at two minutes after eleven. No one would ever know how many stood watching a parachute falling peacefully toward earth. At ground zero, those who bore witness to the birth of a star were blinded where they stood, incinerated, then atomized, becoming part of the purple pillar of fire shooting up from the valley.

The pillar of death grew a huge, ugly head of billowing purple smoke and exploding white geysers. Thunderclaps struck across the sky as the sun burned large and red. And then a terrible beauty unfolded as the fiery pillar grew another head and burst into bloom like the opening petals of some cosmic flower, shimmering with the incandescence of rainbow-colored hues.

Shizue had seen the blinding blue flash, like starlight twinkling through the cracks around the basement door. Then the earth shook, and the air seemed to explode with a shudderingly awesome roar that built and built until the sheer magnitude of the sound seemed to assume the mass and weight of solid matter. The child was literally torn from Shizue's arms as a deep sea of sound flooded in against the crumbling walls.

Trapped in the darkness, Shizue shielded her head from the raining debris. Timbers buckled and snapped like matchsticks, while the earth still trembled and buffeted her against the fissuring stone wall. Mercifully, the deafening roar tapered off into a low rumbling, drawn out like one enormous wave pounding the surf. The rumble seemed to go on forever. Then the fury of its sound diminished gradually, and it became a loud hiss, like the sound made by waves being pulled back out to sea on the tide. After that, the sudden quiet registered as a shock.

Shizue was stunned into inertia. The basement was a black pit beyond which nothing else existed, and it was hard for her to breathe. Suddenly, the little girl's screams pierced the quiet. Dust choked Shizue's voice as she called to her. There was little air. Shizue reasoned that part of the basement had caved in, and that rubble must be heaped high against the door. Otherwise, she would be able to glimpse a crack of daylight or feel a draft of fresh air. The old woman moaned for help. All three of them had survived. But Shizue feared they could be buried alive here like the shipyard workers a nurse had told her about earlier that day. She masked her panic with pretended calm. "Talking will waste oxygen. Pick up a stone and tap the floor. I'll find you one at a time. First the little girl."

"Kazuko," the girl spoke her name in a small voice.

Shizue crawled toward the tapping sound and found the girl. "Give me your hand, Kazuko." Both their hands were cold as ice. "What a pretty name. My name is Shizue." A sharp pain caused Shizue to touch the blood-matted hair behind her ear. The thief's blow had raised a painful welt. "Stay very close, and we'll find the old woman together."

"She is near my feet."

Shizue felt the Buddhist prayer beads, then the woman's clenched fingers and her wrist. There was no pulse. "She's dead."

"I want my mother," Kazuko sniffled, pulling on Shizue's sleeve.

"Hush now, soon we'll be outside and I'll take you to her. I don't remember seeing another way out. Help me find the door. Take shallow breaths. Keep one hand on the wall, and it will guide us."

As they inched along the wall, something outside crashed to earth with an impact that brought a slide of debris down around their feet. Shizue coughed, able to see the dust particles rising to slender needles of light. "See, there's no reason to be afraid."

Kazuko made tiny fists and rubbed her watery eyes. "Why is the light so red?"

"I don't know." Nagasaki was on fire, she thought, wishing for stronger hands to help her clear the mountain of crumbled stones. "We must have air. Dig, Kazuko. Climb with me and dig for the light."

The basement door was hinged to open out. Shizue realized that debris might also have blocked the other side. If so, perhaps it could be forced open wide enough for Kazuko to squeeze through and bring help.

Shizue concentrated on reaching the bolt latch midway down. She and the girl slowly removed the heavy stones to clear a space around the doorframe, which now let in reddish light and a steady draft of hot, muggy air. Kazuko bit on her lower lip, bravely moving stones as the light grew brighter. Shizue bolstered her spirits, telling her about little Kimi, the fun they would have when her family visited their farm. Mindless talk. Each stone seemed to grow heavier, and she paused to conserve her strength, searching what she could see of the basement for a tool of some sort.

In the hellish red light, she was able to see the body of the old woman, who must have had a weak heart, for there were no visible injuries to her head.

Shizue spotted a broom close to where the little girl was standing. "Kazuko, bring me that broom. I can use its handle as a wedge."

"Here it is."

Shizue felt dizzy and momentarily lost her balance, reaching for the broom. The welt raised behind her ear began to throb painfully.

"Are you sick?"

"I'm very thirsty. We'll rest a moment. The latch can't be much farther down." Her smile calmed the girl.

The faint patter of raindrops gave way to a heavy shower that cooled the air, and her dizzy spell passed. Even with both their weights applied to the broom handle, the heaviest stones were not easily dislodged. Before long the handle snapped in two and snapped again only inches from the straw whisks. Kazuko lost heart and screamed for help, but no one came, and Shizue weakly struggled on alone, using the handle's splintered end.

"I think I've found the latch."

"Shizue! Oh, there is blood running down your neck."

"It's nothing." The effort had reopened her scalp wound. She strained in vain to dislodge a jagged cluster of stones that blocked the latch. "My hands are too large. Reach between these stones and feel for the latch."

"Yes, it's here."

"Can you lift up on it?"

"I'm trying. The latch is lifting—but it's stuck."

"Think of your mother and try harder." Desire was not enough to make up for what the girl lacked in strength. Shizue picked up the splintered broom handle. "Take one hand away and use the other to help me guide this to the latch as a lever. Once it's in place, we'll count three and push up together hard as we can. Careful of splinters."

On the count of three, the latch was sprung. Rainwater dribbled along the inner edges of the creaking door. Shizue had not expected the latch to give so quickly and she lost her footing, falling hard against the pile of stones, which partially collapsed.

But enough of them had moved to give Shizue space in which to put her weight against the door. Using all her strength, she pushed, and the cellar door opened.

The rain had ended. She stood for a moment, hugging the girl against her as they both looked up at the murky sky. It was a nightmare painted in bleeding reds and mustard yellow. The sun was a red fireball glowing through the unearthly haze.

A twisted oil drum that had rained down from the sky now lay steaming on the cracked stone steps that led to the hillside above. Shizue took Kazuko's hand, unsteady on her legs and listening for planes while they climbed. At once she realized it was a miracle they had lived. The grass on the slope just at her feet was green, but everything directly below was scorched black. Everything on the hill behind her was on fire, every house smashed flat, as was the house whose basement had sheltered them. Shizue could only assume that the curvatures of the slope and its neighboring hillsides had offered some protection against destructive flames. Smoking ashes blanketed the earth, and Shizue's nostrils and eyes stung from the pungent fumes in the air. Below her, she saw Nagasaki in flames. Everything was on fire, pouring more ash and smoke into the dense yellow haze. A great cloud hung over the sky, and it seemed to be growing ever larger.

Kazuko began to sob hysterically. The district where her house once stood was no longer there. Flames shot up from it and the now flattened earth of other residential districts. Shizue looked toward the Yamazato district, where thousands of children lived. Flames and thick black smoke claimed the dwellings. The Urakami River was some walk away. Here and there in the scorched earth leading down to it were isolated patches of greenery, where the rolling curvature of the valley had offered shelter from that brilliant blue flash of light that incinerated everything else in its path. This hillside path was no more: weeds, grass, earth, and stones were a mushy brown goo, no longer resembling anything on the face of this earth.

Kazuko clung to Shizue. "My mother. Please take me to my mother," she pleaded.

Shizue had difficulty focusing her thoughts and concerns for her own family. The way back to them was made impassable by the destructive forces of this holocaust. What she could see of the Urakami River bank showed as a hard black edge of ashes. Kazuko's family might be found there among the dead, she thought. A violent pain shot through her head, and she dropped to her knees. The wet grass was littered with grain. Wheat stored in Nagasaki's exploded grain warehouses had showered down with the rain everywhere across the devastated city's black shroud of hot ashes. Shizue rested back against the soft grass, desperately wanting to avoid the horrors awaiting them near the center of destruction. "I can't go on with you, Kazuko. I must wait here for help."

"No, no! You promised. I am afraid to go alone."

Shizue rolled her throbbing head on the sweet-smelling grass, thinking how peaceful it would be to give in to sleep. "I'm so weary."

"Oh, please get up." Kazuko's small hand prodded her urgently. "The planes may come again. There are bomb shelters near the river."

"All right." She plucked a handful of wet grass and held the cool blades to the welt behind her ear. There would be fresh water in the bomb shelters, she thought, first aid supplies, a quiet corner where she could rest. While the city lay crippled and burning, she was helpless to do more than wait and regain her strength. Shizue stood and took Kazuko's hand. Other survivors slowly came into view, dazed figures who roamed the barren landscape unaware of their surroundings. The haze made it impossible to see for more than a few yards ahead, and the ashes under Shizue's feet were still hot, as if it had never rained.

A young woman climbed the slope. Shizue shouted, "The way up is blocked," then saw that one side of the woman's face was badly burned. Half her blouse was burned away, the blackened skin of one breast and arm hung like melted wax. "Stop! Come with us and we'll find you help." The woman seemed oblivious to her pain. She neither saw nor heard and kept climbing to nowhere. Shizue covered her eyes. The encounter threatened to destroy her sanity, but Kazuko insistently pulled her along, demanding more than she had left to give.

On their journey toward the river, Shizue was certain that Ema, the king of hell, had conjured up these horrific visions of the damned. People had been scorched black as pitch, turned into naked zombies without eyes or hair. Some were so charred it was impossible to tell their sexes. Shizue passed what had once been a mother, who was kneeling down on her arms and legs. Perhaps she had tried to shield her baby, who now lay on the ashes under her bosom, its charred, outstretched arms frozen in time.

There were other human statues of this bomb. What had been a man sat naked watching the sky, fused to the charred remains of a tree. His face still gaped in awe, and directly behind him the blasting inferno had left the bodies of children stacked up in what remained of a playground. At first Shizue thought them stacks of charcoal, but when she saw arms, legs, and heads poking from the grizzly stacks, she began to gag. Kazuko gripped Shizue's arm tightly. They walked on and passed a low wall, where a crouching person had been reduced to a shadow in the stone. Even the stones had boiled, and what must have been a bicycle was melted into the blistered wall. Shizue wondered if it could be hers, and if the remains of a man was the thief who had struck the painful blow that had stranded her in this hell. Nearing the river inside what would later be called "the red circle of death," she saw Urakami Cathedral in flames. She saw a horse without eyes, his flanks seared with red-black burns, blindly nuzzling the cadaver of a dog, whose intestines had spilled from its belly.

She could look upon it all only as a wilderness raised from hell, inhabited only by the mutilated and disfigured forms of humans and beasts. Kazuko whimpered, keeping one arm across her eyes as Shizue led her along. The river was filled with corpses. On its banks they passed charred, distorted bodies with faces that were blown up like balloons. The few survivors were burn victims, disfigured to various degrees. Some filed past like zombies. Others just sat on the ground, immobilized. In their minds they belonged with their dead. To have survived seemed a fate worse than death.

Farther on, naked men and women sprawled dead, their heads bobbing in the river. Shizue stared at the living, who stared back blankly. None of them recognized Kazuko, who jerked away from someone's burned hands and arms reaching up for help. The man was too severely mutilated for Shizue to guess his age. She took hold of his arms, moved by a compassion that suddenly turned to horror while his skin peeled off in her hands like two gloves. He remained seated on the ashes, looking at his raw flesh, and then his head drooped. Rooted there, holding his peeled skin, she felt the thin fabric of her sanity begin to tear apart. Her hands shook violently as she let go of the dead man's skin. There was a sticky yellow fluid on her fingers, and she wiped them again and again across her blouse.

Shizue nearly swooned as a naked, sexless figure ambled by, dragging the burned skin it shed like that of a snake. There was a putrid odor stronger than the fumes of the burning city as the shredding strips of flesh fell from the passing figure's legs and steamed on the smoldering ashes. "Can't go much farther," Shizue managed to say.

Kazuko clung to her sleeve. "Our neighbors must all be dead. But mama is saved. I feel she is near."

Placing one foot after another, Shizue distanced herself from the carnage around them. Farther along, voices pleaded for help, but she was utterly helpless as well, and numbly walked on. "Call your mother's name," she said to the girl. "Call it loudly."

"Ikuko! Mother, where are you?"

Shizue abandoned all hope. Pleas for help sounded all around them, but no one answered the girl's cries. A partially naked woman shuffled upstream, cradling the body of an infant, whose buttocks were swollen to twice their normal size. The woman's blackened skin was patterned with shiny pink spots, and she had no face left to speak of, no hair except for a matted strand that hung down across one unblinking eye. Her eyes mirrored the tortures of hell. Looking into them, Shizue's knees buckled.

Kazuko screamed, "Mother!"

Who but a child could know her mother as this walking corpse? Poised at the river's edge, the woman was deaf to her daughter's terror-stricken screams. Kazuko ran to her mother and began clawing at the remnants of her skirt, but the cloth disintegrated in the child's hands. An instant later the mother and her dead baby toppled forward, joining their bodies with those floating away. And in the next instant, Kazuko threw herself in after them, vanishing beneath the surface without a trace.

"Kazuko!" Shizue waded into the water, but she was too late. There was no sign of the child among the bloated corpses and floating debris.

Shizue prepared to dive, but dizziness forced her back from the river's edge. It had all happened so fast. Even if she had strength enough to swim the current, diving to search for the little girl in these polluted waters seemed futile. Kazuko's death plunge made life itself seem futile, and Shizue sank to the ground, overcome by inertia.

The Urakami became a river of lost souls wending its way through the underworld. In hell a damned soul was handed a mirror in which to view the events of his life, and now Shizue saw hers passing before her eyes with merciless clarity. She had failed to save Jiro, had failed to save Kimitake and her father. Her efforts to prolong Douglas Napier's life seemed doomed to failure. Now she had saved this little girl from the flames, only to watch her slip away in the blink of an eye. By what right had she survived?

For an eternity she sat watch over the river. Finally, she staggered past the mortally wounded. The doomed called to her for help, but Shizue saw herself as one of them and wandered on aimlessly. She neither saw nor heard the man who took her by the hand.

She was in some cool, dark place. It frightened her, and she sobbed like a child, curling up in the fetal position on the muddy floor. Water was being pumped from a well. Its trickling sound evoked visions of the river filled with corpses. Droplets beaded the bamboo dipper placed to her lips, and she drank. Shizue vaguely perceived a round, wrinkled face. "Thank you."

"You are hot with fever."

"I hurt, *ogisan*," she answered the grandfatherly voice, and felt a gentle hand across her forehead.

"Ah, there is a fat bump behind your ear. Lie still, daughter, this is only a cool compress to draw off the heat."

"Such comforting hands." Shizue sighed, unable to bring their owner's face into focus.

"Rest your weary eyes. The well water is sweet and pure. Here, drink a little more. When the fires burn down, I must go into the city to search for my loved ones. Until then, I will watch over you. Sleep, daughter. This cave serves as a bomb shelter. Remain here and you will be found."

Her head was lifted, then rested on something soft and dry. A benevolent spirit had materialized in the midst of hell. Perhaps her mind had only invented him and that was why his shape remained elusive and transparent. A warm cover was drawn around her shivering shoulders. With the unquestioning trust of a child, Shizue smiled up at her phantom friend, then was enveloped in his velvet cloak of dreams.

At twilight, Nagasaki still continued to burn. O-nami slowed his ox cart on a valley road below what remained of the army hospital. Except for the chimney, the entire structure had collapsed in on itself like a house of cards, and its timbers were ablaze. Any survivors trapped beneath the rubble were doomed to burn or die of suffocation. But nearby he found one nurse tending the wounded who told O-nami that she had seen Shizue running from the hospital well before the explosion, and he gave thanks to the gods.

On the farm he had seen a brilliant blue flash of light and had heard a great bang that moved the earth. Instantly he had ordered everyone into the bomb shelter, where they had prayed for Shizue's safe return. He had already combed what could be reached of the neighboring slopes around the hospital, and now many others like him filed ahead of his ox cart on foot, moving toward the city ruins in search of loved ones who might have survived. In the near distance, the smoldering remains of buildings looked like gaping skulls. A crimson glow flickered behind their eye sockets, and O-nami was chilled by the thought of human bones scattered beneath the ashes.

"Oh, she is lost to us," Yufugawo wailed, turning Kimi's face away to protect him from the gruesome sight of burn victims being carried past them on litters.

"Where is your faith, woman? Shizue is unharmed. Her heart goes out to others. She would never abandon the injured and is somewhere here at some aid station doing what she can to nurse them." Standing tall in the slow-moving cart, O-nami cursed his poor eyesight and the advancing darkness. "Open your eyes, woman. Shizue is not among these dead. Use your lungs to shout for her. You as well, Ichiban!" He stood Kimi up beside him. "Ah, he can be louder than the two of us put together. Fill your chest like me and let us hear you."

While everyone called to Shizue, the sky grew darker. Soldiers turned people back on the road ahead. O-nami reasoned that the soldiers could not be argued with and guided the oxen off the shoulder of the road. His plan was to sneak past the roadblock on the higher ground that nestled against the foothills.

"Mommy, Mommy!"

"Be quiet now, Ichiban, until we are past the soldiers." Just then, the cart bounced to a stop. O-nami leaned over the side, squinting at the wheels, which were lodged in a rut. The oxen refused to budge. "Stubborn beasts! Climb down to lighten their burden, and I will encourage them with a push."

Little Kimi skipped down from the cart on his own. Wide-eyed, he looked all around him. "What that, obā-san?" he asked Yufugawo, pointing one finger at an opening in the hillside some yards off.

Tears of grief clouded her vision. "I cannot say."

"Good for hiding. Come see, Grandmother!" Laughing, he ran off to explore the mysterious opening. Shizue had taught him not to fear the dark, and Kimi turned back to laugh at O-nami, delighting in a race. O-nami panted as he ran after Kimi up the steep grade. "O-nami too fat!"

"When I catch hold of you, there will be the devil to pay!" roared O-nami, shaking his fist to no avail. "Do not enter this cave without me."

Kimi heard water dripping from the well pump spout and was intrigued by its echoing plops. "Hello?" He was delighted as his voice echoed back. His keen eyes quickly adjusted to the light filtering inside the cave's yawning mouth. He saw footprints, then a shiny object half pressed in the mud. He hurried forward and began digging it out. His mother's good luck charm spun on its gold chain; one of its links was broken.

O-nami entered to lift him high. "Hah, now I have you."

"Mommy!" he yelled, thrashing with both arms.

There was enough light for O-nami's failing eyes to glimpse Shizue's charm in the boy's hand. But she did not respond to his cries, and the way ahead was black. He swallowed hard, then set the boy down. "We will look for her. I have matches."

Kimi stuffed the charm in one pocket, crying out excitedly as the first match was struck. "Mommy!"

"Do not run off!" The match blew out, and O-nami struck another, cupping the flame between his hands. While he could make out nothing more than shadows on the wall, Kimi saw his mother lying there and he ran ahead. They had found her.

"Thank the gods she is alive. Let her sleep, Ichiban," he told the boy.

A man's suit coat was neatly folded as a pillow for her head. An expensive garment, its silk label bore the name of a tailor in Hiroshima. There was blood on the fine linen handkerchief O-nami lifted from behind her car. Shizue's breathing was shallow, labored, and she uttered no sound as he carried her away in his arms.

Waiting at the cart, Yufugawo dissolved in tears and would have fainted if not for her husband's sharp commands. They had brought water canteens for the journey. Riding beside Shizue on a bed of straw, she ripped off the hem of her kimono and soaked the cotton strip. Shizue's eyelids fluttered violently as Yufugawo applied the compresses to her fevered brow and the swollen area behind her ear.

"She is delirious," Yufugawo said. "I fear the poor child may be gravely injured. The country doctor is too far away. We must take her to a doctor here."

"Look around us. The city doctors have their hands full treating the thousands in greater need. The village doctor who brought Ichiban into this world has nothing better to do than treat colds and coughs. The gods have spared her life. *Hai*, their hands guided Ichiban to the cave. These things are decided in advance." O-nami tousled the boy's hair and Kimi yawned. "The *kami* prompted your mischief. Climb into my lap, sleepyhead. In less than one hour we will be home."

Kimi's eyes grew wide. He had never heard the roar of bombers until now and pointed to the sky. "Big buzz."

O-nami whipped the oxen. "Hungry locusts who have come to eat our crops. We must race to the farm and beat them off with sticks." His invention delighted the boy.

Nothing could be seen of the planes, and people filing along the road appeared not to care. After all, what was there left to bomb? White paper rained down over Nagasaki, whose flames cast an amber glow against the sky. Kimi gleefully threw his hands up to catch one.

"Let me see what is written there," O-nami said. Stopping the cart, he held the white paper close to the tip of his nose. The American propaganda leaflet announced that Nagasaki would be destroyed and urged her citizens to evacuate. O-nami shook his head sadly at the irony of this mistake by the enemy. Then, beneath the paper showers, he whipped the oxen for home.

The country doctor had kept a vigil over Shizue's bedside throughout the days and nights while she lay in a coma. Her will to live was strong, but there was a possibility that the blow to her head had caused permanent damage. She developed an infection where her skin had been lacerated, and some of Douglas's drugs were used to fight it.

On the third morning the fever broke, and the doctor, who sat by her bedside exhausted, saw her move the fingers of one hand. When she lifted her arm to her face, he issued a warning. "Hosokawa-*san*, keep your head quite still. Make no sudden movements and do not try to speak as yet."

She did not see him clearly. When he flashed a bright light in her eyes, she recoiled, recalling a blue flash of light twinkling through the cracks around the basement door. "My baby. Where is my little boy?"

"The boy is asleep. You have been very ill. Now the crisis has passed, and you must sleep as well to restore your health."

Gradually, her bedroom came into focus. Yufugawo hovered tearfully beside O-nami. The household moved on tiptoe, speaking in whispers as one by one their smiling faces appeared at Shizue's doorway.

She was safely at home, Shizue thought. She remembered dreaming that the war had ended, that Max had returned home to be reunited with them, and Douglas was made well again. But how long had she been dreaming? she wondered. "I can't stay in bed. Douglas needs me." Shizue made a faltering effort to rise, but the doctor gently eased her back against the pillows. Everything grew dim.

"See that she remains in bed, or I will not be responsible for the consequences," he told O-nami and Yufugawo.

The doctor followed them into the kitchen. "Never have I known such a willful woman," the doctor said. "Ah, so, this war has made men of our women and has altered our role in the scheme of things. Perhaps women like Hosokawa-*san* will help us endure the unendurable. Surely, after Nagasaki, our leaders will accept the enemy's terms."

Wearing a long face, O-nami poured him tea. "Man to man, I feel there could be more of these bombs in store for Japan."

Yufugawo was weeping as she set the table, and O-nami put his arm around her waist tenderly. "Why these tears? Shizue is out of danger."

"Like you, I fear what is yet to come. I feel useless and old."

"*Hai*, we have grown old together, love of my life. Come, give us a kiss." She kissed O-nami's forehead, and he complained with a groan, taking her face between his hands. "No, a real kiss here on the mouth."

"Great oaf! Oh, why must you carry on so in front of company?"

"Hah, the woman still blushes. She is an obedient wife. With us there is no question as to who is the man."

"Pay no mind to this braggart, Doctor. I do have some say in matters of importance." Bristling with indignation, Yufugawo folded both arms across her chest and admonished O-nami. "Your laughter will disturb Shizue."

The woman's words were like music to Paul's ears. "Thank God, she's alive!" he exclaimed, surprising everyone as he limped through the farmhouse door. "I thought I'd never see you again." His sense of despair had lifted immediately. But after walking for miles, his last few steps caused him to double over in pain. He was grateful as O-nami helped him to sit and the doctor promptly unlaced his shoe. Explanations could wait, Paul thought. His swollen leg required immediate attention and he was put to bed quickly.

After O-nami helped to undress him, the doctor examined Paul's leg. He marveled at the army surgeon's skills. "In my day, an injury of this nature would have required amputation," he said. "How did you come by it?"

"Some bullets I caught in China." The swollen leg was a mass of scar tissue. A wooden one might have served just as well and with far less pain.

Yufugawo entered the bedroom to hand him a cup of warm sake. "Thanks. I tried getting here in time to warn you," he told her. "But it was impossible. The tracks from Tokyo were badly damaged, and my train had to detour time and again. I hadn't made it as far as Hiroshima, when I learned the bomb had been dropped hours before. Getting the rest of the way took days. But I couldn't turn back without knowing what had become of you. Thanks to my press credentials, I was able to hitch rides with the military. Now, tell me about Shizue."

Between them, O-nami and Yufugawo told him of their own experiences. But only Shizue could speak for what had happened to her on that fateful day. Kimi bounded into the room and fell across his uncle's chest, jabbering away in two languages.

Lying there with his arms around the boy, Paul wondered if Natsu's God had answered his prayers or if it had been only a lucky spin on the wheel of fortune. He had also prayed for Douglas's life.

"Keep his leg elevated until the swelling goes down." The doctor opened a flat tin box, selected a half-smoked cigarette from the stubs inside, lit it, inhaled two short puffs, and then feathered out the ember with his fingers. "For after dinner," he said, sighing as he returned it to the box. "When Shizue wakes, feed her broth and rice. Watch for signs of dizziness, nausea, and blurred vision. If there are no further complications, she can get out of bed in a day or so. But see that she avoids any strenuous chores."

Paul closed his eyes, grateful to be safely among friends. "The stations at Urakami and in Nagasaki proper were badly damaged. My train got only as far as Michinoo Station, and I had to walk from there. Nagasaki looked worse than Hiroshima. The rubble is still smoldering. It gives off an intense heat. Most of the hospitals were destroyed. There are no medical supplies, no equipment to treat the wounded. I saw fires burning—funeral pyres to cremate the dead. The main road to Omura is impassable, blocked for miles. Work crews are attempting to clear a path through the debris with shovels, rakes—any tool they can lay their hands on." Overcome by exhaustion, Paul closed his eyes. He wanted only to escape in sleep, to wipe the carnage of Nagasaki from memory and draw a curtain across his mind as he had in China.

Kimi craved the attention of his uncle, disappointed when the sleeping figure did not respond to his playful tugs on one limp arm. O-nami reached out for the boy, who squealed "Want Mama," as he was lifted astride O-nami's shoulders and carried outdoors past the room where his mother lay sleeping. "Wake up, Mama!"

"Be still, or I will eat you up starting with your toes," O-nami whispered.

Shizue stirred to the sound of her child's voice. But his call went unanswered. The traumas of Nagasaki and the ordeal of her fever had killed all desire to raise herself up from the downy pillows. She heard the barking of dogs in the farmyard, her son's giggling while at play, the leaves rustling against her window. The scents of hay drifted on a warm breeze. Familiar, tranquil aromas and sounds of life wafted over her reassuringly, and she surrendered to the peacefulness of a deep sleep.

When Shizue woke to voices conversing in the kitchen, she noticed that her room was colored in the purple hues of dusk, and for a time she lay quite still, as if the farmhouse were a dream. Then she carefully felt the bandage behind her ear and was jolted to reality. What day was this? How had she reached the farm? Somehow she managed to get up, cautiously testing her physical stamina as she walked toward the voices of her loved ones. She saw their faces as fuzzy blurs.

Kimi gleefully ran to her, and Shizue barely had strength enough to pick him up. "When did you bring me home?" she asked.

"Three days ago," Yufugawo said, trying unsuccessfully to pry Kimi loose from his mother; his arms were too tightly wrapped around her neck. "The doctor said you are not yet out of danger, Shizue. He prescribed rest. Give the boy to me and return to bed."

"Let him be. I won't be pampered like an invalid," she insisted. Dizzily, she sank to a chair and hugged Kimi. Her eyes were still blurry, and she could not believe it when she saw Paul. He could not really be here, she thought, confused as everyone questioned her at once. She did her best to relate her horrendous memories, but at that moment everything that had happened seemed so vague and remote. "Oh, please don't ask me for more. I'm just a little weak. What I need is some nourishment and your patience. By morning I'll be fit as ever and we'll visit the prison camp," she insisted. "I do remember securing the drugs for Douglas, and he must have them."

"Walking a few steps doesn't mean you've recovered," Paul argued. "I'm speaking from personal experience, Shizue. You have been through a great deal. Right now you're probably feeling numb. But don't let that deceive you. The aftershock can hit at any time."

"I should know how I feel," she countered weakly. "Honestly, Paul, your father's life is at stake." Indeed, the shock to her brain had temporarily erased much of what had taken place after the bombing. Those blank spaces in her memory permitted Shizue to function. But Paul continued to argue with her, and she became hostile. "Stop harping at me! Just because I can't remember every little detail doesn't mean I've lost control of my senses," she told him. "Your father's life is in jeopardy. The visitor's permit is made out in my name. You won't get past the guards without me."

"I give up!" Paul said angrily, banging the table in anger and frustration. "Since I can't prevent you from endangering your health, we'll visit the camp tomorrow. But tonight you belong in bed as the doctor ordered! Don't argue. I'll carry you there myself if necessary."

Shizue stared back at him on the verge of tears.

Puzzled by the heavy silence, Kimi tugged on his uncle's sleeve. "I'm angry only because I care for your mother," he told the boy. "We often get angriest with those we love," he said quietly.

The look in Shizue's eyes revealed her awareness that his love extended beyond friendship, and Paul took a deep breath, wondering how long she had known. He was grateful for her decision not to speak of it, for it would have destroyed their closeness. "I talk too much." He managed to smile at Shizue. "I'm sick to death of words."

"Yes, words often come between people and their deepest feelings," she answered. "Well, I suppose all of us should go to sleep so we can get an early start."

"It is past your bedtime, Ichiban," O-nami said, swooping Kimi onto his shoulders. Giggling, the boy rode off, holding on to O-nami's topknot.

"Good night, Paul." Shizue retreated from the love in his eyes.

Yufugawo helped Shizue into bed. Once again Shizue's thoughts became confused. Horrible visions flashed through her mind, and she clung to the reality of Yufugawo's mothering hands. "Oh, Nagasaki is like a nightmare. I don't want to remember anything."

"Sleep, daughter."

Shizue sat up in bed. The memories returning to her came out in a jumble of sentences. "The old man called me 'daughter'. He watched over me. Dr. Haefele said there was no hope for Douglas."

"This distress can only make you ill, child. Close your eyes. Give yourself over to pleasant thoughts."

Paul watched from the doorway, thinking how childlike Shizue was in sleep. He decided to go for a walk. The sky was clear. Walking beneath its untroubled canopy, he felt that Hiroshima and Nagasaki belonged to the realm of nightmares, and he prayed for the girl who had once believed in wishes to be spared from remembrance.

Then he felt O-nami's hand on his shoulder. The two men quietly shared a moment neither one could hope fully to understand. They felt a warm kinship and embraced. Both were moved to tears. Soon their long years of struggle would be ended. But their world had died. Peace was destined to test them with perhaps even greater challenges.

They walked for a while longer, followed by the affectionate pack of dogs Shizue had adopted. She was the hub around whom everyone revolved, thought Paul. O-nami settled against a haystack and Paul sat down beside him. There was no need to speak of how Shizue's presence in their lives nourished them both. It occurred to Paul that he had never taken time to enjoy the simple pleasures of life. For that night at least, he had stopped running long enough to smell the earth, to look at the stars, and to feel the stillness of the evening. Shared with a woman, the darkness would have brought him peace, rather than a sad, empty yearning for what could never be.

O-nami snored contentedly. The dogs stretched out and yawned. Puppies ran to be suckled at their mother's nipples, and Paul observed the runt of the litter being pushed away by his siblings. He picked up the small whimpering creature who suffered from neglect. "We're alike, you and I. Mongrels. Loners." The puppy licked his face, hungering for affection.

Drowsy now, Paul stroked the tiny outcast and carried him to the farmhouse. "Things are tough for misfits like us." In the kitchen, he gave the puppy a bowl of milk. After the puppy drank his fill, Paul settled in a chair and cradled it with the tenderness he had learned from his mother. By forgiving Douglas Napier, he had honored her final wish, releasing himself from years of bitter self-denial. Not many days ago he had placed flowers on Natsu's grave. Kneeling there, he had spoken a few simple words. "Father wanted you to have these."

He thought about seeing Douglas in the morning. "Please don't let my father die," he prayed to Natsu's God, and made the sign of the cross.

*   *   *

With the cock's crow, Shizue awoke and dressed. She discovered Paul fast asleep in the kitchen, the puppy cozily snuggled up on his lap. She hated to disturb him, but just then O-nami bellowed loudly.

"Why is breakfast not on the table?" he demanded, entering from the yard. There were wisps of hay in his graying topknot. "Time weighs heavily on my bones this morning. The oxen are hitched and waiting. Where is Yufugawo? Paul, give me that runt and change your clothes. Ah, I dreamed the skies were black with enemy planes."

After breakfast they left for the prison camp. Riding in the cart made Shizue nauseated, and rippling heat waves caused the road to blur, taking her back to a river of corpses, where a little girl had joined her mother in death. She held her son protectively, experiencing a foreboding as the cart neared the prison gates.

Paul was dressed in the peasant garb he had worn before. He knotted his sweaty hands around the walking stick. Black crows circled above the watchtowers. One mile from Nagasaki, another POW camp had been wiped off the face of the earth. In the city, American soldiers forced to labor in the factories had also become casualties of the atom bomb, whose explosion had been felt even here. Shizue noticed that the gate guards looked a bit jittery. There were no friendly smiles, only grim faces when she bid them good morning.

"You will wait here!"

O-nami reined up just outside the gatehouse, where a sergeant cranked the telephone and announced their arrival. They were told to wait. "Wait for what reason?" he challenged.

"Orders from the commandant," the sergeant replied. "His adjutant is on the way to explain things."

Shizue exchanged looks with Paul. A series of barbed wire gates were parted for the camp commandant's adjutant.

"I am Lieutenant Ono," the fastidiously groomed young man announced, clicking his boots and removing his dusty glasses. "Please, bear with me a moment," he said, polishing the lenses with a clean white handkerchief. "This dust gets into everything." Lieutenant Ono put his glasses on, then his eyes went to Shizue. "It is my regrettable duty to inform you that Napier-*san* died in his sleep sometime during the night of August 7, 1945, and was promptly buried in accordance with the rules that govern this camp."

Had Shizue not prepared herself for death, the shock would have proved too much. Little Kimi squirmed on her lap, impatient to see his grandfather. Shizue hugged him tightly, her eyes filling with tears. She looked at Paul's grief-stricken face, which was shadowed by his large straw hat. Tears rolled down his cheeks.

Shizue knew that Inge would need them more than ever now. "We'll visit with his wife," she quietly told the lieutenant.

"I am sorry. But when word of Napier-*san*'s death reached her by the prison grapevine, she stoned a guard and attempted to scale the boundary fence to the male compound." Lieutenant Ono impassively folded his handkerchief into a neat square and daubed the moisture at his temples. "It was necessary to place the woman in confinement under physical restraints, Hosokawa-*san*. As part of her punishment, you are forbidden to visit here again. The commandant is law here. Go over his head by complaining to your important connections in Tokyo, and Napier-*san*'s widow will only receive harsher punishment."

"Idiot! My father's grave is behind those gates. Open them to us, or I'll have your commandant roasted on a spit by the general staff!"

"Your father, is it?" Hands on hips, the lieutenant threw his head back with a laugh. "Sit down and hold your tongue, *ainoko*."

"You, there!" The lieutenant reached up to jab O-nami's arm. "Turn this cart around and be on your way."

"We're not peasants to be ordered about." Before O-nami could stop him, Paul leaned from the cart and brought his walking stick down hard. It barely grazed the cowering lieutenant's shoulder. As Paul raised it to strike again, the guards unshouldered their rifles, waiting for the command to fire.

Aware that his anger was futile, Paul dropped the stick from his shaking hands. The murderous intention burning in his eyes flickered out, and he sat down beside Shizue, dazed and staring through the barbed wire separating him from his father's grave.

"Mongrel. His bark is worse than his bite." Lieutenant Ono dusted his jacket, laughing so as not to lose face with his men. "Give the cripple his walking stick. I would teach him a lesson, but he is not worth soiling my hands. Go before I change my mind."

O-nami wasted no time in turning the cart around. Kimi was puzzled. "Go see *ogisan*," he cried.

"Your grandfather isn't feeling well enough to see us today," said Paul, trembling as the boy's hand brushed the tears on his cheek. "We're all disappointed. But soon you'll visit him again," he lied, then looked back at the closing gate. Douglas's suffering had ended, Paul thought, and there was comfort in knowing that his father had died peacefully in his sleep.

Shizue felt a sense of dislocation. Nagasaki and the prison camp were merely points on the compass while she traveled the isolated road stretching between two horrors. As they arrived home, only the pull of her son's hand carried the weight of reality. For most of that afternoon, Shizue sat alone before the bedroom mirror, staring at the hardened face looking back at her. A wave of nightmarish images floated before her eyes. "Oh, Max, I need your arms around me. But will it ever be the same between us after the horrible things I've witnessed?"

"It is not good to be alone with your grief," said Yufugawo, entering the bedroom.

Shizue beat her fists against her lap. "All for nothing," she cried. "Douglas was already dead, and I risked my life for nothing. All this waiting for the war to end. All this hope and sacrifice wasted. For all I know, Max has been killed in this war, and there's no point in going on."

"What dreadful thoughts. You ask too much of yourself, child."
Yufugawo put her arms around Shizue. "Your efforts have helped keep
Inge alive, and you mustn't lose faith. Max will return to us. Think of him
and your son. You must go on for them both."

"Yes, I mustn't fail my son." She glanced down at her floppy blouse
and baggy trousers. They were unsuitable attire for mourning Douglas,
she thought. Her father and Kimitake had been mourned in the white
dress she kept folded inside the dresser drawer that she now opened. She
looked down at it, recalling the day she had been taken away to prison
wearing this dress. Just touching it sent shivers up her spine.

Shizue closed the drawer on tradition. Long ago it had ceased to play
a significant role in her life. "Max is alive. I'd know if he died, Yufugawo.
Somehow I'd feel the loss. Wherever he is tonight, he's thinking of me,
wondering how much longer it will be until he can set foot on Japanese
soil again and be with me. He'd expect to find us at home," she said,
experiencing a moment of panic. "How will he ever find us if we don't
return home?"

"Come. O-nami has gathered the household to discuss our fate. No
decision can be made without you."

Shizue accompanied Yufugawo to the kitchen, where everyone was
seated around the table discussing the possibility of an Allied invasion that
would turn the countryside into a battleground. She listened to the fears
expressed by those who had come to be her family. Many of them wanted
to return home, to meet whatever fate held in store for Japan on the soil of
their ancestral lands.

"Perhaps it is now too late for Japan to accept surrender," said O-
nami, thoughtfully stroking his topknot. "The enemy may have tired of
waiting for us to answer his terms and may plan to avenge himself by
storming across our shores, killing as many Japanese as he can." He turned
to Paul. "If there is an invasion, we must be prepared to defend our loved
ones."

"In my opinion, the Americans won't waste lives testing your
bravery against bullets," Paul replied, and everyone grew silent. "I don't
think these bombings were a prelude to an invasion. No, that would cost
the Allies too many lives. America chose to take Japanese lives, hoping the
power demonstrated by their new weapon would shorten the war. They
might bomb city after city unless Japan sits down at the peace table."

Shizue protectively cradled little Kimi. "Then we must surrender
quickly."

Paul had run out of cigarettes, and his hands nervously crushed the
empty pack. "After Hiroshima and Nagasaki, it seems that mankind has
the capacity to destroy itself, to wipe itself off the face of the earth. But
speaking from my experience, the powers behind the throne are too busy
arguing among themselves to accept the realities of a surrender."

Even as Paul spoke, America was prepared to drop two additional
atom bombs if Harry Truman gave the order. The Japanese government

was in a state of upheaval. Dissension among its high-ranking officials and chiefs of staff had encouraged the emperor to take command and bring the war to a speedy end. But the palace revolt was being played out in utmost secrecy, and those gathered in the farmhouse kitchen could not know that the Allied surrender terms would be accepted in a matter of days.

"Since the Allies have denied us a negotiable peace with honor, we have no choice but to lay down the sword in unconditional surrender," Paul said wearily. "Otherwise Japan risks annihilation."

"The B-sans could strike again anywhere," said Yufugawo. "Here there is nothing left worth bombing. But the roads to home would be unsafe."

"Yes, we can't simply run home and hide our heads in the sand," Shizue said, rocking her child. "The army must still be in command there, prepared to fight off an invasion. Those of you who long for home as I do may not find things as we remember them. This farm has been a safe shelter. Here we have survived. Here we strengthen each other."

The eldest member of the household shook his clean-shaven head, then wiped one sleeve across his watery eyes. "I have not forgotten the fall of Nanking. After the city was surrendered, our army raped and slaughtered its citizens. Now the Americans put our cities to the torch with this new bomb. What assurance have we they will not avenge themselves on us after Japan surrenders?"

He turned to Paul. "You are someone of importance in the government. We trust your words. But can even you know how the enemy thinks?"

"Yes, I think I do. In our papers, many facts about the enemy were distorted. I saw the combat reports. We were required to edit them in such a way that readers never learned the truth about the enemy."

No one doubted Paul's sincerity as he broke down the propaganda barrier, describing the true accounts of Japanese defeats at the hands of an enemy who had fought an honorable war. "I don't believe the Americans are capable of atrocities like those we committed against the Chinese," he told them. "They've fought well and bravely, earning the respect of our commanders. These recent bombings were an act of desperation. From what I know of General MacArthur, he's a fair-minded shogun. A soldier-statesman who time and again ordered his bombers to bypass the Imperial Palace. I believe he plans to conduct an orderly occupation. He realizes how useful the emperor can be in helping him establish our trust and confidence so that Japan can begin rebuilding. American reprisals would bring only civil unrest, and Japan is no use to anyone in a state of collapse."

Yufugawo heaved a sigh. "It seems our fears are unjustified. Perhaps the gods have chosen this American shogun to spare us more suffering."

O-nami squeezed his wife's hand. "*Hai*, but the threat of more bombs is real enough. So, we stay here to face the conquerors like samurai," he addressed Shizue, then slapped his topknot and grinned. "When the

Americans come, you will go to them and inquire about your husband. Once they are told your story, they will send word of us to Ichiban."

"Oh, yes, surely they'll be of help." Shizue now brightened with the prospect of contacting Max through the occupation forces. Then, looking at Sato's father, she saw the hostility in his eyes. His son had been reported missing in action. Shizue observed that others among her family of friends had mixed emotions regarding her excitement about receiving the conqueror with outstretched arms. Their animosity was understandable, she thought, but wounding nonetheless. She grappled with how her own feelings might be twisted against Max's countrymen, following the horrors of Nagasaki.

Finally, she spoke from the heart. "All of you know my husband would never willingly fight against his Japanese brothers. He was healthy and strong, and I'm sure he didn't escape service in this war. Given his choice, Max would have volunteered to fight the Nazis. But soldiers aren't given a choice. They're sworn to obey orders."

Sato's mother embraced Shizue tearfully. "Forgive us for offending you. Leaders are to blame for this misfortune, not your husband, not my son. Let them both return to us with sound bodies. There may be hard feelings for a time," the woman said, facing her husband. "But it will pass."

"Yes, home must wait until there is peace," Sato's father decided. "Shizue was right. Here we strengthen one another. Here we survive what is to come."

Shizue smiled up at her family warmly. They were united, and everyone joined hands in a bond of friendship that made them tearful.

Dinner was brought to the table and there was the usual hum of voices giving thanks. Shizue placed her faith in Paul's belief that peace would carry no hidden dangers, no tragic surprises, only a quiet end to her trials. But the horrors wreaked by the bomb would forever leave a scar on her mind. Life's travails had turned her away from the cult of ancestor worship, and the obligations of her Bushido were no more. Her eyes rested on little Kimi, who would one day inherit the lands and her father's title. He knew no other home than this farmhouse, and leaving here would be an uprooting experience for him. He knew his American father only from old photographs and her childhood memories told to him as bedtime stories. She had done everything in her power to make his father real to him.

Suddenly Kimi climbed down from his chair at the table and tugged on Paul's arm. "I miss *ogisan*. I miss grandma-*san*," he said with a sad look on his face. "We go see them tomorrow, Uncle Paul?"

Shizue went to lift him in her arms. "A few days from now, sweetheart," she hushed him, reminded of what Lieutenant Ono had said about Douglas's aggrieved widow having to be physically restrained. "What's to become of Inge?" she asked Paul.

"Repatriation by the Americans."

"Repatriation to where? Max and I are her only family. She has no one in America. No one in Germany. She belongs here with us."

Paul stared off into space for a moment, then shrugged and said, "She won't be returned to occupied Germany. Inge's camp records speak for her situation. As a U.S. citizen, she'll have a say in deciding her fate. I'm sure she'll also inquire about Max. And wherever he is, he'll try locating you through military channels as well. There's no better way of getting a message to him." Paul mustered a smile. He knew that his brother would move heaven and earth to reach Shizue, but the occupation of Japan would be governed by strict regulations, and if Max had served in the Pacific, the military was unlikely to write him a pass to go where he pleased.

Rising from the table, Paul kept his thoughts to himself and stood facing out the kitchen window. He glimpsed the headlights of trucks on the main road. "It looks like the government's finally sending emergency supplies to Nagasaki," he said, pacing with his cane. "My leg's fit enough to travel. I'll leave for Tokyo tonight."

"Paul, why go back there?"

"It's my destiny, Shizue. The end of a road I chose long ago."

"But there may be other bombings. Oh, it's senseless to expose yourself to so much danger," she insisted, realizing nothing she could say would dissuade him.

"I'd appreciate a ride as far as the crossroads, O-nami," said Paul. "Those trucks will give me a lift, and I'll find transportation north from the supply depot."

"Hai." O-nami left to bring the ox cart.

"With surrender so near at hand, I can't understand what you hope to accomplish in Tokyo," Shizue argued.

"What better place to witness the events that shape Japan's future? When General MacArthur arrives to accept the emperor's sword, the flag of the rising sun will descend over Tokyo's ruins like a shroud. But the sun will continue to rise over the Imperial Palace, and the conqueror will need Japanese journalists to reach the people."

Paul struck the floor with the tip of his cane, the adrenaline rushing through his veins as it had on that distant night aboard a troop ship, outward bound across the China Sea to adventure. Then he had looked forward to exciting times, to a clean slate on which to write off the bitter past. He had seized a particle of power, but he had never risen above the stigma of mixed blood except in the most superficial way. Not a fair exchange for having sacrificed his ideals to the tides of war, he thought. But now a new sense of purpose fanned the embers of his youthful idealism. That night he felt the pull of some noble cause awaiting him in a defeated Japan. "America will bring democracy to Japan," he announced, his eyes burning with zeal. "Social reforms will be founded on the ashes of defeat. Maybe the Americans will discount my past sins and use my talents in establishing their new order. Yes, I'm still a journalist. The press will have to make room for me. Japan would be crippled, its people in a state of chaos if the Americans silenced the newspaper presses. Without the right words to support it, the mechanisms of a new government would grind to a halt. I belong in Tokyo."

Being a journalist was Paul's identity, his strength, Shizue thought. "I'll ride with you to the crossroads," she said, resigned to letting him go. "Kimi, it's your bedtime. Say good-bye to Uncle Paul. Then I'll tuck you in."

"No, no! Go with Uncle Paul," he cried, rushing out the door.

Paul laughed. "The boy's inherited a stubborn streak from both sides of his family."

Suddenly, the dogs began barking. "They sense that you're leaving us," Shizue told him. Everyone bid Paul good-bye and wished him luck. When Shizue stepped outside with him, Kimi was standing in the yard anchored between two of the largest dogs.

O-nami appeared in the ox cart that squealed to a stop. "We should go quickly before the trucks pass us by," he announced.

"Come along, Kimi," Shizue said. "You can ride with us." Kimi shook his head. A moment ago he had been eager to ride in the cart. Now the boy cried for his uncle to stay. "You can't have everything your own way," Shizue said. She tried to pick Kimi up, but he began shrieking, triggering a howling throughout the pack.

Paul came to the rescue. "Quiet down, young man. Making such a racket won't give you the last word."

Bending down, he lifted a brown-and-white spotted puppy by the scruff of its neck to dangle it before his nephew. "I was going to take this little fellow home with me, but he's better off staying with you. His name is Runt. *Chibi*. The other puppies won't give him a fair chance. Here, take care of him for me. Not much to look at now, but give him love, and he'll soon grow bigger and stronger than the rest."

Kimi giggled as the puppy licked his face. "Runt, I love you. Give him to me, Uncle Paul. I'll take care of him for you."

Shizue stepped back with a look of amazement. "Paul, it's the first time he's spoken in complete sentences."

"Don't count your blessings. Before long you'll be plagued with questions. Why is the sky blue? Why are Daddy's eyes like the sky and Mommy's dark like mine? I didn't mean to sound like such a cynic. You've nothing to worry about, Shizue. The boy's led a sheltered existence. He hasn't been poisoned by the ugliness I was exposed to even at his age."

"Children are so vulnerable," she said. "I've done all I can to prepare him, but Kimi might not easily accept his father."

"Oh, he's strong enough to make the adjustment. Once he sees Max, everything will work itself out." Hiding his sadness behind a grin, Paul observed how adversity had changed the dreamy-eyed girl he had loved to this mature mother whose helping hands steadied him as they climbed into the cart. Shizue sat beside him with Max's son on her lap, who hugged the puppy in his sturdy little arms.

Paul realized his role as Shizue's protector was ending. "Surrender isn't far off." He reached down, massaging his aching leg. "I feel it in my bones, Shizue."

"I hope you're right," she replied, watching him fold both hands across his cane. He had a special way with her son. He might help the boy to accept Max as his father, and she struggled with the temptation to plead with Paul to stay for Kimi's sake. But she remained silent, aware that for Natsu's son, Tokyo was home. She thought of the tea shop on the Ginza, so far removed from the Napier mansion. Was that familiar old house destroyed in the bombing? she wondered as the ox cart bumped along the rutted dirt road. Paul's years of devotion to her had Shizue fighting back tears. She saw the yellow eyes of truck headlamps flickering on the main road ahead. To her they were like the lights of ships that sailed on the ebbing tide of a long and costly war.

O-nami stopped the cart, waving his arms at one truck heading away from Nagasaki. "Someone of importance with the government in need of transportation," he called to its soldier driver.

"Well, here's my ride," Paul said, trying to sound cheerful. "No tears, Shizue. I'll turn up on your doorstep again. Haven't I always?" He kissed her hand, then the cheek of his drowsy nephew. "Take good care of your mother."

"And Runt," the boy said sleepily, burying his nose in the puppy's ball of fur.

"Come back to us soon." Shizue thought of all her hurried farewells and wanted to hold him there. *"Sayonara."*

Her arms were full with Kimi, and Paul's embrace seemed too short. She watched him limp off and saw him hand the truck driver some form of identification. The driver nodded. Without so much as a backward glance, Paul walked to the tailgate and soldiers hoisted him aboard.

"Smile and wave good-bye to your uncle," Shizue said.

Kimi waved at the slow-moving truck. *"Sayonara,* Uncle Paul. Thank you for Runt!"

Shizue waved with her son, who had suddenly outgrown his baby talk. As O-nami urged his oxen back to the farm, Kimi fell asleep with the puppy pressed securely against him, and she wanted to preserve his innocence. Kimi had as yet no concept of death or of the differences between races. For now he saw everyone as being the same. In the months ahead, it would be necessary for her to explain many difficult realities to him, and she wished his innocence could be preserved always.

Rocking her baby, Shizue saw people being turned away from the door of a neighboring farm. The three figures stood huddled together at the side of the road. "O-nami, stop and see what they want."

"Dressed in city clothes," he observed, then bid the strangers a good evening. *"Komban-wa.* If you come to buy food, we have none to sell."

"Komban-wa." A handsome woman of perhaps forty bowed and introduced herself as Mrs. Kano, wife of a doctor at the University

Hospital. It and her home had been destroyed in the bombing. She, her elderly mother, and her ten-year-old son carried a few bundled belongings. "My husband sent us out of the city," she explained. "He remains there doing what he can for the wounded. Some medicine and emergency food supplies began arriving only today. But the situation remains grave. Even fresh water is scarce. My grown daughter is among the missing. We seek lodging, to wait here until the rubble cools. Then we'll return to continue our search for her in the ruins."

"How sad for you," Shizue responded. "We've no room in the house, but you're welcome to stay in our barn."

"So kind," Mrs. Kano and her family bowed, and they wearily trudged behind the cart to O-nami's farmhouse, just a short way down the road.

Yufugawo greeted the city visitors at the kitchen door. She was hospitable but concerned that their presence might kindle Shizue's memories of the bombing. "Here, give Kimi to me and rest," she said to Shizue. "I will put him to bed."

"Let him sleep with the puppy."

Shizue invited her guests to sit at the table and eat what food was left from dinner. "Our household retires early, Mrs. Kano. They'll welcome you in the morning. We'll all gladly share what we have with your family."

"I can never thank you enough," the woman said, visibly relieved to be off her feet and in the company of friendly faces. "Many people are moving outside the city. Cremation fires burn day and night for the many who have died since Terrible Thursday."

"I was there on that day. I saw their burns." Shizue trembled. August 9 had now been given a name, and the homeless survivors of Nagasaki bore witness to its continuing horrors. "Forgive me for saying this, Mrs. Kano, but death was a mercy for those poor souls who were burned beyond recognition. Yes, a mercy."

Mrs. Kano stared blankly at the wall. "That is so. Yet, the deaths I've witnessed seem beyond mercy. I do not speak of the badly burned," she said, pushing away the food set before her. "There is a mysterious illness that strikes down people who are visibly uninjured. Hundreds of them each day. Oh, some do have minor burns. But for the most part, the dying are as unblemished as you and I. Every day more victims wander into temporary hospitals like the one in which my husband serves. They complain of no appetite, of bleeding gums. The early symptoms of the illness are always the same. Then there is loss of hair, fever, and bloody diarrhea. Infants were among the first victims of this invisible killer."

"How horrible." Shizue felt chilled. "Is there no hope for these people? No treatment?"

"None of the doctors can diagnose its cause. My husband lacks the knowledge to ease their suffering, but the dying plead with him, in great pain and half out of their minds. He believes it may have something to do with the distance one stood from the blast. All the victims in Nameshi Village had black spots on their skin. Before the end, others also develop these spots, which mark them for certain death."

Shizue examined the unblemished skin of her arms and hands. "What you describe sounds like the plague."

"Yes, a plague that strikes suddenly, without warning. No doctor can say who it will strike next or how many others will be marked for death in the days ahead. We examine our gums and watch our skin for those spots." Mrs. Kano raised her hand and traced the gray in her hair. "I count the hairs in my comb. There was no gray in my hair before the bombing. Only four days have passed since Terrible Thursday, but it seems years."

O-nami looked at Shizue; he saw the fear in her eyes. "But you took safety underground," he told her. "I say these victims were unable to find shelter as you did. Your fever would not have passed if you were marked by this illness."

"Perhaps you're right." She felt the bandaged area behind her ear. Sweat had loosened the adhesive tape, and its gauze came away in her hand, clean of any fluid. The injury was healing. Would her wound caused by the thief's blow have healed if she were not sound in every way? The illness struck without warning. How could she be sure death's invisible hand had not reached down to touch her in the basement shelter? Shizue cringed at the thought. For a moment she studied Mrs. Kano and her family, visibly healthy suvivors like her, and yet perhaps all of them were living on borrowed time. "Are the wounded being helped? Can many of them be saved?"

"Yes, with proper treatment. The doctors are receiving the necessary tools, but some like my husband lack trained nurses to assist them."

Yufugawo read the look on Shizue's face. "No, I forbid you to go into the city. You belong at home caring after yourself and Kimi."

"I'm an experienced nurse. You heard Mrs. Kano. There are lives to be saved," Shizue answered firmly. She glanced out the window and saw the headlights of trucks moving to and from Nagasaki. She would get a ride on one of them. "I'll volunteer to help your husband."

"He will be so grateful. Please, carry a message to him that we've found shelter with you."

"Yes, in the morning." Suddenly she felt drained of strength. Mrs. Kano regarded her with a look of grief, and Shizue knew she was thinking of the missing daughter she could not search for until Nagasaki's rubble had cooled.

Shizue covered her eyes. Her mind had erected a wall of protection against the memories of Nagasaki. Now all at once the wall crumbled, and she could remember every detail of Terrible Thursday. "I must think only of the living," she said loudly, as if to shock herself back to the reality of the moment. "Yes—I must do all I can for them."

Yufugawo made their guests comfortable in the barn while Shizue retired to her bedroom. Kimi lay sound asleep beside his puppy. Quietly

Shizue opened the bottom drawer of the clothing chest and fluffed up some old clothes to make a bed for her son's pet. After gently placing him there, Shizue turned, and her eyes went to the *omamori* resting on the night table. One link of its gold chain was snapped. She must have torn it from her neck with a strength born of her anguish and thrown it to the muddy entrance of the cave, which she now vividly remembered. Max's glittering talisman had acted as a beacon, pointing the way to their son. She might well have died if not for being found that night. But had she escaped the nameless, invisible death Mrs. Kano had spoken of? Perhaps the *omamori*'s blessing had spared her from that awful fate.

Going over to the chest of drawers, she took out a pair of tweezers and began to pry open the tiny gold loops between the chain links, removing the broken piece and mending the chain so it could be worn. All she had of Max was this keepsake and his slumbering child. She never wanted to part with Kimi again, even for a single day. But there was a desperate need for trained nurses, and she could not take Kimi with her, could not expose him to the aftermath of holocaust.

She fastened the *omamori* around her neck once more, and her sense of purpose grew firm. The fabulous bird Hōō was a symbol of hope, a phoenix rising from the ashes of Nagasaki who would help insulate her against its dead and the dying. Staying at home would only magnify her personal fears; caring for the sick would make her vigil pass more swiftly. Soon the occupation forces would arrive. Then she would rush to tell them her story.

She recalled Max giving her the *omamori*, telling her to think of it as part of him going home with her, promising they would not be separated for very long. Now four years had come and gone. Nestling beside her baby, she held the passing years in her embrace. So like Max and yet so Japanese. When she returned with Kimi to the happy place of her own childhood, how would she answer for the graves of his namesake and his Japanese grandfather? When the prison camp was liberated, how would she answer for his beloved *ogisan*'s death?

Unable to sleep, Shizue imagined hearing the mournful wails of Nagasaki's dead whispering through the trees and taking flight with the evening mist. But unlike the *kami* voices heard in her childhood, there was no laughter in their haunting presence.

The agonizing chorus of voices was mercifully dispelled by the whimpering sounds of a puppy. Frightened to be alone, he scratched at his bed in the chest drawer until Shizue rescued him with a hug. How warm he was, how tiny and vulnerable. Life was a precious gift, but it was as fragile as this puppy she cradled safely in her arms. No one could foresee beyond the moment, Shizue told herself, and she gave thanks for another day.

CHAPTER 43

Soon after dawn, Shizue rode to Nagasaki in an ambulance stocked with medical supplies. The young private at the wheel complained of the duty that forced him to enter what he called "that city of ghosts." He shivered, lowering his cap against the glaring sunlight, wishing he had a cigarette to calm his frayed nerves.

Although Shizue had hardened herself to meet Nagasaki's ugliness, the shock of seeing its vista slowly unfold took her breath away. She wanted to scream, but no sound came out. She put her fist to her mouth, able to remember walking the city as it burned on Terrible Thursday, when much of the devastation lay hidden in the smoke and flames.

Viewed in the unsparing scrutiny of broad daylight, the gutted landscape was beyond imagination. It was as if the earth had suddenly tipped upside down, hurling everything built upon it into the heavens, where the sheer weight of it all had stormed down as a crashing rain. Nagasaki was much like a salad of masonry, twisted steel, and ashes tossed in the bowl of its longest valley. Little remained standing in the graveyard of rubble and the blackened skeletons of buildings, which still smoldered. The debris-choked foundations of collapsed buildings and the caved-in networks of tunneled bomb shelters had become underground furnaces, which had burned for days.

Shizue felt shaken once again. She relived the cataclysmic explosion that had battered her against the fissuring walls of a pitch-black cellar, tearing the little girl she had carried to safety from her arms. "Kazuko." She spoke the girl's name aloud and saw her tiny hands clawing the debris with her, fighting to reach the air and the light that glowed red through cracks in the cellar door.

"Have you family here?" the ambulance driver asked, steering a downhill course on the one-lane road that was open to traffic.

Shizue shook her head, then gazed at what remained of the army hospital, abandoned except for work crews searching the ruins, their sweating faces protected with surgical masks. She covered her mouth again, sure the American doctor must be dead and fearing a possible encounter with Colonel Sekino. She wished him dead, perished in the inferno as just punishment for his cruelty.

Although that monstrous man no longer held any power over her, she gasped and dug her fingernails into her arms, as she saw a figure in uniform stumbling through the rubble. He was followed by women of the rescue corps bearing the wounded on litters to a makeshift hut, one of many such shelters being erected.

It was Colonel Sekino. Shizue's heart pounded up in her throat as he faced the ambulance. One eye and half his gristly face were swathed in bandages. His exposed eye fixed on her, but he showed not the slightest sign of recognition before he turned away. His jacket sleeve was scorched black, and the stump of his bandaged hand dangled limply as he stumbled off again, leading the procession of stretchers. She knew then that Nagasaki was the blind leading the blind to live or die in the crowded shelters built upon the ashes.

As they drove on, Shizue forced herself to concentrate on the good she might accomplish caring for the survivors in this barren landscape of windblown dust and cinders. From what she could see, there were a number of makeshift treatment centers staffed by a handful of doctors, nurses, and young girls from the rescue corps. A medical team was operating in the ruins of the Nagasaki First Branch Hospital. Mount Kompira rose up behind its demolished rooftop, and the ambulance driver told her that no widespread damage had occurred in Nagasaki's old city, located in the shortest valley on the other side of the mountain's steep slopes.

The Urakami Valley had been decimated by the blast. There was no electrical power, no water. There were few survivors of the public works crews, whose efforts to restore water had met with failure, since the pipes were too badly damaged to be used.

They drove past the civic hall of Iwaya. Sections of its bombed shell had been repaired to serve the wounded, and the same was true of the Shinkosen Hospital set up in what remained of the old school building, where Mrs. Kano had said her husband would be found. Both the facilities were woefully inadequate, and the area surrounding them reeked of human excrement. Most of those who had not been wounded still suffered from a shock-induced inertia. Cremation fires burned for disposal of the dead. Otherwise, sanitary conditions beyond the treatment center were nonexistent.

"I'll get off here," Shizue told the driver, who stopped at the open shell of the partially destroyed building.

She walked inside and immediately recognized Dr. Kano from his wife's description. A short, slender man, he was dressed in soiled trousers, and his shirt sleeves were rolled up. He moved among his patients who had been laid side by side on tattered mattresses, straw mats, beds made of rags.

As Shizue stepped through the motionless sea of victims, she was struck by the quiet of what appeared to be a morgue of bandaged corpses.

The frozen orbs of their eyes stared up as though she did not exist. "Dr. Kano, I've come to help." She addressed him in a hushed whisper. Quickly she told him of her nursing experience and that his family was being sheltered at O-nami's farm.

His drawn face momentarily brightened with her news. Then he placed both hands on Shizue's shoulders and related the dire situation confronting them. "Several student nurses are assisting me, but their stomachs are weak to the tasks. Many here are badly deformed. I'm grateful to have someone with your experience, Shizue."

One of the student nurses called to him. The young girl was pale and seemed about to faint. She dropped the bedpan from her trembling hands and spilled bloody diarrhea across the floor. A woman volunteer rushed to the scene carrying a bucket and dipped her mop into some strong-smelling disinfectant that turned Shizue's stomach. Dr. Kano bowed over a small boy not much older than Kimi, who was withered up against the mattress like a bent twig. The exposed parts of his skin were covered with black spots. She averted her eyes, but the ill lay all around her, and she watched Dr. Kano's fingers pass across the boy's eyelids, closing them to death.

Vaguely, she heard the doctor say that the dead must be removed quickly. Unsanitary conditions threatened those who could be helped. And so Shizue's work began with this devastating introduction to the bomb's invisible killer. It would stalk Nagasaki's ruins for weeks to come. There would be many others like the boy, whose body was carried outside in her arms to men wearing face masks who stoked the cremation fires.

This child orphaned by the bomb had no family to offer prayers for him, and for a time Shizue bowed her head and prayed for him as she would for her own baby. Then she dried her tears, rolled up her sleeves, and resolutely made her way back through the debris to assist Dr. Kano.

Working beside him, she learned not to dwell on those who died, not to shed tears as their remains were taken to the funeral pyres, not to think she might also be struck down. Throughout that first day, Shizue ministered to those who were not beyond hope, whose pain and sufferings could be eased. Any faintness of heart was soon forgotten with the reward of her patients' grateful smiles—the victims of Nagasaki, whose sufferings had brought the war to an end.

No one would ever know exactly how many had died, how many people had left no remains to bury, no survivors to mourn them or to list their names among the missing. Early on the morning of August 15, 1945, a hot, sultry day, it was announced that the emperor would address the nation at noon. One of the nurses brought a radio to Dr. Kano's treatment center.

Emperor Hirohito spoke to his subjects from Tokyo on the NHK station. Reception was poor, and much of what the emperor said was lost to those who gathered near the radio listening with bowed heads: the charwomen with their pails of disinfectant, the men wearing face masks who abandoned their cremation fires, and the young nurses who were growing hardened to their tasks.

To Shizue's ears, the emperor's nervous, high-pitched voice sounded unreal, an unearthly singing vibrating on the air waves. His wording was difficult to understand. At best his speech was a garbled message of Japanese surrender, an anticlimactic moment for Shizue while many wept in the silence that followed and dropped to their knees, stricken with grief. As Japanese they all shared the dishonor of defeat. But Shizue did not suffer their loss of face. She had wanted no part of this war and stood erect, clasping the *omamori*. There would be no more bombs. Paul was safe now, and Inge's release from prison camp would soon come to pass.

But peace had not ended her exhausting work. Six days had now passed since Terrible Thursday, and people continued to be marked for death by the invisible killer. It was nearing dusk, and that day alone some twenty new patients had entered the treatment center, displaying symptoms noticed only the night before. Dr. Kano had no room for them all, nor did the other aid stations who reported hundreds of new cases. These poor souls could be given shelter only in the city's makeshift huts, where all of them would die.

Dr. Kano believed the Americans would know how to treat this illness. "When they arrive, the dying will stop," he told Shizue, and put her in an ambulance, ordering her home to rest.

She felt perfectly healthy, but as darkness fell she began to weep, racked by the private fears she had stifled while giving comfort to the disfigured and the maimed. Even if she were to be spared, perhaps the war had ended too late and at too great a cost for her ever again to embrace life's joys with Max.

While the reality of peace settled in gradually, Shizue could not know that the man she loved was separated from her by only a short span of wrinkling sea, the same East China Sea that fed Nagasaki Bay. On that very night, Max bore witness to a fireworks display of tracer shells lighting the skies over Okinawa, where the American forces were celebrating victory by firing off their guns. The jagged, wave-battered coastline where Shizue waited was almost within his reach. The ships of the fleet anchored in Okinawa's deep water bays would sail for Japan in a matter of days. But those in command would order Max to bypass the bombed city he had circled on the map as his goal. His destiny and his destination were as uncertain as Shizue's fearful doubts that she had more than that night to tuck her son into bed, lulling him to sleep with stories of his father.

Shizue rested from her work in Nagasaki's ruins to watch American MP's patrolling the city streets. Glimpsed through the rippling curtain of heat caused by the cremation fires, she saw the military police cruising by slowly in Jeeps, their spotless white hats like mushroom caps, the polished brass of their uniforms set ablaze by the sunlight of another day without news of Max.

Oh, how she had counted the days following Emperor Hirohito's surrender address to the nation. The first occupation troops had entered Nagasaki on August 18, 1945. Then she had rushed through the streets, searching their clean-shaven faces, hoping to find Max among those quiet young men dressed in their combat fatigues. But he was not there.

Now the month of August had ended, and the days had stretched on to the middle of September, while U.S. troops continued to arrive by ship. Shizue went to the dock, but guards kept her at a distance, and she could not distinguish the faces of GI's landing ashore to board trucks destined for duty elsewhere.

The conquered Japanese were ruled by strict regulations, and American soldiers were forbidden to fraternize with the enemy. Although Shizue had pleaded with them in fluent English, no one listened or had been moved by her tears. She was barred from entering their military installations to tell her story to someone in command. She had also been turned away from visiting the prison camp where Inge was being repatriated. The Americans saw her as the enemy they had fought. As a Japanese she had no voice, no rights. Even if someone in authority would listen to her story, she had no papers to back up her claims to U.S. citizenship as Max's wife.

Not for years had she thought of her term in prison and the price paid for her release. A Japan at war had forced her to renounce her American husband in order to save her baby. Now the prison at Urakami was a barren plot of earth, and her records there had been destroyed. If only she could pass through the camp gates, Inge would testify that she spoke the truth, give testimony to her efforts for the Allied prisoners. Then Max would know where to find her and their son.

Shizue resumed her care of the wounded. One woman reached up with bandaged arms and hands, asking for water, asking for drugs to kill the pain, demanding more of Shizue than she had to give. The man lying next to the woman was near death. He was all skin and bones, too weak to ask for anything. At any moment, Shizue thought, he would be claimed by the invisible killer that seemed to stalk her more closely with each passing day. Several times each day she disrobed to examine her body, relieved to find no black spots like those on this dying man, who writhed in pain.

Stooping down, she held a cup of water to his cracked, fleshless lips. But he could not swallow, and the water dribbled off his contorted face. He had wandered into the treatment center only the day before, already consumed by the last stages of this dreadful illness and unable to remember his own name.

Shizue wanted to pray for his soul, but to what gods? She took the Buddhist prayer beads from her pocket. She carried these and a Catholic rosary, which she had taken from the hands of a dead woman in order to comfort others who embraced that faith. Nagasaki once had a large Catholic community. Now its famed cathedral lay in ruins, within walking distance of the Hosokawa–Napier weaving mill that was leveled to the ground. "Are you Catholic?" she asked the man.

She half-turned away to call the Catholic priest, who knelt, giving last rites to another doomed victim. Then she felt a chill run through her as one grave-cold hand reached up to touch the hand in which she held the Buddhist prayer beads. The man's bony fingers closed around the beads as she prayed for both their souls. His was quickly set free, while hers remained earthbound as she now prayed for life. If she was claimed by this invisible killer, let it be in Max's arms, she prayed. Let her be spared until he returned.

"This poor man is gone. Release him and come away," said Dr. Kano, helping Shizue to her feet. She looked out across the sea of patients. Many of the blistered wounds she treated showed no signs of healing. Every day hundreds more died. No trace had been found of Dr. Kano's missing daughter, and he had quietly accepted her death, never once complaining or losing courage. But the occupation forces had as yet sent no aid, and the hopelessness of their situation caused him to grow angry.

"The Americans keep their back turned to us. The supplies we receive limit us to treating only minor burns and broken bones. Surely their doctors must know what's causing all this suffering." His voice rose. "How much longer must we wait before they give us the means to prevent these deaths?"

"Help will come soon," said Shizue, trying to hold out hope to him while hiding her utter despair. Only Japanese doctors cared for the victims of the atom bomb. Food, desperately needed plasma, and blood for the burn victims came from the Japanese supply depot in the town of Omura. Both the conqueror and the defeated had teams investigating the after-effects of the bomb, but it seemed nothing helpful had come of their efforts. No medical procedures to heal the badly burned. None to offer those who had been poisoned weeks ago. Shizue wiped the sweat from her brow. "Perhaps it's too late for those being struck down, even if there were some treatment."

Suddenly there was a commotion on the street outside. A dusty convoy of U.S. Army vehicles roared past, but one Jeep screeched to a stop. An army private entered alone. Tanned and freckle-faced, he seemed in a great hurry and consulted a pocket dictionary before asking in Japanese who was in charge. Dr. Kano announced himself and was handed an official-looking envelope.

"Wait," Shizue called after the soldier, following him into the street. "Please, I must talk to someone in command," she pleaded. He looked back at her, surprised by her English. "My husband is an American. He may have served with you in the Pacific, and I'm desperate for news of him."

"No Jap-Americans fought with us," he answered shortly.

"My husband is Caucasian."

"Oh, I see." The soldier's expression revealed his distaste for mixed marriages. "I've got to rejoin my outfit, ma'am. Colonel Blume is the CO in charge of most everything hereabouts," he said while climbing behind the wheel of his Jeep. "The colonel's a fair man and might be of help—if you're telling the truth."

"How do I get to see him? Where do I go?" Shizue cried out above the Jeep's roaring engine.

"The supply depot in Omura!"

She fought back tears. At last someone had shown her kindness. As the Jeep sped off, she saw other convoys carrying supplies for the conqueror, who was spreading inland from the sea.

"This is good news, Shizue."

She responded to Dr. Kano's hand on her shoulder. "Have they found a cure?"

"No. But we're being relocated to the Omura Naval Hospital, and the facilities there are excellent. It's a sign the Americans haven't forgotten our needy after all." Dr. Kano smiled.

"When will we be moved there?"

"Sometime this afternoon."

The Americans would give her transportation to Omura, twenty miles away, she thought. She was determined to let nothing stop her from seeing the American colonel.

Shielding her eyes to cinders blowing out from the smoking cremation fires, Shizue wondered how many others must die before the flames were extinguished. More people were making their way through the ruins to Dr. Kano's makeshift hospital, and she recoiled from the face of death mirrored in their glazed eyes. Suddenly she was overwhelmed by her personal fears.

"I feel faint," she told Dr. Kano, running both hands through her hair. "I had no appetite this morning, and now I feel nauseous. It's the illness." She nodded toward the newest victims, marked for death. "Soon I'll be just like them."

"I'll be the judge of that, Shizue. Open your mouth. Open it wide," Dr. Kano ordered firmly. "Your gums look healthy, and your eyes are clear. No fever."

"This morning there was hair in my comb. Far more than usual."

"Emotional stress can often cause some loss of hair," he said, taking her pulse. "A little fast, but not abnormal considering your fears. Exhaustion brought on your nausea. Fatigue is responsible for your lack of appetite. A good rest is all you need. Now, you mustn't be frightened." He smiled and patted her hand. "One doesn't have to be a doctor to see that you're a very healthy young woman, Shizue. This notification promises an experienced nursing staff at the naval hospital. I'll need you to help our patients get settled in. Then you really should go home to your son and family." He sighed heavily. "I could do with a long rest as well."

Shizue felt reassured by Dr. Kano's fatherly embrace. "I've neglected my son. He's at an age where every moment spent with him is precious."

When the doctor let her go, she placed one hand across her forehead and gave in to exhaustion. She had kept her hands soft for Max by wearing cotton gloves while harvesting the crops on O-nami's farm season after season, wearing through at least a dozen pairs. This afternoon her work here would come to an end. But people were still in need of her comforting voice and gentle touch, so she returned to her patients. Her nausea and the faintness she had felt passed as she used the skills she had learned to nurse her brother in the isolation ward of another war.

Late that afternoon, Shizue, Dr. Kano, and their patients were driven off in trucks bound for the naval hospital at Omura. The Americans had given Nagasaki's homeless little aid, and her citizens were forced to call upon their own resources as they labored in work crews to resurrect the city from the ashes.

The work crews sifted the ashes for human bones, fragments of bodies, jewelry, any clue to identifying the missing. The monumental task of clearing Nagasaki's rubble would take many months. The debris had cooled, and workers were tunneling underground, searching for those who had perished in basements and bomb shelters. Countless thousands had been wounded, and it was doubtful that the number of dead would ever be known.

People walked the streets with heads bowed respectfully to the conquerors in their midst. Once Shizue's sword-bearing samurai ancestors had ruled these streets. Only they had enjoyed the right to bear arms. Now the people made way for American samurai bearing rifles. But weapons were not necessary to maintain the peace. Nagasaki's occupation had taken place without incident, and her survivors toiled with a quiet acceptance. The transition from hated enemy to a rather benign conqueror seemed complete. Emperor Hirohito had bowed to conquest, and his subjects' loss of face, their defeat, was total, only to be endured.

As the truck Shizue rode in drove on, she saw people searching the ruins of what had been their houses. She saw grief in their faces over what had been lost. However, their eyes showed no animosity toward the armed soldiers patrolling the remains of a residential neighborhood. Children had once run to school on the sidewalks between now-flattened lots. The schoolyard swings were fused into grotesque chunks of metal and char-blackened wood. She remembered passing this schoolyard with Kazuko, and quickly turned her eyes away.

Despite the ban on fraternizing with the Japanese, American fathers dressed in uniform stopped little children to offer them candy bars. Children were the same the world over, and the soldiers reached out against the ugliness, hoping to bring smiles to the faces of children like those waiting for them at home. But these children had lost their looks of innocence. They had lost the gift of laughter, and few of them smiled. They snatched the candy bars and bowed politely before running off.

Omura Naval Hospital was sparkling clean, with beds spaced out enough to offer Dr. Kano's patients room to breathe. He seemed cheered while Shizue assisted him for several hours. Bidding good-bye to him and those she had cared for was emotionally draining. Improved hospital conditions would not end the dying, and she could feel no relief.

The buses were running again, and she rode one to the supply depot. The American army colonel's office there was under guard, but she saw Japanese civilians working at the loading docks, and pretending to be one of them, she approached the guard.

"I seem to have forgotten my pass," she told him, and feigned tears. "How will I feed my family without a day's work?"

"Do you help in the mess hall?" he asked, impressed by her bearing and command of his language.

"Yes."

"Okay, go on in."

Shizue bowed low, quickly walking past the guard with her eyes submissively to the ground. Her next encounter might not go so well, she thought, halting before the door to a wooden hut. COLONEL MORRIS BLUME was painted on its sign. After taking a deep breath for courage, she knocked and entered to confront a WAC lieutenant at the reception desk. "I must see the colonel."

"Must?" The young woman grew stern-faced, her penciled eyebrows arched threateningly at the Japanese woman so nobly staring back at her. "You meant *please*, of course. Your kind must learn to keep your place."

Shizue humbled herself as she bowed low. "Please, forgive me. Might I see the colonel, please?"

"On what business?"

"I seek news of my husband, who is an American," she answered with extreme politeness, keeping her temper in check. "We married before the war. We were separated on the day of Pearl Harbor. I feel certain that he served his country. His name is Napier. Maxwell Napier."

The WAC lieutenant snapped her manicured fingers. "Let's see your work permit! Well? Do as you're told and be quick about it!"

Her short-tempered tone angered Shizue. "I've forgotten it. But that's no reason to address me so rudely! I'm not an animal, Lieutenant."

"No, you're the enemy!" The woman rose up indignantly, and she grasped hold of the campaign ribbons pinned to her blouse. "We didn't start this war. My brother was killed at Pearl Harbor, and I would have gladly fought beside the men who died taking Saipan and Okinawa. So far as I'm concerned, you Japs deserve what you got."

"I'm sorry for your brother," Shizue replied, shaking with emotion. "But nothing Japan has done can justify the atrocity of your bomb. Nothing can justify setting fire to innocent women and children."

The young woman's hands began to tremble as she lifted a pack of cigarettes from her desk and struggled to light one. "War nerves," she said, coughing on the smoke. "I'm not a hateful person. After seeing the wounded of Nagasaki, I broke down and cried. I didn't ask to be assigned here, but they said that I was needed. Now I'm trying hard to forgive what I've seen in three years of combat against the Japanese. Even what I've seen of the bomb doesn't make it easy to feel compassion for your people. But I'm trying to do the Christian thing—Mrs. Napier. Looking at you or any Japanese—well, I can't help seeing my brother trapped aboard the *Arizona* when it was blown apart by your bombs."

"It's difficult for us both," said Shizue, watching this woman fight to regain her equilibrium. Who could speak for which side had suffered the most? Her fingers traced the Buddhist priest's blessing engraved on the back of the *omamori*. The lieutenant wore a small gold cross on a delicate chain. In the silence, each clasped the symbol of her faith, sharing an unspoken understanding of what each had endured. Just then their eyes met in a womanly bond. For the briefest moment they were only two women who longed to be reunited with loved ones, who longed for the secure comforts of their childhood homes.

"I'll go and speak to Colonel Blume. Wait here."

The lieutenant vanished behind the door to the inner office. Framed photographs of Harry S Truman and General Douglas MacArthur hung on the wall. Shizue had never seen their faces until now. The American president who had ordered the bombings of Hiroshima and Nagasaki had such a surprisingly open and pleasant face, she thought. The American shogun Paul had spoken well of appeared to be the strong, silent type. He was younger and more handsome than she had imagined him. His hawklike features were reminiscent of the Napier men, except that their features were softer. She wondered how the years had altered Max's face, able to think of nothing else but reaching him. She grew taut with expectancy as the lieutenant came out and said, "Colonel Blume will see you."

Colonel Blume gestured for Shizue to sit in a comfortable upholstered chair. Although she was put to ease by his relaxed manner, she feared losing this opportunity to contact Max and waited for him to invite her to speak.

Colonel Blume stretched up from his desk to massage his spine. "Well, I'm told you're married to an American."

Shizue nodded. Her throat was very dry, and she eyed the coffee decanter warming on his hot plate.

"Coffee?" he asked. "Relax, Mrs. Napier. I've been assigned here to establish some rapport with the Japanese. Vengeance is the Lord's work. Mortal men can only sigh and hope to mend the broken pieces. Do you take your coffee black?"

"Yes, please." The cup wobbled between Shizue's hands as she sipped. "I haven't tasted coffee like this in years."

"No need to rush yourself. When you feel like telling me your story, I'll just lean back here against my desk and listen." He smiled. "I pride myself on being a good listener."

"How understanding you are." The years all at once poured from Shizue's lips in an unbroken stream of words. Reconstructing her life for a total stranger was a profound emotional catharsis. The sacrifices, the waiting, the petrifying unknown now choked her voice. "I must reach my husband," she said at the end. "Won't you help me?"

"In every way I can, Mrs. Napier." His eyes moist, Blume pressed her hands as a friend. He was a Jew with relatives in Germany. What she had told him about the escape route provided by her husband gave him hope that some of his relations might be among those who were spared the Nazi Holocaust. Shizue appeared startled by his look of gratitude, and Colonel Blume decided not to speak of what lay behind it. "If your husband served in the Pacific, we'll get word to him. You've my promise," he said, then lifted the telephone. "Let's see what I can learn about your mother-in-law."

Shizue was far too overwhelmed even to thank him. His name did not register as Jewish to someone Japanese and she had no idea the work that had separated her from Max now lay behind Blume's eagerness to help reunite them.

The colonel took immediate action on her behalf. The Army Signal Corps had strung phone lines to the prison camp. Inge was contacted there and put on the receiver.

The two women wept at hearing each other's voices. Overcome by emotion, they could express little in words. Inge said she was being well cared for, but the American camp commander had refused to send word of her to a Japanese. She had tried getting some word of Max, but the Red Cross was so busy processing similar requests from the other prisoners that nothing had come of it as yet.

Shizue promised she would visit Inge the next morning and was devastated when Colonel Blume took the receiver and said their reunion must wait.

"Until your claim to U.S. citizenship is confirmed," he said, and smiled reassuringly. "The U.S. Army runs on paperwork, Shizue. I want you to understand that locating your husband and getting him here won't be accomplished overnight. Military priorities come first, and I can't honestly say how long it'll be until we get some reply through the chain of command. But I'll notify you once we have."

"There's so much my husband doesn't know," she replied, clasping the *omamori*. "His father's death will come as a blow. But there's little Kimi and Inge to give thanks for. You've been so kind. I can't understand why your country hasn't done anything to help stop the dying, Colonel. Forgive me, but I'm afraid I'm among those who were poisoned by your bomb. America owes a responsibility to every man, woman, and child who survived, and they can't just let us die." She burst into tears, and Blume gently placed his hands on her trembling shoulders. "Surely your doctors must know of some treatment."

"I'm sorry to say that we don't have much to offer, Shizue." The colonel leaned back against his desk. "Had our medical team arrived here days after the bombing, we might have helped save some lives with plasma and blood transfusions. But we're even in short supply of that after fighting this war. From what we know of things, X rays rippled outward from the bomb's hypocenter much like a pebble thrown into a pond. In the blinding blue flash of light, many of Nagasaki's survivors received lethal doses of radiation. The Urakami Valley's hilly terrain bent the atomic light to strike at those who are dying now. X rays reflected off the hillside slopes and turned corners, penetrating the shelters and dwellings that were hardly touched by the fires. Radiation poisoning attacks the blood corpuscles. I'm afraid there's no hope for those who received lethal doses. We can't stop the dying or predict when it will end."

Blume had just given the invisible killer a name, and Shizue stared down at her hands, which were tightly clenched together. "Radiation poisoning," she said in a choked voice. "I took shelter underground." Although she had not seen the mushrooming cloud on Terrible Thursday, now she could hear its roar and feel the earth trembling around her once again. "I carried a little girl to safety after we heard the B-*sans*. Seconds later there was a brilliant flash of light. I could see it through the cracks of the basement door."

"That doesn't necessarily mean you were exposed to the X rays," Blume said, trying to offer hope. But he could not bring himself to smile away this young woman's fears. "You've had a rough time of it, Shizue. The best place for you now is with your family. I'll have my Jeep take you home to the farm you spoke of."

Shizue felt dazed as she walked from his office. Only a thin crust of earth had protected her, and there was no cure if she had received a lethal dose of radiation.

Colonel Blume's driver had some documents to deliver in Nagasaki. It would be the last time she would return there; her work was done. While counting the days since Japan's surrender, she had served amid these ruins, not really seeing much beyond the patients in her care.

As they drove, Shizue was suddenly aware of a miracle taking place. Nature had begun to reassert itself. Green buds were emerging on the scorched limbs of trees and plants. She saw stalks of wheat sprouting up everywhere; the wheat showering down on the hot ashes from Nagasaki's exploding grain storehouses had taken root. And by some miracle, a field of clover was growing near the ruins of the medical college. New life rustled in the breeze across what had been ash-blackened earth. The scorched land had become fertile again.

Still, Shizue shuddered. Even with the green hand of nature reasserting itself, the decimation of an entire city stretched out for miles, dark and bleak even under the blazing sun. Only crushed bricks marked the site of Hosokawa-Napier, Limited's, weaving mill, where a dynasty had begun. Douglas Napier's gigantic machines had been silenced forever by a mightier roar, and not so much as a blade of grass struggled up through the rubble. It seemed nothing would ever again take root in the mortally wounded soil at the center of the blast. Shizue feared building so much faith on a future life with Max while so much of Nagasaki remained barren and lifeless. Still, the greenery blooming up against the Urakami hillsides gave her hope.

Her hair flew free in the cooling sea breeze, and the fresh air smelled of spring. Nagasaki's clocks had been stopped on one terrible summer's day, but now the clocks had begun ticking once again, turning back time to the season of growth, the season of renewed hope. She saw one fragile marigold pushing up its brightly colored head through the gnarled black roots of a charred, dead tree. That fragile flower risen from the ashes was to her a symbol of triumph over the poisonous X rays whose touch had killed everything within the scope of their path. The marigold's seed had survived harm, sheltered underground as she had been, and so she, too, must live to witness another spring with Max at her side.

A cluster of gingko trees now marked the turnoff to the rutted dirt road Max would travel someday soon. It was here they would meet again.

Dogs barked in the yard where Kimi ran out to greet her, calling, "Mama!"

Shizue thanked the driver and climbed down from his Jeep. Was it only stress that caused her falling hair, her wearied step, her nausea? Or were they the first symptoms of illness? Shizue lifted her son, who had grown so heavy. "I have good news. An American colonel has promised to help us find your father," she announced, carrying her baby toward O-nami and Yufugawo, who had heard her and were smiling.

Little Kimi seemed upset while everyone made a fuss over his mother's news. He clung to Shizue possessively as if sensing his dominance was about to be threatened.

With Colonel Blume's promise of help, Shizue resigned herself to accept whatever came to pass. Her appetite improved. But preparing for bed at nights, she counted the hairs on her comb and watched a thinning spot form on her scalp. The spot on the crown of her head was no bigger than a coin, but it held a larger threat, one she could not bring herself to speak of. Otherwise her dark hair remained thick and kept its healthy sheen. She combed it over the spot to hide it from the household. Nothing asked of her in the years of waiting demanded the courage she now brought to bear. She smiled and spoiled her son with an outpouring of love, and lavished affection on all those around her. She lived each day to its fullest as if it might be her last. Caring for the wounded had made it possible not to think of herself. Now her hands, kept soft for Max, were idle. Next season's sweet potato crop had already been planted, and there were few chores to keep her mind occupied. Time passed slowly as she waited, from sunrise to sunset, for news of Max, waited for permission to visit Inge, waited in the hope that she was not poisoned—not living on borrowed time.

CHAPTER 44

It was a bright autumn morning, and Shizue took her son to the village marketplace, just to help pass the time. The first weeks of October, 1945, had dragged on without any word from Colonel Blume. The market was noisy that day. Food had become more plentiful. Tea and coffee, cakes of soap, and cartons of cigarettes were displayed by the merchants, mostly at black market prices. The villagers haggled at the stalls, trying to set a bargain. The sun was hot, and Shizue set Kimi down, watching him take everything in with his large eyes. Her fingers touched the balding spot at the crown of her head. There had been no hairs in her comb that morning.

She looked at several villagers gathered around a frail old woman dressed in city clothes. "Come, darling. Mommy wants to hear what that woman is saying." Taking Kimi by the hand, she joined the others, who stood there listening.

"*Hai*, I watched my daughter and grandchildren grow ill," the woman bemoaned, rocking in grief. "Why them and not me, I asked myself. Now I am alone, except for cousins here, who were kind enough to take me in. When I left the city, the cremation fires no longer burned. No one has died of this terrible illness for many days now. *Hai*, it would seem the worst is over." She noticed Shizue grow pale. "Are you ill?"

Shizue could only shake her head, tears of relief streaming down her cheeks as she hugged her son tightly. The gods had spared her from death. Her life was all at once redeemed, and she hurried for home to relate this good news to those who had silently shared her private fears.

Within sight of the farm, Shizue held her ears against the roar of airplanes. American C-47's were swooping low across the fields. The occupation forces were pushing farther inland, their troop trucks kicking up dust on the country road under the supply planes' winging shadows. Before that day the countryside had remained quiet, and now everyone in Shizue's family gathered outside to watch the conquerors' parade of military might, which brought Japan's defeat to their front doorstep. She recognized the driver of Colonel Blume's Jeep. He blasted his horn and zigzagged past the advancing army convoys as she rushed to meet him at the farmyard gate.

"Your husband's been located!" he shouted to be heard above the roar of swooping planes. "Major Napier's outfit was stationed on Okinawa until one day ago, when they were shipped out for duty in Tokyo."

Shizue listened breathlessly, her pulse racing.

"Your husband's ship was nearing the coast of Kyushu when Allied headquarters contacted him by radio at sea. Sorry, no personal message from him that I know of, ma'am. Could've gotten lost in the shuffle at headquarters. But it seems Major Napier carries weight with the top brass. He's waiting for permission to be put ashore here and could arrive at the farm by sometime late tonight."

Shizue went numb from head to foot. After all her trials, the day had brought too much joyful news for her to experience more than shock. "Does my husband know about his father? That he has a son?" she asked, and received a nod.

"Colonel Blume wanted me to say that you aren't to worry. He'll personally see to it your husband finds his way here once he's put ashore. No confirmation on your U.S. citizenship as yet. But Major Napier can get you inside the POW camp to visit your mother-in-law."

Lacking the voice even to thank Blume's driver, Shizue turned away, walking in a daze. Her husband was safe and sound—an army major. Her beautiful husband was coming home.

"Your father is coming home, Ichiban!" O-nami shouted, lifting Kimi onto his shoulders and prancing him around like an old stallion who was all heart but had little wind in his lungs. "Your father is a *rikugun shosa*. A samurai you will come to love and respect," he panted, while the boy cried for his mother.

Shizue did not hear her child and wandered off alone to stand in the fields, shaken by the roar of planes whose swooping wings were like the shadows of clouds passing across the face of the sun. At any hour that night Max could appear on this very road dressed in the uniform of Japan's conqueror. Had he killed? she wondered. Had war changed him, or was he still the sympathetic young man she remembered? Suddenly fighter planes streaked across the sky. Oh, she wished for an end to the awful sights and sounds of war that continued to invade the peace.

She had kept faith with Max's safe return. Now his homecoming would put them on the threshold of a new beginning. There was no telephone at the farm, so he would appear without any warning. Shizue pictured him pushing open the squealing front gate, resplendent in his officer's uniform, the ends of his hair bleached frosty white and his face deeply tanned by the tropical sun. She thought back to their romantic reunion in the charming cottage at Beppu, of sailing the crystal-clear waters as she oiled his muscular body, his smooth skin bronzed. What they felt for each other could not have been diminished by time, she told herself, and picked up a straw basket lying in the field. Memories of love took Shizue into the hillsides, where she picked wildflowers to decorate her hair and to brighten the farmhouse rooms to welcome her husband's return.

Oh, how she once planned their reunion, wanting everything to be perfect. Now he might come to her at any hour, and everything must be left to chance. Now she was the mother of his child, a noblewoman forced to live and dress as a peasant. Max would come to the humble farmhouse where she had experienced the pain of giving birth to their son, where she had tilled the fields keeping her hands soft for Max with cotton work gloves.

Now the wildflowers she gathered turned her thoughts back in time to the Hosokawa lands, to the place where the kerria bloomed. She had last returned to that sheltered oasis with Max in the days following their wedding. She recalled the fragrant yellow roses that had seemed to bloom just for them. Had the kerria bloomed in the years while they were apart? she wondered, longing for home.

Setting down her basket of flowers, Shizue gazed out across the far hills to where Douglas's widow was being well cared for in the prison camp, now guarded by American soldiers. There was triumph even in her failure to save Douglas, Shizue thought. She had brought light into the darkness of his confinement and breath into his failing lungs. She had brought him the gift of his grandson and the gift of Paul's forgiveness. Through her, Douglas had been able to share precious hours with Inge, which had helped sustain them both. Yes, she had not merely survived. She had emerged triumphant.

As she walked back to the farmhouse, Shizue sighed, enriched by the understanding that her years of struggle had not been in vain. She had achieved the goals expected of her bloodline. She had inherited great beauty, high station, and wealth. But those were gifts she had not had to earn. Max had left her as a woman not yet fully emerged. She had been pampered and spoiled. Now the war years had taught her humility, had divested her of youthful vanity, and had given her a new set of values to live by.

She plucked one straw of sweet-smelling hay from a mowed stack in the fields, musing as she brushed the silky straw across her cheek. Perhaps some things had been sacrificed to the ripening of her womanhood. She was now too womanly for girlish flights of fancy about how it would feel when Max took her in his arms, or how she would appear to his eyes attired in her mannish blouse and baggy pants. She had no proper dress to wear, no cosmetics, and could only scrub her face clean, pinch her cheeks for color, and groom her hair with the simple flowers gathered in her basket. And yet it seemed fitting Max should see her unadorned, just as she was now, just as she had looked throughout their years apart.

All at once she recalled abandoning her son, and she ran to him across the fields.

Kimi sulked just outside the farmhouse door, ignoring the affection-ate proddings of his puppy, now grown plump and rather spoiled like his young master. Shizue bowed to the child's needs and said nothing more about his father's return. Despite all her efforts over the years, her son was clearly at odds with how this event might change things. He had grown up having Shizue all to himself, and Max's return was like bringing another child into the household.

Excitement crackled through the farmhouse as everyone worked to spruce it up for a welcoming feast. Everyone was in such high spirits. Max's homecoming symbolized an end to their trials, and they spoke of soon being reunited with old friends the war had scattered to Kyushu's cities and villages. Sato's parents wondered if any Japanese soldiers were being released and were hopeful the postman would deliver official news of their missing son, news that he had been found in some Allied prison camp and would soon be returning to them as well.

O-nami brought homemade sake from the storehouse, as well as jars of pickled vegetables and other delicacies he had hoarded for just such an occasion. Shizue watched, lacking the heart to ask those dear to her for privacy.

She grew radiant with joy while artfully arranging displays of wildflowers and counting the hours until nightfall. Finally, the sun was going down. Shizue bathed to prepare herself for Max. She wanted him all to herself on this glorious night. But that would be insensitive to everyone else's feelings, she thought, listening to their excited voices coming from the kitchen.

Relaxing in the bath water, she reflected on how little her figure had changed. Her breasts were still firm and shapely following the months of nursing her baby. Her waist was almost as slim as it was before she had given birth to him. But she longed for feminine clothes, yearned for the sensuous touch of silk against her skin. She hated the coarseness of her mannish clothes. The material evoked hardships, and she did not think it was vain to wish for womanly things such as satin lingerie and silk hose. She had once taken such luxuries for granted, frivolously scattering them on her bedroom floor while complaining to Yufugawo of having nothing to wear that would dazzle Max when he saw her again.

That night Shizue posed before her mirror haunted by the phantom of her girlish vanity, wondering if romance had passed her by, if maturity had altered the boundless passions of youth. Perhaps she and Max would need time in which to recapture the intimacy they once had known. For so long he had stirred her feelings as a woman only in her dreams, she mused, combing her hair to cover the bald spot that had ceased to threaten her future.

Shizue smiled to herself, thinking how this day had swept away all her fears. She had no need to pinch her cheeks for color. There was a healthy blush on them as she walked into the kitchen, where everyone was seated at the table. The welcome-home feast lay stored in covered baskets.

Only soup and rice were put on the table. Everyone watched the door, alert for the slightest sound.

The gate squealed on its hinges, and Shizue ran to investigate. "Only the wind," she announced to everyone. "Max isn't likely to arrive until very late."

Her son grew drowsy-eyed. Those seated around the table yawned, hard pressed to keep their eyes open but determined to wait up with her. Yufugawo cradled little Kimi, rocking him to sleep.

Crickets serenaded the full moon loudly as Shizue strolled outdoors alone. Moonbeams tinted the countryside in silvery hues. She spun with outstretched arms, celebrating the gift of life under the sprinkled stardust of the Milky Way and remembering the castle gardens, where she had held Max's hand beneath showering fireworks at the festival of Tanabata. Those who had once been her father's servants began to file outside. She was surprised to see them all carrying their rolled-up bedding, lighting their way with lanterns in a silent procession to the barn.

Yufugawo appeared with Kimi asleep in her arms. "He will stay with me," she whispered. "It was decided that no one should disturb you, Shizue. Even the boy will be kept quiet as a mouse."

O-nami tarried for a moment, putting his arm around Shizue's shoulder. His round face was like that of the man in the moon as he smiled down at her. His eyes lined by age had lost their keenness, but not the spirit twinkling behind them as he said, "Now it is for you and Max to choose the path that lies ahead for us all. The baron and Douglas signed papers that dissolved a business partnership, but the bonds between our two families were not written on paper to be signed away with a scratch of their pens. Kimi continues the unbroken line of firstborn sons, and his parents are wedded to the Hosokawa lands and its silk as surely as they are wedded to each other."

"Dear O-nami, tonight is all that matters. I can't think of anything but Max. Oh, how much longer must I wait?"

Her old friend offered a sympathetic smile, then bid her good night and melted into the darkness. His lantern was a flickering firefly as he entered the barn.

At that very moment, Shizue thought, Max could be debarking from a ship anchored in Nagasaki Bay, eager as she was to close the short distance between them. Night would veil his eyes to the devastation. She was right to wait for him in the untrammeled countryside, where the peace he had fought for had not been so bitterly won.

It was hot for October, and Shizue brought a chair from the house. She sat near the gate, lulled by the chirping crickets who were believed to bring good luck. They had always congregated around O-nami's house as if fleeing the unfriendly neighbors' yards.

She rested her head against one arm. The hills grew darker under a waning moon. There were no headlights flickering on the main road. Now and then she caught herself nodding off.

"Wake me if I fall asleep," she instructed the dogs gathered around her feet. "The stranger coming here is my husband, so don't bite him, or your dinner pails will go empty." Their upturned eyes seemed to understand, and she laughed. The grass was moist with dew. Shizue curled both legs up on the chair, and her eyelids grew heavier, her weary mind at last resting.

Crisscrossing beams of searchlights swept the night sky over a surrendered Japanese airbase some miles inland from Nagasaki. The planes landing there were American; they roared down past row upon row of Japanese trainer planes still parked off the runways. Before Hiroshima and Nagasaki, Japan had staged a desperate last-minute effort to convert thousands like them into fighters to repel an invasion of the islands. Bomb fittings had been welded to their underbellies and machine guns fitted to their boxlike canopies. Flying these gerrymandered trainers against American Thunderbolts and P-51's would have been a suicide mission. But they had never left the ground, and emblems of the rising sun glistened bloodred on their fuselages as Major Maxwell Napier urgently walked the landing strip from the carrier-based plane that had winged him there moments ago. To date, no Japanese soldiers had fired on the occupation forces. But if there were any renegades who refused to accept defeat, night offered them cover. And so Max was assigned an armed escort to transport him through the sleeping countryside.

He swung his gear aboard the lead Jeep, then quickly sat beside the driver. "How far is it to the farm?"

"About forty miles, sir," the corporal answered, impressed by his superior's youth and the numerous campaign ribbons pinned on Max's chest. "Seen a lot of action, Major?"

"Some." Max wiped his sweating face with a handkerchief, overwhelmed by what had happened to him that day. Only hours ago he had been at sea, steaming for Tokyo, when Allied Supreme Command radioed the news of his father's death, numbing him to the announcement that Shizue was alive and that he had a son. Then he had been catapulted off the deck of his carrier aboard a pursuit bomber. The plane had landed with a swiftness that left him breathless, and now the Jeep he rode in plunged downhill, divebombing along a paved road neglected during years of war.

It was a jarring ride. The wind slapped Max's face, waking him to the end of his hard journey. It had begun while he was stranded aboard the rolling deck of a freighter, watching her propellers churn a twisting road of white spume far out across Yokohama Bay. He had fought his way back along those same Pacific waters, but now there would be no more bloody beachheads. He had traveled full circle back to Shizue, and there would be no more lonely yesterdays, only tomorrows, with his wife safely nestled in his arms.

His eyelids blinked against the mesmerizing effect of the Jeep's headlamps punching holes in the darkness ahead. "I was told the POW camp is somewhere nearby," Max said.

"Not half an hour's drive, sir," the corporal replied, pointing to the yellowish glow appearing through the roadside trees.

"Take me there first," Max ordered sharply. The prison camp's brightening lights pointed to Douglas's final resting place and to Inge's presence there. But he had only two days leave from duty in which to make up for the years lost with Shizue, and he was suddenly possessed by a vision of her face as he had last seen it, framed in the floppy-eared leather flight cap that had made her look like a little Eskimo.

"I've changed my mind, Corporal. No detours." Torn by allegiances of the heart, he locked his hands tightly together while he felt the pull of those dear to him, as if their voices were calling him to detour up the side road marked by a dingy wooden sign. "Can't you get this damn Jeep moving any faster?" he shouted, feeling his resistance weaken.

"Steep grading here, Major. My foot's to the floor."

As the Jeep steadily climbed, Max glimpsed the prison camp's illuminated compounds. He pictured Inge dressed in tattered clothing, her beauty faded, his father withered by illness but clinging to life in the dismal POW camp, which showed itself below this steep road. Their long confinement suddenly became a tangible reality. He much preferred the saving grace of memories to the blazing reality of barbed wire fences that saddened his homecoming. Fighting tears, he was overwhelmed by grief, torn by the need to share it with Inge, who had stood by his father until the end, who could tell him his father's last thoughts, who might have heard his last words.

He almost ordered the driver to turn back. But any delay in reaching Shizue would seem an eternity, and Max looked away, telling himself Inge would understand. Visiting there must wait. He did not want to come to Shizue drenched in grief after visiting his father's grave. She, too, had stood by Douglas, had aided other unfortunate souls given cruel treatment by the Japanese. Little distinction had been made between civilians and soldiers held captive throughout the Pacific. His father was another casualty of war. But a grandson had survived the holocaust, and one ship of their final mission for the Jews had sailed from Japan to spare hundreds the concentration camps of Nazi Germany.

By some miracle Shizue had survived the atomic bomb. He had feared she was still behind bars in Urakami Prison, which had been wiped off the face of the earth. Weeks ago, Max had viewed aerial films of the devastation and lost all hope of ever finding his wife alive. While serving on Okinawa, his efforts to locate his loved ones through military channels had met with failure. Most of the records on Nagasaki's citizens and POW's had been destroyed. The dead and the survivors were still being counted, and the names of those he sought had not appeared on any of the lists made available. He had requested to be assigned duty in Nagasaki, but his request was buried in army red tape, and he could get no one to take action on it. Orders had suddenly put him out to sea bound for another destination. Only the day before, he had stood on the deck of an American carrier, once again stranded from those he loved. Then fate had altered his course. Thanks to his army service record and the efforts of Colonel Blume, Shizue had found him.

Slowly the lights of a Japanese prison camp flickered out on the road behind Max. The numbing effects of being wrenched from utter hopelessness slowly gave way to feelings of gratitude and joy as his spirit stirred because of what lay ahead.

"I'm a father!" Max exclaimed, at last able to celebrate the birth of his son and gleefully slapping the driver's shoulder, then slapping everything within reach. "Burn rubber, Corporal! Dammit, I've got a son waiting just down this road." He gripped the windshield and stood on his feet, giving vent to the laughter that had been submerged for years.

Wind blew the cap off his head. It was caught by the armed soldier riding behind him, who was also holding the kit bag Avery Bullock had pushed into Max's hands. It was stuffed with chocolate bars, nylon stockings, a cornucopia of gifts.

"Can't go home empty-handed," Avery had said. Good old Ave had pulled strings with MacArthur to get him this short term of leave. The fate of Avery's missionary parents remained unknown, but Avery had stood on the carrier's bridge, his corncob pipe in hand, undaunted and waving as he sent Max off with a smile.

Avery was a rare friend, indeed, promising to cut through the red tape so Max could bring his family to Tokyo soon after reporting for his tour of peacetime duty. His outfit would assist in reshaping Japan's government along democratic lines. After centuries of military rule, the generals and admirals had been toppled from power. On the first of September, they had boarded General MacArthur's flagship anchored in Tokyo Bay to bow with hats in hand before putting their signatures to a formal declaration of surrender. Then the victorious American shogun's motorcade had driven through bombed-out Tokyo, the city of Max's and Paul's births. No news of his brother had been radioed to Max at sea, but Natsu's son was a tough and wily survivor, Max thought. He anticipated seeing Paul again, unscathed and riding on the crest of peace to carve some niche for himself in Japan's future. Yes, Paul was too resourceful to be lost in the reshuffled deck.

The driver swerved to avoid clusters of potholes, throwing Max down into his seat. Before long the road leveled off and the sky overhead was a black velvet dome decorated with bright baskets of stars. The landscape around him was unfamiliar, but these same constellations shone over the Hosokawa lands far to the south. Even knowing that her ancestral lands had been confiscated, for all these years he had dreamed of returning to find Shizue waiting for him there in the castle gardens, her beautiful face unchanged, her touch melting away the years. He recalled Shizue once saying that home was wherever they could be together, and his pulse quickened as the distance between them grew shorter. His Jeep sped past the soft fuzzy shapes of gingko trees, but he saw them as the gnarled old pines marking the mountain pass to the Hosokawa lands. He was thrown forward as the Jeep braked to a sudden stop. Max watched his driver fold back a map and begin reading it with his flashlight.

"Must've passed the turnoff, sir," he said. The Jeeps all backed up to a dense clump of trees, where their headlights scanned across the wooden sign half hidden under branches. "Yeah, this is it. Farm's just up the road a piece from here, Major."

Max consulted the luminous hands of his wristwatch. "I'll go the rest of the way on foot," he decided. The hour was late, and he had enough presence of mind to know that the Jeep convoy would wake O-nami's household. Everyone would rush out to greet him. Instead, he wanted to enter the farmhouse on tiptoe and find the room where Shizue and his son were sleeping. This moment belonged to them alone. Max got out of the Jeep. "Give me your flashlight, Corporal."

"Orders were to stay with you," he said rather meekly, glancing back at the other noncoms in the escort whom he outranked. "It could cost my tail, Major, sir."

"Negative! I can look after myself." Max patted his holstered .45. "These farmers aren't likely to take a shot at me. Hand down my gear. Leave one Jeep parked here under the trees and give me the keys. I'll need transport to the POW camp. You have your orders, Corporal. Thanks for the ride. Dismissed!" He fired off a salute, then shouldered the kit bag by its strap, and rushed up the dirt road, aiming his flashlight beam at gates identified with family names.

O-nami's farmyard grew noisy with barking dogs, and he halted just outside the gate, paralyzed at the sight of Shizue curled up asleep in a chair, undisturbed by the barking. "Be still. Quiet down," he whispered. The dogs obeyed him. They poked their noses between the gateposts, tails wagging at the stranger riveted there unable to move a muscle.

Caught in the beam of his flashlight, Shizue seemed an illusion that would evaporate if Max stepped close enough to touch her. He saw the flowers that adorned her hair. Her lovely face was half-turned away, resting on her folded arms. Her beauty outshone his memories.

Someone had been wakened by the barking dogs. Max saw the barn's hayloft doors opening. In the lantern light he saw O-nami, still larger than life, clad only in a loincloth. The man's great belly heaved like an inflated inner tube, and he stifled his excitement by clamping both hands across his mouth. Max smiled as Yufugawo appeared at the door beside her husband. She was about to cry out when O-nami promptly drew her away and closed the hayloft doors. Shizue stirred. Her blouse fell open, exposing the *omamori* he had fastened around her neck to insure her safe journey home an eternity ago.

The instant Max quietly opened the gate to her, he ceased to live on memories. As if their parting had cracked an hourglass, he felt not one grain of sand had trickled away since their bodies had last touched, and he knew that all they had been to each other was now waiting to be released in the moment when they touched again.

Max reached out to take her in his arms. But suddenly he stopped, feeling weighed down by the .45 strapped around his waist, his constant companion in war. He had never fired at his Japanese brothers even while his life hung in the balance. All that was behind him now, and he could not embrace Shizue while he was chained to this instrument of death. He unholstered the weapon and removed the bullet clip. In a gesture not unlike that of a samurai wearily laying down his sword after surviving a bloody conflict, he hung his webbed gunbelt on the sweat-blackened handles of a rusting plow.

Years of abstinence made him awkward as he bent over the woman of his dreams. She was simply gorgeous, he thought. The natural scent of her skin was enhanced by some faint trace of perfume, which evoked their summers together when love had first blossomed from the green buds of childhood friendship. How innocent they had been then, like flowers opening their petals to the sun.

Shizue's hand brushed at the silky strands of hair trailing down her brow, and she smiled. Was she dreaming of him? No matter. In that instant he fell in love with her all over again.

To wake his sleeping beauty with a kiss seemed the act of an incorrigible romantic. But one kiss would lead them away from the confusion of words. One tender kiss would gently awaken them both from the limbo of dreams. At last his lips touched hers, and that sweet sensation brought a weakness to his knees.

Shizue's eyelids fluttered open. Max was just as she imagined he would be, his handsome face bronzed by the sun. She ran her hands through his sunbleached hair while she deliriously murmured his name. "Max, oh my darling, I've waited so long." She wept for joy. There was no one else on earth but the two of them, greedily in love and smothering each other with kisses. "Darling Max, I'll never leave your side again. Not for even a moment."

"I love you." Max exalted in voicing these words. For so long, he had spoken them only in his dreams, and now the woman of his desires mixed her breath with his on a sigh. "Thank God for you, Shizue. Thank all the gods for keeping you safe." He lifted her up in his arms, then carried her across the farmhouse threshold. Oil lamps burned dimly and she guided him to her bedroom, whispering in the husky voice he remembered so well.

Shizue clung to his neck, feeling as if her heart might burst. At last they were together, and nothing else mattered, nothing more needed to be said as Max lay her down on the bed. Her husband was like a god descended from the heavens, and she felt blessed by his strong yet gentle hands, which made her come alive as a woman. Death could never touch her now. She and Max had years to make up for, years in which to grow old together. Her husband's caresses played on the strings at the center of her being, and she experienced an aching sense of release.

Only that day she had been given back her life, and that night Shizue's flesh burned, ignited by passion as Max yielded her up from the empty years without him; years in which she had merely existed, merely survived. Throughout it all, she had never given herself to another man. Max was the fountainhead at which she drank. He was the source of the unending stream, whose purifying waters once again united their souls. Only the weight of their mortal bodies still anchored them to this world and kept them from soaring high into the heavens. Gradually, they were set free of earthly bondage, and the ugly face of war was erased by the miracle of their love.

Shizue sighed in pleasure as Max kissed her breasts and explored her body with his hands. The intensity of feeling made her cry out as Max entered her. He seemed inexhaustible, and a dazzling array of shooting stars flashed before Shizue's eyes. Then they both cried out, like survivors of a mighty storm being swept ashore. There would never be another union such as this perfect moment, she thought. It was unbounded and limitless—measureless by any laws of the universe.

And, finally, after the zenith between them had been reached, the feelings rumbled on inside them like the thunder of a storm slowly drifting off into the distance. They remained locked together, tracing the features of their bodies. With lingering caresses they briefly drew apart to lie side by side just holding hands. Max turned his head on the pillow to look deep into Shizue's eyes. Then quite suddenly they were holding on to each other once again, and the joining of their bodies formed a private universe.

Max had journeyed far and alone, while Shizue's roots had been securely planted among loved ones. She was now the wife of a soldier who had not rested in years, and the fatigue of his long march home laid claim to him as he closed his eyes. His long lashes were bleached white by the tropical sun, telling her of the many islands her husband had helped to win back from the Japanese.

Shizue silently marveled over his maturity. There were shallow lines etched across his smooth face. Sympathetic lines, she observed, glad to find no traces of hardness in his face. His tanned skin was unblemished except for a shiny pink scar along one shoulder.

Oh, she was jealous of his sleep! She longed to know so many things, to listen to Max's mellow voice for hours and gaze into his clear blue eyes. Throughout her years of waiting, little Kimi had slept quietly beside her like this. Now she reflected on the warm glow of motherhood and of a woman's love for her man. Shizue lightly brushed the downy blond hairs on Max's chest. She had never before felt so complete, so content, and at peace.

The daylight would wake Max gently, she thought, leaving the window unshuttered and covering her nakedness with a faded cotton robe. He had always risen hungry for breakfast. In the kitchen she prepared a meal for them to share. Decorated with flowers and with the sunlight streaming through its square little windows, the farmhouse kitchen was not so very different from that of the charming cottage in Beppu, whose garden overlooked the sea. Shizue smiled to herself, reminiscing over that special place they had promised to share again one day. As then, she artfully arranged eggs, rice, and pickled vegetables on her best dishes and decorated the tray with flowers that had survived the night. She placed this gift of caring next to the *futon* where Max slept. He groaned, crossing one arm over his eyes.

Shizue quickly took a flower from the tray and pinned it in her hair. "Welcome home, my dearest darling," she murmured, planting kisses across his forearm.

Suddenly he sat upright, his expression stunned as he cupped Shizue's face between his hands, searching her out in the first light of day. She felt unattractive, certain that she was a disappointment to him by daylight. Then Max kissed her hard, and she realized it was all in her mind. Giddiness set in as he playfully pulled her down on top of him and grinned rather boyishly. The way his rumpled hair poked out in every direction made her laugh. It was hearty, robust laughter the two shared. Neither one had laughed so openly while apart, and laughing together erased the intervening years.

He and Shizue sat cross-legged on the bed facing each other over the breakfast tray. It might have been her childhood room in the castle, where Max had carried her across the threshold as his young bride. They took turns speaking, but Shizue avoided describing the horrors of Terrible Thursday, and Max avoided saying very much about his combat experiences. She said little about Douglas's hardships, deciding this was best told by Inge. Instead, she drew a happier picture of the hours she spent with his father as a family, and of Paul's act of forgiveness, which had brought a ray of light to Douglas Napier's final hours. Their emotional conversation weaved back and forth in time, broken with passionate embraces and lingering kisses. Baron Hosokawa and Kimitake had been buried on the eve of war, and years had softened the grief of their loss. But Douglas had died on the eve of peace, and his absence was felt the most.

Once more they made love, celebrating life, survivors whose grief was temporarily laid to rest. Afterward, Shizue rested her head against Max's chest. His beating heart was like the cadenced voices of temple drums celebrating the rhythms of the seasons, promising bountiful crops at harvest time. More than anything she wished to have more babies. She dreamed of a healthy little girl, a sister for Kimi to play with and to love. Smiling, Shizue drifted into a sleep, where all her dreams came true.

*   *   *

Later, Max woke to a child's laughter. For the first time, he heard his son. O-nami shouted at the boy to behave, and it seemed as though a chase were taking place in the yard.

Shizue uttered a whimper of complaint as Max left her side. Their son's giggling took him to the window, and it was love at first sight for Max as he watched O-nami hoist the small boy onto his shoulders. Shizue observed the look of wonder on her husband's face. His chest swelled out, and he grinned proudly. With all the awe of a brand new father, Max watched his son riding on O-nami's shoulders and he marveled over the existence of this tiny human being. Turning to Shizue, for the first time he saw her as a mother. As she took his arm, her worried face spoke for problems that Max had not considered. He was a stranger to this boy, he thought, and a father in name only.

His son was some yards away near the barn. Max could see that Kimi had inherited his mother's dark hair, her honey skin, but he could not discern any resemblance to himself, other than the boy's sturdy physique.

"Why is Mommy still sleeping?" his son demanded of O-nami in English. "Why doesn't she wake up?" he demanded in Japanese.

"You ask too many questions," O-nami bellowed, wheeling the boy around as if on horseback. "I will ride you into the fields to play."

Max was shocked to hear the boy expressing himself in words. "O-nami!" he shouted from the window. "Keep my son there. I'll be dressed in a minute!"

"*O-kaeri-nasai!*" O-nami waved, welcoming him home as he ran toward the house. "Ah, you see, Ichiban! Your father has come home, and that is why your mother sleeps so late. Wave to him!"

"No, no," Kimi shrieked, pulling O-nami's ears. "I want Mommy!"

"I'm coming, sweetheart."

Seeing Max's nervousness, she smiled and said, "Oh, dearest, you mustn't worry. Kimi's had me all to himself, and it's only natural for him to be a little jealous of you."

"You're my first love," said Max, jealously wrapping her in his arms. "Our son is part of us both. I think I understand his fears. I'm a stranger to him. I'm not a Japanese father, and I can't help thinking how Paul turned against our father because of that."

"Max, he sees everyone as being the same. I've done my best to make you real for him. Even when he was only a baby, I talked about you and our childhood together. He's still just a baby living in a child's world, and you can easily win him over with a loving hug," she insisted.

But her son's angry shrieks added fuel to her husband's concerns. It might take more than a gesture of love to bridge the years lost between father and son, Shizue thought, while she maintained a smiling front.

"Despite what you say, it's important that I don't start off wrong," Max worried aloud. "I'm afraid he'll feed off you, play one of us against the other unless we make it clear his place isn't being challenged."

"Just follow your heart, dearest."

As the two of them dressed, Shizue observed how different Max was from the boyish-faced youth in the old photographs she had showed their son. Black-and-white snapshots had made his father's blond hair and luminous blue eyes appear darker. Their son might have outgrown the innocence of seeing everyone the same. Kimi might find this tall, imposing figure a rather fearsome sight. Years of being a soldier had imbued Max with a commanding presence, which was enhanced by his tailored khaki uniform, the gold oak leafs pinned on his starched collar, and the rainbows of campaign ribbons he had won in the war against Japan. "Kimi can be so stubborn," she confided to Max. "He was confused and upset about your return. Darling, I should go to him alone. Give you both more time to adjust."

"No, it can't be put off." Max smiled, linking his arm with hers. "We'll go to him together, Shizue, and hope for the best," he said.

The entire household had gathered in the kitchen to greet Max. Shizue watched bitterness flashing across their faces. Yesterday they had eagerly awaited her husband's return. But now these people who had known him as a child stared at the uniformed conqueror, momentarily estranged from what he had meant to them in the past. Then Yufugawo flapped her pudgy arms, too choked by tears to speak as she rushed forward to embrace Max. Suddenly there was an outpouring of affection. Max evoked memories of carefree times. He was the sole surviving son of a dynasty they had kept alive in their hearts, and there were tears as each took turns welcoming him home.

"Give the man room," O-nami called to them from just outside the door. "There is a son waiting to meet his father. Do not be a crybaby, Ichiban," he scolded the boy, setting him on the ground as Shizue stepped into the yard with Max. "There is nothing to fear. Remember that you are a samurai. Go to your father bravely."

"Mommy, Mommy," Kimi sobbed, running to hide his face in her baggy pants. "Make him go away."

"Sweetheart, you don't mean that." Shizue could not pry him loose and searched her mind for the words to open his heart. "Daddy's traveled to us from very far away, just to see his little boy."

"Hello, son." Max felt like a giant looming over him. Kimi sneaked a look, but his tiny hands remained firmly anchored to his mother's trousers.

Max knew that if he appeared too eager to win the boy over, he could set them further apart. He squatted down to appear less overbearing. "I didn't want to leave your mommy. We were separated in a big storm, and I couldn't find her again until it was over," he explained in terms a child might understand. Reaching out one hand to touch the boy's hair, he said softly, "I love you, son. I'd give anything for your smile."

Kimi shook his head from side to side. A puppy toddled forward to nuzzle his young master.

"Is this your puppy?"

"Yes," the boy answered coldly. Tight-lipped and unsmiling, he turned to face Max. "Uncle Paul gave him to me." Kimi scooped up his pet. "He's my friend. You go away."

Shizue tried sternness. "I'm so ashamed of you. Give your daddy a big hug. This instant, young man!" Her desperation only encouraged an act of defiance.

"No!"

Max watched his son run off as fast as his short legs would carry him. Kimi ran inside the barn and used all his strength to shut the door with a resounding bang. "Well, it seems I've lost the first round."

"I'm guilty of spoiling him terribly," said Shizue, feeling wounded for her husband. "Paul said things would work themselves out between you. Now I'm at a loss for what to do."

"Our son's got a lot of spunk!" Max exclaimed. "I'm more frustrated than hurt."

O-nami laughed and seized Max by the shoulders. "Do not worry. Blood will tell. The idea of having a father will soon grow on the boy." His eyes filled with tears. Max's decorated chest spoke for having fought Japan with valor, and O-nami's expression shifted between pride and sadness. "Your gun still hangs where you left it, Ichiban. I will not ask what you have done to earn these medals. Your eyes tell me that you are still a man of honor, and I thank the gods for your safe return. Ah, what a sight you are!"

"And you, old friend." No homecoming would be complete without O-nami's bear hug to welcome him, and Max grew tearful as well.

"I brought gifts for everyone," he suddenly remembered, and took Shizue by the hand.

O-nami followed them across the yard to Max's kit bag, which sat on the ground near the rusty plow on which he had hung his gunbelt the night before. "I brought chocolate bars, American coffee, and some other things," Max said, unzipping the bag.

"Kimi has a sweet tooth. You should go to the barn with a peace offering," O-nami suggested.

"I don't want to win his smile with a bribe." Max looked down at the chocolate bars in his hand. "Too bad Paul isn't here to put in a good word for me. Kimi seems very fond of him."

"Yes. But your father was his favorite, and Inge means a great deal to him as well." Shizue faced the barn, where their sulking son had fortressed himself. The day was waning all too quickly. Max had only what remained of it and the next day before he must report for duty in Tokyo. "It must be awful for Inge, still closed up in that camp surrounded by its memories. We must go to her, dearest. Maybe when Kimi sees the love she feels for you, it will open him up."

"All right. I have a Jeep parked down the road." Max scrubbed the growth of beard on his face, deciding he needed a shave. He dug inside his bag, surprised to find a woman's dress neatly folded under his shaving kit. "Good old Ave. He must've requisitioned this from one of the nurses aboard ship," he told Shizue, unfolding the flower-print cotton dress cut in the short-skirted style popular during the war years. "I must've described you to my army buddy a thousand times over. Looks just your size."

"Oh, it's perfectly lovely." Shizue excitedly held up the dress against her, crossing an arm around its waistline and raising the skirt as she turned in a small circle. "I've forgotten what it's like to wear a dress."

"These go with it," said Max, holding out a pair of flesh-colored stockings. "Nylon. Synthetic silk. Our parachutes were made of it."

Frowning, O-nami rubbed one stocking between his fingers. "There is nothing to this imitation."

"Don't run it!" Shizue quickly took possession of the nylons. She also preferred the touch of silk. But the synthetic material had placed her in contact with a new era. Its feel was like the touch of the future waiting for her and Max beyond the farm's dusty fields.

"Wash Kimi and dress him in his best clothes," Shizue told Yufugawo. "Say we're going to visit his grandma-*san*. Oh, I'm so happy."

She kissed Max on the mouth and ran off, eager to try on her new clothes. America had not neglected its women's need for feminine things even while at war, Shizue thought. She halted at the farmhouse door. "America must be a wonderful place! Will we live there?"

"I haven't given it any thought." Hands on hips, Max smiled back at his wife, taking delight in her girlish enthusiasm. Kimi's rebuff had dampened his spirits, and the imminence of visiting his father's grave now caused him sadness.

Max shaved at the well. The uniform he wore made him feel alien in his homeland. But as he watched O-nami splash water on his face and groom his silvery white topknot, he soon began to feel at home again on the soil of Japan.

Yufugawo smilingly carried a water basin to the barn, Kimi's small shirt and short pants draped over one arm.

"Kimi, I am going to dress you for a visit with Grandma-*san*," she called to the boy, who came out of hiding only long enough to stare gloomily at Max. Kimi had both arms wrapped around his puppy.

Now he retreated, stomping his feet as if announcing no possibility of a truce. While Max shaved, everyone in the household stood around the well offering words of advice on being a parent. As he looked at the friendly faces from his past, Max experienced the warm feelings he associated with his boyhood summers. He gave them all chocolate bars, which no one bothered to unwrap. The baron's former servants all seemed content to watch him shave and comb his hair as if it were some festive event. Sato's parents were cheered by his account of crossing paths with Koichi, the old gardener's grandson, who had received medical care and had been treated humanely.

Sato's father questioned Max, asking how long he would serve the occupation forces in Tokyo, and if he thought the climate was right for them to journey home to the valley of their ancestors.

"I'll inquire about the situation there and let you know," Max promised them. The army had not specified when he would be discharged, and his hands went up to signify that his future was left up in the air. Everyone laughed and bowed.

All eyes went to Shizue as she walked toward them wearing the stylish American dress. Its skirt trailed midway across her knees, and gathering up its material, she glanced down at the back of each leg to check the dark seams of her nylons. She had no high-heeled shoes to wear, only a scruffy pair of thonged sandals. But to Max she had never looked lovelier.

"I'll bring the Jeep," he said.

Shizue felt lighter than air as she glided to the barn. Her son would benefit from being reunited with Inge. Shizue was sure that once Kimi realized that Max was Douglas's son, he would accept Max as his father. She found Kimi well behaved but withdrawn and impatient while Yufugawo struggled to get his legs into the short pants he was already outgrowing.

When Kimi heard the sound of an engine nearing the barn, he scurried away to peek outside at his soldier-father seated behind the wheel of the Jeep. His eyes grew larger as he watched Max work the stick shift that caused the engine to make a powerful noise. Kimi jumped up and down as his father sounded the horn. Before that day he had ridden only in the ox cart. Clearly he was impressed and eager for a ride.

"Come along," said Shizue.

"Runt, too," he insisted, and shrugged off her touch. Lifting the puppy in his arms, he marched from the barn.

Max observed the excitement in his son's eyes. "Would you like to sit here on my lap and help me drive, Kimi?" The boy appeared about to leap at the invitation, and Max revved the engine to entice him. But Kimi shook his head.

Resisting temptation, the boy refused to sit up front on his mother's lap and climbed into the backseat hugging Runt. Max assured Shizue it was safe for him to ride there. As he threw the Jeep into gear, Kimi giggled at the new sensations of riding in a motor car.

"We're going to visit *ogisan*," he cried, waving at the stoic-faced neighbors who lined the dirt road.

Shizue snuggled up against her husband. Max honked the horn to further delight their son. Each time he turned to look at Kimi, his son's smile became a scowl. Once on the main road, the boy was fascinated by everything in the Jeep. He tried to stand and look over his father's shoulder, but the Jeep moved too fast, bouncing him as he held to the backseat. He shrieked like a child on a roller-coaster ride.

Max drove the unfamiliar road he had traveled the previous night. Shizue gave him directions and spoke of O-nami resting his weary oxen on this steep hill. The Jeep climbed easily to a spot overlooking the prison camp. The compounds of dingy wooden buildings and watchtowers looked even grimmer viewed by the light of day, Max thought.

His son cried, "*Ogisan*," and stood up in the slowly moving Jeep.

"We'll visit your grandma-*san* first," said Shizue, hoping that Inge could find the right words to make her son understand the death of his grandfather. As Max braked the Jeep in a cloud of dust, Shizue looked up at the deserted watchtowers. She felt chilled by the memory of Japanese soldiers with machine guns who had once stared down at her. She saw that the series of gates leading to the inner compounds had been removed, but she observed that the sense of confinement remained unchanged.

American marines appeared from the guard house, asking to see Max's orders.

"The camp's off limits to Japanese," the sergeant-of-the-guard stated bluntly.

"My wife and son are American citizens," Max fired back emotionally.

The sergeant raised an eyebrow. "You'll have to get authorization from Captain Brace, sir."

"Fine with me." His Japanese family was ordered to wait in the Jeep while Max was escorted to the marine officer in command, who asked to see his orders.

A rigid man, the captain did everything by the rule book. "See here, Captain," Max said. "I didn't fight this war to have my family turned away by your stupid regulations."

"I'm not disputing your rights, Major. But no Japanese are permitted inside the compound. I'll have Mrs. Napier brought to you here," the captain grumbled, and handed back Max's orders.

"I don't care for your tone of voice," said Max, pulling rank on him. "We've come to pay respects at my father's grave, and we'll go to his widow as a family. Now I'd like to visit my stepmother without further delay."

Captain Brace stood at attention. "Well, since your orders come from Supreme Command," he said through a forced smile. He bent over the roster of names on his desk. "Mrs. Napier is in barracks number ten. The sergeant here will show you the way."

Max did not bother returning the captain's salute. This had been his first encounter with the stigma of being married to a Japanese in occupied Japan, and it left a bitter aftertaste.

Holding Shizue around the waist while their son excitedly skipped along pulling her by the hand, Max followed the sergeant. His gaze roamed the jagged corridor of barbed wire, and he envisioned his father ravaged by illness, shuffling on this same barren path of earth to the squalid wooden building Shizue pointed out. It was there she had visited

Douglas and Inge. Tears ran down her cheeks as Kimi ran up the warped wooden steps calling for his grandfather and pounding on the door that was now padlocked.

No pets were allowed, and after some coaxing, Kimi reluctantly surrendered his puppy to the care of friendly soldiers at the guard post.

Max felt grateful that Inge had survived. But as he crossed the barren yards of the oppressive confines to be reunited with Douglas's widow, nothing could fill the void created by his father's death. "How much of a walk is it?" he asked the sergeant.

"A few minutes, sir. Just past these buildings where the military prisoners were kept."

Inge was mindlessly carrying a laundry basket under the clothesline strung in the yard outside her barracks. The barbed wire to the men's compound had been torn down, but she still saw it standing there to keep her apart from Douglas. The repatriation process was excruciatingly slow. Only the military prisoners and the very ill were being taken to better quarters somewhere outside the camp, to await ships bound for their homelands. Tuberculosis had widowed other women in her compound, and they, too, silently hung their laundry up to dry. The Red Cross provided clothing, but Inge had chosen to mourn Douglas in the faded cotton dress of her long confinement. Friendly American soldiers had replaced the stoic Japanese guards, but to her the bleakness had not been lifted. Shizue was still refused passage through the outer gates. She imagined the Jewish colonel was occupied by more important matters. No word had reached her of Max, whom she feared was dead in this war. For Inge it was just another day of feeling homeless and forgotten. As she bent over the laundry basket, she noticed a ladybug crawling on her arm. "Ladybug, ladybug, fly away home." She gently coaxed it with her finger. "*Nein*? You wish to stay? *Ach*, what of your children waiting all alone? Perhaps you are lost like me."

"Inge."

Inge looked up and gasped as she saw the tall soldier standing over her. "Max!" She was suddenly in tears. Blinded by them, she did not see the faces of Shizue and Kimi. Max held Inge against him tightly, while they shared the grief and the joy, one inseparable from the other.

"Grandma-*san*!"

Inge's body went limp, and she sobbed. "*Schatzkens*." Kimi and Shizue rushed forward to hug her. "My dear ones, I feared never seeing you again. Please, help me sit or I may faint." Max walked her to a bench shaded from the sun by one scrawny tree, the only thing growing in what seemed a desert of dust.

"Where's *ogisan*?" Kimi's eyes searched everywhere for Douglas. The other women sadly watched this small boy, who skipped under the clothesline looking for his grandfather. Some of Inge's prisonmates had not seen their own children in years, and they tearfully reached out to touch him. "Have you seen *ogisan*?" he asked them, on the verge of tears, begging for some reply.

"Your grandpapa has gone away from here," Inge found the strength to say. She turned to Max, observing the changes in his handsome face. "Give me your hands. Let me feel them so I know you are really here," she pleaded.

As Max took her hands, his son stood apart, and Inge saw the gulf between them. Everyone began speaking at once, and she laughed through her tears. Her sad-eyed friends now mutely filed past her into the barracks.

"They have no one," Inge whispered, brushing the soft hair at Max's temples. "The Japanese would not let me go to your father's grave. Now I have planted flowers there and sit there talking to him for hours on end."

"Our reunion is incomplete without Dad," said Max.

Inge twisted the plain gold wedding band that his father had placed on her finger one long-ago spring day in Paris. They had found love in their marriage of convenience, Max thought, a love born of needs that had given new meaning to both their lives. Inge Karlstadt's escape from Hilter's death camps had turned the war in Europe into Douglas's war. Not long after their return to Japan, his father had been imprisoned because of this terrible war. Now his father could not bear witness to the safe return of his soldier son, who reached out to the woman who had survived him. Max kissed Inge's wrinkled brow for them both, and she sighed as if his gesture had healed the wounds of her long confinement. "I'd like to visit Father's grave."

"*Ja*, what we feel must be shared with him. I will take you there."

"Lean on me, Mother." The word came from Max's heart, and he was moved by her fragility as her pale lips tremblingly formed the word *son* and she gripped his strong arm.

"Where did *ogisan* go?" Kimi demanded, skipping along the dusty path to the prison camp graveyard. "When can we see him, grandma-*san*?"

"In your thoughts, *Liebling*. Only as you remember him last."

Shizue picked up her son. "Do you remember what I said about the *kami*? How their spirits share a place beside us for always?"

"Yes."

"Well, *ogisan* is with the *kami*, and he's watching you now. Don't try and see him. Just listen for his voice in the breeze."

Max dropped his head. The graves were close together. Napier, D. was painted in white on a bare wooden stake, and he knelt beside it, placing both hands on the earth as if in search of his father's heartbeat. This stake driven into the parched earth was a poor tribute to the man he had loved, and bitter tears rolled down his face as he pounded the sandy soil with his fists. Never again to feel those strong hands and to be called son. "Dad, it isn't fair."

Shizue sank to the earth at his side, cradling their son against her. "Your grandfather is watching over us, dearest." Kimi's lower lip trembled. Although he did not understand death, the tears shed by his parents moved him to feelings of loss. Her son regarded Max as though he glimpsed some resemblance to his grandfather. *"Ogisan* was your father's daddy," Shizue told him. "When your daddy was small, he would climb into *ogisan*'s lap and hug his neck, just as you did when he was alive."

Kimi tearfully twisted free of his mother. "Make him come back, grandma-*san*," he sobbed, throwing his arms around Inge's neck.

"Hush, now hush. Your grandpapa's face is there in your teardrops," Inge said. "Our memories will always keep him alive for us."

"Memories aren't enough," Max said angrily. "Peace is a rotten cheat without Dad here to bring us all together again. It won't ever be the same without him."

"That is so. But your father would not want to be mourned with such bitterness in our hearts. Until the last, he forgave his persecutors and spoke to me only of living for this day of your return." In a frail, quiet voice, Inge related Douglas's painful struggle for life. "Paul's forgiveness brought him peace. Death cannot take away the love your father gave to us, Max. You three are all I have. Without you, I would have given up on life." She rocked Douglas's grandson, thinking there were other graves to be visited, those of Heinz and Angela. *"Liebergott,* what a gift you are. Foundlings. We are foundlings who must never be parted again."

"Very soon we'll all be together in Tokyo." Max looked at his son. Kimi rubbed the tears from his eyes and looked back with an expression bordering on affection. It was obvious that he recognized something of his grandfather in Max's sad blue eyes.

Max looked down at the blooming autumn flowers Inge had planted on the grave. Taken in the prime of his life, Douglas Napier had never once raised his fists to curse the heavens. By giving to others, his father had redeemed himself for the selfish mistakes of the past. A child of wealth, he had died a pauper, but he left a fortune in memories that would always shine in the thoughts of his loved ones. *"Namu Amidadutsu,"* he spoke an ancient prayer. "May your soul remain untroubled," he translated for Inge.

"This is a beautiful thought," she said.

To Max, Inge's beauty was as faded as the old dress she wore. But her expressive blue eyes reflected the warm depths of an inner beauty he had always known. They shared a look that spoke for everything that had passed between them over the years. "I'll arrange to have father's remains shipped from this barren place," he said, "and we'll give him a proper burial in Tokyo."

Inge took his hand. "Max, do you remember how gay we once were—so long ago. Will life ever be gay for us again?"

Max nodded. "Yes, I promise you that." He rose on the shallow path between graves with Inge's hand in his. It was trembling and cold. "Take heart. My army buddy is hard at work on the red tape so we can be a family again. Housing in Tokyo is scarce. If the old mansion's still standing, I'll requisition it for my tour of duty there. Maybe Paul can be persuaded to move in with us. I just can't wait to see him again."

Kimi dug both hands inside the pockets of his short pants. "I want Runt," he announced, marching off toward the compound's guard post alone, kicking at the ground.

"Come, I have something to give you that may help with the boy." Inge linked arms with Max and Shizue, walking them to her barracks. "Douglas carved a toy from scraps of wood. A labor of love. He wanted to finish it for Kimi's birthday, but he simply lacked the strength. He finished it on the night of his death. The men of his barracks kept it hidden from the guards, and I wrapped the toy for safekeeping."

"Oh, I'd forgotten." Shizue cheered with the recollection. "Your father worked on it for months. I brought him glue, oil paints, a number of things."

"It is kept under my cot," said Inge, halting outside the barracks door. "His grandfather's gift will bring you close, Max. You will see. I feel you must share this with your son as a surprise. Come inside."

"Yes, I'll wait here and keep him occupied." Shizue walked to the guard post, where her son was at play throwing a stick that his puppy only yapped at, too young to understand he was to fetch it. A friendly soldier on guard retrieved the stick and instructed Kimi on how to train his pet. While her son played near the squalid building where he had spent so many hours with his beloved grandfather, Shizue gazed back on the separate paths Inge and Douglas had always returned along, following each visit.

Max walked toward her from the women's compound alone, carrying a rather large cardboard box tied with knotted string. "Inge felt her presence would be too distracting," he said, weighing the toy Douglas's talented hands had fashioned during the last weeks of his life. "Son, I have a surprise for you. A present from your grandfather."

Kimi abandoned his pet and raced over to look at the package in Max's hands. "*Ogisan* went away to live with the *kami*," he said, suspicious and pouting.

Max ventured closer and smiled. "Yes, but before leaving he made this toy for you. 'Be sure my son gives this to little Kimi,' he told your grandma-*san*. My daddy would be very sad if you refused to accept his gift."

"Go on," Shizue encouraged, giving him a gentle nudge. "Accept the gift, then bow politely and thank your father."

The boy stepped forward, and all at once surrendered to temptation. "*Arigato!*" he said excitedly, and grabbed the package with both hands.

Chased by the puppy, Kimi ran to the steps of the deserted building and sat there eagerly opening his surprise package. The puppy fought him for possession of the string. "Oh, all right, Runt. Take it and play," he said, mimicking his mother's adult tone of voice.

He was far too preoccupied to notice his parents standing there hand in hand, sharing his delight as Kimi took the fanciful toy out of its cardboard box. A white stallion and a brown bear carved from wood faced each other on a square stage decorated with painted wooden trees. The stage was joined to a box open on three sides to expose the intricate clockwork mechanism of colorfully painted wooden cogs and gears. Clearly, Douglas had engineered his creation with some movement in mind. Kimi turned the box this way and that, poking its gears, shaking it, frustrated when his efforts failed to make the toy perform. "What does it do?"

"I honestly don't know," Shizue said. "Maybe your father can make it work."

"Yes, I think so." There was a round hole in the sealed end of the wooden box, and Max saw a tiny wooden crank lying inside the cardboard box Inge had given him. "Here's the key to open its magic. Would you like me to share its secret with you, son?"

"Yes, show me, Daddy."

Little Kimi was all eyes as his parents sat beside him. "Give me your hand and we'll work the magic together," said Max.

Guiding his son's hand, Max snapped the crank in place and slowly turned its handle clockwise. The white stallion and brown bear reared up against each other on their hind legs, heads moving side to side. Douglas Napier's genius for invention had once served the guns of war. He had devoted his last hours to delighting a child with a masterful machine carved from scraps of wood. It was his final statement, his epitaph, that was voiced in his grandson's laughter. The horse and bear went down on all fours and half-turned away from each other, one to the left, one to the right, then both reared up again shaking their heads. Cranking the wooden handle faster made the combatants appear more ferocious and lifelike as they spun back and forth.

"Let me work it, daddy."

"Sure, Kimi." Max mussed his hair, then put a fatherly arm around his son's shoulders. As a boy, his father had fashioned him a delightful rogues' gallery of jack-in-the-boxes. But none was the match for this charming labor of love. The toy's mechanism churned out a special magic that opened doors between the surviving generation of father and son. Tears came to his eyes. Shizue snuggled closer. Kimi soon tired of playing. He squirmed into a nook between his kissing parents, and they were three.

"Daddy, Mommy, don't I get a kiss?"

"Yes, sweetheart," said Max. He stood and lifted his son high off the ground and planted kisses on his smiling face, making up for all the lost years between them. "Your mother wants to invite brothers and sisters to live with us. What do you say to that?"

"I am Ichiban! Number-one son." Kimi laughed, unable to comprehend anything beyond his father's dizzying ride as he was lifted high in the air.

Shizue contentedly watched her men. Her husband's flood of loving kisses led to masculine play. Their son brought out the eternal boy in every man, and Max roughhoused with Kimi, indulging the boy's whimsy with extravagant gestures as they played a game of tag in the dust of this prison camp yard. She imagined she saw Douglas standing here now, straight and tall, the virile man of the childhood she had shared with Max. For a time he stood beaming at his son and grandson while they played, and then Douglas Napier slowly turned to walk away in the lowering afternoon sun.

Shizue cranked the marvelous toy Douglas had left behind, a labor of love that would always speak for their triumphs. She felt an inner tranquility. There were healing powers in the union of another generation. As her men at play stirred up the dust, the prison camp seemed to melt away before Shizue's eyes, and she saw herself in the castle gardens, where the faces of the missing now passed in review, looking as they had in happier days gone by. Angela Napier, who had never grown accustomed to Japan's steamy climate, walking with Sumie Hosokawa, shielding her smooth complexion against the sun under a frilly silk parasol. Kimitake, the athletic youth, flexing his muscles to impress everyone while Shizue laughed with Max at the serious expression on her brother's handsome face. And finally, she saw her father coming toward her through the flowering jasmine, his warmth and humor shining through the steel of his samurai armor.

What a marvelous youth she and Max had led. There had been great love to balance the tragedy and the death. What a marvelous future yet lay in store for them and their sturdy firstborn son.

Shizue rushed to hug them both, thinking how the future was inextricably joined to the past. One day they would return to the Hosokawa valley and its mist-shrouded peaks. But for now home was a mystical place of the spirit, and one had only to follow one's heart to be there forever.